Praise for

"Wheeler has done for . . . [   ] -
ester did for the sea s[   ] -
—*Rocky* [   ]

"Wheeler is a master storyteller." —*Library Journal*

"Wheeler captures the roughneck atmosphere of the mining town and brings to life the social problems of the Gilded Age. . . . A multilayered world as versatile and enduring as the copper that inspired it."
—*High Country News* on *The Richest Hill on Earth*

"Passionate, intelligently written, thoroughly entertaining historical fiction." —*Kirkus Reviews*
(starred review) on *The Richest Hill on Earth*

"One of the best Western writers around today. He doesn't rely on epic battles or gunfights to tell his stories, relying instead on fascinating characters, vivid imagery, subtle a[   ]
[   ]*kly*

"W[   ]
[   ]*ost*

"W[   ]*rn*
no[   ]*er*

"N[   ]*ry*
w[   ]*ly*

DATE DUE

PRINTED IN U.S.A.

719.2

BY RICHARD S. WHEELER FROM TOM DOHERTY ASSOCIATES

CHERYL'S BOOK NOOK
104 Main Street
Canon City, CO 81212
719-275-4964

Anything Goes

{ AND }

The Richest Hill on Earth

RICHARD S. WHEELER

A TOM DOHERTY ASSOCIATES BOOK / NEW YORK

NOTE: If you purchased this book without a cover, you should be aware that this book is stolen property. It was reported as "unsold and destroyed" to the publisher, and neither the author nor the publisher has received any payment for this "stripped book."

This is a work of fiction. All of the characters, organizations, and events portrayed in these novels are either products of the author's imagination or are used fictitiously.

ANYTHING GOES AND THE RICHEST HILL ON EARTH

Anything Goes copyright © 2015 by Richard S. Wheeler

The Richest Hill on Earth copyright © 2011 by Richard S. Wheeler

All rights reserved.

A Forge Book
Published by Tom Doherty Associates
175 Fifth Avenue
New York, NY 10010

www.tor-forge.com

Forge® is a registered trademark of Macmillan Publishing Group, LLC.

ISBN 978-0-7653-9170-4

Our books may be purchased in bulk for promotional, educational, or business use. Please contact your local bookseller or the Macmillan Corporate and Premium Sales Department at 1-800-221-7945, extension 5442, or by e-mail at MacmillanSpecialMarkets@macmillan.com.

First Edition: December 2016

Printed in the United States of America

0 9 8 7 6 5 4 3 2 1

CONTENTS

Anything Goes

TO MY WIFE, THE ONE, THE ONLY

SUE HART

ONE

The silence was deadly. The show might as well be playing to an audience of cigar store Indians. Half the seats were empty. August Beausoleil hoped that Helena would be one of those cities where people habitually arrived late. But he wasn't seeing any new arrivals pushing their way along the rows. The opera house seemed a giant cavern. Opera houses were like that. They seemed largest when they were empty, more intimate when they were jammed.

From his perch at the edge of the proscenium arch, he studied the vast gloom beyond the hissing footlights. Ming's Opera House, in Helena, in the young state of Montana, was a noble theater just up the flank of Last Chance Gulch, where millions in gold had been washed out of the earth just a few feverish years earlier.

And now, opening night, those who had braved the chill mountain winds were sitting on their hands. Who were they, out there? Did they understand English? Were they born without a funny bone? Why had a sour silence descended? A miasma of boredom or ill humor, or maybe disdain, had settled like fog over the crowd, what there was of it.

The show had opened with the Wildroot Sisters, Cookie, Marge, and LaVerne, strutting their stuff, singing ensemble; Sousa marches melded into a big hello, we're starting the show. And all it got was frostbit fingers tapping on calloused hands. Beausoleil could almost feel the dyspepsia leaking across the arch onto the wide stage.

The show was his. Or most of it. Charles Pomerantz, the advance man, owned the rest of it. He had done his usual good job, plastering Lewis and Clark County with gaudy red playbills and posters touting the event, booking hotels, hiring locals, stirring up the press, handing out free passes to crooked politicians, soothing the anxieties of clergymen with bobbing Adam's apples, and planting a few claques in the audience. Who weren't doing much claquing at the moment.

Beausoleil doubled as master of ceremonies, and that gave him a chance to stir the pot a bit, sometimes with a little jab, or a quip, or even a hearty appreciation of wherever they were.

He grabbed his cane and silk top hat and strutted into the limelight, Big City man in gray tuxedo, in the middle of arctic tundra.

"Ladies and gents," he said. "That was the Wildroot Sisters, the Sweethearts of Hoboken, New Jersey. Let's give them a big hand."

No one did.

"LaVerne, Cookie, and Marge," he said. "Singing just for you."

Dyspepsia was in the air. Time for some quick humor.

"Citizens of this fair city—where am I? Keokuk? Grand Rapids? Ah, Helena, the most beautiful and famous metropolis in North America—yes, there you are, welcoming the Beausoleil Brothers Follies."

Well, anyway, waiting for whatever came next. No one laughed.

"We've got a great show for you. Seven big acts. Please welcome the one, the only Harry the Juggler, who will do things never before seen by the human eye."

Harry trotted out, bowed, and was soon tossing six cups

and saucers, breaking none. And when it was time to shut down, he pulled one after another out of the air and set the crockery down, unharmed. He bowed again, but the audience barely applauded.

"And now, the famed Marbury Trio, Delilah, Sam, and Bingo, from Memphis, in the great state of Tennessee, doing a rare and exotic dance, a lost art, for your edification."

It was, actually, a tap dance, and they did it brightly, the dolled-up threesome syncopating feet and legs and canes into rhythmic clatter that usually set a crowd to nodding and smiling. But the applause was scattered, at best. This crowd didn't know a snare drum from a bass drum.

"Next on our bill is the monologuist and sage, the one, the celebrated, the famous Wayne Windsor. Welcome Mr. Windsor as you would a long-lost brother fresh out of the state pen."

They didn't.

Wayne Windsor trotted out in a soft tweed coat, a string cravat, and a bowler, which he lifted and settled on his balding head. He would do his act in front of the silvery olio drop downstage.

Another bomb, Beausoleil thought, retreating into side-stage shadows. Windsor was also known as The Profile, because he thought he had a handsome visage from either side, with a good jut jaw and noble brow and long sculpted nose. He had contrived to take advantage of this asset, speaking first to the left side of the audience, giving those on the right a good look, and then when that portion of the audience had absorbed his famed profile, he shifted to the other side, treating the viewers on the left to his noble nose and jaw.

The act was a good one. The Great Monologuist always began with an invitation.

"Now tonight," he said, "I'm going to talk about robber

barons, and I want anyone who is a genuine, accredited robber baron, or any other barons, to please step forward so we can have some fun at your expense."

That was good. Robber barons were in the news. Helena had a few. The Profile had a knack. Beausoleil thought it might crack the ice this sorry evening, but it didn't even dent the silence. The Profile fired off a few cracks about politicians, added a sentiment or two, and finally settled into one of his accounts of bad service on a Pullman coach, while the Helena audience sat in stony silence. It was getting unnerving.

Was something wrong? A mine disaster? An election loss? A bribery indictment? Nothing of the sort had shown up in the two-cent press before the show. The trouble was, the week hung in balance. A bad review, three bad reviews in the three daily rags, and the Beausoleil Brothers Follies would be in trouble. A touring show bled cash.

He eyed the shadowy audience sourly, and came to a decision. He talked quietly to two stagehands, who told him there were few tomatoes this time of year in Helena, but plenty of rotten apples, which would do almost as well.

"Do it," he said.

They vanished, and would soon be sitting out there in the arctic dark, surrounded by surly spectators and bystanders little comprehending the subversives in their midst.

"I knew it," said Mrs. McGivers. "I saw it coming. You should pay me extra. It grieves my soul."

"I didn't know you had one," he said.

Mrs. McGivers and her Monkey Band would follow, after The Profile had ceased to bore his customers. Like most vaudeville shows, this one had an animal act, and the Monkey Band was it. Mrs. McGivers, a stout contralto, would soon take the stage with her two obnoxious capuchin monkeys, Cain and Abel, in red-and-gold uniforms, and an accordionist named Joseph. Cain would pick up the miniature cymbals, one for each paw, while Abel would command two drumsticks and perch with a little drum in front of him, looking all too eager.

And then the music would begin, with Cain clanging and Abel banging, and Joseph and Mrs. McGivers setting the pace and melody, more or less. It was usually good for some laughs. And sometimes the beasts would add a flourish, as if they were caffeinated, which maybe they were. The result was anarchy.

August Beausoleil loathed the monkeys, who usually spent their spare time up in the flies, careening about and alarming the performers. The Profile had complained mightily when something had splatted on his pompadoured hair. Beausoleil sometimes ached to fire the act, but good animal acts were tough to find and hard to travel with, and Mrs. McGivers usually gave better than she got. It was better than any dog or pony act he'd seen.

But he had one surefire way to turn a show around, and this was it. When at last The Profile had ceased to bore and offend, the master of ceremonies announced the one, the only, the sensational Mrs. McGivers and her Monkey Band. Quick enough the olio drop sailed into the flies, revealing Mrs. McGivers, the monkeys seated beside her, one with cymbals, the other with drumsticks. And Joseph, the accordionist, at one side. The audience stared, lost in silence. Would nothing crack this dreary opening night?

Mrs. McGivers had come from the tropics somewhere, and the rumor was that she had killed a couple of husbands, but no one could prove it. She used a jungle theme for the act, and usually appeared with a red bandanna capturing her brown hair and a scooped white blouse encasing her massive chest, below which was a voluminous skirt of shimmery blue fabric that glittered in the limelight. She looked somewhat native, but wasn't. She wore sandals, which permitted her smelly feet to exude odors that offended performers and audiences alike.

Her repertoire ran to calypso from Trinidad and Tobago, mostly stuff never heard by northern ears, which usually annoyed the audience, which would have preferred Bible songs and spirituals as a way of countering the dangerous idea that man had descended from apes. There, indeed, were two small primates, wiry little rascals dressed in red-and-gold uniforms, making dangerous movements with drumsticks and cymbals in hand.

She turned to Beausoleil.

"You're a rat," she said.

Joseph, the accordionist, took that as his cue, and soon the instrument was croaking out an odd, rhythmic tune, and she began to warble in a nasal, sandpapery whine stuff about banana boats and things that no one had ever heard of.

Mrs. McGivers crooned, repeating chords, giving them spice as she and her monkeys whaled away. The capuchins gradually awakened to their task, led by the accordion, and soon Cain was whanging the cymbals and Abel was thundering the bass drum, with little attention to rhythm, which was actually intricate in Trinidadian music. The whole performance veered toward anarchy, which is what Mrs. McGivers intended, her goal being to send the audience into paroxysms of delight.

Only not this evening in Helena, in the midst of stern mountains and bitter winters.

Were these ladies and gentlemen born without humor?

Abel rose up on his stool and began a virtuoso performance on the bass drum, both arms flailing away, a thunderous eruption from the stage. And still those politicos out there stared across the footlights in silence.

Very well, then. Beausoleil quietly waved a hand from the edge of the arch, a hand unseen by the armored audience.

"Boo!" yelled a certain stagehand, now sitting front-left.

"Go away," yelled another stalwart of the show, this gent sitting front-right, four rows back.

The capuchins clanged and banged. Mrs. McGivers warbled. Joseph wheezed life out of the old accordion.

The two reporters, front on the aisle, took no notes.

"Boo," yelled a spectator. "Refund my money."

The gent, well known to Beausoleil, had a bag in hand, and now he plunged a paw into it and extracted a browning, mushy apple, and heaved this missile at Mrs. McGivers. It splatted nearby, which was all Cain needed. He abandoned his cymbals, leapt for the mushy apple, and fired it back. Any target would do. It splatted upon the bosom of a politician's alleged wife.

This was followed by a fusillade of rotten items, mostly tomatoes, but also ancient apples and peaches and moldering potatoes, drawn miraculously from sacks out in the theater, and these barrages were returned by Cain and Abel, who were born pitchers with arms that would be the envy of any local baseball team.

Mrs. McGivers was miraculously unscathed, the war having been waged by her two capuchins. Joseph, too, was unscathed, and continued to render calypso music, even imitating a steel guitar with his miraculous wheezebox.

It was a fine uproar. Suddenly, this dour audience was no longer sitting on its cold hands, but was clapping and howling and squealing. Especially when Abel fired a soggy missile that splatted upon the noble forehead of the attorney general. The Helena regulars enjoyed that far more than they should.

After a little more whooping, Beausoleil, in bib and tux, strode purposefully out onto the boards, dodged some foul fruit, and held up a hand.

"Helena has spoken, Mrs. McGivers," he said. He jerked a thumb in the direction of the wings.

She rose from her stool, awarded him with an uncomplimentary gesture barely seen on the other side of the footlights, and stalked off, followed by the capuchins, and Joseph, and finally some hands who removed the stools and instruments.

"Monkey business! Give them a round of applause," Beausoleil said, and immediately the audience broke into thunderous appreciation.

The two bored reporters were suddenly taking notes.

All was well.

The rest of opening night was well nigh perfect. Indeed, Mary Mabel Markey, the Queen of Contraltos, got a standing ovation and repeated demands for an encore, which she supplied so abundantly that Beausoleil almost got out the hook to drag her offstage. Mary Mabel was getting along, was fleshy, and used too much powder to hide her corrugated forehead. She was sinking fast, and Beausoleil had hired her mostly out of pity, since she could no longer find work in the great opera houses of the East and Midwest. But she was also becoming impossible.

There were more acts after the intermission and, finally, the patriotic closing in which all the acts combined with a great huzzah for the waving flag.

The rotten vegetables had rescued the show, once again. It annoyed August Beausoleil. It meant his acts weren't working. It meant financial peril. It hurt the reputation of the Beausoleil Brothers Follies. There were neither brothers nor follies in it, but that was show business. The audience had gone home happy.

August Beausoleil stared at the greenbacks and coins in the battered lockbox. The evening's take was a hundred forty-seven dollars and fifty cents. Forty-five were gallery seats, sold at fifty cents. The rest were dollar seats. There were also some free passes, given to local bigwigs and press and bloodsuckers.

That was not even his gross. He owed Ball's Drug Store, seller of advance reserved seats, two percent. And he owed Ming's Opera House seventy-five. And he owed the Union Hotel for the rooms. And he owed the printer who did the playbills, and his partner Charles Pomerantz, who ran up expenses as the advance man, his costs. There were other costs, too. Chemicals for the limelight, chemicals for the footlights. The publicity spending he had to do, drinks for guests.

Running a variety show through western towns was a tough proposition, and it required near-sellout bookings. He usually had seven acts, too many for small-town vaudeville, but he hoped that the size and depth of the show would start tongues wagging and purses opening. It was folly, but it was also a bet, and August Beausoleil didn't shy from a good bet.

Ming's had emptied, and the lights were mostly doused. But the evening was far from over. He had been in the business all his life, ever since he was a hungry boy edging his way through the theaters of Manhattan, making a nickel here, a dime there. His instincts told him that this night was going to bring trouble.

Indeed, a gent in handsome attire worked through the shadows to the arch, climbed to the stage, and found the proprietor of the Beausoleil Brothers show in the wing.

"Your show, is it?"

"Hope you enjoyed it, sir."

"We did until a rotten apple landed on my wife's dress, ruining it. She wishes to be reimbursed, and tells me the cost is fourteen."

"I see," said the proprietor. "And you have some evidence, do you, that the dress is beyond repair, can't be restored, and of course you have a bill of sale, and all that?"

"Now see here. The dress is ruined and one of those infernal monkeys did it. The show was so bad that it got all the spoiled fruit in Helena tossed at it."

"I agree, sir, that monkey act is really beneath our standards."

"Beneath your standards! You hired it on. Now you can pay the piper."

"Ah, but the monkeys were entertainment. There wasn't a smile all evening until the monkeys took offense. And after that, sir, the show was a great success."

"Well, fork over. I don't have all night. My wife waits in the hansom cab."

"Who did you say you are?"

"I didn't. I'm the attorney general, Carruthers, and that's all I need to say."

Beausoleil digested that. "Here, sir, are two tickets to tomorrow's performance, absolutely free. Give them to your friends."

"Two dollars."

"Well, then, four reserved front-center orchestra seats, something only a well-connected person can hope to acquire without paying a premium."

The gent stared. "It's late. I'm tired. My wife is angry. Otherwise I'd be digging into that cashbox."

"Here. My compliments. On the house. Enjoy the show tomorrow."

The dandy vanished into the gloom, clutching some prize tickets, and in the distance a door opened and closed.

Beausoleil thought that the monkeys had saved the show. When the barrage of spoiled fruit sailed in, no one out there expected Mrs. McGiver's capuchin primates to return the fire. Yes, it was worth it. The whole audience erupted with glee. The show would have a good run in Helena. A few free tickets wouldn't hurt anyone. Give them anything but cash.

He contemplated the hotel, the awaiting bed, but he knew the night was not over. She would show up. She always did on a night like this. So he waited, and in a couple of minutes there she was, storming across the dark boards, the ultimate, the memorable, the sublime stage mother. He would listen, she would storm, and he would wind up his day.

"Fire that act," Ethel Wildroot said. "I don't want to be in a show with Mrs. McGivers. It's a blot on my name."

"I think you're right," he said. "Of course the monkeys saved us."

"Saved us! They drove everyone out of the theater. The show's dead in Helena."

"They broke the ice, Ethel. They returned the compliments. After that, it went perfectly."

"I'm putting you on notice; we'll leave the show unless you unload that immoral woman and her tropical parasites."

He yawned. "That it?"

"I'm just getting started."

"Pull up a stool."

"No, I'll stand, and you will sit, and you . . . will . . . listen."

August had succeeded in the business by being agreeable, but now he knew she was going to discover his limits.

"LaVerne's ready to move up. She's been rehearsing. She's got the songs, and she's ready for the big time. The East Coast circuits big time, not here. I thought you might want to show her off. Get rid of the deadwood around here, like the monkey act, and that fat old Mary Mabel Markey. She makes me want to screech. I won't even be in a theater when she opens that cavern of hers and bats fly out."

Ethel was alluding to the star of the show. A little shop-worn, but still capable of packing them in.

"I hadn't thought of her songs as bats," he said. "They're said to carry rabies."

"She's got a thousand bats nesting in her gums. But La-Verne, she's young, shapely, and she can wow the crowds. She has her own teeth."

"And you want to pull her out of the Wildroot act?"

"Certainly not. She holds it together. The girls are stupid, she's not."

This all was odd. LaVerne was actually a niece, and the other girls, Cookie and Marge, were Ethel's daughters. Ethel was a stage mother in reverse.

"She's got the songs. 'Sweet Rosalie.' 'Empty Stockings,' and 'You're a Daisy.' You've got to listen. Better yet, throw her in as an olio act. She'll show you a thing or three."

"Nice to have your counsel, Ethel."

"I'm not done yet. You think you're getting off easy? Not this opening night in this dumb town. It's worse than Peoria. And Peoria's the end of the line. Now that hotel room, it's impossible. There's four of us and two beds. La-Verne needs her own room, and since I'm her manager I'll join her."

"One room, one act," he said. "That's how it is."

"What a cheapskate."

"And I'm getting rich by mistreating you," he said.

She laughed. There was that about her. "Make LaVerne a separate act, and then she gets a room."

"You've got three salaries in your act. Buy a room for her."

"If we don't walk out on you first. This show, it's an embarrassment."

He didn't say they were welcome to.

She whirled into the gloom, and he heard the theater door snap shut.

Everybody wanted something. He felt the lonely, dark theater around him. In rare moments it was bright-lit, packed with cheerful people, a certain mysterious joy rising from the crowd. But mostly it was like this, a hollow place waiting for those few minutes.

He wanted things, too. A show on solid footing. A hit act or two.

He'd been at it since age nine, when he hung around theaters, wanting the pennies or the occasional dime he'd collect to run an errand, get a sandwich for a showgirl, take tickets to someone, carry a stagedoor Johnny's bouquet to his dream girl. He never knew his old man. His ma started raising him fiercely enough, in a basement cubbyhole, but then she would go away for days, and then show up and feed him, and then go away for weeks, and he had only his wits and a little knowledge that at stage doors people wanted something or other, and he could run it down and get a tip—sometimes. Sometimes not. Sometimes he spent a hungry night atop a steam vent in the big city, the dank warmth the only thing between himself and bitter cold. But there was always the next show coming in, and actors who wanted stuff, and he got good at getting it, and got good at understanding how it worked. And there came a time when people on the streets would ask him if a show was good, somehow trusting in a boy's verdict, and there came a time when he had actual jobs, sometimes taking tickets, sometimes doing the books, sometimes working as a stagehand. By the time he was eighteen he was a veteran of show business, and by the time he was twenty-three he was doing his own variety shows—not big time, but on the roads of rural America.

He'd never done Broadway; he'd made his way in smaller venues. And now the new thing, vaudeville, cranked out by Tony Pastor, clean stuff, good for ma and pa and the brats. His shows were a little more gamy. He was playing to miners and cowboys and their silky ladies. But it was vaudeville, the new thing, and it drew crowds.

He turned down the lamp and watched it blue out. The theater was black and yet he knew his way. He'd been in so many that they were no mystery to him. Some of these opera houses had towering flies, where curtains whirled up out of sight. Some had draw curtains, flooding across the stage. Those were the cheaper deals, and they slowed the show.

He felt the rush of cold air, and eyed the empty street for footpads. The hotel was four blocks distant, but the editorial sanctum of the *Independent* was two blocks straight down the gulch, and next to it was the *Herald*. He'd go see. Sometimes he could get a good idea of how the show would go in a town by reading a review.

The *Independent* was well lit. Light flooded the street. He saw within a couple of compositors, someone in a sleeve garter who was reading proof and a walrus-mustache man who looked to be the one putting the morning edition to bed. He entered. The place was hot.

He headed for the one who was poring over some hand-written pages.

"I'm Beausoleil, from the show. Have you a review I might look at?"

"Suit yourself," the gent said, not moving.

August Beausoleil had been in plenty of printing plants, and knew something about ink. It leapt out at you. While you were protecting your front, it nabbed you in the rear, and sometimes ruined a coat or a shirt. He edged gingerly toward the compositors, who were garbed in grimy smocks, which did little to protect their hands, which looked like they'd never wash clean, and in fact they didn't wash clean.

"Got a review for the show?" he asked one.

The man nodded. The review was sitting in a half-filled form consisting mostly of pre-cast advertisements. Beausoleil couldn't read the backward type, but he knew what to do. On a spike next to the form were the galley proofs, so he gingerly tugged his way through until he found what he wanted. It was lacking a headline. The compositors would add that later. He yanked the galley proof free and smeared a thumb with sticky ink. He laid it on an empty stone and read.

"So-so show at the Ming," was the opener. It started with an all-out condemnation of the monkey act, but then had a kind word about The Profile, Wayne Windsor, whose humor was "piquant." It announced that Mary Mabel Markey was so-so, and looking a little shopworn. But it had a good word for the opening act, the Wildroot Sisters, who were "fresh and maidenly and a delight to the eye."

It praised the other acts readily enough, and even encouraged readers to lay out a little for tickets and an evening of good fun.

Well, no disaster there.

The *Herald* was less active, but there was one duffer setting type.

"Got a review?" Beausoleil asked.

"Review? Nah, he went to bed. Try about nine. We hit the alleys about eleven."

Beausoleil stepped into deep dark, not having the slightest feel how the Beausoleil Brothers Follies would fare in the cold capital of Montana. There would be three more shows: Friday, Saturday matinee, and Saturday evening. And a lot of bills to pay.

THREE

Wherever Mary Mabel Markey went, she hunted for a confessional. She always had a lot of confessing to do. She was guilty of the sin of vanity, which was a version of the sin of pride, which was one of the Seven Deadly Sins.

The Vicariate of Montana did not have large congregations, except in Butte, which was Irish and Italian. But there was a nondescript redbrick church in Helena, off the gulch, which she soon discovered. She needed to confess for the good of her soul. Being a big draw in vaudeville was something that needed forgiveness.

Late that morning, the top-billed performer with the Beausoleil Brothers Follies found her way to the Church of Saint Helena, and discovered an empty confessional and a waiting priest on the other side of the screen.

She plunged in and settled herself.

"Forgive me, Father, for I have sinned," she said.

This was the familiar ritual. She was an Irish girl. Her name wasn't really Markey; that was a theater name. It was O'Malley. Her birth name was Mona O'Malley.

"I have committed vanity," she said.

"Well, the Lord requires humility," the priest said. "But I don't quite grasp what it is that gives offense."

"I am too proud. I'm in show business. I'm in vaudeville. I'm at the top, and proud of it. I fought my way up, and now there's no one better."

"Ah . . . I wonder a little about this, my daughter."

"Pride is the worst sin. It excludes God from my life," she said. "I confess it whenever I reach a new town."

"Ah . . . I'm sure the Lord is most merciful, but perhaps you could say a little more about this."

"Father, show business is wicked. And I've climbed the

ladder. The higher I've gone, the more wicked things I do, so I need to confess them all and be forgiven."

"I wonder if you could tell me a little more," the priest said, sounding a little confused.

"I insist that the posters and playbills put my name first."

"Well, that's wicked, all right, if you don't deserve it."

"But I do deserve it. The company wouldn't be profitable without me."

The priest paused. "I think it might be wicked to think it if it's not true, or if you attach more importance to your presence than is merited, my daughter. But I find no sin in assuming your rightful place."

"Well, that's just for starters. I make a point of abusing my rivals. I'll never say a good word about anyone else in the company."

"Yes, that's a venial offense," the priest said. "You would do better treating others as you wish to be treated. Yes, there's something that needs repentance. But I don't quite see it as one of the Seven Deadly Sins."

"Well, I do. Take my word for it. I could spend twenty minutes giving you a list, but there must be others waiting. I've done it all. I'll do whatever you say. Just give me my absolution and penance and I'll be gone."

A pained silence exuded from the other side of the screen.

"Daughter, penance for what?"

"For all of it. For being in vaudeville."

"How is being in vaudeville sinful?"

"I put myself on display and sing."

"Do you sing things that offend our Lord?"

"No, but maybe He thinks I do."

"Do you behave in a manner that evokes lust or evil thoughts?"

"No, but who can say?"

"Are you dressed modestly?"

"Mostly. But the corset's so tight I have no breath."

"You've examined your heart and believe there is wickedness in the very business? Vaudeville? It compels you to sin?"

"Yes, Father, that's just it."

"Then it would seem you should leave vaudeville. But you can always be forgiven, even in vaudeville. Temptation is one thing, sin is another."

"I knew you'd say that. Thank you, Father. I'll say a few extra prayers."

More odd silence, a sigh, and then the mumbled absolution in Latin, the words strange and puzzling, strangulated as they passed through the screen. It felt just right.

She enjoyed that. He would never forget it. His first encounter with a vaudeville star. Tonight, he would be mulling it in his mind, confused and unhappy. Hers was not the usual act of contrition. That was how she affected people. She departed, knowing she would feel just fine until the company reached Butte, the next venue. Then she'd have to find another confessional and unload. Meanwhile, she thought, she was free to be whatever she felt like being. Whoop-de-do!

She had grown up in the jammed tenements of Gotham, the daughter of desperate Irish parents who had fled the Famine, traveling steerage to the New World and hope. The cold tenements were worse killers than the famine. One in five died each year of consumption, and indeed, the lung disease soon took her mother. But little Mona O'Malley, as she then was known, survived, and so did her father, who first swept streets and then delivered bags of coal for the parlor stoves of the comfortable classes.

There was one bright thing about Mona's mother, Eileen. She could sing. She brought from Ireland a whole repertoire of ballads, lullabies, and sometimes strident songs full of pride and fight. And these she sang, and these did Mona absorb, somehow delighting in each song. Her mother sang until her last hours, sang even after consumption had ravaged her throat and her voice was a hoarse and crackling rumble and there was blood on her lips. And when she died, Mona's father said it had to be; everything had to be. He was a fatalist, and whatever happened had to happen, and Mona kept wondering why her mother's death had to be, and why her father didn't grieve.

Mona was very thin, and sometimes weak from not getting anything to fill her, and she took to wandering the bustling city, a pale child of ten, looking for anything to snatch for her stomach. Even the seed some people fed to birds. One day she saw a street entertainment: a man with an accordion and a monkey with a cup, looking for pennies and dimes. And she saw people listen to the man, who had great mustachios, and put coins into the monkey's cup. Mona hastened back to the tenement, a room she and her father shared with five other people she barely knew, and there she found a cup that no one had stolen. She took it.

She hastened uptown to a place where there was a little park and people strolling, and they looked clean and pink compared to everyone in the tenement, who was waxy and gray. She set her cup on the grass, back from the paving stones, and sang. She didn't mind it if people stared. She had utterly no self-consciousness. She knew her mother's songs, so she sang them, and soon people listened, and some smiled and drifted on, but sometimes someone put a coin in her cup. Later some boys stole the coins, but her career was launched in that hour, and she sang the ballads, and when mothers with perambulators came by, she sang lullabies, all six her mother had sung, and the women listened and studied Mona and sometimes added a coin. She learned to empty the cup frequently, and slide the coins into a pocket, and after that she kept what had been given.

Then she bought things her body cried for. She bought pastries at a bakery. She bought an apple. She bought some potatoes to take to her father. She presented them to him proudly when he returned at dusk after a day working for the coal and ice merchant. He eyed the potatoes, and her, and flew into a rage.

"Stealing are you, shaming me are you?" He smacked her.

She didn't reply.

"You get what you deserve," he added. "That's the way of things."

She had an old sweater and a couple of pinafores, and these she gathered, tied into a bundle, and walked away. It wasn't cold, not yet. She never saw her father again, though once she saw a wagon like his, with a man like him, driving across a street ahead. She had no wish even to find out whether it was John O'Malley, the fatalist who thought everything was meant to be except that his daughter had earned an honest living.

She was not yet eleven.

Now she patrolled the crooked streets of Helena, blotting it up. It was a city in flux, barely a state capital, without a capitol building but with a good commercial district that hemmed the winding gulch that had turned a few miners into rich men and spawned a busy city. She saw bureaucrats in suits, and far more men in dungarees. She saw few women, and wondered why. Up a hill was a modest governor's residence, only slightly larger than a comfortable private home. She wondered where the legislature met, and where state offices were housed. Maybe it scarcely mattered. Montana was a work in progress.

She liked to get a feel of a place, but Helena was eluding her. She thought she would do better in the saloons, and that was where she was headed anyway. It was a bright fall afternoon, and the saloons would be empty, but that didn't matter.

Most of them lined Last Chance Gulch, and some bore the usual names she had encountered in the West—The Mint, Stockman, Pastime—but some carried evocative names: O'Leary's, The Shamrock, Harrigan's.

She chose O'Leary's, pushed into a wall of sour odor, and let her eyes open to the gloom. A wide barkeep with a soiled apron eyed her.

"Sorry, lady," he said.

It was not customary for a single woman to pierce these male sanctuaries.

She saw only half a dozen patrons, all with mugs of ale before them. Not a whiskey glass was in sight.

"I will sing," she said.

"Lady, I said, there's the door."

"I'm Mary Mabel Markey and I will sing."

"Who's that?"

"You can buy tickets. Seven at the Ming."

"Mark, let her sing," a gent said.

She placed her portfolio on the bar and withdrew some sheet music. There were several titles, which she fanned out.

"Fifty cents, signed by Mary Mabel Markey," she said.

She stood back a bit, selecting a spot where all six of the guzzlers could study her, and then she paused, drew a breath, and sang. This one was a lively jig, one of her mother's, rhythmic and rollicking. Her voice carried outward. The barkeep scowled. She knew he was thinking it'd soon be over and she'd be gone.

But now, as always, she caught them nodding, feet tapping, shoulders swaying. It always was like that. She finished the jig.

"There now," she said. "I'm Irish, and I'll sing a medley, every one of them learned from my ma. She died of the lung disease long ago, and left one thing behind. The songs of the old country."

She sang once again, needing no backup, no instrument, just a cappella to half a dozen working men—hod carriers, dustmen, who knows? Her voice was untrained and hadn't changed in all the years she had sung on street corners. She sang without elegance, no vibrato, no finesse, no punctuation to catch a breath. That voice had never been shaped by a maestro in a music academy, but it was sweet, and better still, it was earnest; more than sincere, it was honest and true. She sang the way her mother did, daughter emulating mother, and she saw that they liked that, and even Mark, the saloonkeeper, liked it and allowed a small smile to lift the corners of his mustache.

When she had finished she let silence settle.

"It's my pleasure," she said, not defining just what pleased her. "The sheet music sells for fifty cents, and I will sign each one."

First one old bloke ambled over and laid out two quarters. She lacked a pen, but she had a good pencil, and she signed the name that the customers knew. Little did they know that she was Mona and that she was an O'Malley, and some of them, if they listened closely, could name the county where she was born. Then the next one bought, and another, and she sold five in all, with one sour holdout.

"I'll give you a kiss instead," she said, and planted a kiss on the old duffer's dandruff-caked brow.

She hadn't changed at all. She was the ten-year-old girl with the cup.

FOUR

At noon, August Beausoleil pounced on the *Independent,* only to find that the paper had pounced on him. He found no review, but on the front page was a lengthy article, or rather, an outburst. A deacon in a local congregation had not liked the show, and had voiced his complaints to a friendly reporter, who had written them up and added the weight of the paper's concurring opinion to them.

The show, it said, was an affront to decency. And morals. Most especially, a certain act featuring monkeys.

> The act featured certain musical material from the tropics, with morally objectionable rhythms and offensive appeal to the baser instincts of the sort not on display in more northerly climes. That it had a corrupting influence on the audience is beyond cavil. What started as stern rectitude in the silent viewers soon turned into lax and ludicrous amusement as the ugly little beasts, devoid of human dignity and spirit, began to maul melody and inject anarchy into the proceedings.

That for starters. But the deacon and the paper were not content to trash Mrs. McGivers.

> The songs rendered by the opening act, known as the Wildroot Sisters, were not of the sort to elevate moral and ethical sensibility, but to debase both singer and listener. The catchy rhythms were quite the opposite of what might be rendered by a trained and spiritual church choir, offering melodic praise to the Almighty.

Neither did the operators of the show escape.

The very name of this abomination, at the Ming Opera House, The Beausoleil Brothers Follies, tells the entire tale. It is an effort to Frenchify and Latinize good American tastes, and as such it subverts all the efforts of the Founding Fathers, guided by their respective congregations, to create a nation that would truly be The City on the Hill.

Wayne Windsor didn't escape, either.

There was a monologue, rendered by a vain eccentric who would turn from one side to the other, which lacked both humor and grace, and poked ridicule at the better classes of people, the empire builders who are subduing this continent and turning it into something close to paradise. The callow, shallow fellow doesn't hold a candle to the builders of the Republic.

And one of the early acts, The Marbury Trio, who performed with metal taps on their shoes as they did complex routines while dressed in tuxedos and silk top hats, came in for some of the worst of the assault.

To put a woman in men's clothing, with two men beside her, and have her do pirouettes and rattle the boards with the metal on her feet, debased not only the woman who was subject to such public gaze, but also the audience, unused to seeing such coarse violations of whatever is sweet and retiring and fair in American womanhood.

The piece recommended that the show fold and depart the precincts at once, or failing that, that no one should purchase a ticket, and in any case the chief of police should be on hand at all performances to step in and cover wanton dancers and issue summons for all infractions.

Beausoleil sighed. The show was a long way from Manhattan. For decades, variety shows had been somewhat racy, or deliberately offensive, often mocking anything that might be considered traditional. But in the early eighties, a New Yorker, Tony Pastor, had cleaned it up. He was the godfather of vaudeville, and every show he put together was considered suitable for any viewer. That careful approach had been picked up by Keith and Albee as they built their vaudeville circuits. They enforced the rules relentlessly. An act that violated certain standards got pitched out.

This wasn't a Keith circuit show, and Beausoleil had no contractual arrangements with the kings of vaudeville, so he and Pomerantz were free to assemble whatever acts appealed to them and to their audiences. Maybe someday the vaudeville magnates would swallow all the small shows like his, but not yet. There was plenty of room in vaudeville.

He read the material once again, and liked it. He'd sell out tonight, and for the rest of the run. He couldn't have written a better review.

"Boy," he said to the kid hawking the papers. "Here's two bucks. Put a paper in every saloon and barbershop in the gulch, and keep a dime."

"Holy cats," the kid said, staring at the two greenbacks.

"I'll take another," Beausoleil said, and hurried toward the hotel, hoping to catch most of the acts.

He was lucky. There in the lobby stood Delilah Marbury.

"Get a load of this. Do your worst," he said.

"Skirts or pants?"

"Show some leg," he said.

"You worship the golden calf," she said.

"Mainly yours. And whatever else is attached."

"So does my husband."

"Which one?"

She laughed. The act was new, and tap dancing was new, and some people thought it should be done in black-face. In all of variety there were only a few tap acts, and he had wanted to try one out. He soon discovered that these people were dancers, day and night, cold and hot, and a stage was nothing but an excuse to tap and click and drag a foot and rattle the boards. He hadn't made up his mind about them. He usually ran them third, between two stronger acts. This was their first tour. The three were from Memphis, where they had picked up the motions and the rhythms on the waterfront. They made a good olio act, and that was proving handy whenever he was having a tough time with sick performers, or boozy or hungover ones. But the jury was out on the Marburys.

"August, we've got a new routine, and tonight's the right time to try it. I'll be in a skirt."

"Wear a tutu," he said.

"If you post bail, I will."

"Delilah, don't let them slow you down. Don't let me slow you down. If you've got something to give to those people out there, they'll know it and they'll buy it, and they'll clap, and I'll back you. I like talent. I like whatever it is that catches people in their seats and brings them to life, and brings them to cheering for you. That's why I'm here. That's what I'm looking for. It's not just the show, it's the magic. It's what makes some acts grand, and some acts flop. If you've got it, you've got me every step of the way."

She gazed at him, almost like a frightened doe. "I guess we'll find out," she said. "We're going to tap a love story."

Tap dance a love story. What would it be? A triangle, the three of them tapping away?

"The hall might be empty tonight."

"We'll see about Helena," she said. "Maybe there's a lesson or two in an empty hall."

He liked that.

He returned to sunlight and headed up the slope on Broadway, looking for city hall and the coppers. He didn't know the name of the chief, but he would learn it. He found the place, most of a square block set aside for local government but not yet built up.

The top constable was named Will Riley, and he was in, chewing on some junior constable for something or other. August never caught what.

But in a moment he was free.

August pierced the cigar smoke–coated room, and offered a hand to a man who had been feasting too much and too long and now had trouble holding his trousers up.

"August Beausoleil, sir. I own the show."

The top cop grunted, licked his lips, and waited.

"I thought you and the missus might enjoy the show, so I brought you some tickets. Front-center, third row, best in the house, perfect for variety. You get to look up every nostril."

He laid a pair of green tickets on the battered desk.

Riley eyed the tickets and grunted. He studied Beausoleil a little, and smiled.

"We'll be there. Behave yourself."

That was all there was to it.

"If you want two more, for tomorrow, matinee or evening, let me know," Beausoleil said. "Courtesy of the whole troupe."

"I bet," Riley said.

Beausoleil headed for fresh air, but then realized he was next door to the Lewis and Clark County Attorney. So he entered.

The gent was as skinny as a weasel, but mostly bald.

"Beausoleil, here, sir. I run the show at the opera house. A quick question. Is there some ordinance or local law I should know about?"

"Ask me after you've broken it."

"We want to give people a show they'll all enjoy. Especially women."

The skinny man yawned. "Good afternoon," he said.

"Would you like a couple of tickets?"

"I knew it. Soon as you walked in. You're here to grease the skids."

"Thought you might enjoy the show. We're proud of it. There's something for everyone in it."

"Time is precious, sir, and I don't squander it on entertainment."

"You have a list of the pertinent ordinances?"

"In the ledger." He jerked a thumb toward a gray ledger book. It was thick. The city fathers had been busy.

It wasn't hard to see where this was headed.

Beausoleil lifted his hat and headed for the pebbled glass door. The man stared, measuring the impresario for a black-and-white–striped costume. Walking through that door into the hall was like stepping out of a bat cave.

You never knew what you'd find when you and your company hit a town. The chill weather brought bold blue skies and a pine perfume off the mountains. There was an early dusting of snow up high, making the world virgin. He liked Helena as a place to visit but he'd never live there.

He'd done what he could. It was up to the acts now. The newspaper assault had made the rounds by now, and everyone in the company knew that there might be trouble. Some places didn't like to be entertained. Or they thought anyone in show business rose straight out of some devil's lair. But sometimes it was the reverse: show people sensed a holier-than-thou town and resented it. And their resentment showed up in the acts, no matter how professional they were. Some things couldn't be hidden. Beausoleil had occasionally gotten rid of an act because there was something about it that caused trouble. Sometimes nothing more than an attitude. Something that was a little like spit-

ting on an audience. Take this, you rummies. Like it or
leave.

But that was rare. More common was simply that each
venue was different. Some acts played well in some towns
and not others. Some acts bombed in a town that enjoyed
variety and welcomed any company that rolled in. What
prompted these shifting welcomes was a great mystery,
and August Beausoleil had tried out every theory he could
come up with, without getting anywhere. Running a road
company was largely guesswork and instinct. But there
was one thing he could always do: stay alert and try to
head off trouble.

He stopped at Ball's Drug Store to see how advance
sales were going, and wasn't surprised to learn that ninety
reserved seats for the night's show had been sold, and
more for the matinee and finale. Maybe his instinct was
right: that newspaper piece had stirred things up.

As the day faded and the lamps of evening were lit,
Beausoleil found himself in an anxious mood, which was
unusual. He was a veteran showman, a veteran with road
shows, and he usually took trouble with aplomb. But not
this evening. There was nothing but a hostile, even nasty,
newspaper piece between him and an ordinary show
night, but somehow this article, with its brooding menace, threatened him, threatened the show, threatened trouble of a legal and political sort, trouble that could mean
jail and fines and ruin.

He ate lightly, a bowl of soup, and could stomach no
more. At the opera house he found the acts were tense and
silent. So the newspaper assault had affected his people the
same way. As showtime approached, it became plain that
the evening would be a sellout. Crowds waited their turn
at the ticket window, plunking down dollars, picking up
green tickets, entering the quiet opera house a block above
Last Chance Gulch.

He stirred through his people, who were dressed and

waiting, ready for the curtain to sail into the flies and the Follies to begin.

"We're going to be just fine, just fine," he said. "A grand crowd. Enjoy yourselves."

A few grinned. Others didn't.

"We'll bail you out," he said.

Only Mary Mabel Markey smiled. She looked like a woman who had just been shrived.

FIVE

howtime. As always, seven minutes after the appointed hour. The limelight was lit, casting brilliant white illumination across the center of the stage, creating an anticipation of good things to come.

August Beausoleil, in his tux and stiff white bib, appeared suddenly, waited for the packed house to quiet, and welcomed these Helena people to the Follies.

"We are delighted to be in this handsome city, among such fine people," he said. "And now, to open our show, please greet the Wildroot Sisters."

The curtain flew up, and the limelight caught the girls in bright pastels, crouched together, and then they exploded out and into their first number, a lively heads-up song about big things coming.

August studied this crowd from his perch at the wing, and thought it looked good. Every seat had been sold, and now the crowd was settling in for the evening. In the third row was the police chief, and next to him what appeared to be a twenty-year-old wife, or a mistress or daughter. That was good news. The gals strutted, the accordion wheezed, and the girls won a quiet round of applause from an audience that seemed content enough.

Next was Harry the Juggler, who soon was tossing bowling pins, then tea cups and saucers, then baseballs, and then a mix of them all. Harry's act was short. People could take only so much tossing, even when the items were likely to break, which is what the audience waited for. He got polite applause. He'd do a second stint in the second act, juggling two knives and two scimitars. He was missing a finger, and August always wondered if that had been a juggling disaster. Harry was a loner, spoke Latvian or something, and sent his pay somewhere.

Next came the Marburys, one of the acts that was criticized in the press for violating womanhood.

"It's my delight to present, for the first time in the great state of Montana, the tap-dancing Marburys, who will show the world what's new."

They tapped out from the wing, Delilah in a calf-length frothy skirt, short by most standards but definitely female attire, and they soon were in an arm-in-arm pirouette, or buck-and-wing. August never knew the terminology, but the trio's obsession with bright dancing and intricate tapping was captivating the audience. And no one was complaining.

But August Beausoleil had a feel for things, and he knew that this crowd was waiting, and he knew what they were waiting for, and he hoped there wouldn't be another rotten fruit fight.

She was next. He sprang out into the limelight, feeling the heat of the device, bowed, and waited dramatically until there was deep quiet.

"And now, ladies and gents, one of the great attractions, brought to you from far across the Caribbean seas, in the tropics, in a world that few of us have ever known. The one, the only Mrs. McGivers and her Monkey Band."

The olio rose on the old gal, with the capuchin monkeys Abel and Cain on cymbals and drum, and her sagging accordionist wheezing his bellows to life. This was what they were waiting for out there, something scandalous. She let them absorb the rhythms, study the cheery little monkeys, and then she began singing, her corpulent body rising and sagging, her melodies hoarse and alien. The cymbals clanged, and the drum got banged, at first in an orderly manner, but the anarchistic monkeys were soon improvising, and leaping up on their seats, their arms gonging and hammering, even as the music became dissonant and at war. It was not a good sale for calypso.

Helena's theatergoers hardly knew what to make of it. But there was no flying fruit. And he heard an occasional chuckle. They were getting it: this began as languid tropical music, and was turning into anarchy, and that was the fun of it. She was the conductor of the Chaos Symphony. And some of those people were grinning.

Mrs. McGivers stood and swayed, formidable, like a tropical banana queen. The audience began to enjoy it. It didn't matter what she sang; no one could understand a word of it anyway, and the monkeys were more entertaining than the singer.

And no fruit. No rotten tomatoes.

Then the accordionist switched to a new tune, one Beausoliel hadn't heard before, a little like an organ grinder's street corner music, and sure enough, the monkeys pulled out tin cups and leapt into the two aisles, shaking the cups, which had a couple of pennies in them, soliciting coin from the audience. And the gents out there indulged the monkeys and pleased their wives by dropping nickels and dimes and even quarters into the cups, while everywhere people stood or craned necks to watch the rascally little monkeys extract boodle from pockets. And then, as fast as the accordionist had started this monkey business, he switched to another song, new marching orders, and the monkeys bounded for the stage and presented the loaded cups to Mrs. McGivers. She stood, bowed handsomely, accepted the coins like a priestess accepting a sacrament, and made her queenly way off-stage.

There were some chuckles out there. This audience had gotten its money's worth. Beausoleil watched Mrs. Mc-Givers, just offstage, empty the cups, slide the coins into a pocket, and go back for an encore, which was strictly calypso, restoring the tropics to Helena's Ming Opera House once again.

"Wasn't that fun! That was the famous Mrs. McGivers and her Monkey Band. Let's tell the world about her talented act." He waited for the final ripple of applause. "And now, my friends, the woman you've been waiting for, the one, the only, the celebrated Mary Mabel Markey."

She swept in, her posture erect, her shoulders thrown back to make her look a little more svelte. She had started to sag, but now, in the limelight, she exuded a brassy command of the whole world.

The audience clapped, glad to see the star of the show, the legend, the top-billed singer, with her accompanist, who played a flute. And then an odd thing struck Beausoleil. His star seemed distraught. Maybe that wasn't the word. He had no word for it, but she was taut and uncomfortable, this woman who was totally at ease singing in any place, for any group. It passed, but when she launched her first song, to the counterpoint of the flute, it wasn't as serene as usual. He couldn't say what was ailing, only that even though she seemed the same as ever, she wasn't. And listening carefully, he decided her voice was troubled. He suspected that two decades of singing on a stage, or maybe a street corner, had coarsened her vocal cords. He didn't know. But something wasn't right.

She sang a ballad about mothers, and another about sweethearts, and a final one about courage, and when she was finished, she bowed, and the audience clapped politely, and that was the heart of it. Polite clapping.

It troubled him more than he cared to admit. He was

suddenly worried about her; she was the most stable person in the company. She was the one he could count on in any emergency. If half the acts took sick, she could fill the bill. But there she was, a shadow over her as she slipped into the wing. He caught her hand, and she pulled it away. There was no encore.

It was just a passing moment. She'd be fine. But it would not vanish from his mind, even as he strode out to introduce the final act before intermission, which was Wayne Windsor, The Profile.

"Ladies and gentlemen, welcome the king of comedy, the legendary Wayne Windsor," he said, hastening the show along to cover the odd mood left by Mary Mabel Markey.

The Profile trotted out, bowed to the right audience and the left audience to give everyone a fine view of his noble brow and jut jaw, and then addressed the multitude:

"Now, I have it from the local paper, the excellent *Herald,* that there's some people of the better class in town. That's good news. I should like to meet you. Are there any people of the better class out there? Please wave a hand, and maybe we can all gather right here, in front of the footlights."

Beausoleil did not spot any waving hands out there. It was going to be a good evening. The Profile would say kind things about the better class. Some smiles were already building up.

"Surely," he said, "there are some better-class people in Helena. I'd be disappointed if there is not one person in this beautiful city who is not of the better class."

There sure was a lot of silence out there.

"Actually, the paper got it right. There is one person of the better class in Helena. Can you guess who?" He paused. "I'll give you a hint." He pointed a finger at himself.

The crowd laughed. Windsor smiled, and posed for a Napoleonic moment.

"Now I reached this status by inventing a form of accounting, a method widely used to keep the ledgers of both government and commerce. This accounting has a new feature, which directs one percent of all revenue into a certain charity, with offices in Kentucky, Argentina, and Australia, as well as the Principality of Monaco. . . ."

The audience had settled down to some good times, and was listening sharply for heresies and scandals. The Profile was doling out scandals slowly, making sure to shift his feet, giving the lucky listeners another view of his visage.

Beausoleil hurried to the Green Room looking for Mary Mabel, and found her alone, staring sternly at the wall. He knew better than to ask if she was ill.

"I'll sub LaVerne Wildroot for the last," he said.

"You will not."

"She won't hold a candle to you; it's just that you need a break."

"I don't need a break, and if you sub her, you can put me on the next train to New York."

"You're a little out of breath."

"What do you expect? Helena's not sea level."

"Yes, and Butte's much higher. You might have a bad time of it. You'll be up a mile, I understand."

"I will be out front, singing, every day, every performance."

"Mabel, you'll have top billing on this show. You don't need to worry. I'm giving you a break. You're worn-out. There's some young talent that can fill in."

"I am who I am. I am no one else. I have been the same all my life. I sang on street corners, and I'll sing until I can't. And when I can't you can put a yellow rose on my coffin."

He knew he had to ask the hard question. "All right, Mabel, but what if you can't sing well? Bad tonsils. Nothing comes out."

"Not sing well? That will be the day I die."

She sat there glaring, as granitic and unmoving as Gibraltar. He reached across, plucked up her icy hand, and squeezed it. She didn't respond.

He hurried up to the wings, wondering how the monologue was progressing. One thing about Wayne Windsor: every night was different, and sometimes there were a few jokers in his deck. He peered out from the edge of the arch, and saw exactly what he hoped. This crowd was devouring every word, sometimes anticipating Windsor ahead of his punch lines. The various acts hung around in the wings, just to scoop up whatever he was dishing out. He offered fresh talk in a show loaded with routine.

And there was Ethel Wildroot, over in the opposite wing watching The Profile. August Beausoleil sometimes wondered if the old gal had set her cap for the man. She rarely missed an act. August made his way behind a rear curtain, found her listening raptly, and summoned her back into the darkness.

"I may need the new act," he said. "Is LaVerne ready?"

"But you've given me no notice!"

"It may not happen. Mary Mabel's sick. Or at least she's off her form. I want to be ready."

"I'll go tell LaVerne and the accordion."

"Ethel. I'm not saying it'll happen. It's to be ready. Clear?"

"You could make it happen. You're the boss."

"I respect my talent, Ethel. Try to, anyway. All these years, I've respected my talent."

She glared. "Well, make up your mind. If I tell the girl she should be ready, then she's going on, whether or not Mary Mabel quits on you."

He took a chance. "Then don't tell LaVerne anything,

Ethel. Mary Mabel's an old trouper, and she can put the sun into a new orbit."

"She can't stop old age," Ethel said.

"Well," said Wayne Windsor, winding it up. "I will go forth and tell the world that there's no one of the better class in Helena, Montana."

People chuckled, and then clapped. Windsor awarded them with both profiles.

SIX

Mrs. McGivers sat comfortably in the wing, watching the second act. Unlike most of the performers, who retreated to the Green Room or out the side door for some air, she preferred to watch the performers. Sometimes it was instructive. More often, she caught mistakes and blunders and had something to enjoy.

Her act would be on soon, and she and Joseph would do things a little differently. He would use a guitar, and the Monkey Band would be racier than the first act. She was very good at undulating to Caribbean rhythms. And the end of the act would be anarchy when the monkeys took over.

Just now, though, the Marbury Trio was leading off, a sudden switch by August Beausoleil. He sometimes did that, when he was not entirely confident the variety show was doing well. One indicator was empty seats. If people returned after the break, that was a good sign. If some had abandoned the theater, that wasn't so good. But Mrs. McGivers' own peeks upon the sea of faces had led her to believe they had a happy crowd that cold Helena evening.

But now the audience was quiet. The tap dancers were tapping, a fiddle was making music, and the routine was going well. This time, though, Delilah was in a tuxedo and pants, like her two dancing partners, and all three had a gold-knobbed walking stick they used as a baton, and sometimes to punctuate a musical verse with a rap on the boards.

Mrs. McGivers thought it was just fine. Three great dancers doing great footwork, the taps clicking and rattling out into the dark, beyond the limelight. But not even the perfection of the act, the astonishing footwork, toe and heel tapping, the rattle of taps on boards, was loosening up the crowd for the second act.

Cain and Abel sat beside her, leashed, watching the tapping, which was new to them. They were imitating what they saw on-stage, making their monkey feet go, swaying the way Delilah swayed.

Messing with other people's acts was taboo, but Mrs. McGivers didn't care. There had never been a rule that contained her for long. She turned the capuchin monkeys loose.

"Go wiggle your butts," she said.

The little devils could hardly believe their good fortune. They eyed her, eyed the trio in the spotlight, and sprang out. The dancers, to their credit, didn't falter. The monkeys leaped right in and imitated the trio, while a ripple of delight rolled back through rows of seats. It took a moment for those at the back of the opera house to catch on. In the bright light were five, two monkeys and three tap dancers, all rat-tat-tatting along. Delilah, never one to miss a chance, handed her black walking stick to Cain, who went into paroxysms of joy, hammering the boards in perfect rhythm as the fiddler speeded up the game.

Now the crowd was undulant, whispering, tapping feet, and pointing. Cain and Abel were so integrated into the line of dancers that they seemed a part of the act, as if it had been rehearsed that way from the start. But it hadn't.

"What's this?" asked Beausoleil.

"A little pepper," Mrs. McGivers said.

"They got loose, eh?"

"Smart little devils," she said, which won an arched eyebrow from him.

He watched the tap dancers bow and exit, tapping their way off the stage, led by a pair of delinquent primates. Then, as the clapping subsided, he hastened out to introduce the next act, which was Wayne Windsor, doing another monologue.

Delilah Marbury stormed straight at Mrs. McGivers, who sat quietly.

"You ruined it. You wrecked the act."

"Probably needed wrecking, girl."

"We're dancers. Not some Punch-and-Judy show. Don't ever do that again."

"You have a good act, sweetheart. Just needs a little spice."

"Spice! We're dancing, and that's all we do. And we're good at it. I'm going to have it out with August."

"Guess you will, sweetheart. And don't be surprised by what he says."

Out front, the boss was introducing the next act. "And now, for your delectation, the finest comic in the country, the one, the only Wayne Windsor!"

The finest comic in the country hastened out for his second appearance, caught the light, allowed it to shine upon his left profile, and then his right, and smiled.

"I certainly enjoy Helena, Montana," he began. "It has great newspapers. I'm especially taken with the *Herald*. I was talking to one of its reporters a while ago, and I said, 'Sir, what are your qualifications? What makes you a good reporter?' And he eyed me sternly and he said, 'A quart a day.' Now I immediately knew I was in elevated company . . ."

Beausoleil returned, unbuttoned his tuxedo, and stood, listening.

You never knew about Windsor. Once in a while he caused a ruckus. Mrs. McGivers had seen moments when the audience was ready to lynch him. The man was a phenomenon. He did have a standard routine, but most of the time he improvised, somehow coming up with good quips and funny anecdotes that had a local flavor. He was superb at his craft, which was tickling the funny bone of audiences wherever the show performed.

When there was music out front, people in the wings could talk a little, but not when there was a monologuist or a silent animal act. So she sat and watched and listened, as interested in Beausoleil's responses as in the performance. And in truth, the boss was listening carefully, because Windsor was on perilous ground. Reporters got the last word.

"I asked this fellow what a reporter's job is, and he said a really good reporter hunts around for the truth and then hides it. I said, 'How do you hide it,' and he said, 'By printing it on the front page, where no one believes it.'"

That seemed to evoke a chuckle. Windsor decided that his other side needed exposure to the limelight, so he shifted and let the white glare fall upon the left-side view, with the high brow, fine long nose without a wart, and jut jaw tapering into a handsome neck.

The limelight flickered a bit. It was achieved by training a hot flame upon a block of quicklime, which threw out the eerie light that performers loved. In Windsor's case, he somehow became incandescent himself, throwing brightness out upon his rapt listeners. It was some trick, and sure wasn't anything she had picked up in the tropics. Some performers had all the luck, and he was one of them. Audiences enjoyed him even if they didn't love him. His comments were usually barbed, and while that evoked a few laughs, it sometimes evoked some rotten tomatoes. Either was just fine.

She saw the juggler waiting his turn. If juggling baseballs and cups and saucers was entertaining, the next stint with sharp blades would be riveting. How he managed to keep those knives and scimitars in the air at once, without cutting his hand off, was something of a mystery, though once he said that the knives were heavily leaded to the exact weight of the big scimitars, so he didn't have to vary the throw. One of these days, a scimitar would crash down on his neck like a guillotine, and that would be the end of the act. The audiences always hoped to see it, but he disappointed them. She scarcely knew him. He ghosted about, not really part of the company, and barely making friends.

Meanwhile, The Profile was having a fine time. "So I asked this reporter from the *Herald*, I say, 'Who edits your stuff? Who decides what goes on the page? Who corrects it?' And he says, 'The advertisers do.' He says, 'Peruna Tonic wields the blue pencil.' He says that the editor whom every reporter dreads is Mrs. Stewart's Bluing. She wants to get the yellow out of every story, and make it perfect blue-white, with no yellow tint anywhere. 'I tell you,' says he, 'there's no editor in the business like Mrs. Stewart's Bluing.'"

She heard an appreciative chuckle. The Profile was steadily scoring, pushing back against the local paper. Even as Delilah Marbury had gotten back into her tuxedo and pants just to affront the paper, so was The Profile nibbling away at the paper. And it wouldn't stop there. The whole vaudeville company would, in its own way, even the score.

The boss was enjoying it. A show that fights back is a show that gets itself an audience, and if Wayne Windsor wanted to even things up with the *Herald*, that was just fine.

When Windsor was done tickling their funny bones, he awarded them with left and right profiles, and trotted off. A fine round of applause lured him back for a bow, a quick right and left, and then he was done.

"Now how about that, ladies and gents? The incomparable Wayne Windsor," said Beausoleil. "And now, the one you've been waiting for: the world's finest juggler, straight from Vienna, Harry Drogomeister. Please welcome the one, the only man who will put himself in harm's way to show you his unparalleled skills."

Harry trotted out, armed with a lot of blades, including steel knives with heavy handles, and scimitars, curved swords with slasher edges on the interior curve, useful for beheadings. He didn't speak much English, so he simply bowed, this way, that way, accepting the ovation, and then he picked up the knives, two lethal weapons, and casually flipped one upward, and another, and another, deftly catching each as it descended, his hand clasping the handles, never touching the blades, faster and faster, until the limelight glittered off of flying steel. Then he caught them, set them down, and picked up a scimitar, ugly, sinister, menacing. He slashed air with it a few times, ran a finger along its wicked edge, and finally pitched it upward, where it rotated slowly before descending blade-first, and the juggler caught the handle and sent it looping up again.

The audience was rapt. What reckless thing were they seeing?

He added a second, each one requiring that it be caught by the handle and deftly tossed upward. People studied his hands, looking for missing digits and scars, but they saw none, or at least none was visible across the footlights. He whirled his swords faster and faster, making the loop smaller, a prodigy of deft maneuvering, and then collected the scimitars and bowed.

But he was not done. His next feat was almost beyond imagining. He started with the knives, adding them one by one, and slowly added the scimitars until he was juggling six deadly instruments, each one treacherous, each one requiring the most delicate propulsion. How he did it no one knew, but it always impressed Mrs. McGivers as something that required voodoo. It was simply beyond human sensibility.

But there he was, out there, in front of hundreds of people, some of whom hoped to see a disaster, while others feverishly prayed that the juggler would not shed gouting red blood all over the stage.

Which he did not. Somehow he plucked the scimitars out, set each one down, and then the knives, and never let any of them clatter to the boards.

He had worked up a sheen. He bowed, and listened to polite applause. Mrs. McGivers had never heard wild applause or huzzahs or bravos following this act. It was the applause of respect and relief, and maybe thanksgiving. For that is what she always felt when the juggler was done. There he was, whole, not dripping blood or writhing on the boards, killed by accident.

It was not just the audience. The whole company breathed relief when the juggler walked safely into the wings, while a stagehand picked up all his sinister hardware in the limelight. The audience had turned somber, and she spotted a few customers abandoning their seats. It was not, she thought, an act for children.

Mary Mabel Markey would be next. But Mrs. McGivers didn't see her. She was usually stationed in the wing, ahead of her act, ready to bloom onstage, somehow flowering sweetly as she paced into the brightness.

August Beausoleil was looking for her, too. He was ready, but where was the star of the Follies?

Where indeed? The best quick sub would be the Wildroot girls, but they were lounging in the Green Room. Beausoleil nodded to Mrs. McGivers, the unspoken gesture meaning to go look for the leading lady. So she abandoned her comfortable seat and lumbered toward the stairs, and only then did she encounter Madame Markey, panting, heaving her way forward, her face white and distraught.

She pushed right past Mrs. McGivers, and nodded to the master of ceremonies, who studied her briefly, nodded, and stepped into the light to welcome the top-billed singer and star of the Follies, who looked strangely chalky and afraid.

SEVEN

Mary Mabel Markey hurried to escape, feeling out of sorts. She slipped on a plain street dress, found her shawl, and headed through the Green Room hoping no one would waylay her.

But there was August, and she was trapped.

"Want to take a walk, Mary Mabel?"

"No, I'm tired, I'm going to bed."

"I think we'd better talk."

"Tomorrow," she said, heading for the stage door and the velvet cold of Helena at about eleven at night.

"I'll come with you," he said. "I like to escort a lady to safety."

"I'm not going to talk about it, so forget the gallantry."

She was alluding to the evening's performance, which she had struggled through, barely completing three songs, out of breath, off key, her stage presence lost, and that ineffable quality that had made her the queen of the vaudeville palaces utterly gone. The audience had welcomed her, then grown restless, then silent, and when it was over, the applause was tepid. She had smiled, stormed offstage, and neglected the final bow.

But as she stormed into the night, momentarily disoriented, not sure where the hotel was, he stuck with her. The last of the theatergoers were drifting away. Some of the cast had switched to street clothes and were heading for the nearest saloon. There were several lining Last Chance Gulch.

August Beausoleil would not be put off, and he caught her elbow and navigated down the steep grade.

"The air is thin here, and a singer can't get enough of it," he said.

"I told you I wouldn't talk about it."

"I was thinking some rest might help. We all wear ourselves to shreds on tour."

"I will not leave the show, and the show needs me, and you'd fall flat on your face if it wasn't for me."

"You are quite right, Mary Mabel. Absolutely. You're the draw."

He helped her down a long stair that took them into the gulch, where there was a little light spilling from windows. The quiet air bit at her cheeks and ears. Helena was cold and hard.

"But," he added, "I'm thinking you need a few days' rest, and we'll manage. Some time with your head on a warm pillow should give you more air."

"I don't need air. And I have no intention of letting La-Verne Wildroot substitute for me. She'd drive the crowd right out the door. You'd be paying refunds."

"I haven't heard her. She has some songs worked up, Ethel says."

"Ethel has a tin ear."

"The mothers of entertainers tend to have tin ears, yes. Mary Mabel, your slot is yours. I'm simply hoping that a little bed rest will put you back where you belong."

"You won't get rid of me that easily, August Beausoleil."

"It's my object to keep you."

"Then we won't talk about this again."

"We may have to if your act continues to weaken your hold upon your admirers."

She relented a little. "I won't be toyed with," she said.

He nodded. They both knew he wasn't toying with her. He was a discreet and sensitive impresario, with a knack for placating unhappy talent. She would give him that. He said no more, but she knew it was far from over. She felt out of breath; the mountain air didn't seem to satisfy the craving of her body for more oxygen. Her pulse raced, and she ached. She wondered sometimes why she was a performer. No one in the business lived quietly, safe and rested in a nest somewhere.

If Helena did this to her, how would she survive Butte, which was much higher? She felt dizzy again, and felt his firm grip on her elbow, steadying her. They headed up the Gulch, found the dim-lit door to the hotel, and entered. It wasn't much warmer inside the tiny lobby, but somehow it was welcoming.

"I will see you to your room."

He never did that. It alarmed her. She ran through the reasons, and concluded that he was escorting her to her door for the worst of them: he feared she would collapse before she got to her room. He had read her well. She was wobbly on her pins, rasping for air, and she hurt. Her vocal cords hurt. They often hurt a bit, but not like this. Her voice had thickened. During her act, the sweetness that had won ardent admirers had vanished, and what emerged this night was thick and nasal and without the maidenly quality that had made her a celebrated singer with a silvery high range.

He paused at the door, while she dug for a key.

"You've given your all to the Follies, Mary Mabel. I know you'll continue."

"If that's a warning, lay off."

"I need to do some accounting," he said. "We had a full house."

He tipped his hat and vanished. She was angry with him for no good reason. She'd had a miserable night, sometimes so faint onstage that she wondered if she should sit down and sing from a chair. All those Mary Mabel Markey admirers had been disappointed. It wasn't blatant. She had pushed air through her throat, forced her lungs, delivered every ounce she could, even as she grew horrified and desperate at her own performance up there in the limelight.

She'd had a few bad nights, sick nights, nights when the stage was so cold, or so hot, it made her dizzy to sing. But nothing like this night, which is what terrified her. She slipped the skeleton key into the door, and swung it open. It wasn't the fanciest place in Helena—show people didn't live like that—but it had a soft bed, a taut red blanket drawn over it, and a good white pillow in a slip that wasn't yellowed. Tonight any bed would be paradise.

She slipped down the hall to the water closet that served six rooms, found it empty, and prepared herself for the night to come. She washed her face in cold water, studying it. She was still young, or at least not seamed and gray. She had a dozen more years at the top of the heap if she wanted that. But she didn't like this dizziness, or the aching arms and chest and neck, so she hastened to her room, slipped into her white flannel bedclothes, and tumbled into the bed.

But the weariness wouldn't release. Her racing pulse wouldn't slow. She lay angrily, not wanting to know what was troubling her, and not wanting to learn about it from stupid doctors who didn't know, either.

In the morning she sought out Marcus Aurelius Flannigan, MD, who practiced in the front parlor of his home on the other side of Last Chance Gulch. It had to be a morning appointment; she had a matinee that afternoon, and an evening performance. There were two doctors in Helena, so she chose the one with the most imposing name, on the theory that he knew more.

He welcomed her and led her to his parlor, fitted up as an examination room, with square bottles lining the walls and instruments of torture lying about.

He wore a gray swallowtail coat, and had a closely cropped beard, and hair in his nostrils.

"I am Mary Mabel Markey," she said, but that elicited no response. "If you are overly familiar with me, and talk about it, I will consider it an offense against me."

"I practice medicine," he said, and nothing more.

"I may have the vapors. Find it out at once, and give me some powders. I have a matinee this afternoon."

He pursed his lips, registering that. "What powders do you have in mind?" he asked.

"You're the doctor. Take twenty years off me."

"Well, if you'll take twenty off me, I'll take twenty off you," he said. "Sit right there and tell me what's ailing you."

She seated herself on an examination table, eyeing him suspiciously. She was fussy about who did what with Mary Mabel Markey.

"I'm waiting," he said.

"I am dizzy. My strength vanishes. My neck and arms hurt. My left arm. My chest hurts. I have no air. I can't get enough. It's the altitude. I'm cold at night. My throat bothers me, especially when I sing 'Sweet Lover Be Mine.' My throat's a little better when I sing 'Wayward Girl, Whither Goest Thou?' But I have trouble with the high notes, and the lowest ranges seem a little coarse. Not like me at all. And I almost fainted, twice. And they were all waiting in the wings for me to keel over, but I foiled them."

"I am going to see about your circulation," he said.

"I don't circulate."

He had one of those listening tubes in hand, and pressed it on her chest, suspiciously close to her bosom, but she let it pass. He listened carefully, moving the instrument about, being all too familiar, but what could you expect of a man named after a Roman emperor?

"Breathe in and out," he said. He was listening at her side, her back.

He took her pulse, his hand firm on her wrist, his eye on a pocket watch with a second hand. He poked around in her mouth, the fountain of her fame, with a tongue depressor, using a carbide lamp for illumination. Tongue, gums, nostrils. Neck glands. He also peered into her eyes, one by one, with some sort of lens, which annoyed her. That was all the apertures she intended for him to examine. Knee tap. He checked her ankles for swelling, his hand lingering there, probing.

He asked the usual questions. How long have you felt this? You get faint standing up? How about sitting down? What powders are you using? Have you had any other examination?

She was inclined not to answer him because he was becoming personal, and she was Mary Mabel Markey, and doctors who wore swallowtail coats were obviously suspect. Clothing could cloak incompetence. Where did he go to medical college, and what was he doing in a raw, tawdry town like Helena, full of politicians and miners and crooks?

No one in his right mind would live in Montana except to get rich quick and get out.

"Your pulse is high, ninety-five, and erratic. Your heartbeat's erratic and not regular. Your left ventricle's misfiring, is the way I could best put it. You have heart trouble."

"I do not. It's the altitude."

He sighed. "That'll be three dollars."

"What do you mean? Are you done with me?"

"You just announced that my diagnosis is wrong, and it's altitude. Three dollars, and you may head for your matinee."

"Of course it's wrong. So why should I pay?"

He stared out the window for a moment. "You're in great peril of an attack. You've had some small ones. There's not much to do for it but lose weight. You would profit from losing ten or fifteen pounds."

"I am Mary Mabel Markey and I won't listen to malicious talk."

"You would also do better at lower altitudes. You'll breathe better at sea level. And certainly live in less peril."

"I knew it. My rivals have paid you off. I'll want some powders now."

He contemplated that. "I saw no major problems with your throat. But it would take special lighting equipment, incandescent light beamed in, to tell you more. Until Helena's got electricity, I'm limited. But I would suggest temporarily retiring from your company, and spending a few months at a seashore."

"I want powders."

"Any powders I might prescribe would have no effect on your heart, nor would they improve your breathing, and they'd probably weaken your voice."

"But they'd stop pain."

"Dover's Powder, opium, would stop pain, and so would any of the cough syrups with opium in them. They would all damage your voice. And the longer you use them, the higher the dose you'd need to subdue your demons."

"I want powders."

He eyed her gravely. "I'm sure you do. And they would be your ruin. When you sing 'Sweet Lover Be Mine,' you may not receive the ovation, the response, you expected."

She saw that he was not going to budge, so she pulled out two dollars and slapped them on the examination table.

He eyed the two dollars, eyed her, and nodded. An odd amusement filled his face. But he didn't argue.

She left in a tantrum, headed for the nearest apothe-cary shop, purchased a bottle of Dover's Powder in tablet form, and some Williams' New England Cough Syrup, opium in an alcohol solution, and headed for the matinee.

EIGHT

The house was filling up. August Beausoleil eyed the rough crowd, wondering what brought them to the matinee on a bright autumn afternoon. They were miners. The matinee price was seventy-five cents and two bits for gallery seats. They would enjoy the show, have money to spare for a few drinks before heading for the outlying gold mines. Or so he was told. They were not gentlemen in cravats, and there were few women out there.

That was unusual. In most places, matinees were for women and children, who could see the show and reach their homes safely before dark. But not this crowd. He saw bearded men wearing bib overalls, pale men who worked far from sunlight. Men with big, rough hands. And one or two with a flask in hand. Many of them lived in remote barracks and hadn't seen a woman in a week.

A quiet descended as curtain time neared. These were men starved for company, starved for entertainment, ready to lap up whatever was put on their plate. It would likely be the best sort of audience, generous and happy and forgiving, if one or another performer failed.

All right, then. The audience had settled. He nodded, and the curtain rolled skyward, revealing himself, center stage, in the bright white light of the lime. This would be a dandy afternoon. A faint foreboding skittered past him, and he ignored it.

"Ladies, gents, welcome to the Beausoleil Brothers Follies," he said. "We're here in beautiful Helena, the proudest town in Montana. Now, to welcome you, meet the Wildroot Sisters, Cookie, Marge, and LaVerne. Let's give them all a big hand."

Indeed, applause rose upward as the three young ladies danced out, in the order by which they had been introduced. And quickly, they broke into song, "Yankee Doodle Dandy," always a good opener that swelled up a little national fervor.

Beausoleil discreetly abandoned the stage, and waited in the wings.

The girls wore shimmery taffeta, rose and turquoise, which rippled with light and movement and added to the luster of the opening. It was all fine, fine, another opening, another matinee.

Several acts appeared, juggling, tap dancing, and the audience delighted in them, and waited for the one that had brought them. Beausoleil knew they were waiting, didn't quite know why, but knew he'd soon find out.

Mary Mabel sat quietly, almost remote, dressed in her show costume, her corset giving her a wasp waist and pushing her bosom high. She was oddly serene. Usually, as her turn loomed, she was blooming with energy, some inner fires heating up for the performance. But now she watched, distant, all too quiet.

"You're fine, Mary Mabel?" he asked.

She replied with a little wave of her hand. It was a white hand she rubbed with sheep lanolin daily to hide the wrinkles. Now it was soft and languid. She peered up at him with enormous eyes, and smiled. Her quietness disturbed him almost as much as the agitation that had given a ragged tone to her act the day before.

"The show is a king," he said. "It commands us."

She nodded, still strangely quiet, the shadowed light hiding her from him.

"All right, here we go," he said.

She stood, languidly.

He adjusted his tuxedo, made sure the attached white bib was reasonably clean, and plunged out just as the applause was fading. He was always conscious of pace, and hated dead moments. So now he strode into the shocking light even as the clapping echoed through the hall, and waited for all those miners to settle into the next act, the big act, the one he knew had brought them, the one for which they had laid out seventy-five cents and slipped into a theater seat.

The light momentarily blinded him, as usual, but soon enough he could make out those rows of males before him. And he could smell them. This was not a perfumed crowd, not for this Saturday matinee.

"And now, the lady you've been waiting for, the one, the only Miss Mary Mabel Markey! Welcome our sweetheart!"

Some of those miners cheered; most clapped amiably, and settled into their seats. She moved languidly past the arch, into the light, and somehow instantly quieted the crowd. Some performers could do that. Her mere presence was all it took.

She smiled right and left, almost a Wayne Windsor performance, letting all those lusty men have a gander at that hourglass form.

This would be good, he thought. He guessed she'd sing three. Usually it was two, but a little adoration sometimes stirred her juices.

She would sing a capella. She usually did. That was one of the qualities that had made her a legend. She smiled, took a breath, and began. But she produced only a squawk. She smiled, nodded, touched her throat, and plunged in again, and that yielded another throaty rumble. She seemed puzzled. The whole house was watching, transfixed.

She smiled, captured a breath, and tried again, this time landing heavily on a note, until it died. She seemed utterly bewildered. How could this be? She peered right and left, and offstage, and there was no help. She smiled helplessly, cleared her throat, and tackled her opening of "Blue Eyes" once again, only to have it strangle in her mouth. She seemed utterly befuddled.

Beausoleil was just as befuddled, but he was a veteran at rescuing beached acts, and hastened out, blinded by light.

"A bit of laryngitis, is it?"

She nodded.

"We'll see if things clear up. Ladies and gents, our beloved Miss Markey is out of voice, at least for the moment. This is most regrettable, but can't be helped. We hope our favorite singer will be fine for the next act."

But she was shaking her head.

"We'll count on it," he said.

That crowd slowly absorbed it. They wouldn't be hearing their favorite, Miss Mary Mabel Markey. Not this afternoon. The miners stirred, restless, uncertain about something. Mary Mabel bowed, meandered offstage, in no hurry, and with no particular concern about all of this. He glanced her way, puzzled, wondering who to run next. Probably the tap dancers. The show needed something lively just then, something to wipe away this odd interlude.

And then some fellow out in the house was talking. He stood up.

"You mind if I come up there? We have a little something for the lady," he said.

"After the show, sir. Time to roll out the next act."

"It's a gift for Miss Markey, sir. We came here to present her with something. It's gotta be now, or we'll lose our chance."

August Beausoleil was flexible. You had to be flexible, sometimes bending backward, to run a variety show. He'd always argued that every town had a surprise waiting for him. And so he waved the man forward, with a flourish, and then hastened backstage to find Mary Mabel, who was standing numbly in the wings. There was something plenty strange about her.

"Come," he said.

She strode out obediently, ahead of him, and won a lively round of applause, even as the miner, a black-bearded fellow, clambered up a stair to the boards.

He was carrying a little white box, and seemed perfectly at home on the bright side of the lights.

Beausoleil steadied Mary Mabel Markey, who seemed as slippery as soft butter, and steered her around so she was facing the gent.

He grinned, nodded to some of his friends out there, and plunged in:

"Ma'am, me and my crew, we got to thinking that you're the girl we'd like have serenade us. We saw your picture in *The Police Gazette,* and one of us heard you in St. Louis, and said you're a nightingale, and you can sing for us any time. Anyway, we've decided you're The Montana Nugget, meaning no offense of course, and we got together to give you a nugget, one of the biggest ever hauled out of the ground around here. This one's over an ounce, and it's all for you."

He handed her the box. His crew cheered. The rest clapped. She slowly undid a blue ribbon, pulled open the pasteboard, and spotted an irregular blob of native gold.

She smiled, lifted up the shining gold for all to see, and then planted a big smack of a kiss squarely on his hairy lips. And she added another and a big squeeze for good measure. And one more to make the point.

"You're my boy," she said, in a voice bordering on basso.

Beausoleil shook the man's hand. "And your name, sir?"

"Aw, just call me Fandango."

"All right, Fandango, you've brought blessings to Miss Markey, and pleasure to the Follies. We all thank you. What a fine audience! Montana takes the cake."

Fandango retreated to his seat, Beausoleil welcomed Wayne Windsor, and hastened to the wing, looking for Mary Mabel. He found her meandering back toward the Green Room, and steered her in. They were alone, with just one lamp lit.

She plunked herself in a chair.

"What's the story?" he asked.

"Oh, I'll get past it," she muttered, still basso.

"Your throat?"

"The cough syrup. And the pill."

"Show me."

She found a handbag and handed it to him. He opened it, found the brown bottle of Williams' New England Cough Syrup, and the pasteboard box of tablets. The labels didn't say much, but he didn't need to learn what he already knew.

"We'll sub for the evening show, and your second act," he said.

Then she was crying. He knelt beside her, pulled her close, gently wiped her flushed face, ran a hand through her uncombed hair, and kissed her softly on her forehead.

"You're my star, and you always will be," he said.

"I was born that way."

"Come out for the curtain call," he said.

"I'm so dizzy."

She seemed almost inert as he held her, and he wondered if she would ever grace his stage again. He could feel it, something ebbing within her. He wondered how ill she was, and how deeply the pain ran through her body.

"Wayne's winding up," he said. "You rest."

He trotted upstairs, and found Windsor showing his right and left profiles to all those miners. He had managed to win them over, and now they were chuckling regularly. He was still mining the *Herald* story.

Ethel Wildroot aimed straight at him, and it was too late for him to escape.

"She was drunk!" Ethel yelled.

Beausoleil thrust a finger to his lips. Talk in the wings was forbidden during the silent acts; you could whisper something during the musical ones. Yelling was a felony.

"Drunk as a skunk," she added, deliberately loud enough to reach the first few rows.

Beausoleil shook his head, and grabbed her elbow, and steered her away, finally reaching a rear corner of the commodious backstage.

"No, she wasn't. She's sick."

"Sick, my eye. Why are you covering up?"

She still was loud enough to disturb Windsor's act, so he just pressed a finger to his lips, and to hers.

That turned her into a hissing teakettle.

"The woman's an old drunk," she whispered, loud enough to rattle windows. "I don't know why you put up with it. Treating you that way. Her voice's gone to seed, and the way she abuses it, it's done. She's a has-been. Yet you stick with her, mollycoddle her. What's the matter with you? There's talent, there's good voices, there's people like LaVerne, ready to step up, to fill the stage and shine, but you stick with that derelict."

"Later," he said softly. "Not now. You're out of line."

"You don't even give LaVerne a chance. She could turn this around. She could knock all those miners out of their heads."

"That isn't what we have in mind, Ethel," he said, softly enough so maybe she would get the message. He could hear Windsor winding up. It was odd how rhythm played a role in his monologues, and the faster the laughs lapped each other, the closer he was to finishing.

"Gotta go," he said, abandoning her. But she boiled right along beside him.

"That whole business. She doesn't have laryngitis. She has whiskey-itis. And it's wrecked her voice. And you pay her three times more than she's worth. She's thirty-nine!"

"Ethel—stop."

She smiled suddenly and patted his arm. "You know what you're doing," she said.

NINE

Ethel Wildroot was elated. LaVerne would do a solo at last. Ethel discovered LaVerne in the Green Room, playing solitaire.

"Get ready. You'll sub for Mary Mabel second act."

"Who says?"

"He's got no choice. You get yourself gingered up and be ready."

"What did he say?"

"He said Mary Mabel's sick, and if she's better, she'll go on. Actually, she's drunk."

"I haven't done the songs in days."

Ethel glared at her. "Now's your chance."

"I should be happy?"

That was the trouble with LaVerne. She didn't come from theater family. Not like Ethel's daughters. Marge and Cookie looked too much like their father, the comedian Wally Wildroot, which was why Ethel brought her niece LaVerne into the act. LaVerne actually looked like Ethel herself, halfway pretty. Marge and Cookie had inherited all the wrong features, and they weren't going anywhere in vaudeville. Rotten Wally Wildroot had sired two jut-jawed girls with bad voices that were beyond redemption,

even though Ethel had paid for lessons. They were doomed
to be blues singers in Memphis, but Ethel wasn't ready to
tell them that. Not yet. They had bad teeth, too. LaVerne
could sing when she felt like it, but she didn't care if the
audience was ten people or two hundred. It sure was hard
to create a good act.

"What'll you sing?"

"Whatever you want."

"You'll sing 'Waltz Me Tonight,' and 'Ta-Ra-Ra Boom-
Dee-Ay.' And for an encore, 'Warm My Hand.'"

"All right," LaVerne said, and returned to her cards.

"LaVerne, I've brought you into the act, and given you
top billing. You owe me a performance that they won't
forget. This afternoon. Now. Get ready."

"Sure, Ethel."

"I'll get you more money. You'll reach the top. All I'll
want is an agency fee."

"Sure, Ethel."

"The second act's coming right up. Shouldn't you be
talking to the music?"

"Just tell him."

The music was any of several people in the show. The
Wildroots borrowed an accordionist or a fiddler, or sometimes a clarinetist, and gave him a couple of dollars.

"I'll get Willie," Ethel said. Willie made music for the
tap dancers.

LaVerne was no Mary Mabel Markey. She needed
backup. Ethel hastened to the stage door, where Willie
usually smoked cheroots and watched the pedestrians
during matinees, and there he was, fingers stained brown,
sucking a fat nickel cigar.

"LaVerne's subbing for Mary Mabel, so be ready," she
said.

"It's LaVerne's big chance," Willie said.

"It's only a matinee, Willie."

Willie smiled. "Have her show some ankle."

"You would say that, wouldn't you?"

"Bunch of miners out there."

It wasn't a bad idea. She'd advise LaVerne to appeal to the male animal.

"Vaudeville's elevated and spiritual," she said.

Willie grinned maliciously.

The second act rolled along, the Helena afternoon bright and chill. Harry the Juggler put on a good show, but nothing compared to a sword swallower. There were only a handful of those, and they all played the big circuits back east. Imagine slowly lowering a double-edged sword, right to the hilt, down your gullet. People always waited for the sword swallower to eviscerate himself. But so did they wait for Harry to behead himself with those flying scimitars, and that was almost as good.

She had seen Harry lose a scimitar only once, when a gust of air hit a playhouse back in St. Louis, pushed open a double door, sending a gale straight across the stage. It also blew out some footlights. Harry had picked up the scimitar, smiled, and did the deal all over. Except for the missing finger, Harry was unbloodied even after a dozen years in variety shows. But he was so quiet that some people thought a stray knife had cut out his tongue.

The miners clapped politely, and Beausoleil introduced the tap dancers again, and the trio did that strange loose-jointed clatter that Ethel couldn't call a dance, and couldn't call gymnastics, and probably came out of some plantation somewhere down south. Oh, well. Vaudeville was always trying out new acts, and sometimes one clicked. Not this one, though. Ethel knew it was doomed. Tap dancing was a passing novelty, and there wasn't enough to it to catch an audience.

LaVerne stood quietly in the wings. She had on a short green skirt and scooped blouse, mostly because Ethel had told her to wear that outfit. Willie's accordion sagged across his belly.

Beausoleil trotted into the bright light.

"And now, ladies and gents, something special. Mary Mabel Markey, once again."

It was as if an anarchist had thrown a bomb under the duke's carriage.

"Mary Mabel Markey, the world's sweetheart, is going to hum her songs tonight, gents and ladies. You know the words. She knows the words, but they're locked up in her throat this rare afternoon. So may I present, the world's sweetheart, Mary Mabel Markey."

Mary Mabel swirled out of nowhere, head to toe in pale blue velvet, with only a strand of pearls to relieve the sky blue gown.

She would hum, sore-throated, a capella.

And she did. She started softly, so softly the audience strained to hear her, but slowly Mary Mabel Markey triumphed over lyrics, and let melody steal her act, melody rising from her throat, low and soft as velvet, sweet as whispered love.

The effect was unearthly. Ethel was enthralled, in spite of a wish to tear the opera house to pieces. Mary Mabel swayed softly, small and vulnerable, yet powerful and sweet. Not a word was spoken. Her lips never formed them, but only formed a soft aperture. When she finished, and the opera house was caught in quiet, she bowed. And her audience leapt up and cheered.

LaVerne, across the stage in the opposite wing, stared. The accordionist yawned.

Mary Mabel started another, soft as a lullaby, her throaty voice rising from some new place in her body, almost down in her stomach. It never broke. It had innocence in it, somehow transforming Mary Mabel Markey into a woman waiting for her lover. Beausoleil watched from the wing: The other acts, drawn to this phenomenon, were watching too, the Green Room abandoned. And then when it was done, Mary Mabel took her sky-blue bow, and bowed again, and vanished.

It was not a tumultuous applause, but one suited to the mood, warm and polite and affectionate. Somehow, Mary Mabel Markey had triumphed over her sore throat. She disappeared, not pausing to stand offstage, gone for the rest of the matinee.

August Beausoleil looked pensive. He was thinking about all this. They all were. But finally, after an unduly long pause, he headed into the white light, nodded at the miners, and very quietly introduced Wayne Windsor, The Profile.

"I'm the two-spot following the Queen of Hearts," Windsor said.

Ethel listened a bit, curious about the miners out there, wondering whether they would simply shut out Windsor, but he soon was digging up chuckles. Windsor had his own gifts.

"Be ready," Beausoleil said.

"LaVerne?"

"You've been asking."

He was shuffling the acts again. She hastened to the Green Room, found LaVerne at her solitaire, bullied her to the stage, and collected Willie from the alley behind the opera house.

"Ladies and gents, something special now, direct from Brooklyn, New York, the Miners' Heartthrob, LaVerne LaTour. Welcome Miss LaTour."

"The what?" Ethel asked, pushing her niece into the limelight. She heard scattered applause as LaVerne stumbled out, smiled, waited for Willie to crank up his squeeze box; then she bowed, did a little pirouette, and plunged into "Waltz Me Tonight."

She wasn't half bad. She kicked up a little, displayed

that slim ankle, worked at seducing the crowd, and sailed through without winning any hearts. She knew it, and worked harder at "Ta-Ra-Ra Boom-Dee-Ay," which somehow didn't work on this crowd, either.

Ethel watched, revelation opening her mind, aware that this niece of hers lacked talent, would never have talent, and no amount of rehearsal and revamping the act would give her talent. She was adequate as one of the Wildroot Sisters, buried in three-part harmony, but not solo.

Ethel glanced at Beausoleil, who stared impassively. The impresario had seen plenty of nondescript acts come and go, and this one just went and wouldn't return.

He smiled at Ethel, and that smile spoke a million words.

There was no encore. LaVerne could read applause as well as anyone. She and Willie retreated to the wings, and Beausoleil trotted out.

"Give that lady a big hand," he said. "LaVerne LaTour. The Brooklyn siren."

The crowd didn't.

It was odd how careers ended in vaudeville. One day you're on, in the white light, the next day you're barely someone's recollection.

LaVerne looked relieved.

Mrs. McGivers and her Monkey Band were out there, and the crowd was already buzzing with delight at the sight of the capuchin monkeys in gold-and-red uniforms. Suddenly the whole stage was tropical. That was the thing about Mrs. McGivers. The audience just knew it was about to have some fun.

Ethel caught up with LaVerne, who was returning to her card game.

"He shouldn't have put you so close to Mary Mabel," Ethel said.

"I can figure it out as well as anyone," LaVerne said. "So quit knocking me."

That's how the new act vanished. Not a word of rebuke, not a word of regret. In truth, LaVerne didn't really care. But Ethel cared. The Wildroot Sisters act didn't earn much; it had to feed three singers and their manager. And pay a musician. LaVerne wasn't a bit disappointed, but Ethel was.

She rebuked herself for luring her niece into the business. The girl would have been happier living in prosaic wedlock and motherhood somewhere, rather than on the circuit. And this tour had barely started.

Ethel heard the raucous sounds of the Monkey Band, the erratic cymbals, the crazy drumming, the rowdy Mrs. McGivers. That was a good act; vaguely scandalous, though it was hard to say why. It was Mrs. McGivers herself who oozed impropriety of some sort, looking loose and wicked.

Ethel remembered when she and Wally Wildroot were an act. He was a mean comedian, the sort who jabbed and sneered and stabbed. And she was his foil. She in her blond wig. He would ask a question, she would reply, and he would have fun at her expense. She played the dumb blond lady, and he played the superior sophisticate. That was okay, but what wasn't so much fun was the offstage relationship, which was no different from what went on in front of those heckling audiences. After two baby girls and years of abuse and comedy that wore thinner and thinner, she had quit the act cold. She walked out. And it turned out his act was no good alone, without some female to ridicule, and he hated her for it. They never bothered with a divorce, just drifted this way and that, and he disappeared. Last she knew, he was in New Orleans in some steamy dive, making a two-bit living. And she had put together the Wildroot Sisters, which barely survived, even in two-bit shows like this one.

She needed a new act. She knew the entire art of making a joke. She wondered whether she could make it as a comedienne, making fun of some male oaf. Turn the tables. Would these miners enjoy the switcheroo? Could she pull it off? She sure didn't know, but she needed an act, and she knew how to do an act, and it would work if she could find the right foil, a male who'd be her punching bag. There had to be somebody in the outfit, but she couldn't think of anyone. Could she make wiseacre comments as Harry juggled? Could she and Mrs. McGivers trade insults? Could she work out a comedy routine with August? She sure didn't think so. August was practically a saint. She'd never heard him give offense to anyone. Too bad. That was one reason it was a third-rate show touring weary little burgs out in the West, far from the big time. Really big-time operators always wounded everyone around them.

TEN

Ginger. She would never be anyone else. She would have no surname. She would be known only as Ginger. She was not sure she liked the name, but it was as far removed from her real name as she could make it. Her real name would be buried this day, all three parts of it, and never again spoken. That part of her had ceased to exist.

Some of it was to conceal herself from her family and its minions, who would be watching hawk-eyed for the young woman with the birth names she had abandoned. By choosing to be Ginger, she was escaping a velvet prison. She was taking great care not to be discovered and forcibly restored to her mother and father. She was an only child, and that had been part of the trouble.

Weeks earlier, she had bought coach tickets that would take her to Butte, Montana, on a roundabout route. She hoped to meet Destiny there in the mining town, but there was no assurance of it. She only knew she had to do this, was desperate to do it, and would have no regrets, no matter what the outcome.

Her father was the supervisor of the Union Pacific division that probed from Utah up into the mountainous reaches of Idaho, and served the mining towns scattered across the state. She had lived most of her life in a generous home in Pocatello Junction, a haven of space and sunlight and comfort, even as the rude town bloomed into a civilized city serving ranches and reservations nearby.

There, in sunny circumstances, her parents had doted on her, and turned her into a musical prodigy, through constant employment of the best tutors. She could sing sweetly, and with all the nuance of an educated voice. She could play the family's Steinway as masterfully as she could sing ballads, opera, light opera, and hymns. She was a prodigy, a marvel for her eighteen years, a peer of anyone ever taught in the salons of New York.

She had practiced dutifully, performed for her parents and their affluent friends, won the attention of choir directors and orchestra conductors. Her mother doted on her, found vicarious delight in her, boasted of her, demanded that she continue her musical career, and insisted that she surrender everything else in her life. All of which was seconded by her father, who offered to spend whatever it took, bring in whatever tutor was required, to turn her into the most accomplished daughter in all of Idaho, if not the West.

All of which had grated more and more upon her as she realized how totally she was her parents' puppet, the rag doll who was permitted no ambition of her own but was simply the hope chest of every dream her mother harbored. That she was an only child only made matters worse. That she lived in a small town, just setting aside its rude frontier beginnings, only threw a light on her, and made her much more visible than if she had been a prodigy in, say, San Francisco, or Chicago.

But this nightingale in the gilded cage had discovered that the attention lavished upon her was a prison, that no one had ever asked her what she would like to do with her life, that no one had noticed the deepening melancholia as she watched the world through barred windows. She had few gentleman friends; her parents would not allow her to cultivate any.

She had struggled to carve some liberty out of her schedule, but all these efforts, timid at first, and then more urgent, had been sloughed aside, dismissed with a maternal smile, a small joke, a wave of a ring-encrusted hand. Somehow, in the preceding months, she had realized that she had to escape or die. Yes, she believed, die. If she stayed longer, her mother would own this daughter, possessing everything.

Ginger, a chosen name, was as far removed from her nature as she could imagine. Ginger was sharp and bright. Ginger was spunky. And there never had been a Ginger in her father's family or her mother's.

She had to escape. Vanish and never be found. She hadn't the faintest idea of what to do, and didn't even know how to make a plan and execute it. But as adulthood approached, so did desperation. One day, while reading the Pocatello paper, she discovered a tiny story about a vaudeville company traveling through the Northwest. The Beausoleil Brothers Follies would play in Helena that November, then Butte, then Philipsburg, then Missoula, and then head for the coast. She barely knew these places. She barely knew what sort of acts appeared in a vaudeville show. But they employed singers, and she could also play the piano with virtuoso skill, or so they said. And she had secretly mastered a few ballads, not just arias or hymns, but songs real people sang. Ballads about love.

She wished to audition in Butte. In vaudeville! The

Union Pacific would take her to Ogden. The Utah & Northern would take her to Butte. She knew something about railroads; her father ran them. She was not lacking in cash. She had always been free to indulge herself in dresses and suits and skirts and shoes and parasols and gloves. Cash was there for the asking.

She knew a little about vaudeville, or at least variety theater. Small shows had come to Pocatello, gotten a crowd, and left. Her parents had disapproved of them. Barbaric entertainments, not suited for people of substance. She didn't know whether she approved of them, but now she saw the Beausoleil show as a vehicle, a carriage to a new life, whatever that life might be.

Of course she could say nothing, not even express a wish. She would horrify her singing coach, her piano teacher, her other tutors, and her parents. Vaudeville? That would be like throwing away her life.

One day she bought a coach ticket to Ogden, and another from there to Butte. She would need to intercept the vaudeville company and audition for it. Her heart was not aflutter. She would plan and execute this escape, and if it failed she would find something else. She would be unescorted, and she knew that could pose dangers, but there was no point in worrying about anything. She was not anxious. The day she decided she would no longer be a prodigy, she ceased worrying. She accumulated greenbacks, eventually acquiring a hundred dollars, which she concealed in various pockets.

She wondered whether she might feel a pang upon slipping away. These were her parents, after all, Will and Mazeppa Jones, and they had nurtured her, given generously to her, developed her skills. She knew she would miss her father; he always distanced himself from her mother's obsessions. Her mother she would not miss. She bore no love for her daughter, who was little more than a shell to carry a bag of ambitions.

When the cold day arrived, she marveled at how calm she felt. Anything at all would be better than the oblivion she faced at home. She dressed discreetly, not wishing to call attention to herself. She shipped one bag ahead, via express, and would collect it in Butte. The other bag she nonchalantly carried with her. An inner voice whispered that all this was harebrained, but what did it matter? It beat being a prodigy. She had given little thought to what she would say when she contacted the vaudeville company. Nor had she created an act, a performance. All that would come.

She was, at eighteen, handsome. Thin but not slight. A warm-eyed oval face framed with brown hair. She lacked the curves gentlemen liked, but it didn't matter. She could sing, and she would get paid for it, and that mattered. What she would do with herself if she got on board the show, she didn't know. That was part of the pleasure of it. She hadn't the faintest idea how she would live, who she would befriend, and what her future might be. She supposed she was all innocence, given her cloistered life as a prodigy, but she knew she wasn't. Her parents were urbane people who lived in a wide world, and she had a good idea of what lay ahead.

She boarded the train unobserved, settled into the green horsehair seat, and felt the engine yank the couplings and roll the wheels of the coach under her. The conductor, stern in blue serge, took her ticket and smiled.

"We're on time. You'll connect," he said.

She murmured her thanks. She realized, too late, that she knew many of the conductors in that division; they knew her father. But she was lucky this time. In Ogden, she boarded the Utah & Northern, a plainer coach with wicker seats. And again, no one knew her, the red-nosed conductor was no one she had ever seen, and soon she was rolling north, to the mysterious copper mining town of Butte, and Destiny.

She watched the untouched wilderness tick by, caught whiffs of smoke from the engine ahead, heard its mournful whistle, and waited to begin a new life.

Butte finally rose up ahead, a haze of gray smoke, a sloping city, the largest in Montana, surrounded by breathtaking alpine vistas. It bristled with life and grit. When the train finally squealed to a halt, and its engine shot steam from its valves, she clambered to the gravel station platform, bag in hand, wondering what came next.

She corralled an open hack, driven by a skinny gent in a stovepipe hat, and in turn received a once-over from the man. She realized she was an unescorted woman.

"I wish to be taken to a proper hotel," she said. "Near the opera house."

"That would be the Butte—if you can stand the tariff," he said, still puzzling her out.

She nodded. He slapped lines over the croup of his dray, and the bony horse clapped its way up a gentle grade, which grew steeper as the roadway headed toward the forest of headframes ahead, where shafts plunged into the hillside, taking men into the darkness below and bringing rich copper ore up by the carload.

So this is where she'd meet Destiny, she thought.

"You in show business?" he asked, impertinently.

"I'm not in any business."

"Butte Hotel, it might not want show people."

He annoyed her. He was fishing. She kept her silence and let him wonder about her.

He turned, at last, and halted at a smoke-grayed structure.

"This is East Broadway. The playhouse's west, West Broadway, almost in sight," he said.

The hotel seemed nondescript, but so did all of Butte. She paid the man his thirty-five cents and added a dime, and headed into the hotel, where a clerk looked her over with pursed lips. It puzzled her. Butte was famously un-inhibited.

But a dollar and a half in advance put her in a gener-ous room with a water closet down the hall. Butte was electrified, and she enjoyed the novelty of incandescent light when she pushed the switch.

It was deep in the afternoon. She didn't know what to do next, but saw no virtue in mooning about, so she de-scended two flights of creaky stairs, reached the cold street, and headed west on Broadway, looking for Magu-ire's Grand Opera House.

It was not hard to find, its pretentious front shouting its importance. It was dark. A playbill on its side advertised the Beausoleil Brothers Follies, beginning the next eve-ning. Mary Mabel Markey was the top-billed act, and half a dozen more were listed, none of them familiar to her, but she knew they soon would be. There was an empty box office with a small sign that said reserved seats were available at several places it listed.

She spotted a side door, found it open, and started up a gloomy stair. Far above, she saw warm light. Well, noth-ing like asking. She headed upward, reached a second-floor foyer, and found a small reception area, and beyond it an office, where two men were conversing beyond an opened door.

She knocked boldly, and they eyed her. One of them was the nattiest dresser she had ever seen. He wore a pur-ple broadcloth suit coat, fawn trousers, a starched white high-collar shirt with an ascot tie, a black pearl stickpin, and spectacles.

The other gent was plainly dressed in a dark suit, but he had a sharp, hawkish gaze.

"Yes?"

"I'm seeking to audition for the variety show tomorrow, and I wish to know how."

"Audition? You mean, as an act?" the natty man asked. "I'm afraid this isn't the time or place. You'd need to do that when a show's assembled."

"I'm Ginger," she said. "And I sing. I'm trained."

"Well, young lady, I'm John Maguire. This is my theater. Ginger, is it?"

"That's it, first and last and middle name. I sing, and I wish to be given an audition. At least tell me who to contact when the show arrives."

The other one, the hawkish one in the dark suit, answered her. "I'm the man," he said. "Charles Pomerantz. It's my show."

"You're early?"

"I'm the advance man. Ahead of the show. Making sure it's promoted, boarded, fed, ticketed, and all that. You are, you say, a singer? What's the act?"

"When I sing for you, you'll see. I'm a pianist, too."

There was a long assessing gaze. "Ginger, my dear, I was just thinking about a libation and dinner. May I invite you to dine?"

ELEVEN

Pomerantz steered her to the Chequamegon Café, a fancy joint. The locals called it The Chew Quick and Be Gone, but it was often patronized by the copper kings. And the food was tasty.

"So, Miss One Name, what'll you have to drink?"

Ginger hesitated. "I'll let you order for me," she said.

He got the message. She didn't know one drink from another. For that matter, she probably had never been in a saloon or an eatery like this one.

"You old enough?" he asked.

"I wouldn't know," she said.

That was honest enough. He ordered a bourbon and water for both of them. His gaze told him a lot about her. Her clothing was well made and tasteful. Her manners were cautious. Her clear-eyed gaze suggested that she was not afraid.

"So, you want to leap in, join the show," he said.

Now he caught a flash of agitation. "I would like to try."

"You ever seen a variety show? With acts? You got an act?"

She stared, registering that. "I'll let you decide," she said.

"I don't do the deciding. August Beausoleil does."

"He's one of the brothers?"

"There's only one. The name, Beausoleil Brothers, that's for appearances. The more brothers, the bigger the show."

"I guess I've learned something," she said.

"In vaudeville, everything is for appearances. Why are you here, looking to get into vaudeville?"

She stared, dreamily. "I thought I might enjoy it."

"You running away from home? There likely to be cops and warrants and detectives chasing you—and making life hard for me?"

"I'm Ginger now. That is enough. I won't say any more."

The waiter served the drinks.

"Cheers," Pomerantz said. He sipped.

She sipped, grimaced, hid it, and sipped again, coughing slightly.

First one.

"You tell me," he said. "What kind of trouble are you running from?"

"None. And I'm Ginger, and that's all you'll know."

"You come from people with some money. You're wearing it."

"I am Ginger," she said, sipping again. But she smiled. There was something feisty in her.

He ordered lamb chops for both of them, with a Waldorf salad and mashed potato.

"Okay, now it's my turn," she said. "What's the top act in your show?"

"Mary Mabel Markey."

"She sings. I sing."

"And she wouldn't want a rival around, Ginger."

"I wouldn't sing what she sings. I . . . would learn other songs."

"Such as?"

"Sentimental favorites, things like that." She straightened up in her seat. "I'm trained for opera. But I wouldn't sing it. That's what they wanted, but not what I want. I'll use what I've learned—but I'll choose the songs. I'd sing ballads. I know lots of ballads. When I gargle, I gargle ballads."

He smiled. That was funny. But none of that was a bit promising. He was slowly getting the picture now: a girl on the brink of adulthood, in a gilded cage, the canary chirping for her parents. She had fled. This is where she hoped to begin anew, and far away from her cage. He sighed. It wouldn't happen. He'd occasionally dealt with people who wished to audition for the show, and it all came to nothing. A girl would dream, and the dream would crack apart. But he wasn't prepared to shatter any dreams. Not yet, anyway.

She ate quietly, employing her tableware with daintiness and discipline. She had gotten manners somewhere. She sipped the bourbon carefully, in tiny measures, determined to master it. And she probably would. Anyone who could sip an unfamiliar and fierce drink like that must have an iron will. She seemed oddly innocent and yet formidable at the same time, which intrigued him.

"I'm simply the advance man," he said. "I'm usually far ahead of the show, but Butte's the big one. The opera house has a thousand seats, and we mean to fill them. If we make money here, we'll be in better shape for the rest. And we're scheduled to extend our stay if it's worth doing."

She was listening, eating slowly, and carefully observing everyone else in the place. He could only imagine what she was studying. She was the best-dressed woman in the café, and she probably knew it. He wondered if she had ever been out after eight o'clock.

"I'll be staying for the opening, ready to plug holes," he said. "Then I'm off to Philipsburg and Missoula. I have a simple task: making sure that it all goes right. Philipsburg has no electricity but a nice new opera house. Not well equipped. So I make sure we've got lamps, footlights, and all that gear, and the oils we need. You never know. Our hotel may be far from the theater, and we need means to get our people back and forth. A sleigh, a buggy, a wagon. I have to find bed and board for twenty-some people. Sometimes I can get a bulk rate. Sometimes I have to pay in advance. Sometimes something goes haywire, and there are no rooms, or an eatery closes, or the owner decides to charge more for a breakfast because show people are supposed to have lots of money. Or a printer didn't print our tickets, and we need some, and fast. Or they didn't paste up the playbills and no one knows we're coming. That's what I do. I make it all work, and there's no room for error."

"You don't decide what's in the show," she said.

"That's my partner's job, and he's got the judgment for it."

"And everything's going to be all right in Butte?"

He hesitated. "On my end, yes. But not on the other end."

"Trouble with the show?"

He smiled. "Nothing for you to worry your head about. And nothing to start you dreaming. Show people all have that fantasy. You hope you'll fill in, be discovered, do better than the act you're subbing, and then you're on your way, audiences worshiping you, stage-door Johnnies waiting to escort you, all that. It's the dream."

"All I dream about is making my own life," she said.

He'd heard that, too. From runaways like this girl, escaping something unbearable, risking everything just to flee their homes. Usually with good reason, if not good sense. More often boys, escaping fathers. He watched her sip and eat, always dainty, always trusting. She trusted him, foolish girl. She brimmed with quiet strength, and the more he sat across from her, the prettier she became. And it wasn't the bourbon speaking. She was uncommonly lovely.

There was an impenetrable wall about her. Whatever he had garnered through a dinner had been gotten from intuition. She was Dresden china.

"There's nothing I can do for you," he said.

She smiled. The Chequamegon was noisy. Butte was noisy. Every shift change amounted to a racket, with shouts, chuffing steam engines, bells, whistles. The city never slept.

"What comes next?" she said.

He wasn't quite sure what she meant. She was gazing, unblinking, at him.

He arched a brow, and stared at the mustachioed barman.

"This part I know nothing about. Except what I've read in trashy novels," she said.

"How old did you say?"

"Old enough."

"You are reckless, and it will get you nowhere."

"I am unaware of it. No one has instructed me."

"And you want to be taught."

"When I left my home I left everything behind."

"And you suppose you can discover a way to become an entertainer. No, my little canary, you cannot do it. You must have an act."

She laughed suddenly. "I don't even have stage fright," she said.

He thought for a moment about the delight of being her instructor, opening the curtains, awakening her to a new world, the limelight where it had never shone. She was waiting, and he had only to pay the tab, collect her on his arm, and escort her a short distance, and close the door behind them. For her, there would be mysteries upon mysteries, revelations and maybe moments of fear, but no regrets. Not just then, anyway.

He could not fathom what was inhibiting him. Not scruple. He had none. But then he knew. She was too innocent. She was too sheltered and utterly unaware of traps, of cliffs, of slippery slides into hopelessness. She might fall crazily in love with a man who could not return it. More likely, she would pack up in the morning and head back to wherever she came from. And for once in his life, he would harbor regrets.

"Sing for me," he said.

"Here?"

He saw the flash of fear upon her. "Where else? An audience you must capture. They're eating. They're with friends. They're drinking."

The restaurant hummed. People conversed. Dishes clattered.

It amused him. She stood, gathering courage, and faced him. "It is called 'Cielito Lindo,' " she said.

"De la Sierra Morena,
cielito lindo, vienen bajando,
Un par de ojitos negros,
cielito lindo, de contrabando."

She sang it sweetly, but with voice enough to catch the restaurant. Heads turned.

"Ay, ay, ay ay,
canta y no llores,
porque cantando se alegran,
cielito lindo, los corazones."

A strange quiet settled now. What was all this? Charles Pomerantz confessed to being surprised, which was, for him, a major concession. His vocation was to prevent surprises. Her French horn voice caught his ear. It was not the sweet and virginal voice he had expected.

"Ese lunar que tienes,
cielito lindo, junto a la boca,
No se lo des a nadie,
cielito lindo, que a mí me toca . . ."

A dark youth busing dishes quietly joined the chorus. "Ay, ay, ay, ay . . ."

So did several patrons. They were swaying in their seats. Was this one of those songs that drew people into it?

And they clapped when she was done. She smiled serenely at them and rejoined Pomerantz. Patrons turned away. The evening's amusement had passed.

"There are many verses," she said. "And people create their own. It's much enjoyed by mariachi bands."

He hadn't the faintest idea what such a band was, and wasn't about to confess it, but he would find out sooner or later. She was somehow annoying him. She was exuding superiority. She was better bred and letting him know it.

"If you have an act, you'll need your own music. Not someone else's. Not a folk song," he said, gently.

She looked bleak. "I have none of my own. I know almost every ballad that's been caught on paper. I know Stephen Foster. Lullabies that came across the sea. Songs my grandmother sang, and songs I learned from music teachers. Songs they got from their home countries across the sea. The songs have come together, and we learn Irish lullabies and English sea shanties. I have all those, but nothing that would suit your show."

"Put them into an act, and try out somewhere," he said.

She stared, smiled, and nodded. The crowd was thinning.

"I'll walk you to your hotel, wherever that is."

"The Butte. And I can manage."

He ignored her, paid the tab, helped her throw a shawl over her shoulders, and walked beside her, filled with odd thoughts. He wished she would pack up and go home, stop being Ginger and start using all her real names. She was too sheltered to be out in the hurly-burly world, especially show business. People didn't just get hurt; they nosedived, they sank, they made bad choices. They tried powders and pills. They trusted the wrong people. She had no idea. She'd been raised in a garden, high walls around her, kept that way by protective parents who didn't want their little girl to grow up. And they no doubt congratulated themselves.

"So, Ginger, I enjoyed the dinner. And I wish you success," he said as they paused at the door. Inside the door, and up two flights, was her room, rented for one night.

She was hoping for more, but he made no commitment. He would introduce her to no one. She should get the hell out of Butte, and out of her dreaming.

"Thank you. I've never done that before," she said. "Singing for my supper."

"No, I was just curious. Not for your supper. Just curious."

She eyed him, sudden mischief in her eyes. "Odd how evenings end," she said.

He thought maybe she was a lot more experienced than he had supposed.

She entered, digging for her room key, and that was the last he saw of her.

The show would arrive in Butte around eleven, barely in time for an advertised matinee, and the telegram from Beausoleil indicated there was trouble.

TWELVE

M ary Mabel Markey was enthralled. Butte lay before her, stretching up a long grade, its stacks churning smoke into blue skies, the busy city glittering and shimmering. She loved the thought of all those people, people who might show up soon at the opera house. Butte was Irish. Her own.

She had spent hours traveling through wilderness. There was hardly human habitation between Helena and Butte, and the view from the coach window was monotonous forest and anonymous emptiness. Give her a bright city anytime, especially a brawling, sprawling one like the copper mining city with all its miners and millionaires.

Butte was high, hugging the continental divide, and an island of purpose in a lifeless land with nothing but mountains and forest. At the crest of the city were scores of headframes, the mines that tore copper and silver and a little gold out of the earth. The place deserved an opera house and deserved a great variety show like the Beausoleil Brothers.

The train screeched to a halt, huffing steam and pouring ash upon the platform, as brakemen opened doors and set steel stools on the gravel. They all must hurry: it was eleven thirty and they had a matinee at two. She spotted Charles Pomerantz waiting with several open carriages and two wagons, ready to speed the company to the opera house. He was a fine advance man, knew what was needed and got it there at the right time. The acts and props would go straight to Maguire's Opera House. The bags and trunks would go straight to the hotel, where performers would find them in their rooms, later.

She spotted August Beausoleil, first off the car, in earnest conversation with his colleague, no doubt about her. She was the problem, and enjoyed it. August had persuaded her to abandon the narcotics, especially the cough syrup with opiates, and that had restored her voice—a little. Enough to permit her to do the opening act of the final show in Helena. But she was dizzy, reeling, her heart flip-flopping, her chest hurting, her left arm aching, and she barely reeled off the stage after one song. The audience clapped only politely and thought she'd imbibed. Little did they know she could barely stand up, much less dish out a lively song.

Let the two of them worry out there in the smoke. She was the top-billed act, and she'd sing or they'd carry her out. They were frowning, earnest in their exchange, occasionally glancing back at the enameled green coach that was, even then, discharging a steady stream of the show people.

Beausoleil had settled quietly beside her on the trip to Butte.

"I think it's time for you to get some bed rest," he said. "Skip Butte. There's a hot springs near here, chance for you to soak and get better. Fairmont, it's called. Hot water, right out of the ground. Just sit in hot water and get strong."

"Over my dead body," she said, and meant it.

"That's nearly the way it worked last eve," he said. He

had helped her off the stage when it appeared she would keel over at the end of her first song. She had suddenly lost breath and balance, and he caught her just before she tumbled.

"I'm singing. Every performance. I wouldn't miss Butte for anything. This is my city. These are my people. Right here, buster."

"Mary Mabel, Butte's higher than Denver. Up against the continental divide. You'll not get enough air in your lungs to sing. I'd prefer to see you strong and with bellows pumping down the road. Sing for us on the coast, at sea level."

"I'm top billed. They buy tickets to see me."

He had hit a wall of granite.

That had ended the exchange, but it wasn't over. The two owners were talking earnestly in the cold wind on the platform, while carriages were wheeling the acts up the hill.

She stepped down to the platform, the brakeman offering a hand to steady her, and headed straight toward the owners.

Charles Pomerantz lifted his derby and nodded.

"Miss Markey, how good to see you," he said. "Your admirers are awaiting you, and in Butte, they're legion." He smiled. "And I'm at the top of the list."

"Someone around here wants to cheat them out of the price of a ticket," she said. "And it won't be me. I'll be on that stage. The first performance is what gets reviewed in the dailies, and they're going to review me."

"You're an admirable lady," Pomerantz said. "And you're ready, of course, and fit to sing?"

She eyed him. "I'll be on that stage, singing." She was going to add, even if it kills me, but decided that would not be politic.

"Air's smokey here," he said. He glanced at August.

"We're prepared to give you paid leave, Miss Markey. We want you full of zip when we reach the West Coast."

"If you reach the coast without me."

She had played her ace. They couldn't survive without her. This second-rate company would fold, the acts wouldn't get paid, and there'd be a lot of talent trying to hitch a ride back to civilization, And they knew it.

They didn't like it. But she had them. There was no way they could push their top-billed act out of town and let some little songbird pretend to put on a performance.

August smiled suddenly. "Take the carriage," he said. "You'll be dropped at the opera house. Rest before the show."

She eyed the carriage, ebony and open to the November chill. The hack driver was eyeing her as if she were a piece of hanging beef. She entered and settled, drawing a robe over her, and the hack driver slapped his nag into motion.

Her heart was tumbling again, and she didn't like it, but she wouldn't give in to it. It had all come down to stark options now: do or die. A few minutes later the hack turned onto Broadway and pulled up before a fancy-fronted opera house, all noble pretense, except that it would seat a thousand, and was as big as any, anywhere.

She wondered about paying the man, but he shook his head, helped her out, and pointed toward a side door. She found herself in a huge, dark auditorium, but there were incandescent lights on the stage, and people moving about. She grabbed a seat-back to steady herself. Her pulse was racketing around again.

She made her way to the bleak stage, where hands were putting the props in order. And there, watching, was a man whose reputation preceded him, John Maguire, dressed just as she had known he would, in a purple swallowtail.

"I believe I have the great honor of meeting one of the finest names in variety theater," he said. "Miss Markey, Butte welcomes you."

He not only clasped her cold hand, but reached down to plant a kiss on her cheek. She already liked Butte, and now she was filled with sublime delight. The most admired theater man in the West, kissing her cheek. Her heart skipped.

She peered out upon row after row of seats, a wide stage, majestic wings and flies, everything on a grand scale. It suited her. This was the great city of the Northwest, and these were her people, and here she was known and celebrated. She would sing to them, lullaby them, awaken them to love, stir ancient memories of a greener land, poke them with humor, smile and feel them smiling back. She had waited long for this, a Celtic celebration, a communion with all those lonely men, imported from across the sea by the copper king, Marcus Daly, and put to work in those terrible pits thousands of feet below the sunlight.

It made her heady, dizzy, and she retreated to the Green Room, passing people who were putting their act together. Mrs. McGivers had loosed her capuchin monkeys, and they were swinging about, looking for trouble. Harry the Juggler was unloading scimitars, and the Wildroot girls were opening a trunk, digging at costumes. There wasn't much time. The matinee crowd would flood in soon.

Mary Mabel Markey careened to a dressing room, found it solitary, lit by a single incandescent light hanging on its cord. It was as quiet as a confessional, and she wished there would be time to find a real confessional, in this city teeming with Irish, and confess to the sin of pride, the sin of having an act, of being in variety theater, so she might assuage her pride. But there was no priest here, and no church anywhere near this opera house, and her yearnings would have to wait for a while. Maybe between the matinee and the evening show.

She tried her voice, just a bar or two, and didn't like it much. But it would have to do, and what she lost in hoarseness she would make up in sweetness. She knew how to sweeten music, make it sugary and honeyed. Today she would slather honey on all those off-shift miners. She would give the most memorable performance of her life, there in Butte, there before the men from County Clare, or County Kilkenny and County Cork.

It was cold. The great barn of a theater carried a chill wrought by icy air flowing out of the mountains. It might warm with a packed house; it might not bother other acts, but it bothered her. She chose her sky-blue velvet dress because it was warm, and because she looked smashing in it, and she would woo her miners in it, and she would feel their longing, as they sat out in the dark, peering up at her, lit by incandescent spotlights.

She spotted John Maguire in the wing, and approached him.

"Miss Markey, what an honor. Rarely has this house seen the likes of a singer of your reputation," he said, plucking up her cold hand again.

"It's the Irish in me. I'm singing for an audience that'll pick it up," she said.

"They'll let you know it," he said. "But not loudly. You'll bathe in it, my dear."

"I've never bathed in anything but water," she said. "This will be a novelty."

August Beausoleil approached, looking stern.

"I've talked to the fiddlers, and they'll cover for you, see you through if your voice cracks."

"My voice is fine, and I'll chase them off the stage."

"Alone, then?"

"This is my town, and this is my hour, and this is my act."

He didn't like it. He was preparing for the worst, and fiddlers were good backup, carrying a song if a voice

vanished. That was a veteran showman for you, anticipating trouble and dealing with it ahead of time.

But he annoyed her. She felt a great thump in her chest,
and she meet his steely gaze with one of her own. Maguire watched intently, missing nothing.

"We'll have a sellout," Maguire said. "Nine hundred
advance, and the rest being picked up right now." He led
her to the arch and drew the curtain aside. The house was
starting to fill up. Miners, but more. Wives and children,
old men, and plenty who didn't look Irish at all, because
Butte was Cornish and Italian and Slavic and Norwegian
and Russian and Spanish and Greek.

"Good crowd, since it's snowing."

"Snowing?"

"All the time, all winter, in Butte."

"We were lucky to get in, then."

"It was close."

Then, somehow, it was curtain time, and the house
lights dimmed, and the footlights cranked up, and the
spotlights threw their beams, and there was August Beausoleil, all gotten up in his tux and bib, striding out there,
welcoming the crowd, urging them to enjoy the show, and
enjoy the famous Wildroot Sisters, and their medley.

The curtain flew upward, and the gals plunged in,
bright and saucy, with plenty of flounce.

The Butte crowd enjoyed them, and enjoyed the acts,
and laughed at The Profile, and clicked right into the tap
dancing, and howled at Mrs. McGivers and her Monkey
Band, when the unruly little devils went into their anarchist mode. It was a grand show, and Butte was a grand
city, and they were in the grandest opera house in the
region.

"And now, the one you've been waiting for, the lady
who gets a hundred proposals a day, the one, the only
Mary Mabel Markey," August was saying.

Her heart tripped. That was a new one, a hundred proposals a day. She glided out, feeling the spotlights, feeling a thousand gazes watching her, the blue velvet, the smiling Irish eyes. All that warmth made her dizzy.

She welcomed them, and told them she would sing for the best audience ever, and then, in the hush, sang "Your Big Blue Eyes." She was in fine voice, and her honey spilled over the footlights, and when she was done, there was a pause, and an affectionate swell of happiness, just as John Maguire had predicted. She waited for that outpouring to ebb, and then sang "The Cradle Song," and again her people sitting in row after row loved it, and she was dizzy with love, and she volunteered a third song this opening in Butte, "The Ribbon on My Finger." Oh, yes, they loved that, too, and everything was perfect, and the world whirled.

She bowed, and the world turned white, brighter than limelight, brighter than sunlight, and she felt herself floating, carried up through the flies, out into the snowy heaven, into the blinding white until she could see no more.

THIRTEEN

The headlines said it all that afternoon: "Markey's Finale"; "Singer Dies"; "First Act, Last Act." The newsboys hawking their two-cent tabloids on the corners put it in their own vernacular: "Croaks on Stage," one was yelling. "Read all about it."

For August Beausoleil, it was a moment of anguish, one he foresaw, and one he was helpless to stop. Mary Mabel Markey had simply dropped dead. One moment she was concluding an oddly tremulous act, the next, she toppled, slowly, flailing, to the boards, convulsed twice, and lay still. He knew in a paralyzed moment that she was gone, that her heart had quit.

Strangely, his first thought was to forgive her. Those in the wings watched, galvanized by the moment, unsure of what to do. He knew.

"Drop the olio," he said. The olio was a canvas backdrop that lowered downstage, permitting olio acts to perform in front of it while scenes were changed upstage. After a long moment, the tan curtain descended, even as a first stirring of the audience caught and spread.

His performers rushed to the fallen singer, turned her onto her back, sought life, and stared helplessly. She was gone. The clock was ticking. Harry the Juggler was patting her, pumping her, but life had fled.

There was a terrible instinct in August to continue the show, keep it rolling. Just a seizure, folks, and here's the Marbury Trio. But he could not. These people had just witnessed death. His people were huddled over Mary Mabel Markey, staring at him, waiting for something, and that something was up to him. Even John Maguire, restless in the wing, waited for him. And so did his colleague, Charles Pomerantz. All waiting for him.

In his gray tuxedo, stiff bib at the neck, he stepped into the bright glare of the footlights, and walked to the center of the stage.

"We grieve Miss Markey," he said. "This show is over. We will honor your ticket stubs at a special matinee tomorrow. We will cancel tonight's show in honor of our beloved Mary Mabel Markey, and will honor tickets at a future show. Thank you, good people, for coming this afternoon."

The audience sat, restless, unable to begin its exit.

John Maguire stepped into the light.

"My friends, I will be at the box office to refund the price of your tickets," he said.

The two of them hastened offstage, even as the shocked

audience stirred. August knew he had done the right thing. If he had tried to keep the show going, his performers would have faltered, and the audience would have ached.

"There will be very few refunds," Maguire said.

But August was already absorbed with the things he must do. First, to arrange her burial, to deal with any officials, to find her relatives, if any. Death brought sudden tasks. It all fell upon him. And he still had to keep the show going, keep his company afloat, fill those seats or perish.

There, backstage, the Wildroot Sisters stared, frightened. Mrs. McGivers sat beside Mary Mabel Markey, holding the dead woman's hand. Ethel Wildroot, on her knees, stared, looking for signs of life. Wayne Windsor sat beside the singer, patting her occasionally, as if to wish her back to life. Others—musicians, stage hands, performers—all watched desolately, deep in their own thoughts. Mary Mabel Markey's white face, distorted when she fell, now had slipped into serenity. Her wrinkles somehow vanished. August thought that she had run her course, had succeeded, and was content even as her spirit drifted away.

A whiskery doctor with a Gladstone bag appeared, knelt beside the fallen, and listened with a stethoscope, and shook his head.

"Mr. Maguire got me," he said. "There's nothing I can do. She was gone even before she fell down. I'm so sorry. I don't think it could have been prevented."

He stood.

Two burly men in dark suits appeared. "Brogan Mortuary," one said.

Maguire had been busy. Beausoleil was grateful. It was Maguire's city, and he knew what to do. They all watched silently as the mortuary men lifted Mary Mabel Markey into an ebony handcart and wheeled her away. The stage, lit only with one overhead lamp, was gray.

Then it was all back to August.

"No show tonight," he said. "Matinee tomorrow, and the evening show. We may make other changes in the schedule. I want to honor our great lady. But I don't yet know how, or about a funeral, or any of that. You're free this evening."

"August," Mrs. McGivers said, "God bless you."

That was it. Somehow her benediction completed the moment. The knots of people gradually abandoned the boards, and vanished into the late afternoon.

Charles Pomerantz corralled him. "We should talk to the papers," he said.

"And say what?"

"That Mary Mabel Markey could hardly wait to play Butte," he said.

"You know what, Charles? That's exactly right. Play Butte, almost a home to her. Her town. Play Butte, no matter how she hurt."

August had the sense that there were things undone, decisions looming, but for the moment he couldn't think of any. He found John Maguire sitting quietly in the box office, and paused to thank him for the arrangements.

"No one wanted a refund, August. Not one," Maguire said.

"We're doing a matinee tomorrow, and the rest, I don't know. What would you say?"

"Extend here. I'm dark for three days after you've booked me." He smiled wryly. "You have a publicity bonanza."

"I hadn't quite thought of it that way," he said. "But Mary Mabel would like it. She loved Butte. Charles and I are off to talk to the papers."

"There's the *Daily Post,* the *Evening News,* the *Inter-Mountain,* the *Miner,* the *Montana Standard,* and the *Reveille,* which is an obnoxious rag. Each copper king has one or two."

"Any to start with?"

Maguire smiled. "Get their slant, and use it." He added that they were clustered a couple of blocks south, gaudy rivals, keeping a sharp eye on one another.

The two principals of the company headed into a wintry evening with overcast skies and icy knives of snow in the wind

"You can handle this, August? I'm off to Philipsburg tomorrow, but I can hold off a day."

"We've both been around the block," Beausoleil said. "There's a hole in the show, and you'll need to patch the playbills."

"Just some white paper. Unless you've got something up your sleeve."

"White paper," Beausoleil said. "A show without a top act. We're a week from a replacement. Someone from Chicago if we're lucky, New York, more likely."

"There's local talent."

"Mary Mabel was the draw. They knew her. They lined up to see her."

Pomerantz conceded it with a nod.

They turned into the first paper they came upon, *The Standard*. Beausoleil was glad to meet a wall of heat after two grim blocks with alpine cold jamming into his flesh.

He spotted four compositors plucking up type and filling a stick. And two reporters, scribbling on sheets of newsprint. Compositors were wonders. They created lines of type, one letter at a time, working upside down and backwards, then slid the completed line into a form that would print the page. Even more wondrously, reporters and compositors were often one and the same. A man would get the story and then compose it as he plucked up the type.

But now a redheaded young man in a thick waistcoat rose and headed toward the visitors.

"We're from the show," Beausoleil said. "Would you like something on Mary Mabel Markey?"

"We're pushing deadline, but a bit, sure," the newsman said. "Jake James here."

He escorted them to his battered oak desk. "Now then?" he asked.

Beausoleil made the introductions and then plunged in. "Mary Mabel Markey was our top-billed act, you know. We thought she was marvelous. That voice, that presence. She drew crowds wherever we went, because she was sweet. And tender, like a mother singing a lullaby. And she was Irish, and that's why she was so eager to play Butte. This was homecoming for Mary Mabel. This was the most important engagement of her life." He paused. "And at least for one act, she enjoyed the thing she dreamed of, the thing she pined for. Singing in Butte."

Pomerantz continued. "We're in shock, let me tell you. After that olio drop rolled down, the rest of us crowded around her, wishing life into her, holding her hand, but she was gone. There were tears, sir. There was the deepest silence and respect I've ever witnessed. We just want you to know, officially, that the principals and the acts here all grieve the greatest lady in American vaudeville."

The young man scribbled away for a bit, and then eyed them.

"Any plans?"

"We're working on them," Beausoleil said. "We're going to have a funeral. She's going to be buried right here, in the city she loved. And we'll put up a stone, knowing all her admirers will be looking for the grave, and we'll have a funeral in a big place, a place where people can come, which we'll announce."

"What about the show?" James asked.

"We're dark tonight, of course. And tomorrow, we've scheduled a matinee for those who didn't get to see an entire show this afternoon. And beyond that, we're working things out. We'll extend our stay in Butte for two performances, to be announced."

"You think you'll draw without Mary Mabel Markey?"

"We think people will flock to the show, just to honor her," Beausoleil said.

Jake James grinned suddenly, as if this were some sort of private joke, but he dutifully got it down. "This is a good town to make a buck," he said.

"You know what I'd like?" Pomerantz asked. "I'd like people to bring bouquets to put on her grave. Mary Mabel's spirit would rejoice."

Jake James let his pencil hover, and set it down.

There might not be a story.

"Mr. James," Beausoleil said. "Let me tell you a bit about show business. Those of us who survive in the game don't know from month to month whether we've got a job. We ache to see those seats filled, because if they aren't, we're done. We ache to entertain, to make people laugh, or smile, or chuckle, because if we don't, we're done. If there's a lot of empty seats, we're done. Or maybe we just worry ourselves down to nothing. We have bills to pay: hotels, meals, railroads, and rental of halls. And if we don't pay them, we're done.

"So, sir, we do what we can to stir up interest. Mary Mabel Markey really did like Butte, and really did dream of playing here, because Butte's Irish. We really do want to honor her, because she topped our show, and because we were her friends, and we cared about her. She was always doing things for us. And there were real tears shed among us, when she lay there, on the boards, gone from our lives. And as for a funeral, we want a big one, because we really think she would have wanted a big one, one that people will remember. And the two of us, we own the show, we want her to be celebrated, and we think Butte's the perfect resting place for her. This is what she would have asked for.

"So, sir, you're right to think we want to fill our theater seats, and right to think we're making what we can of this, but that's not the whole deal. The whole story is that this vaudeville company grieves Mary Mabel Markey. Every one of us has memories, thoughts of Mary Mabel's many kindnesses and, yes, quirks, the things that make us mortal, stumbling along in a world we don't always understand. And it's going to be hard for our players to perform. And Mr. James, you can print up all of this if you want to. I'm talking straight, and you're welcome to put quotation marks around every word."

Jake James stared out the window into the dark November dusk, and nodded.

"It's a good story, Mr. Beausoleil, and if I don't write good stories, I might lose my thirty dollars a week, and if all those people who buy the paper don't read what I wrote, then I won't last as the top-billed reporter around here. You'll see the story in the morning."

FOURTEEN

Ginger pounced. She had been waiting in the opera house. When she spotted August Beausoleil, a somber man who seemed to be carrying a heavy load, she addressed him.

"Mr. Beausoleil," she said, stepping up. "I would like to audition."

He studied her a moment, saw a handsome young woman, and shook his head.

"I'm Ginger," she said. "I've a trained voice and a good repertoire."

He smiled. "Not now," he said. "I couldn't be busier. I'm burning up the wires, trying to get some box office."

"I sing," she said.

"I know you do. My partner told me about it. But Ginger, my dear, even if you sing like a nightingale I wouldn't hire you. I need more than a singer; I need a draw. I need a name. I need a top-billed show-stopper."

"When you're less busy, sir, may I sing for you?"

"Oh, I don't know. It's all a waste of time. I need seasoned people."

She felt the tide ebb from her. At least he wasn't simply brushing her off.

"I—I have one question. May I sing at Miss Markey's funeral?"

That startled him. He smiled. "Look, you go talk to Brophy Mortuary. They're doing all that. Tell them I said you could sing your song. I don't know a Catholic funeral from a Hindu one, so I don't know what they want. But tell them I said it's okay. Can't do any harm."

He tipped his hat, and hurried off. She stood in the darkness of a wing, a single bulb throwing a little light across a mysterious darkness.

She paused, studying the great expanse of stage, the curtains that sailed up and down, the props in the wings, ready to roll out in an instant, the upstage, the downstage, the footlights, the spotlights, the row upon row of stern seats, canted upward to give everyone a view. There was not a soul in any of them.

She had been nurturing a fantasy: She would sing into the dark theater, unaware that there was an auditor watching from some distant row, and the auditor would stand after she was done, and tell her that she was hired. That it was utterly beautiful.

But it was only a fantasy. She studied the empty barn of an auditorium, seeing no life at all. But she stood down stage center, and tried an American ballad she loved. She liked being on a grand stage, all those seats, row upon row, fading away into darkness.

"Oh Shenandoah,
I long to see you,
away you rolling river.
Oh Shenandoah,
I long to see you,
away, I'm bound away,
'cross the wide Missouri."

She liked the silence. Her voice felt silky. She tried another.

"Oh Shenandoah,
I love your daughter,
away, you rolling river—
Oh Shenandoah,
I love your daughter,
away, we're bound away,
'cross the wide Missouri."

There was no one to hear her, and that was fine. The opera house itself seemed to welcome her, and tuck her song into its walls, and that was fine. She sang two more verses, and it all was good, and no one heard a word. Then she wrapped her shawl about her, and headed into the blustery November day, and soon found the Brogan Mortuary, where Miss Mary Mabel Markey lay, waiting for the last act.

The place was quiet, and dark, and smelled of incense. She found a small silvery bell, and rang it. And out of the gloom a bearded man rose up, black as the River Styx.

"Madam?"

"Are you Mr. Brogan?"

"I am. Are you in need?"

"Mr. Beausoleil suggested that I come. I would like to do a song, 'Ave Maria,' at Miss Markey's rites."

"I see," he said. "You are?"

"Ginger."

"Ah . . ."

"First and last, Ginger."

"A stage name, then. Well, come along, and let's talk."

He led her to a small office, lit the overhead lamp, and motioned toward a chair.

"Mr. Beausoleil suggested that we do what we could, by way of a service. We've asked Monsignor Murphy to officiate, and there immediately arose some questions. Is the deceased a Catholic, and in good standing? A theater person, you know. That's how it is. We've been unable to find out, so Monsignor has reluctantly concluded that the proper course is for him to assist in a simple prayer service. He'll open, Mr. Beausoleil will eulogize the late departed, and the monsignor will offer a prayer for her salvation. And of course, yes, your song would be fitting and sacred. We'll fit it in. You're talking about Franz Schubert, of course?"

"Yes."

"Yes, fitting. How kind of him to send you along. Now, we've scheduled it for tomorrow at eleven. It must not interfere with the matinee. They're scheduling matinees each day, in the hope of recovering what they lost yesterday. One today, of course. But you must know that. How shall I list you in the program?"

"Ginger."

He smiled suddenly. "Ginger it is, then. Please be here ahead of eleven, so we can seat you in the first row. Now, will you need accompaniment? We will have a pianist."

"I will sing a capella."

"I take my hat off to you theater people. I would want to hide behind a pipe organ."

"Where will Miss Markey be buried?"

"Mountain View. Immediately following the ceremony."

"How will I get there?"

"It's a long way. The cast won't be there; they have a

matinee. But I believe Mr. Pomerantz will represent the troupe. Maybe he'll take you."

She worried it all the way back to her hotel, where she had engaged the room for another night. Couldn't they respect Mary Mabel Markey enough to set aside the matinee? Was that show business, or just the Beausoleil Brothers Follies at work? Bury their top act on the run? Well, she knew what she would do. She would sing the beloved Mary-song in a way that honored the woman they had come to bury; sing it in a way that it had never been sung.

Was it the right song? Would a song honoring the Virgin be the thing for a vaudeville singer? Maybe she should choose something else, something more suited to Mary Mabel Markey. She had mastered it in Pocatello but had never sung it at a recital. It wouldn't have been suitable there.

Much to her surprise, the service was at the Maguire Opera House. Long before eleven the next morning, every seat had been taken. The cast, Miss Markey's only relatives, filled the first rows. And Ginger, dressed in white, was among them, at an aisle seat. The crowd waited expectantly, in deep silence, not so much as a cough disturbing the quiet. An upright piano stood at one side, downstage. The curtains were open. At eleven, the stage lights came up, shining down on Miss Markey's simple coffin, which rested on a pedestal draped with gilded cloth.

The monsignor appeared, wearing a black suit with red piping, and addressed the silent throng. "We are here to celebrate the life of our beloved Mary Mabel Markey, and to hasten her ascent to an eternal life with the angels," he said. "Now let us pray."

Next was August Beausoleil, this time in an immaculate black suit, entirely at home on that stage, before that quiet crowd.

"I will talk a bit about our dear departed. Every member of our company is grieving this hour for a remarkable woman who was the backbone of our show.

"She was intensely private, but once in a while shared bits of her past. Mary Mabel was not her name; I don't know what it once was. I know that she was Irish, that she grew up in New York, and from earliest childhood found a way to survive by singing the songs her mother had taught her. Songs she remembered after her mother had died. Singing as a girl on street corners for a bit of loose change. Singing for passersby. Singing for her supper, for those songs would give her the only food she had, and the corners of the city offered her the only shelter she had.

"But out of it came a miracle. Her very life depended on pleasing people, and that was her salvation and her secret road to success. When someone liked her song and gave her a generous tip, that was a clue. When someone listened to a song, walked away, and never looked back, that was a clue. So she was in the hardest school of all, and failure was not a grade, but death or starvation. But gradually, being a woman of courage and intelligence, as well as a woman who learned without help how to employ her voice, gradually she turned herself into an instrument of beauty and joy for countless admirers. Mary Mabel Markey wrought the raw material into the most successful female singer of our times, and not one step along the way was easy."

Beausoleil talked of the way Miss Markey had become the single thing she wished to be, a singer, and how that had shaped all her life, to her last hour, when she sang because she had to, sang against the wishes of the show's managers, sang because she was there, in Butte, among her people.

"Mary Mabel Markey gave the world songs that linger in our hearts. Tomorrow, a year from now, and when you are old and gray, you will be hearing her songs in the concert hall of your memory," he concluded.

It was amazing how that crowd devoured August Beausoleil's eulogy. They were starved for Miss Markey; they wanted every intimate detail, and he gave them whatever he knew of a woman who was largely private and distant from them all.

After he sat down, the monsignor invited Ginger forward.

"And now, a sacred song in honor of all womanhood," he said, judiciously.

Ginger had never faced a crowd like this. She made her way to the stage and peered out upon the sea of quietness, brushed her white dress, folded her hands together, and began.

> *"Ave Maria,*
> *gratia plena,*
> *Maria, gratia plena,*
> *Maria, gratia plena,*
> *Ave, Ave, Dominus . . ."*

Ave Maria, full of thanksgiving, Maria, full of thanksgiving, Maria, full of thanksgiving, Ave, Ave, God . . .

And so began her solo. There alone on the stage, she let her voice soar far out into the great opera house, soar to every corner, soar to every heart.

Then a strange thing happened. Joseph, Mrs. McGivers' accordionist, quietly stepped away from his seat in the first row, made his way to the stage, and settled at the piano, and soon was adding its notes to her voice. She was momentarily flustered, but he was perfect, and the piano only amplified the moment, and the words, and sent them sailing on the wings of white keys and black.

> *"Benedicta tu in mulieribus,*
> *et benedictus, et benedictus,*
> *et benedictus fructus ventris . . ."*

And then it was done, and the last sound from the last key faded into the hall, and there was only the deepest silence. She waited for a moment, and then retreated to her seat, and the pianist quietly returned to his. There were gazes upon her. She settled in the safety of her seat, and waited.

"Let us pray for the departed," said the monsignor.

And they did. And then the priest blessed the crowd and sent them on their way.

She watched, suddenly alone, not part of the company, unknown to them all. The Butte crowd collected quietly outside, where an ebony hearse, drawn by four jet horses with black plumes, stood waiting. By prearrangement six of the troupe gathered about the coffin and carried it outside to the hearse and slid it inside the glass-paneled chamber. And then, with a stately clop of hooves, its driver, in a black silk stovepipe hat, steered the ebony hearse toward the cemetery, far away.

She watched. Her part was done. She felt oddly lost.

Then Charles Pomerantz approached her.

"I will give you a ride, if you wish," he said.

An enclosed hack, armor against the Butte wind, awaited, its bundled-up driver eager to move.

The crowd was watching him and her. The company gathered on the street was watching. They would not be going. They would be snatching a bite if they cared to before the show, and preparing for the matinee that was looming just ahead. Charles Pomerantz and the girl in white, the girl unknown to them, would represent the company at the graveside service.

He held her hand, to help her up, and soon she was seated, with a buffalo carriage robe about her, while he settled beside her. The carriage rocked gently down a rough road.

"Ginger, that was magnificent."

"Well, thank you, but most sacred songs are like that."

"Your voice. Never have I heard such a voice, and such an offering, in any opera house. Or any concert hall. Or anywhere else."

She glanced at him, suddenly shy. He was gazing intently.

FIFTEEN

A biting wind hastened the monsignor through the burial rite. Two employees of the funeral home were on hand, no one else from Butte. Ginger shivered in her summery white dress, with only a shawl to turn the cold. Charles Pomerantz stood patiently, the representative of the touring company.

He was the only person present who knew Miss Markey. Ginger had not met her. The priest wasn't sure Mary Mabel was in good standing, but he was offering her the benefit of the doubt, and gently laboring through the burial, though he was blue with cold. He was doing as best as he could, because death was the greatest mystery.

It was an odd end for a nationally known and acclaimed performer, Charles thought. Burial in utter obscurity, no friends gathered at the grave. The company would pay for all this, and a headstone, too, and it would carve a hole deep into the working funds that supported the tour. He lacked even a flower to lay upon her plain pine coffin. She would be buried as anonymously as she had started, a girl struggling to survive on the streets of the city, not unlike August Beausoleil. She deserved more.

Then it was over. "Ginger, go wait in the hack," he said. "I'll thank the priest."

The monsignor was climbing into a black topcoat.

"Those of us who were Miss Markey's only family thank you, Father. She is lost to us, and found above."

"We may all trust in it," the priest said, and hastened toward the mortuary hack, which would hurry him back to his rectory.

Ginger fled to the thin protection of the hack, where the driver huddled against the cold, and moments later Charles climbed in and pulled the lap robe over both of them. A great quiet settled upon them as the driver steered the reluctant dray straight into the wind. Pomerantz had a sense that things were unfinished, that Mary Mabel was waiting for more. Maybe what was needed was a wire to someone back east, announcing her death. But who? She had lacked a family, and found one in her admirers. Maybe that was the thing: let the press know, and the world would know.

The hack rolled up the gentle slope toward the opera house. The chastening cold had vanquished traffic, and Butte seemed almost deserted. There were more dogs than people on the sidewalks. Smoke scraped the streets.

"Where to, Ginger?"

"It doesn't matter," she said.

"You're at the Butte Hotel. I'll drop you there."

She peered out of the breath-silvered isinglass window. She was no longer shivering, the carriage robe warming her.

"I want to thank you for singing. I've never heard a finer voice. And not just a voice, either. I've never heard a more accomplished voice, a voice that was tutored by someone, wherever you came from."

"Thank you."

"You're at the end of your tether. You don't know what to do."

"I will make my way."

"You came to join the show."

"Yes."

"I never saw anything so compelling. You, dressed in white, with your wavy hair, mahogany colored, like my mother's, all alone, without so much as a pianist, standing there poised, your hands folded together at first, wholly absorbed in the gift you would give us."

She eyed him, her brown eyes wide.

"Franz Schubert, was it not? Is your repertoire mostly classical—opera?"

"It's everything. It was the wish of my . . . mentors . . . to be able to entertain them for any occasion."

The hack driver pulled up at the hotel. She pulled the carriage robe off, thanked him, opened the flimsy door, and stepped down.

She started toward the hotel.

He threw open his door.

"Ginger!" he said.

She paused, orphaned, in the cold.

"Please join me."

The driver looked impatient. He wanted to escape that crushing air.

She turned back, shivering again, the blue shawl a poor defense against the bitter wind. But she clambered in.

"The Chequamegon," he said, and the weary horse once again lugged the hack along hard-frozen streets.

"Ginger, will you marry me?" he asked.

It shocked her. It shocked him even more. He had no idea why he had asked. The thing had simply erupted.

She could make no sense of it. She stared at him, stared at the cold city, stared ahead, even as he tucked the carriage robe around her.

She smiled. "I'm not your ward," she said. "And I don't know anything about you. But it was sweet of you. It was the nicest compliment."

He was beginning to think he didn't know anything about himself, either. The question hung between them, like a light throwing illumination in all directions. What was it about her? Her looks, something like his mother. Her bravery. She volunteered to sing at a funeral all alone, with no help, for people she had never seen before. Or something else. Only now, as the hack climbed another grade, did he realize that she had knocked him over. Theater men were immune to all that. Especially womanizing ones like himself. He could not fathom what had made him so reckless. Now, if she began to smile, he'd have to retreat from that precipice.

They reached the restaurant. It was midday. He hurried her in, paid the driver, and led her toward warmth. They settled into a booth in deep silence, the moment oddly choreographed with nods and smiles and courtesy. She still was cold. He settled his topcoat over her lap. The impulsive question was forbidden turf now. And yet it governed everything they said and did. He supposed it had been a lapse, a folly, something that had escaped harness.

He ordered tea for her, a whiskey for himself, and still she sat in silence.

"You asked. I will tell you about me," he said. "I'm Polish. My parents brought me here at age two from Warsaw. I'm Jewish. There were troubles in the old country and promise in the new. I'm thirty-three. I'm from Brooklyn. I've been in this business since eighteen, when I sold tickets. I did accounting. I managed acts. I speak Polish, Yiddish, English, and some others. As you probably guessed."

He was referring to the slight accent that rolled up some letters and words.

She nodded, her warm gaze registering everything about him: The combed-back hair, starting high on the crown of his head. The sallow flesh, the dark eyes, peering out from bags.

The plainness of his features. He could never pass for dashing or handsome.

"No one has ever proposed before. Especially not an older man."

He was almost twice her age. "And who is Ginger?"

"She is what you see before you, and all else has passed and will never be seen again."

"So I have proposed to a new woman."

"I am eighteen. That is the age of consent, I believe."

"And, you have had male friends, boys?"

She shook her head. That was the past. He could see the curtain sliding down.

"How do you live? Where is home?" she asked.

"Home is my suitcase. I live in hotel rooms ahead of the show, or sometimes with the show, and at the end of the tour, I rent a room until the next tour."

"And what would you do with me?"

"The same."

"I would have to like the business," she said. "That's why I left . . . where I grew up. Why have you proposed to me?"

"I don't know. I have no idea."

She colored a little. "I can imagine. You've had many women."

"Yes. A few. Ah, more than a few."

"And you're an accountant!" She had turned merry.

"A thousand women, and none of them got into the show."

"Would this marriage last one night, one week, or one month?"

He shrugged. "I don't know why I asked, and I cannot see into the future. I apologize. It was an impulse. I shouldn't make light of it."

"Yes," she said. "Neither can I see ahead. But never say never."

"I don't audition acts," he replied.

"It's the best offer on the table," she said. "And now and

then there'll be a piano. I need a piano in my life. A piano's more important than singing. So you're stuck with it."

He sat, nursing his drink, oddly cheerful, confused, wary, curious, regretful, and even afraid, all at once, which was too complex to sort out.

"Cheers," he said, lifting his glass.

They toasted it.

"I think I like you," she said. "But we'll see."

He knew he would remember this moment as the jackpot play of his life. But what would he take off the table?

"Where and when?" she asked. "I'm ready right now."

He hadn't thought about that. Down the road, maybe. This would take some getting used to. He could live with her for a while, see how it might go.

"Shall we find a justice of the peace?" she asked.

"In for a dime, in for a dollar," he said, not quite believing any of this.

"Over the cliff," she said, a quirky smile building.

"The matinee's playing? You want to wait for the company?"

"You're already weaseling out," she said.

"I am not! I just thought we might invite the acts. Witness the follies."

"You've got thirty seconds. Now or never."

He lifted her hand, squeezed it, and kissed it gently.

"My white dress is fine, but I'd like my coat," she said. "And you can buy me a bouquet."

It took an hour or so. Ginger checked out, they caught a hack to the courthouse, they completed a license, she as Ginger Jones, and they scouted up a justice of the peace who said he'd do the deed in half an hour after he was done with an assault and battery case. It was odd: instead of doubts, Charles had only delight coursing through him. There were no but, but, buts. He could not explain why a normally cautious man was stepping over a cliff believing he would land safely. He could not imagine what he would tell August, his confidant, when the deed was done. And he was curious about what Ginger thought, whether she was having a flood of doubt. How little he knew her.

"Do you have doubts?" he asked.

"No. The time when I had doubts was when I left my home, took a new name, and headed here. I don't have a single doubt. There's no turning back."

"Do you love me?"

She ignored him. "Should I call you Charles or Mr. Pomerantz?"

"Suit yourself. Shall I call you Ginger or Mrs. Pomerantz?"

The judge invited them in, eyed them skeptically, and studied the bride. "Where'd you run away from?" he asked.

She paled for the smallest moment. "Make me a proper woman," she said. "And be quick about it."

The judge laughed. So did two smirky clerks serving as witnesses. He extracted a hidebound text and rattled it off, enjoying the embarrassment when Ginger and Charles could produce no ring, and continued on, amusement in his bearded face. An older man, a younger woman of great radiance, and some adventures ahead. They cheerfully repeated the vows. Stuck with each other for life, until one or another croaked. The judge pronounced them man and wifey, his little joke, and they shook hands with him, and Charles handed him a fiver.

"I don't suppose you'll have a reception or banquet," the judge said. "If you do, I'll come and toast the happy couple."

"You're not invited," Ginger snapped. She hadn't liked the ceremony, and Charles didn't blame her. Marriage wasn't frivolous, even if the judge treated their union as a joke.

The judge nodded, grinned, and saw them out.

They headed into the late afternoon, both of them in a funk. The matinee was over. Miss Markey was buried. The Butte wind whipped. And now they were strangers in paradise, scarcely knowing how to cope with their union. He took her hand, squeezed, and was rewarded with a smile, and then a flash of delight in her eyes.

"You ready to tell the world, Mrs. Pomerantz?"

"Call me Ginger," she said. "I have no other name."

SIXTEEN

The act was a disaster. August Beausoleil was auditioning local performers, hoping to plug the hole in his show. But Cohan and McCarthy, from the Comique, in the nearby smelter town of Anaconda, were about to get the boot.

This was an Irish act; the vogue in vaudeville was acts that made fun of the various peoples flooding to America. Most of these were performed by the very people who were being ridiculed. Blacks were doing blackface acts. Irish were doing drunken Irish acts. Like this one.

Cohan did a somewhat drunken Irish clog dance, and McCarthy showed up to insult him, and soon enough there was a brawl, with the pair whaling away at each other, both of them in well-padded suits to take the whacking of canes.

Some people apparently found this hilarious, especially the Irish audiences in Butte and Anaconda. Actually, there were some amusing moments, but the proprietor of Beausoleil Brothers Follies hoped to find something better.

With the help of John Maguire, who owned the opera house, he was looking at local talent. He'd wired agents on both coasts and Chicago, and had not come up with anything to fill out his show bill, especially an act that would draw crowds. And Butte was a long way from anywhere.

"Thanks," he said. "We'll let you know shortly."

"We're filling the Comique every night," Cohan said.

"Comedy, that's the trick," said McCarthy.

August nodded. They paused, expectantly, and then quit the stage.

"Any more?" Beausoleil asked.

"You could try skits," Maguire said. "One-act comedies, ten or twelve minutes. There's a show at Ming's we might get down here."

Beausoleil had seen the ads in the Helena papers: Mr. Roland Reed, in *Lend Me Your Wife*. On other nights the actor starred in *The Woman Hater*: "Reed as the Misogynist; Reed as the Bigamist; Reed as the Lunatic," read the ad in the *Helena Independent*.

Good fun, at least around Helena.

The stage was empty, lit by a clear glass bulb. The matinee was over, the evening show a way off. He had put LaVerne Wildroot into the matinee against his better judgment, and the crowd was neither inattentive nor delighted. That had been plain to Ethel, and she was no longer promoting her niece. She hinted that she was putting something else together, but he discounted it. That was show business talk. Everyone was working on a new act.

The afternoon crowd had been good enough. Not a sellout, but not bad. The aura of Mary Mabel Markey still hung over the show, and over Butte. There were seats available for the evening show, but the next shows were not selling advance seats. And without her, unlikely to sell, even in a great theater town.

"Well, maybe I'll go out and do a two-step," Maguire said.

"Knock 'em dead," August said.

He stared into the cavernous theater, deep in shadow, a place that could crush dreams as well as make them come true. "Any dog shows around here?"

Dogs were always welcome. Dogs jumped through hoops, caught anything thrown, did their own ballet, howled in unison, and bowed to audiences. Dogs, ponies, tigers. An animal act was a good deal.

The stage door popped open, boiling cold air through the darkened house, and Charles Pomerantz appeared, with that mahogany-haired girl at his side, still in white, but bundled up in a blue scarf and wooly hat and gray mittens. They made their way across the bleak stage, and down to the orchestra, where August was nursing his melancholia.

"Tell me you just hired a great act," Charles said.

August sighed.

"You've met Ginger. She sang. She is now Ginger Pomerantz."

Ginger looked pretty solemn.

"Congratulations, Charles. It's number thirty-three, right?"

"No, this is real. This is serious. A justice of the peace, an hour ago. You're the first to know."

"Oh, number seventeen!" August said.

"You want me to show some paper?"

This had to be some sort of joke, so August grinned. "Well, miss, you want to audition now?"

"No, I won't sing for you," she said. "Anyway, you've heard me." She turned to Charles. "But this is my husband." She caught his hand and held it.

It was dawning on August that this was real, or at least an improvement on most of the theater jokes he was familiar with. Maybe the punch line would show up in a few days. Maybe this was one of those endless gags.

"Ginger, is it? Forgive me. I've been rude. If this is your wedding day, permit me to wish you all the best."

Charles was enjoying it, even if Ginger was not.

"We'll want to celebrate," August said. "Maybe after the show this eve?"

"Yes," said Maguire. "Please allow me to host a gathering. And my congratulations. This is all a surprise. But show business is nothing but surprises, right? And we'll want to toast the happy couple. Will you be putting an act together?"

There it was again. Not even an emergency marriage could trump the business.

August stared at this unlikely couple, noting that they were smitten with each other, serious, and somewhat mysterious.

"Tell me the story," he said.

"She propositioned and I proposed," Charles said.

She reddened, but said nothing.

"It was a lost cause. Her hair's the color of my mother's. That lowered all my resistance, and after that, she was driving and I was along for the ride."

She eyed him nervously, and eyed August and John nervously. But she caught the crinkle of flesh around their eyes, and smiled herself.

"And what are your plans?" John Maguire asked, closing in on the question that August had been too polite to ask.

"She'll travel with me, and with the show, and we'll see," Charles said.

"And will there be a home somewhere, like Brooklyn?"

"Wherever he is, that's my home," she said. "I'm not a performer, but I'd love to be in the company. And I'd love to be with Charles, wherever he goes."

Something sweet in her caught August.

"A trouper! Well, Ginger, welcome to the Follies," he said, and clasped her hands in his own. The glacier had melted. But he was still waiting for a punch line.

"I don't know who's more surprised," Charles said,

"You, me, or her. None of this was by design, and all of it is pure good luck."

"I believe in omens," Maguire said. "Who can explain these things?"

"We're off to Philipsburg," Charles said. "When we can. The local train leaves at dawn, alas."

A flash of a smile, and a surrendering gaze from the bride, and they vanished into the afternoon.

"Who can explain it?" Maguire asked.

It was two hours to showtime. August wasn't hungry. He had no more auditions. He eyed his pocket watch, considered the stern weather, and decided to risk it. He bundled up, hailed a hack, asked the driver if he could reach Mountain View and return by seven, and hopped in. The horse, whipped by wind, hastened south, the enclosed coach rocking gently. Night was crawling down, and he'd return in full dark.

The cabby knew exactly where to go. Death and Butte were familiar with each other. He pulled up at the naked grave, raw earth shoveled over Mary Mabel Markey's tomb. The bleak twilight revealed a hastily filled grave, the clay not yet smoothed, and patches of snow dotting the yard.

"Give me five minutes," August said.

"I'll bring a lantern, sir."

"Thank you; I'll be all right, and won't be long."

A rim of last-light lay on the western horizon.

The cold air off the mountains took the breath out of him. There on the grave was a wreath of pine boughs. Someone had remembered.

"Well, Mary Mabel," he said. "Here's where it ended. In a town that loved you. Buried by your friends. You came out of nowhere, and touched the sky. I just wanted to say good-bye, and tell you that you've got a corner of my heart."

He had nothing to give her, and then remembered the

new Indian head penny in his pocket, and this he placed at the top of her grave. Even in the near dark, it shone oddly bright, a bronze coin in a copper town.

"Good-bye, sweetheart," he said. "We've played a lot of towns together, you and I."

The ride back deepened his melancholia, and he knew that he must banish all that before the show. He was no good at concealing his feelings, even in tux and topper, ready to open the show. He paid the cabby extra, thanking him for braving the wind, and walked through the stage door, feeling better for having the communion he needed with his old friend and occasional nemesis.

Butte was the coldest place he had ever been, and the opera house was slow to warm. He wondered whether people would show up this evening, braving the relentless wind and the smoke from the boiler stacks that was whipping along the streets.

The stage felt like an icebox. He spotted The Profile hurrying his way, a grimy rag in hand.

"The catarrh and a bad throat," Wayne Windsor said, his voice a growl. "I should shorten the act—if you're willing."

"Fever?"

"Feels like one."

"Go to bed," August said. "Whenever I push too hard, we pay for it."

Windsor looked shocked. "I'll do the act. I can't let you down."

"Rather have you away from the rest."

"Two of the Wildroot girls have it, and Harry the Juggler, he's wiping his nose. Got a faucet running from both nostrils. Hope he doesn't sneeze when those scimitars are flying."

The juggler was a silent act. August could use the silent acts to fill in. The tap dancers, too. They didn't sing.

The Marbury Trio had several routines. LaVerne Wildroot could sing, if she was up to it.

"Which of the Wildroot Sisters? Is LaVerne sick?"

"No, she's good. Cookie and Marge caught it, Marge with a cough."

"What about Mrs. McGivers?"

"Who knows? Maybe it'll be a monkey night," Wayne said. "They're our ancestors."

"They can catch what we catch," August said.

He headed for the Green Room, hoping to find ways to put a show together. He wouldn't cancel. Never cancel. Work it all out. He found Harry the Juggler there, and asked him to do a third, maybe a fourth act if he could. Harry listened closely; August never knew if Harry was grasping words, or just nodding. But yes, Harry would add the cup-and-saucer act. Drop one and it'd break; drop several, and there'd be a lot of ruined pottery on-stage. The deal was, break the whole lot. It was an amateur juggler act, and usually got some laughs. But pottery was costly, and that act didn't come cheap.

"Break it all, Harry," August said. "We'll buy more in the morning."

He corralled Ethel Wildroot next. "What's the score?" he asked.

"The girls are ready. LaVerne'll sing. Cookie and Marge'll squawk a little, but they'll do it. They'll do the job, and no one will guess."

"Twice? Second act? And LaVerne can solo?"

"They grew up in the business. Speaking of that, dear boy, I could do the Dumb Dora act if I had to. That's what the act was, before the girls took over. I'd put on a blond wig and he'd deliver the questions and I'd deliver, and the crowd got a chuckle out of it."

"Well, not tonight, Ethel."

"You could do it. Just slide me questions, like where

are we, and who's on first, and what day of the week is it?"

"We'll work on it. Not tonight. We'll go with whoever's here."

"Break a leg," she said. There was something tender in her response.

He found Mrs. McGivers in the wing, fussing with the capuchin monkeys.

"Run long if you can. About half the acts are sick."

"Sweetie pie, I was just thinking Cain's not looking so hot, but Abel's fine. Don't worry. We can add the organ grinder routine; the little buggers squeeze some coin out of the crowd while Joseph cranks the accordion. That can get juicy."

Somehow they'd put on a show. It had been the longest day in memory.

SEVENTEEN

Somehow or other, the company delivered that evening. That was the thing about veteran troupers: they could fill in, make do, improvise, put on a show, get out there in the limelight and keep the songs and laughs coming.

Ethel Wildroot watched the girls perform, not once but thrice that evening, and they managed somehow. But just barely. Truth was, she was disappointed in them. They'd grown up in the business, knew the ropes, and still didn't quite deliver whenever something was amiss.

It annoyed her. She'd spent years teaching, cajoling, demanding, encouraging, and the best they could do was get some pleasant applause. She wished that her late husband, rat that he was, could hammer something of the business into their heads. She would even prefer their old stand-up comedy, rat that he was, to this. At least they were an act, and it got laughs, rat that he was. It was called a Dumb Dora act, because she made sure to be the dumbest dame up there that anyone had ever seen. She was good at it. She picked up his cues, his questions, and her responses guaranteed that every male in the audience felt superior to every female ever born on this earth. Rat that he was.

But that was long ago. If she could put a comedy routine together, it would be the reverse of the Dumb Dora act. She'd feed questions to some old goat and let him dither. She'd looked around the company some, but no one qualified. Even the accordionists were smart.

The company headed for the hotel, and sleep, and maybe better health in the morning, but Ethel was ready to roam. She often stayed up late, never got sick, and sometimes had fun. Especially in Butte, with a saloon for every nationality and taste. What's more, most of the places didn't mind a lone woman, even if the precincts were entirely male. And it helped when she said she was from the Follies. Where else could one get a drink from barkeeps like Butt Bean or Dago Jim or Stuttering Alex or Big Jerry or Whistling Sammy?

Butte was the best town she had ever played. It was lit up all day and all night, and there was nothing like it outside of New York. That night, half frozen, she burst into a saloon with the mysterious name of Piccadilly, which offered few clues about its clientele. It turned out to be a haven for Englishmen, especially those who wouldn't rub shoulders with the Irish, and would cross the street before tipping a hat to the Italians.

Decorum ruled. She feared she wouldn't be served, but this was Butte, after all, and pretty soon a barkeep with a soiled apron supplied her with a rye and water. Well, fine. She would listen to the galoots. Maybe she would get into an argument. Maybe she would huff out, into the cold night.

There was one particular gent who interested her. He had a kingly way about him, and for some reason people kept buying him drinks. He was carefully groomed, but shabby, the sort who had seen better days but still got into his boiled shirt and cravat, even if his attire was worn at the sleeves, even soiled. But there he was, often with a crowd about him, listening intently.

She caught the attention of the barkeep. "Buy the gentleman a drink," she said.

"He's got four ahead of you, madam."

"He's good for a quart," she said.

The keep poured some amber fluid and set it before the gentleman, nodding in her direction.

"This is a portentous event, and history will remember you kindly," the man said.

"What have I done?"

"You have wet the whistle of a man destined to be remembered throughout the ages," the man said. "It's my fate to be the Shakespeare, the Newton, the da Vinci, of the ages."

Several of his auditors were listening now, following every word, plainly enjoying the exchange. She had walked into something, maybe a running joke at this saloon.

"What have you done?" she asked.

"Done? Done? I am recorded on the pages of history. I am the Napoleon of empire, the Hannibal of ancient times, the Julius Caesar of modern times. I will be remembered as the conqueror of Asia, the Lord High Chamberlain of India, the Christopher Columbus of all the oceans, the conquistador of Argentina, the man who raced his sled dogs to the South Pole and lived to tell about it. The British Isles are in my rear pocket."

"What haven't you done?" she asked.

"I have not yet set a record for wives," he said. "I've had a few, disposed of many, but so far, I'm no match for a typical Italian."

"I'll marry you if you want."

"Madam, you are already touched by history. My numerous biographers will remember this fateful day when you bought me a drink, thereby entering that select world of those who will be read about a thousand years from now."

"I gather you're important," she said.

"Important! I disdain the word. That suggests merely a berth in the first rank. I leave that to the multitudes who toil and sweat. In truth, madam, I am unique. Throughout the history of the world, of all the civilizations, in the jungles and deserts, on the steppes of Asia, and in the frigates of navies, there has been none like me."

She took the plunge. "Would you like to tell it to the world, sir?"

"There's nothing to tell. I'm already known from pole to pole, and clear around the equator."

"But not everyone's seen you, sir. I think you should be granting audiences to those who have admired you from afar."

His gaze bored into her. "What's the proposition, eh?"

"First tell me your name, sir."

"If you don't know it, you are grossly deficient."

"Here's the proposition, sir. I will display you. I'm with the company at the opera house in town, and I will put you in front of large crowds, who then may catch a glimpse of your genius, and remember it the rest of their natural lives."

He mulled it.

"You will be fed, clad, sheltered, and will have your choice of beverages at any time."

He turned to the rest. "There, you see? It took a woman to recognize the unique person before you. She wasn't content to offer me a drink or two; she has offered me sustenance worthy of my unique calling."

"I'm Ethel. We'll call the act, The Genius and Ethel. All right?"

"Madam, I'm your liege lord," he said.

"Come along now. I'll get rid of some girls and put you in the Butte Hotel, where it's warm."

"Madam, genius has met its match," he said.

"And we'll tour Philipburg and Missoula next."

"Abominable towns, but I will suffer cruelties until the whole world has gathered at my feet."

The observing crowd was smiling. That was the deal. He was half the act. She would need to be the debunker and skeptic, and puncture the gasbag now and then, and if it all worked, she'd have a comedy routine.

She got him out of there, fed him some soup at an all-night café, and stowed him in her room. He was not fragrant but that could be dealt with. She moved in with the girls, who didn't want another in their two beds, but so what?

"I've got an act, The Genius and Ethel," she said. "And don't ask me his name."

Her tone was belligerent enough to quell questioning, so they grumbled instead.

The next morning she pushed some porridge into him, found August Beausoleil, and arranged for an audition at the opera house.

"Who's the genius?" he asked.

"I haven't beaten that out of him yet."

Beausoleil's smile spoke loudly.

She insisted on some spotlights, and the olio drop, since this would make a good olio act. And she wanted the focus on The Genius.

Beausoleil sat about four rows back, looking impatient. But Ethel was an old hand, and he'd give her careful consideration. She wished there could be a small audience, able to pick up on details, but August was as much a veteran of auditions in empty theaters as she. She settled The Genius in a wicker chair with a high back that looked vaguely like a throne.

"All right, Genius, away we go," she said. "Who are you?"

"I'm the greatest man who ever lived, from the beginning of time," he said.

"What have you got against Napoleon?"

"Utterly incompetent. Now, if I had been in charge, Waterloo never would have happened."

"Have you ever served in an army?"

"That would be an utter waste of my talents," the Genius said.

"What about Shakespeare, Genius?"

"Pedestrian, madam. I could write circles around him. Hamlet's the worst bit of stagecraft ever written."

"So are your plays better?"

"Good Lord, woman, why bother? Plays are an inferior form of storytelling."

It went along for a while like that, and she didn't see Beausoleil crack a smile. That wasn't good. She put more heat on the Genius, making fun of his windy assertions, but it wasn't softening up Beausoleil any.

"Ethel, that's enough," Beausoleil said. "I'm going to say no to this, for several reasons. Thank you, sir."

"You mind telling me what?"

"You have the germ of an idea, but it's not going anywhere. It's not building. It's not an act, with a finish. But there's more, I'm afraid." He eyed The Genius. "The audience may be discomfited by you picking on this fellow. If he were an entertainer, that would be one thing, but he's not."

"Well, sir, I am an entertainer, and I'm glad you've put your finger on it," The Genius said. "First, let me introduce myself. I'm Cromwell Perkins. I don't use my name much, so as not to embarrass my family. Let me explain. I grew up in comfortable circumstances in the East, and got a good education, but I was born with a fatal flaw, at least a troublesome one. I have a great aversion to honest labor, and I'll find any wretched means to avoid toiling as a grocery clerk or a surveyor or a shoe salesman. The thought of practicing law, like my father, makes me faint. I sank deeper and deeper into want, and then figured out my salvation. I became a barstool entertainer. I am a frequent visitor to saloons of all sorts, and the places eventually gave me my living. I learned how to collect a crowd.

"It was there, sitting on more stools, or putting a foot on more brass rails, than I can remember, that I evolved into The Genius. I learned how to startle and amuse. I learned how to shock and dismay. People bought me drinks. They fed me lunch. They gathered around. They brought others in to hear The Genius. It didn't matter which saloon; I could wander into any, and pretty soon I collected a crowd, and sooner or later, they'd be buying me drinks, or offering me a tip. Not much of a living, I declare, but one that allows me a bunk in a basement, and a little heat in winter, and the chance to make a fool of myself day by day, to avoid honest toil."

He stared at Beausoleil, who stared back, and chuckled.

"So you're in the business after all," he said.

"It beats working for a living, sir."

"You know, this could turn into something. Not today or tomorrow, but soon, if you and Ethel turn this material into an act, something that doesn't sputter and die every other minute. I can do this much: I'll give you a free ride for a while, bed and board, but no pay until you've got an act that we can put on the boards with some confidence. And then we'll talk pay. Does that make sense to you, Cromwell?"

"It sounds suspiciously like toil," The Genius said.

"Take it. I'll work with you daily. We'll work up some

material. We'll make this into the best comedy on the circuits," Ethel said.

It was strange how it worked out. August was dead right. The act needed some refining. And in two minutes he had gotten the man's name and history out of him, and put a halt to the idea that Cromwell Perkins was half mad, or delusional, or that he was being paraded in front of audiences just to make fun of him.

"Come along, Cromwell. We'll have a bite, and then we're going to work, and I mean work, whether you like that idea or not."

"The thought makes me dizzy," The Genius said.

EIGHTEEN

Mrs. McGivers had two sick babies. Cain and Abel lay on her hotel bed, listless, their nostrils lined with phlegm, their long prehensile tails limp. They wore diapers. Their red-and-gold band uniforms had been brushed and set aside for the next performance. But now it seemed unlikely there would be another performance anytime soon.

She scarcely knew what to do. She wondered who might help, or whether it was useless to consult with anyone. She already knew what the trouble was: both capuchin monkeys had pneumonia. They were tropical animals, living in lowlands mostly, moist and warm, with good air. Not like Butte, over a mile high and numbingly cold, no matter how much heat warmed the room.

She had asked the Butte Hotel to summon a doctor, and wondered if the man would flatly refuse to treat a pair of sick monkeys. She could only wait and see. She rarely had trouble keeping the monkeys in her hotel room. In fact, the hotels usually enjoyed the prospect of a pair of primates in diapers in a room.

They were the only babies she had. She fed them, nurtured them, played games with them, and occasionally practiced the act with them. She had fitted them out with custom-made cymbals and a small bass drum, and had shaped them into an anarchistic band, with each song spinning off into chaos until the audience howled.

But she had nurtured them, too, brought them fruits and various vegetables, beverages, sweets. Monkeys had a sweet tooth. And sometimes, when they were unsettled, she took one in her arms and held it close, felt its little monkey arms wrap around her neck. She was mother and counselor and teacher to Cain and Abel.

Joseph, the accordionist who actually put the melody before audiences, had a room of his own, and lived oddly separated from the rest. And yet he was as sensitive to the monkeys, and the act, as she was. Indeed, he had been a street-corner organ grinder, and both of the monkeys had once been his wards until Mrs. McGivers bought in and reshaped the material into an act for the vaudeville stage.

Now she sat and fretted. She was more than worried; she felt panic, which she ruthlessly suppressed.

At the knock she leapt up, opened, and found a bearded man carrying a black Gladstone.

"Dr. Mortimer, madam. You are ill, I take it?"

"Ah, not me exactly, sir. There." She pointed at the small primates on her bed.

He stared, registering that, and smiled. "I'm afraid that's outside of my competence, madam."

"I thought you'd say that. They have colds, coughs, rattling in their throats, and maybe worse. Pneumonia, I'm thinking. Any help—well, they're my babies."

He peered at her, at them, at the small bed filled with two beasts with long tails.

"All right, let's see what I didn't learn in medical college," he said.

He settled on the edge of the bed, while Cain and Abel eyed him listlessly. From his Gladstone he extracted a listening horn, and placed it on Cain's chest, and paid close attention to what he heard. Then he placed the horn on Abel's chest, listening closely. He dug out a tongue suppressor.

"Will he bite?"

"He won't like it."

"I'd like a look."

"I'll hold him, and hold his tongue down, and you have your look."

It worked pretty well. Dr. Mortimer lit an electrical torch and got a good look inside the mouth of each.

"It's a pulmonary disease, certainly. As for a name, that is beyond my competence. Pneumonia, bronchitis, catarrh, common cold, sore throat, cough. Not that naming it would do much good. This is not the healthiest climate for a pair of tropical animals. Your best chance is to get them lower and warmer and dryer as fast as you can."

"And where might that be, sir?"

He stared into space. "Salt Lake City. I'd not trust them to survive the trip if you took them any farther than that."

"Any idea when they'll get better?"

"You're with the vaudeville show, I believe. I can hardly hazard a guess. But diseases come and go faster in smaller animals."

"Are there any remedies, sir?"

"I would hesitate to dose an animal with anything. The best I can suggest is a trip to a climate more suited for these little fellows."

"Are they dying?"

"They have a lot of fluid in their lungs. Especially that one there. I can hear it."

"I have some cough syrup with opium. . . ."

He shook his head. "I wouldn't."

"These monkeys, I love them. They're my act. My life depends on them."

The monkeys watched intently from their sickbed, somehow knowing this was all about them.

"See if you can get some honey in them," he said. "A little warm whiskey and honey, or tea and honey. It has mysterious powers."

"The whiskey or the honey?"

"Tell me about it," he said.

He charged her two dollars, two for the price of one, he said, and wished her success.

She closed the hotel door, and eyed her sick babies, and felt a wave of desolation crawl through her. There wasn't much hope. She couldn't get them to Salt Lake City; she lacked the means to rent a Pullman compartment, and they'd die before she got there. She couldn't leave the show. She couldn't stay in the show. She hardly dared leave the little capuchins alone, but she had to deal with this.

She found August Beausoleil in his room.

"Cain and Abel are sick; maybe pneumonia. I got a doctor, and all he could say was that it was in the lungs, and the monkeys were far from home. He thought the nearest dry and warm place was Salt Lake."

"No act, then?"

"No act."

He seemed to sag, and then straightened. "What may we do for you?"

"Keep us in the company for a while."

"Of course."

"The doctor said diseases come and go fast in smaller animals."

"Did he say whether the monkeys would recover soon?"

"No, he said that was beyond his competence. He said

I should try to get some whiskey and honey into them; it has properties."

"Drunken monkeys," he said. "I'll send someone for some honey. There's no shortage of whiskey in Butte. Madam, I'm so sorry."

He hugged her. It felt comfortable, his gentlemanly hug, and reassuring. She was almost beside herself. The monkeys were all the children she would ever have, and they loomed so large in her life that she couldn't imagine a future without them.

In due course she mixed some steaming water, some honey, and some whiskey together, and coaxed first Abel and then Cain to swallow some, which they did listlessly, accusation in their dull eyes. She gave them as much as they would swallow, and kept trying every few moments, until they rebelled and spit out anything she coaxed into their mouths. Then she sat, the bedside vigil, even as the next performance, another matinee, cranked up.

She couldn't imagine how August could fill the bill with so many acts disabled—or dead. But that was the business. Limp along, improvise, and hire claques to laugh and clap.

She clung to the room, even as the capuchins slept peacefully. Maybe it was the whiskey, she thought. Once she placed her hand on their fevered brows, but they barely stirred. She made room between them, and settled herself on the bed, her babies on either side, her rough browned hands clasping her little ones, until she dozed the afternoon away.

She was awakened by a knock, and opened to Ethel Wildroot, and welcomed Ethel even though they'd not gotten along, and Ethel was brimming with schemes and plots.

"Those poor little things," Ethel said.

"I've got them whiskeyed up," Mrs. McGivers said.

"That's as good as any," Ethel said. "We got through

the show. LaVerne did it. Three solos. There's hope for the girl in spite of bad blood on her father's side."

"Someone comes through, and the show limps along," Mrs. McGivers said.

"You want some monkeys? We can come up with monkeys."

"In Butte, Montana?"

"Don't I look like a monkey? And I've a friend I can turn into one."

The thought of it alarmed Mrs. McGivers at first.

"I can follow a beat; I can whale away at the cymbals when the moment comes. I can do monkey business. I can turn into an anarchist. I'm half monkey myself."

Mrs. McGivers stared, speechless.

"I have a new friend, a natural-born monkey we can put on the drum. Cromwell Perkins. He'll get the idea in no time. We can climb into some costumes, something evil, something that speaks of jungles, and we can do your monkey act without Cain and Abel."

"I could never leave Cain and Abel alone in the room."

"We could get a nanny. Cookie, my daughter, she likes monkeys. She's a little slow. I'll send Cookie over after the matinee, and we'll practice for tonight between shows. Get Joseph, and I'll get Cromwell, and we'll see what happens."

And that was how it played out. About five that afternoon, Mrs. McGivers and her new monkey band assembled at the opera house, under the skeptical eye of August Beausoleil, and soon were hammering out the revised act, this time gradually sliding from disciplined calypso music into utter anarchy. And then Mrs. McGivers shouted imprecations, and the culprits returned to rhythmic calypso, only to have that born rebel, Cromwell, begin to foul up the music.

And August Beausoleil was laughing.

"I don't know why I'm saying this, but I'll put you on. Be ready fourth slot in the first act, and we'll see."

Cromwell was a natural subversive. He caught the idea instantly—start with disciplined music, veer into anarchy, give it a tropical twist. Mrs. McGivers wondered about him. He almost looked like husband material to her jaded eye.

That evening, with Cookie Wildroot nursing the sick monkeys, Mrs. McGivers got her act costumed, absurd hats and gaudy pants, and then they were on.

"Gents and ladies, the one, the only, the sensational Mrs. McGivers and her Monkey Band," August intoned to a good crowd that had braved the dark cold evening.

It was a funny thing; she had a way of seeing success or failure in advance, and now the eve was bright with promise. The costumes were outlandish enough so the audience chuckled at the very sight of them. Joseph wheezed away on the accordion. Mrs. McGivers plunged into exotic calypso, strange rhythms from distant places. Ethel Wildroot whanged a cymbal at just the right moments, an odd sound against the tropical beat. And the insidious Cromwell was poking along on the bass drum, perfectly attuned to the music, until they had finished the first stanza. Then everything began to fall apart. Ethel whacked the cymbals. Joseph wheezed the accordion. Cromwell loosed a thunderous volley that rumbled out upon the crowd.

The crowd was discomfited. Something was wrong. And then Ethel loosed a clatter of cymbals that shook the rafters, and that monkey Cromwell battered the bass drums mercilessly, and now the crowd was chuckling, then laughing, then howling. The whole act tumbled into chaos, with Mrs. McGivers screeching, in turns, at Joseph, at Ethel, and at Cromwell. She grabbed a drumstick and beat Cromwell on the noggin with it.

The crowd howled. Mrs. McGivers' band had deserted her, poor old dear.

And August Beausoleil stood in the wing, delighted.

"How was that, ladies and gents?" he asked, when the crowd had quieted a bit. "Mrs. McGivers and her Monkey Band. Come out and take another bow, Mrs. McGivers! And the rest of you, come out and face the music! You're all fired!"

They did. People laughed and clapped. It was a different act, not a monkey act, but it worked. And August was smiling.

NINETEEN

Wayne Windsor hated to get out of bed before ten, but there were tasks to perform. Butte had ignored him. In fact, the papers had been silent, the coverage abysmal. He made a point of getting into every paper in every town the company played. On this cold morning he pulled the blankets away, fled their comforting warmth, and prepared himself for an excursion.

He scraped away the day's whiskers with his well-stropped straightedge. He took special care not to nick his cheeks, because the profile would be under close observation within the hour. He was an immaculate man, taught the virtue of cleanliness and grooming by his immaculate family. Unlike most people in vaudeville, who rose from the depths, or arrived on an immigrant boat, Windsor had grown up in privilege. He had achieved a bachelor degree, and he ascribed his success as a monologuist to the fund of wisdom and knowledge that he had acquired in New Haven. And, of course, his career had started in those hallowed precincts, the debating society.

After tea and a poached egg and muffins dripping with jam, he ventured out upon Butte's cruel slopes, after ascertaining the locations of several newspapers. He found *The Inter-Mountain* first, which was fine. By all accounts, a good, sober paper, not given to conniption fits.

He discovered a squinty gent in a sleeve garter at an oaken desk; behind him was the inky plant, where skinny compositors toiled at their typesticks, and half-formed pages were spread on iron tables known as stones. He had been in many a plant, and knew the language.

Sleeve-garter took notice, and approached the counter.

"Yes, I have a story for you, sir," Wayne said. "I'm Wayne Windsor, top-billed at the Beausoleil Brothers Follies, at the opera house. I've stopped by to give you an interview."

"An interview, ah, yes, some publicity."

"Well, look what I have here, sir. Here's an attractive portrait of me, from the side of course, which is the most flattering vantage point when it comes to depicting any vaudeville performer. Precast, ready to drop into your forms. And here, sir, is a complete interview, precast in type metal, so all you need do is drop it in your forms, and you've a story without further labor. Very handy when you're rushed. We'll be playing two more days, extended engagement because of the fine reception we've received, and I thought you'd like to run it in the afternoon edition. A good way to sell copies."

Sleeve-garter eyed Windsor, eyed the portrait etched in metal, and the two-column interview.

"Sir, if you want to run an ad, you have to pay for the space," he said.

"It's a balanced interview, finest journalistic tradition.

All you need do is write a headline mentioning that I'm at the opera house these two days."

Sleeve-garter sighed. "We could use some news today. I tell you what. I'll run that image of you, and interview you myself. We'll have to hurry, though."

Windsor was delighted. He followed the reporter to his grimy desk, and settled in for a good talk.

"I'm Bruce Key," he said, grabbing a pencil and a pad. "Now then, you're with the Follies, and you do what?"

"I'm a monologuist. I spin stories. You might say I'm a Mark Twain drifting through Butte."

"Who's that?" Key said.

"Tom Sawyer? Huck Finn? Never mind. I like to tickle funny bones, and I do this by poking a little fun at people."

"Ridicule, then?"

"Oh, nothing so blatant. There's plenty of people who beg to be examined. You might say I like to throw some light on their foibles."

"You amuse people on a stage. How'd you get there?"

"Debating societies, college, you know. I am among the fortunate, having a well-rounded schooling. I'm from an old Massachusetts family, textiles, shipping, slavery, rum, and various learned professions. A good name is worth a lot, of course. Here from the early seventeen-hundreds, prominent in Boston. Not quite up to the Cabots and Lowells, but certainly a peer, as families go. You know, that gives me a vantage point to view this country. I must say, sir, the tide of immigrants coming in now is very inferior. Not up to snuff. Half can't even speak English. The other half do nothing but breed. I'd support laws restricting immigration to the English, and no one else."

Key was busy scribbling all that, to Windsor's great satisfaction.

"You'd exclude the Irish?" Key asked.

"They don't really speak English, do they?"

"Dutch, Germans, Norwegians?"

"Yes, the stock would improve if they were kept out."

"What about those in your vaudeville company? Are they all English?"

"Well, you have to understand there's exceptions to any generalization, sir. Some people succeed, in spite of their genetic and social deficiencies. That's show business. Home of the mentally defective."

Windsor was enjoying it all. And Key had opened him up and was mining Windsor's richest veins. It turned out to be a fine interview. Even brilliant. Windsor explained that the country's strength was based on good English genetic stock, and the more it was diluted and debased by the hordes of people flooding through Ellis Island and spreading out across the continent, the weaker the republic became. These new people didn't understand the common law and tradition that had gone into founding the republic, he said. And they were lazy by nature.

Key cheerfully recorded all that, and then explained he would have to rush to get the story into the afternoon paper, but it should be on the streets around four. Windsor debated whether to take his interview material to other papers, but decided he had done a good day's work, and he would enjoy a leisurely tour of the town, if it wasn't too cold, and then prepare for the evening show.

He never knew which of several monologues he would employ, and he often sounded out his audience a little before plunging in. Maybe he would talk about future janitors and farmers pouring through the golden gates, and see where that would lead him. The ethnic roots of pig farmers fascinated him.

At four, he bought the paper, hot off the press, and was delighted to see his interview prominently displayed on page one. Good. That would help to fill the opera house that evening. The troupe would be pleased with the publicity he'd managed to get on his own.

But in fact no one said anything. Beausoleil was more concerned about having enough acts to run a normal show. The monkeys were sick, and that was a blessing as far as Windsor was concerned, but so were half the acts. And there were some strange faces around; some dubious sorts filling in, which made Windsor irritable. Beausoleil must be desperate.

The Profile saw it all as golden opportunity. During his first stint, in Act One, he had some fun with the copper kings of Butte, getting rich off the sweat of thousands of miners toiling deep in the pits. That got him a lot of nervous laughter. In fact, he was the real star of the Follies, since none of the other acts were drawing the sort of applause and delight that he was enjoying.

Mrs. McGivers was working with two human monkeys, and they weren't half bad, but it wasn't as bizarre as when the capuchin monkeys were whaling away. And the Wildroot Sisters were all sniffling and sick, and their stuff wasn't up to par. And Harry the Juggler wasn't up to snuff, either, especially when a scimitar fell to his feet. But the tap dancers, the Marbury Trio, were in good form.

All of which made Wayne Windsor glow. He was the top act, and the audience knew it. He did even better in the second act, with an improvised monologue about trying to converse with people who didn't speak English. He had a knack, and soon was imitating Norwegians, Italians, French, Bohemians, and Eskimos, much to everyone's delight. The new stuff was so good that he resolved to polish it up and make it part of his standard repertoire.

The show ended with the usual patriotic finale, and The Profile was looking forward to a drink or two, and bed. But John Maguire approached. "Windsor, you've got four admirers at the stage door, wanting to take you out for a beverage or two."

"Women?"

"No, miners, unless I miss the mark. They said they

wanted to treat you to a few, and hope you'd accept. They said you're the man they'd like to visit with."

"Tell them I'll be there in a bit, soon as I get into street clothes."

Sure enough, there were four gents waiting for him, two of them burly, one tall, one short, and all grinning.

"Windsor, is it? We're looking forward to a visit, sir. We'll take you to a miners' pub, and buy whatever it is that wets your whistle."

"I'd be pleased to bask in your admiration," Windsor said, wondering if these louts heard him praise himself. But they didn't.

"This is Martin Murphy, and that's Will McNamara, and this is Robby Toole, and I'm Mike Hoolihan," said one of the burly ones. "We all work the Neversweat. We'll share a toddy with you, if you're inclined."

"Of course. I relish time with my admirers," The Profile said.

They headed northeasterly, toward the great complex of mines that seemed to be the heart of the city, and in that zone where the downtown fell away and dreary streets with mining shanties and flats spread darkly into the night, they paused at an obscure saloon, ill-lit and strangely lonesome looking.

"Pile on in, Mr. Windsor," said Hoolihan.

Windsor found himself in a long ill-lit saloon with lithographs of horses tacked to the walls and only two lamps illumining the place, front and rear. Pipe smoke hung thickly in the air; most of these cobs had a pipe stem clamped between their teeth. Twenty or thirty silent men nursed ale or a shot of something.

"What'll it be?" Hoolihan asked.

"Some Jameson's, if it's to be had," The Profile said. That was good Irish whiskey, and this saloon might not stock it. But a bottle promptly appeared, and was set before the guest, along with a tumbler. He could pour his own. That was all fine with The Profile, who awarded his hosts with a long look at each side of his visage.

"We all work for Marcus Daly, and his Anaconda," Hoolihan said. "He brought us across the sea, by the thousands, and put us to work here. There's more of the Irish here than anywhere else away from the old country."

Windsor was beginning to see what this was about. He'd finish the good whiskey, and duck away.

"You know, my friend, it's mean work, and it wears a man down, and it's work few Yanks want to do, because it'll kill a man quick. Now, we thought you might like to see how it's done. You know, we're only a little hike from the Neversweat, and we'd like to take you down and show you men knocking rock. I'm a shift foreman, and I have the right to go where I want. You'll see men working in their underdrawers, it's that hot. They're all sheened up with sweat, and have to sip on the cool water they send down the shaft. But we keep on. The muckers break up rock and load it into the one-ton cars, a little noisy for your tastes, and those get pushed or pulled to the shaft and taken up. Others, they're using pneumatic drills on the face, to pound holes and set the charges. There's a lot of dust, and nowhere for it to go, and a lot of men get silicosis, miner's lung, or maybe consumption, because over the years they breathe a lot of that busted-up rock into their lungs, and they die young. So maybe all these immigrants are being led to their doom, wouldn't you say?"

"I'm sure you're very strong, sir."

"But maybe dumb, too, wasting our only life down there, far from the sun, breathing killer dust, and getting laid away at age forty-two. All so you can have copper to make wire to light your cities. Take that opera house. It's wired, and you get to do your show with incandescent lights, courtesy of mostly immigrant miners like these boys here.

"We were thinking, boyo, that there aren't many as

strong as us or brave as us. Mr. Daly, he couldn't hire enough Yanks to fill his mines, and so he went and fetched us, and brought us here. What does that say about all the ones living here, boyo?"

The Profile smiled. "Thanks for the drink, fellows. I'm worn-out from the show, and looking forward to bed. You've been most entertaining."

He rose to leave, but a strong hand clasped his shoulder and pressed him into the bar again.

"Not so fast, boyo. We've decided to take you down the shaft. You ready to go?"

Windsor laughed. "I must say, sirs, it's not my line of work, and it's time for me to head for the hotel, with thanks, of course, for your hospitality."

"You're staying a while, boyo. We're not done with you—unless, of course, you wish to show us that you don't enjoy our company."

They were itching for a fight. Well, Windsor hadn't been on his college sculling team for nothing, or the baseball team, or the tennis team, either.

He grinned, tucked a leg behind Hoolihan, shoved and twisted at the same time, and unbalanced the miner, who toppled with a mighty thud. The Profile headed for the door, but only to run into several fists. The others closed in. One caught his left profile with a jab; the other caught his right profile with an uppercut. Hoolihan bounced up and landed a hairy fist square in Windsor's mouth. He tasted blood. He felt his lips swell. He knew he had bitten his tongue. His mouth was a ruin. He could hardly form words. He fled into the night as they smiled.

TWENTY

Augustus Beausoleil clutched the yellow flimsy with the bad news: GEO PARSONS BARITONE AVAIL BUTTE THREE DAYS YOU PAY FREIGHT.

That was from a Chicago booking agent, Abe Stoop. Even if August added the Parsons act, it would be too little and too late. And he didn't have the cash to buy a two-thousand-mile ticket to Butte, Montana, from St. Louis, where Parsons was doing a club.

No, not Parsons.

That morning Wayne Windsor had shown up with a battered face, swollen lips, purple bruises, saying he couldn't work. His speech was slurred. All he would mumble was that he had been beaten by hooligans, and Butte was a dangerous place. He'd be out of the lineup until he could speak, and that would be a few days. The Profile had gotten himself into a jam somewhere. Beausoleil had a good idea how it had come about, but he didn't push the issue. That Butte newspaper with the interview sat on his hotel room table. It was a reckless interview in a mining town teeming with people straight off the boats.

That left a major hole. Windsor was good for two monologues a show, always richly humorous, and always an audience pleaser. But that wasn't all. Mrs. McGivers had come to August that morning with more bad news. Cain had perished from pneumonia but Abel lived on. Cain had died in the night, his prehensile tail wrapped around Mrs. McGivers' ample arm. He'd coughed and stopped breathing. Butte's brutal altitude and cold had overwhelmed the tropical monkey. Mrs. McGivers, in her night robes, had carried the dead monkey around and about the hotel, haunting corridors, until someone in uniform had finally steered her to her room and took the dead creature away.

Maybe that act was done, too, but for the moment, if Mrs. McGivers was up to it, the act could continue with a pair of humans playing monkeys. It didn't look good. He worried less about the substitute monkeys than about Mrs. McGivers, who was suffering a mother's loss of a child, and might not be able to open.

Suddenly the follies was falling apart. He could manage a short performance, with extra work by the Marbury Trio, and possibly get by. Or he could cancel, lose the box office, but still owe the theater. It was morning; he had a few hours to decide.

He would need to wire Pomerantz. If they were too crippled to play Butte that night and the following, they were likely to be too crippled to play Philipsburg. He wondered if he could even reach Pomerantz, who was off honeymooning after a reckless marriage. Dream girl. Ginger was her name, girl in white, singer of opera and ballads. Funeral singer. Did a good job at the service for Mary Mabel Markey.

He hiked to the telegraph office in the next block, and hastily fashioned a message: NEED GINGER TONIGHT TOMORROW.

Maybe if there was passenger service, he'd have a singer.

But not an act. The girl would just sing some songs. But she was good at it, and that counted.

The odds weren't good, but he sent the wire anyway, and hoped for a quick reply. It wasn't anything he could count on.

Catching all the acts in their rooms would be tough, but he could spread the word. He found a Marbury in the hall.

"Delilah, wait."

"More trouble, I suppose. I hear The Profile got beat up."

"You know more than I do," August said. "But yes, he's out for a spell."

"The word is, some miners didn't like his piece about immigrants, and let him know it."

"He hasn't revealed the source of his affliction, only that he's lacking the means to talk."

"I heard it at breakfast. They wanted to take him into the mine, and show him where copper comes from. It doesn't come from people with social connections and college degrees."

"I think he learned that last night."

"In spades," she said, grinning.

"Delilah, we're short of acts. Mrs. McGivers' little monkey died of pneumonia, and she's not fit."

"Oh no, oh no."

"We'll see. She's a phenomenon."

"Tough old performer."

"The thing is, Delilah, can you and your gents do three different deals tonight?"

"We've been working on one. This house has hardwood on the aisles. We're thinking of a deal tapping our way through the audience, and up and down some stairs. But we've barely tried it."

"You're on, and you've rescued me."

"We'll work on it this morning. Which monkey, Cain?"

"You know, I don't remember."

"Poor Mrs. McGivers. She might kill husbands, but she loves monkeys."

"Delilah, get the word out."

He headed to the opera house, braving a smoke-choked morning. The north wind drove the acrid mine and mill smoke straight down the slope of the city, burning up lungs and tempers. He marveled that anyone lived to be forty in this miserable city. He wondered whether this mean city would be the ruin of his company, whose ranks were thinning by the hour.

He found John Maguire in his office, staring at the horizon.

"I've heard," Maguire said. "Word gets around fast. You have some acts?"

"Maybe cancel; have to make up my mind."

"Tonight and tomorrow?"

Beausoleil just shook his head. Butte had defeated him.

"The Profile sure chose the wrong place to tout his ancestry. Frankly, August, I'm surprised he got away with it as long as he did. This town's famous for saloon fights; I mean, the Cornishmen invade an Irish saloon, and bust it up, or the Irish and Italians tangle over some alleged insult. So Windsor simply walked right into the middle of it. I know who did it, and they were kind to him. He could have been busted wide open."

"You have any ideas, John?"

"Headline: Wayne Windsor not in show tonight. Turn it to good use. In this game, turn everything to good use. Fill the seats, one way or another."

That was it. One way or another. "Thanks, John. I'll see," August said.

That was a novelty. But so was Butte. And by now, Windsor's fate was the gossip of the whole mining town. It was a town that enjoyed rough humor. August weighed what to say, and finally decided that the gaudier the story, the better. He bundled into a thin coat—he hadn't fathomed how early cold weather would descend here—and headed for *The Inter-Mountain*. He'd get it into all the afternoon rags if he could, but he might as well start with the paper The Profile visited.

A stern gent in a sleeve garter greeted him at a counter.

"Beausoleil here; I own the show. Have an announcement," August said.

"I imagine you do," the gent said.

"One of our acts, Wayne Windsor, won't appear this

evening or tomorrow. But the show will be better than ever."

"That's what I figured," the gent said. "Incapacitated? On both sides of the profile?"

This gent knew a lot more than August had imagined.

"Yes, he's a bit out of sorts."

"And how did all this happen, sir?"

"He didn't tell me. Maybe he ran into a doorknob."

"I'll quote you."

"That's what I want. Tell your Butte readers that the star of the Follies ran into a doorknob and won't appear."

"Beausoleil, you're a genius," the gent said. "Is this a scoop?"

"No, I'm going from paper to paper, varying the story considerably. Whoever gets it out first will have all the advantage."

"I might improve upon the story, sir."

"Good. You'll sell more papers and I'll sell more tickets."

Impulsively, Beausoleil shook hands with the dour reporter. He counted it one of his best interviews ever.

He braved the dank cold and arrived at the *Miner,* owned by one of the copper barons who rode herd on the town. This time, the reporter who met him was stern, gray, with wire-rimmed spectacles. He oozed skepticism.

"So, what's the story?" he asked.

"Why, sir, our lead performer may not appear this eve."

"So why are you telling me this?"

"So our customers will know in advance; it's the thing to do."

"Why won't he appear?"

"He's been injured, sir. He hasn't told me how. But it impairs his performance. Now, of course, he may change his mind and appear; one never knows. In that case, he would bravely do his monologues even while words don't form easily on the tongue. The audience might be treated to a performer's courage."

"Word is, he got whaled in an Irish pub. Yes or no?"

"He hasn't told me, sir."

"Are you weaseling?"

"I have heard the rumor. But he hasn't told me. I also heard that the assault was a response to Wayne Windsor's comments about immigrants of all descriptions."

"Maybe you're square after all," the man said. "I might run something. Maybe not. It's not the hottest story in town."

"Read all about it," yelled a newsboy on the next corner. "Actor loses his teeth."

That was *The Anaconda Standard*, published in the next town by copper king Marcus Daly, but a lively presence in Butte. It was Daly who had imported Irish by the thousands to work in his pits.

Beausoleil laid out his two cents, and examined the sheet. Sure enough, on the front page, was the Wayne Windsor story.

Some gentlemen who worked at the Anaconda Company's Neversweat Mine invited the performer at the opera house, Wayne Windsor, to tour the pits with them, which the performer declined, and in the process of escaping the hospitality of these gentlemen, ran into a few knuckles.

It was an elegant story. The Beausoleil Brothers Follies were mentioned more than once, along with the opera house. But the story's real focus was Wayne Windsor's observations about new immigrants, their deficiencies, and the virtues of solid, old American English-speaking stock.

So it was all over town, both the rumors and now a story on page one. But it went on to discuss the performer himself.

"Mr. Windsor is enamored of his countenance, according to our sources, and is known in the company as The Profile, because he turns one way and another as he addresses his audiences, so each half of the crowd may admire his noble brow and aquiline nose and jut jaw.

"By all reports, he has a good line of repartee, mostly poking gentle fun at assorted groups. He does a whole routine based on trying to talk to various Norwegians, Swedes, Irish, Bohemians, or Italians, and this is said to amuse not only the English-speakers in the audience, but the more recent arrivals on our shores.

"We await word as to when The Profile will be back in commission. There's been no one quite like him in Butte."

August had the odd sensation that this evening's performance would be well attended. That was the odd thing about publicity. Even the most negative would draw a crowd.

When he reached the Butte Hotel a flimsy was awaiting him: NO TRAIN UNTIL TOMORROW GINGER READY FOR LAST BUTTE SHOW.

Tonight, then, his beleaguered company would sing and dance themselves into exhaustion. He headed for Mrs. McGivers' room, wondering if madam would perform this cold evening.

She opened to him, with an apparently restored Abel on her shoulder. The little criminal looked lonesome for his lost pal.

"You have an act?"

"You damn betcha," she said. "We're going to put on an act, one way or another. Work or starve, that's my motto. We'll crank something out. Abel, he'll pick pockets, the organ grinder act. And I've got that fake monkey

Ethel pulled out of a saloon. Hey, it don't take much to keep Butte happy."

She was smiling broadly, but there was a sadness around her eyes.

TWENTY-ONE

harles was waving a yellow paper. "Hey, sweetheart, you wanted to sing? You get to sing."

"What, Charles?" Ginger asked.

"August needs you, right now. He's got sick acts."

"But he said I'm not, what was it? Not a draw."

"You put on a show or you cancel. And if you cancel, you return the ticket sales, and you still pay the house, and you still have expenses, and people waiting for their money. So you do the show, baby."

This was dizzying. These days had been dizzying. She had recklessly plunged into a universe she knew nothing about, and that included much more than a sudden marriage.

"What do I do?"

"You take the train back to Butte. I'll go with you partway, but then I've got to go to Missoula. We're nearly done here anyway. You go back, try out your tonsils, and knock 'em dead, twice, first and second acts."

"I haven't practiced."

"Neither have half the acts. You put a smile on your mug, you go on out there, and you do what you can do, and maybe you'll score, maybe not."

"What do you think I should sing? You know better than I ever could."

He eyed her cheerfully. "Here's where you're the boss, baby. I don't know what's stuffed in your head; I've barely heard you. We've got an amateur marriage. Singing, you're the pro. So you pick the numbers, and you dish the numbers, about three each act, if August wants to stretch it out a bit. And have an encore ready."

"Who'll accompany me? I often sing at a piano."

"Improvise, baby. If it bombs in the first act, do something else in the second."

"But what should I wear?"

"Nothing."

She reddened. She'd been wearing a lot of nothing in the hotel room in Philipsburg. She'd gotten the whirlwind tour of marriage. She'd expected a lot of sweet nothings, a lot of whispered kisses, a lot of hand holding, and instead, she'd been carried to a mountain top and hurled into space. She hadn't had time to figure it out. She was plunged into a river of impressions, feelings, odd loneliness, yearnings for the home she had fled, aching for whatever might come next. And her first real awareness of her lithe body.

He'd been furiously busy. Apart from making arrangements to house and feed the company, an advance man was involved in publicity, first and foremost. Tell the world about the show. Get three-sheet playbills up on barns, ads in papers, notices in cafés; start barkeeps gossiping, start editors muttering. Hire someone to hand out flyers.

He was off and gone all day and half the nights, so she barely knew her husband, and knew even less about the marriage she had contracted, and had spent a lot of time cloistered in the room, waiting for him. She had felt like some useless baggage, and maybe that's all she was. But then he'd burst into their room, beaming, and the world was aglow again.

One thing she knew: this world was nothing like the bourgeois one she had escaped. And she wasn't sure she liked this one at all. What was the axiom? Act in haste, repent at leisure. But there was this about it: She had made good her escape. She had fled the world that was crushing her and arrived in a world rife with possibility. And somehow, she had left no trail. They wouldn't be coming after her. She was free!

He was eyeing her. He had been curious about her, curious about how she was taking all this. He had learned to read her, and she marveled at it. She'd barely known boys; now she had a man. A stranger. More of a stranger than the day they had met. The odd thing was, she liked this jittery life. Even when she was scared, she liked this business. She was ready to hug the world.

"The shuttle leaves at seven; we reach the mainline at eight; Helena by nine; Butte by ten thirty. You'll have the afternoon to work up an act. It's the last show there. That makes it easy on you. If you flop, you won't let anyone down. But you won't flop. You've got the goods, babe."

Philipsburg lay at the end of a long spur off the Northern Pacific. A short smoky train carried freight, ore, passengers, and hoboes each way, each day.

She couldn't remember where she had put her sheet music. Or what dress to wear. Or what she should do out in front of people. She had given recitals, but this wasn't a recital. And after the company was together and well, she'd be back with Charles, Mrs. Pomerantz, out in front of the troupe, living in hotel rooms. Well, she had bought the ticket, and now she would see where it would take her.

She had barely gotten some sleep that wild evening when he was awakening her.

"Up, baby. This is your big day."

Big day? For what? As she went through her ablutions, she understood. They all thought she had wanted to be a vaudeville star, that she was some stagestruck girl with ambitions. Well, there was that, but the thing that had driven her to this point was simply a passion to escape.

She hurried into gray woolen travel clothes, and they hastened to the small barn-red station where several other people huddled in the morning cold. The ancient coach wasn't much warmer, but steam from the engine gradually wrought a measure of comfort.

For a change, every train was on time. They boarded the lacquered eastbound NP express, and were soon in Helena. Charles left her there with a kiss and a squeeze, and caught a train to Missoula. She boarded another local and rattled through a mountain valley to Butte. A hack sent by Beausoleil was there to meet her and carry her and her several bags to the hotel. She had been billeted with the Wildroot girls, for lack of any other room. And no sooner had she dropped off her bags than August was at the door.

"We'll go to the opera house. You'll want to work out an act," he said.

She realized he hadn't welcomed her, hadn't made small talk, hadn't engaged in pleasantries. He had brusquely commanded her presence. Keeping a touring company afloat was serious business.

"I don't have my music," she said as they walked along Broadway.

"Sing from memory or tell me you're not in," he said. "And right now."

"Is there a pianist?"

"We've got a fiddler, an accordionist or two, but not a pianist. We can't be hauling a Steinway from stage to stage."

"But doesn't the house have one?"

"They sometimes do. John Maguire probably does."

"Can someone accompany me?"

"What are you, some opera diva?"

This was not going the way she had hoped. Charles had vanished; he always seemed to have more business than he had time. There were shadowy things in this new life she was leading.

He pulled open the side door to the opera house, and

steered her toward the stage, pulling a switch that lit a single spotlight that flooded a downstage area with white light. Then he clattered down some steps and into the cavernous darkness, filled with row upon row of empty seats, and settled in one, about five rows back. He made no effort to find a piano for her, or an accompanist, or Mr. Maguire, the boldly dressed gentleman whose place this was.

Then Beausoleil's voice softened. "Warm up a little, Ginger, and when you're ready, give me music."

She ran a few scales, a few high C's, and nodded.

"Introduce yourself and your song," he said.

It frightened her. "I'm Ginger," she said, tentatively.

"No, no, tell the audience how fine they are."

"I'm so pleased to see you good people this cold evening," she said. "I'll do a few ballads, songs that tell stories."

"Okay, okay, not exactly riveting," he said. "But you'll figure it out. If they yawn, try something else."

"Here's a favorite of mine, from Old Mexico," she said.

Dead silence out there. At least Beausoleil wasn't barking at her. "It's called 'Cielito Lindo.'"

That was greeted with a long silence.

She sang, her voice sailing into oblivion, swallowed up by the cavernous space in front of her. She was tense, and then relaxed a little, and caught the complex rhythm, and made it Mexican bright.

"Give me another," he said, afterwards.

She did.

"This isn't a recital," he said. "Sing to someone. Sing to me. Make contact with your audience."

"I don't understand."

"Tonight, pick out some gent in the fifth row, and sing to him. Make him think you're up there for his sake. Get him in your vision, and keep him there. Like he's a lover."

She hadn't the faintest idea why she should do that, but she nodded.

"If that bothers you, pick someone else. Sing to the old gal in the third row with the hearing horn. And that brings up another thing. Your voice is weak. Make it strong. Make it bounce off the rear wall, behind me."

"You don't like my voice?"

"Sure I do. Nice for operas and recitals. This is vaudeville, show business. It's not a voice for that. Not like Mary Mabel Markey. She could deliver, know what I mean?"

She did, actually.

He softened again. "Glad to have you here, Ginger. You'll do. You'll be fine tonight, and maybe we'll use you some more, if the acts stay sick. I'll borrow you from Charles for a while. Once you get the hang of it, you'll pick up some steam. Mostly, you need to connect with people. At recitals, you just sing. Onstage here, you have a different task. You'll seduce every male and enchant every female."

"But that's—not . . ."

"It's show business, sweetheart. See you a half hour before showtime. Might have other things to tell you. Get gussied up so you look like everyone's favorite girl."

That was it. He wandered off to talk to Maguire. She stood there, in the spotlight, feeling two things at once. She seemed to be soaring, and she felt crushed, and she couldn't reconcile the two.

Charles wouldn't be in the audience that evening. She wouldn't be singing for him. She wouldn't have his assurance. If she failed, there'd be no hug, no arm around the shoulder. Now she was in the troupe. She was a performer. She had crossed some sort of bridge. She realized, suddenly, that show business could be the loneliest profession, and sometimes the loneliest moment of all would arrive when she was surrounded by well-wishing people, and a warm audience, and a happy manager.

The Wildroot girls were annoyed by an addition in their crowded room. It meant they would all be sleeping two to a bed, and any disturbance in the night would keep them all awake. But they were veteran troupers, and would joke it away.

"How'd it go?" asked LaVerne, the one who seemed most caring, even if she was a rival with a singing act of her own.

"I don't think Mr. Beausoleil was very happy," she said.

"They're all like that, sweetheart. It's not the managers and coaches and any of us you should worry about. It's the crowd. It's those folding-money folks who lay out the moolah, come in out of the cold, and sit down and want you to give them something good, something that they enjoy, in the bright lights. You pay no attention to us, to me, to the owners. Just ignore us. Go ring their bells. You listen to the crowd. You listen to their clapping. You listen to their smile. Yeah, sweetheart, listen to that. When they're smiling, the sound is different. When they ain't smiling, you'll hear something else. And sweetheart, don't give up after one bad show. It's a big ladder, and not very many climb to the top. Keep trying. Keep working new stuff. But if you get a few rungs up, that's fine. We're out here on a rinky-dink tour, not big time. No big-timers do Montana. This is the end of the earth. Beausoleil couldn't afford them. He can barely afford our two-bit sisters act. But now you're in the business, and you'll have a good time—mostly."

TWENTY-TWO

Wayne Windsor watched dourly from the wing. Harry the Juggler was tossing teacups and saucers in perfect form, a blizzard of pottery flying in perfect arches. The audience was rapt. Harry was doing things people had never seen and could hardly imagine.

The opera house was full. That spate of publicity had filled it. Windsor had read the articles grimly, aware that Butte was rubbing it in. He was in a foul mood, and August Beausoleil, dressed in his majordomo tuxedo, was eyeing him carefully. Windsor was not beyond causing trouble, and took some pride in it.

His lips and cheeks were swollen, his tongue bore some lacerations, and his noble visage was in ruins. The latter, more than his inability to enunciate clearly, was what kept him in the gloom offstage.

He envied Harry the Juggler, who needed only to smile, gesture, and plunge in. The man was actually billed this time as Harry Wojtucek, The Exhibitionist Extravaganza. He spoke enough English, after Polish, or whatever, to get along, but he remained a mystery to the company, and chose his own lonely ways. Harry didn't need to say a word. Harry could mesmerize audiences with the dash and daring of his skills. Wayne was always a little contemptuous of all that. Wayne Windsor had to go out twice an evening, fathom his audience, tickle their humor, and adapt his monologues to all sorts of conditions. Now that took mental skill. That took finesse far beyond what Harry the Juggler possessed. It was another case of the gifted American standing above the crowd.

Wayne wearied of it. Wearied of being in shadows, ignored, distrusted, and even laughed at by the company. He knew they were laughing. He truly did have a noble visage, a stunning profile, but no one much cared, and a few rubes were ready to make fun of him. The Wildroot Sisters were ready; silent acts were followed by noisy ones. And after that, who knows? This was an odd show, patched together. Maybe that girl in white, the one Charles Pomerantz wanted to bed badly enough to turn himself into a sucker. The girl who was standing rigidly in the shadows, far from anyone.

Beausoleil turned to the girl in white next. He was dealing with a cheerful crowd, but a quiet one. Nothing had ignited them this eve. Windsor watched the majordomo stride out to the spotlit center, peer out to the crowd, and lift his top hat.

"Ladies and gents, a new voice, the sweetest voice I've ever heard, a young lady I'm proud to present to you, as a farewell gift, the one, the only Ginger!"

He paused there, awaiting her, and she finally strode out, smoothing her dress as she went.

He nodded and left. She bowed, deep and long, and smiled. She had borrowed Joseph, on his accordion, and he struck a tentative note. And then the lively "Cielito Lindo," a bright tune up from the lands below the border. She sang well. Windsor watched, fascinated. She received polite applause, and he knew why. She wasn't connecting. In vaudeville, you play your audience, you nearly reach out and touch those people. Her voice sailed straight over their heads, and died at the farthest walls.

Two more ballads, same response. Not bad. She really did have a sweet voice, and a discipline rarely seen on the variety stage. Not bad at all, just not a success, and not really vaudeville. For her, it had been another recital.

But Beausoleil had filled some time, kept his patched-up show out there, in the limelight, everyone digging deep to entertain this Butte crowd. Windsor watched the girl, wondering if she could read the performance, and decided she could. She left the stage quietly, even as Beausoleil led the crowd through a final round of applause. And then she was alone again, hugging the dark, while the rest of the crowd steered away from her because that was plainly what she wanted.

"The one, the only Wildroot Sisters," the majordomo was saying.

Windsor headed her way. "Good start, sweetheart. You'll get the hang of it soon."

"I forgot to sing to the gent in the fifth row," she said, smiling suddenly. "The bald gent with the big wife wearing fake pearls."

"Yeah, I try to talk to the wiseacre in the seventh row, the guy who's going to head for the saloon and tell the town my act was lousy." He had trouble saying that, but it didn't matter. This was whisper time, with the three girls out there, getting primed to wail away.

"It's not like I thought it would be."

"It's better, sweetheart. Wait until you connect. Wait until that guy in the fifth starts nodding or grinning or mouthing words, until his wife elbows him and the couple behind him catch the fever."

"I hadn't thought of that. I'd thought of a perfect high C, or a slight pause, or a gentle fade, or making sure I didn't betray the composer."

"You've been trained, right?"

She seemed to freeze up a moment, and then nodded.

"Throw it out. Make use of it, but throw it out. Next time you sing a song, put a stamp on it. It'll be yours more than whoever wrote it."

"That would be—a sacrilege," she said.

"Then commit sacrilege."

He swore she turned pale, there in the shadows, as she absorbed that, while the sisters out front were doing a high step. She smiled, excused herself, and headed toward the safety of the Green Room.

She'd never make it. She should go back to giving recitals at tea parties. They came, they went, they had a round or two on-stage, and they disappeared. He'd seen a thousand, each hopeful, each with stars in her eyes or a smile on his lips, and they didn't pass muster, and after a few tries, they knew it. And left the stage.

Windsor listened a while. The audience wasn't exactly giving the Wildroot girls the big huzzah, either, but they were professionals, and they could even turn an act around in the middle, picking up a better beat.

Beausoleil didn't look happy. But this was the last shot in Butte. What did it matter. Openings, those counted.

Windsor found himself itching to escape. They wouldn't use him this eve. He thought of Butte, raw, cruel, teeming with ruffians who had muscle and no brains, and not enough schooling to fill a third-grade classroom. He pulled a coat over himself, slid out the stage door, and into a black night while arctic winds caught his sore cheeks and tugged at his bowler.

Any saloon would do. No one knew him. A drink or two or three would comfort him. He needed several to quiet the pain. And he could watch the animals, watch them sip ale and tell stories. He drifted upslope and east, and found himself at the edge of the commercial district, staring into a well-lit eatery. It looked to be crowded, the patrons all male. He suddenly realized he was starved. He had eaten little; his lacerated tongue and lips and mouth simply hurt too much. But now a ravenous need propelled him into the warmth and cheer.

These were rough men, ruddy, and cheerful. And he didn't understand a word they were saying. It seemed to be English, but he swore it was some dialect beyond his fathoming, with broad yeowls and mews and barks. But the fragrance of food caught him squarely. These men were mostly buying a single product, a warm pastry served in a paper wrapper. The customers collected one, sat down at trestle tables, and devoured the fragrant thing, eating it straight out of the paper.

"What'll she be, boyo?"

"That," he said, lacking a name.

The server wrapped one up, handed it to him, and muttered a price, some amount he couldn't understand.

"Two-bits," said the customer behind him. "Beef pasty, a quarter."

Windsor paid.

"New here, eh? These are Cornishmen, and their English is so thick you need to slice it with a knife."

"I hope I can eat this. I need something soft," Windsor said.

"Half the miners in Butte lack most of their teeth," the man said, as he picked up his own pasty. "Have a seat, and I'll tell you a little about this town."

They found room at the trestle table, and settled on its bench. Windsor bit gingerly into the hot pastry, and was rewarded with some tasty, soft mixture within, mostly beef that had been reduced to small pieces.

"Your first one? It's cubed beef, onions, and potatoes, baked in a pastry shell. Miners love them, take them into the pits, call them 'letters from home.' They're a filling meal, no fork needed, usually still warm in their lunch buckets. And a Cornish delicacy."

Windsor swallowed gingerly, having no trouble working the tasty food past all his wounds.

"Good," Windsor said.

"Lots of Cornish here, sir. They were miners in Cornwall, had the knowledge to help over here. They're often shift bosses, or people with special skills, putting all they know to work."

The pasty filling was warm and fragrant, and slid down easily. Windsor thought he might like a little more spice, but this was a good hearty meal, and he was filling his empty stomach with little bits of pasty.

"We've got all sorts flooding in. Norwegians, Finns, they're the ones to work with wood, and they do the timbering of the mines, employing skills they seem to have been born with. Seems like just about every corner of Europe is sending people here, each with a specialty."

"And you, sir?"

"Shift foreman, actually German."

"You'd come here into a workingman's restaurant?"

The German stared at him. "In Butte, sir, everyone's a workingman. Including the owners."

"But there's no plates and napkins and silverware and all. Why come here when you can enjoy better?"

The foreman eyed Windsor, somehow assessing him, and smiled, a recognition.

Windsor was suddenly aware of his battered face, the notoriety, the papers, and knew he'd been found out.

"And all you get along?" he asked.

"No. The Irish jump the Cousin Jacks; the Cornish wreck dago restaurants; the wops bust every mug in an Irish saloon; the bohunks heckle the norskies, and once in a while someone gets hurt. Like you. It's a matter of national pride."

"What are Cousin Jacks?"

"Cornishmen. Half of them are Jack, so that's the name for them all."

Windsor watched the foreman polish off his pasty and wipe his hands on the paper.

"I saw your act," the man said. "The best was when you were mimicking the immigrants, when you had Norwegians trying to talk to Hungarians in rough English, and everyone got a little crazy."

"That didn't bother you?"

"Windsor, that's Butte humor."

"I thought you kill each other when you can."

"That's in between laughing at each other."

"Then why did the Irish do this to me?" Windsor pointed at his bruises.

"You've got to understand the rough humor here. If you'd just laughed, they'd have bought you a mug of ale."

"But they were going to take me into the pits."

"Just to see you soak your pants, my boy. All you had to do was grin back. Now, it's getting on to shift time, and I'm heading toward the Anaconda to put in my hours. Want to come along? See how it is, a thousand feet down, and hot as the tropics?"

"Sir, I'd be scared."

"Well, fella, I'd be scared standing up in front of an audience and spinning out jokes and stories. I think I'd be the one staining my britches, my friend. Whenever I tell a joke I forget the finish, and feel like an idiot. It's what you're used to, and what you can bear. I couldn't stand it, myself."

The gent clamped a shapeless fedora over his head, headed into the night, and left Wayne Windsor sitting alone at the bench, contemplating a world he little understood, but had suddenly started to appreciate.

Maybe he'd be healed up by the time they opened in Philipsburg, a booming mining town a little ways away. Another pasty, and some more good company, and Windsor would be ready to go once again.

TWENTY-THREE

The Butte box office wasn't bad. August Beausoleil sat with the opera house owner in John Maguire's dim-lit office, counting out the singles and two-spots and change. There was hardly a fiver or a ten in the lot.

This final night they had filled most of the seats; another seventy would have packed the house.

"Pretty good," said Maguire.

"Nothing to complain about. Are we even?"

"Far as I know. You want to stow it in the safe?"

The troupe wouldn't be leaving Butte until mid-morning. "Best place," August said.

"You'll be the first road company to play Philipsburg," Maguire said. "Let me know how it went."

"Three-hundred-fifty seats; matinee and evening."

He and Maguire knew the Follies would need to fill the house both performances to come out ahead. And there would have to be no surprises. That was the thing with a touring company: no matter how carefully you worked out the arrangements, the acts, the accommodations, the travel, there always were surprises. And the only thing between you and disaster sometimes was the cash box.

"Enjoy Butte?" Maguire asked.

"Not enough people speak English."

Maguire smiled. "They know how to count. And miners make a good day wage, usually three and a half. And they spend it."

They did spend it. Unlike people in a farming town. There was a lot of cash circulating in Butte. And miners were not the sort to save and scrimp.

"August, I'm pleased you booked the house." The natty Maguire, in his dove-gray waistcoat and tailored coat, offered a hand, and Beausoleil took it.

"You helped us through some troubles, John."

"That's the biz," Maguire said. He slid the cash box into a small safe and spun the dial.

The house was dark, save for a single lamp high up. Beausoleil was feeling that odd loneliness he always experienced upon finishing an engagement. No sooner did he have a relationship with a town than he was torn from it. He couldn't explain it, and it made no sense. The next town would probably be better. The future was always better than the past.

Out on the cold reaches of Broadway, he discovered Mrs. McGivers waiting patiently for him. "Caught you. You're not going to bed yet. The night's halfway along."

"Mrs. McGivers—I'm worn."

"We have business. And I'm buying you a drink and a supper."

She stood there, formidable, the wind whipping her thin coat, the monkey nowhere in sight. He knew what the business was. Her act had been a disaster this eve; it never caught the crowd, people yawned. Ethel Wildroot and what's-his-name were no substitute for the monkeys, and messed it up. Calypso had an odd beat, an odd secondary syncopation, and this evening nothing worked. It hurt just to watch the disaster unfold on his stage. She was going to apologize, or maybe propose changes, or who knows?

"Okay. We don't have to get up early," he said. "Ten o'clock at the station."

She steered him south, the wind at their backs, while the commercial district faded into nondescript two-story shops, and then into something else entirely. She was taking him straight into the district. Butte's bordellos were famous and sprawled over several square blocks, and did a booming trade with a few thousand miners on the loose, shift after shift. He eyed the area curiously. Lamplight from windows spilled on the cobbled street. Which street, he wasn't sure. It didn't matter. She steered him past hurdy-gurdies, noisy saloons, dark and quiet buildings with a single lamp at the door. There were few pedestrians, all male, braving the night air eddying off the peaks above Butte.

"Here," she said. "Number fifty-two."

She opened upon a well-lit saloon, with a small stage, and an adjoining eatery to the left. And a stairway along one wall, leading upward to whatever was going on up there in Butte, Montana, in November, 1896.

The bar was doing a trade; keeps in soiled aprons were serving up what probably was rotgut. But these precincts were not all male. Here and there were gaudy serving girls, in wrappers, who seemed available for anything a customer desired.

"We'll eat," Mrs. McGivers said.

"I could use a bite."

"They serve stew out of a pot, two-bits, and drinks are one bit."

He knew the stew would be bland, and without flavor, but it would do on a cold night. Butte's food matched its weather, he had discovered. A lady with peroxide hair, in a blue kimono that hung loose, took their order, and brought him a bourbon.

"You like it?" Mrs. McGivers asked.

"It's as good as any, I guess."

"I bought it this afternoon."

That stopped a lot of conversation. She smiled, lifted her glass, and touched it to his.

"I've got seven girls upstairs, a suite to live in, me and Joseph and Abel, a stage to play on if I feel like it, a bar, and this eatery. How's that, do you think?"

"Well, your monkeys knew how to rattle the tin cups, didn't they?"

"Hell yes," she said. "Some shows, twenty, thirty dollars. Who could resist giving a dime to two monkeys, more on matinee days?"

He sipped the bourbon. Or whatever it was. It tasted like varnish. He remembered sipping stuff like that on State Street in Chicago.

"Okay, what?" he asked. This all had sudden implications.

"Crappy act today."

He nodded.

"Ethel Wildroot, God love her, she's no damned monkey. And neither is whatever his name is, Cromwell. And Joseph, he wasn't caring, and Abel, he's in mourning. So you got the worst performance on the tour, from an act that flew apart and can't be put together again."

He grinned. It was all shaping up.

"You saying adios, are you?"

"If you need me, August, I'll play a few shows until you can get another act."

"I'll miss you, Mrs. McGivers."

"I'll miss you, too, August. It was a great tour. You're a great manager. We had some good shows."

"Long way from home, I guess."

"Not so long. I was born in Scotland. Cold weather, it's not something I've never seen."

"I know nothing about you."

She smiled. "I guess you never will. But now I'm a madam, with a dive in Butte, and some commercial ladies upstairs, and a monkey who's ready to retire and entertain the customers. Joseph gets in free. So do you."

"I'd sure like to know more about you."

"If I started confessing, they'd lock me up."

"Do they know you here? These people?"

"Not yet. They will tomorrow. . . ." She let it remain a question.

"Tonight, if you wish," he said.

She laughed suddenly. A big, hearty, meaty yowl. "Maybe I'll move in. Joseph's got the itch. And Abel's telling me he's half froze. That hotel is not tropical."

"Mrs. McGivers, I'll be leaving a piece of myself here. The show, it'll be leaving a lot of itself in Butte. I suppose we should celebrate, but the truth of it is that I'm feeling blue."

"August, you need to get laid."

The kimono-clad bleached blonde showed up with gray stew, which August ate delicately, fearful of an upset stomach. But the stuff settled amiably in his belly, and he supposed he would survive Mrs. McGivers' famous and maybe dubious hospitality. He wondered if the blonde was a working girl. They probably were all working girls.

"I'll have Joseph bring the stuff, and the monkey," she said. "We've got a big square room at the back, upstairs where I can keep an eye on the ladies."

"You stay; I'll tell Joseph," he said. "He can bring the monkey and your stuff."

"I got a woolen scarf," she said. "The little guy wraps it round and round, and pretty soon there's nothing but wool and a tail."

She laughed, big and booming again, and reached across the table to kiss him.

He sat there, amazed. He had just lost an act. A woman he loved, and her entourage. Life flowed on around them: men at the bar, ladies serving stew, stairs leading to quieter precincts. The loss of a monkey had killed her act, but maybe Butte had killed it, too. Butte was where everything happened. A troupe might arrive in Butte for a run at Maguire's Opera House, and it wouldn't remain the same company for long.

She knew what he was thinking, and patted his hand.

"Whenever you come here, everything's free," she said. "On the house."

They laughed.

"You won't get rich," he said.

"There's always a way, a door, a future, if you're willing," she said. "Lots, they aren't."

"Well, if I'm free . . . ," she added, pausing, waiting for a nod, "I'd better move in. And tell the bunch here. They don't know."

He nodded, stood, and welcomed her hug.

"Thank you, August. Not everyone would do that."

That was true. But he had learned a few things about acts, and one of them was that unhappy acts made bad vaudeville. He smiled, clapped his hat on, and sailed into the night, not looking back.

The air was still and crisp, and it was an easy hike up to the hotel. He liked Butte. But he kept a wary eye for footpads. One could never know, around Butte.

He found Joseph, the accordion, some packed bags, and the monkey in the hotel room.

"It's fine," August said.

"Yah, good," Joseph said. "Hey, it's auf Wiedersehen, eh?"

"I'll fetch a cab if I can. The city never sleeps."

Abel perched on the rumpled bed, subdued. The star of the Beausoleil Brothers Follies seemed mournful since his pal had vanished. August realized he had never touched the little fellow, and was more inclined to cuss him. But suddenly everything had changed.

"You mind?" he asked Joseph, reaching for the monkey.

Joseph grinned. He was watching closely.

August picked up the little fellow, feeling the surprising weight in his arms. The monkey snuggled right in, his little paws clasping Beausoleil's arm. It was an odd feeling, holding this creature so like a child. He held the monkey for a bit, found the long gray scarf, and wrapped it around the monkey, who helped him with it. There was a blue child's receiving blanket, too, and August caught it up and wrapped that around the monkey, who rewarded August by pulling the blanket up over his monkish head and burrowing into it.

Beausoleil had never had children. He had lived a while with a Latvian woman, Katrina, who had drifted away, or maybe he had drifted away, and he knew he was a stranger to hearth or home. He had grown up on the streets and scarcely knew what a quiet, serene home might be. There had been two or three other women, mostly very young and worldly, but never a home. Never a quiet refuge from the world. Never a Christmas tree, with strings of popcorn on it. Now, with Abel snugged deep into wool and bundled in his arms, he suddenly longed for the thing he had never had: a warm hearth, a home, a welcoming wife.

Joseph wrestled bags and accordion down the narrow hall, down a flight, to the lobby, while August followed with the bundled-up monkey, who curled trusting in his arms.

The deskman summoned a cross-eyed boy, who braved the night to find a hack, and after a few minutes one rolled up, the back of the dray horse frosted, the driver's breath a haze in the deeps.

The monkey shivered. The hack driver loaded bags and the accordion, and then Joseph climbed into the cold interior. August handed the bundled monkey to Joseph, feeling as if something had been torn away from him. Joseph gathered the bundle, and pulled the monkey tight against his massive chest, his big hands cupping the blanket.

The cab door snapped shut. The driver clambered up, slapped the lines, and the cab, carrying the best act, carrying a creature August hadn't realized he loved until that very moment, slipped into the hushed Butte night.

TWENTY-FOUR

August Beausoleil woke up to a grim day. He had to move his troupe to Philipsburg, a miserable U-shaped route involving two transfers, and at the same time revamp his broken company. There would be a matinee and evening performance the next day at the new opera house there. He collected his company at the Butte station, told them that Mrs. McGivers had departed, and that he would be revamping the show en route.

"Not her," said Delilah Marbury. "She held it together."

"Her act died when Cain died," August said. "She was brave enough to keep on trying."

"What is she doing now?"

"Running a joint."

He spotted some smiles. Wayne Windsor announced he'd be fit to perform the next day, and that helped. But the company was still strained to the breaking point. They boarded a short train, a baggage car and two cigar-stink coaches, that would take them back to Helena, where they would transfer to a westbound Northern Pacific train. The stubby engine soon wrestled them out of the toxic smoke of Butte, and into a serene valley.

The coach had banging wheels, which added to the travel headache, but August didn't have time or energy to lament. He found Ethel Wildroot, sitting with the new man, Cromwell Perkins. The sisters were huddled together in the seats ahead.

"You have an act yet?" he asked.

Perkins started to reply, but Ethel cut him off. "We've tried to come up with something."

"In other words, no." He stared at Perkins. "This one won't get you any drinks. But sometimes things work. Could you insult everyone in Philipsburg—the town, the miners, their kin, and anyone else around there?"

"Mr. Beausoleil, sir, I am in a class by myself when it comes to insult." He turned to Ethel. "Just ask me what I think of the locals."

"You sure you want to do this?" she asked August.

He smiled. "It's practice. We're out of there after one day. What I want is to get him cranked up for Missoula. It's a college town. Be merciless."

"I loathe college students, miserable parasites bleeding

their fathers of fortunes, learning how to ruin their own lives."

August thought he could like the man.

"We'll try an olio act, three or four minutes, for the matinee. Expand it to seven or eight in the evening. If they don't threaten to put you in the hospital, I'll call it failure."

"At last, a chance to enjoy life," The Genius said.

"It's a small house. People halfway back can toss the tomatoes. It's also new. We're the first big show." He smiled. "Maybe the last. If you don't rile them up, I'll hook you."

Perkins was mystified, so Ethel explained. "It's a big hook on a stick, to drag off people who are boring the house half to death."

"As long as I can use it on you, I'm fine with it," The Genius said.

That was a novelty. August wondered whether there were moments when he should be hooked. He headed down the aisle to Ginger, who sat alone, staring out the window. She wore a gray teacherish suit, almost as if it were armor. The coach was chilly. She had been almost aloof since joining the troupe, and August could only guess at the reasons. Maybe show business wasn't the lark she had imagined when she fled from somewhere or other.

"May I?" he asked, sliding in beside her before she responded.

"I'm revamping the show," he said. "You know. What act follows what act. How do you think you did last night?"

She looked uncomfortable. "I tried to do what you asked," she said.

"And?"

"There was, I don't know how to describe it. An

invisible wall. A glass wall between me and the audience. It's as if my voice stopped traveling."

"Your voice reaches the rear. I checked."

"Then I don't know. They applauded."

"Yes, they did," he said. They applauded politely, waiting for the next act. There were all types of applause, and they all sent messages, and the message they sent Ginger was indifference.

"No one wanted an encore," she said.

"Maybe you could experiment some. Different songs. You must have lots."

"But I haven't practiced them."

"It's not a recital, Ginger."

She brightened suddenly. "It's not at all like I thought. I mean, I'm trained. My voice is good. I was considered a prodigy. They all said so. I always thought that was it. I was at the top, the whole world would see it." She smiled. "Some joke."

"I wish you could be a saloon singer. Up close, getting something back from the people watching you, people with drinks in hand, and you a few feet away, trying to entertain them."

"Entertain them?"

"Of course. Entertain them."

She seemed puzzled. "But I perform."

He grinned. "Ginger, try something different. A nice, sentimental ballad or two. Don't worry about getting high C or B flat right. Just wink at some gent, and see if he winks back."

"I don't know how you put up with me," she said.

"I know some reporters," he said. "They tell me about their training. How to write a lead that's interesting. How to make sure the story has a who, when, why, where. The four Ws, they call it. How to catch a reader's attention. How to be spare, not waste words. Good reporters, with years of training, years of mastering the art, the lore. And you know what? One or two of them switched to writing novels, and they crashed. They said it's different; they had to unlearn everything they had mastered as newsmen. The lore didn't help them write a novel. They lacked voice, the personal thing a novelist puts into his work. Maybe it's that way for you."

She stared out the window at the passing slopes. "Maybe I was naïve," she said.

"I'm not giving up on you, Ginger. Let's just see what you do. Let's see what part of yourself you put out there."

"Oh, well," she said, not believing.

"Philipsburg is a good place to try something new. Brief engagement. Then on to Missoula, and big crowds."

"Maybe this is a train to nowhere," she said.

The engine lurched around a bend, the bad roadbed bucking the coach, and August patted her hand and left her there. Show business wasn't whatever she had dreamed long before. But she was flexible.

They were passing through anonymous forest that largely blotted out the scenery, so the train seemed to crawl through a place of no beginnings and no endings.

Wayne Windsor was sitting on an aisle seat, but there was space across the aisle, so August settled there. Windsor was no longer masking his damaged face with high collars and scarves.

"You'll play tomorrow?"

"One act, maybe two for the matinee. I'm talking, anyway."

"Small house," August said. "But we don't know much about it. No big show's played there."

"I didn't think I'd ever love a monkey," Windsor said. "But I do. She had a great act, Monkey Band. It loosened people up. I always wanted to follow her, because everyone would be in a cheerful mood."

"Butte air's hard on monkeys."

"She bought a joint?"

"Whatever it is. With a little stage. She's still got some box office. Along with a bar and some working girls."

"I never thought she'd end up in Butte. Cuba, maybe, but not Butte."

"Where will you end up, Wayne?"

"In a big city, full of people. Not Montana. This is the hardest tour I've been on."

"Yeah, and a lot still left. Thanks for sticking with me, Wayne. You're the draw now, always were."

Windsor sighed, rubbed his wounded profile, and stared at the anonymous forest. Montana was a lot of nothing.

August managed to visit with each of the people in the company, as the train huffed north. The Marbury trio were doing fine; Harry the Juggler was as surly as usual. LaVerne Wildroot was cheerful. The other girls were a little blue. It would be their last tour, and they knew that, though nothing had been said about it.

"Your music's holding it together," August said. "You're out there when I need you."

They probably didn't believe it.

Butte sliding away, minute by minute. Mary Mabel Markey dead and buried there, lying beside a thousand miners who died young. Mrs. McGivers and the remains of her Monkey Band running a joint there. One monkey left. He felt an odd pang. Ever since he had carried Abel down to the waiting hack, swathed in wool, he had known that Cain and Abel were the true stars of the Follies. It took death to give him some insight.

They waited in a sturdy frame station off Last Chance Gulch for the Seattle Express, which would whistle its way to Garrison Junction, and another square-wheeled local that would shuttle them down to the sprawling silver camp that would soon see the first touring variety show ever to show up there. He hoped Pomerantz would meet them and settle them there. He knew the turf.

By the time the troupe finally boarded the train to Philipsburg, which consisted of three box cars, a gondola, an ancient coach, and a caboose, everyone was ready to crawl under two blankets and into bed. August could not remember a more grueling and bone-cold trip in all the years he had been on the road with a touring company. He had an odd thought: it was no place for monkeys. Mrs. McGivers had saved the little guy's life, staying back there in that bustling city. Abel and Butte were made for each other.

They chuffed in at dusk, noting a snowy landscape. They had come to the end of the world. If Butte was isolated, Philipsburg was on another planet. The train halted shy of the gravel platform, leaving passengers to wrestle their way along the roadbed after a long step off the coach stair. Whatever was in those boxcars was more important than mere mortals.

But there was Charles Pomerantz, collecting his crowd, opening his arms to his bride, who fell into his embrace as if it were the only comfort left to her. The engine hissed steam, which enveloped them and smeared grit on them.

"There's no hacks here, but the hotel's over there. And I've got some boys to help you," Charles said. "The opera house is around the corner, a block beyond that."

Indeed, there were four boys in knickers and leather caps, ready to help. Pomerantz steered the boys to the larger trunks and satchels, and studied the troupe.

"Am I missing something?" he asked.

"We've got a lot to talk about. Including changes in the playbills," August said.

"Where's the show? I mean, the acts?"

"We've got a show. Just not the show we had when you left Butte."

"Mrs. McGivers?"

"Dead monkey. She pulled out, opened shop in Butte. Don't ask what she's selling."

Something heavy settled on Pomerantz. "Okay, we'll work it out. The paper wanted to interview her." He stood on the platform—the town had an unheated station—counting his company, act by act. He seemed almost to forget his bride, who clung to his arm, her face strained in the dusk.

They walked slowly toward the clapboard-sided hotel, two stories with barracks windows in a military row. Pomerantz finally turned to Ginger.

"How did it go, sweetheart?"

She didn't answer at first, choosing her words. "All right. I guess."

"She's off to a good start," August said.

He and Pomerantz exchanged a glance. "And how's the advance?" August asked.

"We've got a good house. We'll sell out the matinee. Maybe the evening."

They passed a building with a playbill plastered to it. Mary Mabel Markey, it said. Wayne Windsor. Mrs. McGivers and Her Monkey Band. The juggler. The trio, the Wildroot Sisters.

"Who's that?" Pomerantz asked, pointing at Cromwell Perkins.

"New act, The Genius and Ethel," August said.

For once, Charles smiled. "Where did he come from?"

"Ethel collected him from a saloon. He's a bar rail comic."

"What'll he do?"

"Insult the crowd, I hope."

Charles Pomerantz wheezed, laughed, and steered his weary bunch into the small hotel, which at last offered a modicum of comfort. "We'll put on a hell of a show," he said.

TWENTY-FIVE

Mrs. Charles Pomerantz lay abed homesick. The hotel room was small, mean, and cold. Barely enough morning light filtered through a listless curtain for her to see her quarters. Her husband had hastily abandoned the room, en route to Missoula again, to publicize changes in the show.

Her brief moment with him had been melancholic. From the moment he met the troupe, stepping off the bone-jarring coach, he and August Beausoleil had been consulting, and he had barely given her a kiss on the cheek, much less the warm embrace a newlywed woman might expect.

He had, finally, unlocked the door and entered, long after she had pulled the covers over her and tried to banish the chill. He lit a lamp, eyed her, kept his long johns on, and slipped into the narrow bed beside her.

"Glad you're here, sweetheart," he said. "Sorry to be so busy. But we'll have some time in Missoula."

"Oh, Charles . . ."

"I hear good things about your act," he said.

"That's more than I hear."

"We've had to change the billing. You'll be on the playbill. How's that?"

Oddly, she didn't care. "That's more than I expected," she said.

"I'm worn-out. Nothing but troubles these days, losing our biggest draws. I'll be out of here before you're up; see you down the road."

He squeezed her cold hand, turned his back to her, and swiftly fell into a soft snore.

She didn't sleep. The cold made the wooden hotel snap and creak and pop, startling her. The stranger she called husband lay inert, not caring, not holding her tight, not kissing, not even wondering how she fared, or how she had spent the long, hard day. Everything for him was the show.

She turned away, on the cold pillow in the cold room under the cold blankets, next to a cold husband, and wished she were somewhere else.

Like home.

A handsome, spacious, secure home. Her family. Comfort. They cared about her, showed her off. Pocatello was clean and gracious, with grand vistas in most directions. She had never shivered in bed in her life. Even the thought of her intense mother, who treated her like a windup doll, didn't seem so awful, the way it had a few weeks earlier.

She wondered if she should go back. She could disappear back to her home, just as she had disappeared from her home, took a new name, and left no trail. She could abandon Charles Pomerantz, abandon the show, abandon Ginger, and walk through the door as Penelope, virginal, unmarried, a prodigy who was the wonder of southern Idaho. Not say a word; just return to her own home, her own spacious bedroom, resume the name she had abandoned, and let them wonder where she had been.

If she was not pregnant. She wished she knew.

She didn't know much about anything, and there was no one she could ask. Maybe she couldn't go home again; maybe she couldn't be a vaudeville player, either. Maybe she would be a mother whether she wanted to or not, at age eighteen. She corrected herself. Nineteen, if it happened. That made her all the more homesick. Maybe she couldn't go back home. Maybe she was doomed, a castaway of some worldly impresario, who probably had more women than he could remember.

She watched him awaken, get up, vanish down the hall to the water closet at the end. She had barely seen a man do his morning rituals, scrape away beard, comb his hair. Men were mysteries. One moment he was fawning over her, kissing and seducing, and the next he was doing business. He would soon return, dress, abandon her without a word unless she lit the lamp and waited for his morning greeting.

She did that. She lifted the glass chimney, struck a match, and lit the bedside kerosene lamp. It slowly bloomed to life.

When he returned, he was shaven and combed.

"Well, well," he said, discovering her staring, the lamp spilling yellow light over her and piercing into the dark corners of the room.

"Are we married?" she asked.

"I'd have to check," he said.

"I don't think I like this business, and I might go away somewhere."

He paused. He was buttoning a clean shirt, but he stopped.

"Ginger, this is rough on you. Some people aren't cut out for it. Some people try hard, and it defeats them. I hope you'll give it a chance. As for marriage, it's for you, not for me. You're a girl from a proper home, and marriage is the way you feel comfortable in a hotel room with a man. It's what you need." He smiled. "But I'm glad we did it. I'm glad you're my wife."

"I guess that's your declaration of eternal love," she said, and from somewhere a big laugh boiled up in her.

He didn't say a word, but leaned over and kissed her. She tasted mint on his lips.

"I'll stick," she said.

"After Missoula, it's Spokane, and then a few days of down-time. Just right for us to figure out who we got married to," he said. "Damned if I know."

"If I don't find another gentleman first," she said.

That startled him more than it startled her. "I think you're gonna fit right into the business," he said, but she thought there was an edge in his voice.

She watched him tie his blue polka-dot cravat and straighten it, shrug into his fawn waistcoat and button it, climb into his gray woolen suit coat, and eye himself. These theater men were natty dressers; they were careful with appearances. He looked to be a man of substance, no matter what condition the show was in.

"We've got a big rendezvous in Missoula," he said. "It'll knock your socks off."

"We'll see whose socks come off," she said.

His eyes lit up.

He lifted his black bowler, saluted her with it, collected his bag, and vanished. She stared at the door. That had been her husband and now her husband was going away to a town she knew nothing about, but was probably evil since it harbored the state college.

She wasn't homesick anymore. In fact, she wanted only to find a place to practice, to try some other songs she knew, to see about hugging her entire audience. The hour was early, the sun not yet sailing, but she could not bear her hotel room another minute. It took only a little while to don her gray travel suit and slip outside, discovering an oddly mild day and an orderly city in a broad valley, built around a smelter. Philipsburg lay in the heart of a silver mining district, but the mines were well away from the town.

She saw hardly a soul on the streets, and certainly did not expect to discover any of her troupe. Show people rose late and retired late. But she had always flown into each day from its very start, because that's how she was. She would soon sing to those who lived in this place. Who were they? What would they enjoy? Could she please them? The one thing she had garnered from her brief visit was that this town was orderly and its cottages well kept.

But what did that imply for her performance? She felt a little foolish for even wondering about it. What was she? An eighteen-year-old prodigy? A genius, able to fathom an audience and respond to it? A canary in a cage.

She was amused by her own presumptuousness. She felt the weight of her parents' expectations, and knew it was a millstone on her back, and she should escape that burden once and for all. That was one thing about vaudeville: she wasn't in a concert hall singing grand opera.

She spotted a well-lit café, and decided it was time for breakfast. Uneasily—she had yet to live life on her own terms, her own volition—she entered, discovered an all-male patronage, with one exception. Ethel Wildroot sat at a table, a coffee cup before her. Ethel saw her at once, and hailed her. Hesitantly, Ginger joined the mother of rival singers, wondering where all this might lead. Discomfort, probably.

"You're up early. A rara avis in show biz," Ethel said. "Park your little rear in the chair, and tell me about it."

There was always something a little edgy in Ethel, and it made Ginger smile. She settled in the chair, and soon was ordering a bowl of oatmeal and tea. Ethel was demolishing a breakfast steak that a smelterman would have considered large.

"So, how do you like the Beausoleil show?" she asked, sawing a piece of pink meat loose.

Ginger was discreet. "I don't think I'll be in it long," she said. "All I really want is to be a good mate to Charles."

"Oh, horse apples. Your act isn't catching on, and I can tell you why."

"August wants me to sing to my audience, and I'm doing that."

"Well, that's half of it," Ethel said, sawing another slab of meat off the steak. "You've got everything you need. Great voice, fine training, poise, all that." She waved a knife. "But you can't just be the goddess, singing songs."

Ginger braced herself. Something was about to knock over the tenpins.

"Girl like you, you should talk to them. You go out there, smile, start a song, and you never talk to them. That's a killer. You come from a concert background. I can tell. Concerts, you just stand there and sing. Or start playing the piano, or whatever. Well, that's what the fuddy-duddies want. Hold your hands together, stare at the far wall, and sing. But this is vaudeville, sweetheart. Quit being the Virgin Queen."

The waiter arrived with a bowl of cereal, and Ginger made a great show of spooning it.

"Talk to them, dammit. Don't just clasp your hands together and start warbling away. Hey, they're people, just like you. And don't be so polite, either. Don't thank them. August, that's his job. He thanks them for coming. You, though, that's not your job. You need to connect with them. Just get it through your head. Be their best friend."

"What would I say?"

Ethel masticated the beef a little, and then smiled. "Hey, that Mexican drill. Don't just sing it. Say it's cold around here, and maybe the way to warm up is to sing something south of the border, and maybe something about a señorita. And tell all those miners, they'd like to hear something about a señorita."

"I'd need a script, Ethel."

Ethel waved her spoon. "If you need a script, you shouldn't be in vaudeville. All you do is introduce the song, tell them about it, about yourself a little."

"Myself?"

"Tell 'em you've been singing all your life, and it's much more fun singing for a lot of grown-up men. You've been waiting for the chance!"

"That's too forward, don't you think?"

Ethel sighed. "You probably shouldn't be in the business, sweetheart."

The curtain rolled down, or so Ginger thought. But Ethel wasn't done. "You've got the best voice in the company. Sure beats my girls and LaVerne. That kind of voice, you can wind a man around your little finger. It's sweet and sultry."

"Sultry?"

"You haven't been married long enough to figure that out, Ginger."

"I haven't figured anything out yet," Ginger said.

"Charles, he'll be a good husband if you keep a leash on him."

"So far, it's been a few hotel rooms. Neither of us know why we did it. It sort of bubbled up. But he just smiles and says it'll be fine."

Ethel eyed her assessingly. "Beautiful, naïve, innocent maiden."

Ginger pulled into herself. Somehow, marriage, show business, this new world, were full of shoals that could sink her. These were worldly people, and she knew she was nothing but a small-town girl adventuring into a hard world.

"Hey, Mrs. Pomerantz, if you need any crystal ball reading, call on me. I know a few things about men," Ethel said.

Ginger was itching just to spill out everything she didn't know, every mystery of marriage, every odd thing about males, why they shaved, what they expected, who they thought they were, and how a wife fit in.

Ethel sensed it, and patted Ginger's hand. "You're the star of the show, sweetheart. You just don't know it yet."

TWENTY-SIX

how day. August Beausoleil hurried through a late November chill to the glistening opera house operated by Marshal McFarland. It stood a block from the hotel, seven or eight from the smelter grounds. The hotel had been cold, and his body felt numb. He found the place, noted that it was devoid of ornament, a utilitarian frame and fieldstone structure washed white. A playbill in a case at the front touted the Follies. He found a side door and entered, only to meet with a blast of icy air. A side corridor opened on the auditorium, also bone cold and dark, and led to a small cubicle where, August hoped, he would find the proprietor.

That office was as cold as the rest, but at least McFarland was present, wrapped in a woolen waistcoat, gray woolen pants, and a woolen coat. A loose scarf lay about his neck and fell down his chest.

"Beausoleil, is it? You're late," the manager said. His mantel clock announced the time as 9:15.

"Sorry, the hotel was slow to serve."

"There's some messages for you, sir," McFarland said, all business. "The Methodist women wish to conduct a bake sale in the lobby before each performance. I said I would let them know as soon as you appeared."

"Bake sale? Breads, muffins, tarts?"

McFarland glared at him. "They raise money for injured miners."

"What are the buyers supposed to do? Sit with an apple pie in their lap during the show?"

"Usually, they throw whatever's in hand at the performers, sir."

"No. No bake sale."

"Then there's Mrs. Wall. Josephine. Wife of the general manager of the Granite Mine. That, sir, is one of the finest silver mines in the country. You would do well to accommodate her."

"Which is what?"

"She wishes to play her harp during the intermission."

"Harp? It takes a couple of strong men to haul a harp around."

"She has footmen in abundance, sir."

"What will she play?"

"She tends toward light airs, sir."

"Is she good?"

"I reserve judgment."

He didn't want her, but knew that rebuffing powerful people might have consequences. "Are you going to start heating up the building?"

"Firewood's dear in Philipsburg, Mr. Beausoleil, and it's a habit in town to get along without it."

"I will want the building fully heated as soon as possible."

"Your footlamps will do it, sir. Light the lamps, and your limelight, and you'll have plenty of warmth. That and a full house, warm bodies."

There was some reality in it, but not much. "Mr. Mc-Farland, our contract provides that you'll supply a house suitably prepared in all respects. And that includes heat."

McFarland looked annoyed, but finally rang a bell, and soon a lackey appeared. "Start the stoves," he told the man.

He turned to Beausoleil. "There are two potbellies flanking the stage."

"I have new acts, and people wish to rehearse, and disease has already damaged my show, sir. We had a death, and the loss of an animal, and that meant two acts down."

"So I heard. We're hardy people here, sir. We don't need all that coddling. Miners are used to having bad lungs, so cold air makes no difference to them. That's reasonable. I'll add a firewood surcharge."

"Surcharge! The contract calls for suitable conditions."

"You're in Montana, Beausoleil. What's suitable here is not suitable for hothouse flowers."

A great clatter interrupted them. McFarland leapt up, opened the door upon two footmen hauling a great, gilded harp on a dolly. And they were followed by a formidable woman, swathed in layers of gabardine formed into a high-button suit.

"That stair there leads up," she said, steering the liveried footmen toward the stage. She spotted McFarland and Beausoleil. "I shall be with you directly, once we station this up on the platform," she said.

Beausoleil wondered how much choice he had in any of this. He watched silently as the experienced men slid the great gilded harp up and onto the dark stage.

"There, that's done," she said. "Marshal, put the heat down. It will affect my arms when I play. I don't want droopy arms."

"This is Mr. Beausoleil, whose company will perform today," McFarland said. "And this, sir, is Madam Wall."

"Mrs. Wall, I'm pleased to meet you. I only now heard of your proposal to play during the intermission, but I'll have to decline your generous offer. All the acts are paid, of course, and the budget doesn't permit the slightest change. But it's most generous of you."

Her face pinched up. "Then put me on. I will play for you, sir."

"I'm afraid that's impossible. We have a regular troupe, you see . . ."

She reached out and patted him on the arm. "My dear sir, you'll accommodate an old lady. Your audience will forgive you, knowing that my husband can fire the whole lot of them."

She lifted a thick handful of skirt, and climbed to the stage, and settled beside the harp, which she began tuning, sometimes letting her fingers trill out a chord. The notes were throaty and lingering. She was a gray presence on a dark stage.

"It will only be during the intermission, in front of the olio," she said. "The rest of the evening is yours to ruin."

August sighed. Philipsburg had a few surprises, but so did most of the towns he booked. He said nothing. Perhaps the dowager queen of the mining town could stumble through some music. Most of the audience would be out in the lobby, or visiting the water closets, or next door downing a fast one at the Quail saloon. On the other hand, she could chase the crowd away, and the second act would play to a few survivors.

But then, after she had fiddled a little, and ran nimble fingers—probably numb with cold—across the strings, she slipped softly into melody, the name of which he didn't know, but it was sweet and lyrical, and not at all painfully wrought. She was playing on a dark stage, barely lit by light spilling back from the lobby.

It depressed him. Keeping some sort of lid on his show was the hardest of all his tasks.

She was accomplished. He confessed to that. And she was playing sentimental ballads, the sort of thing a miner might appreciate.

He resolved to say nothing at all. He wouldn't approve; he wouldn't get into a predicament about pay. This was between the formidable lady and McFarland.

"Count me out of it," he told the proprietor. "It's not my show. She's not an act. I don't know what she is."

Marshal McFarland grinned. "She owns the town."

"And I'm not paying for firewood. I'll have my people in here shortly to set up footlights, the limelight, and stow the props. There may be some people practicing. Especially Charles Pomerantz's wife."

He had barely spoken the name when he heard her singing, picking up on a ballad the harpist was playing. Her voice, the harp, the sound was gold. The harp was made for Ginger, and Ginger was made for the harp.

And that meant trouble.

"Now sing one I don't know," Mrs. Wall commanded.

Ginger launched into "Cielito Lindo," singing it in Spanish. Flawlessly, Mrs. Wall added chords and flourishes, creating an eerie beauty even though the song was intended for brass, for a mariachi band. It was a tender thing, this accord between Ginger and the dowager empress of Philipsburg.

August knew when to bend. "All right, Mrs. Wall, you're hired for two performances," he said. "I'll have cash for you after the second show."

"Oh fiddle, I don't want money. I want this child to savage the hearts of those knuckleheads, the smeltermen in the audience. And with a few flourishes from me, she'll do it."

"How shall I introduce you, madam?"

"You won't. Every man and woman in that audience will know who I am. If you introduce me they will applaud, for fear of not applauding. I could wear a mask and they still would know who I am. I could play badly and they would still applaud. They believe my husband knows all, and punishes his critics. They believe he has snitches in the mine, who report to him. Maybe Marshal Mc-Farland is a snitch. Let them think it. In fact, I play quite well. So let them gossip and worry. That's how it all works, you know. Some gossip rescues all enterprises."

Beausoleil gently entertained the notion that Mrs. Wall was a godsend. But swiftly dismissed it. He tended to be superstitious.

A thin warmth began to welcome mortals to the opera

house. Ritually, August began a tour of the place. It always helped to know everything. He eyed the olio drop, and lowered it himself, making sure it fell behind the harpist and singer. He walked out to the rear of the auditorium and listened. Ginger's voice carried well. This was a small house. It would likely carry well even when packed, but there were always surprises.

The seats were hard and uncomfortable, rising in slightly canted rows. McFarland had not concerned himself much with comfort, but perhaps he was right. He had the monopoly on entertainment in this place, and his customers could take it or leave it.

They would need footlamps here. He surveyed the front of the stage and found a shallow metal trough intended for the lights. Each light burned inside a hood that threw the light onto the performers and hid the flame from the audience. A mirrored interior assured that the light would be reflected forward, upon the artists. The company carried eight of them, and a limelight, which was also a hooded device, larger, that directed a hot gas flame upon a cylindrical column of quicklime until it threw brilliant white light. He would use that, also. Most of the acts would be as far downstage as he could manage them. Upstage was poorly lit. He could burn a lot of fuels in a single performance. Running a show in an opera house that had not been electrified was far tougher than one that relied on incandescent lights.

Even as the morning quickened, his two hands placed the footlights, made sure their reservoirs were filled, and set up the limelight. He watched Mrs. Wall and Ginger shape an act, and hoped it would work. Instinct told him it might. But who could say what a notional, powerful woman might do?

Around one, his troupe drifted in. The house was almost warm; the footlights and crowd would do the rest. Some had eaten lunch. Others would wait. A few wouldn't touch food until both shows were done. He eyed The Genius, Cromwell Perkins, and hoped for the best. He hoped Ethel, a veteran of the stage, could steer the man away from shoals. An old professional like Ethel was a comfort and consolation to him. She was capable of marching The Genius off the stage if things erupted badly.

A boy showed up with a wire for Ginger. She read it and beamed. Break a leg, it said, and it was from Charles, who was working the advance in Missoula. She was puzzled, momentarily, and then smiled. Well, this would be one hell of a show. New acts, untried talent, new town, cold weather. But that was the business. You bent, you ducked, you stood tall, you improvised, you wrestled the dragons, especially illness, the thing that caused more cancellations than anything else. Especially in cold weather like this.

Outside, a thin layer of cloud softened the sun, but the Saturday was bright and the air was quiet. The smelter-men and their mates and families drifted in. He stood quietly near the box office, watching the crowd, largely male, almost all young, dressed in work clothes for the want of anything finer in their wardrobes. Mostly men, lonely men, bored men who had only a few saloons in this isolated town between themselves and dreariness. Their wives, if they had any, were far away, in the East, in Europe, across the seas. Not here, not in the wilds of a new state. This opera house, where no large company had yet appeared, was the magnet. But they laid down their greenbacks and settled in the hard seats. He did spot a few women, mostly the wives of managers, he guessed. They would be looking for anything that would color their isolated and slow lives.

He saw a reporter, brandishing a pass, come in. There'd be a review, but it wouldn't appear until after the second show, the morning they pulled out. Even so, August itched to read it, and thought to hunt down the twice-weekly paper to see the verdict.

He hoped to give them a memorable time. And if Mrs. Wall said to clap, they would, and if she didn't raise her hands in applause, neither would they. August thought it was the damnedest bind he'd been in.

TWENTY-SEVEN

August eyed the crowd. The house was full. McFarland had sold some standing-room tickets, and now twenty more stood at the rear. Philipsburg was flocking to the new show in the new theater.

He nodded. A stagehand stepped out, lit the footlights, struck a match to the jets that fired up the limelight, and retreated. It was six minutes past two. The acts waited quietly in the wings. He signaled a stagehand and the curtain parted. This house had draw curtains, and no flies. The limelight caught him in his top hat, tuxedo, white bib, a gold-knobbed cane in hand. Before him, a dim-lit gulf of pale faces peered upward.

"Ladies and gents, welcome to the Beausoleil Brothers Follies," he said. "It's our pleasure to play here in Peoria—or is it Altoona?" He glanced toward the wings, awaiting an instruction, an old joke. "Ah, forgive me, it's the noble city of Philipsburg, Montana. The finest town on the continent!"

They laughed.

"Thank you for coming this cold afternoon. And now, ladies and gents, those gorgeous and talented ladies, the one, the only Wildroot Sisters!"

The girls trotted out along with the accompanist, and

away they went. They put their hearts in it; Ethel had drilled that into them. And they always had a good opener to warm up the crowd. They hugged the limelight, a trio of bright-lit songstresses, a stage full of butterflies.

"What a trio! Give them a hand, ladies and gents. You'll be seeing more of the beautiful Wildroot girls. And now, as a special treat, the country's finest monologuist, the gent who'll tickle your funnybones, the gent who taught Mark Twain how to do it, the one, the only Wayne Windsor!"

He led the applause as Windsor, still a little rocky from his laryngitis, stepped out and was met with polite acceptance. This crowd was male, and it was looking for female entertainment. Windsor had a little spring to his step, no matter how he felt. And a wry smile that anticipated some delicious bon mot. He faced right, then left, letting the crowd admire him.

"I'm pleased to be here, in this great, rich, jewel of the Rockies—at least that's what the mayor says," he began. "I think I'll talk about robber barons today. I'm all for robber barons. Are there any out there? If so, stand up, sir, and take a bow."

He peered out upon a quiet crowd.

"I don't see any. A pity. I was going to heap praise upon him. The world needs robber barons. They clean out pockets of ore; they clean out workingmen's pockets. They clean out the till of every merchant in town."

August watched from the wing. The gifted Windsor had his audience, and that act would be fine. There was always an edge to his humor. He did best picking on someone or something. He rarely reduced an audience to fits of laughter, but his sly humor worked its way through the crowd, gaining chuckles and smiles. And today he was in good form, his voice holding up, bouncing off the rear wall, where those standing customers lounged.

August rolled out the Marbury Trio next. "Ladies and

gents, this afternoon you'll see something brand new. Some incredible footwork, called tap dancing, that will make you snap your fingers. It's all the rage in Memphis, and now it's flaming in all directions, conquering audiences everywhere. This is talent, my friends. This is music as you've never felt it. I'm proud to offer you the one, the only, the sensational Marbury Trio."

The trio tapped their way out from the wing, their rhythm perfect, the gents in black dinner jackets, Delilah in a daringly short red skirt. These miners had never seen the like, or heard a dance done with tapping of shoes, and they sat silently, blotting it up, and finally smiling, and even laughing at one of Delilah's extravagant solos. Her partners peeled back, turned her loose in the limelight, where the dress shimmered in the brightness, and her feet lifted into a staccato that was broken now and then by a whirl of the skirts, and a new rhythm. August was suddenly aware he was watching a virtuoso. That was the thing about the business. Something grand always cropped up.

When they took their bows, he applauded along with the happy crowd.

"Weren't they a sight? That was just magnificent. The Marbury Trio. Take that home and tell the world about it." He paused a moment, letting the crowd settle down. "Next, ladies and gents, is Harry the Juggler. He's got three names I can't pronounce, and all I know is that he is not from the South Pole. And he's the best juggler on the planet. It's a miracle he doesn't break all the china in Montana. The one, the only . . . Harry."

That went fine, too. And then it was time to try Ginger. She was waiting quietly in the wings, wearing that white dress of hers that made her all the more girlish.

He signaled, and Josephine Wall's men rolled the golden harp out, but kept it away from the limelight. Mrs. Wall wore a glittering brooch on her bosom.

"And now, friends, a special treat for you all. The loveliest singer you've ever heard, with the voice of an angel. Miss Ginger, my friends, Miss Ginger."

Ginger floated out gently, and settled herself in the limelight, which caressed her white gown. She smiled, took her time.

"I see many faces before me," she said. "I know you come from many countries, far across the sea. And many of you remember the lady you left behind, the one you dream about, the one you hope to bring to the New World . . . someday soon. I will sing 'Far Across the Sea' for you, and for your sweethearts."

She started gently, alone, her voice indescribably rich, rising from some heartland within her, and then Josephine Wall picked up the chords on her harp, instantly catching the melody and mood, not so much playing as adding resonance. Ginger sang to those men, her gaze slipping from one to another, and sometimes to those who stood at the back.

A different sort of applause greeted her. It was respectful and firm, polite and glad. Beausoleil listened knowingly. This was exactly what he had seen in her. A tremor coursed through him. She had added an introduction, and now she had an act.

She sang two more. First, "Frost Upon My Garden," a gentle song about love lost before it could ripen. And once again, Mrs. Wall added the melodic company of her harp, this time with more flourishes than before. It was as though they had practiced this over and over, getting it right. But they hadn't. Mrs. Wall was gifted in her own right, and the honeyed voice and gentle harp seemed made for each other.

There was, oddly, no applause. No one wanted to break the spell Ginger had cast over the darkened theater.

"It's cold outside," she said. "And I think you just might

enjoy something spicy and warm, from Old Mexico. Of
course it's a love story, too. It's called 'Cielito Lindo,' and
it won't be in English, but I think you'll know just what it
means."

And that was fun. This one was lively, the middle song
had been sad. And after the first chorus, she invited her
rapt listeners to join in.

"Ay, ay, ay, ay,.
sing and don't cry, heavenly one,
for singing gladdens hearts . . .
Ay, ay, ay, ay,
canta y no llores,
porque cantando se alegran,
cielito lindo, los corazones."

Now they loved her. With each wave of applause,
Mrs. Wall added a resonant flourish of her harp, somehow deepening the acclaim. August watched, feeling
the glow work through him. He chose a moment to return to the stage, swept a hand toward Mrs. Wall, who
rose and bowed, and then Ginger, who lowered her head
a moment, as if saying grace, and then slowly exited the
limelight.

That closed the act. The curtains rolled. The cheerful
audience drifted out. A hand extinguished the limelight.
The footlights soon revealed Mrs. Wall, before an olio,
playing intermission music, pale hands plucking harp
strings, and plainly enjoying her moment. August looked
on, entertained. In the business, who could ever predict a
thing?

August led off the next act with the Marbury trio again,
this time all three clad in tux and tails, each with an ebony walking stick that doubled as a baton. He had never
put them in that spot before and he wanted to see if they

launched the second act with gusto. They did, and he moved easily into the rest of the afternoon's entertainment.

"And now, ladies and gents, a brand-new act, The Genius and Ethel. I'm not sure which of them is The Genius, and which of them is Ethel, but you'll figure it out. We found The Genius in a saloon in Butte, and life hasn't been the same since he joined the troupe. I give you the one, the only Genius on the planet, and the one and only Ethel."

The Genius showed up in a brown tweed jacket and a deerstalker hat, and Ethel followed in a dowdy dress that turned her into a sort of pyramid, even as the olio drop closed behind them.

"Well, sir, how did you get to be a genius?" she asked.

"It's my vocation, madam. Some people choose to be carpenters. Or miners. I chose to be a genius."

"What makes you a genius, sir?"

"My natural superiority, madam. I am the world's greatest expert. I know more about everything than anyone here."

"Well, you don't know much about women," she replied.

The audience enjoyed that.

"Ask me anything, madam, and I'll prove it."

"Okay, genius, tell me how many people are out there watching you."

Perkins swelled up and gave her a withering glare. "More than you or anyone out there can count, so there's no reason to be specific."

"How do you know you're smarter than anyone out there?"

"Madam, that's simple. They live here."

"You don't think much of Philipsburg, do you?"

"Madam, being a genius is lonesome. If there was even one genius out there, one genius equal to me, I'd be happy to live in Philipsburg. Until then, though, I'd have to consider the place poor and deprived."

"I like Philipsburg," she said. "They came to our show."

"That's why they're not geniuses," he said.

The banter went along like that, pretty entertaining, Beausoleil thought. It would be fine if they didn't run too long, or let the joke get pretty thin. It made a light act, a diversion. And they'd probably improve it as they worked the audiences. Maybe Cromwell Perkins could be a little more outrageous.

They quit after a few minutes, and got a good hand. That sort of braggadocio was a novelty, and the miners out there were entertained.

"The Genius and Ethel," Beausoleil said. "Let's hear some applause for Ethel."

That won more cheer.

He ran the acts in order. Harry did his juggling act with knives and scimitars. Wayne Windsor did a brief monologue on misbegotten English, which the miners appreciated, since they were misbegetting English constantly.

And then it was Ginger's turn, and once again Mrs. Wall's men rolled out her golden harp, and Ginger appeared, this time in a powder-blue dress that glowed in the limelight.

"I love ballads because they tell a story," she said. "So I'll sing three ballads now, ballads that seem to rise right out of the longings of people who are far from home. The first is 'Shenandoah.' Across the wide Missouri. I guess a lot of you have left your own Shenandoah behind."

That surely was true. The old American ballad evoked tender thoughts. Beausoleil could see it in their faces. These were men who had come some vast distance across a virgin continent to find a new life here, in an obscure corner of the Rockies.

She sang that and "Swanee River," and "Down in the Valley," and then "My Old Kentucky Home" for an encore, and the hush that followed was more eloquent than applause. She had won hearts here.

It had been a good afternoon, and bore the promise of a fine evening, and in spite of a small opera house, they would do better than break even.

"My dear sir," said Mrs. Wall. "After the evening's show, I would like to invite your entire company to my home for a late supper, and a farewell from the grateful people of Philipsburg," she said. "It would be our farewell."

"I'm sure our people will be delighted," he said. "I'll tell the company."

"It's the house on the hill," she said. "You can't miss it."

She was right. No one in Philipsburg could possibly miss that house.

TWENTY-EIGHT

The Steinway grand piano in Mrs. Wall's music room caught Ginger's eye. Near it stood the golden harp. Both instruments seemed out of place in Philipsburg, a raw and hastily built mining town. But there they were, in one of the few brick buildings, a fine Georgian home overlooking much of the town. She had seen only one other Steinway grand piano in the region, and that one was in her parents' house, and she had spent hours at its keyboard. The nearest piano tuner was in Salt Lake; it was journey enough to Pocatello. Bringing a tuner here would require an arduous journey.

The piano evoked memories, and she fled into the spacious parlor and dining area, where the entire cast and crew of the Beausoleil Brothers Follies congregated around a buffet supper, with Mrs. Wall presiding as a vivacious hostess. It was a grand farewell party, even though the company had played Philipsburg only one day. Few in the company had ever been in a home like this.

Ginger saw no sign of Mr. Wall, and presumed he was away somewhere. The Granite Mine lay several miles distant, and by all accounts was a superb producer of silver ore. Mines rarely lasted long, and most mining towns were built with that in mind. But some sort of optimism had embraced this district, and now the Walls were living in a solid home built to last for generations.

Mrs. Wall spotted her and bloomed before her.

"Ah, there you are, Penelope. Come with me to the music room for a little visit."

Ginger's world stopped cold.

"Mrs. Wall, my name is Ginger. Ginger Pomerantz," she said, the words hollow in her dry throat.

But Mrs. Wall steered her into the quiet music room. "I think not," she said.

"I'm married," Ginger said, feeling her life fall into pieces.

"Of course you are, my dear."

"But I want to thank you for your interest," Ginger said. "Your backing with the harp worked well, I think."

"Would you like to play the piano?" Mrs. Wall asked. "I remember when you were the child prodigy, playing in Pocatello, your hands so small they didn't stretch across an octave. But you played marvelously. Of course you had tutors, brought from distant cities by your parents, to impart the best that the world could offer you."

"I am Ginger, madam, and I'm sure you are thinking of someone else."

"No, my dear. Your father and my husband were classmates and close friends. They still are in touch." She walked to a bric-a-brac and plucked up a portrait in oval gray pasteboard, the gilded name ADAMS BROTHERS, POCATELLO, embossed in its base. The portrait had been taken when the young pianist was sixteen, a time when she was past girlhood and taking lessons from another set of tutors to develop her glorious voice.

"I think it's grand that you are engaging in show business, even if it's not what your parents expected."

"I think I'm ready to go back to my hotel," Ginger said. "I do want to thank you for the evening."

"Yes, of course. But first you must play me Chopin's Polonaise," Mrs. Wall said. "Here, I'll collect some of your colleagues."

The Polonaise had been Penelope's triumph. Mastered at age fourteen, her body still growing, her hands still maturing. A prodigy. To play it would amount to an admission, but she could think of no way to escape.

Even as Ginger was braving herself to bolt, Mrs. Wall returned with several of the troupe, and then more, and finally August Beausoleil, who eyed her contemplatively, obviously not sure what to make of this.

Very well, then. Ginger seated herself. She would make no apologies. She hadn't played it or practiced on a piano for as long as these people had known her. They would understand. Still, this was something strange, some facet of Ginger they knew nothing about, and now they settled quietly, some of them with hors d'oeuvres in hand.

She glanced at August, wishing he would intervene, send his singer home to rest, but he didn't.

She played, the soft introductory measures, and then the great theme, so familiar to all, played as if she had never stopped playing, her fingers dancing, the Steinway leaping to respond. She played out of desperation, not looking at anything, played in a crowded room lit by a dozen kerosene lamps that lifted heat and light and a faint odor. She played grandly, even as the troupe absorbed this surprising skill in the young wife of Charles Pomerantz.

They didn't applaud, but smiled when her fingers caught the last notes, and the sound lingered.

"Thank you, Mrs. Pomerantz," Mrs. Wall said.

Ginger felt her body sag. The worst had passed. But who could say what might come next?

"That was spendid, Ginger," August said, an odd smile upon him. "I had no idea."

"It isn't often that this piano is put to such good use," their hostess said. "Mining towns—well, they come and go." She smiled. "I'm sure you could offer us a concert, my dear."

"Thank you," was all Ginger could manage.

Was Mrs. Wall implying that all of Ginger's training, and tutors, and practice, was being wasted? Yes, probably.

But maybe this would be the end of it; in the morning they would all be on the shuttle to the Northern Pacific mainline, and then to Missoula. She would leave Mrs. Wall behind. But maybe not.

Nothing more came of it. Mrs. Wall did not corral her. And her name continued to be Ginger Pomerantz. And yet the evening was wreathed with worry, and she knew it would not easily slip away; a night in her hotel bed would accomplish nothing to allay her fears.

Later, carriages and footmen conveyed the troupe to the wooden hotel, and only then did her friends in the company pour out their admiration.

"I had no idea," Ethel Wildroot said. "You have kept it all a secret."

Ginger bobbed her head uncertainly. There were hidden shoals here. She had risked everything to escape the gilded prison her parents had built around her.

"Thank you," she said, and turned away. She did not welcome questions.

August collected them all in the lobby. "Train leaves at seven forty-five. Be here at seven fifteen. Sorry to cut into your beauty sleep."

"Where in Missoula?" asked Windsor.

"Bennett Opera House, second floor of the European Hotel, downtown. It seats five hundred. We're there four nights, Saturday matinee, but tomorrow's free."

"Lumberjack town, bad for business," Ethel Wildroot said.

"We have a good advance sale," August said. "Prosperous town. It supplies timbers to the mines. Also a school. Helena got the capital, Missoula the state college."

"We'd better play it while we can," Ethel said. "Students want comedy; faculty wants symphonies."

"You'll be awakened at six," he said. "Eat before you leave or wait to get to Missoula."

Ginger had discovered that managing a troupe took a lot of work, including herding the company to train stations on time. None of it was effortless, and often it involved smoothing ruffled feathers.

He turned to Ginger and handed her a yellow flimsy. "From Charles," he said.

HEARD YOU WERE SPLENDID SEE YOU SOON, it read.

She longed to be with him, and now there was something new about it. He was her husband, and protector if trouble followed her from Pocatello. Her mother would stop at nothing.

August grinned. "I second that."

That night she lay abed in the room she shared with two of the Wildroot Sisters, but sleep eluded her. She dreaded what might happen soon. So willful was her mother that anything could happen, even a kidnapping. The morning arrived with a knock, and soon the troupe was settled in the sole passenger coach of the mixed freight train that would carry them to the mainline. She was soon watching the forested slopes drift by. She had never been east, to settled country, where farms surrounded towns, and forests mingled with pastures and plowed fields. This was different. She had a sudden impulse to catch the next train to New York, and try a new life once again. But the moment died. She sat passively, with the company, and transferred passively to a westbound express with plush maroon seats and a tobacco odor. She stared anxiously from the window as the train screeched to a halt at the Missoula station. She ached to see Charles.

The line crawled slowly to the end of the car, and then the conductor was helping her down the steps, onto the stool, and then the gravel platform. And there he was, a bouquet of yellow roses in hand, his derby cocked on his head, his gaze feasting upon her. She swept toward him, and he gathered her in, and pressed her tight, and she felt the brusque warmth through his gray topcoat, and then he was placing those roses, wrapped in green tissue, in her hands, and smiling, an odd sadness in his eyes.

"Oh, Charles . . ."

"It's himself," he said. "I've been hearing about you. And now you're going to sing for me."

"Private concert?" she asked.

He liked that. He squeezed her, pulled her back, looked her over, and helped her collect her stuff. A trainman had deposited her travel bag on the platform. A small trunk would follow, delivered by expressmen.

A hack stood ready to carry them to the Florence, near the opera house, where they had rooms on the ground floor. He waved at August.

"I'll see you at the hotel," he said. "There's things."

August nodded. The cryptic message eluded Ginger, but managers were like that. They always had things to resolve. The hack driver, dapper in his ankle-length black coat, steered the dray horse over to Higgins, and set a fast

pace. Inside, the Wildroot girls were jammed in beside
Charles and Ginger, and also Harry the Juggler, who sat
impassively, studying the city.

It seemed a harsh place. Wood smoke layered the city
and there were no breezes to carry it away. But that didn't
matter. Charles, her husband of a few days, sat comfortably beside her, his quietness suggesting that there would
be intimate conversation only when they were free from
company. Maybe at dinner that evening. Yes, surely then.
An odd anxiety wormed through her. For some couples,
this would still be a honeymoon.

The hack driver unloaded them quickly, intent on collecting more customers, and Charles escorted her inside
and straight to a room she realized was his. The bags
would catch up, somehow. He let her in, flipped a light
switch—Missoula was electrified—and a table lamp
burned inside a Tiffany shade.

He caught her close and kissed her.

"Long time; too long," he said. "I tell you what. Rest a
little, and I'll be back in time for dinner. We'll have a
grand evening."

"You'll be back?"

He looked apologetic. "There's some things to talk
about with August. You know, business interferes with
everything, and it's interfering with us, with our rendezvous." He smiled woefully. "It can't be helped. The company, you know, is on the road, and things shift and
change, and we need to adjust, or work out details."

He sure wasn't telling her much. "What is it, Charles?"
she asked.

"Nothing for you to worry your pretty head about."

She didn't like that much. She'd had some notion that
marriage would bring them a complete sharing. But
now . . . she didn't know.

"Make yourself beautiful," he said. "And we'll go out
and have a fling."

"When will I see you?"

He sighed. "Hard to say. But don't worry; I'll be back soon."

He pulled free, kissed her on the cheek, smiled, and pointed at the roses. "Put them in water," he said. "Keep them fresh."

And with that, he opened the door, stepped into the hall, and closed the door behind him. She peered around the comfortable room, peered at his things hanging in an armoire, peered at the bed, and then sat down on it, hardly knowing what to do, or why she was there, or who her husband was.

TWENTY-NINE

Charles Pomerantz knocked and was let in instantly.

"We've got this," he said, placing a yellow flimsy in August's hand. It was from the manager of the Spokane Auditorium, and it canceled the booking.

August stared. "Why?" he asked.

"I don't know much. It's been sold. New owners aren't honoring bookings. They own the Orpheum, San Francisco."

"You argue with them?"

Pomerantz shook his head. They both knew what good that would do. And a lawsuit would only throw money away and take a year to settle. "It gets worse. I picked up a little from the bill-poster there. When I tried to start him pasting up the playbills, he wired back that a combine in San Francisco was buying up houses up and down the West, a chain. It'll be a new circuit called Orpheum."

"What else do you know?"

"There's no other houses anywhere near Spokane. None

in northern Idaho. In other words, we don't have options near there. Can't book another house. Spokane was our bridge to the coast."

"We saw this back east. Combines, buying up theaters, controlling the acts, moving acts from stage to stage, new show every week, shows twice a day, nonstop. I hoped we might escape that here."

"There's another option, August. We can duck south, try to book the houses at Pocatello, Boise, and maybe more towns around there. Good houses, and a good chance they're dark. Pocatello, the Grand Opera house, town of five thousand. Boise, eight thousand, Columbia Theater. But we'd have to get down there. That means backtracking to Butte, and taking the Utah and Northern south. And booking rooms. But we could do it, and fill the two weeks before we do Seattle, Tacoma, and Puyallup. And start down the coast."

"Charles, are we still booked solid out there?"

"No word otherwise."

"And Oregon?"

"We're still booked."

"And California?"

"We're in."

"So we have only this one hole in the schedule?"

Charles wished he could say so, with some finality. "I don't like this. I'd better wire. Get some confirmations."

"Find out fast. We may have a lot of dodging ahead."

Charles' thoughts raced ahead, to ticket refunds, new tickets, reserving rooms, booking alternative houses. But they'd done all that before. And they had a five-day run in Missoula, time to squeeze it out.

Money. They needed to fill the house every performance. They had payroll. Those brown envelopes they doled out each Saturday had to hold greenbacks. Most players got fifty a week. A three-person act like the Marburys, a hundred fifty a week. Some favorites, like Wayne

Windsor, collected more. Seventy-five a week for him. Mary Mabel Markey had gotten eighty. The billing order, who got top billing, and who was stuck at the bottom, usually set the pay. Larger companies did it differently. Their home office paid the agents, who paid the players. But August had no home office.

The troupe was working toward San Francisco, where the show would disband. Some would be hired on the eastern swing a few weeks later, across the middle of the continent, to Chicago, the terminus as well as the starting point. The Chicago agents were booking the return east, burning up the telegraph lines. Now he would have to let the agents know about this. They got a cut of every booking. Everyone wanted a cut and usually got it.

"All right, Charles. Wire Pocatello and Boise tonight. Book what you can. Tomorrow, tickets and rooms, if we're going there. And wire Seattle, Tacoma, and Puyallup—confirm our bookings. And we'd better look at Portland, Salem, Eugene, and keep on going. Yuba City. Sacramento. Stockton. Oakland. Berkeley. Confirm bookings all the way. But tonight, deal with the dark two weeks."

It was a tall order. Shifting a schedule en route, with no time to settle the details, was rough.

"How are we fixed?" Charles asked.

"If we have a good draw here, we should be able to weather it."

"I put out extra playbills."

"I've never played a lumberjack town before. Have you?"

"They eat a lot of pancakes; that's all I know."

August smiled. "We'll do what we always do."

But Charles didn't like the weariness he saw in the manager's eyes.

He hiked up Higgins in a mean wind, and found the Northern Pacific station empty, save for the telegrapher in his cage behind a grille. A clear-glass lightbulb lit his wicket and the empty ticket counter. Missoula had juice. The man bolted upright with a start. He wore a white shirt with a sleeve garter, and had removed his celluloid collar.

Pomerantz found a pencil and filled out forms. One to GrndOpHs Pocatello. Booking Dec 2–10, ASAP Beausoleil Follies Pomerantz, Florence Hotel Missoula. The next would go to Columb Theat Boise, booking December 12–16.

The telegrapher eyed them and counted, and yawned. "Four fifty," he said.

Charles winced. He had it. He had to have it. An advance man operated on cash. The show did, too. Payroll was greenbacks, and part of Charles' job was to deal with banks along the way. Suppliers wanted cash from road shows; most wouldn't take a check or send an invoice east.

"These'll take a few moments," the mustachioed operator said. "You gonna stick around for replies?"

"No, they won't reach their destinations until morning when things open up. But we'll be here four days."

The man nodded. He took his time, reading each one, and then hunched over his brass key, the device with which he tapped out coded messages, usually in a flawless and fast staccato, the device clicking and chattering as it hastened its message out upon miles of copper wire.

Charles did stick, making sure the wires went out, watching the skinny, bored telegrapher depress the key in some sort of rhythm, letter upon letter, word upon word, space upon space, his concentration total.

That was it. An SOS shot into a void. He would be sending more wires in the morning. More and more, a pile of yellow paper the next few hours and days. The show was dark, and putting it into houses was up to him now.

He nodded to the telegrapher, who had returned to a Horatio Alger novel, and headed into the eve. His thoughts were on Ginger. She would be pleased. She had been his

wife a few days, and he had barely given her a kiss. Tonight would be fragrant in their memories.

She was waiting for him, sitting primly in the room's
only chair. She had waited a long time.

"Put your coat on, sweetheart, and we'll eat."

She looked a little pouty.

"Hey, in this business, you'll spend your life waiting for
someone. Namely me. Managers have to put out fires."

He steered her into the breeze, which had a hint of snow
in it.

"There's not a decent eatery in town. Believe me, I
know. Advance men know everything. But there's a hotel, down the street here, that's got something edible."

Missoula wasn't his favorite place. He had his doubts
whether all those sawmill men and timber cutters cared to
be entertained, but he'd soon know. The state college
would only make it worse. Academics never cared about a
feed, and sat long-faced through a show, right to curtain.

He steered her into a folksy place named Mrs. Williams' Appetite Chastener.

It chastened appetites, all right.

Its walls were jammed with embroidered samplers,
most of which flaunted biblical verses, or mottoes encouraging rectitude of one sort or another. Charles had been
there a few times during his advance forays, and had offered to buy the samplers to hang temporarily in the Green
Rooms of the houses they played. But Mrs. Williams had
declined. He had thought to instill virtue in his troupe,
wherever they played. His favorite sampler, and one he
really itched to own, was "Let us eat and drink, for tomorrow we die." But Mrs. Williams would not even
take a five-dollar greenback for it.

He had the sense that Ginger had been in better restaurants, but she kept her silence. That was one of her becoming traits. He talked and she listened. The perfect
wife. That separated her from almost all other females.

"Want me to order for you, sweetheart? I can separate the good, the bad, and the ugly."

She smiled at last.

He ordered something or other she had never heard of that sounded southern. Like grits.

"All right, tell me. What took you away from me this afternoon?"

"I need a double rye to unload all that on you. But the chances of getting one from Mrs. Williams are slim."

"I will ask her," Ginger said.

When Mrs. Williams returned with some bread and butter, Ginger caught her.

"My husband would like a double rye, on ice if you have it," she said.

Mrs. Williams stared. "In a Limoges teacup, and it'll cost a dollar. And don't let on."

Charles stared, amazed.

"Maybe I know some things," Ginger said. "Now tell me what happened."

He waited until the rye materialized, sampled it, and found it was the real stuff.

"We're not going to Spokane. New owner canceled us."

That troubled her. "Can they do that?"

"Easily. They didn't buy the old contracts. They bought the house. We could maybe sue the previous owner and get two cents next year if we're lucky."

"But why?"

"Vaudeville's changing fast, sweetheart. Shows like ours, a complete company on tour, we're being beaten out by the new chains and associations. Circuits. The owners of theaters think they can make more money with continuous shows, or at least two shows a day. And the shows are all acts, booked from one town to the next. It's acts, like yourself, or Windsor, or a magician, or a trio like the Wildroots. The contracts don't include us; the Beausoleil Brothers are being squeezed. But it's not all bad. It takes big towns with big houses to keep a circuit going. This is how it is back east, where there's people. And now, maybe the West Coast."

"But wouldn't the acts prefer a company like ours?"

"Money talks, sweetheart. Those acts are getting a hundred a week, some of them."

"Dollars?"

"It's a tough life: shows all day, moves each week. The circuit's a treadmill."

"What's going to happen to us, Charles?"

"Not over, sweet. Not by a long shot. We've got a few aces. We can make money in smaller houses. We can get talent for less."

She smiled wryly. "Which reminds me . . ."

He reached across to her. "I'll talk to August. You were, well, tentative. Now you're not. I'll get you something. Maybe not a lot; you need to be a draw before you can start dickering with August. But you've got a foot on the rung, and you can climb the ladder."

He sipped his rye from the teacup, and smiled, even as Mrs. Williams brought two plates of sliced beef and mashed potatoes mixed with chives, called Le Grande Eau de Cologne.

She ate tentatively, but dug in after a bite or two. The dish had seemed off-putting to her. He sipped from the teacup, thinking the Limoges improved the rye.

"We're going to try another route," he said. "We've a two-week gap to fill, and I'm heating up the wires looking for bookings. We've got an option worked out. Pocatello, Boise. I sent queries this eve. That was what delayed me. If the houses are dark, we can detour. It's a pain. We'll need to print a lot of playbills and slap them up. . . ." He stared. "Something wong?"

She was staring into space, her knife and fork down.

"I'll be all right," she said. "It's just a spell."

"Anyway, it's a tough haul. Backtrack from here almost

to Butte, go south on that UP branch, Utah and Northern, and then move through southern Idaho. Pocatello's got the Grand Opera House, town of fifty-five hundred, good enough for a stay. Boise's got the Columbia Theater, eight thousand there, good potential. And I'm looking at Moscow, even though there's no direct route. It's got five thousand, and the G.A.R. Opera House. Grand Army of the Republic. I guess we know what side the owners were on. But that's way out of the way."

She had quit eating, and sat rigidly in her seat, staring.

"Vapors or something?"

She smiled, woodenly. "I'll get over it," she said. But she didn't eat. And said not a word.

After that strange meal, he took her back to their room, anticipating a delightful renewal of their honeymoon. But she lay rigid and pale, her mind drifting somewhere, and he wondered what the hell sort of marriage he had gotten into.

THIRTY

Ethel Wildroot, Wayne Windsor, and The Genius were exploring Missoula, having first settled in their rooms. Their first stop was The Woodcutter's Bowl, which had but a single dish, beef stew, all drawn from a pot. A large bowl cost two bits. It wasn't bad if one didn't examine the meat closely. That done, they ventured out once again, this time southerly, and found themselves at the Bennett Opera House, which occupied the second floor of the Hotel Europa.

Some event was unfolding there that eve. The lamps were lit.

"Want a look?" Windsor asked.

Of course they all did, so they entered, climbed a gallant set of stairs, and found a placard on an easel announcing the evening's fare: a lecture by Mrs. Amelia Woodcock of the Women's Christian Temperance Union. It had started at seven, and was no doubt mostly over, unless Mrs. Woodcock was particularly windy.

They entered, found the place lit by electric lights. Mrs. Woodcock, a handsome woman in a gray suit with a jabot at the neck, stood at a walnut lectern. She was flanked by two other ladies and some gents in full white beards, suit coats, waistcoats, with gold watch fobs dangling across their middles. They were all paying rapt attention to the speaker. The three vaudevillians settled quietly at the rear. When Ethel's eyes had adjusted to the light, she discovered several of the acts had slipped in. Show people liked to do that: see the house, see what was playing ahead of them.

Her daughters and LaVerne were sitting nearby. The Marbury Trio, too. Harry the Juggler.

The opera house was a third full, the listeners gathered forward. An olio drop behind Amelia Woodcock barred a view of the large stage behind.

"The rising tide of drunkenness comes from lax immigration laws," Mrs. Woodcock was saying. "There are, of course, certain nations and cultures that actually welcome intoxicating beverages and even use them in religious rites. Even small children are permitted to sip wine, a sure way to begin them upon the road to ruin. It doesn't matter whether it's wine or ardent spirits; they are all evil, and destroy the character and decency of those who take the fateful step of drinking them. The Woman's Christian Temperance Union is staunchly opposed to imbibing alcohol of any sort, in any circumstance.

"We are, of course, opposed to lax immigration laws, which have opened the gates of this great nation to morally loose people, especially those gathered around the

Mediterranean Sea. They tend to be people of darker hue, a sure sign that they are vulnerable not only to drunkenness but also to social disorders, crime, cruelty, and wantonness of all sorts. But wine drinkers aren't the only problem. Head north and we find the Germans, celebrating life in beer halls, drinking all sorts of ardent spirits, and delighting in it. Such people can never make good citizens of our republic; neither can the Irish, another race imbibing ardent spirits. Look at Butte, a city lost to inebriation, a city in perpetual turmoil because moral bonds are loosened, and widows and orphans suffer.

"This organization is devoted to curbing promiscuous immigration, and maintaining a civil order intended from the beginning to reflect the ideals and cultural traditions of its founders. That means, largely, those who cannot speak English ought not to be welcomed here."

Ethel listened closely, peering at her vaudeville colleagues, wondering if they felt what she felt. Her alienated husband's name was not Wildroot but Wildenstein; he was German. Ethel herself was Irish. Her daughters were a mix of both peoples and would not meet this speaker's approval for citizenship in the United States.

Harry the Juggler was Polish, or at least from some country around there. Who knew which? The Marbury Trio, golden-fleshed, were mostly Italian, from the boot of Italy. Charles Pomerantz was a Polish Jew. August Beausoleil was French, and who knew what else? Mary Mabel Markey had been Irish. Heaven only knew what Mrs. McGivers was, all told, but only part of her could have been Scots.

And that was true of the whole business. Vaudeville was a creation of recent arrivals, people distinctively different and not on this lady's approved list. Not native, but arriving in immigrant boats from Italy, Ireland, Germany, the Continent. And they were giving these native people like Mrs. Woodcock the best entertainment and humor they had ever seen.

"Now, then," said Mrs. Woodcock, "to sum up, the community can cleanse itself of tragedy and grief and loss and financial ruin, all of it wrought by spirits, if it quietly removes and destroys all the drinking parlors, making it impossible for the weak to appease their ravenous appetites, or bring further sorrow to their families and friends and colleagues. How great is the ruin they visit upon their loved ones, friends, associates, and neighbors.

"We calculate costs, which go far beyond the financial sort, and include children denied food and shelter and the loving paternal hand; we calculate that the presence of spirits ruins an entire city and county. The solution does not lie in Washington, or in the Montana capitol, but right here. In your village ordinances. In your county laws. Make this beautiful county dry. Make it a crime to operate a saloon, or a store where spirits are vended. Drive out the demonic presence of spirits, which corrupt a whole community until it bleeds with tragedy, and no household is spared.

"Yes, begin here, and then take the issue to the state, and then to the nation, so that at some future date the United States Constitution will forbid the sale or possession of intoxicating spirits. And then, dear people, we will see safe and secure communities, sober and industrious fathers, each neighborhood dotted with white churches watching over the flock. Then we will see the orphanages empty out, the work of constables diminish, the available jobs increase because a sober workforce is far more productive than a dissolute one. Yes, we will swiftly see all these things come to pass. Not all at once, but as a tidal wave rolling toward shore, carrying a clean and bright new world on its crest.

"Start here, dear people. Start right here in this opera

house. Make it the home of lectures, enlightened musicales, uplifting sermons, exhortations to achieve a good life lived in quietness and service. Ah, dear friends, begin right here in this theater, and choose carefully what might be played here. Let it inspire and reward."

She paused, collecting the polite applause, and sat down.

A gent with a massive white beard stepped up to the lectern.

"We do thank you, Mrs. Woodcock. We all have profited from your inspiring talk, and your vision of the future, and the remaking of America. And now, as always, I invite inspirational comment from our audience."

A matronly lady in blue arose at once. "Mrs. Woodcock," she began. "We're all inspired by your lecture, and also by your guidance. We know now what to do, and how to do it. The WCTU has a great history of picketing saloons, but also picketing undesirable places that endanger public morals. I do believe I know of some places right here, in Missoula. In fact, this opera house tomorrow will be turned over to a troupe called the Beausoleil Brothers Follies. That's the word, *Follies*. That says it all. It's time for us to drive pernicious influences out of Missoula, wouldn't you say?"

"Madam, you have caught the letter and spirit of my lecture, and if that's what's coming here, then let the world know. A firm line of picketers has been known to drive such company out of a town."

"Count on us!" said the lady in blue.

"We'll organize the event right now," said someone else. "Those of you wishing to join us, have a sign ready. I believe the Follies starts at seven."

Ethel watched, fascinated. And so did the rest of the troupe.

The crowd around the stage stirred, and the lecturer and her contingent abandoned the stage. Few people were leaving; most of the Missoulians were collecting around the woman in blue, who was plainly organizing the surprise party for the vaudeville company.

"I guess we'd better talk to Charles, or maybe August," Ethel said.

"I've been in a couple of these," Wayne Windsor said. "And I'm English."

"I bet," said Ethel. Windsor laughed.

"This place sure isn't Butte," The Genius said.

Some of the company, notably the Marbury Trio, were drifting forward, boldly intent on listening in, while others, such as the juggler, were quietly donning coats and pulling out.

LaVerne Wildroot eyed her aunt. "What are you going to do?"

"Talk to August if I can find him."

"He'll know what to do?"

"I think so. He can turn something like this into box office."

"I'd never thought of that," LaVerne said.

"Any publicity works," Ethel said. "If it's put to use. All right, Genius, let's hunt down the boss. You coming, Wayne?"

"No, I'm going over there and listen in. I might have a new monologue ready when we open."

"You coming, LaVerne?"

"No, I'm going to volunteer to picket us."

"I always knew you had talent," Ethel said. She eyed the rest of the company, including a couple of musicians and stagehands who obviously didn't know what to do.

"Go listen," she said. "Make a picket sign."

They smiled.

Ethel headed into the evening, Genius at her side, passing a knot of dignified men in topcoats, waiting for their wives within.

"Scandalous," Ethel said to one, who sputtered something that vanished in the wind.

She tried Beausoleil's room at the hotel, but no one responded, so she headed for the nearest saloon, and entered, with The Genius, against a wall of frowns. Sure enough, there was August, nursing a drink, maybe his third or fourth, in one of his melancholic moments. She knew about those. Sometimes the remembrance of an abandoned youth, desperately surviving on tips around theaters, caught at him, even now, and sent him reeling into a bleak private world.

Beausoleil smiled slightly as Ethel plowed down a long bar. An oil portrait of Cleopatra, thinly veiled about the loins, was prominently displayed above the handsome, mahogany Brunswick back bar.

Beausoleil nodded, even as a serving man showed up.

"I can only serve the gentlemen," he said.

"Then your life is half as valuable," The Genius said, ordering a rye.

"We're going to be picketed tomorrow," Ethel said.

August stared, sipped, and waited.

She spilled the story swiftly, and he absorbed every word.

"What set them off?" he asked.

"Follies."

"That's why I use the name," Beausoleil said. "I almost used *Scandals,* but the times aren't ripe for it."

"Those ladies were all Presbyterians or Baptists or something like that," she said. "There wouldn't be a Catholic in the lot. Probably not an Anglican, either."

"WCTU—ban the spirits, along with Italians, French, Germans, Irish, and the rest," he said. "Missoula isn't Butte. All right, we'll give them something to picket about." He nodded to Ethel. "Have the girls show an ankle. I'll want the Marbury Trio in blackface."

"Blackface?"

"Biggest acts back east are blackface. Burnt cork's selling tickets. And tap dancing's straight out of minstrel shows. I'll go talk to the newspaper. The minstrel show's arrived in Missoula."

"LaVerne's been itching to show a lot more than some ankle, August."

"Let her rip," he said. "A girl needs to make good use of her assets."

The waiter delivered the drinks, and The Genius shoved his glass at Ethel, who downed it neat, in three coughs and two sputters.

"I'm a case history for the WCTU," The Genius said. "Maybe I can turn it into something."

"Give it a shot, and if it bombs, I'll give you the hook. You play something like this for all it's worth."

August finished up the dregs in his glass, reached for his black topcoat and black derby, and swept into the night, with Ethel and The Genius in tow. The newspaper, the *Missoulian,* was just a block or two away.

THIRTY-ONE

Charles Pomerantz opened his room door to August, who bore news.

"We're in luck. The WCTU's fixing to picket us tomorrow."

"What's their beef?"

"Follies. They don't like follies, so they'll get more than they bargained for. I've asked the Marbury Trio to go blackface, and they'll be the Marbury Minstrel Dancers. And LaVerne's going to show a little limb and chest. And The Genius says he'll try to work the theme. I headed over to the paper and bought a small ad, program change, minstrels, etc. With some luck, we'll get a lot of picketers."

"How'd you get wind of it?"

"They were at the opera house. Lecture by some temperance lady or other. She doesn't like spirits or Italians. She doesn't like Catholics or Episcopalians or Latvians or Norwegians. Half our company was there, enjoying the show. It could give us a few sellouts. Speaking of which, what's the word?"

"Won't know until morning. Wired Pocatello and Boise. We're covering two weeks, and need two theaters or a long run in Boise, which is big enough."

"Let me know fast."

"I'll wire the houses in Washington and Oregon tomorrow to confirm our dates," Charles said. "And California. If a circuit's buying houses out there, we need to know, fast. While we can still maneuver."

"I sure get tired of the scramble," August said. "What a business. Nothing's firm. We need houses that won't cancel us. We need acts. I'd pay good money for an animal act, but where do you find one in Montana?"

"So we stir the pot," Charles said. "Got any more scandals?"

"I'll invent some."

Charles thought that August looked drawn. Road managers careened from crisis to crisis, and this tour had been full of them. It had always been hard to read August. He was the loneliest man Charles had ever met, keeping everything to himself. He was always affable, always affectionate—and distant. There was an interior life in August that no one knew, or would ever know. A man without intimates carried a terrible burden, especially in critical moments.

"I will do something," Ginger said, suddenly. "I have assets."

"That's sweet of you, but you just keep on the way you are," August said.

She smiled suddenly. "The way I was. I'll never be that again."

Charles sensed something that he couldn't quite fathom. She had been almost rigid, silent, withdrawn all evening. Something was burdening her. And then suddenly, this. Her assets. He wished he could fathom what was inside of her. And what she meant. Whatever it was, she wasn't spilling any beans, not now.

"You'll be the draw," he said.

"Not if I stay the way I was."

This was beyond him. August stared flatly, nodded, and a moment later the door clicked shut.

She sprang from the chair where she had sat in locked silence, raced to him, and crushed him in her arms with an eagerness that astonished him. She clung fiercely, and only after a long moment did he respond to her, drawn ever closer to her pliant body, which for the first time seemed to shape itself to his.

He felt the rush of need, and returned her kiss. But still this sudden change in her very nature bewildered him.

"There, now," he said, softly. "What is this?"

She didn't respond except with her eager hands. And he was discovering a Ginger he hadn't known, a woman of such intensity and passion and willfulness that he simply surrendered to her, a circumstance as strange to him as marriage itself. He was married, and he hadn't ever grasped how it happened, or why. A crazy impulse.

Their brief honeymoon was fraught with tension, and she had surrendered piecemeal, unloosing bit by bit those parts of her that no man had ever known, and always a little removed from him, even analytical as if she were an observer. And when they had at last achieved union, he had no sense of whether she enjoyed it, or whether it repelled, or perhaps made no inroads upon her heart at all. Maybe it didn't matter. And in the end, before he was compelled to leave Butte, he had concluded that he knew little of her, and might never know much about her, and least of all about their union. He had married a woman far removed from anyone—from him, but also from the world, a woman with a chest of secrets she shared with no one.

Still, as he thought back, there had been tenderness, and tentativeness, and experiment, and she had not resisted as she experienced his caresses, and weighed his advances. But she had been a mystery, and now in her passion she was even more so, the heat in her shredding the moment, hurrying their bodies along.

It took little time, actually, a great tugging of clothes, rending of buttons, yanking of stockings, and he discovered a different bride this time, one he had never fathomed. And was it tears he was finding on her cheeks in the midst of passion? When, finally, they lay spent in that narrow hotel room, it seemed that this really was the first of their matings, that all that had gone before was little more than removing locks from doors.

Then she was there, her tangled hair nestled into his shoulder, an utter stranger in bed with him. And along with his peacefulness was curiosity; who was she, and why?

"Who are you?" he asked.

"A bird out of her cage."

"And what cage?"

"My mother's cage. What she expected of me."

"Which was?"

"Charles, you can't possibly know. It's beyond, I mean, there's no words. A clockwork doll. A windup toy. A prodigy to be displayed and put back on her shelf. A prisoner. A girl whose will was trampled, stolen, who could never be herself. My mother has no self, so she invaded me, possessed me, stole me. She doesn't even see me as a person."

"Your father?"

"He went along, bought the tutors, paid for it all, and

never questioned it, or objected, or asked me. But he always, oh, it was like he was the law."

An old story, he thought. And no doubt all out of proportion, an eighteen-year-old woman who had yet to see the world. In a year or two, she'd see it differently. Mothers against daughters. Daughters against parents. Escape, somewhere, anywhere, even into vaudeville, so impossibly distant from her quiet, bourgeois life.

"Ginger, where was this?"

She didn't speak for a long time, and he felt her stir in the comfortable dark. "I'm afraid to tell you," she whispered, and then pronounced it: "Pocatello."

No wonder, he thought.

"My father's superintendent of a Union Pacific division."

"And has railroad muscle behind him," he added, finishing her thought. "So, you don't want to perform there."

"You don't know my mother," she said.

"You're married. So what's going to happen?"

"If you knew my mother, you wouldn't ask."

"Ginger's not your name, right?"

"It's Penelope."

"And lots of people there would spot you the moment you walked into the limelight. And you're hoping we don't book Pocatello."

She clutched him and buried her face in his shoulder. Her fear was palpable.

"Penelope, there's no reason to worry about anything. We're married. You're old enough."

"Please, please, don't ever call me that. Please."

He pulled her tight. "You're Ginger to me; that's who I married."

He felt her quake, and felt the heat of her tears in the hollow of his shoulder.

"Hey, it'll be all right, Ginger. For one thing, we haven't

gotten a booking there. Maybe they're running something. For another, we need two. If I can book Boise, we've got most of what we need."

"My mother would pull the ring off my finger. My father would send railroad workers to take me away."

That seemed wildly unlikely to Charles. The woman he'd taken to wife was brimming with feverish fantasies. "Ginger, brace up. You go out there, on that stage, on any stage, and you bowl them over. You've got it; you'll strut it."

"They'll take me and lock me in my room. They'll charge you with things. They'll say I was stolen."

"Ginger, you're of age. You have a right to your own life."

She burrowed closer, and clutched him desperately. It amazed him. Rampant fear had caught her even though the company was not yet booked in her hometown. He didn't know what to do. Terrified people made bad performers. He'd seen performers quit the stage in the middle of an act. He doubted she would even walk out there, smile at the crowd, and offer up something they might like.

But there was this: A long run in Missoula, time to get used to the idea of playing Pocatello. Time for her to grow a little, pitch out the demons, collect herself. And time for him to work out a schedule.

"Hey, sweetheart, you're a long way from home," he said.

"You don't know," she replied.

The dread was there, alive, lashing back and forth like a lion's tail.

He hadn't known the woman he married. Marry in haste, repent forever. But the thing was, he had no regrets. This half-girl, half-woman enchanted him. There was a dimple in her cheek that he loved. It somehow doubled her smile.

Her quietness signaled sleep, or at least those peaceful moments of surrender to sleep. But he was starkly awake. The troupe was suffering for the lack of acts. Markey and McGivers gone. You couldn't just add a new one, not in Montana. He and August were pinning their hopes on this girl in his arms, hoping she would soon be a draw, have the magic, the power, the reach, that would bring crowds to their show. All the signs were there, but she hadn't quite connected yet; still too much recital, and not enough performer, or whatever it was called. Magic, that's how he described it. She needed magic, and they needed her magic, and so far there was no magic.

He'd know more in the morning when he heard from the opera houses in Idaho. What houses were dark, what houses weren't. A two-week break in the tour could be fatal. He had to book something fast, in the sparsely populated Northwest. He'd avoid Pocatello if he could, but even as he considered that prospect, he knew he couldn't avoid any house that was dark. Any house where the Follies could light up the stage, perform, and bring in the crowds. And cash.

The next morning, long before she stirred under the thin gray hotel blanket, he dressed quietly, braved sharp cold, and hiked to the railroad station. He didn't expect responses until the managers began their own quotidian routines and saw what Western Union brought to them. But it turned out he didn't need to wait; the managers had received the wires in the evening and had responded.

"I was just going to send a boy out to find you," the telegrapher said.

The news was good. Pocatello was dark the first four days, booked two days, and dark the next days. Boise was booked the first four days, dark the rest.

Pomerantz knew what he had to do. He booked the Grand Opera House at Pocatello for four days, with two travel days following the Missoula run. He booked the

Columbia Theater in Boise for the next leg, one travel day after Pocatello. After that the Follies would head west, Washington and Oregon, solid cities, big houses, some safety. And then California.

From the *Julius Cahn Official Theatrical Guide* he carried, he wired Pocatello for hotel rooms, Boise for hotel rooms. Then he wired the bill-poster at both sites, saying three-sheet bills would be expressed. The bill-posters would need to add a paste-on with the date of the appearance. They were skilled at that. They would get the sheets, post them on barn sides, walls, structures beside the roads, add the dates. There was more to do: wire the papers with small ads, wire or mail publicity material, find out from the house managers what worked best in their towns.

That's what an advance man was for. He would have to leave Ginger behind, set up the shows in Idaho, and hope for the best.

THIRTY-TWO

Two redoubtable ladies, armored against the evening cold with thick woolen coats and oversized hats, hoisted picket signs that evening. One sign said AMERICA FOR AMERICANS, and the other said KEEP US FROM FOLLIES.

They stood placidly in front of the Bennett Opera House, drawing only idle glances from those planning to see the show. August Beausoleil was, in a way, disappointed. A rowdier, snaking picket line would have been more to his liking. But these respectable matrons, armored in the attire of their bourgeois lives, generated only mild curiosity. And they were polite enough to stand to one side, not interfering with theater patrons.

He knew what the signs were about. The Woman's Christian Temperance Union was not just about removing every last ounce of alcohol in the states; it was also about immigration, and about a variety of other sorts of conduct it deemed immoral. It did not open its membership to Catholics and Jews, and was actively opposed to immigration of these groups, as well as Germans, French, Italians, Irish, and most everyone from Eastern Europe. Show business was the peculiar realm of these people, such as himself. So show business itself was the target this cold eve.

In 1882, a New Yorker named Tony Pastor had turned variety theater into vaudeville. The old variety shows had been racy, and Pastor had reasoned that their bawdiness was keeping women and children away. He could lure them into theaters with the promise of clean, cheerful shows. He called his new variety shows vaudeville, a little French, and swiftly turned them into a bright success. August Beausoleil, along with countless others in the business, had learned the lesson. Especially Oscar Hammerstein, whose shows soon outdid anything that Pastor put onstage.

August Beausoleil adhered to the new variety forms, but with a small caveat: he believed a little bit of spice could draw people into the theaters. He would even generate a little bad publicity if it improved his sales. But these polite ladies would only disappoint.

He headed toward the ladies, confronted them with a slight bow, and waved four tickets at them.

"My show," he said. "Please be my guests. You and your husbands."

"Over my dead body," said one. But she pocketed the tickets.

Beausoleil smiled, bowed once again, and headed

inside. The ladies probably wouldn't attend, but they would find friends to "report" what they saw inside.

He found Pomerantz backstage, looking worn. The other half of the Follies had spent the day in the railroad station, keeping the telegrapher busy.

"Where are we?" August asked.

"Looking good. Booked Pocatello December one to four; Boise seven to eleven with two holdover days reserved. I've got hotels in Boise and Pocatello. I've got the paper hangers alerted; they'll get playbills tomorrow, and they'll print paste-overs locally. I've got rail schedules and worked out the backtrack from here to Butte to Pocatello. I'll be leaving here tomorrow; got to be on hand forward. But it should get us through the gap, in time for the year-end stuff around Seattle."

"Any trouble I should know about?"

Pomerantz sighed. "My wife."

August said not a word. He studied the dark wing, offstage, empty of performers. Stages are sad, bleak places except for the few explosive moments they come alive with light and song and magic.

"Pocatello is where she's running away from," Charles said.

"And she doesn't want to return."

"Mother-and-daughter deal; sounds bad but I've seen a few daughters swear their mothers were straight out of hell."

"What's the deal?"

"I don't know. She's silent. She's a lot of things, but you know what? I'm tied to someone I'm just starting to know. So, all I can say is, coax her along."

"We're short of acts. She's getting better. We need two more acts, and can't get them fast around here."

"I'm away from here after the show; milk run to Butte. I've got more to worry about than mothers and daughters. If I don't get publicity out, it won't matter that we're booked across Idaho. So," he said, sounding amused, "she's your cookie."

"All right, what's your guess? At Pocatello?"

"She's got a stage mother, nah, call this one a recital mother, and Mama's spent a few thousand tutoring her little prodigy, and Mama's gonna drag her out the door."

"You married her, right?"

"Yeah, to a girl named Ginger. Her name's Penelope. So it's your guess."

"Showtime," said the stage manager.

Swiftly, August donned his tux with the snap-on bib, and stole a look out there. The house wasn't full, but there were people drifting in. And there were four empty seats where the temperance ladies would never sit. Seating in the gallery was spotty. But there were a pair of reporters out there.

What was it about showtime? Everyone who'd been in the business felt a galvanic current run through him when the moment arrived when the curtain would roll away and the performers and audience would greet each other. At each curtain time, not a few performers were sucking spirits from flasks. Beausoleil checked his acts; the Marbury Trio had applied the burnt cork this time, and looked lean and lanky. That would be one to watch. You never knew how a minstrel act would work. The Genius looked ready to go. He'd improved his line, making himself more and more outrageous, and at the same time more vulnerable to Ethel's little asides. He would probably pick on the WCTU. Harry stood quietly, waiting for his turn, and the Wildroot Sisters were ready, this time in the shortest skirts in their wardrobe, which showed plenty of white stocking at the calves. Strangely, Ginger had a new dress this time, one borrowed from somewhere, with a bit of ankle showing, and a scooped neckline. That should please the gents, if not their ladies. And there was Wayne Windsor, the old professional, a slight mocking in his face, as if to say he'd reduce this audience to fits, the way he often did.

Let it roll, then, August thought.

Then he was out there, introducing the Follies, waving the curtain up, thanking the crowd, and introducing the Wildroot Sisters.

Another show, another town, another audience to please, one of a thousand or two he had stood before, welcoming them, and welcoming his show.

The girls knocked them dead. What was it, the air? The perpetual smoke? The frowning ladies with their posters? He didn't know. He only knew that Cookie and Margie and LaVerne were singing, shimmying, and showing a little ankle out there, and Ethel was looking smug. The crowd warmed up. You could feel a crowd warming. It wasn't applause, it wasn't laughter, it was something else. Everyone in vaudeville knew what it was, but no one could put a word to it, or explain it to someone not in the trade.

Had Ethel reworked the act?

That proved to be a great opener, and the audience was ripe and warm.

He introduced the Marbury Minstrel Dancers next, and Delilah and her gents clattered out in blackface, their faces pitch black and shiny, the hands encased in white gloves, the men in tuxedos, Delilah in a loose glittery gown that bared some calf. That drew a ripple from the crowd as the trio clattered into the limelight. Minstrel was new to most of them. It had been a part of variety theater for many years, but this was frontier Montana. No one knew just where tap dancing came from. It seemed to combine English clog dancing with the movements and rhythms of southern blacks, and it had swiftly become a staple of vaudeville, with many blacks in blackface as well as whites.

The trio clattered and dodged and set the audience to swaying. They leapt and split and tiptoed and whirled.

This was a controlled dance, small gestures, intense and disciplined, and Delilah and her gents were masters of it. The clickety-clack, the explosions of Gatling-gun chatter, the slow and syncopated taps of six shoes with metal cleats toe and heel; it caught an audience that had barely experienced any of it. They used the limelight, working into it, retreating from it, and then, finally, rattling down to a finale, three statues, halting, finally, in the white light center stage, hiding the pumping of their lungs.

That won a surprised gasp, and applause.

They danced two more, the second loose and louche, the accompanist on the accordion discovering ways to coax New Orleans out of his squeezebox. The third round was quite the opposite, the dancers barely moving about the stage, but their legs and feet working in syncopation, bright and chattery.

That won a great and steady round of applause, as August finally strode out and introduced The Genius and Ethel. A quiet act following an expansive one.

The pair bowed.

"Well, Genius," said Ethel, "is it true that you're the brightest man in Montana?"

"I wouldn't want to exaggerate," he replied. "No doubt the brightest in North America."

"What makes you so bright, Genius?"

"I didn't buy a ticket to tonight's show," he said.

That got them laughing. It was a good act, getting better as the pair worked out their patter, August thought. The Genius would make outlandish claims, and Ethel would puncture them. And the fun was, the audience usually ended up on the side of The Genius. They didn't stay long in front of the olio. The joke wore out fast.

They got a cheerful round of applause, and August strode out once again.

"Ladies, and usually gents but not always, I'm pleased to introduce Harry the Juggler. He's got a last name, but

I can't pronounce it. He comes from one of those little nations near New Jersey. Here's the Juggler!"

Harry came out, followed by a stagehand pushing a cart loaded with stuff, and after some bowing and scraping, Harry pitched a couple of saucers up, and soon added enough tableware to seat four at dinner, and somehow managed not to break so much as a teacup. The crowd enjoyed that. He bowed long and low, and trotted off.

Then it was time for Ginger. He introduced her softly, conversationally. Some acts he introduced with fanfare, but not this young woman. She floated out on polite applause, wearing a borrowed dress this evening, with some of her golden shoulder and neck glowing in the light.

She seemed different somehow, though August could not say how. Only that she had never seemed more tender.

She sang alone, without accompaniment, her voice floating out upon a quiet crowd. She always chose familiar ballads at first, Stephen Foster or "Shenandoah," and let the familiar strains find their home in a hundred hearts. The crowd listened quietly, blotting her up. She was reaching them this evening. She seemed a little older, perhaps. August couldn't tell exactly, but he knew that she was connecting, and that she had the whole crowd in her grasp, and that it was a sweet and memorable moment. She finished her first one to polite applause, slipped solo into another, and finally a third, and after the last note died, she bowed.

Her auditors clapped politely, and kept on clapping, and she bowed again, and they clapped on and on, not letting her leave the stage. August finally rescued her, striding forth and lifting a hand.

"Miss Ginger, that was the most beautiful singing I've ever heard," he said.

The crowd enjoyed it, but finally let her go.

August caught her eye, and winked. She smiled and retreated, the respectful clapping still echoing in that house. It had never happened like that. August made note of it. That performance, Ginger had transformed herself into the biggest draw in the show. There would be some out there who would return for the next performance and the next, just to listen to her.

Wayne Windsor wound up the first half, turning right, turning left, treating the crowd to his profile. His monologues always had a good-humored edge to them, and August knew the crowd would enjoy some good times.

"I understand that Missoula captured the state college," he began, and paused a moment. "What a pity. You should have applied for the state prison."

They liked that. He managed to do ten or twelve minutes on the shortcomings of students and professors, with a few asides about how colleges subtracted more from the local economy than added to it, and then he was done, and the audience headed for a halftime break in a very good mood.

The second half went just as well, and the crowd seemed especially eager to hear Ginger sing. But the moment she was done, she vanished into the Green Room, and August knew that the booking at Pocatello was tormenting her. The small bare room was empty, save for her. The show wasn't over, and he had more introductions, but maybe he could listen and learn in one quick interlude.

"You were great this evening, Ginger. You'll have top billing."

She looked haunted, and stared away from him.

"We've had to make a few quick changes," he said. "But once we get to the coast, we have the best houses lined up. Big ones. I just want you to know that, and know how much Charles and I like your act."

She pushed her golden shoulders back and met his gaze. "Mr. Beausoleil, after Missoula, I'm leaving the show," she said.

THIRTY-THREE

The opener in Missoula was a success. A good box office. A dandy show. A profit. August could meet payroll.

He lingered in the opera house office long after the building had emptied, doing payroll under a naked bulb. He carried with him a stack of small brown envelopes, which he filled weekly with greenbacks and hand-delivered on Saturdays, the last day of the week, when pay was due. All his transactions were cash. His players didn't want checks they couldn't redeem. They wanted spending money, and that's what he gave them. Each show night brought in a load of small bills from ticket sales.

He kept his accounts in a small vest-pocket notebook, often using cryptic initials rather than writing entire entries. Now, in the creaking quiet of the Missoula house, he doled out bills and stuffed them into the envelopes. A hundred fifty for the Wildroot Sisters, who would pay their mother and manager. Eighty for LaVerne, who had a separate act, and would give thirty to her accordionist. A hundred for Wayne Windsor. Seventy for Harry the Juggler. Greenbacks, carefully counted out, stuffed in the envelopes, and an initial or name on each envelope. Fifty for Ginger. He hesitated a moment, and then pushed the folded fives into the envelope. She had earned it.

There were four musicians in the company, paid by the various acts. A guitarist, a banjo player, an accordionist, and an all-around percussion man. He did not pay them. He did pay his sole stagehand, Vince Leo, thirty a week.

He finished the payroll, stuffed everything into the opera house Mosler safe, and swung the door shut. Those safes, used by each company, were common accouterments in opera houses, and resolved a dilemma for touring companies: where to store their cash. The other options were the hotel safe, if one was available, or keeping the cash in his hotel room, under the mattress as a bonus for the chambermaids.

It added up. This payday would eat up the evening's take, and then some. The take of other matinees and evenings had to pay for train, hotel, theater rental, playbills, advertising, Charles' expenses, and sometimes payoffs for officials who threatened trouble of one sort or another. All cash. All grubby greenbacks, in heaps, collected at the box office or the drugstores that did advance sales. Arrangements varied from theater to theater. Some simply rented, but others wanted a percentage, and their owners usually hung around through the counting. Keeping it all straight was a headache.

On the road, with its ups and downs, he careened from confidence to panic. There was never enough cash. Sometimes he had to struggle to buy fuel for the lamps, where there was no electricity. Light your own spots, and buy the kerosene. Once in a while, at the end of a tour, there was actually some cash, and this he split with Pomerantz. It was the only salary they ever got.

He sometimes wondered why he did it. It wasn't because he loved show business or was infatuated with the players and the acts and the excitement. It was because this was the only thing he knew how to do. He had been a part of it, squeezing dimes out of it, since he was a boy, cadging tips and trying to fill the hole in his stomach and quell his loneliness, when he had no home to go to and spent a night in a trolley barn or railroad station. But it had taught him the business from the ground up.

He was slipping deep into the blues. He had lost Ginger. And much more, there were things that filled him with foreboding. The cancelation in Spokane heralded more cancelations. Someone on the West Coast was putting together a circuit. That was the new thing: own a string of houses, put acts out on the circuit in rotation, keep the lights lit with two shows a day. And drive out competition. In New York, that meant building a rival house across the street from whatever house was holding out. The whole vaudeville business was coalescing into a few owners and a few circuits. And the casualties were the touring companies like his own.

There wasn't much he could do about it unless he had an act so top-dog that he had some power to book his show wherever he wanted. But Ginger had folded her hand for some reason known best to a young woman barely out of school. Show business was a tough game and what she was doing would get her booted clear back to her hometown, but she was his partner's new wife, and in any case she was wrestling with something no one else could fathom. So he'd just let it go. And his show would be stuck with one less act.

He didn't feel like going to bed. The opera house was dark, hollow, and as bleak as his own feelings. He was lonely but didn't want company. He could never make sense of it. The very times when he starved for friends and lovers, that was when he turned solitary. Like now.

He wore a gray cape, a utilitarian garment that could double as a blanket on the road. And now he wrapped the cape about him, pushed his plug hat down low, and departed, switching off the light, locking the opera house doors. Any saloon would do, and he found one a few yards from the hotel. He smacked into a wall of heat, picked up the scent of hot wool and rank armpits, and settled in a dark booth.

"You serving food?" he asked the pimpled man who loomed over him.

"Chili, that's all."

"A bowl, and a glass of red wine."

"This is a timber town," the youth said, which translated to the absence of wine.

August would have liked a glass of Beaujolais, but settled for Old Orchard, one of Kentucky's more lethal products. He had inherited a French palate, and that didn't include whiskey of any sort.

Too late he spotted Wayne Windsor at the far end of the bar, entertaining some rummies there. Even as Windsor spotted him and waved slightly. The monologuist would stay on his stool, indulging himself with his favorite narcotic, conducting a discourse to an attentive crowd, winning their chuckles, their smiles, their nods. Windsor was doing exactly what he enjoyed most, both onstage or off. With some spirits in him, his monologues edged toward the bawdy, especially late in the evening.

August nodded, slipped chili into himself slowly, savoring the spice, washing it all with sips of bad bourbon.

But then Harry the Juggler materialized, looking as alone as usual. He was by far the most isolated and distant of his acts.

"Have a seat, Harry," August said.

The juggler did, at once, in a way that suggested that Harry had something in mind.

"I yam working on a new act," Harry said, his peculiar accent barely discernible. "Maybe not for this tour. The next."

August smiled. He welcomed new acts, especially by someone with the skills of Harry.

"There's an illusionist, magician, escape artist back east. Just a boy, not yet twenty, but already causing a lot of talk. His name is Weisz, but he's calling himself Harry Houdini, same first name, like me, and he's on the vaudeville circuits in the East."

"I've barely heard of him."

"His big act is to invite the local police in, tell them to cuff him, manacle him, put on leg irons, and give him a little time behind a curtain, and soon he's free and walks out. They can't lock him up."

"But the audience doesn't believe it, I hear."

"Now they do. He's thrown away the curtain, and they see him wrestling with it. He's strong. He's double-jointed. He can move his bones in and out of their sockets. He can somehow compress his muscles, shrink his wrists, like he was India rubber."

"That's a good act."

"Yes, and now he's adding to it. He's putting himself in jeopardy. They're putting him manacled in a tank of water, and he's got to get free before he dies."

August pondered that. "Not sure I'd like that on my stage."

"Houdini never fails," Harry said.

"Well, that's the sort of big-time act I can't afford, Harry."

Harry stared, checkmated by August's dismissal. "I am working on such an act," he said. "I will keep the audience transfixed."

"You already have one. The scimitars. Drop one, catch one wrong, and you're likely to lose a finger. And they know it. You can tell. There's not even a sneeze. It's so quiet out there, you know they're waiting, waiting, waiting for blood."

"Yah, it is good. They're waiting for me to behead myself. That's going to be the new act. You think this one is waiting for mistake, wait until you see my guillotine act."

"Your what?"

"I will juggle lying in a guillotine, my head on the block, facing upward. The blade above, held in place by a small cord. If a scimitar drops and cuts the cord, the guillotine falls and my head rolls. That will keep the audience on the edge of their seats, eh?"

August stared at Harry, stared at the soaks along the bar, stared at Wayne Windsor, whose jaw was rising and falling, and stared at his empty chili bowl.

"Harry," he began delicately, "this is a road show. We

can't be hauling a guillotine around from house to house. Not even if you pay the freight."

"Houdini has big tanks of water, and derricks, and hoists to lower him in."

"Yeah, and a thousand-seat house in New York."

"I will perfect the act. And join you on the next tour. I could do something like it even now. A small guillotine and a rabbit in it. I make a mistake, and it's rabbit for dinner."

"Ah, Harry . . ."

"That's the trouble with acrobat acts. Sing and they love you. Talk and they laugh. But acrobats, jugglers, the silent acts, all we can do is worry them. Scare them. And when the bad doesn't happen, everyone applauds. It's a small pleasure. That boy, Houdini, he doesn't talk. It's all silent. But he does great things. I hear even coppers are amazed. They think they've got him locked up solid, but they don't. Audience likes that. Nothing like a red-faced copper."

Harry smiled. A rare moment.

August didn't want blood on his stage. Drama, fine. Getting out of manacles, that was Houdini's game. But no guillotines. "Harry, there's something you might do. Magic. Combine juggling with some magic. I've always wanted a magician, but they're hard to find, and don't like road shows so much. But if you can do some magic, pull rabbits out of an empty top hat, put your assistant in a long box on sawhorses and saw her in two, until she steps out of the box, that stuff would work fine, and I'd put you on."

"So it is fine for me to saw a woman in two, in a box, but not to put myself under a guillotine blade, eh?"

"The one's an illusion, Harry. Every person watching the magic act knows the young lady will be just fine, and what interests them is how it's done, the illusion. But you're talking about something else, the possible horror if something happens."

"So? What does Houdini do, eh?"

Harry won that one. But August was damned if he'd put a potential bloodbath before people, and ruin his company and maybe vaudeville in the process.

"That's my decision, Harry."

"Magic, that's not the real thing, eh? I do the real thing."

"I'm in the entertainment business, Harry. I want people to go home happy and come again the next night."

"Well, I'm thinking about another act. The Firing Squad. Latin America, sombreros, bandannas. The soldiers drag a prisoner in, white shirt, tie him to a post, lift their rifles, all aimed at his heart. The *capitán*, he lifts his hand holding his sword . . ."

"Then what?"

"A beautiful girl rushes in, waving paper, a pardon."

"Then what?"

"*El capitán,* he lowers his hand, the sword drops, the line of soldiers fires."

"And?"

"The victim, he smiles, takes the big sheet from the girl and holds it up. It says, *Intermission,* and he kisses the girl."

August laughed. And in the wash, his melancholia vanished. He loved the business. It owned him.

THIRTY-FOUR

J. J. Sharpey, manager of the Pocatello Grand Opera House, proved to be a fountain of useful information. Charles Pomerantz had contacted him immediately upon arriving in the southern Idaho town, and was welcomed at once.

It had been an exhausting trip, clear back to Butte, and

then down to Pocatello on the Utah and Northern, and he was ready to call it a day. But on the road, anything can be urgent. He needed to know whether the bill-poster, J. W. Kelly, was putting up the posters, and pasting the new billing in. With his wife, Ginger, getting top billing.

"You have a concert grand piano here. Is it available?" Charles asked.

"Unusual, right? A gift, sir, of the Joneses. He's the superintendent of the Idaho division of the Union Pacific, and a prominent man here. They have a daughter, Penelope, you see, and employ the house for regular recitals. But of course they had to give that up. She was a prodigy, you know, trained by masters, but no master can make a hand grow large enough. Hers didn't span an octave, the minimum for concert pianists, which disappointed the family. I once heard the mother, Mazeppa, inform the young lady that she had to grow her hands, fingers half an inch longer, an inch for the thumb, and no ifs, ands, or buts. But the dear young lady, Penelope, wasn't able to accommodate her mother, though no doubt she tried. Growing one's hands is a tricky business. So the piano goes unused. A Steinway, too. We charge two dollars a night, simply to pay for the piano tuner. He comes clear from Salt Lake to keep it right. We can also put on an orchestra if you need one. Six people."

"So the young lady gave up her career?"

"Oh, no, not at all. Thwarted by small hands, the mother, lovely but firm lady named Mazeppa, put the girl into voice. A sweet voice, that girl. A parade of voice teachers reached town, one after another, and before long the young lady could not only play the piano, but could sing. A nightingale, they call her. Two great skills in a girl not yet an adult. Oh, she slaved, she sang, she comes here for recitals, with her proud parents front center, sir, front center, best seats in the house for the man who more or less runs Pocatello. Front center, to see their precocious daughter sing."

"Her parents sound a bit ambitious for her, sir."

"Oh, they are capital people. I would never say a word otherwise. But they do have a program for that girl, an only child, the vessel of their dreams, it seems."

"What does she think of it, Mr. Sharpey?"

The manager sighed. "She is a dutiful girl, but sometimes I see something, almost haunted, yes, haunted. That's the mark of genius, you know."

"How old, sir?"

"Late teens, out of school now. A whole life on the concert stage ahead. I'm sure the parents are arranging it, but I haven't heard recently."

"I've met a few stage mothers in my day," Charles said. "We even have one in our show, managing her daughters. They are, well, impressive, most of them. But sometimes I feel sorry for the child, the one who's a vessel of someone else's dreams."

"Actually, that girl, she's fortunate. Her folks laid out a fortune, brought in the best teachers. Did it all here in a growing town, too. I've heard tell they've spent seven thousand on her. They could have sent her off to New York, some academy, but now Pocatello, Idaho, has a top-notch talent to boast about."

"And it is all fine with this girl, Penelope?"

"She puts her heart into every performance."

"Does she have any other life? A young gentleman?"

"Nope. None that I ever heard about. I think her parents discourage it. The music is the beginning and end of everything, that's how I figure it. Must be a quiet life, everything depending on a B minor or a C flat."

"Why here in an opera house? Why not a small hall, or someone's parlor?"

"Fame. We seat six hundred. That's a corker of a number for a town this size. Penelope's fame. It rubs off on the parents, I think. And this is the best place in town for all that. She sings and it rubs off. You should see her mother, just waiting for the compliments. Like the compliments were meant for her, and not the daughter. They always have a reception afterwards. Poor girl has to shake a thousand hands."

"These people, they seem to own the town."

"Well, sir, let me put it this way. He runs the railroad. He can hire or fire most of the people here. And a suggestion to the city fathers, well, you get the idea. Their house is on a little rise, and it gives them a view of Pocatello. You'll see it when you step out."

The manager suddenly reined in his comments, caution restoring his decorum. "You saw the playbill coming in?"

"I did. It's just what we want."

The playbill filled a varnished frame at the front of the opera house. The Beausoleil Brothers show was well displayed. Not like a big-city marquee, but that playbill would be noticed by anyone passing by.

"You going to Boise after us? And what's after that?"

"Reconnect with our West Coast bookings. Three around Seattle, then Portland, Eugene, Corvallis, Klamath Falls, on down, Sacramento, Stockton, Oakland, Berkeley, finish this tour in San Francisco."

"Yeah, if it happens, sir."

"You know something I don't?"

"The new circuit. Everything's changing. The Orpheum man out there, Leavitt's buying every West Coast theater he can put his hands on."

"With what?"

"He's not asked me so I don't know. But he's offering stock in his company, all of that. He's got a couple dozen, and he's locking up the talent now. He'll move the talent city to city, once a week, or hold it over, it doesn't matter. The talent's mostly back east, so Leavitt's got a hold on what's here. He can give an act a forty-two-week contract, good billing, and good pay, and mostly playing big towns. Most show people would snap that up."

"Is that what happened in Spokane?"

"I heard so. And every day now, I hear something new. It's like falling dominoes. Get a few and the rest fall. They threaten, you know. If you don't sell out to them, they'll build a house across the street and steal your patrons. It's not what you'd call a genteel game."

"We're booked solid," Pomerantz said, suddenly wondering whether that was still true.

Sharpey just grunted.

"And there's a hundred smaller houses. And we're a name show."

"The new vaudeville, there's no show at all, just acts, catching trains from town to town, connected by telegraph. Even phone sometimes. Lots of trains, take you anywhere, fast service, some with sleepers."

Pomerantz had a bad moment, and pushed it aside. "We're booked. We've got good acts. We're paying our freight."

Sharpey didn't argue. Instead, he went upbeat. "Lots of smaller towns, like this one, each with a house that's dark too much, and the ones putting the circuits together, they don't pay attention to us. What do they care about Pocatello or Boise, when they can have Portland?"

"It doesn't make sense to run circuits in places where they can fill a house just once a day," Charles said. "That's for us. A few matinees, but the cash comes in after dark."

"If you can get talent," Sharpey said. "They're locking that up, too."

"We've got a young sweetheart, Ginger, she's going to the top," Charles said. "And she's not going to jump ship." He smiled. "She's my wife."

"Ah, a syndicate," Sharpey said.

Charles smiled. He wondered what Sharpey would be saying in a few days.

There was business to be done. Sharpey had ordered the tickets, a set for each night, with the bulk of them on sale at Ransome's Drugstore. The store got a nickel an orchestra ticket, two and a half cents for a gallery seat. The newspapers had been contacted. Ads purchased. Tickets sent to the reviewers. Some handout releases had been given to the papers. Sharpey was as good as his name. There was a good handout of Wayne Windsor, and a fine one on Harry the Juggler. The stuff that Ethel had printed up about LaVerne Wildroot was embarrassing, but it didn't matter.

Pomerantz yawned. "What hotel?"

"Pacific Hotel. Just a hop away. Dollar seventy-five single, two dollars double."

"I'd better book us in," Pomernantz said.

He stepped into a velvet evening. The town's commercial district was solid, permanent, and bustling. He could begin to like a place like this, if it weren't so far from everything. Sure enough, on a rise to the north was a house that lorded over the town, a light shining from most of the mullioned windows. It was not a mansion, just a spacious house with a regal view over the town and the valley.

His parents-in-law. He wasn't sure he wanted to meet them. But then he decided they would soon relax, maybe take some pride in their daughter's new career. Maybe welcome him. He could hope for the best. Ginger was a miracle he couldn't explain. She had slipped into his every thought, and the sheer joy of her colored his days.

He got a room, payable in advance, and then sought to book the company into twelve rooms, doubles, four nights.

"This a theater outfit?" the clerk asked.

"Yes, the Beausoleil Brothers Follies. We'll be playing at the opera house, then off to Boise."

"Theater company, is it? That'll be in advance, of course. Twenty-four times four, that's ninety-six."

"I don't have that much. But the company will, when it arrives, sir. How about a deposit, to be applied to the tariff?"

The clerk, a thin fellow in wire spectacles, slowly shook his head. "My instructions are, sir, enterprises of your sort, they all pay cash on the barrelhead."

"Is there a reason?"

"Certainly. Skipping town with bills unpaid. That's one. But this town, we have certain standards. I'm sure you'll understand."

"No, I don't. Tell me."

"I will leave it to your imagination, sir." He pushed his spectacles upward. "Cash up front, that's it."

"Is there another hotel?"

"I'm sure you'll find that out."

He kept his room for the night, but bowed out. The European was down the street, and he soon had rooms for his company, four nights, doubles at one-fifty, five percent discount. Payable on arrival. But the place smelled odd. And it had no plumbing in any room. That was all down the hall.

The clerk there was just the opposite of the one at the Pacific: short, garrulous, and bursting with cheer. For some reason, he wore a battered bowler, even behind the check-in counter.

"People go to the opera house much?" Pomerantz asked.

"Depends on whether you empty a pay envelope or fill one," the clerk said. "Them that fill the envelopes, the proper ones, they don't much care for entertainments."

"Is there a reason?"

The clerk eyed Pomerantz. "There's an idea around here that this nice place, it should keep out a lot of people and just welcome some. And the easiest way to do that is to run a watch and ward, looking after morals and such. There's some, want to take the town dry. There's others, want to make tobacco costly, put a big tax on. There's others, they want some people to live in certain wards, and other people to live in other wards, all sorted out.

There's some, they want to have the public schools, they won't take anyone that don't speak English. We got some railroad workers around here, they're from all over everywhere."

Pomerantz was filling in the blanks fast. "Suppose we do a minstrel act. How'll that go?"

"Blackface?" The clerk grinned, baring a snaggle tooth. "You sure don't know Pocatello."

"We've got some gals singing. They show a little ankle."

"Yeah? They'll get hauled away, likely. Two-dollar fines."

"We've got a monologuist. You know, like Mark Twain. He pokes a little fun."

"Who's this Twain?"

"Man with a sharp tongue, wrote some stories."

"He'd best keep his trap shut," the clerk said. "Take my advice."

That was good to know. That's what advance men did, and why advance men worked ahead of a show. Pomerantz felt the burden. It was his task to keep the show out of trouble, and trouble often came from the least-expected corner. But this time, he thought, Pocatello would run him through the wringer.

THIRTY-FIVE

Ginger read the telegram she had just received. It was printed in capital letters on porous yellow paper, the blue ink blurred.

SING AND THE WORLD SINGS WITH YOU STOP MISS AND LOVE YOU CHARLES

She clutched it. A boy had knocked at her door and handed it to her. It seemed a marvel, something bright and new in her life. Charles was such a worldly man, and each hour with him had brought riches to her.

A wire, just for her! The yellow sheet diverted her, if only for the moment, from the looming menace that was threatening her life. Pocatello. Her parents. Or rather, her mother, ready to impose her will at whatever cost. She hoped that she could simply hide in her hotel room there, not appear, not let anyone in her town see her or know she was there.

She hoped she might return to the stage in Boise, having escaped the confrontation she dreaded. She hoped she might just continue, Charles' wife, then the cities around Seattle, then Oregon, each show, each day one step farther away from Pocatello. She had told August she would leave the show, but she hoped she wouldn't. She hoped she could just slide through. Or maybe go with Charles on his advance tours, putting things together in Boise, far, far from her home.

That afternoon she had ventured into the bright November sun, strolling Higgins, looking for some small token to give to Charles. And in front of a chocolate shop a well-dressed couple had waylaid her.

"Miss Ginger, is it?" the gentleman said. "Ah, we saw you, and simply want you to know what a delight. A treat. I wish we could see more beautiful girls singing."

"Me?" she asked.

"Yes, young lady. You are the beau ideal."

She wasn't sure about that beau ideal business, but she nodded.

"I teach rhetoric at the college, and if you should ever like to address my class, I'd be pleased to have you. Just six students, just getting the college under way, of course. Beaumont, my name. Sterling Beaumont, and my wife, Clarice."

"A lovely performance, Miss Ginger," the lady said.

"Our students will be so pleased to learn we encountered you."

Ginger nodded. Her first admirers! So many people had come to her recitals, and they were quick to say how well she had mastered Chopin or whatever. But she had never considered them admirers, as this couple were.

"Well, goodness, thank you," she said.

Beaumont tipped his felt hat, and the couple proceeded on its way.

She bought a small paper bag of chocolates laced with almonds for Charles, and retreated buoyantly to the hotel.

If this was show business, she was all for it.

She was noticed. They liked her singing. The whole world lay just ahead. All she had to do was sing, sing, sing, and everything life had to offer would be hers. She hastened back to the hotel, looking for August Beausoleil. She needed to talk. He was not about. She hastened to his room, knocked boldly, and after a moment the door swung open. He was half-dressed. He stared, no warmth at all in his face.

"I want to talk to you, sir."

"I will not have my partner's wife seen entering or leaving my room. I will be in the lobby in five minutes."

With that, he pressed the door shut. She found herself staring at the blank door instead of his flinty face. Well, then, the lobby.

It wasn't much of a lobby, and this wasn't much of a hotel. It was an enlarged corridor, the registration desk on one side, and a bench on the other. It seemed all too public, with all the hotel's traffic walking straight past her. But she had to explain. She had to try it again.

He appeared in less than five minutes, nodded to her to step outside, and she followed, having to exert herself to keep up with him.

"What is it?" he asked.

"I was hasty," she said. "I want to sing. Just not in Pocatello, that's all. I'm sorry I was hasty."

"No," he said.

"No what, sir?"

"You're done. You'll not come to me one day, wanting out, and another day, wanting in. Every such choice turns my show upside down. I don't care who you are, or how you're married, you're through."

There was wrath in him. She'd never seen it, never imagined it, because Beausoleil was a man firmly in command of himself.

"Go to Pocatello or not, but not on my stage," he added. "Travel with Charles if you want, but not in my show. Sing on the streets if you want, but not in my show."

"Could I rejoin in Boise?"

"Never. The best thing for Charles to do is ship you back east. Are we done?"

She felt a wave of sorrow steal through her. Everything had gone wrong. She had fled her parents to find a new life, and now she had thrown away that new life, and there was nothing ahead. Not even if Charles loved her, not even if her sudden marriage bloomed, would it make up for what she had just done.

"I deserve it," she said. "But you deserve something, too. A warning. My father is a powerful man, and he and my mother can make trouble for you, and will. I was seen by a friend of theirs. They may know I'm in the company."

"I'll deal with whatever comes."

But then he relented a little. "What should I expect?"

"I don't know. But it could be courts and lawyers."

"They're like that?"

"My mother . . . she's poured all her ambitions into me, and the least of her ambitions is to join a vaudeville company. For her, that would be like—getting a bad reputation."

"I'll deal with it. I've dealt with worse. I've opened in towns with officials who wanted to bust the company."

"What for?"

"They see a company come in, make some good money, and leave town with a bag full of greenbacks. To them, it's almost like we stole it. So they think of ways to break the company. Get the money before it skips town. Fines, jail, lawsuits. I've dealt with them all. And I'll deal with your family, if it comes to that. Are we done?"

This was a different man than the quiet one she had met only a few weeks ago.

"I will sing tonight and each show in Missoula."

"I will expect no less of you."

"I will sing better than I ever have."

"I expect that from every person in the company. Those who don't, they don't last. I've hardly ever ended a tour with the same company I started with. And this is no exception."

He was softening a bit. But she knew better than to think that would affect her fate.

"I've said what I wanted. Now I'll go warm up," she said.

He grunted and left her there, and she made her way into the darkened theater. Not even a bare bulb lit the stage, but there were two small windows on the left-side corridor casting gray light into gloom. The place echoed and its hollowness caught her. Why were theaters so sad, so much of their lives?

Backstage she found a simple light switch on the wall, and pressed the button. A lamp glowed up at the top of the flies. A deep chill weighed upon the dark interior.

What would this be, a recital or a vaudeville act? Recitals barely needed an audience. The performer was looking for perfection, and if the audience assented or approved, that all was fine but not critical. There wasn't a soul in the cold theater. She peered into the gloom, somehow comforted that no one was sitting there, not a single soul. That gave her liberty. She could experiment. She could perfect a note, a breath. Until recently, she had begun recitals with barely a nod to the auditors before her. Her task, her mother's wish, was to prove to the world that her daughter was a prodigy.

She would sing to the audience that wasn't there. Not long. Even at her tender age, she could wear out her voice. She would have to pretend. She imagined that the opera house brimmed with gentlemen in tuxedos with slicked-back hair, the women in gowns and tiaras, all aglitter. She imagined that these people out there were urbane; they had seen a thousand performances and were hard to please. And her task would be to pleasure them, an eighteen-year-old girl wishing to triumph over all the jaded minds waiting for something to happen worth applauding.

She pulled off her coat, letting the chill reach her. In a moment it wouldn't matter. She ran a few scales, knowing that her vocal cords were muscles that needed warming, just as an athlete's body needed warming.

Then she sang this or that; pieces of song. She would try one, try another, discovering only the emptiness of the cavern that swallowed her voice. She sang her folk songs, not forgetting Stephen Foster. She was in good voice, the notes liquid and sweet, but they sailed into a great hollow, where each word was instantly doomed. It would live in no one's memory. She sang an aria. It didn't matter. The place was empty. She felt dissatisfied, and knew at once that she needed the audience. She could never return to recitals. Not until this quiet, hollow place was filled would she find what she was looking for.

She left the building, having gotten more from her singing than the exercise. She had gotten a need and vocation. She had walked into the cold edifice a girl still fleeing her family; she had walked out changed. She was a vaudeville trouper. Nay, a vaudeville star. She might be married to Charles, but in fact her spouse was her audience.

She didn't know how it would work out, but she knew she had a destiny. And she was no longer afraid of going to Pocatello. Or having it out with her mother. If trouble came in Pocatello, her mother would find not a servile daughter, but a firebrand.

That evening in Missoula, once the opera house had warmed, and the crowd had packed in, and the bright lights of the show were burning, she rocked the house. Whatever it was—and who could say?—she owned the stage from the moment she set foot before that crowd. She walked straight to the light, an arc light serving as the limelight, and there she poured out her ballads, some old and familiar to the heart, and then a little of *Carmen,* and finally a couple of love songs, the verses settling like velvet upon all those good people there.

It was a dandy show. Ethel and The Genius finally found their stride, with The Genius insulting everyone in Missoula, and Ethel deflating The Genius at every opportunity. Just as surprising, LaVerne Wildroot was working a new repertoire, a little swing to it, and she was sporting a new smile, too. She was so good that Ginger felt a moment of envy—and fear.

Wayne Windsor went hunting for robber barons in Missoula, and when he couldn't unearth any in the audience, he settled for city council members who were saying smoke was good for the city, proof of its vitality, so what did it matter if it irritated the lungs? He punctuated all that with lingering left and right profiles. And the Marbury Trio, in blackface, tapped minstrel music into the receptive ears of an eager audience that eve.

When Ginger had completed her second-half gig, to rolling applause and an encore, she discovered August Beausoleil staring from the wing, his gaze dark and maybe even bitter.

She smiled but he stood rigid, in his master of ceremonies rig, scowling.

"Well, August," she said, "if you'll let me sing in Pocatello, I'll knock 'em flat."

He glared angrily, and walked away.

THIRTY-SIX

Cromwell Perkins waylaid August Beausoleil after the curtain call.

"Want to talk to you, old sport. Did you notice? The wind has shifted. Ethel and I got thirty-seven good laughs. Thirty-seven belly-whoppers, in a few minutes. Quite a bit better than Wayne Windsor, I'd say. He got twenty-something."

"Yes, you're coming along. I like it."

"I'm the top dog now, better than Windsor, but it's not reflected in my pay."

Beausoleil caught the drift of this, and said nothing. Around him, people were packing up, heading into the night.

"The Genius is your top draw now," Perkins said louder, as if August were deaf. "And I'm not getting top pay. Windsor gets his hundred, plus top billing. The Genius gets fifty, split with Ethel, and fifth billing." The last was almost a shout.

Beausoleil chose his words carefully. "You're coming along well. But Windsor is known, and draws crowds, and a veteran, able to change his act for any audience. That comes only from experience. This is your first tour. We're proud to have you, and it's my good fortune to feature you and Ethel."

"I'm requiring a pay of a hundred a week henceforth, sir. Ethel will get twenty-five."

He had used that unusual word, *requiring,* deliberately. It was a demand.

"I see," said the manager. "I'm afraid I can't afford that even if there's merit."

"Then you can't afford the best talk act in the business. You can lock me in for the tour, or not. There's never been a contract. You're so short of acts that I'd think you would go out of your way to keep each act satisfied."

"Then the answer's no."

Beausoleil was being a lot tougher than Perkins had expected. It obviously galled him. For weeks, he and Ethel had worked on their drill, spiffing it up, jumping on each other's lines. It was not only rich comedy, it was also becoming a hit. Actually, Beausoleil had been delighted with the improvement.

"You would also need to give me top billing, starting right now, sir."

"Then we are at a parting of the ways. I trust you will finish our Missoula appearance?"

"I shouldn't. I'm just giving away talent. The Genius part of it is real. Can you name any other act that comes close? Of course not. We can pick up any theatrical agent and soon have work at four or five times what you're paying. Fifty dollars in a brown envelope for two. That's called cheap."

"And Ethel would go with you?"

"Ask her. She's tired of her daughters. And LaVerne doesn't need her. And she likes my, shall we say, bed and board. I'd rather be a barstool entertainer again than earn ten percent of what I'm worth."

"I can add ten dollars, make it sixty, and move you up to third billing, but only if you and Ethel commit to the entire tour, ending in Frisco in March."

"Not nearly enough. We'll pull out when we close here."

Beausoleil smiled. "Your choice," he said. "Your act means a lot to me, and I'm hoping you'll stay."

"Your loss," said The Genius.

August thought that Perkins' head had expanded several hat sizes.

"I'll wire New York for an act starting Pocatello," Beausoleil said.

If The Genius was disappointed, he hid it well. "And we'll wire an agent ourselves," he said.

"You're done with me? Definitely?"

The Genius hesitated. "I have to talk it over with Ethel. She doesn't always appreciate my contributions. Let you know."

"I'll bring in an act," Beausoleil said. He needed one in any case, with Ginger out. He was stretched way too thin.

It was a costly option; he'd have to pay the freight. But when the opera house had emptied, he braved a cold night, hiked straight north to the rail station, found a sleepy telegrapher with muttonchops, composed his message to theatrical agents in Chicago, Weill and Branch, who used the wire address BWELL: NEED COMEDY OR ANIMAL ACT OPEN POCATELLO DEC 4 TOP SIXTY BEAUSOLEIL.

"Thirteen words, twenty a word," said the agent. "Two dollars and sixty cents, please."

"I should buy some Western Union stock," Beausoleil said. And coughed up.

He probably would be covered. Train to Pocatello took three days. He'd probably greet some eccentric with two talking dogs. Or a raucous parrot. Or a cat with two heads. Or two midgets with top hats taller than themselves. Who could say?

He stepped into a harsh night, feeling the old melancholia again. He was alone; he had been on his own for as long as he could remember. Sometimes he caught

glimpses of families, children at the table, the girls in pigtails, the boys happy and well fed. He had no family at
all, but he had a good substitute for one, the talents who
came and went. Just like The Genius and Ethel, and just
like Ginger. All of them quitting at the end of the booking. Well, Ginger was a puzzle. Now she was saying she'd
play Pocatello. Suddenly she was ready to take on her
family and quit running. He'd think about it. He disliked
talent that signed on, signed off, couldn't be steady and
reliable. But in spite of himself, Ginger's new feistiness
brought a little cheer to him.

He headed back to the dark opera house, let himself
in, headed for the safe with the evening's take in the cashbox, lit the overhead bulb, and did his usual count, sorting
the grimy bills and adding them. Five hundred and forty-
seven this evening, very good. He made a small notation
in his vest-pocket ledger, slipped the cashbox back in the
Mosler safe, and locked it tight, giving the dial an extra
spin. Hartley, the manager, would change the combina-
tion after Beausoleil Brothers pulled out. Each visiting
troupe got its own strongbox.

Payday was coming, and August would spend the next
eve filling brown envelopes. One with fifty for The Genius. Same pay as most of the acts. The Genius was
unique. There wasn't another act like it in the business,
some knucklehead turning himself into a genius, scorning everything, everyone, every hero or saint in history,
all for a surprise and chuckle out there among those folks
who often sat on their hands. August was tempted to add
ten more to his offer, seventy, try to keep the act around,
but he knew what the result would be . . . unless Ethel laid
down the law. It really was Ethel who turned Perkins into
an act. She figured it out, became his foil, sometimes
puncturing him with a wild riposte. And that inspired an
interesting idea. He would offer Ethel a fifteen-dollar
raise, but nothing for The Genius. She might take it. And

then The Genius would discover whose act it really was. The Genius was her prisoner, a thought that entertained August.

It was late. Gust's Saloon stood kitty-corner across from the opera house, and August headed in that direction. After each show, the place was packed. And before the show, too. It was a long, narrow place with a few tables and a dartboard at the rear, and a homespun bar and back bar forward. All pine cabinetry, made from local wood. No Brunswick mahogany bar furnishings here. The rear overhead light had been turned off.

Almost empty. One old soak in a white shirt and corduroy coat occupied a seat. The saloon man was polishing glasses. He looked annoyed, probably because he wanted to close.

"Make it fast," the barkeep said.

Moments later August was nursing a bourbon several stools away from the old soak.

"You're with the show," the soak said. "I can tell."

"Manage it."

"We're in the same business," the soak said.

"You? Variety shows?"

"No, I teach rhetoric at the college. My task is to entertain about twenty bored students and stuff them with what they don't want to know."

"How does that make us alike?"

"I am a showman." The soak sipped amber juice from his glass. "The enemy is boredom. They are eager to be entertained, but not educated. But if I fail to educate them, then it reflects on me just as bad box office reflects on you. No paying customers, and you're done for."

"I can fire an act," August said. "But you're stuck. At least until grading time."

"No, no, I'm talking about my failings, sir. Some academics inspire students, draw them to their courses, turn them into good scholars who get good grades. But, sir, you are not talking to one of those. I'm the sort who drones through the hour, and the students avoid rhetoric the rest of their unnatural lives. I envy you. Entertaining well is a rare gift. Not one person in a thousand can entertain others."

He downed a mighty slug of amber.

August scarcely knew what to say.

"This is our fourth academic year, sir. A new college in the sticks. We're missing an ear, have six fingers on one hand, and webbed toes. But we're open. No scholar in his right mind would voluntarily come to Missoula. That says something about me, correct?"

"Yes. It says you had the courage to come and build a university, sir."

The old soak laughed. "And everyone has a fairy godmother."

The barkeep set down his towel. "Drink up, gents; I'm closing in five."

"Professor, I'd like to give you two tickets to our show," August said, digging into his vest pocket for the front-center seats he always carried.

"Have I earned them?" the man asked.

"Anyone who survives classes of daydreaming students year after year has earned them."

The old gent stared, plucked them up, and smiled. "This is the best thing that's happened to me in Montana," he said.

The professor tucked the tickets away, swallowed the dregs, nodded, and left.

August was about to follow, but the keep suddenly poured another shot into his glass.

"That's for making the old sob-sister happy," he said. "He's got a cloud over him and leaks rain every time he comes in."

"We've all got troubles."

"Sure we do. And professors got more troubles than

anyone else. If I had to deal with a lot of wet-behind-the-ear squirts I'd be a souse. You know what? You've got the best business on the planet. You open the curtains, and you make people happy. They forget their cares for a bit; you run your acts out, and they take us away from ourselves, and for just a little bit, the world is good."

"Well, you do that here, just listening to your customers."

"Nah, I just get them soaked enough so they quit complaining. No big deal."

"Life's mostly drudgery. You open up your pub, and they come in and tell stories or make friends, and they go away content."

The keep didn't argue. "That's what pubs are for. And you're what opera houses are for. I keep an ear out, you know. My regulars, they see whatever comes into town, and they're talking about just one thing. The girl. The one in white. She comes out, into the limelight, and she's just right. I mean, not brassy, not glittery, but like the girl most lads dream of, and she starts to sing, and she's smiling at them, and she sees them, and she sings to them, and that's how she's got about half the men in Missoula in love with her."

"Ginger."

"That's the one. She's giving every lad in town a dream, including the married ones. You know what? They talk about her. They say they'd trade any two women for one Ginger. They say they'd never have a chance with her, because some millionaire's gonna snap her up."

"Yes, she's a great one. And she came to us just a few weeks ago. Out of the blue. Wanted to audition. I wasn't even going to do that. She sang at a funeral; we lost one of our acts, and this girl sang. And my partner got interested in her, and here's the thing. They got married. I thought it was just because she wanted a ticket into the business, but the thing is, she loves him. She's got that, you see. That innocent beauty."

"And now she's your draw."

"For the moment," August said.

He found two more tickets and proffered them, but the bar-keep shook his head.

"Gotta work," he said. "We all gotta work."

THIRTY-SEVEN

August read the terse wire from Weill and Branch, theatrical agents. An act, The Grab Bag, would be in Pocatello December third. Good. August had not seen it but knew about it. The act was the work of Harry and Art Grabowski, acrobats, and it featured a stooge. Art would sit in the audience and insult Harry, who would begin with some indifferent acrobatic stunts, and sometimes fail to execute them properly, landing in a heap.

That's when Art would start yelling insults, and Harry would take offense, and Art would boil up to the stage and there would be a comic brawl. Harry would throw a haymaker, and Art would do a cartwheel or a flip-flop. The mock fight was a work of acrobatic genius, each blow resulting in a comic response. That was all good. Sixty a week, two hundred twelve to get them to Pocatello. That was painful. He was lucky to collect six hundred a night to support his entire company.

But it was necessary to put them in the lineup. Who knew what The Genius and Ethel would do next, or whether the girl would sing, or who'd get sick. The whole tour had been like that. The Grabowskis were insurance, and could vary their routine. They could do a variety of straight acrobatic acts, some combined with music.

This was closing night in Missoula and he was eager to put the show on the road. They'd had enough of smoky air, and were hoarse. The night was going to be hell. An eastbound express rolled through at ten thirty, and he was tempted to cut the show short and board it; but he refused. It had been his cardinal rule to give every audience its money's worth. The next train was a milk run, stopping at every crossroads, and leaving Missoula at two in the morning. And when it got to Butte there would be another wait for a southbound Utah and Northern local to Pocatello, and the company would not get a wink of sleep.

They would spend night hours in the Missoula station, sitting on its varnished pews, waiting. They would spend hours more in Butte, waiting in the dimly lit waiting room, waiting, waiting, wanting only the comfort of a warm bed.

It was all because of an improvised schedule through Idaho, upsetting the careful planning that smoothed a tour. Still, these were troupers, used to it, and he was satisfied that the company would hold together and that they'd soon be in the footlights.

But it was an oddly listless show that eve, before a house only two-thirds filled. There were two bright spots. Ginger sang eloquently, and caught the crowd once again, and The Genius and Ethel topped everything else. His two departing acts had saved the night. Then it was over. The troupers climbed into winter coats and left the darkened theater. Their bags had already been carted to the station; they had only to walk the seven blocks through the gloomy city and begin the long wait.

By eleven they had all settled on the hard pews in a semiheated building, and began a three-hour wait, always assuming the local was on time. Wayne Windsor seemed resigned; he had done this a hundred times on the road. The Marbury Trio were restless, pacing the room, sliding outside, letting in gales of cold air, wishing the train along, peering down the empty rails, and seeing nothing. A freight at midnight stirred them all. No one was saying

much. No one was reading. They had all sunk into their
private worlds. Or wishing hellfire upon the new operators of the Spokane opera house. Or trying to sleep sitting up. Or wishing for a stiff drink.

Why were they there? What bleak turn of life had
brought them to this stern waiting room on a wintry night?
Why were they patient? He stared about, seeing not performers but wounded people driven to the performer's
life, just as he had been from childhood onward. Most
were first or second generation. Harry the Juggler was a
new arrival, and wrestled with English; what had driven
him to abandon a quiet life in Europe, cross the sea, and
find a living in vaudeville?

Most had arrived in the business because it was the
only door open to them. They certainly hadn't come from
bourgeois families; they were outcasts, prevented from
walking through polished doors that might lead to law or
medicine or political office or academic life. Some had
changed their names, shedding the one that imprisoned
them in favor of something bland and English. August
could guess the origins of most of his troupe. He knew of
only one who had arrived in his company from the upper
crust, and that was Ginger.

She sat alone, encased in a shroud that seemed to iso-
late her. He watched her, knowing that the trip back to
Pocatello would be a trial, but also her passage to independence. He didn't know just what awaited her there, but she
had chosen to confront it, and if she won the forthcoming
battle with her family, she would bloom.

She was not inviting company, and there was something in her face that suggested a private ordeal. The rest
of the troupe, sensing something, had left her to her imag-
inings.

August approached gently. "Want to walk?"

She nodded. He led her into the quiet dark. The air was
harsh but not moving, and they could ease their way along

the streets, which were largely devoid of paved sidewalks in the area.

She seemed almost companionable, though she was utterly silent.

"Going home's going to be hard, I imagine," he said.

"I knew you wanted to talk about that. If I don't find the courage, then I'll be afraid the rest of my life."

"You left your family?"

"My jailers."

"I have good friends in the business who escaped, like that."

"You do?"

"Sure, in the East. One's the son of a cantor in Brooklyn. His father wanted him to sing and taught him all the sacred music; he was going to have his son become a cantor, too. Except the son couldn't stand it, and bolted. Flat ran out. He's singing in vaudeville now. All that training, it's making him a living."

"My mother wants me to be a singer, like in concert halls. First she wanted me to be a pianist, and when my hands didn't grow enough, she wanted to stretch them every night."

"She has ambitions for you, Ginger."

"Ambitions, yes. But for her, not for me. She sees me as a vessel for her dreams."

"And that's why you need to confront her now."

"At first I fled; I'd never look back, but when I learned we'd play in Pocatello, I suddenly had to face the music."

"Do you think you can? May we help?"

"It's something I've got to do, Mr. Beausoleil."

"Ginger, I like it. Most of us in the business are running from something. We ended up in the business because it's the only open door. Our families fled the old country, where we were shunned or outcasts or desperately poor, or trapped in a life without hope. You fled, too, and now you're willing to finish up, return, and face them, if that's the word for it. You've got some things on your side: eighteen, employed, married."

"I'm christened Penelope, and you'll hear that name if they come, and I know they will. But I'm Ginger, and I won't let them take Ginger from me."

"Everyone in the company will help, if you need help."

She stopped walking. "I need to do it myself," she said. "But thank you."

He admired that. "Ginger, there's not a man in the company who isn't in love with you," he said.

She didn't know how to manage that, and slid into quietness.

"Call on us if you need us," he said. "The whole company."

"You don't know my mother," she said.

That was all. They strolled back to the station through lonely darkness.

They welcomed the local when it finally chuffed in, two boxcars and an ancient coach, just in case someone wanted to travel somewhere through a long night. They boarded, put all their show baggage in the coach, and soon the engine was wailing through the blackness, with pea snow clattering against the grimy windows. The train was literally on a milk run. At Deer Lodge it stopped to load casks of raw milk, destined for a Butte creamery, along with a ton of potatoes destined for the mining town.

Then the local cranked its way east, its weary passengers swaying through the wee hours and the very late hours of night. Butte, perpetually alive, seemed quiet at four when they wearily debarked, heaving all their show stuff to the platform because there were no teamsters or cabbies to help them.

August eyed his company; they were shell-shocked with weariness and lost in silence. The only one who seemed impervious was The Genius, who had been working the contents of a flask through his innards. The Utah and Northern, a branch of the Union Pacific, loaded them at dawn, this time into a clean coach that was warm, and soon they were en route to Pocatello.

Ginger was staring at nothing, lost in her own world, but the rest brightened at the thought of a hotel room and sleep. The Grand Opera House in Pocatello would be dark that eve; the next day, the Follies would be up in lights.

Beausoleil lost track of time, but in the middle of the next morning the train chugged into Pocatello Junction, a mountain-girt town of about fifty-five hundred. The troupe wearily collected bags, and discovered Charles Pomerantz waiting for them with two hacks and a dray to carry luggage and equipment.

August peered about, looking for signs of trouble, and found none. The whitewashed station rested peacefully in the bright sun, indifferent to those who flowed through it day and night. He watched Ginger step onto the conductor's stool, and then the gravel platform, peer about cautiously, discover Charles, and race to him. He greeted her with a sweeping hug that lasted a long moment, and then led her to a hack. He had business to attend to: getting the weary troupe to its hotel, along with all their baggage.

The hack carrying Ginger was soon loaded, and Charles sent it on its way, and then the rest, until the company had been cared for.

That left just August and Charles, partners in a precarious enterprise, standing there.

"So far, no trouble," Charles said. "I've learned a thing or two about the Joneses, her parents. They are well liked and greatly respected here. But I haven't met them, haven't heard a word about trouble. They may not even know their daughter's here. But we'll see."

"Ginger's holding up. She's not running; she wants to get it over, so she can quit running."

"That's my girl."

"New act in?"

"Yes, at the hotel. The Grabowski boys. They seem fine, ready to go."

"Tickets moving?"

"Yeah, good news, sold out tomorrow. Filling up the next nights. You want to walk? It's a few blocks."

"Do me good," August said.

They walked through a bright and comfortable town, well set in its valleys, which branched outward into arid slopes. Maybe a good place to visit, but not a place to live if you enjoyed variety.

"How are we in Boise?"

"They're pasting the bills up, they say. I think we're set. But I'm not hearing from our bookings on the coast. And it's been three days since I wired Seattle. The manager in Boise says he's heard a rumor or two about buyers offering good money for houses up and down the coast, but he said it's just talk. Things are going along."

Charles had booked them into the Bannock Hotel, white clapboard place next to a Mrs. Wilson's Pancake Parlor. It would do, even if they charged two dollars, a steep price for a small room. The opera house was half a block away.

The Grab Bag boys were waiting in the small lobby. Art looked like a muscular boxer; Harry was a slim gymnast.

"We're ready to roll," Harry said. "Art's the stooge. He's twice my size, which works real good. Sets up the crowd. He's gonna get up on the stage and flatten me. We're ready for a few laughs."

"Can't wait to see it," August said. "We'll run you twice, before and after the break. I hope you've got several routines."

"Oh, we got a bunch," Art said. "We can knock 'em senseless. You mind paying us in advance? We're flat."

"I'll lend you two bucks," August said.

"We eat that in a day," Harry said. "Acrobats chow down."

August sighed, and forked over two singles. "Earn it, then," he said.

THIRTY-EIGHT

G inger had been in this building before. Twice she had played her parents' Steinway grand piano on this stage. The piano had been carried down to the opera house from her parents' home on the heights. Three times more she had sung at this hall after her mother had switched her from piano to voice. There had been other recitals in more intimate venues, but this was the stage where her mother had presented her to the world.

After a few desperate hours of rest at the Bannock Hotel, the weary troupe was gathering at the opera house ahead of its opening in Pocatello. They had rattled along silver rails, finally settling in their rooms around eleven for whatever rest they could extract from an early December afternoon with the low sun brightening the streets.

It soon would be dark. The Grand Opera House loomed solidly in the dusk. In Pocatello they built things to last, in part because her father insisted on it. Pocatello Junction, as some still called it, was no fly-by-night railroad construction town, but a durable city of brick and stone with spacious houses of well-cured pine. The Union Pacific was going to put this town on the map to stay.

Ginger was oddly passive. She had come to accept that she could not thwart a confrontation if her parents chose to have one. She had her majority, a wedding ring, Charles and August to shield her, not to mention a performance contract with Beausoleil Brothers Follies. Still, her parents were a looming presence, and she could hardly take a step onstage without imagining that they were watching and waiting.

Charles had mercifully let her rest. Marriage was still a puzzle to her; she hadn't been at it long enough to learn how to live with a man she barely knew. He, the urbane showman, seemed a lot more comfortable with it than she was.

"This is where you'll be the star of the show, baby," he had said.

The troupe soon collected there in the cold building. Theaters were never warm except when they brimmed with people. The stage was lit by one bare bulb, casting sickly light upon the gathering company. She met The Grab Bag act, thick Harry, slim Art, gymnasts with a streak of comedy.

"Miss Ginger, all I've heard about you is true," Art said, which made her curious. "Here's my greeting card."

He leapt upward, did a complete back flip, landed on his feet, and bowed.

"Do I shake your hand or your big toe?" she asked.

"I'm your slave for life," Art said.

"Have you met everyone?" she asked.

"Not if I can help it," Harry said.

"He's the stooge," Art said.

The term was beyond her, but she would soon figure it all out. She watched the Marbury Trio, looking just as tired as they did in the morning, loosen up. And Wayne Windsor was loosening his tonsils, sipping something she decided was a private brand of tonsil tonic. But what startled her the most was The Genius, who was singing scales, *do re mi fa sol la ti do* . . .

"Genius, why are you singing the scales?"

"The train ride wrecked my voice."

"But you could just talk to Ethel."

"Ethel is in no mood for talk. All she wanted was her

matrimonial rights. No sooner did we get off the train than she attacked me."

"I think I will go say hello to Harry the Juggler," she said, escaping the hand that shot out to stay her.

"Once a genius, always a genius, at all things large and small," he said.

Harry was unpacking his trunk, filled with lethal knives, scimitars, and cups and saucers.

"Did you sleep, Harry?"

"I am working on a guillotine act," Harry said, his voice thick. "Soon I will have it. A guillotine, the blade above me, suspended by a cord. If I drop a knife on the cord, I drop my head in a basket."

"That would make the front pages," she said.

"It would be an India rubber head. I will work it like the magician who puts a girl into a box and saws the box in half."

"Where would your real head be?"

"I haven't figured that out yet, but I will. Then I will show the act to Monsieur August."

"I think at the end, you should stand and hold your head at arm's length," she said.

"I'm perfecting it," he said.

She greeted the Wildroot girls, who seemed none the worse for wear. They were from an old theater family, and somehow knew how to get through exhausting times. She discovered August eyeing her, and knew he was keeping close tabs on her.

"I will be all right," she said. "There's nothing they can do."

"But will it upset you?"

"Maybe. But Mr. Beausoleil, I left home. I did it on my own. I made my plans, got some cash together, figured out an escape, and did it, and they never found me. That was harder than this. Now I have friends."

"My empty stomach is what started me," he said. "Get into the business or steal."

Then she was alone. She had to see what was least wrinkled in her trunk, and put it on. She slipped down the steps into the orchestra, three hundred and fifty seats stretching back to a perimeter that defined the lobby. A balcony curved overhead, with another two hundred fifty seats. This was a fine, solid house for a small town. It had 110-volt alternating current, the latest type, and the company would not need to light foot lamps or fire up the limelight. It had a skilled bill-poster, who had pasted up the notices all over town, notices that placed Ginger in second billing, behind Wayne Windsor. One of the bills graced a cabinet at the front of the opera house, between two sets of double doors. And Charles had not neglected the press. There in *The Tribune,* that day, was a story, and a paragraph about her, Ginger, wife of the co-owner, Charles Pomerantz. Maybe that was a form of insurance, she thought. Charles would do what he could to keep her from being molested.

She selected a bottle-green velveteen for the first act, a tailored dress that flattered her and also seemed suited for the American ballads she planned to sing her first round. She had exploited familiar songs, old songs children had learned from their parents. Her second act was often classical, sometimes operatic. And she welcomed encores.

Showtime.

August had donned his tuxedo and top hat, the white bib a little worse for wear, but no one would notice. She caught him gazing at her. He waved gently; everything would be fine.

Backstage, the acts readied themselves. The new one would be different. One of them was seating himself on an aisle seat. The other, Art, was wearing blue tights, a gymnast outfit, and looked pretty snappy, she thought.

The Wildroot girls were looking glorious, as always; they were the real troupers in the show.

Ginger slid the curtain aside a bit so she could peer out from the edge of the proscenium at the gathering crowd. She couldn't make out faces, nor did she see her parents. If they came, they would be front center, but they weren't. Still, there were people she knew, people who knew her, who would puzzle at the transformation of Penelope Jones. They would know her voice, her style, her face, her walk, and her parents. She could not hide that, nor would she try. If there was trouble with her parents, she would cope—somehow. She wasn't sure of it. The thought made her jittery. But she had songs to sing, and a voice to warm up, and she concentrated on readying herself. A few quiet scales, anything to loosen the tightness in her throat and body.

Then the moment came. An opening was always electric. It was just as electric to veterans of the stage as it was to new arrivals. An opening, new town, new audience, caught in the throat and held, as the curtain parted or rolled upward.

And there was August, his stride confident, pushing out to center stage as the crowd quieted.

"Ladies and gents, good evening. The Beausoleil Brothers Follies is proud to play in, what is it? Peoria? Billings? Ah, Pocatello, in the great state of Idaho, home of the potato," he said. "And now, to warm your evening, the one, the only Wildroot Sisters, sweethearts of song."

And away they went.

August returned to the shadowed wing, smiled at Ginger, and the show rolled ahead, one act upon another, a clockwork procession of song and athletics and talk. Wayne Windsor warmed up the crowd. The Marbury Trio did a jaunty tap dance. Harry the Juggler tossed his scimitars. And then August announced a new act, the one, the

only Grab Bag. Art Grabowski sailed on, found the brightest spot, did a few flips, walked on his hands, did several
cartwheels, and whirled around the stage on a monocycle. But there was a fellow out in the crowd who didn't
like it.

"What's this, a joke?" he yelled.

Art stopped. "My good man, if you don't like my act,
you can always leave."

"Leave? Then all these suckers would have to sit here
for another ten minutes."

"You're interrupting the show, sir."

"I'll show you what it means to interrupt a show, pal."

Harry, in street clothes, bulled up the aisle, found the
stairs, pushed out onto the stage, while the audience
waited breathless at what looked to be a fight.

Harry was about twice as big as Art. Harry pushed on,
while Art backpedaled on his monocycle, a precarious retreat. And then Harry charged, but Art cycled out of the
way, abandoned his one-wheel bike, and stood his ground.
Next time big Harry swarmed in, Art unloosed a haymaker, and Harry did three backflips and a cartwheel.

Suddenly, the audience chuckled.

The act turned into a choreographed brawl, the little
guy against the big tormentor, with the pair tumbling and
rolling. Every time the big guy swarmed in, he overshot,
or the little guy tripped him and he ended up doing cartwheels.

The audience soon was laughing, then hooting, then applauding each time the little guy foiled another assault
and sent the big guy to the floor. But the moment came
when the little guy won the fight, and stood with a foot
on the big guy's chest, and then the Grabowskis were up
and bowing and looking a little sweaty.

This was a world that Ginger knew nothing about. She
had never seen anything like it in her gently raised life,

and at first she recoiled, but then the audience's enjoyment tugged at her, and from her perch backstage she began laughing, too. The Grabowskis were not only acrobats but gifted comics, and their act was winning a lot of laughter from the crowd.

She knew something then: Vaudeville was for all people. It wasn't a bit like her high-toned recitals for cultivated people whose tastes had been schooled and refined. Vaudeville was broad, earthy, universal, and fun. Which is perhaps why her parents were not out there; vaudeville was beneath them.

It had almost been beneath her, too. But in the few weeks of her touring, she had come face-to-face with thousands of working people, miners and shop girls and clerks, all of them laying out their dollars for an evening of fun.

She watched the two grinning acrobats slip off the stage, even as August, looking chipper in his top hat, trotted out as the applause faded.

"The Grab Bag, come out for a bow, boys," he said.

And Art and Harry hurried out for one last bow, and then cartwheeled away.

"And now, the lady you've been waiting for, the singer with the voice of a silver bell, the one, the only Ginger! Please welcome our new nightingale, Miss Ginger."

And then she was on. Her heart pattered. She heard an immediate buzz, the whispers, the questions as she made her way to the bright-lit center stage. Some of them knew her. Another name, an earlier time. She paused, knowing she looked good in that green velveteen.

She smiled. She bowed gently. There were three of the company's musicians in the orchestra pit. An accordionist, a guitarist, and a banjo player. They would simply pick up whatever she started.

She filled her lungs. She chose some ballads first. Stephen Foster. "Jeanie with the Light Brown Hair." And the more she sang, the more she knew that all those people were dreaming of Miss Ginger, and wildly curious about the girl they knew as Penelope.

THIRTY-NINE

S tanding in the wings, Charles Pomerantz thought that maybe this show, this evening, was the finest the Follies had ever wrought. The performers, exhausted from the hard trip, had somehow drawn from their last reserves to delight the audience.

His surprising bride had done even better after the intermission, turning to ballads that evoked generous applause. And it was her audience. These were people who knew her, who were speculating about her new life and name.

She knew it. She sang with a warmth he had never heard in her. It was almost as if she had minted a new voice for this event; as if the new Ginger-voice would separate her from her Penelope self. Was she seeking their approval? It occurred to him that, yes, she wanted it badly. She was offering herself to them.

And still no sign of her parents. But the run in Pocatello had just begun, and if word had not yet reached them, it soon would. He thought she just might cope with it. But it worried him. He hoped to be on hand, to help, to defend, to encourage, and if there were tears, to wipe them away.

But it wasn't just Ginger who was transfixing the crowd that night. The Genius and Ethel had them chuckling. The Marbury Trio was introducing tap dance to a lot of people who had never seen it, and they were swaying in their theater seats, and enjoying the svelte athletics. Even

LaVerne Wildroot, doing a solo or two in front of the olio, was catching waves of applause.

August seemed to know the evening was rare, and fairly strutted out to introduce the acts, choosing to be conversational and quiet. And so it went on opening night in Pocatello Junction, Idaho. When at last the curtain rang down on a generous evening, the performers stood quietly, aglow. How long had it been since any of them had enjoyed an audience like this? A perfect show, like this? Even the newcomers, Ed and Harry Grabowski, who had contributed much, listened to the happy crowd in wonder.

It was only after a peculiar pause that the performers began to drift to the dressing rooms. Ginger looked oddly restless; whatever she had been expecting hadn't happened. Not yet, anyway.

Charles watched a bespectacled man work through the performers and close in on Ginger. He was a skinny drink of water with a polka-dot bow tie and gummy lips.

"Parkinson with *The Tribune*," he said. "Like a word."

Charles caught the flash of uncertainty in Ginger's face, and watched her stiffen and nod.

"Okay, miss, you're Penelope Jones, right?"

"Sir, I'm not *miss*. I'm Mrs. Pomerantz, and this is my husband, who's an owner of the show."

"How do you spell it?" the reporter asked.

Charles obliged him.

"Okay, the word is, you're the same as left here a while ago, dodging the old lady, and now you're an actress. Right?"

"I am Ginger now. I am not an actress."

"You saying you aren't the Jones babe?"

"I'm saying that I left her behind me."

"So, your parents, they approve of it?"

"I haven't talked with them."

"So, you mind telling me how this happened?"

ANYTHING GOES   277

"I am of age; I chose to leave. I chose to make my way in the world, and I did."

"You defying them, are you?"

"Thank you for your interest, Mr. Parkinson. Are you done?"

"Hey, relax, sweetheart. I'm just getting at the nitty-gritty. Word is, you flew the coop, and the old lady's having a conniption fit."

"I wouldn't know, not having talked to them."

"The buzz is, they put a fortune into your training, and now you're wasting it all on, what is this? Sideshow. Carnival stuff."

Charles was ready to barge in, but Ginger smiled at the reporter and touched his arm. "Thousands of people have enjoyed my singing since I joined the show. I'm proud and pleased that I've had the chance to sing for the whole world."

He liked that, and scribbled it into his spiral-bound notepad.

"I'm grateful for the training. It gave me my chance to fulfill my dreams. Mr. Beausoleil, and my husband, here, have opened doors for me, given me a chance, brought me along when I was learning the ropes, and here I am."

"Yeah, but sweetheart, your old man and old lady, they had different plans for you."

"Yes, my mother did. And I'm sorry to disappoint her, but it's my life, and my choice to enter vaudeville. I love vaudeville. I love the company. These are the sweetest people I've ever known. They have great gifts. They entertain. They have, well, a knowledge of how the world works, and what pleases an audience, and I've learned more from them than I ever learned from voice coaches and tutors. Singing is more than hitting the notes."

"Holy cats, lady, that's a mouthful," the reporter said, scribbling away.

"Get it right. Write what I said. I've learned more about

singing, and voice, since joining this company, than I ever did through my girlhood. These are my teachers."

"Man, you're gonna tick off a lot of people."

Charles started laughing. Ginger was a champ.

"Get it right, Mr. Parkinson," she said.

"Or what?"

"I like your bow tie," she said. "I'm all for polka dots, but I prefer blue. Really good reporters get the facts."

The skinny bird laughed. "Hey, you're a story and a half," he said.

He hurried off. Charles caught her elbow, and winked.

The company was too exhausted to head for the usual watering holes, and Charles quietly walked Ginger back to their hotel in a darkness that seemed almost ominous. She wrapped her cape tightly about her, and then they were safe in the thin warmth, and soon entered the quiet privacy of their room.

He helped her out of her cape and then hugged her.

"You're my star," he said.

"You're my heaven," she whispered.

"I'm still trying to figure out how we ended up hitched," he said.

"Destiny," she said, and kissed him.

He hugged her, and she melted into him.

"I need to lie down a little," she said.

He helped her to the double bed and eased her down. She smiled up at him, her eyes full of promise, and she clasped his hand and held it.

And fell asleep.

It took him a moment even to realize it. One moment, full of promise, the next, surrendering to exhaustion, the conclusion of one of her hardest days. Her body seemed to sink into the mattress, and she was gone, her breath gentle, the rise of her chest steady and quiet.

He undid some of her buttons, giving her room and air,

and stared down upon her, his miraculous bride of just a few weeks. There were dark circles under her eyes.

"My shooting star," he said. "A comet across the dark."

He was disappointed. He had been looking forward to this night, for many nights. But there would be more nights, each more delightful, and for now, sleep was best. The kindness of the quiet night was the best tonic for the long trip and the brave front before the people of her hometown.

She wasn't dozing; she had slipped over the cliff, her weariness at last compelling her young heart to rest. He felt closer to her than he had ever felt, and marveled at it. There she was, exhausted and asleep, and he was watching over her, keeping her safe from harm. He had never been in the guardian angel business, and was liking it.

A sharp rap on the door halted his reveries. The rap soon became a clatter.

"Tomorrow," Charles said at the door. "Whoever you are."

"Police. Open up."

Charles stood, knowing what this was about. He eyed Ginger, who had barely stirred, and opened the door. There indeed was a large, blue-uniformed policeman. And a hawkish, small woman with blazing eyes. And a tall, lantern-jawed man with a stern look to him.

"You have my daughter," the woman said, pushing in.

"My wife," Charles replied.

She ignored him, pushed to the bed, where Ginger was stirring.

"Penelope, you're coming with me," the woman said.

"Madam, who are you? You are talking to my wife."

"If you interfere we'll throw you in jail and toss away the key," the woman said.

"Jones here, and that's my daughter and we're taking her."

"Taking her? She's my wife."

"She's not anymore, if she was at all," the woman said.

She reached over, grabbed Ginger's left hand, and swiftly stripped it of her wedding ring, and tucked the ring into a pocket. "Get up," she said.

"Now just a minute. This is my wife. She's of age. She's committed no crime. And she's staying right here. You're in my room. Get out. Right now."

"Get up," the woman said.

Ginger, groggy still, finally realized what this was about. "No," she said. "You can't do this. You don't own me."

"We're taking you away from this filthy carnival. They abducted you and we're taking you away. We've sunk a fortune into your career, and they're stealing you from us."

"I'll stay right here," Ginger said, sudden ferocity in her. "It's my life. My choice."

The woman turned to the cop. "Carry her out."

"Get out! You're kidnapping her," Charles said.

"I'm me!" Ginger cried.

That was the most poignant cry that Charles had ever heard.

A crowd had collected at the door, among them the reporter, Parkinson.

"Hey, what's the deal?" he asked.

"None of your business," Jones said, "and if you print a word, we'll sue."

"You kidnapping her? How come you got the right to do that?"

"Get away from here, Parkinson."

Outside the door, the Grabowskis were watching, and so were Harry the Juggler and The Genius.

"Go on, get away from here," Jones said.

"You gonna kidnap her in front of all these witnesses?" the reporter asked. "That's front page. We'll use the war type."

"She's coming home, and that's that. Pick her up and get her to the carriage," Jones said.

The cop slid his arms under Ginger, who refused to cooperate, and lifted her from the bed. She lay inert, resisting.

Charles saw how it was. The prominent Joneses had the cop on their side. Nothing else mattered, including wrong or right.

Ginger suddenly struggled. "What are you going to do with me?" she asked her mother.

"You're going to return to the concert hall."

"No. I'll never sing again. Not as long as I'm your slave."

"A few days of bread and water will cure that," the mother said. "We've spent a ransom on you. We'll get it back."

"I'll never sing again," Ginger said, and there was something so strong in her voice, in the forceful way she said it, that it sent a shiver through Charles.

"Don't think this is over," he said, directly to Jones. "You'll be dealing with me every day of your life."

"Hey, copper, put her down," The Genius said. "Or you'll spend a few years behind bars."

"And who are you?"

"I'm the voice of conscience, the whisper in the night, the wrath of the gods."

The cop ignored him, and pushed through the crowd carrying Ginger, wrapped in a sheet that pinned her like a straitjacket.

"Holy cats," Parkinson said. "Stop the presses. This'll sell a lot of papers."

The big cop bowled through the door, into the hall, scattering spectators like tenpins, and carried Ginger away. She was squirming now, struggling, no longer sleepy, fighting to break free. The parents followed behind, the hawkish woman glaring at everyone, her gaze withering, while the Union Pacific superintendent Jones, with balled fists the size of hams, walked behind, daring anyone to resist.

Outside an enclosed carriage waited, and the copper stuffed Ginger into it, the parents climbed in, the father slammed the lacquered door, and a hack driver pulled away with its human contraband.

Charles followed the carriage, step by step by step, before it vanished in the darkness.

FORTY

T he big copper carried Ginger, under the watchful eye of her mother, to her room in the spacious house. The copper left. The maid, Maude, stripped away Ginger's clothes, without Ginger's cooperation, and finally got Ginger into a nightdress.

There was nothing to say, so Ginger kept her silence.

The maid removed every bit of clothing from the armoire while Ginger's mother watched.

"There," she said. "There's not a slipper or shoe or coat or dress anywhere about. Just in case you try to leave. There's snow on the ground, and it's cold."

"You have taken my life from me."

"Exactly."

"Where's Father?"

"He's off at the paper, putting out fires. The paper will understand that you were abducted by the vaudeville company, and we have rescued you and restored you to your rightful life. That will quiet that reporter."

"It's not true."

"Now it is."

"I will tell everyone it's not true."

"You won't be here. Tomorrow you will be on a private car, carrying you to the American Academy of Symphonic Arts in New York, where you will study voice. It will take some arranging, getting a car here isn't easy, and a chaperone and a guard. But he has ways."

"I will never sing a note as long as I am not free."

Her mother smiled, her lips curling upward. "Time will tell," she said. "And by the way, never use the name Ginger again. That's gone and buried. It'll take some effort to escape the blot on your reputation—vaudeville! Vaudeville! Cheap shows, cheap people, mostly off the immigrant boats."

"They're the best people I've ever met."

"Who assaulted you, demeaned you, and exploited you. Like that fake husband."

"Charles . . . ," Ginger started to defend him, and gave up. Whatever she said would be ignored.

Her mother suddenly turned cheerful. "Good night, Penelope. You're back."

She clicked off the electrical light. Penelope lay in fragrant darkness. Her mother was a great one for sachets, and the house always had a pleasant scent of exotic spices.

So there it was. In the space of an hour or so, she had been abducted, imprisoned, returned to the life she had fled, and reduced to nothingness. No amount of fragrant spice in the air could conceal the odor rising from this house overlooking Pocatello. The blankets covering her felt like shrouds.

She was weary beyond words. The night of travel, the new town, the show, the longing for sleep, deep sleep, sleep until she might wake rested, all of it weighed her down. The temptation was to crawl under those clean, fresh covers, and fall instantly into oblivion, and accept whatever fate awaited her.

But she couldn't. And there was no time. A private car, actually a prison, carrying her away, carrying her to a distant place across a continent, silencing her, forcing her into the life her mother planned for her. Even now, her father was out in the night, summoning a railcar, wiring people in New York, putting it all together.

She crawled wearily from bed, drew aside the curtain, and stared into the wintry night, the snow cover giving ghostly light to the scene. It would be a long way to the hotel. In a nightdress. Without a scarf or coat or anything for her bare feet. And she might be picked up and returned by that big copper. And when she got to the hotel, she would be wearing her nightdress, and they would stop her.

She could freeze to death. That was one way to die. But she would die a worse death in a railcar under the eyes of an armed guard.

The house was not yet quiet. She heard her mother, and the servants. They were making sure she had nothing to cover her feet or body, making very sure, making the wayward daughter a slave once again. Even as her father was busy at *The Tribune* giving them a monstrous lie, quieting the sensation.

She would wait an hour. And she would freeze her feet, if that's what it took. And she would wrap herself in her Hudson's Bay blanket, which covered her bed. And she would find a way to wrap bathroom towels about her feet.

So she waited. She heard her father return, and the houseman take away his hack, and the doors click shut. She heard muffled voices. She watched the moon rise, turning the snow silver. She waited in the silence. She discovered she had no good way to wrap towels about her feet, so she would go barefoot, and if her feet were frostbitten, she would pay the price.

She wrapped the blanket about her, headed downstairs, and gently tried the door. It was bolted, and she could not grasp how to release the lock. She tried the rear door, and found it was locked also. She gently pushed the sash on a downstairs window, and it wouldn't move. The generous house was more a fortress than she had known or imagined.

She returned to her room, opened the sash, which slid upward easily, and crawled out on the roof of the generous verandah, wondering if she could find the courage to jump. She could hurt herself badly. But her liberty was worth the risk. She edged through patched snow, down the slippery shingles, and reached the edge. The frozen ground was a long way down. It was bitter cold. Her feet were already numb. Doubts flooded her. And a renewed weariness. A bed would be so welcome.

"Ginger."

The voice floated upward.

"Ginger. Harry Grabowski. Me and Art, we came to help out."

"Oh!"

"You sit down on the edge, feet over the edge, and I'll be ready to catch you. Then just push off."

She needed no invitation. She slipped to the edge, sat slowly, slid her bare legs over, discovered massive Harry, dressed darkly, waiting, a welcome shadow.

"All right," she said, and pushed off.

He caught her easily, so easily she marveled. One moment she was falling, the next, his strong hands caught her at the waist, and gently settled her.

"Barefoot, are you? It figures," he said. "In the old country, keep 'em barefoot. That's how they ruled."

"All clear," said Art, who was keeping watch.

Harry lifted her up, tightened the blanket about her, picked his way carefully to the drive where broad carriage tracks would obscure footprints, even as Art whisked away the footprints in the snow around the veranda, obscuring everything.

"Hey, Ginger, you mind walking in the snow a while?" Art asked.

"I would be proud to."

Harry eased her to the ground, and she felt the snow bite her bare feet, and she walked artfully, now and then in the carriage tracks, but now and then leaving small, feminine prints which Art did not touch. She wanted each print in the snow to be an indelible record, a signature, of her will. For all the world to see, including the reporter at the paper. So she walked, and walked, and oddly her feet did not go numb because it was a record of her flight, a record of her determination.

And then, when they reached the end of the drive, Harry swept her up and carried her along moonlit lanes, and into the slumbering town. Near the hotel, Art eased ahead, checking things out. He entered the hotel, looked around, stepped out, and nodded. A few moments later, Harry tapped on a familiar hotel door, and Ginger found herself peering into the face of her distraught husband. His gaze ran deep and gentle.

Charles reached out, touched Ginger's cheek, and nodded.

Harry gently lowered her to the bed, and drew the red blanket tight about her.

"We were right," Art said. "Nothing holds this lady in a cage."

Charles shook hands heartily with The Grab Bag, and the brothers slipped into the peaceful corridor, clicking the door behind them.

Then he held her, warmed her, pressed her to his solid body, and finally eased her to the bed and settled her in it.

She told him about the escape. And about her parents' plans for her. And about the barefoot prints she left in the snow, a mark of everything she was and intended to be.

"Those prints may tell the world the truth," Charles said.

He found her feet and began massaging them, warming them, awakening the circulation in them, and she enjoyed the sensation.

"Your father went to the paper? With a story that we abducted you?"

"Yes."

"I don't like it," he said. "I'll talk to August."

"I'm so tired."

"We have one matter to decide," he said. "Shall we slip you out? To Boise?"

"I've already decided it. I'll sing tonight. I will sing right here, before this city. I want the world to know it's my choice."

He smiled. "I knew it. I knew it when I proposed," he said. "Who you are. I saw it."

Sleep crept up once again. And this time, she slept the night through. And there was no one hammering on the hotel door. She didn't hear Charles, who was up and down, and she didn't hear when he got dressed and left the room in the night, or hear him return at dawn, or feel him slide into the double bed beside her.

And yet when sunlight at last teased her awake, she sensed at once that her new husband was taut with worry.

Yet he smiled. "How's my girl?" he asked.

"I could sleep for days." She watched him pull out fresh clothing from his satchel.

"You're worried about something."

"Worried about your parents, yes."

"What is it?"

"He's been telling the paper that we abducted you, and they rescued you."

She was puzzled.

He didn't elaborate. "There's trouble in it," he said.

Indeed, when they saw *The Tribune* that morning, the headline read, "Singer Rescued," and the story was about the Joneses and their success in rescuing their daughter, Penelope, from a notorious vaudeville company that had captured and exploited her. A vivid description of the rescue, penned by their ace reporter, Studs Parkinson, put Miss Penelope Jones back in her ancestral home, with help from the city police. She was reported to be at rest in the bosom of her home, grateful to be freed from vile servitude. And Jones was reported as saying he intended to take legal action against the vaudeville company.

No wonder Charles was restless.

He sipped coffee and sighed. "It's the lawsuit part that's worrying August and me," he said.

She felt blue. Her flight had triggered all this. And yet, maybe some good would come of it. "I'll sing tonight, Charles. Just put me on, and let me sing. Let them see me, singing. Let them see me smile. That'll say what needs saying."

"Lay low today?"

"No. I'll be here. I'll be with the troupe. And if anyone asks, I'll tell them I left, of my own free will."

He smiled suddenly. "What else did I marry?"

"Most of an iceberg's below water," she said.

"You're more of a volcano," he said.

It proved to be a quiet day. She moved freely about, window-shopped, looked at ready-made dresses, lunched with some of the troupe, and showed up early at the Grand Opera House. But it wasn't quite normal; a line of people stood at the box office, thirty, forty, plunking down cash to see the show. And not a one recognized her. She wondered how that could be, and remembered that any publicity, good or bad, would sell seats.

Backstage, August eyed her sharply, noting her new blue dress, purchased that afternoon.

"We've got a full house," he said. "Thanks to you."

"Are my parents out there?"

"No one's seen them, and the word is, they wouldn't set foot in the opera house as long as we're billed."

She thought that was true. Maybe it was all over. But when she thought of her mother, she thought it wasn't over.

FORTY-ONE

August Beausoleil couldn't remember when he had felt so melancholic before. He was often a little blue; that was his nature. The melancholia was a sort of thermometer that registered how well his life was going. He had learned that when he was particularly blue, something bad was looming. He had an intuitive understanding: the blues heralded trouble.

As they did now. He shouldn't be melancholic at all. The young star of his show, Ginger, had weathered a brutal confrontation with her family. All her fears had been justified; they were quite ready to imprison her and deny her the life she had chosen. And somehow, at a tender age, she had weathered it. She was singing with a richness that he ascribed to adulthood; the girl had vanished in a leap from a roof; the woman was now walking out on the stage.

All the uproar had been duly chronicled in the Pocatello paper, *The Tribune*. At first readers were treated to a colorful story about a girl from a prominent family who had been abducted and used by Beausoleil's Follies. And how her enterprising parents had freed her from her degraded estate and returned her to the bosom of her family. But the story hadn't ended there. Next, readers learned that she had been kept a prisoner in her family's home, deprived of clothing and footwear, but had escaped barefoot, with only a blanket against the wintry night, to return to the life she had chosen on the variety theater stage. "Jones Girl Returns to Stage," was the first headline. "Married to Owner," was the subhead.

All of which generated intense interest. The Joneses were Pocatello's first family; he ran the railroad. Their daughter was a prodigy, destined for great things. And then, it seemed, she wished to live a life of her own. And she was packing the house. There was not a ticket to be had to any performance. Lucky people got to see her twice, thrice, if they could find the tickets. With each performance, August looked out upon a jammed house, with standing room only. It was all a miracle.

Charles had left for Boise after making sure his bride was well and weathering the worst ordeal of her tender years. He had the usual advance work to complete, and could delay no further.

Then, one bright December morning, a man with a sheriff's badge pinned to him thrust some papers into August's hand. It was a summons issued by Bannock County District Court. *Notice! You Are Being Sued*, it said. It was accompanied by a complaint. The Follies, Charles Pomerantz, and August Beausoleil were being sued by the Joneses. The complaint was a lengthy one, and August skimmed quickly over it. It had to do with damaged reputation, theft of property, alienation of a family member, and a lot more. It was a legal mishmash, likely to be dismissed, but that was not the real purpose.

The defendants would need to appear the next day. The court would place a heavy cash bail on the vaudeville company to prevent flight.

The real purpose was to wreck the company, prevent it from playing its next engagements, and require surety so drastic that it would drain the company of its last cent. It was a very old game. Want to destroy a traveling show? Lower an enormous performance bond on the entire show and its performers. Lawsuits like this were the Achilles' heel of any touring company. It didn't matter if the complaint had merit; the idea was to disrupt the show's schedule, destroy its income. In most cases, the odds were stacked against a touring company being sued by a local citizen, with the case heard by a local judge.

Suddenly August Beausoleil needed a lawyer, and a lot more money than he had in his cashbox. More than those things, he needed liberty; the freedom to move his company to its next billets, keep the income rolling in, day after day, town after town.

The sadness that engulfed him was old and familiar. It harkened back to the days when he was a boy so alone he scarcely knew his mother and had never known his father. He could go find a lawyer, or he could go to the Joneses' lawyer. He had, actually, a stronger suit than the Joneses did. They had kidnapped his star, the wife of his business partner, who was of age, and they had done great damage.

But he knew better. Lawsuits would mire the company. The Beausoleil Brothers Follies would be stalled in Pocatello, and swiftly starve to death, its players unpaid, its bills unmet, its credit run into the ground. A company on the road had to fix its troubles in other ways.

Charles had gone ahead to Boise. August would wire him; they had a code word, *RED,* which meant emergency, return at once. But that would be tomorrow. And the Follies was due to open in Boise in three days. Tickets were on sale there. August was on his own, alone, as he had been from his earliest memories. The stage-door errand boy would depend on his own resources once again.

Jones himself operated from his superintendent's office in the railroad station. Their lawyer, whose name was Brophy, was also a Union Pacific lawyer in the same offices. August could go there, three blocks distant, and endure the test of manhood.

Instead, he collected his worn topcoat, hoping it would do against the sharp cold, and headed toward the generous house on the heights, the house that overlooked much of Pocatello, and was meant to be seen from below, by lesser people.

The long driveway up the grade was caked with ice, and treacherous, so August walked carefully, as much in snow beside the road as on it. But he did not fall, and eventually found himself stepping to the front door, located at the center of a broad verandah.

The door opened even before he knocked. A manservant, tall, with slicked-back hair, confronted him.

"Mrs. Jones said to talk to their lawyer, if you must," the manservant said.

"Please tell Mrs. Jones I'm not here to argue, but to listen. I wish to know what her grievances might be, and how I might be of assistance."

The manservant debated that, and finally vanished into the gloomy interior.

When he returned, he had a simple message: "Madam says you cannot be of assistance, and good day."

"Very well, tell her I'm on my way, but I'd hoped to hear all about her daughter. A remarkable young woman, sir."

The door closed in August's face, and he turned to leave, his next stop being Superintendent Jones himself. But then, suddenly, the door opened. It was Mazeppa Jones, looking thin and waspish.

"I will give you ten minutes," she said.

"I will listen," he replied, as she waved him in and escorted him to an ornate parlor done in reds: red plush horsehair, red velvet drapes, oriental rugs. She took a seat but let him stand.

"You are French," she said.

"Mostly orphan, madam."

"Penelope was destined to be the finest concert pianist in the world, but her hands never grew. You need an octave, you know. So I switched her to voice, a good soprano that altered downward as she matured, but not perfect. It was such a blow to me. But training can perfect a flawed voice, and I was about it when all this girlishness happened."

"What did happen?"

"You destroyed her reputation. She's ruined."

"Ah, I am not following, madam."

"Of course you wouldn't. And I'm not going to explain it."

"What of the future, madam?"

"Penelope is dead. Let her lie in an unmarked grave."

"And you, madam?"

"My daughter took my life. I will spend the rest of my days scrubbing her from the world. Until nothing's left of her. Not a memory."

Beausoleil became aware of a ticking clock, a mantel clock over the fireplace.

"Is there anything you want from me, madam?"

"Put her on the streets. Here. She must never sing again. Do that, and I will drop the lawsuit."

"Is the suit yours, rather than your husband's?"

"My intentions entirely. Now I have given you your salvation. You are going to snatch at it. One could not expect more from your sort. You may leave."

"She is married to my colleague, madam."

"You heard me. On the streets. After that, your company will be free to go."

He bowed slightly; the manservant materialized at once from behind velvet, escorted him to the door, and moments later he was in fresh air, under a cloudless sky. He edged carefully down the icy drive, and into town. He stepped around ice, avoiding black patches, checking each step before putting weight on that foot. And so arrived back at the hotel, unscathed by broken bones.

The price was a glowing young woman, whose talent was larger than any he had ever known. The day was still young. He headed for the chambers of the Union Pacific lawyer who was also handling this matter for the superintendent. Pierce Brophy, according to the signature.

August was ushered in the moment he gave his name to the clerk. The office was far from opulent, but the railroad preferred oaken muscle to show when it came to legal affairs.

"Mr. Brophy, what sort of surety will you seek in court?"

"Five thousand."

"And is the judge likely to set bail at that?"

"Always."

"Thank you, sir," August said.

"Just a minute, Mr. Beausoleil. Mrs. Jones required me to supply you with another option."

"I was just there, and heard it."

"Well?"

"Mrs. Jones will not succeed."

"I think I like you," Brophy said.

"Then ask the court for a more appropriate surety."

Brophy stuck a finger in his left ear and twisted, apparently gouging out wax. August thought Brophy hadn't heard the expected.

"Ten thousand?" Brophy asked.

"I will be there at eleven tomorrow," August said.

He left, somehow knowing he had gained ground. There were lawyers who did not like to do what they were commissioned to do, and he sensed that about Pierce Brophy.

He was done. Fate would play out in the morning. A weariness settled through him. He might not be the proprietor of the Follies for much longer. But he had weathered worse, and the Follies was actually the second of his variety companies. The first had collapsed under his own mismanagement, which had been instructive.

The show went splendidly that eve, with every seat filled and thirty people standing along the rear wall. Again, Ginger was the attraction. The battle with her parents, flamboyantly described in the paper, had ignited the curiosity of people for miles around, and all eyes were on Ginger, who did not fail to sing her golden songs, in her golden way.

In the morning, Charles showed up on the first train in from Boise, and August filled him in. Charles looked stricken. At eleven, the pair showed up in the chambers of Henry Rausch, district judge, and waited for events to unfold. The courtroom was empty, save for a clerk and a bailiff. And *The Tribune* reporter, Parkinson.

The bored jurist eyed the defendants cursorily, and Pierce Brophy petitioned the court to set bail at one thousand dollars, that being a reasonable estimate of the presumed damages suffered by the complaining party.

Judge Rausch, from the bench, set the trial date as January third, and set bail at the thousand dollars, August agreed to provide it forthwith, and that was the end of the proceeding.

"Can we do it?" Charles asked.

"Yes, and with a little to spare."

"I don't know how you managed that," Charles said.

"I don't know, either," August said. "But it had to do with honor."

FORTY-TWO

Parkinson trailed them out of the Bannock County courthouse, annoying Charles Pomerantz. Ginger had suffered enough from *The Tribune*'s sensationalism.

"What was all that about?" the reporter asked.

"Ask the Joneses," Pomerantz said.

"It's a public document, a complaint. You may as well tell me."

"Read it, then. We have nothing to say."

"You posted bail. That cuts you loose, right?"

"We will lose a large sum unless we appear in this court in January."

"What have the Joneses against you?"

Parkinson was amused by his own question.

"Look, sir, talk to them. We have a show to put on tonight."

August was listening as the reporter dogged them, walking back to the hotel. But suddenly he intervened. "Here's your story, sir. You tell the Joneses there will be two seats, front center, for them this evening, and the company would be pleased to host them, and let them see their magnificent daughter perform."

"Holy cats, that's a story, all right. Who do I talk to?"

"I gather that Mrs. Jones makes all the decisions, sir. At least she says she does."

"I can work this into a great story either way. An invitation and two empty seats tonight. Or the Joneses, bitterly opposed to their daughter's entry into vaudeville, show up for a gander."

Charles smiled in spite of himself. It reminded him that reporters often manufactured news, especially when there were no good headlines at the moment.

"Go ahead, Parkinson, fill our house for us," Beausoleil said. "Here's a pair of tickets. Give them to the Joneses."

"Hey, this is a story and a half. And if I can't unload them?"

"Bring your lady and enjoy the show. But let me know if the Joneses accept the tickets, all right?"

"Yeah, sure, I'll give you the word."

Actually, the last performance was nearly sold out. The hurly-burly reportage of Ginger's tussle with her parents was filling the opera house. So far as Charles or August were concerned, any publicity was good publicity. But Charles worried about Ginger, whose courage was being tested each hour in Pocatello. How would she feel, singing in front of her mother?

He found Ginger lying on the bed, looking worn.

"Bail was a grand. We can manage, sweetheart. We'll be opening in Boise."

"I've cost you a fortune."

"Hey, sweetheart, you're our new star."

"You'd be better off . . ."

"If we hadn't found you? Nah, you're our fortune cookie. But there may be something going on tonight you should be ready for. Like maybe your parents in the audience."

"They are?"

"We don't know. August sent some prime tickets to them."

She stared up at him, looking forlorn.

He sat down next to her. "Maybe some good will come of it," he said.

She just stared, and he could only guess what torments were flowing through her now. August had been impulsive, the fixer making things good, but maybe this time he had overstepped. The gulf between Ginger and her mother could not be bridged, much less fathomed.

"I've come this far. I'll go the rest of the way," she said, and squeezed his hand.

She was tough.

That afternoon, Parkinson reported that the Joneses' attorney, Brophy, had accepted the tickets. Parkinson had gotten nowhere with Mrs. Jones. He didn't know who, if anyone, would claim the seats.

And that's how they went into the final performance. Pomerantz hoped it would be a door-buster. That surety for the court appearance came to the entire income for two shows. And that meant they'd barely make payroll and expenses, going into Boise. But that was nothing new for the Follies.

By seven, the troupe had assembled at the opera house. Ginger was costumed early, and spent her time peeking out at the empty house, looking for her parents. And then, at the first signs of people arriving, the Joneses appeared, he in ordinary business clothes, but she in black taffeta, with a black hat and black veil, looking funereal from head to toe. Mazeppa Jones made a spectacle, which was plainly what she intended. They took their seats as the opera house began to fill. There was whispering out there, but nothing untoward, as show-goers slipped in, found their seats, and settled down for the evening. Mrs. Jones sat immobile, wrought from stone, not so much as a finger moving inside its black glove.

Oddly, Ginger smiled.

"It figures," she said.

But by then the whole troupe was curious about her, about her parents, about the quiet hubbub out there as this final audience in Pocatello realized the sort of drama playing out right there between the wayward daughter and the rejected parents. As far as Charles could tell, the town was divided, many siding with the parents but some standing up for Ginger. It had all played out in the paper, and people had rushed to their own conclusions no matter whether they knew the Jones family or not.

She stood quietly, a wall of privacy around her, waiting in the wings. Charles couldn't say what was passing through her then, only that she was composed. She had stopped peeking from the edge of the proscenium. Her parents were there, a pool of darkness in a festive crowd, and then it was showtime.

The curtain rolled up; August Beausoleil, jaunty and eager, a spring in his step, sailed into the center of the stage, the bright place, and began all his familiar routines, welcoming the ladies and gents to this, the final performance of the Follies.

And then, to everyone's astonishment, he changed the order. It would not be the Wildroot Sisters opening this time.

"Ladies and gents, I bring you the star of our show, the one you've been waiting for, the beautiful, the sublime, the engaging Miss Ginger!"

Ginger was caught utterly unprepared, and in the ticking seconds, she processed this shocking thing, collected herself, and plunged out to a warm applause, once again in her bottle-green gown, looking as heavenly as Charles had ever seen her. She paused, center stage.

There was a great hush.

She bowed, she smiled at the balcony, she smiled at the orchestra, and she smiled at her parents.

"I wish to dedicate this performance to my mother and father," she said, into the deepening silence.

Charles, from the wings, ached for her and rejoiced in her, all at once.

She began with "Jeanie with the Light Brown Hair," which she sang sweetly, and with the warmth that Stephen Foster had intended.

Mrs. Jones sat motionless.

•

Soon, Ginger was singing her repertoire of American ballads, one after another, while her mother sat like a gravestone, and the crowd was craning to see how the Joneses were responding to their daughter. Something was happening. Ginger was pouring beauty and joy into these familiar songs, transforming each of them into something magical. She was singing as she had never sung before.

But they saw nothing. The pair sat silently, a black pool in front-center seats.

She bowed and abandoned the stage, and August swiftly continued the show, bringing on the Wildroot Sisters, and Harry the Juggler, and then Wayne Windsor, who had worked up a new routine.

"I'm going to tell you about a railroad man who figured out how to get rich," he began. "This fellow knew where the traffic was, and found a way to make his fortune. His secret was simple. He built a railroad to Hades. A high-speed state-of-the-art railroad, that hauled multitudes down the slope. At first he thought coaches would be all he needed, but he soon discovered that parlor cars were in great demand. The more luxurious the better. He was catering to clientele of the better class. So he began adding luxurious and roomy cars, one after the others, and his business improved. . . ."

The audience was plainly enjoying this, enjoying Windsor's attempt to entertain the railroad man in their midst. There were chuckles and cheer, but not from that bleak little pool of darkness front center.

The performers were watching from the wings, watching to see if the couple would ever smile, ever settle in and enjoy the show. And gradually, it all became a contest, with each act striving to entertain the Joneses.

Harry and Art Grabowski put on a fine show, choreographing a brawl that set the crowd to howling. Every time Art threw a haymaker, Harry did cartwheels, until laughter rippled through the opera house and continued almost nonstop. Then the Marbury Trio tapped out to center stage, tapped intricate steps, did a buck and wing, delighted the crowd—except for the two who could not be entertained, and who didn't move a muscle.

And August had never been better at introducing his acts, one after another, each given a special send-off that wrought eagerness in all those people out there in the dusky seats.

The Genius and Ethel wrought good cheer that eve. The Genius was especially outrageous and superior, comparing Pocatello to Butte, scorning everything and everyone, while Ethel bled the hot air out of the blowhard. The crowd chuckled. Many of them had run into self-serving people bent on letting the world know how superior they were. And still the Joneses sat, immobile.

Ginger watched them anxiously, and was so restless backstage that Charles finally caught her hand and held it quietly. She looked stricken at first, but his smile wrought one in her, and she was all right.

When intermission came, the performers watched anxiously to see whether the Joneses would rise, retreat to the lobby, and vanish. Instead, they sat silently, unmoved, unmovable, while the patrons refreshed themselves and drifted back to their seats.

The second act was much like the first, with the crowd enjoying the performers while Ginger's parents sat sternly, revealing not so much as a smile or raised eyebrow. They did not clap. They did not nod, or share their delight with those in neighboring seats.

When Ginger returned, she told her eager listeners that she would sing more ballads, and invited the crowd to sing along. She offered them "Careless Love," "Swing Low Sweet Chariot," "Clementine," "Down in the Valley," and concluded with "Buffalo Gals."

Nothing could be further from what her mother intended than these old songs, and Charles knew that Ginger was carefully, deliberately, staking out her independence. He watched them closely, but saw not the slightest shift of a muscle. They had been cast in bronze.

Ginger was watching them, too, as she sang, and registering her mother's every movement. And then it was over, and the crowd clapped politely, almost as if these people were afraid to appreciate the wayward daughter.

The show ended that way, the crowd subdued, as if the stern disapproval of the Joneses had triumphed over their own appreciation of a happy evening. They had seen good vaudeville, and had enjoyed top talent, and yet when the curtain rang down, they left quietly, soberly, defeated by Ginger's parents.

Charles watched them rise, stretch a little, and make their way to the aisle, and up the lobby, and vanish into the night, where their enameled cabriolet was waiting. He could not fathom what they were thinking, and no one else could, either. The performers felt blue; they had turned the whole show into an effort to break the ice, win the good cheer of those two people. And had failed.

Ginger was inscrutable, too. Whatever she felt, she was not sharing.

This was the end for Pocatello. He watched the performers pack up. There were accordions and guitars to put into cases, a few props to bundle, Harry the Juggler's array of cups and saucers and knives to box up, costumes to return to trunks, and they did these things in deep silence, unsure of themselves. It was as if Ginger's mother had not only thwarted the entire audience, but thwarted each performer who had sought her approval. She had approved of none, and now it lay like a blanket over the company.

But there was always tomorrow. They would catch a train for Boise early in the morning, and would be setting up shop in the opera house in the state capital late that afternoon. Another opening. Another crowd, this time more likely to enjoy the talent.

Charles walked back to the hotel with Ginger, both of them lost in silence.

He was worn, and crawled into bed ahead of her. She took her time washing up, and when she did emerge she was in a bright crimson wrapper.

"Let's leave Pocatello behind, forever," she said, and reached for him.

FORTY-THREE

B oise was surely the place where good things would happen. It was a bustling state capital, with plenty of cash. It had a fine, large theater, the Columbia, with a thousand seats. Fill those seats for several performances and the troupe would bridge the gap in late December, and start along the West Coast with the new year.

Charles Pomerantz brimmed with hope. He had done everything it was possible to do. In a short time, when Spokane canceled, he had put together two Idaho dates, looked to all the details, and somehow managed to move the company, which was now quartered at the comfortable Overland Hotel, close to the theater. The Union Pacific had delivered them on time. The trip was restful. The performers were lodged, and spreading out to look at the handsome town. And they had a day of rest. The first show would be tomorrow eve.

There was one worrisome puzzle. Only three hundred seats had sold for opening night, and a handful for other nights, and none for the matinees. He contacted the owner and operator of the Columbia to find out a few things. The man's name was Pincart, James Almond Pincart. Maybe Pincart could point to something that needed doing.

The man had not been helpful. He charged a flat rent, not a percentage, which gave him little incentive to fill the seats. He was of the crafty, calculating sort, always with an eye to protecting himself and his property. In the early negotiations, Charles had learned to expect nothing, and to follow through on everything, from printing of tickets to making sure the bills were posted and the ads scheduled in the daily *Statesman*.

He found Pincart peering at his ledgers in the small office at the back of the Columbia Theater.

"Well, you're not selling seats," Pincart said. "I knew it. You'll have empty houses."

"What's not working, sir?"

"The ads in the paper. They buried them, back of the classified. They like to do that."

Charles pushed an issue of the daily across the prim desk, and thumbed it open to the inside of the rear page, where the announcement of the Beausoleil Brothers Follies was buried.

"The publisher, Wool, he doesn't like money leaving town. He says every cent taken out by a touring company's a cent that Boise merchants don't get, so he buries ads like yours."

"But not locals?"

"Nope. When the Boise Marching Band advertises a concert here, Wool runs the ad on page two, prime spot, where it gets seen. A Boise band, the ticket money stays in town, you see."

Charles stared. "I wish you had told me. We could have insisted it get better play in that paper."

Pincart shrugged. "No skin off my teeth," he said. "Wool's right. Keep the money in town, not let it ride the next train out."

"I was called away, couldn't be here, and now these ads are buried. And you let it ride?"

"Small crowds, it's easier to clean the house," Pincart said.

"What else isn't right?"

"Bill-poster, name's Thompson, he never got them up. You got cheated."

"What?"

"Cold spell, he didn't feel like going out, got only two, three pasted up. Don't know what he did with the rest. Hid them, I guess. Here's his invoice, sixty playbills up, eighty-seven dollars."

"Say that again?"

"He didn't paste up the playbills, worthless sort, and here's his charges."

A desolation stole through Charles. "And you didn't wire me, or inform me?"

"No skin off my teeth," Pincart said.

"Where are the sheets? Who can I get to paste them up? Can you show me the walls where they go up?"

"Thompson's probably used them to start fires in his stove by now. They're evidence against him, you know, so he no doubt burned the whole lot."

Charles stared. "I've got no ads anyone's seen, and no playbills around town, and no seats sold. And you let it pass?"

"Saves me work, cleaning up. I hate to fill the theater. Janitors complain and want overtime. People are all swine, leaving stuff on the floor. I ought to charge a clean-up fee on top of the tickets."

"Are the tickets all printed?"

"Here's the invoice."

"May I see them?"

"Printer's holding on to last three nights until you pay him."

"Steer me to Thompson. I want to get the bills and find someone to paste them up. He must have a sub."

"Now, you don't want to disturb a sick man, and I'll say absolutely not. He'll catch the pneumonia."

"Where can I get flyers printed fast? And boys to pass them out?"

"I despise flyers. People bring them in, drop them on my floors, and I have to cart all that rubbish out."

"What is the other paper?"

"*The Evening Mail,* just out today."

Pincart looked almost triumphant.

Charles snapped up the Thompson invoice. It had a street address. He stuffed it in his pocket.

"I'll expect rental from you for the next five days, before showtime tonight," Pincart said. "Or the curtain doesn't go up."

Charles wrapped his coat and scarf around him, bolted through the cold theater and out into bright light, and waylaid the first man he came across. The capital was serene.

"Pardon, sir, looking for an address. Can you direct me to Myrtle Sreet?"

The man could and did, and Charles raced in that direction. There was no time. No time at all. But maybe he could prevent disaster. Four blocks later he found Myrtle, and a shabby bungalow at 400 south so poorly marked it was all guesswork. But he bolted up two stairs, rapped on the white door with peeling paint, and soon confronted a whiskery man in his grimy union suit and britches.

"Ah, you've come to pay up," Thompson said, looking Pomerantz over.

"Maybe, maybe not. It depends on whether you do your job, now, this afternoon, every bill up."

"Too cold," Thompson said.

"How many were you to put up?"

"I dunno. The usual."

"How many did you post?"

"Two, three."

"I want the playbills and you can give me the name and address of a sub."

Thompson yawned. "You sure are making a fuss."

The man was soaked in rotgut, and exuded it.

"You mind if I come in and look around?"

"Well, truth to tell, the bills are at the theater. Pincart's sitting on them."

"You mind if I look?"

"There's two, three here."

"Why is Pincart not putting them out?"

"He doesn't like vaudeville, but doesn't mind renting the stage."

"You mind putting up the bills you've got, and any you can find?"

"It sure is cold, old boy."

He saw three or four large playbills lying in a corner. "I'll take those," he said, and tried to edge past the owner of the manse, but a hard arm shot out and blocked him. "They'll cost you a dollar apiece," Thompson said, a smirk building. "Lay out five."

"I'll find the ones in the theater," Charles said. "If Pincart's got them."

The door turned him back to Myrtle Street. It was too late to paste up three-sheet playbills around Boise. He needed a printer. In the space of an hour he had gone from optimism to utter desperation. It was time to get August and the performers in on it. They could hand out flyers as well as anyone, and it might generate some interest in the show.

The job printer on Fourth Street turned out to be a gruff old pulp-nosed codger in an ink-stained smock. Charles sketched out his needs: Beausoleil Brothers Follies, Vaudeville, Columbia Theater, December seven to thirteen, featuring Ginger, Wayne Windsor, Harry the Juggler, The Wildroot Sisters, The Marbury Trio, The Genius and Ethel, The Grab Bag. Each evening at seven, two o'clock matinees on the eighth and twelfth. Advance sales at Rubachek's Pharmacy. Fifty cents to a dollar fifty. The biggest show ever.

"Small flyers, you choose the size, a thousand, as soon as possible, an hour or two if you can manage it."

The printer eyed Charles as if he were daft. "An hour or two! Have you the slightest knowledge of my art? An hour or two. Judas priest, where have you been all your life?"

"Sir, you can set that type in twenty minutes, I can proof it in one, you can make corrections in five, and crank out a thousand in an hour on that flatbed right there."

The printer's eyes gleamed with malice. "Supposing I can. What makes you think I will?"

"I'll pay extra. Half again your charge."

"Oho, bribing me, are you? You can pick up the first hundred at noon, day after tomorrow, and wait for more stock to come in before I print the rest."

"Sir, I see all sorts of sheets on your shelves, different sizes, but they'll do, if you don't mind. We can hand out all sorts of flyers. Whatever's in stock. Colored paper, too."

"You think that, do you? And has it never occurred to you that those sheets are reserved for printing jobs ordered locally, in time for Christmas?"

"There's a paper cutter, sir. Sitting right there. I'll cut large sheets myself, and ready them for you."

"Just so you can walk the cash out of town. That's the trouble with you travelers. You think you can come in and skim the cash from good folks here and catch the next train out with a pocketful."

Charles had heard that before. "You own this job shop, sir?"

"Nope. I run it, but the *Statesman* owns it."

"Is there another job shop here?"

"I leave that to you to discover, my good man. Now, if we're done?"

Charles plunged outside, into an icy wind, the sort of wind that withered and killed anything fragile. Boise, a bustling, prosperous town, didn't know the troupe was about to open, stay a week, and generate marvels, laughs, musical delights, and amazing feats of dexterity. If there were any playbills up, Charles had not seen them, but some tickets had sold even so.

He hurried back to the Overland, against the arctic wind, and hunted down August, who was in his room with the cashbox, filling brown pay envelopes.

Tersely, Charles outlined the events of the past hour, sparing his colleague nothing. August stared at his pay envelopes, at the declining stack of greenbacks in the cashbox, and nodded. The show was in peril again.

"And Pincart wants the balance in advance," Charles added.

"Anything left?"

"*The Evening Mail*, we might persuade to print flyers. Or some sort of extra edition. If it's not too late."

August seemed almost to fold up. "I suppose we could just tell them what we're up against and see what happens," he said. "We could bring some acts with us. They've got stories. A good reporter could make something of them. Maybe we could give the weekly a scoop—if they'd go for it. But we're down to the wire, Charles."

There weren't many of the troupe in the Overland Hotel that hour, but they found Wayne Windsor, Ethel Wildroot, and Art and Harry Grabowski. That would do.

The weekly, it turned out, was near the capitol, and survived largely by publishing legals, the endless public notices that emanated from a seat of government. Its editorial content was sober, with business stories dominating. It seemed the last place for a special edition about a vaudeville troupe. But who could say?

Its owner, Harvey Pelican, greeted the visitors cordially. Considering that he published a weekly loaded with legal notices, he seemed almost jovial. Nothing so exotic as a vaudeville troupe had ever penetrated his sanctum sanctorum.

"If you've time, sir, I'd simply like to tell you our story, and our dilemma," Charles said.

"Have a cup of cold mean java, there, and spill the beans, Mr. Pomerantz," the owner said. He plainly wished to be diverted. And that's how it went, the next hour. They diverted him. They told him their tale of woe. And asked for help.

"You tickle my funny bone," Pelican said. "Let's whip up a few and see how it goes."

FORTY-FOUR

The Western Union boy found Ginger in the lobby of the Overland Hotel, and handed her a yellow envelope. A telegram? Who could be sending it? She pulled it open and found the message printed in block capitals: MAZEPPA JONES DEAD OVERDOSE TODAY PARKINSON.

She could not fathom it. Her mother? Dead? Overdose? Suicide? The reporter had swiftly sent word. And probably had another sensational story. She read and reread it, trying to unlock its terse message, more and more shaken. Her mother did have laudanum and used it frequently for whatever ailed her. And it was dangerous. But overdose?

Her mother? Had Ginger's flight from her family anything to do with it? Of course, of course. Disobedient daughter, mother gives up living. Her mother's revenge. *You failed me, so I will give up my one, my only life. You are what I lived for, and now I have nothing, except the blue laudanum bottle and a teaspoon.* A flood of something unfathomable flowed through Ginger. She could not say what. Her mother was hanging a crown of thorns upon her, and she felt the thorns cut into her heart.

She felt no rush of sorrow or loss; that was impossible. Maybe sometime, a few years away, she might. She didn't feel weighted; quite the opposite. Her spirit seemed to float free. No longer was her mother trying to work her will upon her daughter without the slightest thought of what Penelope might want from life.

And yet, somehow, Ginger felt sadness steal through her. There was love, too. She suddenly understood how starved Mazeppa was for attention, how hollow was her mother's passage through the days and years, and how desperate her mother had been to find a reason to live, finally settling on shaping her daughter.

Then Ginger couldn't think at all, and sat numbly, the yellow telegram in hand, her mind a jumble of conflicting feelings. She did not know the passage of time, only that she was paralyzed, in the hotel, and that was how Charles found her some while later.

"Where've you been, Ginger?" he asked.

She handed him the yellow sheet. He glanced at it.

"Oh, Ginger," he said. "Oh my God."

She nodded.

"Let me take you back to the room," he said.

She let him lift her out of her chair, and let him guide her down the dark hallway, let him unlock the door, let him guide her in, let him guide her to the bed and ease her down upon it, she looking upward at her husband.

He shut the door, and sat beside her.

"You don't have to make any decisions," he said, which puzzled her.

But then it grew upon her that there were decisions that needed to be made. Whether to sing that opening eve. Whether to go back to Pocatello, the funeral, her father.

But she could not make them. She felt small and helpless, and just wanted to lie quietly, without decisions.

But he made one for her, then and there.

"You won't want to sing at this time," he said.

She wasn't so sure of that. She thought she might, she might sing a canary song, a bright song, a song of her own. But his decision had foreclosed that.

"I'll talk to August," he said. "Change the show around. This would be a good night to do it. Small crowd."

"Small crowd?"

"Yeah, a lot of trouble. The bills didn't go up; no one knows we're here. But tomorrow we'll have flyers to hand out, and maybe make some money."

She understood none of it.

He vanished. She stared at the ceiling. Oddly, she could barely remember her mother, or anything about her. She could draw her father's image into her thoughts, but not her mother's. She liked her father; she was not afraid of him. But mostly, she just lay quietly, uncertain, uncomfortable with any thought or plan.

When Charles did return some while later, he handed her a train ticket. "There's an eastbound express at seven, gets you to Pocatello before dawn. Lousy schedule, but that's all I could do. You'll have a room at the Bannock Hotel there for as many nights as you need. I can't go with you. There's trouble here, so you'll be alone. But I know you'll be all right, and secure, and doing what needs doing."

"I don't know what needs doing."

"You'll want to be at your father's side, for your sake, for his. And to quiet the newspaper, which is likely to make much of this. Be thinking of what you'll say to that reporter, Parkinson."

"What to say?"

"He will want to know if your mother, ah, abandoned life because of you. Your departure."

"I think I should stay here. I have nothing left in Pocatello."

"You have ghosts, and they need to be laid to rest, Ginger. Memories . . ."

"But I'll miss the show. Several shows."

"Yes, and the shows will miss you."

"But Charles . . . ," she said, knowing she would go. Knowing it was something she had to do.

"You'll regret not going, and always be grateful you put your mother to rest," he said.

She wasn't so sure of it. He could not know what her mother was like.

The talk ended that way, she uneasy, he firm. But she welcomed his firmness. It was as if he was, momentarily, more father than lover.

She whiled away the afternoon, packed a small valise, grew fretful when the performers headed for the Columbia Theater and she was not among them. But then Charles escorted her to the Union Pacific station, and waited with her until the eastbound local huffed in, sending up clouds of steam in the chill air.

"You have everything? Money?"

She nodded, and he escorted her to the coach, gave her a squeeze, and helped her up the stool, and onto the steel step of the coach. And then he was gone. He didn't linger. He didn't wait on the platform while she settled in a seat, but was gone, and it reminded her that something was amiss, and he was trying to deal with it.

The train lurched eastward, its whistle mournful in the inky dark. Beyond the lights of the city lay nothing at all, and nothing but night lay beyond the windows. The coach was mostly empty, the passengers mostly male, and all were keeping to themselves. The coach exuded an odor, and she wondered what it might be, whether a leaking water closet, or ancient sweat, or scratchy wet wool, but most of all the odor was despair. It was the train to no-where.

She sat quietly through the night, occasionally passing a flash of light that signaled something, perhaps a town. But mostly she was tunneling toward the unknown. When at last the weary conductor announced Pocatello, she collected her wits, pulled her satchel off the rack, and waited for the train to squeal to a halt. Then she stepped into a cold night. There were no hacks. She waited for someone, anyone, and found no one. The two others who left the train vanished.

Well, this was her hometown. The bag was heavy, so she left it on a luggage shelf. She would send someone from the hotel for it. And then she walked toward the Ban-nock Hotel, through the wee hours, a time so devoid of life that not even footpads would be about. When at last she turned into the hotel, its entry barely lit, she found no clerk, nor did ringing a counter bell bring one.

But a while later, she didn't know how long, a skinny man appeared, apologized, put her in her room, and vol-unteered to go for the bag himself after she had signed in as Mrs. Charles Pomerantz.

"Never see anyone at this hour," he said.

"Here's a dollar," she said.

"Holy cats," he said, fingering the bill as if it were a thousand-dollar note.

Fifteen minutes later, he was knocking on her door with the bag, looking like he wanted to come in and see where the waning night might lead.

"My mother died," she said, and closed the door.

She lay inert, dressed, on the bed until midmorning, when a thunderous thumping on the door galvanized her. She rose, slowly, feeling unwashed, knowing who it would be. Parkinson, the reporter, who regularly read hotel reg-isters.

"Please wait," she said, and without listening for a reply from the other side of the flimsy door, she found a washbasin and pitcher, poured water into the basin, and wiped away the travel from her face with the cool water.

"Hey, it's me," Parkinson said.

She took her time, all the while wondering what he might ask, and how it might hurt her, or how it might inflame Pocatello. When she felt more presentable, she opened, but did not invite him in.

"Saw you were here," he said, doffing a fedora. "Ask some questions?"

"Thank you for wiring me," she said.

"Yeah, and that's the story. You came back to bury her. How come, given the little spat or two? And escaping from her upstairs window?"

"I came to bury my mother."

"Yeah, but why?"

"I think that is my business. Now, if you don't mind, I'll try to nap."

She started to close the door, but found his foot blocking her. "Not so fast, sweetheart. Now, here you are, even before your old man's set the funeral day. You regret ditching your old lady?"

"They sent me," she said, and regretted it.

"Who's they? The Follies? They want to keep their nose clean, right?"

"I came because it was the thing to do, and now please remove your foot. I need rest."

"Naw, my foot in the door's gotten me more stories than my pencil in hand."

"Then your foot will feel what comes next," she said, and swung the door hard. He yanked his fancy shoe away in the nick, and the door clattered shut.

"That's how you treat the man who wired you?" he asked in the hallway.

"I will talk to you after the funeral," she said.

He tried a few more gambits, and finally left, and she

was back on her bed, engulfed in the silence of the morning, and an odd sense of loss for her mother. She understood her mother at last, and the understanding freed her. For Mazeppa Jones, marriage had been a prison.

But she was allowed no rest. When she opened to the next knock, an hour later, she discovered her father, in black, solemn, his gaze gentle. She hesitated.

"May I?" he asked.

She nodded. He stopped in, eyeing her quietly. "The reporter, causing trouble," he said, trumping her question. "I'm grateful you came."

He saw her weariness. "If you'd like, I'd like to take you out. I have a club, and we can dine quietly, away from prying eyes."

She nodded. "Let me freshen," she said.

He met her in the lobby, and he walked briskly toward the river, and a brick building there he said was the Bannock Club. In short order, he was seating her in an obscure corner. They were left to themselves, the dinner courses arriving.

"I'll tell you about it, if you want. If not, I'll just have a quiet meal, and be on my way."

She nodded.

"Mazeppa always had dreams for you," he said. "I never paid heed until you left us, and never really understood. I think I do now. I didn't understand, and went along with it, paid the bills, thought we were simply giving you the best that we could give a gifted daughter. I missed the other. Until your barefoot escape . . ."

"Thank you," she said.

"I make no apologies," he said. "Not for me, not for her. No matter how you add it up, you had a privileged upbringing."

"But it wasn't me," she said. "I didn't count."

He quieted, dabbled with his potatoes, and stared.

"Let bygones be bygones," he said. "I need you. The

house is empty. I'd like you to stay on, live as you choose. I will make sure you have everything. I'd be pleased if you resumed your life as a concert performer, but wouldn't insist on it."

Oddly, the arrangement tempted her. The person who had tormented her, driven her to flight, was gone. Her father, well, she could manage life in the same house with him.

But the yearning for that vanished.

"I . . . I'm afraid not," she said. "I love my husband, I love the stage. I'll catch the next train to Boise. But thanks."

He grinned unexpectedly. "Now I'll have to deal with that rascal reporter," he said.

FORTY-FIVE

The Boise opening went badly. The cavernous Columbia Theater was mostly empty, as bad an omen as there was. August peered out upon row after row of blank seats, each a rebuke to his company. Out there in the darkness a couple hundred people were scattered about, many of them in cheaper balcony seats. The hollow theater subdued them as much as it subdued the performers.

August was used to bad shows, but somehow this one abraded him. His ceremonial posture was too jaunty. His apology for not offering the star of the show, Ginger, was too forced. His easy humor, intended to put the people out there in a good mood, fled him.

"And now, ladies and gents, the one, the only Laverne Wildroot," he said, and she bounced out to the limelight in the middle of silence. And trilled her songs in a vacuum.

"And now, ladies and gents, the masters of acrobatics, The Grab Bag," he said, but the act fell flat. Harry, out of what should have been the audience, was off. Had he bulled his way onstage from a packed house, it would have been comic. Instead, it seemed like a ritualized rehearsal. But they tried. August gave them credit for that. They careened about like demented gladiators.

Wayne Windsor's monologue fell flat. He tried several tacks, trying to pick up a thread that would delight those scattered people, and he couldn't. They didn't chuckle. They didn't appreciate. And they didn't clap.

Harry the Juggler performed flawlessly, and no one noticed. The Marbury Trio tapped and two-stepped as elegantly as ever, and the tapping sounded like hail on the window, and the audience stared. The Genius gave it a try, insulting Boise, insulting the audience, insulting Idaho, insulting men, women, and children and dogs, and no one howled.

At the intermission some of the audience vanished, leaving even fewer to enjoy the second set. From the wings, the company watched inertly, knowing they were witnessing something as bleak as they had ever seen onstage. Ethel Wildroot stood there, shaking her head. LaVerne Wildroot looked to be ready to weep.

August himself was about ready to weep, too, with cash receipts for the show running about two hundred dollars, and bills piling up by the hour. He watched the critic from the *Statesman* clamp his felt hat over his slicked hair, and slouch his way toward the exit. No telling what would be in the paper, if anything. The ultimate thumbs-down was to say nothing at all.

The show seemed to end with a whimper, and after a scattered clap or two, the remaining patrons wound their scarves around their necks and vanished. The theater was large, quiet, and empty.

August noted a fair-haired man in a topcoat working

his way through the performers, who were standing mute in the wings, reluctant to call it quits.

"Where may I find LaVerne Wildroot?" he asked, politely.

The Genius jerked a thumb in her direction, and the local gent headed her way, hat in hand, and introduced himself as Stanford Sebring. It was easy to see he wasn't poor.

"Miss Wildroot, I just had to come back here to tell you how enchanted I was, and how much I liked the opening song," he said.

A stage-door Johnny. That was the last thing August anticipated on a night like this, when there were no stars in the sky.

"Why, I'm so glad," she said. "You came all the way back here to say that? My goodness. You've surprised me."

"It took some doing," Sebring said. "I thought, if I don't try, she'll never know. So I found an unlocked door. In fact, I think you are the finest songstress I've ever heard."

August had never seen a stage-door Johnny flatter the cast after a debacle like tonight's. But that was fine. If there were stage-door Johnnies around, all wasn't lost. LaVerne was swiftly turning into a coquette, and August heard her say she'd like to get into street clothes, and yes, she'd love to do a turn with him, and yes, wait in the Green Room.

It gave August odd solace. It was still show business, even in Boise, in the worst opening in recent memory. He glanced bleakly at Charles, who was holding a strongbox with the night's take, which was going to be pathetic.

"Bad, right?"

"Worst ever," Charles said.

"Well, maybe we can make it up when we get out to Seattle."

"August, I wired them days ago, and haven't heard a word."

"Carelessness. It's December, and people have other things in mind."

"I'm glad you think so," Charles said.

August didn't like the sound of that. But there were pressing things, such as paying bills, keeping the theater open, and in a couple of days, another round of payroll for the acts.

They repaired to an alcove off the Green Room and counted the take, which came to a hundred ninety dollars and change. Pincart wanted two hundred just to keep the doors open for the remaining performances.

"Guess we'd better shovel it all his way. We can add the rest. If you have it," Charles said.

"I was keeping it for the flyers."

"Better tell the acts they'll be out pushing flyers all day tomorrow."

Harvey Pelican over at the weekly would do a thousand flyers, gussied up with a few stories about the acts. He thought it would be fun, and a way to needle the daily. But the flyers wouldn't be ready until morning. And then August intended to push them into every store and restaurant and bar, hand them to people on the street, drop them into government offices, leave them on counters in stores, tacked to electrical poles, stuffed into mailboxes, and pushed under doors. He would have his entire ensemble at it, including the hands, the musicians, the acts, and Charles and himself. One way or another, Boise would be given the message: The Beausoleil Brothers Follies was in town, at the Columbia, and tickets were going fast. See Ginger! See Wayne Windsor! See the Marbury Trio! Laugh with The Grab Bag. Enjoy The Genius and Ethel. Get your seats fast at Rubachek's Pharmacy, open all day, every day.

"What was the takeout?" Windsor asked.

"Under two hundred."

"And how long can this keep up?"

"About another hour," Charles said. "Or maybe a half hour."

"Never fear. LaVerne's new Johnny will fork over. He's not wearing cheap rags."

August had entertained fantasies like that in years gone by, and had never seen one materialize. Maybe someone would like to own a piece of a vaudeville company.

"I should have been a barber," Windsor said. "You get to talk to the guy while you're shaving him and he can't talk back, and if he does, you nick him. He's in the chair and he's gotta listen. I'd like that. Captive audience every time, and if he whines he bleeds. And barbers have a regular income."

August didn't contradict him.

"I live high, never worry about the future. There's no point in show business if you don't live life to the hilt," Windsor said.

"Then you'll do better on the big-time stages."

"Hey, August, here I'm top banana."

August made some notations in a pocket ledger, and closed his cashbox.

"Hey, what are you going to do with that?" Windsor said.

"Add eight dollars of my own, making it two hundred, and then I'll give it all to Pincart. He wants cash in advance to keep the doors open the next four performances. Fifty a day."

"Out of our paychecks, right?"

"We have to fill a lot of seats starting tomorrow."

"This company is sitting here without a dime?"

"And a stack of bills. Like the hotel. Maybe that'll inspire you to get the flyers out tomorrow."

"Nah, it'll inspire me to wire my agent about work."

"I've had the same idea," August said. "If we make it to the coast, we'll be okay. But that's a ways off. I don't know who'd employ me."

"Is this secret?"

"Anyone who has eyes can see it. No, it's not."

August left the rent money in the manager's strongbox, and headed into a bitter night. The acts had been alerted. Show up at ten for duty on the streets. The show needed a jolt, and fast, and flyers were the only route open. There had been very little grumbling. Anyone who had looked out upon all those vacant seats, each with its bleak message, knew something needed to be done. He'd send men into women's stores, and the show girls into men's stores, and see what that did for sales.

He debated whether to spend something on a nightcap, and decided against it. His early life had taught him a few things. Just now he was wondering whether that would be his fate once again. But not if he could help it, and he thought he could.

In the hotel lobby he ran into Charles, who was bundled up for a cold walk.

"I got a wire from Ginger's old man. She's on the westbound ninety-seven, due here in a few minutes. Want to come?"

"He wired you? Did he wire you about canceling that suit?"

Charles stuffed the yellow sheet into August's hands. It was terse.

"I'll come along," August said. "Maybe she'll have full pockets."

They braved the whipping air that scoured warmth from Boise along with smoke from a lot of chimneys. They walked grimly, straight into the wind, and that's how life was in Boise, so far. The station was cold, but a relief from the wind. The ticket window was shut. Anyone boarding here would need to buy passage from the conductor.

But the express train did roll in on time, and first off was Ginger, carrying her satchel, and glad to be wel-

comed. Charles pecked her cheek and grabbed her bag.
There was no hack in sight, and August was glad of it. A
dime saved was a dime to eat with.

"So, what happened? Did you bury your mother?"

"No, but I did go to a private visitation with my father.
I said good-bye, and he put me on the train again."

"You contacted your father?"

"That reporter was busy. He's still looking for stories,
like a runaway singer who scorns her mother's funeral. He
told my father I'd arrived, and my father came to me, and
we met privately."

"What happened, if I may ask?"

"He asked me to stay on, take my mother's place in the
house, and resume a concert career."

"And?"

"I told him I loved my husband and I loved show business. He accepted it, and that was all. He upgraded my
ticket; I came back in a palace car."

"Did he talk about the lawsuit? Like dropping it?"

"We talked about honoring my mother."

The wind blew them back to the hotel, a gale gently
pushing at their backs.

"Tomorrow, Ginger, we have work for everyone in
the show, handing out flyers. But Charles will tell you
about it."

She nodded. August left them there, in the lobby, and
headed into the night once again. He had one more mission, which was to drop in at the *Statesman* and see what
sort of review the critic had penned. You never knew.
Dour critics, sitting three rows back, sometimes wrote
fine reviews. Other times, the affable critic, looking plumb
happy, would butcher the show. Most reviews were mixed.
That was all right. It was vaudeville, variety, and no one
had to like every act.

The paper was easy to get to, in the shadow of the capitol. He entered a well-lit pressroom, found a live body,

reading proof, introduced himself, and asked to see the review, if any.

The gent, in a stained vest, wire-rimmed spectacles, and a green-billed visor, nodded, pulled off galley proofs from the spike until he found what he was looking for.

"Dull," was the tagline.

"The Beausoleil Follies opened last eve to a sparse, cold, and bored crowd, a condition that didn't change an iota the entire evening, except the audience diminished as the evening crept onward."

There was more of that, and a concluding line. "Keep the cash in Boise, and spend it locally," it said.

Beausoleil read it carefully and handed it back.

"Thanks," he said.

"Glad to be of service," the proofreader replied.

FORTY-SIX

The telegram, this time from Chicago, made Charles Pomerantz's knees go rubbery. It was from an acquaintance named Martin Beck, who was now employed by the Orpheum circuit on the West Coast. It announced that Orpheum had bought the Olympia Theater, the Puyallup Opera House, the Seattle Theater, the Tacoma Theater, and was negotiating the purchase of Reed's Opera House in Salem, Parker Opera House in Eugene, the Marquam Grand Opera House in Portland, Cordray's New Theater in Portland, and Park Theater in Portland. And bookings made by the previous owners would be canceled immediately. Circuit vaudeville on the coast would start in January.

There went the tour.

He should have guessed. Circuits were fast replacing

individual vaudeville companies. Circuits put individual acts on tour forty weeks a year, moving from city to city, providing constant fresh entertainment along the circuits. The arrival of a rail network offering swift transport from town to town had made circuits possible. New shows, on the move.

Charles stared at the offending yellow paper, feeling the clutch of despair grab his chest. Of those on Beck's list, five had been booked by the Beausoleil Brothers Follies. Nothing in the telegram said anything about Northern California, but the Orpheum was already strong in San Francisco, and the outlook there was just as bleak.

Charles paced his room, knew he must find August, and fight—if there was any way to fight anything.

He found August in the lobby, handing out stacks of gaudy flyers to the show people. The whole troupe was there, save for The Genius, who refused to demean himself with anything resembling work, and had wandered off looking for a saloon that served pretzels for breakfast. Oddly, The Genius' loutishness didn't affect the rest. They had seen the empty house, and knew what needed to be done.

"On the streets, to anyone who'll take one," August said. "Don't neglect children. In stores, to any that will post them in the windows. In restaurants and saloons, any livery barn, on any counter, in any office, in any station of public place, state office, on any tram, in any seat of any hack—it all depends on you," August said, quietly. "Hire a newsboy to hawk them."

"What if we run out?" Ethel said.

"There'll be more here. We ordered a thousand. Eight thousand people live here."

"Why didn't the bills go up in time?" LaVerne Wildroot asked.

"That's complicated. The bill-poster claimed it was too cold. The house manager seems to enjoy embarrassing touring companies. The newspaper's gospel is to keep all cash in Boise."

Several laughed. Boise was cleaning them out of their last nickel.

"What happens if no one buys tickets?"

August smiled. "I hope you don't mind selling apples on street corners."

The whole crowd was pretty serious. They each collected an armload, arranged among themselves what areas they would cover, and hastened into the biting wind. There wouldn't be many people lounging along the streets this December day.

August watched them go, and grinned at Charles. "There's always a way," he said.

Charles did what he hated to do, and placed the telegram in August's hands. August read it slowly, reread it, and seemed to turn into marble. He said nothing for a while, stared into the distance, even though they were in a warm hotel.

"We were running from this," August said.

"It came faster than we thought."

"Do you have a *Julius Cahn Guide*?"

"In my bags."

The *Official Theatrical Guide* listed every opera house in every state and in Indian Territory, with all relevant contacts.

"Maybe we can reroute the tour," August said. "Wherever the rails go. Nevada, who knows?"

"Not much in Nevada," Charles said. "But there's houses on the coast not bought up. We'd have competition from the circuit."

August laughed shortly. Operators of the new circuits knew how to deal with competition, including buying up opera houses, cut-rate ticket pricing, bringing in big-name talent, bribing suppliers such as printers, paying off bill-posters to do bad work, stealing acts. Their inventiveness knew no boundaries.

"Wire Graeb. We need cash. Two thousand. Book us straight down the Rockies, Wyoming, Colorado, starting now. If we can."

Bland Graeb was the company agent in Chicago, the man who usually cut deals, booked theaters, auditioned acts when needed. It would have to be Graeb's money, and he would be the naysayer.

"There's no north-south rail in the Rockies. We're heading for the coast. Like Portland, there's the Park Theater, and the Baker. Smaller places. Not bought up—yet."

"Right into the circuit. But that's the game."

"What have we got?"

"Bills. Printer, hotel, payroll coming up."

Charles grinned. August grinned back. It helped to grin when your neck was in the guillotine.

"How are we gonna get out of here?"

"Sell The Genius to the nearest medical school for a cadaver."

It would be up to Charles. He was the wizard with the telegraph, and could say more in fewer words. He wondered how he'd pay Western Union for the amount of wire traffic he would launch.

"I'll go push some flyers," August said. "We've got to fill the house tonight."

With that, Charles headed for his room to get his *Theatrical Guide,* and then to the Western Union office, at the station. He had the sinking feeling that it was all for show, all to be able to say that they tried every avenue, every angle.

But August had a firsthand acquaintance with miracles, and scrambling on the streets of Gotham had taught him a thing or two. They had booked this area because the circuits hadn't started up here, and a touring company could still schedule its route. Back east, there were cut-throat syndicates, swiftly turning the entertainment business into a few fierce rivals. Some of them would even throw up a new opera house across the street from the competition, and then get into price wars to cop the trade.

He collected his treasured copy of the *Julius Cahn* directory, with all its resources, along with ads on most every page pushing theater products, makeup, costumes, lighting, baggage. Charles would need to consult every Oregon and California page to put a schedule together.

There were plenty of houses in Oregon and Northern California. But he had no way of knowing which ones the Orpheum circuit was buying. Graeb would know, and would know how to set up a tour down the coast. Compete with the circuit.

He composed the most important telegram of his life:
ORPHEUM CANCELING FOLLIES COAST TOUR REBOOK FOL-LIES COMPETING HOUSES JANUARY FEBRUARY ENDING FRISCO WIRE TWO THOUSAND REPAY WITH BOOKINGS URGENT POMERANTZ

Twenty-one words. Reroute the tour, send money. Twenty-one words that could start the wires humming with bookings and confirms and credit. Graeb would know what to do—if he chose to do it.

He took it to the Western Union office, paid the per-word tally, and watched the grouchy telegrapher start tapping on the brass key. Everything rested on it. If Graeb could set up a tour, and send money, Pomerantz could book hotels and passage. It had to be. He didn't like to think of the alternatives.

He watched the man finish up, knowing the SOS would reach Graeb swiftly, and a reply would come swiftly from across the continent. He had an odd, hollow feeling as he braved the cold.

It was odd how Ginger intruded on his thoughts just then. Ginger's father had made an offer. Return to Pocatello. Prepare for the concert stage. And, unspoken, get rid of her husband. But she had rejected all that. And if Graeb didn't produce, she might find herself broke and stranded. But she had plowed ahead with all the optimism of an eighteen-year-old, a trait that Charles Pomerantz no longer possessed. The thought opened something tender in him.

Graeb replied with breathtaking speed. Sorry. He was now contracted to book acts for the Orpheum Circuit and could no longer operate as booking agent for the Follies. He would be glad to book acts into the Orpheum circuit.

Graeb was throwing the dog a bone. He'd rescue the acts but not the show.

Somehow Charles had sensed it. He hadn't heard from Graeb for a while.

So this is where it all ends, he thought. The flyers wouldn't do much, maybe fill a few seats, and then there would be bills unpaid, the acts unpaid, the Follies falling apart. Maybe even before they had finished their run in Boise. You had to deal squarely with the acts. Not ask them to work if you had no way to pay them. Maybe there would be no shows, not the one tonight, not tomorrow, not the next day.

He guessed that this evening's performance would be the last one. And then what?

Maybe the end of his marriage to Ginger, too.

He hurried back to the telegrapher, this time with a reply to Martin Beck. Book Follies in Orpheum Circuit? Buy Follies? Need answer fast.

He sat down on a hard bench in the rail station, hoping for a fast reply, and one clattered in twenty minutes later: NO.

The *Idaho Statesman* was next. He corralled the manager, who stared flinty-eyed at the offending visitor from the dubious world of theater.

"We'd like to do a free Christmas show at the Columbia,

a matinee the day after tomorrow. Absolutely free, to celebrate the holidays. Would you give it push?"

"An ad costs the same for out-of-towners as for locals,"
the manager said. "Three columns, ten inches, twenty-
seven fifty."

"Ah, I'm talking about a free show, a Christmas show,
for all the good people of Boise, and we need a good story
in your paper tomorrow."

"You could have a column-inch in the classified section for eighty cents. A bargain, given what it's worth."

"Ah, we're not talking business, Mr. Hardesty, we're
talking a free show. Good, lively variety, free to men,
women, children of Boise."

"We don't give anything away, especially at Christmas,
Mr. Pomerantz," Hardesty said.

"That I believe," Charles said.

"You sell theater seats; we sell advertising space,"
Hardesty said.

"Merry Christmas," Charles replied.

Charles clamped his hat down, and ventured into the
cold. At the hotel he discovered some of the troupe, cold,
rosy-cheeked, and cheerful. They had unloaded every
flyer, and maybe it would fill those seats. But in his pocket
were wires that would wipe away that cheer in an instant.
He spotted August, who was looking cold and gaunt, and
with a nod, summoned August to an alcove.

August read the wires, and seemed to sink into himself.

"I just offered a free matinee, Christmas matinee, and
asked the paper to push it, and guess what?"

"Eighty cents an inch in classified."

"You were there?"

"Same idea. Ahead of you. Fine fellow, Hardesty."

"You want to tell the acts?"

"We're a square outfit. The worker deserves his pay. My
earliest lesson in life."

"Now or before or after?"

"Not before. It colors the show. Not now; they've headed for their rooms. After the show. I'll keep the acts around for a few minutes."

That's how it would be. Charles found himself peering straight into August Beausoleil's soul just then. He knew August's story, at least in general terms, and what he saw then, he swore, was the abandoned boy, get tips or starve, cadge a nickel here, a nickel there, buy candy, live on, find a basement warm enough to keep from frostbite, watch the people, the ones who never noticed a starving kid watching them. August was still young, or would have been if fate hadn't broken his body. But now his face was the color of whey.

There it all was, radiating from August's worn face. But there was more. August Beausoleil had survived from his eighth or ninth year by his wits.

"Come on up, Charles," he said. "We have things to talk over."

Charles was glad to. It was fine to be in a warm hotel room, proof against the cold streets of Boise, drawing up a last will and testament for the Beausoleil Brothers Follies.

FORTY-SEVEN

No line formed at the Columbia Theater box office. August watched a few people, hurried by a bitter wind, buy tickets and scurry inside. The flyers had little effect. The weather wasn't helping. The sarcastic review in the *Statesman* didn't improve matters.

Beside him stood the manager of the Overland, a Mr. Poole, who wanted cash immediately or the troupe would be evicted forthwith. August had persuaded him to wait for the box office receipts. There were twelve rooms to pay for, at two dollars each.

Minutes before showtime, August slipped into the box office, extracted the cash, and handed it to Poole, who smiled maliciously and hurried back to his hotel. The troupe would sleep warm one last night.

August hurried into his tails and top hat, and peered out upon a sea of darkness. There were so few people they seemed to vanish. And more were in the balcony than in the orchestra. He focused hard, and counted fifty-something. They sat in deep silence, and one could swear that there was no audience at all. Not even a sniffle or cough to signal human presence.

The performers were oddly quiet. They knew. And just because they were performers, and proud, they'd do their best this night. They had already figured out the rest: There was no brown pay envelope awaiting them. And no more Beausoleil Brothers Follies. And no tickets back to Chicago or New York, where they might scrape by until they could find a job. They knew that at the end of this show, he would gather them on the bare-lit stage and apologize, and tell them it was over, and he had no remedy. He hadn't said it, not yet, but they already understood it. Some would be angry, some bitter, some blue, and most would put up a false front, joke, and wonder what the next day would bring.

He eyed his pocket watch.

"Throw on the footlights, and lower the olio," he said.

A moment later, he stepped onto the narrow downstage strip, peered out into the silence, and tipped his hat.

"Ladies and gents, I'm August Beausoleil. This is my show. I want you to enjoy it. You all gather right here, in front. You up in the balcony, come down and have a seat right here. We're about to give you the best show we know how to do, and we're all hoping you'll have a fine time this eve. We'll start in a few minutes."

With that, the curtain rang down, and he watched the handful gradually filter in, and settle in the rows just a little back. Those were the best seats. No one sat in the first row. Just a few people settled there, many solitary, leaving empty spaces between them and the next person.

At a nod, the curtain rose, and he welcomed them, and introduced the Wildroot Sisters, who did just fine, lots of sparkle and smiles. August relaxed. Every performer would do whatever it took this evening. Do it from the heart. Do it without pay. Do it without knowing what would happen on the morrow.

The crowd clapped tentatively, a small, hollow chattering of hands, and then August headed into the next act, and next, and next, and the show glowed, and the audience had a good time, and no one left at the intermission. And when the show ended, the audience clapped, stood, and left, braving the Idaho winter.

Everyone in the show, including the musicians, simply waited on the stage, in the dim light of a naked bulb above. August wouldn't be surprising them. "I'm sorry," he said. "It's over. We had enough to pay your rooms tonight. We don't have pay for you. Tonight's take came to fifteen, after the hotel took its cut. Each act and hand gets a dollar. It buys a telegram or a meal."

"What happened?" Wayne asked.

"Orpheum Circuit bought several houses where we were booked, and shoved us out. Our agents won't lend us cash. One went to work for Orpheum."

"You owe us," The Genius said.

"Yes, I do."

"Then shake what you've got in a sock and pay us."

"You gave people a lot of fun, sir. You added to the show. That's all I have in my sock."

"What are we supposed to do?" asked Art Grabowski.

"Wire your agent," Wayne Windsor said.

"Orpheum is hiring," August said. "Wire Bland Graeb in Chicago. Our agent. Or Martin Beck, who's running the circuit from Chicago."

"Oh, God," said Ethel Wildroot.

"I'll help," Wayne Windsor said. "This is show business. I've been there. Most of us have. Anyone wants to send a wire, tonight, tomorrow, I'll pay. Anyone needs a meal, I'll arrange with the eatery next to the hotel for tomorrow."

No one thanked him.

"If acts want to send a joint wire to Graeb, I'll word it," Windsor added. "One wire, several signing it."

The odd thing was that no one agreed. The theater was growing cold. The manager didn't burn an extra nickel's worth of coal.

"This is a badly run deal," The Genius said.

August didn't argue. If there was justice, The Genius would soon be back in Butte as a barstool entertainer, cadging drinks and sleeping in cellars.

The whole company stood paralyzed. For a loquacious band of performers, they were oddly mute, struggling with fear, maybe anger, maybe helplessness. And there was the cold, the piercing, bitter cold worming straight into them.

That's when LaVerne's stage-door Johnny, Stanford Sebring, showed up, warmed by a black alpaca topcoat.

"Hey, baby, I'm taking you for a nightcap," he said.

"I don't think so, Johnny."

"Hey, what's this? What's the trouble?"

"We're closing, Stanford."

"Well, we'll have a party. I'll spring."

It seemed surreal. At the last, most of the company repaired to Darby's Saloon, down the street, to make merry, and lift a glass to the Beausoleil Brothers Follies, though a few including Harry the Juggler and some accordionists headed back to the refuge where they would welcome one last warm night. A familiar thought passed through August's mind: eat and drink, for tomorrow we die.

Charles helped Ginger into her coat, and donned his own. They would go, of course. August could almost name the ones who'd go for the last hurrah; the ones who were less anxious, who'd weathered storms, who'd fallen from peaks, climbed out of troughs, figured out ways, make compromises, bandaged hurts, smiled at life. He would go, too. No matter what he felt.

He wanted to soak in guilt, but wouldn't let it happen. He had not let anyone down. But some stern executioner in him was surveying his neck. He had wrestled his demons since boyhood, wrestled the Accuser who blamed him for his misfortunes. It was the Accuser lurking in him, condemning him, even now, with a new tragedy unfolding by the hour.

"I will join you," he said.

Darby's proved to be a politico's saloon, redolent of cigars and sharp with whiskey. The place was almost empty. Boise was not known for its nightlife. The keep eyed the women unhappily; this was the home of sovereign males. But when the performers were at last seated at what was probably a poker table, the keep eyed the clock, which said ten thirty, sighed, and approached.

"Closing in half an hour, but I'll serve up a quick one," he said.

Bourbon neat all around, except for their host, Stanford Sebring, who settled for a sarsaparilla. August thought the Wildroot girls were exploring new ground; LaVerne, though, seemed at home with the amber fluid before her.

Most of the troupe looked ready for a drink. The Marbury Trio, Delilah and her brothers, sticking close as usual; Ethel Wildroot; the girls, Cookie and Marge; Cromwell Perkins, The Genius; the Grabowskis; Wayne Windsor; Ginger along with Charles; and even Harry the Juggler, who had changed his mind and joined the company. August wished the rest could be present at this farewell: Mary Mabel Markey, Mrs. McGivers. The musicians and hands, too. Sebring was putting a fitting ending on it, lubricating a sad moment, giving them all a memory. A small company, doubling their acts to fill the bill.

The keep eyed them all sourly; he preferred politicians.

Sebring rose, suddenly. "I must say, ladies and gents, I'm honored to be included here. All this talent. All this grief. If I'd known, earlier, what awaited you here, I could have done something. I have a few resources. At any rate, you fine people, I wish to raise a toast to the Follies, and may you all prosper."

He lifted his sarsaparilla.

"You won't raise a glass of spirits with us, sir?" Windsor asked.

"No, not for me, friend. I'm L.D.S."

August didn't have the faintest idea.

"Latter-day Saint?" asked Windsor, turning to expose his better profile.

"Why, yes, so of course I must abstain. At any rate, here's to you all, to the Follies, to your success."

They sipped gingerly. August was some while sorting it out. A Mormon, toasting them. Boise was an odd place.

"And here's to our benefactor," Charles said, raising a glass to Sebring.

"It's not over, not by a long shot. Here's Act Two," Sebring said. "It's my one and only chance. You shall all be witnesses."

He stood, turned to LaVerne, and took her hand. "La-
Verne Wildroot, my nightingale, will you marry me?"

LaVerne startled, spilled some of her bourbon, and
stared.

Stanford Sebring was smiling.

The clock ticked. She eyed her mother, her sisters, the
troupe at the table, the company she had kept all her life.
She gazed at Sebring, in his costly suit and cravat, his
alpaca coat nearby.

"Yes," she said.

"Ah, ah, a great moment for us all," Sebring said. He
gently collected her, drew her close, and raised his glass.

There should have been congratulations, but no one
in the company could manage them.

"I should add, friends, that if any single lady here
wishes the security and happiness of a good marriage, I
know of many fine and virtuous men who seek to start a
family."

No one spoke.

"And of course, if any gentleman wishes, we have jobs
and opportunities open. Here and in Utah. Say the word,
and your future will be secured. Our people know what
it's like to struggle, to be outcasts, to build our own Zion.
And now we offer a helping hand."

No one spoke for a few moments.

"Thanks, Mr. Sebring, but I'm addicted to coffee,"
Windsor said. "My left side favors java; my right favors
bourbon."

With that, everything eased. They ordered another
round, courtesy of Sebring, stayed way past the keep's
closing hour, and finally drifted into the streets, to
the hotel. Sebring accompanied LaVerne to the hotel,
where he kissed her cheek and promised to collect her
in the morning.

The next hours proved to be the strangest in August's

life. He stood in the Overland lobby, watching his troupe head for their rooms that last night, wondering if he'd see them again. He didn't. After a restless night, mostly awake, he headed for the lobby and found no one he knew. He knocked on the doors of his troupe, but no one answered. Strangers wandered through the lobby, checking in, checking out.

He looked for his company in the adjacent restaurants, and saw no one. He was alone. He didn't know where Charles was, or Ginger. He couldn't fathom how his colleagues could simply vanish, leaving no word, no trace of their existence in Boise, Idaho. There were no messages left at the hotel desk. He had several trunks of gear stored at the express office of the depot, and after an arduous search, he found a secondhand dealer who would buy the stuff for a few dollars. That was all he had; he had shared the last receipts with the troupe. He wandered through the stuffy Overland one last time, his raging curiosity pushing him into every corner, wanting to reconnect with his company. But the Follies were dead; his acts had vanished.

He had enough cash from the sale of trunks and costumes to take him to Butte, where he hoped Mrs. McGivers would shelter him a brief time, or where he could wait tables or serve drinks or run errands. The lamps were always lit in Butte. He carried his sole remaining satchel with him to the Union Pacific station, purchased coach fare to Butte, and boarded an eastbound back to Pocatello, and a change of trains to Butte. If Mrs. McGivers could not help him, he would have to think of something else.

EPILOGUE

Only the Wildroot girls remained in Boise. LaVerne married Stanford Sebring that very day, and never returned to show business. Sebring graciously provided shelter and sustenance for Cookie and Marge, and introduced them to eager young men in woman-starved Idaho. Years later, long after they had started families, they enjoyed roles in Christmas pageants and reenactments of pioneer life. LaVerne named her second son August, even though Stanford was not enchanted with the name, preferring Brigham. Her cousins, Cookie and Marge, raised happy families and gradually concealed their vaudeville past and their father's profession, but once in a while, at a graduation or school play, they would lead an audience in song.

Delilah Marbury, her husband Sam, and brother-in-law Bingo immediately wired their agent, Morrie Gill, and he booked them in the expanding Orpheum circuit and advanced them ticket money to Seattle. They caught the next train west. They had mixed success on the West Coast. Some inland towns didn't like to see her dressed in tux and tails. Other towns thought that tap dancing was corrupt and degrading. But mostly, audiences delighted in the rat-a-tat and clatter, and enjoyed the trio. They toured the vaudeville circuits for many years, and opened the way for other tap-dancing acts, including blackface ones. For a while, blackface tap dancing was all the rage in vaudeville.

Harry the Juggler was booked instantly by the Orpheum circuit, but they changed his name to King of the Jugglers, and had him dress in a glittery gold costume festooned with fake rubies. He succeeded brilliantly for the next two years, but one day a train whistle caught him just as he was juggling his scimitars; he slipped—one scimitar cut his wrist to the bone, severing nerves and ending his career. He did attempt a one-handed juggling act, but it never caught on as well as the original. He ended up a celebrity bartender in San Francisco, able to do amazing things with glasses of booze.

Cromwell Perkins, The Genius, made his way back to Butte, and reverted to his former life as a barstool entertainer cadging drinks from amused customers in several saloons. The harsh winters took their toll, and he eventually vanished. Rumors abounded. Some said he was shot by an irate drinker. Others argued, in Butte parlance, that "he woke up dead" one day. He was not missed, but was the source of good Butte stories, some even true.

Ginger never looked back. She never regretted her flight from Pocatello, her escape from the clutches of her mother. She and Charles caught the next Union Pacific train eastward, riding in a Pullman Palace Car in comfort. Charles, veteran of the rails, not only had letters of credit on his personal account in New York, but also a few double eagles salted away in his effects. He found employment with the Keith empire, and later Keith-Albee, applying his endless knowledge of travel and hotels and arrangements to get acts from town to town, on time, and in comfort.

Ginger's career took an odd twist. Ginger found regular employment at Oscar Hammerstein's new Manhattan Opera House, at Thirty-fourth and Broadway. Her success in the Northwest was unknown to New Yorkers, and it took a year before she recouped the billing status she had known far away. She was celebrated in New York for the aura of innocence that somehow clung to her. She was well ensconced in the business, happy with her life, and close to the heart of the world of vaudeville, where Charles governed over hundreds of acts on the road.

August scraped together enough to get to Butte, where Mrs. McGivers immediately gave him shelter. He discovered Ethel Wildroot also there, waiting tables in exchange for shelter. August didn't have a nickel. But in time, he scraped together enough to ride coach to New York, where he soon found work doing what he did best, introducing acts at Tony Pastor's Rialto Opera House, which was doing vaudeville nonstop all day, every day. It wasn't much, but it afforded him a room, and he gradually paid off his debts to Boise printers and restaurants, sending a few dollars from each paycheck.

But the failure, the collapse of his Follies, and the new, ruthless world of competing vaudeville circuits, had taken their toll on him. He was frequently ill, and developed a tumor on the stomach, and less than three years after he returned to his hometown, he lay dying in Bellevue Hospital, his life dwindling as he lay on a narrow cot in a charity ward under an army surplus blanket.

Charles and Ginger found him there, staring upward into emptiness.

"August, we just found out you're here," Charles said, reaching for a cold hand.

"Good of you," August said.

"Are they treating you well?" Ginger asked.

"The one, the only Bellevue," August whispered.

"August, thanks to you, my dreams came true. I just want you to know."

"Same here, August. I took what you taught me and made a life," Charles said.

For a long moment, August didn't respond. Then, quietly, "The business. The business gives us life. It's a refuge."

"I hadn't thought of it that way," Ginger said. "But yes, it puts its arm around us; it put its arm around me, and after that . . ."

August smiled thinly. "Vaudeville's like this hospital. It's for the ones coming in or going out."

He closed his eyes, and his visitors wondered if he had

slipped away, but they stayed, and clung to his hand. The person who had transformed their lives was adrift.

Ethel Wildroot found him then, noted his closed eyes, and her face formed a question.

"Ethel, I'm glad," August said, mysteriously fathoming her presence.

"Oh, August," she said.

"You were my reliable," he said. "Always ready with an act. I'm glad you came for the curtain."

"Oh, August, oh, baby."

The Profile showed up, too, his visage ravaged by age and spirits, but still somehow noble.

"I'm going to talk about showmen tonight," he said. "Is there any showman in the audience I can honor this evening? Raise your hand."

"Never made the grade, and flunked at Boise," August mumbled.

"Never made the grade? You're one of the great ones. You cleaned cash out of a thousand towns. You bankrupted whole cities."

August laughed gently, and then faded into blessed memory.

{ THE }
Richest Hill on Earth

TO ALL THOSE OF INQUIRING MIND,
WHO ABANDONED YOUTHFUL VISIONS FOR
SOMETHING MORE PROFOUND

{ ONE }

John Fellowes Hall fretted about his middle name. He had changed it from Frank. He couldn't imagine why his parents had inflicted that loutish name on him. Frank had such a pedestrian aura about it, but that had eluded them. Fellowes had just the right tone for a person of his stature, so he had arbitrarily switched it. What's more, it was sonorous, unlike a string of one-syllable names. Anyone of any sensitivity knew that there should be different numbers of syllables in one's given names and surname.

He doubted that his new employer would fathom any of it. The man was a bumpkin in a silk hat. John Fellowes Hall had suffered a string of miserable employers who hadn't the faintest idea of his gifts. Maybe this time things would be better, but he doubted it.

The narrow gauge train from Helena slowed as it entered the flat below Butte, and slowly ground to a halt, hissing steam and belching cinders. Hall could see from his grimy window that the Western city was just as ugly as it was proclaimed to be, and maybe worse, but that didn't faze him. Butte was the place to get rich. It wasn't money that Hall was after, though he had bargained for as much as his new employer could manage. It was reputation. Here was the place for a distinguished newspaper editor to turn himself into a legend.

On this cold and windy spring day of 1892, the smoke pouring from Butte's mine boilers and mills scraped downward, catching the city in haze. Far up, on the naked crest of the naked slope, stood a forest of headframes and rude sheds, which seemed to catch the eye because they didn't belong there, and insulted the dark grandeur of the forested mountains stretching north and east. The russet hill was burdened with a cancerous mélange of buildings, cramped into gulches, teetering on slopes, while Butte, as far as his eye could see through the jaundiced smoke, seemed to seethe.

Well, he had been warned. The train, down from Helena, squealed and sighed, while passengers collected their Gladstones and duffel, and stepped down to the gravel of the station yard. There would be a trunk on the express car, but he would get that later at the depot. He had everything he needed in his pebbled leather overnighter.

The sulphurous smoke struck him and irritated his eyes. Was there no escape from it in this mountain vastness? He located a hack, operated by a skinny gent with a full beard, and engaged the man with a wave of his hand.

"You got any more luggage?" the cabby asked in a ruined voice.

"Trunk I can leave in the express office."

"Moving here, eh?"

Hall was offended by the man's familiarity, and didn't reply.

"I can carry the trunk if you want."

"I will send for it when I need it."

"You headed for the company?" the driver asked.

That secretly pleased Hall, but he would not confess it. That would be the headquarters of the Anaconda Copper Mining Company. The cabby had taken him for an executive, as well he should. Hall wore a fine three-piece gray broadcloth suit, a fine polka-dot cravat, a lean shirt with a starched white collar, and polished hightop shoes.

"Call me Fat Jack," the cabby said. "Where to?"

Hall hated to disillusion the man. "I'll be stopping temporarily at the *Butte Mineral*," he said. "Of course, before going up the hill."

Fat Jack eyed the editor, and nodded. The man was anything but fat, just as Hall was anything but a copper executive, even if he looked the part. The editor extracted a dainty handkerchief and mopped his face. The harsh wind had already deposited a layer of soot on it, which Hall noted on the clean white folds of his handkerchief. Ah, well, he thought. To live is to suffer.

"You seeing Clark?" Fat Jack asked, as he steered his lumbering dray north, up mud-soaked thoroughfares.

"Clark?"

"Himself."

The cabby was referring to William Andrews Clark, owner of the *Mineral* and other rags, owner of many of those mines and reduction works up the hill, owner of the street railway, owner of a bank, owner of surrounding forests, owner of thousands of mortal souls, and about to be the owner of John Fellowes Hall.

"I am planning to interview him, yes."

"I think he'll do the interviewing," Fat Jack said, slapping the lines over the croup of the dray to hasten him uphill.

Hall considered the hack man insolent and resolved not to leave a tip.

In a rude part of town below the commercial center, Fat Jack reined the dray to a halt. This appeared to be newspaper row, with the *Butte Mineral* sandwiched between some others. There was no sign of prosperity emanating from the weary storefront. At least cobblestones paved this street; others appeared to be mire.

"Two bits," Fat Jack said. "Want me to stay?"

That was extortion, so Hall simply handed the man a quarter and smiled icily. He lifted his knobby bag and eased to the grimy pavement. Fat Jack eyed the quarter, stared hard, and slapped the dray forward. Hall eyed the

Mineral with vast distaste. No one had washed its windows. There was no brass on the door. The name had been stenciled in black on the windows. There should have been a gilded sign above. The street had not been swept and was deep in dung. A wave of disdain swept the editor. What sort of rag was this?

He would make short work of it and seek employment elsewhere. He smoothed his three-piece gray broadcloth suit, adjusted his cravat, eyed his hightops, and then pushed his way through the creaking door, to the sound of a bell.

The familiar smell of hot lead, and the bitter smell of ink, caught his nostrils. He heard the clatter of Linotypes. That was good. The new machines made quick work of typesetting and printing. No one showed up at the counter, so he hunted for a bell to clang, but found none. The interior was as grimy as the exterior, and he hesitated to touch any ink-sprayed surface, knowing his hand would be smeared. These things were not good omens.

At last a printer emerged and eyed Hall.

"You're the man," he said.

"John Fellowes Hall."

"You'll want to talk to Mr. Clark. The old man's not here. He's up at his bank."

"May I see my office?"

"We haven't got them. But Louis the Louse could steal one."

"Never mind. I'll just look around."

The printer eyed him. "Without a smock?"

Everything in a print shop stained clothing black.

"I'll interview Clark first," Hall said. "Steer me."

"Two blocks uphill, and left."

"Will this bag be safe?"

"For ten minutes. The next bandits are due at four."

Hall intended to fire the man.

He settled his knobby black bag in an obscure corner

and headed into the cold smoke. The spring weather did nothing to improve the looks of Butte. He might have enjoyed the stroll but for the foul wind, which drove ash into him as he toiled upslope. Butte seemed to be a thriving town, with solid brick commercial buildings everywhere, a streetcar system, and electric wires strung in a crazy quilt pattern. He wondered how Amber would react to it, not that it mattered.

He found the bank, W. A. Clark and Bro., readily enough. This enterprise at least was gaudily announced with gilded letters across its brick front. He pulled open the polished brass door, eyed the lobby, decided that Clark would be upstairs, ascended stairs of creaking imported oak, and found himself at a reception desk, with a comely lady in charge. She had a typing machine before her.

"John Fellowes Hall to see Mr. Clark. He's expecting me."

"Oh, the newsman."

"Editor."

She retreated to a corner office, vanished, and then reappeared. "He will see you in a little while," she said. "Do have a seat."

Which was a polished walnut bench resembling a pew, and probably was. The worshipers of this god required pews.

But Clark surprised him. Moments later the dapper man boiled out of his lair, greeted Hall effusively, shepherded the editor into the sanctum, and settled Hall in a quilted leather chair.

"Ah, so it's you, Hall. I've been awaiting this moment with more anticipation than buying a new smelter."

John Fellowes Hall had never been compared to a smelter, and didn't quite know how to respond, but his wit saved him.

"Ah, yes, I get the bullion out of the ore," he said.

"Well, the *Mineral*'s not going to be doing that. I've

hired you to cut off the tentacles of the octopus. You will hack away, one by one, without remorse, and without surcease. You will win the allegiance of the people of Butte and you will support the Democrat Party and you will discreetly remind the public of who it is who wants to keep Montana independent, free, fair, and honest. We will elect Democrats this November and they will make me senator."

"It sounds like a job made in heaven."

"There is divine purpose in it," Clark said. "We must rescue Montana from the octopus. We must not allow a single corporation to own the government, own the governor, own the legislators, own the regulators, own the tax collectors. I'm determined to fight to the last, so that the people of this state are free. I will be honored to become a senator."

Clark was so earnest it surprised Hall. Did the little tycoon actually believe all that?

"I can see you doubt me," Clark said. He headed for a window. "Up there are a dozen properties of the Anaconda Company. The best mines, reduction works, mills, and a little railroad too. Over in Anaconda is the most advanced smelter in the world. That's Marcus Daly's empire. That's his town. He built it. He erected his smelter, platted the streets, started the houses, built his fancy hotel. Now he wants to put the state capital in his backyard. He wants to own the government, just like he owns most of that hill up there, owns his own city, owns half the forests in Montana, owns a railroad, owns a horse racing stable, and owns every Irishman in Butte. He wants Montana's public buildings, its governor, its legislators, under his thumb. He wants to see them from his office windows. He wants to tell them how to tax and regulate. He wants to own Montana. He cares nothing about the farmers and ranchers and all the rest of the people. And he doesn't want me in office. You will stop him. He may own papers across the state, and a deluxe paper in Anaconda, and another here, and more in every town that can support a daily. But you'll stop him, and when you do, God will smile on you."

Hall debated whether to sound reassuring and confident, or whether to sound a little more modest.

"Let me at him. What's a newspaper for? I'll show you what a bulldog is."

"I don't want to own a bulldog. I want a shark."

"You've bought one," Hall said.

"Good. Now, I imagine you'd like to bring your wife and children here, but I will require you to hold off for the time being. You have more important things to do than raise a family. Keep her back East."

That took Hall aback. "But Mr. Clark—"

"And you may consider that your lodging is taken care of, Hall. I will supply it."

"Well, I'll take a room tonight."

"No need. You are going to board with me, Hall."

"With you? I wouldn't want to intrude in your private life, sir."

"Oh, pshaw, you haven't a notion about me, do you? I have a house with so many rooms I've lost track of them. There are rooms for an army. You will stay in my house. You will enjoy the most modern plumbing in Montana. A half dozen indoor water closets. Not even Daly's plumbing can match it. Not that he cares about plumbing. Any old outhouse will do for Daly. But let me tell you, Hall, you'll live in beauty and luxury. You might live there but you'll not see me. Not that I will avoid you, but our paths won't cross. You'll be in the servants' quarters, of course, where life is lived entirely beyond my gaze. If I invite you for breakfast, you'll come, and bring a notepad so you will have my directions on papers. Agreed?"

"I'm your pet shark," Hall said.

Clark stared. "Hall, I am very good at reading men.

You are taking this much too lightly, making smart jokes. I don't know about you. Are you the man I want? Pet shark. I don't know at all about you. A serious man wouldn't make bad little quips. A serious man would know exactly what I mean, and dedicate himself to the cause. I'm going to put you on probation for a month, and then we'll see about a job."

"Well, I'm not sure I'll work under such conditions. I find them rather heavy. If you think you can buy my loyalty as well as my pen, sir, then—"

"Oh, pshaw, Hall. You're hired. Get to work. The miners have ten-hour days, but you don't and never will. I will own you twenty-four hours of every day including Sundays. And call me Senator. Senator Clark. I'd like to get used to it in advance."

$$\{ \text{TWO} \}$$

Hall studied his new digs, more amused than angry. He had been consigned to a monkish cell on the third floor, which was entirely the realm of the household servants. Clark's redbrick mansion rose importantly west of the central city, announcing its owner as one of the grandees of the mining town.

No sooner had Hall climbed the endless stairs to the third floor, from a rear servants' entrance, than his trunk arrived and two draymen toted it up the narrow stairway and deposited it in his austere white room.

Hall discovered an iron bedstead, a washstand with a white vitreous washbowl and pitcher, a wooden chair, and an armoire. An incandescent light hung on a cord from the ceiling. A single toilet served all the servants. The best thing about the room was its dormer window, which opened on a northward view of the numerous headframes and the mountains beyond. That's what Butte was all about. Wealth yanked from the bowels of the city. Those headframes sat over shafts plunging thousands of feet into the mineralized rock below the city, and each day those shafts coughed up a fortune in copper ore laced with zinc, silver, and a little gold. That mass of rock was known as the richest hill on earth, and with good reason. It had already created some of the greatest fortunes in the United States, not least that of his new employer. Even as he watched, the clatter of the mines drifted to him, and he saw moving ore cars, stubby engines leaking steam, and the bustle of fierce industry.

Or master. Hall wasn't quite sure whether he was an employee or a slave. To William Andrews Clark it made no difference. Other human beings were there to be exploited; most for their muscle, but Hall for his brain. Hall was discovering some advantage in all of this: his family could wait. He'd send them some cash now and then, and maybe in a while he would decide to bring them to Butte. But just now, he was furtively and deliciously pleased to be freed from all domestic burdens. If Clark wanted a crusade, he'd get a virtuous crusader—more or less. Hall had heard a few things about Butte.

He hung his spare suit in the armoire, hung some shirts, lined up his older hightop shoes, and settled his small clothes on its upper shelf. The room was oddly pleasant. A manservant had taken him to it and had answered a few questions. Yes, there would be meals there in a separate dining area served by a dumbwaiter from the kitchen below. Breakfasts at six, lunches at eleven, suppers at five. One ate what was served. It was not a restaurant.

The afternoon was already far gone. Hall glanced at his turnip watch and decided to skip servants' supper and head for the newspaper, blotting up the city as he went. By the time he reached the street, a chill had already settled, reminding Hall that Butte was located almost on the Continental Divide. The street teemed with wagons and carriages and pedestrians, swarming this way and that. Butte was alive. Some towns lay inert and sleepy, but Butte seethed with life, and never slept.

The city was only twenty years from being a shantytown, a place of log and frame structures built to abandon the day the ore ran out. But here was a metropolis of stone and brick, with cobbled streets, trolley lines, a forest of utility poles festooned with wire, and gaudy advertising that commandeered the eye.

· Hall thought he knew how to get to the *Mineral,* but nothing looked the same in the spring twilight. It didn't matter. He wanted to see William Clark's city. Marcus Daly's city. The Anaconda Copper Mining Company's city. The city with ore cars rolling through it, sometimes on streetcar rails, pushed and pulled by stubby little engines. Wealth, unending, blasted and shoveled out of the resisting rock. Metals of great worth, and minerals of more dubious value, such as arsenic. Clark had once said that the arsenic in the air of Butte put a lovely blush on the cheeks of Butte's women.

The great schism between Marcus Daly and William Andrews Clark had erupted a few years earlier when Clark was running for the office of Territorial Delegate to Congress, Montana not yet being a state. Daly supported Clark—they were both Democrats—and then, suddenly Daly no longer did, and the vast armies of mill men and miners employed by Daly's Anaconda Mining Company had voted for the Republican candidate, Tom Carter, who won the election in the heavily Democratic territory. Betrayal, treason, perfidy, screamed Clark's paper, the *Mineral.* And now Hall had been hired to sharpen and deepen the feud, and to use his mighty pen to whittle away at the Irish immigrant boy, Marcus Daly, who had learned hardrock mining and made good.

It was going to be entertaining. And no one on earth was better qualified than John Fellowes Hall. At least Hall could think of none other.

Hall paused at a downtown street corner to examine a yellow dog. The mutt seemed to own the corner. People passing by were obviously familiar with the dog, and some paused to pet it. Hall could find no sign of a master, but one probably was around in a saloon or getting fitted for a suit of clothes. But then a man in a white apron emerged from a restaurant with some bones and scraps and fed them to the dog, which yawned, and settled into some happy gnawing. People approved. Maybe the dog belonged to the man in the beanery. Hall thought it was disgusting, letting a dog occupy a busy street corner while its owner was busy. The odd thing was that every passerby seemed to know the mutt and approve of it.

Hall found the *Mineral* easily enough and entered to the rattle of the Linotype machines. A newspaper never slept. Clark had kept it reasonably up to date, which was necessary if it was to compete with Daly's propaganda sheet, the *Anaconda Standard,* financed by Daly's deep pockets.

A compositor in a grimy apron materialized, a question on his face.

"I'm Hall."

"It's the arsenic in the air," the man said.

"I'm the editor."

"That's what I was afraid of. I'll get you a beer."

"Mr. Clark hired me."

"The taller they are, the harder they fall," the skinny man said. He pointed to a cubicle off to the side of the composing room. "All yours," he said.

Hall found another compositor in there, and a copyboy, and a mutton-chopped reporter at a desk in an alcove, hammering on a typing machine.

"Where's the newsroom?" Hall asked.

"Newsroom? Why don't you quit and go back East?"

"I'm John Fellowes Hall," he said.

"The new copyboy?"

"What are you writing?"

"A story about Anaconda's railroad. It'll run ore trains from here to Anaconda."

"Another arm of the octopus. Who'll they put out of business?"

"No one."

"Well, invent someone. Pretty soon the Anaconda will own everything. Say so in the story. The railroad is another sinister Daly business."

The reporter stared. "What's it to you? It's just a virgin little railroad."

"I'm Clark's shark."

"Call me Grabbit. Grabbit Wolf. That's because I grab the story before anyone else, and the name stuck."

"Well, Grabbit, grab this: it's a new monopoly. This is Marcus Daly's sinister new ploy to own Montana. Get the whole story. If you don't have answers, publish the question. How did it happen? Who financed it? Who got paid off? Was the octopus playing some sort of game? And for what?"

Grabbit frowned, and Hall thought the man was a bit dense, but it turned out to be something else entirely.

"Hey, I write news," he said. "This is just a virtuous little railroad."

One of those, Hall thought. The only question was whether to fire him on the spot or wait a few days. He decided to wait.

"Grabbit, get this straight. If you don't have answers, ask questions. I want twenty questions in this story when I see it in the morning edition. You can also tell readers that the *Mineral* was unable to check the facts. Got it?"

Wolf cocked an eyebrow, stared out a grimy window,

and grinned. "I always wanted to write editorials," he said.

"Grabbit, I think I'm going to like you," Hall said. "And so will Mr. Clark. And Grabbit, I only employ people I like."

"I am now a pundit," Wolf said. "I've been promoted."

Wolf was a pale man, so white that Hall doubted he had any acquaintance with the sun. He looked like he had crawled out of an abandoned mine somewhere. But at least the man could operate a typing machine. Half the reporters in the country still wrote in longhand.

"The *Mineral* have any other reporters?" Hall asked.

"A few stringers," Wolf said.

"Who gathers the news, then?"

"You do," Wolf said.

"I'm the editor."

"You're the new gumshoe. Your predecessor wore out his brogans every six months."

Hall wasn't about to spend his life collecting news. That wasn't his job. His job was to shape the news, fit it to Mr. Clark's needs and whims. He decided to talk to Clark about hiring a few more reporters, plus a cartoonist or two. A good cartoon burrowed into numbskulls' noggins better than a lot of words. If Clark wanted an engine of influence, there would be some changes.

Hall thought he'd write editorials, but those weren't important. Anyone could mouth off, and it didn't affect the thinking of anyone else. The whole deal was to shape the news, turn every scrap of information into something that would help Clark.

"Wolf, what do they pay you?"

Wolf stopped his typing and thought about it. "Not enough," he said. "It keeps me in nickel cigars."

"Mr. Clark has political ambitions. How are you going to help him?"

Wolf pondered it. "I could go to work for the *Anaconda Standard*," he said.

"Comedian, are you?"

"So fire me," Wolf said, and returned to his typing.

"You're not worth getting rid of," Hall replied.

Hall examined the cubbyhole that was supposedly the editor's brown study. At least he could keep an evil eye on the rest of the bunch. He'd know every slacker within a week. He meandered through the rest of the place, watching a bald Linotypist compose lines of type, that would be fitted into forms.

He found stacks of back issues, and pulled one off of each pile, wanting to see what the advertising looked like. He found plenty of it in every issue. That was good. A paper without ads had no impact. This was no rich man's toy, but a working newspaper in a brawling and prospering town. There were clothiers' ads, haberdashers, shoe stores, cobblers, wine and beer dealers, saloons, restaurants, doctors and dentists, but not many classified ads. Only two funeral parlors were advertising, and those ads were in the classified section. Tomorrow he would talk to the ad salesman. Lots of people croaked in mining towns, and the *Mineral* should get a lot more business out of it. There should be big ads, listing the departed, with funeral times posted. There appeared to be only one desk with advertising order forms on it. He'd find out who the joker was and put some heat under him.

A boxed classified ad caught his eye.

See into the future. Know your fate. Know the day and hour when trouble might come. Know when illness might strike, and what it will be. Learn if you have a secret beau waiting to meet you.

I have been given clairvoyant powers. I am in touch with the other world. I have the gift of vision. Stop in, and let me tell you how all this happened, how a suddenly widowed woman with only a few pennies to her name was given profound gifts. And how I can help you, share with you what is given to me. I charge nothing but donations are welcome. If I help you see your future, and you are pleased or rewarded, then you might think of rewarding me.

—Agnes Healy,
317 West Mineral Street, rear.

There might be a news story in it, John Fellowes Hall concluded.

{ THREE }

A well-dressed, even natty, man stood at the door. Slanting Agnes eyed him narrowly. She didn't let just anyone into her kitchen. She gave him a closer look. He wasn't even from Butte. No one in Butte dressed like that except the pimps.

"Miss Healy?"

"It's Missus. Are you from the city?"

He seemed puzzled. "You mean, employed by the city? No. I saw your notice and I was curious."

She felt a faint relief. The city kept trying to move her to Mercury Street, but that wasn't her business, and she didn't intend to move there. She was a good woman, period. She did not peddle anything but whatever sprang to mind when someone wanted answers.

"All right," she said, admitting this natty man into her grim kitchen, which was falling apart from neglect. She couldn't help it. A widow didn't have the means to do much, especially one with two grubby boys. He eyed her closely, and she found herself dabbing her stray hair into place. Usually it didn't matter.

"You want something? Advice?"

"What I want is just to listen to you. It might be worth something to you. I read your card in the paper, and it made me curious."

She caught him eyeing the drainboard, the battered table, the sagging yellow muslin curtain at the window, which overlooked an alley.

"You are?"

"Oh, it's unimportant. A newcomer here."

"You're a snoop."

"That's my profession, ma'am."

"I thought so. A detective." She felt better. Snoops were fine with her. "I'm fey, you know."

"You have me there, ma'am."

"Fey. I sometimes see into the next times. Like death. I told Emmett not to go to the mine—the Neversweat— that day but he did. He just smiled and picked up his lunch bucket and that was the last I ever saw of him. He knew I'm fey, but he didn't care. I told him don't go up the drift that slanted like that. Don't go up it because rock will roll down. But he did, and rock came down, and now he's buried in Mountain View. Wouldn't you know? I can see it and tell people but I can't change fate. So now I'm without a man and I'm forced to do this."

"Fortune-teller?"

"I don't tell fortunes! What do you take me for, anyway?"

"I'm sorry. I'm on new ground here, ma'am."

"They called me Slanting Agnes because I told Emmett not to walk up the slanting drift. That's how Butte is, you know. Everyone's got a name. My name is Agnes and now they call me Slanting, and I have lost my dignity."

"How do you foretell these things? Are you a medium? Do you consult with spirits?"

"Oh, no, sir, that would be a mortal sin. I don't hear voices, I don't listen to whispers. I just . . . things come to me in a flash, and I know I've seen something, like lightning in the darkness, a flash of something. That's me."

"What did you think when you saw me?"

"Nothing. You're just a man who doesn't know anything about here."

"That's certainly true, Slanting Agnes. Is that how I should address you?"

"I'm used to it. At least they don't call me Flat Agnes or anything like that."

"You charge something for this?"

"I am a widow with two boys. But I'm not for sale, and make sure you know that and behave proper."

She eyed him. It wouldn't be the first time a man had made advances. But he didn't seem inclined, and spent most of his time glancing furtively about, reading her wants in everything that lay about.

"Who comes here, Agnes? And what do they ask?"

"Why do you want to know?"

"You have had some successes, obviously, or people wouldn't come to see you."

Agnes was secretly pleased. "I won't name anyone, but I'll tell you a little bit. One regular is a shifter, a shift foreman. He comes to ask me if the pit will be safe that day. He lost some men and is very sorry about it, and wants to know beforehand if there's trouble in the rock. I told him one day to get men out of a drift because there would be a gusher, and that's what happened and three men drownded dead from hot water."

"He didn't do anything about it?"

"I see what I see. If a gusher's gonna kill men, it's going to kill men, and there's nothing a shifter can do about it."

"Then why do they come? If it's foreordained why bother?"

"Beats me," she said.

"Who else?"

She knew this was really why he had come, and it made her a little huffy. "Wouldn't you like to know!" she said.

"Do stock brokers and jobbers come calling? Do they want to know what stocks are going up or down?"

She smiled but didn't nod her head.

"How about big-time people? Do mine owners stop by and get a whiff of the future from Slanting Agnes?"

"Aren't you the nosy one."

"Do miners' widows come wanting to visit with their dead men?"

"I tell them to go away. That's wicked. The dead are dead, and I am not a messenger woman running back and forth like that. I tell them to go to church and pray to join them, if they want to get together with them again. Me, I miss Emmett sometimes, but he drank too much and we had to live on three dollars and fifty cents a day, except when he wasn't working, and then we starved. So why should I itch to see Emmett? All he wanted was more babies, but I had too many, two live, three dead, and don't want any more. Just in case you want to know."

"I bet some big shots show up here, sneaking in, too, from the alley so no one sees them. I'm right, aren't I?"

"You sure are nosy."

"Who?"

"I won't say, but they're some as own the Anaconda. I don't like them. After Emmett was killed, they gave me one month's wage. A few dollars. They left me with two boys. The union, it took up a collection, and that was good for another month, but then I was on my own, with nothing at all, just being fey and having a door on the alley."

"Who?"

"You get out of here."

"Who?"

She stood, arranged her skirts, and pointed toward her

door. He seemed reluctant. Not even when she ordered him out of her house was he willing to go.

"I'll call the coppers," she said.

He got up, started out, saw the money jar on the table, withdrew a ten from his pocket, and dropped it into her jar. Then he smiled, tipped his hat, and stepped into the gray light outside.

She hadn't seen ten dollars in a long time. But it wouldn't do him a damned bit of good. People came to her with fears and needs and hopes and terrors, wanting one of her lightning flashes on the future, and she'd never named names, except for Emmett. So let him roast in hell, this snoop.

She could feed the boys and pay the rent and buy some kerosene for the lamps.

She wondered about the man. He wasn't the sort to search out his own death. He would be more interested in stocks and bonds and things like that. She felt some relief. The worst part of her life was telling people their fate. Sometimes, when she saw the doom of a man sitting at her kitchen table, she went faint with grief, and she couldn't speak, and she would shoo the man out if she could. But the persistent ones wouldn't be shooed away, and would sit stubbornly until she told them what she saw, in a clipped low voice. Oddly, the doomed were the ones who tipped her the most. The doomed stuffed the empty glass jar with bills. The rich were the worst; they didn't really value fate, and just wanted to see what stood in their paths. Like Marcus Daly, who rode up in a carriage and parked on Mineral Street, or William Andrews Clark, the heathen who drove his elaborate trap up the alley and parked half a block away and sneaked in at twilight.

So far, at least, she had little to tell them. Clark wasn't interested in death; all he cared about was tomorrow's prices on everything: stocks, copper, art works, real estate, water, mine timbers. He sometimes sat and waited, oddly patient for such a busy financier and great man. He had smoothly tried to befriend her, thinking that he would get at the future if he buttered her up, and she despised him for it. He was another Protestant, and blind to all sacred things. She wished he wouldn't visit her, and ached to tell him some bad news, but mostly she had nothing to offer. It was as if her gift fled her when he came around, yet that never deterred him. Once she did see the stocks of one of his smelters being sold in great amounts and for more than it had been selling for. She told him, and he told her he had profited greatly from her glimpse into what would be.

She began scrubbing the kitchen. The boys were at school. She would have enough now to buy Tommy some knickers. He was sprouting so fast she couldn't keep him clothed.

No one came for a while, and that was good. Then Andrew Penrose came. He was the night shift boss at the Anaconda, suffering miner's lung but gamely keeping on. He was a Cornishman and Methodist but she forgave him for it. Most of the bosses were Cornishmen, even in Marcus Daly's company, because they knew all about mining, having learned their trade in the tin mines of Cornwall.

"It's you, is it?" she asked, pouring some lukewarm tea which she served in a chipped cup. "Going to try your luck again?"

He settled in her kitchen chair and just nodded. He looked more tired than usual. At four, as the mine's whistles blew, he would descend to the eight-hundred-foot level in a triple cage and begin his daily ordeal far from sunlight.

"It's not for me, Agnes."

She knew. He had been haunted by accidents on his shift. Men working for him had died. A cave-in caught five. A runaway cage loaded with seventeen men had plunged a thousand feet and killed them all. A delayed charge had killed three muckers. He had come to her broken and ready to quit. She didn't know whether these disasters were a failing of his; whether he had been careless or let his men act foolishly. All she knew was that these things haunted him, ate at his heart, took years off his life, and filled him with a desperate need to keep his men safe. It didn't matter that when she saw the future, fate was sealed and he could do nothing at all to stop it. He came to her, wanted that flash of light, and hoped somehow to save lives and prevent wounds and spare future widows. Like herself.

She sat down across from him, took his rough hands in her rough hands, and held on tight, and waited for the lightning to strike. It seemed a long time, this transport from the now to the infinite, but she waited, and he waited, and then she saw what she saw.

She didn't want to tell him.

"What?" he asked.

"I saw a coffin, plain wood, and a face in the coffin, and a Dublin Gulch widow in black, and three children, girl and two boys, and if anyone had looked, the face had no legs."

"When? When?"

"Whenever the future comes, Mr. Penrose."

He slumped in the wooden chair. "I must stop it," he said. "That'd be Brophy, you know, two lads and a lass. I'll tell the man to stay away the next shift, I will."

It would do no good, she thought.

He rose, agitated, and headed toward her door, remembered that he had left nothing in her jar, found two quarters and tossed them in.

Then he plunged into the quickening afternoon.

FOUR

Brophy, then. Andrew Penrose fumed. That hag would be wrong. What right had she to point a finger at someone, the finger of doom? It was all nonsense. No one could see into the future. It mocked science.

He wondered why he went to her. He didn't believe in anything supernatural, especially visionaries. And yet he went, helpless to resist his own obsessions. She was just another fraud milking money out of the gullible.

Not Brophy, not the lad from County Clare brought over by Daly himself. The boss had offered to help any of his countrymen cross the seas if they would work for him in Butte, and some came, including that singing man who had started as a mucker four years earlier.

The Anaconda Hill wouldn't claim him if the shift boss Andrew Penrose could help it. He'd spit in the face of Fate. He'd send Brophy topside to work in daylight that day and the next. The man should get some experience unloading country rock.

Penrose scorned his own thoughts. The Hill was getting to him. The Hill killed people so regularly that he could hardly count the dead. He didn't know why these things obsessed him. His task was to pull as much good ore out of the pit as he could each day, as cheaply as possible, and send it off to Daly's smelter in Anaconda. He was good at it. He was the best in the business. Other companies had noticed, and tried to hire him away. But he was a Daly man, an Anaconda man, and he earned enough to buy a few lace doilies for his wife, or take her out to Meaderville for dinner now and then.

His weapons were rarely fists; they were sarcasm and fear. There were all sorts of males in the pits, ranging from quiet and timid ones to bristling damned fools.

There were reckless powdermen determined to blow themselves up, and muckers who itched for a fistfight, and quiet family men who only wanted their three-fifty a day and would work hard for it. Penrose watched them closely. He didn't boss from aboveground, with rare trips into the pit. He stayed down there most of every shift, showing muckers how to muck rock, showing timber men how to brace the drifts, showing other men how to lay a turn sheet. He could do it all, and he took the time to make sure his men were doing it right.

The only thing was, men died. They got silicosis, miner's lung, drawing all that dust and dynamite fumes into their lungs, deadly fumes after each blast, with lethal bits of rock hanging in the air, ready to dig into a man's lungs, including Penrose's own lungs. He was no more immune than the rest. He could hardly count all the ways men died in the pits. He'd seen them all. And fought them all. Every time a man on his shift was killed, it struck him in the gut. Other shift bosses didn't give a damn, but he did. He might be the best shifter in Butte, but he wanted one thing more: to be the safest shift boss in Butte. And he was far from that.

He was still an hour away from the shift, plenty of time to find Brophy and keep him topside. Brophy lived in Dublin Gulch, a warren of miserable cottages jammed between steep slopes, mixed with corner pubs, mining machine dealers, stained trestles, shining rails, and equipment yards. There was always laundry flapping on lines there, absorbing grit and smoke from the mine boilers. That's where a lot of the newcomers collected. They had to start somewhere, and most often they found rooms with others of their kind. And Dublin Gulch was just a skip or two from the mines on Anaconda Hill, including the Neversweat. It all worked out. There were plenty of Brophy's countrymen to lend a hand to anyone in that miserable gulch.

As Penrose walked east, Butte seemed to grow more crowded and tired and worn. Women in babushkas trudged wearily on their daily rounds. By God, Butte was a city of muscular and tough people, and Singing Sean Brophy was just such a one, raising three children and keeping a wife fed, and still finding time to sip some Guinness and throw darts in Shannessy's Shamrock Ale House after his shift.

Penrose wasn't quite sure where the lad lived, but there would be dozens of people to steer him. High above, smoke streamed from the seven stacks on the hill, where boilers powered stamp mills, generators, and hoists. It was never silent in Dublin Gulch, not with the heart of the Anaconda's mining just up the hill. Mines were noisy; stamp mills noisier, ore trains and whistles and the rattle of rock shook the air at all hours.

But the wail he heard was not from the mines, but from a crowd of weary women before a small, well-kept frame house. There were a dozen, not a man in sight, all of them huddled at the stoop of the gray house. Spring breezes drove the mine smoke off this morning, and seemed only to amplify the wailing. Andrew Penrose had a moment of premonition, and savagely rejected it. There was no such thing as fate. He found a boy in ragged dungarees, who was staring at the commotion.

"Tell me lad, where does Sean Brophy live, eh?"

"Him that got killed?"

Something sagged in the foreman. "No, the living man, damn you."

"He cashed in. That's the widow lady in the doorway."

There was indeed a young, rail-thin woman with strawberry hair loose on her head, standing stolidly in the doorway. She wasn't crying. A boy in knickers clung to her skirts.

He approached warily, and halted before the women.

"It's Sean Brophy I'll be looking for," he said.

"You'll not find him now. And you're from the company?" asked a young woman.

"I'm his shifter, and I came to put him topside today."

"He's never going to go topside, sir. He's beyond sunlight now."

"I probably have the wrong man. I'm looking for Singing Sean Brophy, not Walleyed Brophy or Three-Finger Brophy."

"That's Singing's widow there, and don't you be disturbing her. She's got a hat pin she'll stick into you."

"There's no widows here. I want to talk to Sean, my shift man. I've got a new spot for him."

"Are ye blind, man? Can't you see she's not saying a word? Go away," an old crone said.

Penrose stood awkwardly, one foot and the other, barred from further talk with these women by some mysterious unity among them.

"Go talk to him, the copper there," one finally said.

Indeed, a man in blue, with a helmet on his shaggy head, sat nearby, writing something in a pad with a pencil. Penrose knew the man: Big Benny Brice.

Penrose hastened that way, glad to escape the wall of women. "What's all this?" he asked. The copper eyed him warily. "I'm the shifter at the Neversweat," Penrose added.

"Lost a man, then. Got run over by an ore train. Empties going up the hill. He tried to hitch a ride, slipped, and ended up cut to bits. Train run straight over Brophy, cut off his legs like a guillotine had chopped him in two."

"But why?"

The copper shook his head. "Who knows, eh? Going to work, maybe. Things happen. Right on the street. Same rails as the streetcars use. It was Anaconda's train, sir. Taking those empties back to the mines. Who knows, eh? Happens all the time. A man wants a ride, puts a boot on the iron step, misses, and a dozen people watch him tumble under the wheels, and then there's blood all over the cobbles and the ore train halts a few blocks down, and I get to tell the widow."

"It's not fate," Penrose said. "It's not predestined. Nothing happens but by what precedes it. No one wiggles a finger and says it's your turn now."

The copper stared.

"I'm sorry. I need to give my condolences to the widow, and make sure she gets a little, and hire a new man."

"You do that," the copper said. "You fix it all up good."

"It's not fate," Penrose said. "It wasn't ordained."

"He's been taken to Maxwell's," the copper said. "In three pieces. That's as ordained as it gets."

The widow sat mutely on the stoop, surrounded by her neighbors. Conversation had ceased. Penrose approached reluctantly, hat in hand.

"I'm sorry, ma'am."

She stared.

"I'll try to get you something. It didn't happen in the pit, you know. That makes it hard."

"They killed him," she said.

"A company train, yes. Maybe that will do."

"You some big shot?"

"I was his shift foreman."

"I won't get anything," she said.

"He wasn't watching where he was going," the copper said.

"We've lost a very good man," Penrose said.

"Cannon fodder," one of the neighbors said.

"Mountain View's like a battlefield cemetery," another said.

"They don't die for their country, they die for three-fifty a day," the widow said.

"I need your name, Mrs. Brophy."

"What good is that? I won't get anything." She paused. "Alice. Like thousands of Alices."

"I'll see what I can do."

She nodded.

Penrose stood awkwardly, but the mourners had re-treated into their private world, so he tipped his hat and left. It wasn't far to the mine. Brophy should have watched out, he thought. It wasn't fate. There's only cause and ef-fect, one thing leading to another. The more he thought of it, the more agitated he got. He'd not go to see Slanting Agnes again. He'd not succumb to such ignorance and su-perstition, and he hated the impulse within him that had driven him to visit her over and over.

There was a single hiring hall for all the company mines on Anaconda hill, so he stopped there, pulling the creaking door open. The place reeked of tobacco smoke, and maybe vomit. He steered around a battered desk to a rear office, and nodded at the fat walrus sitting there.

"I need a mucker," he said. "And don't send me bad merchandise."

"The union controls it," the walrus said.

"I'll control it," Penrose said.

"Who quit?"

"No one," Penrose said.

He felt weary even before the whistle blew. He hadn't brought his lunch, the usual richly seasoned pasty his wife made so faithfully. But he could fetch a lunch. He wasn't imprisoned in the pit until the shift was done, like his men.

His men collected in the changing room, where they left coats and hats and gear and got themselves ready to descend nine hundred feet down, where no light ever shone but the light of candles or carbide lamps. His men would squeeze into the lifts and plunge with sickening speed down the black shaft, and then the lift would bounce on its cable and the men would spread into the workings.

The shift whistle wailed, and Penrose was reminded of a dirge. Just superstition, he thought. When the shift ended, the whistle sounded like a fire alarm. He couldn't explain it.

He stayed topside, awaiting the new man. He heard the whir of cables and drums in the hoist works, the steam plant that yanked men and ore, and sometimes worn-out mules, out of the earth, and dropped empty ore cars and weary men into the hole in the hill.

The new man came looking for him. He was black haired, squat, with slavic features, and assessing eyes.

"You the new mucker? What's your name?"

"Red."

"Red who?"

"Red the Socialist Gregor."

"You got a first name?"

"That's it."

"Where've you mucked?"

"All over."

"You been fired?"

"Everywhere. I usually last a week."

"Then what?"

"Someone doesn't like me."

"Why?"

"I stand up for the downtrodden."

"You're hired," Penrose said. "If you don't stand up for them, I'd not want you."

"Three dollars is below a just wage."

"You'll get more as soon as you prove yourself."

"Meanwhile you exploit me."

"Don't cause accidents," Penrose said.

"Accidents happen."

"No, accidents are caused. Everything is cause and effect. They don't just happen. It's not fate."

Gregor smiled. "You're the first boss who's ever said that. Maybe I'll work for you."

"Nine hundred level." Penrose watched the man stride toward the lift.

He had to talk to the super about Brophy's widow, and try to get the widow a couple of weeks' pay. Then he'd go give Gregor a close look.

{ FIVE }

Royal Maxwell eyed the brown-soaked remains on his zinc-topped table. One thing about Butte, he thought. He never had to worry about his next meal. Butte was a mortician's paradise. The widow couldn't pay, but it wouldn't matter. Someone else would. There was opportunity in it.

He eyed the stack of pine boxes, and selected one without varnish or handles. The varnished ones cost two dollars more. Handles would add five. This would be easy. He'd load the beloved departed in and nail it down, and save all the work of undressing and dressing the deceased, or patting a little rouge on his cheeks, and all that. The widow wasn't going to see anything but a tight box.

The coppers had summoned him, and he'd gone with his ebony handcart, properly attired in a black swallowtail and silk stovepipe, and the pine box, and with white gloved hands, lifted the three parts of Singing Sean Brophy into his conveyance, covered Brophy with a gray silk sheet, while two or three hundred citizens of Butte watched. Then he had stood reverently, silk hat in hand, the cold breezes toying with his jet hair, and after a moment wheeled the handcart the six blocks to the rear of the clapboard Maxwell Mortuary.

He wouldn't need to wait long for the widow. They usually showed up in minutes, and indeed this one, Alice

Brophy of Dublin Gulch, made her appearance with the sound of the door chime.

She was bone-thin, and had a little boy in tow, and wore a brown Mother Hubbard.

"I'm so sorry to hear of your misfortune," he said.

"What's it going to cost?" she asked.

"Oh, we won't worry about that now. Come sit down here and tell me what you want for your beloved husband."

"I haven't got anything anyway, so you can't stick me."

"He was a splendid man, Singing Sean was, and I know you'll want the best for him."

"When he wasn't drinking," she said.

"I hear he had a fine tenor voice, and a great repertoire."

"He was more interested in lifting my skirts," she said. "Now I'm stuck."

"Ah, yes, your little ones will want to remember their father, and visit his grave one day soon. You'll want a fine headstone, something that will endure through the ages, and you'll want the finest casket money can buy, and a double lot so when the time comes when—"

"I want to see him," she said.

"But that's not possible. You wouldn't want to see him. You'll want to remember him just as he was, loving and kind."

"I want to make sure it's him, and he's not skipping."

"But the casket's been sealed."

"Open it."

"No, madam, it would be too much for mortal eyes to bear."

"I've seen men that fell a thousand feet down the shaft, so I'll be looking at Sean."

"Well, let's deal with that later. We'll want to set an hour for visitors, and get some lots, and choose a coffin, and arrange a service of your choice. Shall I summon Father McGuire?"

"I'm not ordering a thing I can't pay for. Now show him to me."

"Ah, I'll need time to unseal the box, madam, and I don't think this is wise."

This was turning into a standoff, but not anything that Royal Maxwell could not deal with.

"Madam, my heart aches for you, and I think the best thing is to put all this off for a day, and for you to return in the morning when we can proceed in peace. Take this lad to his fatherless home, and think reverent thoughts and blessings and tomorrow we'll proceed according to your every wish."

"I knew you'd not let me see him. He's mine, I own him, and you won't let me see him."

"May I offer you a conveyance back to Dublin Gulch?"

"I'm not yet thirty," she replied.

He watched her sweep out, into the cold wind, and the door jangled behind her. He waited a few moments, found his placard saying he was out briefly, placed it in the curtained window, and slid into the biting spring air. The Butte Miners Union hall was just down the street, and Big Johnny Boyle would likely be right there.

The hall was stark, with cream-colored paint and stained brown wainscot, and a few handmade desks. Plus a lot of wooden chairs. Big Johnny Boyle, head of the Butte Miners Union, wanted it that way, and was oblivious to comfort anyway. He could stand up or sprawl on the floor as well settle behind a rude desk, and not know the difference. Most of the time he was out of the place anyway, but the door was unlocked and any down-and-out person on earth could find shelter there. Boyle's real office was the Trelawney Tavern next door, where he conducted nearly all his union business and received visitors from a chair in the far corner, which may as well have been a throne.

Maxwell found him there, a mug of dark ale before him, staring at the racehorse lithographs on the wall. The place was not quite a restaurant, but there was always enough stuff on the bar, such as hard-boiled eggs and pumpernickel and big salty pretzels, to feed any beast.

"I know, and I've already started a collection," Big Johnny said.

"You'll want to give him a good send-off," Maxwell said.

"You kidding? Singing Sean Brophy, he was a lousy brother, hardly paid his dues, was always complaining. He'll get your pine-box special."

"His poor widow's distraught. You'll want to put the beloved into a good honest walnut coffin, you know. She hasn't got a dime."

"She'll get a month's pay."

"No she won't. This didn't happen in the pits, and the company won't pay a nickel."

Boyle stared, pondering that, blinking his brown eyes. "It's the company's fault. That was their ore train."

"And Sean tried to hop it on the streets of Butte and died under it."

"They'll pay," Boyle said.

"I don't think so. Alice Brophy's depending on you."

Boyle stared into his ale. "I'll shake it out of some pockets," he said. "And I got other ways."

"Enough to keep her going? Three children?"

"That was always his excuse, got to feed my kids so I can't pay dues. He got it exactly wrong. You pay your dues so you've got a union that'll get you enough to feed your kids. So my heart don't bleed one damned bit."

Royal Maxwell saw how it would go. "I'll give him a good send-off," he said.

"I'll send a few brothers over to console the widow," Boyle said.

There was yet another place to visit, but it would take a bit of luck. Marcus Daly was usually available if he wasn't in Anaconda or out at his stock farm in the Bitterroot, and was a soft touch. The top man for the whole Anaconda Company was often in town, working from his Daly Bank and Trust office, though more and more he relied on his cronies to run the company. Still, it was worth a try.

He tracked Daly down at the Butte Hotel, where he was in the saloon surrounded by people wanting something from him.

"You, is it?" Daly said. "Want a drink? How's business?"

"Improving every day, Mr. Daly."

"You're looking for some funeral cash."

"Singing Sean Brophy, yes. He leaves a widow and three children with nothing."

"It didn't happen in the pit, now, did it?"

"No, sir, but it was a company train."

"My shift boss Penrose was here a bit ago. He wanted a month wage for her. I said no, buy her a nice new gown and call it good."

"Gown?"

"She'll remarry in a week or two. That's how it goes. Give her a gown for the marrying."

There were a lot more males than females in Butte, and a new widow was a prize half the lonely miners would pursue even before Singing Sean was planted. The lady would do just fine.

"That's just right, Mr. Daly, but can I count on you to bury the man? The company man?"

Daly smiled. "Good work, Maxwell; I'll give you an A for effort."

"Then you'll accept the bill?"

"I like men who go for a profit," Daly said. "Send me the invoice."

Royal Maxwell worked his stovepipe hat around a little, and bowed. "It's a fine day, sir."

"It's never a fine day when one of my men dies, Maxwell."

Maxwell retreated, plunged out of the hotel into bitter sunlight, and hastened back to his funeral parlor. It had cost him an affront, but now he had some cash from the union and a hundred from Daly, and it had been a profitable spring day. He was lucky the big man was in town.

The newsboys were on the street, hawking the evening papers, so he invested a few cents in all three papers. The only one that interested him, though, was the *Mineral*, Clark's noisy sheet, which always had its own slant on the news. Including the death of an Anaconda miner.

The headline read: "ACM Train Claims ACM Miner."

The rest fit the bill: "This morning an ACM miner, Sean Brophy, perished while trying to avoid an ACM ore train operating recklessly on city streetcar rails. Brophy was unable to escape the train, rolling at high speed through the heart of Butte to return the empty ore cars to the mines on Anaconda Hill. As usual, safety was not a consideration in the operation of the ore train, not even while it was rolling through Butte neighborhoods lying between the ACM mines and the railhead on the flat. Mr. Brophy is survived by his widow, Alice, and three children. The *Mineral* determined that the widow will receive no compensation, because, as ACM officials explain it, the accident didn't occur on shift or in the pit. The destitute widow says she has no plans, nor the means to feed her children."

That's the *Mineral* for you, Maxwell thought. He set it aside and hunted for the story in the *Butte Inter-Mountain,* the Republican paper operated by Lee Mantle, an editor with ambitions.

"Miner Dies Hopping ACM Ore Train," went the headline.

The text went a different direction: "A Butte miner employed by the Neversweat, Sean Brophy, attempted to hop a string of empty ore cars en route to Anaconda Hill this morning, slipped, and perished beneath the wheels of the cars.

" 'Employees are forbidden to hop the cars,' said mine manager Cyrus Wilkes, 'and do so at their own peril.' A flagman riding the lead car waved Brophy off, but the miner ignored the command and attempted the dangerous hop onto a moving train. The Butte police determined that Brophy died instantly. The company noted that the tragic death occurred on off time, and not during Brophy's shift, and not on ACM property, and has declined further comment. Brophy is survived by his widow, Alice, and children Timothy, Thomas, and Eloise. Services are pending at Maxwell Mortuary."

Daly's own paper, the *Anaconda Standard,* which circulated widely in Butte, said nothing at all. Maxwell was annoyed. It meant he would need to buy a funeral notice in the *Standard.* ACM had a large hand in controlling the news in Butte, as well as the rest of Montana.

Royal Maxwell always enjoyed the rivalry, and especially enjoyed the *Mineral,* which was becoming the least scrupulous rag in the city, if not the state. He wished the other sheets would go out of business. But meanwhile, he'd make around two hundred on a hundred-dollar planting, and that always put him in a good mood. He might head for Mercury Street this evening, and spend a little even before he got it.

He scribbled out some funeral notices, setting the time as ten in the morning, two days hence, and summoned a messenger to deliver to the papers. Filthy McNabb showed up, and Royal was happy because Filthy was more reliable than Watermelon Jones. He gave Filthy a dime and told him to deliver the notices to each of the papers in town.

Tomorrow, he would inform the widow that all the arrangements had been made, courtesy of Sean's union, and she would be free from the burden of arranging her husband's funeral. He remembered to set his two grave diggers to work. They would each get two dollars to dig the hole, wait out the funeral, and fill it up again. He'd order a wooden headboard, no sense fooling with granite, and that would take care of things, except for summoning a priest. Alice Brophy would be grateful, of course. Service was what Maxwell's was noted for.

{ SIX }

Big Johnny Boyle stood at the stately door with a small hitch of unfamiliar fear roiling him. He'd never been in the bank. He'd never met William Andrews Clark. In all of his dealings with Clark's mines and smelters Boyle had dealt with Clark's hounds, the cronies who turned Clark's commands into reality. But this time Clark himself wanted Boyle, and had sent Watermelon Jones from the Messenger Service with the message.

Boyle had heard a lot about Clark, and knew much more about the great man than Clark knew about any Irishman named Boyle. Clark was Scots, and that explained everything. Boyle knew exactly what Scotsmen were made of, and Clark was no exception. Clark would be dour, short, thin, and grim. It was not known whether anyone had seen Clark smile, much less laugh. You couldn't be a Scot and smile; that would be a contradiction. It was an odd thing. Scots were Celtic, Irish were Celtic, but the Scots got all the bad Celtic and the Irish got all the good Celtic.

Boyle couldn't understand the fear in himself. He was

never fearful. He didn't rise to the top of the Butte Miners Union being afraid. He was as big as his name implied, big enough to smack grumblers, knock heads, boot whiners, and shake dollars out of pockets. But this time fear roiled him. Well, if worse came to worst, Boyle could lift the little captain up by the scruff of the neck and shake the daylights out of him—and then fight off the dozen goons that surrounded the little Scot.

He guessed what this was about, but he would have to wait and see. He straightened up, plunged through the doors of Clark and Bro. Bank, headed up some creaking stairs to the second floor, and headed for the unmarked pebbled glass door that would admit him to the sanctum sanctorum. The note, written in a fine script, said simply that Mr. Clark requested the presence of Mr. Boyle at once. That's how it was with Clark. At once. Boyle had read it slowly; he wasn't a top-flight reader, having barely finished sixth grade, and he read at all only because he had designs larger than shoveling rock.

Much to his surprise, the owner of a dozen mines and mills in Butte sat alone behind a plain desk, the chair and desk on a platform. There was a door leading to adjacent offices, where his lackeys no doubt did the great man's bidding, but here, in a modest corner office with modest views of the bustling city, William Andrews Clark pulled his levers.

"Mr. Boyle, my good man, do come in," Clark said, extending a hand and offering a smile. So much for the lousy stories, Boyle thought, shaking the delicate white hand of the little fellow, who was most of a foot smaller. Boyle estimated Clark's height at around five seven, maybe eight in platform shoes, and a hundred pounds wet. His eyes were bright, his gaze penetrating, and Boyle felt himself examined from head to heel.

"You're Irish," Clark said. "A noble race."

Another myth tumbled into dust. Boyle had heard that

Clark had nothing but disdain for the citizens of the Emerald Isle.

"Came here direct, and on Daly's dime," Boyle said.

Clark nodded. Butte was heavily Irish. Boyle's union was even more Irish, save for a few bleak and gloomy Cornishmen. Scots weren't popular with anyone in Butte save for the dozen or two Scots themselves.

"You may sit. When you stand you have the advantage of me," Clark said.

Big Johnny settled in a plain wooden chair. That's how this office was. There was not an ostentatious item in it; no gilt-framed oil portraits of fake ancestors, no walnut wainscoting, no velvet drapes, no Brussels carpets, no gold-plated spittoons.

"That's better. Now, let's cut to the chase. In a few months I will be Senator Clark. I'm going to take the seat. That means there are matters to negotiate. Namely, what I can do for you, and what you can do for me. You and your union."

Clark waited for the union boss to absorb that, but Boyle had already absorbed it before stepping into this austere throne room.

"Mister Clark, it's not easy to buy a labor union. Or sell one. And the brothers, we decide things together. Maybe you should talk to the brothers."

"Senator. Call me Senator Clark."

"Yeah, and call me Big Johnny, boyo."

Clark's attentions seemed to drift elsewhere, and settled upon a fly buzzing at the window.

"Kill it," he said.

Big Johnny didn't budge. The fly sailed through space and alighted on another pane.

Clark rang a little ringer on his desk. A plunge of a lever chimed a summons, and instantly a gent in a white shirt materialized.

"A flyswatter for Big Johnny," Clark said.

The weasel in white vanished and reappeared, carrying a wire-handled flyswatter and handed it to Boyle.

Clark was studiously eyeing the window.

"I think the time has come, boyo, to pay my brothers a four-dollar wage."

The going rate in the mines was three-fifty. Daly resisted. That was an odd thing. Daly had been a hardrock miner and spent plenty of his early life in the pits of the Comstock in Nevada, and Utah too. He still drained a mug of ale with his miners, and looked after them. And paid three and a half.

"If I plunge, Daly will follow suit, and then what?"

"The brothers will know who was first."

"Will that obtain their solidarity?"

"Nothing but the union does that, boyo."

"And you won't guarantee a thing, I suppose."

"They're Irish, and they mostly work for Daly."

"I'm American," the boyo said. "I've created thousands of American jobs for Americans. And in the Senate I'll do even better. I'll help repeal the silver law. I'll support eight-hour days. Eight hours for all who toil. If it's federal law, everyone must comply. Even Anaconda. I'll be known as the Friend of Labor."

That silver stuff was too much for Big Johnny to figure out, but Congress was lowering the price of it compared to gold, and that made everyone in Butte mad.

He shrugged. "No skin off my back," he said.

The fly circled Clark's desk and bombed Clark, messing around Clark's hairy face. Some men had handsome beards, well trimmed. Clark's was a mass of long hair surrounding his mouth, with hair drooping over his lips to strain any soup the man spooned into himself. It was a thick, matted, symbolic beard surrounding a voracious hole in the man, guarding his mouth like a forest of needles. The boyo's wife must have suffered.

Clark probably weighed not much over a hundred

pounds, but he liked to eat, and he liked to conceal his eater behind all the shrubbery he could manage. Who could explain it? The boyo was beyond explaining.

"The brothers shouldn't have to go into the pits for less than five a day, boyo."

Clark twitched. His bright gaze fixed on Big Johnny a moment, and then followed the buzzing fly back to the window panes.

"Marcus Daly would take a strike before he'd go that high."

"Daly lifts some ale with the brothers. His company isn't Scots."

"You're a good man, Boyle. If ever you want to work for me, I pay a good wage. Some of my young assistants earn five thousand a year. You certainly have the makings of a man who gets things done, my sort of man. You show me what you can do with your brotherhood, and I'll show you what I do for rising young executives."

The windows blotted out street traffic. Not even the grind of the trolley cars penetrated the rich silence of Clark's chambers.

Big Johnny yawned, picked up the flyswatter, waved it a few times, stood, headed for the bright window, and dispatched the fly. Clark studied the fly on his maple floor. Then Boyle placed the swatter on Clark's shining desk, and stepped out of the sanctum.

An odd breeze lowered smoke from the smelters and boiler rooms over the city, stinging nostrils and throats. It was mostly wood or coal smoke, now that Butte was connected by rail to the coalfields of the state. The mining outfits had quit the open roasting of ores in town. They used to build giant bonfires over heaps of ore, to roast the ore before milling or smelting it. The smoke was laden with arsenic. Everyone in Butte coughed then, and old-timers still did.

Half the old guys he knew would trade a lower wage

for anything that stopped miner's lung. They lived out their short lives panting for breath, every wheeze of their lungs hurtful and sad. They'd hopped the immigrant boats thinking that anything was better than starving in Ireland, but in Butte they put food on their table and rock dust in their lungs and were half dead ten years before the wake. That was mining for you. Long days shoveling rock in the dark, twenty years of being unable to breathe, and nothing much for your widow and babies.

Boyle found Eddie the Pick in the union hall. Eddie was a hothead. His plan was to storm the corporation offices, slit the throats of the big cheeses, take over the companies, and dole out wages instead of profits. That wasn't a bad idea, but Boyle thought the time wasn't ripe yet. In a few years, maybe.

"I think I just sold out," Big Johnny said.

"My price is a million; what's yours, Boyle?"

"I don't know yet. Those Scots have a way of ruining the rest of us. He offered to fight for an eight-hour day once he gets in."

"He's calling himself senator already."

"He had me kill the fly," Big Johnny said. "Doesn't that mean something?"

"You got me there, boyo," Eddie the Pick said.

"I didn't give him any answer, but I killed his fly," Boyle said. "Now he's going to call it a contract."

Eddie the Pick wheezed with joy. He was far gone with miner's lung, and his real goal was to take the world down with him when he went.

"You gonna put it on the table?"

"No. It's no one's business. But maybe I'll see what Daly's up to. I'm thinking politics is good business for the brotherhood."

"Nah, them captains of industry will think of a new way to screw us."

"It's a lever," Big Johnny said.

"Clark, he's a strange one. When he wants something, nothing stops him, including us. He's got no laugh in him. If he laughed once in a while, it'd be different. But he's as grim a man as ever walked the earth, boyo. That kind scares me. What does he want to be senator for, eh? Not to help anyone in Montana. Not for the money. He's got all the money he needs the rest of his life. Not for anything except looking at himself in the mirror and seeing a senator in the glass. He can buy anything, castles, railroads, men like us, women, fancy clothes. But a Senate seat takes some buying. First you got to put your own men in the legislature and then you got to have them make you the senator. That don't come cheap, boyo."

"Neither do I, Eddie, neither do I," Big Johnny said.

"I got the money for the widow," Eddie said. "Enough to pay Maxwell and a little left over. That's work, shaking it out of miners. They don't have but ten cents in their pockets, and that's to buy a pint after the whistle blows. But I got it. Maxwell's bargain burial is ninety-seven and there'll be some left over."

"So give yourself the change, Eddie. You made the widow happy. When is it, tomorrow?"

"Yeah, at ten. Maxwell, he told her to show up, because that's what the notices say, so she'll be there. After that there'll be twenty brothers in line wanting to marry her. I wish they'd abolish marriage. It's the ruin of a man. And what business is it of government? Why should government care, eh? It's none of their business. When we take over, we'll abolish marriage. All it does is ruin men and wreck women and label half the children in the world bastards. Share all and share alike, that's my motto."

"But it doesn't work," Big Johnny said. "I ain't sharing with anybody, ever."

SEVEN

Alice Brophy stormed into Royal Maxwell's mortuary, found the undertaker sipping from a brown bottle, and lit into him.

"Tomorrow is it? And without asking me? Well, it won't be tomorrow. It'll be the next day. I'm sewing shirts and pants and a little dimity dress. I'll not have Sean's own babies going to their pa's burying in rags. I'll get them dressed proper, and you'll just have to wait a day."

"But madam, that's not possible. The notices were published. It's all set."

"No it's not all set, and you'll delay it a day. Tommy's going to get new britches, Eloise is going to get a white dress, and Timmy, he's got a clean blue shirt coming, and that's that."

"Why, I don't see how we can alter a thing."

"Without a word with me you set the day and the hour and now you can set a new day and a new hour."

"But I have another service scheduled."

"Well, that's too bad. I'm not coming to the one tomorrow, I'm not. I'll not bring Tom or Tim or Eloise either. You'll bury my man without the widow, without his children. And then what'll Butte think of you, eh?"

"They'll think nothing of it. They'll think you're being, well, a bit emotional, madam. Now please accept my sympathies, and we'll seat you at the service with a black veil wrapped about all of you, and no one will see a thing."

"And that's not our priest. What right have you to make these arrangements? I've never met this man. I won't be having a stranger blessing my husband, or saying words over him."

Royal Maxwell smiled, gently, out of long experience smoothing out the uproars of last rites. "We'll send a carriage, madam, at a half hour ahead, and you'll be settled nicely for the service."

She stared. "You're going to switch."

"No, madam, these things are settled."

"Go to hell, then," she said, and wheeled away.

She felt Maxwell's bland gaze on her back as she stormed out. She wondered if she could kidnap Sean and bury him on some hilltop somewhere. Let them gather without her. Let them do it without Sean's own widow and little ones. Just let them.

She needed to talk to Sean's shifter, Penrose. If not one of Sean's friends from the pit showed up, maybe that would show Maxwell a thing or two. Finding Andrew Penrose wouldn't be easy, but in an hour the second shift would begin, and he'd be up there somewhere. She headed up Dublin Gulch toward the Neversweat, but didn't see anyone about except for the topside men lining up an ore train.

But there was an office, and she penetrated it. The presence of a woman there startled the clerk, who wore a white shirt with black arm garters.

"Where is Mister Penrose—the shifter?"

"Madam, if you'll turn about, you'll see him behind you."

The shift boss eyed Alice Brophy, a quizzical look on his face. She spilled out her story in swift angry bursts, while he listened restlessly.

"Why, there's a remedy, madam. I'll stand the price of some readymades, not only for your children but for you. Go where you will, and take this," he said. He began to pencil a note on a sheet of yellow payroll paper.

"I can make my own clothing, thank you," she said. "What I want is for you to tell the men that worked with Sean not to go tomorrow; not a one show up. Let Maxwell run his funeral without one living soul."

Penrose shook his head. "I can't do that, madam. I won't discourage any man who wishes to pay his respects from doing so. Those who want to bury your husband, they're free to do so and I'll not stand in their way. They'll go there to honor their friend Sean Brophy, and that should please you."

"But I want Maxwell to suffer."

Penrose simply shook his head.

She knew he was right, but that wasn't going to slow her down. She'd get the funeral she wanted or embarrass Maxwell's Mortuary, and that was how it was going to spin out.

Penrose stood quietly, his note written.

"No thanks," she said, ignoring the note, and whirled into the cold wind.

She'd make Maxwell stew in his arrogance one way or another. She picked her way down the worn trail, and headed straight for the union hall. She knew what she wanted, and she'd have Big Johnny Boyle do it for her.

Johnny was in the pub next door to the hall, which is exactly where she expected to find him. She entered, and won the scowls of the bartender and all the males standing there with one foot on the brass rail, sipping ale. She knew Big Johnny. Everyone in Butte knew him. He made sure of it. And a few had discovered his brass knuckles, too.

She marched straight toward him, but he caught her arm and led her straight out of that male sanctuary and into the bright spring wind. And there she delivered her ultimatum. "Tell your men not to show up tomorrow. The widow won't be there. I'm going to strike, that's what. It's a widow's strike against Maxwell, treating me like that."

Johnny Boyle was grinning. "You got it wrong, dearie. I've ordered every brother who's not in the pits to show up. We're going to give our brother Sean a fine send-off, and maybe there'll be a few you'll want to visit with afterward."

She knew what he was talking about. The Butte Miners Union was a marriage mart, and she'd have her pick of a dozen after an appropriate week of mourning.

"I'll not have it your way, Johnny Boyle. Go ahead, fill up the funeral parlor, but you won't see Sean Brophy's widow or his three children there. Let them celebrate that, and if they're planning to look me over, and making plans without my consent, let them think that I don't love, honor, and obey anyone unless I choose to."

Boyle's black eyebrows arched.

She left him, and felt his gaze on her as she hurried away. They didn't want to help her. All they thought about was politics and money and ale. Well, she'd go back to Dublin Gulch and sew, and if she wasn't done in time for the funeral, too bad.

She spotted her neighbor Kegs O'Leary parking his wagon in front of his house. He operated a beer wagon and there was always a little spillage or a faulty keg that he needed to take care of to keep the beer from going to waste. Now he wiped his hands on his once-white apron and lifted a sweating keg to the dirt.

"So it's you, is it? My condolences to you, Mrs. Brophy."

"They're going to bury him tomorrow and never asked me, and I'm not ready, I'm sewing a dress for Eloise. And shirts for the boys."

"Maxwell's didn't?"

"Not once. They didn't even ask me what priest. Am I supposed to send off my own man with his children in rags?"

"That's a venial sin, I'd say, Mrs. Brophy. Rags at a funeral."

"And the union wouldn't help me and Sean's shift boss, he at least cared a little."

The beer man stared at the smoke-shot sky. "Would you be wanting a wake for poor Sean, Mrs. Brophy? Would you be wanting to bring poor Sean back to his own little cottage one last time, and keep him there until you get the sewing done?"

She stared at him, and finally nodded.

"I think I'll just drive over to Maxwell, Mrs. Brophy. I'll put this keg in your kitchen for future use. And I think I'll let Sean's brothers come and mourn this evening if it pleases you."

Maybe the world would be made right again, she thought.

Kegs O'Leary snapped the lines over the croup of his big Percheron and drove off, turning west toward the funeral home.

"There now, he's a man who knows his way into a woman's heart," she said to Tommy, who was clutching her skirts.

She settled down to sew on the dimity dress, and had just hemmed the skirt when she heard the clop and rattle of Kegs's beer wagon. She hurried outside and found him removing two sawhorses from his wagon, which he carried into her small parlor and spaced about five feet apart. "I don't have a thing to cover them," he said.

But she did. She had two white sheets. By the time she had these draped over the sawhorses, Kegs was settling the plain pine box on the sawhorses, almost as easily as he hefted kegs of beer.

"I'll put out the word, Mrs. Brophy," he said.

"Please do." She couldn't think of what else to do, so she kissed him. He turned bashful and wiped his cheek.

"Maxwell wasn't even there, so I just backed up the wagon, lifted Sean here, and drove off. I think it's Sean. He weighed about two kegs. There was another, but polished oak and all."

"That's Sean here," she said. "Oak is for heretics."

"I'll put the word out, Mrs. Brophy. This evening, will it be?"

"This evening, Mr. O'Leary."

"I'll be stealing a kiss," he said.

She watched him climb onto his beer wagon and haw his horse ahead.

Everything was right. She settled in a parlor chair, a few feet from the pine box, and began sewing industriously. Everything was perfect, as much as a widow could want.

Sean's union brothers would be on shift, but his brothers from across the sea would come, and maybe that was best. County Clare brothers, County Galway brothers. And there was even an untapped keg in her kitchen, so that she could be hospitable. She thought of her good luck, and Sean's good luck, and how the world was a good place. Even Butte.

She sewed furiously, adding a collar and cuffs to Eloise's white dimity dress.

"There now, go try it on, dearie," she said.

"Is that Daddy in there?"

"It is. Sean Padraic Brophy."

"Why is he there?"

"So his friends can remember him and send him off."

"Where is he going?"

She smiled. "He's going to be with the angels. Maybe, anyway."

The girl took her dress and headed for her alcove, where she had a bunk. The boys had bunks in the other alcove. Alice and Sean's bed stood behind two hanging drapes in the corner of the parlor. Alice eyed the brown drapes, and decided to take them down. She didn't need them anymore. She clambered up on a wooden chair and undid the cords, and the weary cloth tumbled. The room looked different somehow with her bed in it. She felt exhilarated, now that she could live without curtains hanging around a part of her life. Suddenly her whole life was contained in one large room: the kitchen and parlor. She could see the boundaries of her life from where she stood.

She fussed with Eloise's white dress for a while, unhappy because one side seemed to dip below the other, and she finally decided Eloise was lopsided, her left side smaller than the other, and she would leave it be.

The boys barged in. What they did out in the gulch she was glad not to know, but they were uncommonly clean this time, for which she was grateful. She fed them some porridge, and had just finished up when the first of her guests arrived. That turned out to be Kegs himself.

"I thought I'd get the keg pouring right, Mrs. Brophy, so the brothers have more than suds to sip on."

"I don't know what I'll do for cups and mugs," she said.

"They'll bring their own, madam."

She watched him tap the keg and screw in a faucet, and settle it on a counter, and try a few golden swallows to draw off the foam.

And then at twilight the first guest came, and she saw through the glass that he was bringing flowers, and she wondered what she would put them in. She opened up, and beheld a man in a gray suit, cravat, and fedora, standing solidly before her.

It was himself, Marcus Daly.

{ EIGHT }

One swift glance told Marcus Daly everything. The coffin rested on its sawhorses with a silken green cloth over it. The Dublin Gulch house barely held a family. Alice Brophy was work-worn, bone-thin, freckled, and with spun-gold hair.

"Sir?" she said, fiercely wiping her hands on her apron.

"Marcus Daly here. I can only stay a bit, Alice Brophy. Here's a few daisies to remember Mr. Brophy with."

She took them timidly, and attempted to curtsey.

"Word came to me that the funeral home wasn't helpful.

Here, take this card. It's a way to reach me. Whenever you say, I'll send a carriage for the remains, and I'll have a grave ready at the cemetery, and if I can manage it, I'll have your parish priest present for the burying. All this will be at the time and place of your choosing. Send a messenger boy to the place here on the card, ask for my subaltern Hennessy, and he'll make it be."

"But sir, how can I repay you?"

"Name your next boy Tammany, Mrs. Brophy."

"But—lord, how did you know? And why me? Us?" She slid her hands over her children, who clustered at her skirts.

"The Anaconda Company has risen out of Ireland, Mrs. Brophy, and we look after our own."

She nodded. "But we've tapped a keg. Won't you stay?"

"You make a bouquet of daisies for Sean Brophy, and I'll be going now."

"Oh, sir . . ."

He smiled and left, walking the bare-dirt path to the rutted grade, where his ebony trap stood, with one of his fine trotters in harness. She watched from the door. Her house had been whitewashed once, but that was gone and what remained was gray wood.

He drove off, through one of the most twisted thoroughfares in Butte, so bleak that nothing but flame could remedy the ugliness. He felt that yearning for which there was no word, something akin to loneliness even when he was surrounded by his closest friends. It was something he couldn't explain. It was that yearning that drove him to the widow's house, and the yearning that had inspired a company that was almost an outpost of Ireland.

He'd heard about Maxwell's affront to the woman soon after it happened. Maxwell treated the Irish as if they were sardines. The mortician would bury Sean Brophy in the morning, keep the flowers, and stage a fancier funeral in the afternoon for someone with another kind of surname.

But let it be said among Butte's Irish that Marcus Daly spared the widow a little grief and shame.

Just up the hill were his three best mines, a ramshackle cluster of headframes, boilers, and sheds, all working the same massive seams of copper, laced with silver. Just keeping them going and profitable consumed his energy and his life. There was no stability in a mining operation. Whatever bad might happen probably would, no doubt all at once.

He had risen to every challenge, expanded and enriched his company even while building an idyllic life for himself raising blooded horses in the Bitterroot Valley. He thrived on the competition, including the competition of horse racing, and his stock farms had produced a succession of winners. He thought he was like his prize Thoroughbred Tammany, who kept his nose ahead of the pack because he had to.

Always trouble. There was pressure in Congress to repeal the Sherman Silver Purchase Act, which provided that the federal government buy several tons of silver each month. Without those purchases Butte would sink into idleness if not depression. Then there was the Montana Union Railroad, charging monopolistic prices to haul Anaconda's ore from the mines to the smelter thirty or so miles away. Daly had his remedy for that, his own Butte, Anaconda and Pacific Railroad, but that wouldn't be finished until next year.

He had erected the enormous upper and lower smelters over there because that was where he found the nearest water, in Warm Springs Creek. Rival companies had claimed all the water around Butte, and every drop of Silver Bow Creek. Then there was the problem of getting timber enough to run his mines and smelters. He needed four hundred thousand board feet a year to fire his boilers, supply mine timbers, and build his buildings. He and various lumber barons had been cutting public forests, mostly sections interlaced with the Northern Pacific's railroad lands, but the Cleveland administration was putting a stop to it. His own Democratic Party was threatening his livelihood and that of all his miners. What could a man do but buy coal anywhere in Montana and Wyoming he could get it, and build rails to get it to Butte and Anaconda?

There was trouble in Butte. To get his ore off the hill he had to share his right of way with the trolley cars. There were apex lawsuits to deal with from rival mining companies. Copper prices were low and declining. There were elections coming up, and he needed a slate of candidates that would look after the company's interests.

And now he faced another effort by William Andrews Clark, the dour Scots genius who was not content to own much of Butte Hill, but wanted to wear a senator's toga as well. Wherever Daly sought to make a move, there was Clark checking him. The election of 1888 had started it all. For business reasons, Daly wanted to form an alliance with certain Republicans and elect someone who would oppose the administration. He and Clark were both Democrats, but there was a difference: Clark was a rigid loyalist, while Daly was a man to go after coalitions that would do what the company needed. And in the end, Daly rescinded his support of Clark, and had his numerous employees vote for a Republican, Tom Carter, who won the seat by a narrow margin. Clark never forgave him, as rigid in his anger as he was in his politics.

Daly never thought of it as a personal struggle, although he didn't care for Clark. The dapper dandy was a distant relative by marriage, so Daly had avoided contention, while quietly undermining Clark's support among the coalitions that owned Butte. It was all for the company, he thought. Just business. Not for himself, not to punish Clark. Just for the company, and all those men he was responsible for, the men whose pay envelopes put food on their tables and sheltered their families from the brutal winters on the Continental Divide.

But that wasn't the limit of his ambitions either. The new Montana constitution had left it to the citizens to choose a state capital. Helena was the temporary capital, but Daly had other ideas. His shining new city of Anaconda had been laid out to perfection, with broad boulevards and generous lots and sweeping views. It was rising at the foot of Mount Haggin, named after the California financier and major owner of the company, who had underwritten the whole expansion of the Anaconda Mining Company into the dominant business in the new state. It was the most beautiful place on earth.

What better place than Daly's own city of Anaconda, with a grand capitol building at the foot of Mount Haggin, and a welcome proximity between state officials and the company's own directing class? But William Andrews Clark had no intention of letting that come to pass. So it was all politics, politics, politics, from mayors and aldermen on up. And Daly had not forgotten that Butte was Irish, and Daly himself had made it so, and the numerous Butte Irish were the key to all the state's elections to come.

And that brought him back to the story he discovered in that evening's edition of the *Mineral*. It was all about the woes of the widow Alice Brophy, whose late husband had been employed at the Neversweat, and who had been denied a pension by the ruthless company that had employed him. And how the Butte Miners Union members had dug deep into their pockets to give the brother a funeral, and how an Anaconda ore train had taken the life of a hapless miner.

Marcus Daly had thought to protest, to tell the editor that a few facts were missing. But he knew better than that. He wasn't quick with words, and whatever he said would be turned into fodder for another twisted story.

Still, he wanted to do something about it, and decided it was time to meet the new editor, the one William Andrews Clark had hired to do whatever jobbery he could do and in any way he wished so long as it tore at the fabric of Daly's company, and Daly himself.

No, he would not get into a sparring match with words. Instead, he would simply meet the bloke who called himself John Fellowes Hall, as if his name were a three-piece suit. He would ask questions. He'd do the interviewing. It was time to take the measure of the thug whose bludgeons were words and phrases, and who stole a man's honor and a company's good name. There would be things to find out: was Hall simply Clark's goon? And maybe he could find out what Clark hoped to get out of this barrage of character assassination.

Daly steered his trap back toward central Butte, which rose proudly on the slopes below most of the mines. The newspapers were all cheek by jowl, and he found a place before the *Mineral* to park the trap and keep the horse tethered to a carriage weight.

He remembered that newspapers were inky places. The ink jumped at you. Leapt from distant presses and typesetting tables, smeared you as you dodged your way through, and ruined the clothing of innocents. He was greeted by the acrid smell of the Linotypes, but he was used to that. His own paper, the *Anaconda Standard,* had nothing but the finest equipment that his money could buy.

Daly eyed a window-lit corner at the rear, and the sunlit gentleman in the alcove who radiated brightness, and decided the man looked like his quarry, so he dodged his way through the smoky plant and presented himself at the gate.

Hall, dressed nattily, especially for a newsman, stared up, recognized the man at his door, and stood.

"Mister Daly, is it?" he asked.

"I'm Daly. You're Hall."

"John Fellowes Hall, yes. What may I do for you?"

"Nothing at all, Mister Hall. I just wanted to stop by and welcome you to Butte. You're new, are you?"

"Not to journalism, sir. I've been editing newspapers in the East for many years."

"Well, that's fine. What papers did you edit?"

"Oh, names you wouldn't know, sir, New York, New Jersey, Pennsylvania, Ohio, all splendid papers."

"What brought you here, sir?"

"Well, I bested the competition. My employer—ah, Mr. Clark, searched widely for the sort of talent he wanted, and finally settled on me, after looking at several dozen applicants. Of course I was greatly honored. He's offered me unusual remuneration, which I have taken to be a sign of his confidence in me."

"I've started up a paper of my own, you know, over in Anaconda, and got a good man there. What did Clark look for in an editor?"

"An ability to penetrate to the truth of things lying just under the surface, Mr. Daly. He wanted a man who'd be a natural skeptic, a good man with words and ideas, and a man who might know how to advance Mr. Clark's many interests in public affairs, business, politics, and theology. He's a devout Methodist, sir, and a knowledge of scriptures was paramount with him. He told me frankly, a man who knew the Bible was a man who would have the inside track to this position."

"What's your favorite verse, Mr. Hall?"

"Why, I'll paraphrase here. Don't stick it to others when you don't want them to stick it to you."

"Very interesting, Mr. Hall, a motto worthy of Caesar. Well, I was just passing by, and thought to take the opportunity to introduce myself."

"I'm happily employed, Mr. Daly, and not ready to accept any change in my circumstances. But it was kind of you to inquire."

Daly stared, and thought to make something of it. "I tell you what, Mr. Hall. You've got splendid credentials. Put your credentials down and send them to me by messenger so I'll know where to look for such outstanding talent if I should need to find someone. I may be buying more papers, you know. Maybe one in Helena, maybe one in Missoula. And probably Great Falls. And I'm always on the lookout for a gifted, loyal man."

Hall seemed to light up a little. "I'll prepare a little package for you, sir. Read it with care."

Daly scarcely knew whether to shake Hall's stained hand, finally did so, and made his way safely out of the building. The air was much better outside.

{ NINE }

The burying was perfunctory, and Alice Brophy was driven to Dublin Gulch in the black carriage and deposited at her cottage. That was fine; the wake had lasted into the wee hours, and that was fine too except that her outhouse stank worse than usual. She only wanted a nap.

Someday she would put a marker on the grave. But she knew where Sean was, and maybe she'd go see him sometime. He didn't deserve it, but she would.

Her children vanished into the spring afternoon, and she settled down in an old morris chair where she could see the daisies that Mr. Daly had brought. She was glad there weren't a lot of neighbors around, trying to solace her. She didn't need solacing. But she had hardly got her feet up when she was summoned to her door by knocking. Wearily she slid into slippers and opened up.

She knew the man slightly. He was Edward Petrovich,

Eddie the Pick, of the Butte Miners Union. She didn't want to invite him in.

"You settled and all right?" he asked, brushing aside her and entering unasked.

"I wish to rest now."

"I'm sure you do, but Big Johnny's got some business with you. You want to come along?"

"Big Johnny Boyle? Me? What does he want with me?"

"He paid for Sean's funeral."

"Mr. Daly did."

"The union brothers did, and now the chief wants to see you."

"I will go some other time."

"No, this is a good time." He grabbed her arm and forcibly steered her out of her home and directed her toward downtown Butte. She tried to work free, but his clamp on her was nothing she could resist, and short of tumbling in a heap there was nothing she could do.

"All right, I'll come, but lay off me," she said.

He nodded and let go. Her arm hurt. She wished she had a handbag so she could whack him with it. He walked beside her, plainly ready to grab her if she bolted. But she knew better than that.

"Fine way to spend this day," she snapped.

A while later she found herself in the Butte Miners Union hall, face to face with Big Johnny.

"The widow lady's here. He's planted, is he?" Boyle asked.

"No thanks to you. Mr. Daly's kindness did it."

"Is that how your treat the brothers? No thanks to the ones that dug into their britches to bury their brother Sean Brophy?"

She thought about Maxwell and all that and decided not to say a word.

"Good news, sweetheart. I've got a husband for you, Alice," Big Johnny said. "He'll take you and the brats."

"I don't want a husband. At least not now."

"Well you've got one. The union did right by you, so you got to help the union. His name is Mickey Metzger. He's got a lot of seniority, and was first in line."

"First in line, is he? Well he's not first in my line."

"Ah, now, you and Sean, the union gave Sean his job and made sure he was treated right, and now you'll want to treat the brothers right. Mickey Metzger is a good man, a little bald and he's got yellow teeth, but otherwise real bonny."

"Is that what you think? I'm union property? Well let me tell you, Big John, I'm not going to marry anyone. Sean, all he did was climb all over me and then I had more dirty diapers to clean. I'm not going to marry any Mickey or Freddie and have him hand me more dirty diapers, and that's that."

She glared at him hard. He might be the boss, and there might be about ten union men for every available woman, but she wasn't going to let him boss her around.

He smiled suddenly. "You owe the brothers for a funeral, sweetheart. I'll come collecting."

"Ha! What do you know about marriage, Big John? Whatever you catch down on Mercury Street, that's what."

He shrugged her off, and Eddie the Pick steered her toward the door.

She stood outside in the wan sun. It wasn't over. They'd come knocking. They'd find a way. There'd be some grimy galoot busting her bedsprings in a day or two. It made her mad. She could probably go complain to Father O'Toole, but he'd likely tell her to do her female duty.

She made her weary way back to Dublin Gulch. The smoke was lowering over town again, searing her throat. She found Eloise curled up inside, staring at the flowers.

"Did Daddy go away?" she asked.

"He's dead and gone," Alice said.

"Are we poor now?"

"Yes. We'll just have to stick together more."

Eloise stared. The sawhorses still stood in the room. "Pa got took away," she said.

The boys burst in, and studied the sawhorses which now carried no burden.

Tom, Tim, you take these sawhorses out. Then you wash," she said.

"He croaked," Tom said. "He got run over and bit the dust."

Alice didn't rebuke him. Let the children work it all out on their own terms.

"Will he go to heaven?" Tim asked.

"If he had a four-leaf clover on him," Tom said.

"Of course he will," Alice said, not at all certain of it.

The boys took the heavy sawhorses out the door, and then poured water into a washbowl from the pitcher beside it, and scrubbed.

There wasn't much to eat, but that was nothing new. She scouted the cupboards, looking for anything, but a tapping on the door interrupted.

She found her neighbor, Mrs. Cantwell, with a basket on her arm.

"I thought you'd not want to be frying cakes on an evening like this," she said.

She pulled away a napkin, revealing a tureen of chowder, the scent savory.

"Oh, Claire," Alice said. "Oh, dear Claire."

Mrs. Cantwell swiftly ladled her chowder into bowls, and set the children to eating.

Alice wasn't hungry but she found comfort in seeing the children spoon the thick soup into their mouths.

"There now," the neighbor said. "That's the way. I knew you wouldn't want to cook. It's bad enough cooking for a man, but worse when there isn't one to cook for, Alice. But you'll find someone. They always do, especially here. I could name a few men if you want. I know one especially, a fine lad, Algernon, and he doesn't even work in the pits. He drives the streetcars."

"I don't need a man, Mrs. Cantwell."

"Why, that's like saying you didn't need Singing Sean Brophy!"

She was right, but Alice thought to keep silent.

The children licked the last of the chowder, Mrs. Cantwell refilled their bowls until the tureen was empty, and then the neighbor retreated into the evening.

It struck her that she needed to make an unusual decision, and one she would never tell anyone about. She needed to decide whether to grieve for Sean Brophy. She wasn't sure she grieved for him at all. Wasn't sure she missed him. Wasn't sure she would ever yearn for his attentions in their bed. Wasn't sure but what he made her life harder. What did he give her but pails of dirty diapers? Sometimes he drank up the pay before she saw it, and then they could hardly feed themselves.

On the other hand, he had a quick smile and a quick hand when it came to grabbing a handful of her, and she liked that. And most of the time he did bring the brown pay envelope home. And he did no harm to the children. He didn't beat them or anything, even when he yelled at them. And once he took her on a picnic, and sometimes they went to a party together. So maybe she should grieve him after all. He was better than nothing.

She decided she would grieve him for a little while. She didn't have anything black, but she could find a black rosette or a black armband, and wear that, and then people would know that she was pining for Singing Sean. She could grieve maybe a week, and then decide about a marriage. It wouldn't be to Mickey Metzger. She'd pick someone. She wasn't going to get shoved into anything. She'd take her time, too. Whoever wanted her could just show it a little, and buy her a ribbon or a hat, or take her to

Helena on a holiday. With any kind of luck he'd be impotent, and she wouldn't have to worry about all that. But she'd been real unlucky on that count. Sean had wanted her about twice a day and three times on Holy Days.

That evening the racket from the mines seemed louder than usual. The stamp mills were thundering, ore dropped down chutes into ore cars, the whistles were howling. There wasn't much peace in an eventide in Butte, and twilight was never a vespers. She got into her nightdress and then invited her children into her bed.

"Come rest beside me, dearies," she said.

Eloise liked the idea, but Tim and Tom eyed her sternly, afraid that she'd get mushy or something. But they settled beside her, the girl on one side, the boys suspiciously waiting on the other.

"Your pa is gone and we've got to stick together," she said.

"I miss him," Eloise said. "I'm going to cry."

The boys didn't deign to surrender to this female sentiment.

"It seems like everyone's got notions in their heads. Just because we've lost Sean, they all have schemes. The company doesn't want anything to do with us. They say, the accident didn't happen during his shift, and he shouldn't have hopped the ore car. They're right. They took his labor and paid him a wage and all is even. The union thinks I owe them something. They got your pa his job, good pay, and pushed for safety too. But I don't owe them anything. Your pa paid his dues so we're even. Your pa gave something and got something from them. But they're pushing on me to find a new man."

"I don't want a new daddy," said Tom.

She sighed. "I'll fight as long as I can. A woman doesn't have much say in it. But here's what I'm thinking about. There's always some work in the hotels. I can make beds and sweep rooms and do laundry. It gets me fifty cents a day. Your pa was getting three-fifty, but the union got some of it and there were others that had their fingers in his pocket now and then. Fifty cents maybe, it isn't enough. But Tom, you're old enough to sell newspapers. You get one cent for each paper sold. If you could sell a hundred papers, you'd earn a dollar a day."

The boy stared at her. This was the first time in his young life he'd even imagined he could earn money, like his pa did.

"Tim, you're almost old enough to be a messenger boy. You need to learn to read better so you know where to take messages. So you work hard on reading, and I'll see whether they'll take you to run messages. That might earn you fifty cents, and maybe a tip too.

"We can live if we all work. And I can sew and mend. I mended your pa's britches and things. Mines, they tear cloth apart, you know, and the miners are in rags. So I can do that, and maybe you can help me, Eloise."

She stared up at her mother, but didn't say anything.

"If we earn two dollars a day, we can live," Alice said. "Your pa soaked up some, and we don't have to feed him or keep him in boots. Oh, and don't forget we can find things that got tossed away. Firewood, anything of value. We'll get that. Timmy, until you're bigger, there's something for you to do every day. Tomorrow, get a sack and pick up coal that's fallen on the tracks. There's always some. Get us enough for next winter. We've got to keep the stove going."

The children stared uneasily, processing all of that. They had just discovered they would have to support themselves, at least in part, the rest of their lives. Whatever anyone felt like saying about Sean, he'd kept his family clothed and fed and sheltered.

"Maybe you should find a new pa," Eloise said.

"Now you mind your own business! I'll decide that! Now you all go to bed!"

She watched the children slide away. They'd had a hard three days, and she had just made the future harder.

She lay in the darkness, mad at Singing Sean Brophy.

{ TEN }

A t last. The messenger boy, Watermelon Jones, had delivered a note to John Fellowes Hall. It was from Clark, his employer.

"I'll catch you next time," Hall said to the messenger.

The boy in the stiff green uniform looked a little crestfallen, and retreated. Hall thought that such louts should not be overtipped, and limited himself to a nickel every third or fourth delivery.

Hall's presence was requested at the Clark bank in an hour. It was initialed by Clark. Good. That would give him time to get a shoeshine and spruce up. Newspaper plants had a way of grinding ink and grit into everything, and the *Mineral* was especially bad because nothing separated the editorial sanctum from the typesetting.

Finally, finally, the talents of the editor were about to be recognized. Maybe there would be a raise. He had discovered that he was not earning as much as Marcus Daly was paying Durston, the editor of the *Anaconda Standard*. That offended Hall right down to his bone marrow. He thought the *Standard* wasn't worth the paper it was printed on.

He had not received a word of praise or encouragement from his employer. For weeks on end, Hall had brilliantly filled the columns of the *Mineral* with items that damaged

Marcus Daly, or raised questions about what the Anaconda Company was up to.

There had been frequent editorials boosting Clark's effort to win a seat in the Senate. He had praised Clark's skills, let it be known that Clark was a friend of the workingman, announced that Clark, in the Senate, would checkmate efforts to repeal the Silver Purchase Act, which Butte relied upon for its prosperity.

He had lambasted the Republicans, supported the Democrat candidates for the Montana legislature, which in turn would elect a senator in 1893. He had warned against the rising Populist movement, with its hostility against malefactors of great wealth, and expressed outrage that Marcus Daly was making common cause with these rural bumpkins.

He knew himself to be a splendid newsman, maybe the only top flight one in Butte. Nothing escaped him. He despised his cubicle in the servant quarters of Clark's brick mansion, but also saw the utility of it. Good newsman that he was, he had befriended the servants, and found out most everything there was to know about Clark. Those political dinners, for example. Clark was carefully wooing the candidates at sumptuous meals, placing a costly favor at each place setting. Some of these were diamond stickpins for cravats. Sapphire brooches for the ladies, although Clark entertained few of them.

The only thing that truly annoyed Hall was that he hadn't been invited to these affairs. Surely he should have been at Clark's elbow, meeting the candidates, sharing philosophy, acquiring valuable insights that he could place in the news columns. He resented being confined to servant quarters, as if he were the equal of a chambermaid. Clark hadn't the faintest idea of the professional skills and experience that went into the making of a seasoned newspaper editor. He seemed to regard Hall as someone on a par with a pipe fitter or deliveryman. What did this idiot of a financier know about editing? What did he know about nuance? The meaning of words? The art of rhetoric? The things learned in schools and in the school of life?

Hall had sent clippings from the *Mineral* to his employer, intending by main force to call attention to his work. But all he received was cold silence. He deserved a raise, too, especially for his reports on Daly's railroad, but no raise was forthcoming. Each week the printers and reporters at the paper would receive their pay in a brown envelope, and that included Hall.

Each day, he had expected a summons to the bank office, where he would receive a word of praise or a little favor of his own. He could use a diamond stickpin for his own cravats. But nothing happened. That's when he decided, as long as he was stuck in the mansion, to learn more details about Clark. It didn't matter what: just details that might someday be useful. And so he collected information wholesale. Who made Clark's silk hats. How many pairs of cuff links the man had. Who bought Clark's expanding art collection. Who paid Clark's bills. And why were they sometimes not paid in a timely manner?

It became routine for Hall to know of every guest, and know the gist of every dinner conversation, and the names of all of Clark's household suppliers and outfitters. He also knew who visited in off hours, the furtive meetings, the names of men who slid into the mansion at odd hours, only to hasten into the dark soon after.

And still not a word of praise. Hall considered himself a loyal man, and knew that he would endure Clark's neglect because he must. But one of these moments, when he finally had a chance to talk with his employer, he'd let slip the fact that Marcus Daly might well want him as an editor at one of Daly's several papers. Maybe that would awaken some sense of Hall's true worth. If Daly wanted him, then Hall's value would go up. Maybe there'd also be a fine Christmas bonus.

Meanwhile, he was busy turning his paper into the most brilliant sheet in Butte. He used a lot of two-dollar words to show his erudition. He wanted to reach the most influential people, not the hoi polloi, who could barely read anyway. So he used elegant words, just to show the world that the *Mineral* had arrived.

Clark had summoned him. So John Fellowes Hall swiftly wiped his hightop shoes, buttoned a fresh-starched collar on his shirt, and headed up the slope to the Clark and Bro. Bank, filled with excitement. On this breezy day he would receive a raise, or at least commendation, or maybe a privately voiced assignment that would propel Clark into the United States Senate.

Butte was a noisy place, and one lived in the midst of subdued roar. Steam boilers hissed, ore rattled down chutes and into hopper cars, whistles howled, trolley cars clamored along their rails. And for some odd reason, everyone shouted. Why couldn't the citizens of Butte address one another in muted tones?

Hall passed a corner where the boys from rival papers hawked their wares, usually by reciting the headlines, or jamming a paper into a passing man and waiting for their nickel. There were plenty of papers in town, so each busy corner was turf to be fought over by rowdy newsboys, and once in a while some poor little bugger got driven off, and had to sell his sheet where there was less traffic.

"Hey! The copper king bought a smelter!" yelled one.

Hall ignored him.

"City faces doom!" yelled another, a red-haired punk. He was smirking. He knew how to sell, and was pushing copies onto people. Hall eyed the headline. "Silver Bill Advances," it said in large type.

"Doom! Three cents, pal," the little bohunk yelled. "Doom for Butte!"

Smart lad. But he wasn't selling the *Mineral*. He was a damned Republican. That was the *Butte Inter-Mountain* sailing out of his freckled paws. But if there was anything people of all parties in Butte agreed on, it was the menace of repealing the Sherman Silver Purchase Act which required the government to purchase a lot of silver each and every month.

Hall escaped, and plowed through the polished doors of the bank, and hastened up the creaking stairs to the sanctum sanctorum. This would be a great day, and he'd remember to write home about it.   •

Clark's shapely secretary, who wore tight pleats this summery day, nodded. She seemed to know who Hall was, because she vanished behind pebbled glass doors, and returned swiftly.

"Mr. Clark will see you now, Mr. Hall."

He wasn't forced to cool his heels, and that was an excellent sign. He straightened his cravat, and plunged in. The great man was waiting. This warm day he wore a brown broadcloth suit of clothes, with tan silk lapels, and a cherry-colored cravat. This was as informal as the mining magnate ever got.

"Sit! Sit!" Clark said.

Hall did, but Clark remained upright in his patent leather shoes. It evened things up. They were eye to eye.

"The paper's losing money," Clark said.

"But gaining influence," Hall said.

Clark looked annoyed. "Influence doesn't pay the bills. The fact is, advertising revenue has declined in every week since you took over. And the paper is selling fewer copies, too."

Hall didn't like the sound of that. "But we've got your campaign going. We're making you the next senator."

"The *Mineral* is not earning a profit. Everything I own earns a profit. If it doesn't earn a profit, I get rid of it. And that includes newspapers."

"Ah, we could put newsboys on more corners."

"Every mine, every smelter, every utility, every water-works, every lumber company, every bank I own shows a profit."

Hall began to itch. "Well, sir, the *Mineral*'s real profit is influence. We are highly profitable if the paper's influence on voters is considered. We have won more votes to the Clark banner than anyone can count. And I'm proud to say that I've engineered a political shift in Butte."

"Advertising," said Clark. "Get more ads. A lot more. That'll be your task. Get ads and make a profit."

"But, sir, that's the province of an ad salesman."

"You are now appointed ad salesman. My good man, each week that you've been at my newspaper, revenue has declined. The paper is now earning five hundred seventy dollars less each week than when you started."

"But that's no responsibility of mine, sir."

Clark sighed gently, his bright gaze boring in. "I will need to instruct you in simple business economics. A newspaper is a product, like everything else. If the stories in the paper don't appeal, people buy other papers. Your news isn't what citizens wish to purchase. If people don't purchase papers, advertisers won't buy ads. Advertisers want circulation. So here is what you'll do. Write stories that people like, so the *Mineral* sells well. And then visit our advertisers and sell them ads."

"Well, fine, sir, but I don't have time for both."

"Then sell ads. That's where skill is needed."

"But someone must write and edit the paper."

"Leave it to your flunkies, Hall. There's no skill in it. Anyone can do it." He paused, bright-eyed. "And maybe the flunkies will bring back what's been lost."

"Sir, that's not the way to build circulation. We need to hire good cartoonists. We need a woodcut artist. We need more reporters. We need to sell issues in Anaconda and Helena and Bozeman. So we need to print more and ship them out."

"Profit, Mr. Hall. Give me a profit and I'll hire more lackeys for you. Reporters are a dime a dozen. Artists are a dime a gross. Plump cartoonists hang from every fruit tree. Editors, why I could hire twenty with the snap of my fingers. But ad salesmen, they're hard to find. Where can I find that sort of talent?"

Hall was certain he had no idea. A salesman was a salesman. A salesman could hardly string a sentence together, much less write a compelling editorial, or create a newspaper page that was compelling and balanced and beautiful.

"Ah, Mr. Clark, you must be aware that Marcus Daly's Anaconda paper loses money by the cartload. It's a rich man's toy. He's let Durston hire away the best men in the country."

"That's what'll sink him, Hall. The minute you put money into losers, you're acting on sentiment, not sound business principles. Nothing owned by Clark loses money for long."

It was becoming clear to John Fellowes Hall that his employer was, in a way, demoting him. Turning him into a drummer, a salesman, doomed to wander with an order book in hand, into every saloon, restaurant, greengrocery, butchershop, harness maker, barbershop, pharmacy, beer hall, clothier, and coal dealer in Butte.

"Mr. Clark, you're about to see a miracle," he said.

"I don't believe in them. I believe in hard work and a keen eye and canine teeth in the throat when necessary."

"A very good way to live, sir."

"We're done then, Hall. I will keep an eye out."

Clark turned away and peered out the window upon his fiefdom. Hall rose, fled, and headed for the paper, without a raise and without a promotion, and without a future.

ELEVEN

It was time to land on the widow. Big Johnny Boyle had run out of patience. Day after day, Alice Brophy had hidden from sight. She didn't answer her door. Johnny wanted to get this over with. He'd taken two sawbucks from Mickey Metzger to deliver the witch, and so far she hadn't been delivered. But this time he would deliver her, from hair to toes, if that's what it took.

He'd hardly made a dime on her. He'd collected a hundred and change from the brothers for Singing Sean's funeral, and that meant he kept only dimes for all his work. Plus the sawbucks. He never had enough money because the brothers didn't pay him much and didn't have half an idea what he did for them. Ingrates, that's what miners were. Maybe it had to do with working in a hole all day. It made them strange.

He'd change that, and quick. Butte was a town that begged him to get rich. Big Johnny headed for Dublin Gulch himself this time. He wouldn't leave it to the Pick. He'd drag her out by the ass. So when he got to Alice Brophy's weathered cottage, he didn't knock at all; he plowed in and found her rolling a pie crust. She took fright, and yelled at him, but he just stood smiling.

"Yell all you want, sweetheart, but now you're going to come with me and you're going to marry Mickey Metzger."

"I will not! Get out of my house!"

He moved to grab an arm and haul her off, and was surprised when she hit him with her rolling pin. She cracked him across the jaw, and caused him to bite his tongue.

"You'll be getting out, Big Johnny, leaving me alone."

He just grinned and spit blood. "Come along, sweetie. You've been promised, and I deliver."

"You'll drag me kicking and howling, is what. You'll have the coppers on you, and they'll be protecting a widow lady."

Big Johnny didn't relish that. He'd drag a man over the cobblestones, but not a woman.

"Deliver, is it?" she yelled. "You're delivering me? You sold my body, did you? A pimp, are you? What was I worth? Twenty dollars, was it? Well, Big Johnny Boyle, I'll tell you something. I'm not for sale."

"I'll deliver you, Alice," wiping blood off his lips.

"You tell Mickey Metzger that he'll regret the day he took me. I'll be a witch. I'll make his every moment miserable. I'll get out my meat cleaver, I will."

"He paid, and I'll deliver," Big Johnny said, halfheartedly. He hated the very thought of refunding the sawbucks. "You got no way to live," he said.

"I'll chambermaid, I'll wash."

"No you won't. You won't get hired in this town. What I say goes with all the brotherhoods."

"That's what you think. Now you get out of here. This is my house."

"It won't be for long, sweetheart."

"Get out!"

He smiled and got out. Maybe he could find some chippy down on Mercury Street and hand her off to Mickey, and keep the sawbucks. That witch. She'd starve to death, and her brats with her. He'd make sure of it. And her from County Clare, too. They sure got uppity when they came across the sea. It wasn't over. He'd get her delivered one way or another.

It wasn't hard to think of some other way to rake in a few bucks. Pissing Yablonski's grave needed a headstone. Pissing was a charter member of the Butte union, and had died when a lift plunged to the bottom of the pit. Pissing was remembered for wetting everything—utility poles, fence posts, trees, cornerstones. If it was there, Pissing wet it. He could wet a bank in downtown Butte in broad daylight and no one would see him do it. Johnny himself had seen Pissing wet the numbers in a cornerstone, the piss dampening the Roman numerals. His widow, Minny, was pleased as punch to get herself remarried, so Big Johnny got her a new husband, Smelly Stuchen, in two days, and pocketed some change. But now Pissing's headstone had vanished from Mountain View. No one knew who desecrated the grave, but it was time for the brotherhood to honor its own. He'd have the Pick send out word. Let every brother ante up, and there'd be a new headstone on Pissing's grave. And more change in Big Johnny's britches.

Butte was so easy to work if one was content with penny ante. But Big Johnny had larger ambitions, and this here wrestling match of the bosses would surely be the way to get serious about a living.

There was a killing to be made from the fight of those copper kings. The union had votes. And that was worth plenty. The Butte Miners Union wanted two things in a big way: four dollars a day for everyone, and eight-hour days. It wanted some better working conditions too. Better air in the pits, more holiday time, pensions, help for the sick and old, and a dozen other items. It would all be on the table when them bosses showed up for little talks.

There were a few other items, maybe more important to Big Johnny than to the mining kings. Like who gets to work and who doesn't, and how the hiring was done, and whether the union could veto anyone it chose. The bosses didn't like it, because they wanted to hire the best men and not get stuck with lazy bums. But Big Johnny didn't see it that way. If he controlled who went down the shafts, he had something to sell. See Big Johnny about a job. Three dollars and fifty cents, a day's pay, in his pocket, and he'd give the word, and the man had a job. There were plenty of unemployed miners around, glad enough to give a little to Big Johnny out of their pay envelope. And there were more coming in from the immigrant boats and wicker-seat passenger cars every day, all of them wanting a job.

Even so, that was penny ante stuff. The best way to advance his fortunes, and keep his girlfriends on the street rolling in joy, was to own the votes. Not his vote, but every vote of the brotherhood. So long as he could keep that Australian ballot out of sight, and make every man's vote public, he could deliver easily. Anyone who voted the wrong way would get himself pounded until his bones broke. And that was worth a lot of money.

He owned a thousand votes and controlled another five hundred, and a word from him would influence several other brotherhoods. So maybe he had three thousand in all. That was a pretty good bunch of votes. That was enough to send some of Clark's favorites to the legislature. Maybe enough to elect Clark a senator. It sure was an interesting proposition. He had a product to sell. What would the buyers pay?

He found Eddie the Pick at Trelawney's and waited for Eddie to buy him an ale. It took only a moment. Eddie's raised finger, a bartender's glance. Big Johnny liked it that way.

"The brotherhood's about to get rich, Eddie," he said.

"Then we'll have to tax ourselves," Eddie said. He was in favor of a graduated income tax to soak the rich.

"Nah, the brothers won't even know it," Big Johnny said.

That raised Eddie's brow an inch or so.

"We got stuff for sale. Three thousand votes."

"Your arithmetic is a little wet," Eddie said. "But two more pints and it'll add up."

Big Johnny didn't want to explain to the knucklehead. "What we've got to do is hold the money in trust for the brothers," he said. "If we give it to them, they'll just spend it. So we've got to keep it safe."

Eddie didn't like that. "You need to trust the common man," he said.

"I do! He'll vote exactly the way we want, or you'll break his arm and then he can't work."

"Yes, there's that. Common men need some guidance, at least until we throw out the captains of capital."

"Eddie, do you know what Clark's been giving the candidates? As table favors? Diamond stickpins for their cravats. Think of that. Those bozos sit down to a fancy feast at Clark's mansion, and right there on the table is a little white box at each place. And those guys aren't even elected yet. No one says a word. Clark ain't making any noises. No one demands or gives a thing, you see? If we got invited and got some diamond stickpins, that doesn't mean we've agreed to a thing, you see? And we'd keep the diamonds safe for the brotherhood. If the brotherhood needs the diamonds, we'd turn them right over."

Eddie the Pick sipped and weighed and sipped. "Why me?"

"Because you're my knee-capper. I gotta have that. What if someone don't vote like we want? If I promise three thousand votes and someone don't come through, I'd be a liar, and I don't want to be a liar. If I say I can deliver, then I'll deliver, and that's where you come in. Got it?"

"Solidarity," Eddie the Pick said. "You're right. We have to have solidarity. We have to speak with one voice."

"Now you're talking. I think what I'll do is go talk to Clark. I'll have him invite us to dinner. You and me, and whoever else he wants. No women. This is a brotherhood, not some sisterhood. So he'll have us to dinner, just like the pols, and we'll see what sort of table favors he's offering us. Not that we have to accept them, you know. If it's not a good favor, we'll just take the brotherhood somewhere else."

"Yeah, solidarity," Eddie the Pick said, and downed the rest of the pint.

"One carat, at least."

"You know something, Boyle? I never wore a cravat in all me days. Keepin' the diamond safe for the brotherhood wouldn't do me any good."

"You have a point, Eddie. I think we need some other kind of favor, one that would fit better."

"I don't need nothing. I just want all the brothers to be happy. Maybe we could get a statue made. How about a statue of you?"

"Me? What would I do with a statue? I'm too ugly for a statue. Now, double eagles, that would be different. We could keep double eagles safe."

"They sure are pretty, double eagles. Nothing destroys gold. It doesn't rust, it doesn't erode, it stays the way it stays. That's what the brothers need, something that won't let them down in the future."

"It would sure take a lot of them. Twenty dollars, that wouldn't keep a brother happy for very long."

"We could give one to each miner's widow. I think every man who dies in the pit, the widow should get one," Eddie said.

"That's a noble idea, Eddie. And you and me, we'll be the stewards and keep the double eagles safe."

"How we gonna do this, Big Johnny?"

The truth of it was that Big Johnny didn't know. But there was always a way. He had votes to deliver, and there were buyers for votes. And he could deliver to the highest bidder. That got him to thinking about who wanted the entire vote of the Butte Miners Union. Clark, he sure wanted it. So did Marcus Daly. And maybe that Republican, Lee Mantle, wanted it. Or maybe one of them crazy Populists. It wasn't just Clark itching for whatever Big Johnny Boyle might have to offer. It was half the big shots in Montana.

TWELVE

John Fellowes Hall concluded he was working for a very smart idiot. The man knew nothing about newspapers. Hall left the bank brimming with annoyance and toying with some sort of spectacular public resignation on his front page. Who cared about Butte? Ugliest and most barbaric city west of the Mississippi. Permanently proletarian. Every man born to fail. So ugly that it plunged people into melancholia. Who ever heard of a happy resident of Butte, Montana?

So Clark wanted a profit. The *Mineral* must make money. The *Mineral* must sell more ads and boost circulation. And it would be the editor's task to achieve that. An idiot. Hall stood on a busy corner, gagging on smoke, wondering how long to stay in town, and how he might fill his pockets before he stormed off.

Sell more papers! Sell more ads! Something was tickling his mind, but he wasn't quite able to pull it up. He hiked generally downhill, which was the direction his life had taken, away from the mines, away from wealth, and toward the teeming hinterlands. Butte was made that way. The mines, sources of fortunes, were highest up; the privileged a little lower; commercial life a bit lower; and below that were the losers, the depraved, the trash heaps, bawdy districts, and cemeteries. Butte put its cemeteries at the lowest level, the farthest away from God that they could be. It made sense.

Hall didn't return to the newspaper, but drifted a little farther, onto Mercury Street, the precinct of the bawds. There were plenty of those, and plenty of males on the loose ready to spend their change on a spasm of the muscles. Mercury was actually rather discreet, almost cloistered, compared to some of the districts he had seen, where the wild side was on display and the ladies sat in windows or on their front stoops, and the pianos rattled in open doorways.

The place was busy, even though it was not yet evening. Mercury Street's parlors were always open, and welcoming one shift after another. He spotted two of Clark's subalterns emerging from a parlor house. They saw him and nodded. He saw that union boss, Big Johnny somebody, wander into a house across the narrow street. The girls rarely turned anyone down. It amused John Fellowes Hall.

That's when the thing he was looking for came to mind. The name that somehow arose at last was Joseph Pulitzer, and the paper he was trying to recollect was the *New York World*. That was exactly the right medicine. The *World* scarcely needed to hunt down advertisers. They flocked to the paper, wanting to buy ads. The *World* scarcely needed to struggle with circulation. It outsold all its rivals, and some days its newsboys sold every copy that had been run off the big presses. Ah, that was it.

Hall knew at once he wouldn't need to go out begging for ads. He wouldn't need to begin desperate campaigns for more readers. He would lift a page from Joseph Pulitzer's *World,* and that would suffice. Cheerfully, he turned uphill, and soon plunged into the *Mineral's* bleak sanctum. The *Mineral* would never be the same.

He was feverish by the time he reached his writing table and grabbed some foolscap and a nib pen. The rich! Scandal! Sensation! The seamy side! Crime! Anything shocking! And one crusade after another, a great thundering noise that would rattle every windowpane in Butte! Did Clark want a profitable newspaper? He'd get one that would earn more than any of his mines!

Ah, but where to start? That was simple. Clark himself. The man would relish the glare of the lamps.

"William Andrews Clark has been holding gala entertainments that are the talk of Butte," he began. "Mr. Clark,

who has announced his availability for a seat in the United
States Senate, has been acquainting members of his party
with festive dinners. Each of his guests discovers a table
favor at his place at the great dining table, where twenty
may be comfortably seated and served gourmet wines and
dinners by a staff of discreet waiters.

"And what do these gents discover when they pull the
ribbons and open the white pasteboard box at their seat?
A diamond-studded tiepin, given as a gesture of Mr.
Clark's ongoing interest in their well-being . . ."

On and on he wrote, describing the black-tie dress of all
the swells, the menus—his room in the servants' quarters
of the mansion was proving valuable after all—the French
wines, the desserts, the Havanas freely passed around the
table, and Mr. Clark's gracious welcome to the manse.

Ah, now Hall was cooking. On the police blotter that
day was a murder of a whore by a customer of hers. Normally, he wouldn't have deigned to publish the story. But
he was no longer the Hall he was the previous day; he was
an acolyte of Pulitzer, and a story like that might be turned
into the day's headline. He discovered his reporter, Grabbit Wolf, at work on an obituary.

"Forget that," Hall said. "We have a murdered whore.
Her name is Lulu the Boiler. Her customer, Bloody Billy
Bones, is in custody. That's going to be our lead story."

Grabbit looked startled. "Lead story?"

"Banner headline. Give it all you've got, and if you
don't have enough, make it up."

Grabbit blinked, once, twice, and slowly exhaled. An
eyebrow shot up. "We're talking lurid, right?"

"Right! I want every father in Butte to hide this edition from his daughters."

Grabbit sighed. "I've waited all my life for this," he
said. "I've gone down to Mercury Street fifty times looking for a story I could publish. But until now there weren't
any."

"Hurry up, man, and let me see the copy."

Ah, a start. He would make Joseph Pulitzer's *World* look sedate. He would make Pulitzer look like an amateur. And thanks to his genius, the *Mineral* would grow fat. William Andrews Clark would smile.

What next? Ah, of course, a Pulitzer-style crusade. That was easy. He already knew what rankled his employer, and that was the town's Chinamen. That would be the crusade. Drive out the yellow heathen. Drive them out of Butte, out of Montana, out of the United States. Cut off their pigtails, stop their tong wars, send them packing. They were stealing jobs from real Americans. Deport them all.

They were, actually, doing valuable things around town, finding employment as launderers, street cleaners, noodle parlor operators, and operators of opium dens. But that made no difference. Clark would go for this. Clark wanted America for Americans.

And that was the name he gave his crusade. For the next month or so, there would be a crusade piece on the front page of the *Mineral*, and when he had worn that topic out, he would find another.

There were things to do. Scandal news required snitches. And that meant having some loose change around to give a chambermaid two bits, or a bootblack a spare dime, or a barkeep a dollar, if the stuff was juicy enough. He knew where to find snitches, and within a few days he would have fifty on his string, and the more enterprising ones would soon be making some real money, courtesy of the *Mineral*. And it didn't even matter how accurate they were.

He headed back to the printers.

"From now on, every lead story gets a headline in war type," he said.

They looked at him as if he was daft. War type was reserved for wars. It was the biggest type a newspaper owned.

"Grabbit's story. Give it war type," he insisted.

A toothless old compositor smirked. He knew the racket.

"Print an extra two hundred," he said.

The *Mineral* missed deadline by a half hour that afternoon, which made the newsboys snarly. They hung around the delivery door with empty canvas bags, making rude noises and misbehaving. Hall saw it as an opportunity.

"You there. Listen to me. This issue of the *Mineral* is going to sell like hotcakes if you know what to do. You can make money. We're printing extra copies. Now what you'll do is yell murder, murder, murder. Or Mercury Street murder. Hold up the front page. It'll say murder, and you'll say murder, and you'll sell every paper you've got and come back for more. Got it?"

"Who croaked?" asked one little punk.

"A whore."

"A whore's murdered," the punk said. "I got it."

"What's her name? She better be good looking," said another brat.

"She was the most beautiful one on Mercury Street."

"I bet," said the brat.

"We're printing extra. You sell out, you come back for more, got it?"

"Bullshit," said the punk.

The papers finally did come off the old flatbed press. Clark was too cheap to buy a modern rotary press, and it took so long to publish some afternoons that the news was out of date.

The little vultures scooped up their allotted papers and trotted off to every corner of town, including the mineheads. There were some, coming up to daylight, that wanted nothing more than a paper.

The press was still churning out the extra copies when Hall returned, and the only thing to do was wait. Most of the news and composing men had abandoned the place and wouldn't show up until dawn. But Hall waited. He wanted to know one thing: whether those extra papers would fly out the rear door.

An hour later he had his answer. They did. Every one of the two hundred spares.

He headed for the stinking washroom, feeling begrimed. He found some abrasive soap, the kind printers used to scrape ink away, and scrubbed furiously, his face, his hands, his wrists. He hated black ink.

Then he clamped his fedora on his well-groomed hair and headed out the door, the last man out of the shop. He headed uptown, looking for newsboys, but most of them were done for the night. One kid from the *Inter-Mountain* was still hawking his wares.

Hall didn't feel like heading for his monastic cell in the servants' floor of the mansion. He felt like a drink. He felt like some good whiskey. He felt like a bout in a good saloon, one patronized by merchants, so he wandered the streets until he came to the Gallows. It was hot in there, but rotating ceiling fans subdued the worst of the heat. These people were brokers, the sort who bought and sold shares in the mines and smelters. Some still wore green eyeshades.

Hall eyed the place for newspapers, and spotted an *Anaconda Standard* on the mahogany bar, and an *Inter-Mountain*. But no *Minerals*. He was faintly disappointed, but then he saw a couple of papers carefully folded with the headlines facing inward, poking from some suit coats. That was good. The gents were hiding the front page.

A saloonman with a walrus moustache served him a bourbon and branch, which he sipped quietly, just listening to the talk. But it was all stocks and bonds, up and down, bull and bear. He drank up and ordered another, and listened. But it was as if the *Mineral* didn't exist. Maybe this was a Republican saloon. Maybe this was a Daly bar.

The more he sipped the good whiskey, the less happy he became. He didn't like his job and despised his employer. He was far away from Amber and the boys. He had always considered himself the finest newsman anywhere, but now he was churning out a scandal sheet. His employer was demanding a profit. Didn't Clark know that great papers never earned a dime? They were great because they didn't spare any expense tracking down the news and presenting it elegantly to intelligent readers.

But the *Mineral* was now a rag. A guttersnipe of a paper. It occurred to him that he was making a coffin out of this job. He'd have no credentials to take to the next position. He could not show copies of his paper to the next employer. He'd sold out. Everything he'd stood for in journalism had been pitched out the door.

He stared morosely at the men bellied up to the bar, men with their feet on the brass rail, men talking prices and politics. He signaled the barman for another shot, and he downed that and downed another, feeling worse and worse. If he had any sense he'd walk away from Butte. He'd take the next steam train back to civilization.

He had one final shot, wove his way out the door, couldn't remember where he was, and finally couldn't remember anything. So he went to sleep.

Some hours later he came to in a dowdy old cubicle with iron bars across his horizon.

"So, you're awake," said a copper. "I need your name. I have to book you."

Hall stared upward, aware that he lay on a stinking bunk.

"Of course you can donate two bucks to the policemen's retirement fund," the copper said.

Hall did, and wobbled back to the mansion of William Andrews Clark.

THIRTEEN

Royal Maxwell loathed the crone, and she loathed him, but that did not hamper the transaction. He was wondering what Agnes Healy, the famed seer, had in store for him. And she would receive her pittance for telling him.

"So you're wanting to see who's going to die, are you? You're looking for business, are you? You're maybe hoping for a wreck, so you can run the bodies through your place like sausages, are you?"

"I'm always interested in death, madam, whether from the mines or simply from old age or some mishap. God bless the departed."

"I'll bet you are. Each one puts the greenbacks in your pocket. Well, maybe I won't tell you what I see. Maybe you can just guess. Maybe you should be surprised. What if I see you're next, eh? What then?"

She did this monologue every time, and he didn't mind. His business was burying people, and he was all in favor of death. But he was looking for anything else of value, knowing that when her lightning struck, it was a valuable glimpse into the future.

"So what about politics?" he asked.

"Why should I know anything about politics, may I ask? I leave politics to crooks where it belongs. I don't listen for answers to politics."

"The elections, then. Who will be our next senator?"

She slid into a trance, rapt, and he knew she was connecting somehow with that other world.

"No one," she said. "There won't be a senator."

"That's absurd. There'll be a senator elected."

"No one. Montana will have one senator."

"Not Clark?"

"Who am I to say, eh? You asked; I listened."

This was certainly odd. "What about a Republican, then?" he asked. Royal Maxwell was ardently a Republican, and found the party soul-satisfying. He wished all people could be Republicans. That would help business. The Democrats were proposing mine safety legislation, and he was opposed because it was bad for business. The Populists were even worse. They were proposing all sorts of sanitation and pure food laws, which would cut into his business. There was only one thing any funeral director could be, and that was a true-blue Republican. With any luck, he could bury a lot of Democrats.

"Who'll win the elections this November?" he asked.

"How should I know? I don't prophesy; I just get hit by lightning once in a while, and then what's to come is clear. There's nothing about elections in my head."

"I want to know how the Republicans will do. I want to know if Marcus Daly's deserting the Democrats and joining the Republicans."

She sniffed. "You sure are a rotter," she said.

"I'd be pleased to bury every Democrat in Butte," he said. "I'd give them the best send-off they ever had."

She closed her eyes and seemed to vanish from the room, but then she awakened abruptly. "It's a mess," was all she said.

"Well? What?"

"I'm just a poor widow trying to bring a little something to people."

"Well, see about this. Where's the state capital going to be? In Anaconda?"

It had been left to the citizens to decide that. Helena was the temporary one, favored by Clark, and most other people around the new state. But Marcus Daly had his own design, a capital in his own carefully laid-out town of Anaconda at the foot of Mount Haggin, the dome dwarfed by the stack of his giant copper smelter. The very thought of a capital owned by the Anaconda Mining Company was as loathsome to Maxwell as putting the capital in Great Falls, which was the other serious contestant. He was a Helena man, but so were most Republicans.

She frowned, stared into space, and shrugged. "I don't know," she said.

There was no arguing with that. She saw or she didn't. She peered somehow through some lens of time, and sometimes the future was there in a glimpse as bright as heaven. But not now. He felt vaguely cheated and thought he'd leave a dime, not two bits. But he thought better of that.

He peered around the shabby kitchen. The woman got barely a life out of her gifts. There was no stored food; no tins of flour or beans or sugar. She looked so thin that he wondered if she was even feeding herself.

"Death," he said.

"That's what you came in for. You can't fool me. Politics, all that, you were just trying to hide why you're here. Death you want. Business you want. If I say twenty next week, you'll order twenty coffins."

"How can I fool someone who sees through veils?" he asked, not unreasonably.

She glared at him. "I hate this," she said. "You make a ghoul out of me."

"Think of it this way, madam. The more I know what to expect, the more I can be of service to those who grieve."

"Oh, horsepucky," she said.

She closed her eyes, opened them, stared into space, and shook her head.

"I have good news," she said quietly. "No one will die in Butte for the next two weeks."

"Two weeks? That's unheard of. There's several poor souls passing to the nether shore almost daily."

"Two weeks," she said.

"Your crystal ball's cloudy today, madam."

"I'm not a seer. I've told you that. I don't commune with spirits. If something comes to me, it's out of the future, like something seen in the white light of lightning."

"Two weeks? Someone in Butte croaks every day."

She turned silent and stern, so he slipped her two bits and headed out the door. This was the worst-ever session with Agnes, and he swore he would not darken her door ever again. No senator in office! Two weeks with no one cashing in! What a lot of malarkey. He peered around, to make sure no one had registered his visit to the witch, and then slipped downhill, not wishing to reveal his presence in that neighborhood. He would have a good story or two to tell his Republican cronies running for various Butte city offices. Oh, Agnes would be good for something, if only a laugh.

But damn, when was she ever wrong? He'd go broke if he didn't have a miner or a bartender or a dead infant on his doorstep that long. She had it wrong. He didn't wish death upon anyone. He merely welcomed death in the abstract; in a statistical sense. He wished good health upon every mortal he had ever met, and those he hadn't. He wished good health upon himself, which he lacked because he had visited Mercury Street too often.

He had thought at one time of calling his establishment the Golden Rule Mortuary: Bury Others as You Wish to Be Buried. That might encourage people to spend more, and of course it was ethically beyond criticism. But too many people were cheapskates, and wanted to plant their loved ones without the dignity of the finest caskets and the most splendid send-offs. It saddened him that the world was so crass.

Two weeks. He could barely survive such a drought. He couldn't keep his pants buttoned that long. But even as he plunged toward his own place of business, a thought began tickling his fancy. A branch in Anaconda. The company was obliging him with accidents in Butte: good cave-ins, fires, runaway lifts, silicosis, rocks landing on people's heads. It could just as well oblige him with business in Anaconda, where the world's largest smelter burned workers to a crisp, polluted the air with arsenic fumes, crushed anyone who got caught in its giant machinery, and emitted pure copper, save for the occasional bits of flesh and bone caught in the furnaces. A branch in Marcus Daly's backyard! There would never again be a two-week drought. Now that Daly's little railroad was shuttling between Butte and Anaconda, there'd be no difficulty getting from one mortuary to the other. And with the telegraph alerting him to need, he could operate both. He could keep a lackey there, whose sole task would be to wire him when needed, and make comforting noises to the bereaved. Yes, he knew of a dozen brats who'd fill the bill, and not cost anything if he gave them a bed and an attic room over there.

The idea appealed to him so much that he spent the rest of the afternoon expanding on it, and kept coming to the thing he could no longer escape. Daly was right. The capitol building of Montana should be built in Anaconda, and then Royal Maxwell would get to bury tony politicians and powerful bureaucrats, and not just riffraff. Yes, with a branch he'd flourish, and he'd get the right sort of clients, the ones with folding money and big houses and estates.

He felt almost dizzy. Agnes Healy had led him to something grand. For the two bits he'd tossed her, he had received a brilliant expansion of his business to a lively new town that might become the state capital. He'd quickly drive out any competition, with the finest funeral parlor in the Northwest, fluted white pillars in front, a fine electric-lit dias for viewing, and cemetery lots to sell. That reminded him he would need to start a cemetery over there. No point in leaving that to others when he could have all the plots to himself.

He was so taken with the whole idea that he checked schedules, found he could spend the whole afternoon over there, maybe put himself into business in very little time. If Agnes was right, he wouldn't be needed in Butte for a good while. He stuffed his check register into a briefcase, walked down to the Butte, Anaconda and Pacific depot, purchased a round-trip, and was soon rattling his way over to the future capital of Montana. He settled into the austere wicker seat of the passenger car, read the *Mineral* and then the *Butte Inter-Mountain*, and by the time he had sorted out the Democrats' lies in Clark's rag and absorbed the truths in the *Inter-Mountain*, the train was squealing to a halt at the foot of Mount Haggin. It was exhilarating. Anaconda was not a claptrap slum, but an orderly, new, well-planned company town. Good for business, he thought.

He perused the town, especially the blocks surrounding Marcus Daly's new luxury hotel on Park Street. He was a sensitive man, and thought it best not to locate next door, even though the hotel and the funeral parlor would fertilize each other's business. Where better to hold a wake than Marcus Daly's great brick hostelry? But close. A few steps would work nicely. No further than Commercial Avenue, and closer if he could manage it. Surely, people died in hotels, and he wanted his parlor to be convenient.

There didn't seem to be the right sort of vacant structure in the new town, but he spotted a store that might do with a noble facade in front. It was narrow, but deep and had a rear room, which he would need. Yes, it would have to do. And only two blocks from the hotel. Even the rich could manage that. He loathed the rich; they were people who were always shifting their loyalties and looking for every advantage and betraying their former colleagues. That's how they got rich. Not like Royal Maxwell, who had an unwavering loyalty to the dead. He was proud of that. His loyalty to those who had passed by never wavered.

He spent the rest of the day arranging for a mahogany altar, a stained-glass window depicting shepherds, pine pews, a pulpit, zinc undertaking tables, a handsome cream pilaster facade for the building, advertising with Daly's paper, the *Anaconda Standard,* and scores of other details. He would need to find a flunkey and install him in the attic. And since there was only telegraph, not telephone, he would need to teach the flunkey to wire him when a customer showed up and then go fetch the departed with a black lacquered handcart.

He caught a late train back to Butte, satisfied with his coup. Within a few days he would be burying two or three a day, maybe more, and expanding his business as fast as the copper kings were expanding theirs. And he would need to formulate some plans to drive off competition, too. The copper kings were wrestling for the bonanza deep in the richest hill on earth, and Royal Maxwell knew he would wrestle for the richest mortician's paradise on earth. For a moment, as he sat in the rocking railroad coach, watching Butte's slope grow close, he felt a certain brotherhood toward William Andrews Clark and Marcus Daly. They were all looking for the pot of gold at rainbow's end. He was one of them, a businessman flexible enough to make a killing.

FOURTEEN

For the moment, Marcus Daly would set aside the weight of the Anaconda Copper Mining Company, and deal with a minor thing, but one that had acquired an odd importance to him for reasons he couldn't quite explain to himself. He summoned his assistant, Dell Ryan, and ordered his carriage.

Soon, he was trotting westward from the smelter complex into the serene town of Anaconda, which he had personally laid out, attending to every detail from the width of its grand boulevards to the perfection of its water and sewage systems. Anaconda was his Paris. It would be more than a city; it would be as close to paradise as anything on earth could be. It would be a place of perpetual innocence and charity, a place for his oppressed people to raise families and populate the virgin world.

As he drove westward he took note of every detail; not even a new storefront escaped him. He could not control everything that happened on the lots he had sold off, nor did he want to. But he did keep a shepherd's eye on his city, named for his company, and devoted entirely to the comfort and safety of his army of smeltermen and executives. He turned on Commercial and drew up at the new mortuary, the former store that was swiftly being transformed into a sort of churchly establishment. It was Maxwell's project. Daly knew the man all too well.

A funeral parlor was welcome in Anaconda. There had been none, and what few funerals the town had seen since its inception had involved an imported mortician. He studied the feverish activity, sensing that the proprietor wanted to get into business immediately and not miss a single death. He parked the carriage a little away, so the activity would not disturb his sleek trotter, and anchored everything with a carriage weight.

He entered, discovering as much activity within as out front, as a horde of craftsmen converted the interior into a chapel, with two viewing rooms and a reception area. Those parts of the establishment not open to public view lay at the rear, and that was where Marcus Daly headed, hoping to find the proprietor.

He was in luck. Royal Maxwell, in shirtsleeves, was stacking coffins in a corner.

Daly's presence startled the mortician, who suddenly wiped his hands on a towel.

"Why, it's Mister Daly," he said, worry leaking from him.

"You chose carefully, Maxwell. A suitable distance from my hotel, a discreet walk from it. You're the first one in my city."

"Why, I'm honored by your visit, sir."

"That will depend," Daly said. He had a way of leaving things hanging, portents twisting in the silences.

"I take it for a welcome," Maxwell said.

"I created this. I laid it out. Named each street. Worried my way through the water supply, sewer system, and all else. I thought some about where it should lie, and chose this place because of its view. See Mount Haggin? It looks over us. It's the source of our water, but also our serenity. It rises up and up, and we can't see the top from here. I thought to myself, this is a good place. This is where my people can live in peace and get a good wage and see their children and grandchildren grow."

"Why, yes, sir, and now I'm glad to provide my services to them," Maxwell said, a smile building.

Daly ignored that. "It took a railroad to get it right, sir. A smelter as large as ours consumes more wood and coal than you can imagine. It burns through heavy equipment.

It handles tons of ore that arrive each day in long strings of hopper cars. It will soon be much larger. The cemetery's small, but it'll fill soon. We're growing by several dozen people a day."

"I hope to be of service, sir," Maxwell said.

"This is the place for the state capital," Daly said. "Helena's fine, but doomed to be a small town. Its placer ores have run out, and it's living on nothing. The people of Montana will decide all that next year, and of course Helena wants to remain the seat of government. But we have other plans. Anaconda is the right place. I know exactly where the capitol building should rise, up that slope there, at the base of Mount Haggin, where its dome will overlook the whole state. It's a clean, new town, not one sullied by abandoned mines and graveyards—of equipment, of course. My company will proudly back this very place and donate the land to the state. That's why I'm pursuing this. There's not a top man in the company that doesn't want the capital right here. We want the best and brightest of the legislators and public servants right here. We want them to enjoy my hotel, the best in the state, and we want them to enjoy fine dining, every amenity, good transportation. We intend to make Anaconda as easy to get to as Helena, even if it's a little further to the southwest. Do you see?"

"Oh, Mr. Daly, count me among those who'll push for it. I'll support it."

"Will you?" Daly asked. "How?"

"I'll give politicians the fanciest send-off anywhere."

"I'm sure you will." Daly eyed the man. "We're working stiffs here, Mr. Maxwell. We're from the old country, and haven't got much put by. Now take Mrs. Brophy, in Butte. Mrs. Sean Brophy. All she needed was a dignified funeral, at the hour of her choosing. The Butte Miners Union paid you once, and I paid you again, and you got two fees for one funeral and still let her down, telling her when it would be."

"Oh, a sad mix-up."

"Maybe. Maybe not. But in Anaconda, there's going to be funerals that will honor the dead, no matter how poor they might be. And there'll be a modest fee, paid once. I don't give a fig about politicians, Mr. Maxwell. If you want to bill their widows six times for one funeral, go ahead. But I care for all my brothers, the ones who shovel coal all day, who empty the ore from the hopper cars, who pull cinders out of the furnaces. As I did. I care for them, sir, and you will too, because if you don't, I'll go into the funeral business, and I'll see to it that every man who works for me is honored the way he should be, and his widow comforted, and his remains put to rest. That's how my new city will be, sir. Anaconda's going to be a city on a hill, and when it becomes the capital of Montana, it's going to shine. Is that understood, Mr. Maxwell?"

The ferret-faced man nodded, offered a hasty smile and a puffy hand, which Daly accepted gingerly.

Maybe Anaconda was a company town, but it was going to be a good company town, he thought, as he lifted the carriage weight and steered his trotter away.

It wasn't far to the offices of the *Anaconda Standard,* where he would talk to Durston.

The paper had cost Marcus Daly a fortune, but he had not tried to cut back. He knew little about these things, but knowledgeable men told him it was one of the finest dailies in the country. He wanted it to be so, and had imported the newest equipment and best men to make it so. It was more paper than a town the size of Anaconda could support, and even with some sales in Butte, it was still costly compared to its circulation. But for the time being, that was fine. He could not expect to curb the ambitions of Clark, or win the votes of electors throughout Montana when it came to selecting the permanent capital with an ordinary rag. So a significant portion of the company's profits ended up in the pockets of some great political cartoonists, great reporters, and Durston himself, the resident genius, with a doctorate in philology, and a courtly manner, and a command of everything associated with publishing.

He found John Durston in his lair, scribbling another editorial, which he usually featured on the front page. The *Standard* was not shy about expressing its opinions, both with editorials and with elaborate cartoons.

"You, is it?" Durston asked. "Are we going to oppose capital punishment? Are we going to come out against the Church? Will we rail against Christmas?"

Daly smiled. The Republican Durston had transformed himself into a Democrat upon joining the Daly armada.

"Have we got Clark where we want him?"

"No. We bloviate and he bribes."

"What will stop him?"

"Woodcuts. Photographs. Images, Mr. Daly."

"That's as good a wrecker as any."

"Clark's a stuffed shirt. Black silk stovepipe hat. French cuffs. Elaborate chin whiskers. Spats. Shoes so shiny they reflect his face back to him. Remember, the average citizen of Montana wears bib overalls, brogans, and a battered felt hat."

"And you're working on it?"

"Every issue. You bought the most expensive cartoonists in the republic."

"Yes, and I mean to get my money's worth. Now, the easier task. What are you doing for my city?"

"Woodcuts. Streetlamps. Cobbled streets. Mount Haggin. Pure water. That's a big one, you know. Rail connections. And there's a little something for you to do soon. Host the Montana Press Association in your fancy hotel, everything on the house. You've got a rail connection now."

"Ah! You're worth your high pay now and then, Durston. Set it up. We'll have the whole Montana press here, and show off a bit."

Durston smiled. "Trinkets, favors, mementos. Ah . . . a quart of Kentucky's finest as a take-home."

"Draft a plan in one paragraph and I'll okay it."

"It should get you a capital," Durston said. "A hundred editorials, a hundred stories, a hundred woodcuts or photos. A dinner plate, ANACONDA, MONTANA, STATE CAPITAL in gothic gilt letters, the dome rising in front of Mount Haggin."

"Durston, what would I do without you?"

"Employ two semi-competent altar boys."

"Altar boys?"

"That's what I am, Daly, your altar boy."

"All right, now tell me where we're weakest."

"The *Mineral*'s game. Their man, Hall, has a certain genius at twisting the news. Does the company build a railroad? That's so it can gouge passengers. Does Mr. Daly desire that the capital of Montana be Anaconda? Then run a series of cartoons, each showing the very top of the dome of the state house below the stack, below your office. With the state flag flapping below the company flag. And then there's the one showing fat Anaconda executives toting bags of boodle out of the state capitol building."

"Well, that's not far off the mark, is it?"

"It doesn't play well in Great Falls."

"Can we checkmate the *Mineral*?"

"I know Hall. He has a past, though I don't know what. Shall I make some inquiries?"

"Cover all the news, Durston. Cover the *Mineral*."

"Mr. Daly, you're a man after my own heart."

"Only as long as I pay you top dollar, Mr. Durston."

"Very true, sir. Shall we accuse Mr. Clark of anything?"

"A man's private life is his own business, but his public life is public business."

"Would you regard unusual gifts to be public business?"

"Check every land transaction from now on. Anyone who makes a large purchase of land, or who is gifted with land, or who is suddenly an owner of any business. Yes, Mr. Durston, let us find out what politicians and what cronies are enjoying Mr. Clark's favor, eh? Not just Silver Bow County. Look into Deer Lodge, Great Falls, Missoula, Bozeman. And see if any Republicans are sporting cuff links and real estate."

"I'll put two men and two cartoonists on it, Mr. Daly."

"Good. If Clark is handing out diamond cuff links and gold watch fobs, let's find out who the happy recipients are, eh?"

Duston eyed his own barrel cuffs sadly. "Nothing but a little ink on these, sir," he said.

{ FIFTEEN }

The Silver Bow Club annoyed William Andrews Clark. It was entirely inadequate. He had founded it a decade ago, and now it was housed on the fourth floor of the Lewisohn Building on Granite Street, far too modest a place for men of substance. But there was little Clark could do about it until a proper clubhouse could be built, suitable for the accomplished men of Butte and their visitors. So these precincts simply irritated the copper magnate, and he fumed away his moments there and hoped not to see his rival Marcus Daly, who was a member but rarely visited the place. Clark wished the man would resign; he didn't belong among the city's elite, the men of vision and discernment, the men who had built and financed the mines and smelters and built up the city and its streetcars and waterworks.

But he especially wanted not to see Daly because the man had ruined the Democratic Party, and was making open alliances with Republicans, and was deliberately thwarting Clark's ambitions. The elections of 1892 had gone badly for the Democrats. The rising Populists had cut into the Democratic majorities and had elected three men to the legislature. The Democrats had lost the governorship and other offices. At least the elections had kept Daly from locating the state capital in Anaconda, and the state was still governed from the temporary capital at Helena. With his own party sundered into factions, and with the Republicans split into a liberal pro-silver wing and a conservative pro-gold wing, and the appearance of the fevered Populists, who had become power brokers because they held the votes that would turn any faction into a majority, the prospects for Clark were dim. But he was no quitter, and if it came to buying votes again, as he had in 1888, he would do it. He intended to become a United States senator, and nothing on earth would stop him. Except maybe the miserable traitor Daly.

"Fancy place," said Mark Bitters.

"Not a bit fancy; an embarrassment. I've had to entertain James J. Hill in here. It was like dining in a henhouse. Can you imagine what Hill must have thought?"

This was the first time he had permitted his bagman, Bitters, to enter these guarded confines and he was not at peace about it. The Silver Bow Club was intended for the rich, not this sort of barbarian who sat in the wing chair across from Clark.

"Is there anything you wish?" Clark asked.

"I don't suppose there's any red-eye," Bitters said.

Clark summoned a white-jacketed attendant. "Bring him some whiskey." The attendant nodded.

Bitters had been joking. He knew what would be on the bar shelves here.

"You're going to repair the mess in Helena," Clark said. "And do it invisibly."

"When am I not invisible?"

Bitters had a point. He was a full-time retainer of Clark's, but not on any company payroll or connected with any firm doing business with Clark's numerous enterprises. Clark paid him in cash from his bank. He thought six hundred a month sufficed to steer Bitters away from all but the most extravagant bribes, and also keep Bitters from skimming cash off the top. He suspected he was wrong, but did not intend to pursue the matter too closely because boodlers had big mouths themselves. Suffice it to say that Bitters was receiving enough every two weeks to ensure his semi-loyalty.

Bitters was from Kansas City, where they knew a thing or two about how the world worked. He was a cheerful sort, and almost handsome save for a pocked face and a swiftly growing paunch. He had graduated from a private high school, St. Elizabeth's, and had more education than Clark himself, which was useful. Clark was never quite sure how to pick up a fork or when to use a spoon or whether it was acceptable to dab his mouth and beard with a linen napkin. In fact, Clark secretly studied Bitters, whose manners were impeccable, looking for small, telling clues about breeding. Mark Bitters was well-bred, even if he had devoted himself to the life of a scalawag. Clark had no such inheritance. He came from a rural Pennsylvania family and had made his way West doing whatever shoveling and chopping and hoeing and sawing could feed and clothe him. So there was much to learn from Bitters.

"Be subtle," Clark was saying, eyeing the stately room for stray ears. "It goes against a man's conscience to receive gifts, but the same gent'll welcome a business partner, or a payment for services."

Bitters looked bored, as well he should. But Clark intended to make his points and establish his boundaries anyway. It was his privilege, and Bitters was his boodler, and subject to his instructions. Clark saw no wrong it it. Every man had his price; it was simply a matter to finding it. That was what business was about.

"I'll buy the whole state, if that's the deal," Bitters said. "I can buy anything except Mormons. I can buy Episcopalians and Catholics and Unitarians. I can buy Swedes, Finns, Frenchies, Italians, Bohemians, and Irish. I can buy New Englanders and Confederates, Abolitionists and slavers. I can buy farmers and dairymen and pickled pigs' feet bottlers. I can buy editors and conductors and teamsters."

"I don't want you to buy anything, Mark. Just make ordinary business arrangements. There's hardly a man in Montana who doesn't need a business partner."

Bitters was smirking. He sipped his amber spirits and eyed the world cheerfully. That somehow annoyed William Andrews Clark.

"The senators of Rome wore white togas, signifying citizenship and office. They were the most powerful and respected men in the republic. They debated each other on the most civilized terms, and so governed the world. You wouldn't know about that. I've made a study of it, Mark. Anyone with some diligence can make a fortune in this country. All it takes is a little rattlesnake juice and courage. Great businessmen are a dollar a dozen. But there aren't very many senators, and once that title attaches to the name, Bitters, the man has a reputation. He is senator. He is Senator Clark. Even after he's served his term, he is still Senator Clark. I have one thing left to conquer, Bitters, and that is high public office. I don't aspire to the purple toga—you wouldn't know about that. The toga of magistrates, and eventually the toga of emperors. I have no wish to wear the purple. But get me the white toga, Bitters, not because I've earned it, but because I insist. This is something you surely will do, daily, hourly, at dawn and midnight, on Sundays, on holidays, on sabbaths, on new moons and during burials and weddings. You will spend your time in Helena, and you will be on the floor of the legislature, and you will be meeting with every elected man in Helena, publicly and privately, and you will have two purposes before you at all times: I will wear the toga, and the capital will not be abducted by Marcus Daly and built in the shadow of his smelter smokestack."

Bitters sipped, smiled, nodded, and sighed.

"We have made the arrangements," Clark said. "I have a portmanteau filled with presidential portraits, mostly Grover Clevelands and William McKinleys. Do not waste a nickel. Do not pay for perfidy. The less you spend, the more will be your reward."

Bitters lifted his glass. "Cheers," he said.

Clark lifted the portmanteau from beside his armchair. It was no ordinary bag, but one with brass furniture at the corners, and knobby rhinoceros-hide sides and bottom, and an unusual brass lock. The black hide looked thick enough to turn a bullet, and the lock covered a large part of the top of the bag.

"Abercrombie and Fitch," Clark said. "A New York outfitter. Opened this year. I bought three in all, and should have bought a dozen, except Africa would have run out of rhinos. British artisans went to work on the hide, staining it black as sin, and rubbing that glow into it. Ebony and brass; it's not a bag one would ever forget, eh? Now you will find loosely attached an umbilical cord, attached to a wrist bracelet. The bag cannot be easily snatched from your limp hand by a footpad lurking under a gas lamp. Given your physical decrepitude, from an excess of ardent spirits, I thought to add a measure of safety."

"I'll squander it," Bitters said. "Should get me to Paris."

"Yes, and squander it well. The bag cannot be returned to me, not ever. Give it to a curio shop when it's empty. Don't keep it. There is no label in it. The source of the bag must remain entirely unknown."

"When I run out, what next?"

"A one-word telegram to me. The word is rhino."

"Ah, good. I hope not to wire you at all."

"Bitters, the serial numbers are all recorded."

"What's that supposed to mean?"

"It means I will have some idea whose businesses I am partnering."

Bitters lifted the bag. "This is heavy," he said.

"Lighter than gold, sir."

"I mean duty. Responsibility."

"That's a new idea to me, Bitters. Whatever could it mean?"

"I've never held a rhinoceros bag before, sir."

"Let's hope it's your last. Now, then, Bitters, you head for the legislature and get a bit in its mouth and tug."

Bitters eyed his drink, downed it, and set the glass on the end table. Within seconds, a white-coated attendant had whisked it away. Bitters stood, hefting the ebony bag, and winked.

That did not appeal to William Andrews Clark. He wished Bitters had noticed the workmanship that had gone into the bag; the riveted brass furniture, the glossy leather, the knobby exterior, the elaborate handles. But all that was too much for Bitters. Why did 99 percent of human beings lack the slightest aesthetic sensibility?

The greenbacks had arrived in the express car safe of Hill's Great Northern afternoon train to Butte, and had come from the Morgan bank in New York, discreetly wrapped in onionskin.

Bitters would lease rooms off of Last Chance Gulch, and begin to arrange amiable meetings with the legislators as they arrived ahead of the January session. They would know him only as a gentleman who represented substantial interests. His business card said only that he was a commission broker. There would be no talk of financial matters, not then. Bitters was an experienced boodler, and would make no mistakes. That's why Clark had trusted him to a degree. He didn't quite trust anyone who lacked aesthetic sensibility, and there wasn't a shred of evidence that Bitters had ever seen beauty or symmetry or grace in anything, except maybe a thousand-dollar note.

The Silver Bow Club was annoying him again.

He rose to leave, but even as the white-jacketed attendant rushed to get his chesterfield and top hat, Marcus Daly emerged from the vestibule. They saw each other, and Clark knew there would be no escape. He also knew he would be up to whatever affability was required, no matter what fires flared and boiled just behind the dam of civility.

"Why, it's you, Marcus," he said, instantly offering a manicured hand. Daly's hand would not be manicured, and might still bear the scars of hardrock mining. Daly didn't look a bit trapped, and shook the extended pale hand, as if it were a gentleman's club seal of peace for the moment. "Won't you join me for a libation?" Clark asked, hoping for the negative.

"Delighted," Daly said.

And there they were, opposed in matching brocaded wing chairs.

"Are you content with the elections, Mr. Daly?"

"No, not at all."

"I imagine you're distressed," Clark said. "I'm less distressed. I'm quite at ease about the elections. Good men in office, that's what lies at the heart of democracy. Now, this may be a legislature that gets things done."

"The wrong things done," Daly said.

Clark always had an advantage over Marcus Daly, who

was slow-witted if not retarded. And now it was going to be fun. The Silver Bow Club seemed to blaze with light, as the copper titans collected all the sun around themselves.

"Well, as civilized men we can agree to promote differing visions of the public good," Clark said. "Now, I'll want a capitol building with a dome that rises higher than any other structure in Montana, and you'll settle for one with a lower dome."

"Why yes, and I want a United States senator who rises above all other men in the state, but not one of short stature," Daly retorted.

That was an insidious and cruel blow. William Andrews Clark drew himself up to his full five foot and seven inches, and smiled.

"Here's to the future," he said. "Nothing short, and nothing low."

Daly laughed.

{ SIXTEEN }

The more John Fellowes Hall contemplated his first name, the more annoyed he became. John was simply not a suitable name for a man of genius. He seriously considered Jon, which seemed more modern and elegant, but he finally rejected that, too. Instead, he changed his signature to J. Fellowes Hall, quietly burying his first name. He knew a man whose first name was Sylvester and whose middle one was Lawrence, and who changed his name to S. Lawrence. It made sense. Who could possibly want to be named Sylvester?

So J. Fellowes Hall was how he signed his name, and how he was listed in the masthead of the *Mineral*. That had a nice ring to it. The paper, of course, had bloomed under his superb management, and now was the most lucrative in Butte. All he had done was move the daily police blotter to the front page. Grabbit Wolf interviewed drunks, murderers, thieves, confidence men, and a wide variety of doxies and punks, and out of it all came the perfect stew to capture readers and nab advertising. And J. Fellowes Hall had done it all without even selling a one-inch ad to anyone.

Of course William Andrews Clark wasn't thrilled, and tended to be a little stuffy when it came to the content of his paper, but the fat profits from the *Mineral* trumped any reservations he had, and he huffily let Hall have his way. The more readers, the more his campaign for office in the United States Senate would prosper. The more readers, the more he could keep Daly at bay.

And now, with the bitter winds of January, 1893, the legislature was collecting in Helena, there to decide several crucial matters, most importantly the naming of Montana's next senator. There were reformers who thought senators should be elected by the people, but they were lacking gravity. The proper way, the constitutional way, was for state legislatures to select them and send them off to Washington.

It was going to be a messy legislature, with the Democrats divided between the Daly and Clark factions, the Republicans divided between gold and silver factions, and there were a few Populists in there who could tilt the voting in any direction.

Hall decided to cover the shenanigans himself, and leave the coverage of Butte to Grabbit Wolf, who was an adept at writing blood, gore, mayhem, immorality, and any news at all rising from Mercury Street. The *Mineral* would not suffer from a brief absence of its guiding genius.

In truth, Hall itched to get out of town. He had not yet extracted himself from the servant quarters of Clark's mansion, and had no prospect of it until Clark headed off to Washington. Meanwhile, J. Fellowes Hall was enjoying a respite from marriage, and regularly wrote Amber to be patient; Butte was an abominable place, cold and cruel, and no place for gentlefolk or children. That was true enough to satisfy Hall's integrity.

So one bitter day Hall climbed into his lamb's-wool chesterfield, wrapped a wool scarf around his neck, put on a formidable black fur cap with earflaps, and had a hack take him to the depot, where he caught the morning train to Helena. He had arranged for rooms, and planned to settle in for the duration of the session. Hot news he would wire to Butte, and damn the cost. Routine stories would go via special pouch on the trains.

The temporary capital was bustling, and there wasn't room for the legislators and everyone with axes to grind, but for a king's ransom lodging could be had at the great redbrick mansions on the west side, the homes of cattle barons and mining kings and railroad moguls, most of which had carriage houses that could be rented for a fancy price from the servants if not their masters. He was worth it. He would charge the cost to the *Mineral,* and Clark would swallow it without a whimper. It would be servants' quarters again, but Hall was used to it.

He knew how to operate; the axe-grinders and legislators would come to him. He was, after all, the editor of choice to approach, the editor who had turned the *Butte Mineral* into a powerful and widely read sheet. He liked Helena. It still had the aura of a gold-digging town, and some of its solid brick and stone buildings were reputed to sit on rich placer ground. Swift inquiry led him to the Georgian Chop House in Last Chance Gulch. That would be the watering hole of the Democrats; across the gulch was the Dreyer Arcade, which would be the club of the Republicans, while the Populists made a great show of being poor and would come only as guests.

At the Chop House he made an arrangement; a certain corner table, clad in white linen and suitable for four, would be his every afternoon and evening, for a price, of course. When the legislature met, Helena's prices and wages tripled, and tips quadrupled. But J. Fellows Hall didn't mind. The paper would pay.

"And put my drinks on a tab," he said. "I'll settle at the end of the session."

"Very good, sir. Mr. Clark is a regular customer of ours. Mr. Daly, too."

"And if anyone asks, tell them I'm Hall, J. Fellows Hall. That's all. They'll know."

"You're a mining man?"

"An editor, sir. Do I look like a miner?"

The majordomo hurried off.

It all would work out fine. There was no need to attend sessions or listen to the mumbling, when everything he needed to know would make itself plain right there at his table, and the people he needed to see would appear, and the asides and jokes he required would slide into his ear.

By the end of the first evening he was on a first-name basis with most of the legislature. At his table was a bottle of good bourbon, glasses, and a bucket of ice straight off the peaks above town. By the end of the second eve he knew Daly's operatives on sight, and sometimes he saw one of Clark's men, a slippery fellow named Bitters that Hall suspected of being Clark's chief of staff here in Helena. Daly's men were all wearing Anaconda buttons. Clark's were wearing copper-colored ribbons with Clark's name gilded in silver on them, a thoughtful decoration.

The voting for a new Montana senator had begun, and it was deadlocked between several Democrats and a Republican or two. None of that was important. No one was close to a majority, and Clark himself was near the rear of the pack. Federal law required that the legislature vote daily in session until a United States senator was elected, and Hall expected it would be weeks before the dust settled. The winner would need some help from the Populists and in Clark's case, from some Republicans too. Daly's men were heading across the gulch more and more, looking in the opposing party for the votes they needed to stop Clark—and win the permanent state capital for Anaconda. As for Daly himself, if he was in Helena, he certainly wasn't dining in the Chop House.

Hall enjoyed the show. The boodlers were busy. No cash ever crossed a linen tablecloth, but it was plain there were deals done and bank accounts fattened. Now and then a calculating politico slid up to his table with some news, or accusations, or scheme, which Hall duly recorded and shipped off to his rag, usually on the morning train. He had a way of listening without taking notes, which usually made people more effusive and less guarded. A question here and there, a nod, a smile sufficed. He kept the *Mineral* well fed with gossip, with whatever was damaging to the Daly interests, and with insinuations of bribery which were carefully tailored to avoid libel but heavy with suspicions and hints. If a legislator suddenly seemed cheerful, that was grist for Hall's mill.

J. Fellowes Hall knew he was a master, and over the days and weeks of the session, he managed to portray the Daly men and the Republicans as rascals, bribe takers, and crooks. He made a specialty of implying that so and so was miraculously affluent, spending vast sums on dining and wine, and sporting new wardrobes gotten up by Helena's busy tailors. Hall never missed a trick, but neither did Daly's rag, the *Anaconda Standard,* whose black headlines and political cartoons depicted the Clark forces in much the same light.

One day a mysterious lady of indeterminate age appeared unescorted at the Chop House, and settled into a corner table opposite of Hall's. It was impossible to ignore her. She was slender and exotic, vaguely Mediterranean, with jet hair. She wore the most demure of woolen suits, gray with a pleated skirt, all buttoned tight from neck to toe, but at the neckline everything changed. Above was pale and ethereal flesh haloed by black, and soft brown lips always slightly open, with a slim nose and warm brown eyes completing the ensemble. If the demure gray dress suggested primness and propriety, everything from the neck up suggested wanton delight in the ways of the world.

Hall eyed her amiably, knowing he'd soon have her secret. The main thing was to see what male joined her. It was not proper for an unescorted woman to remain for long in a reputable restaurant. But no male showed up, and she proceeded to order wine and a salad and with these before her, mostly as a barrier to unwanted male attention, she continued to eye the politicians. She scarcely ate, but did consume some red wine, and then another glass.

That somehow annoyed J. Fellowes Hall, and he toyed with the idea of introducing himself, but counseled patience. He'd soon enough know her designs. But that evening passed without another clue. The lady gazed, sipped wine, eyed the hurly-burly crowd, even as every male in the Chop House eyed her.

Hall sensed she was about to depart, and decided to break with his own habit, and summoned a waiter. "Invite the lady to my table. Tell her I'm J. Fellowes Hall, editor of the *Butte Mineral,* and I will record her every word for posterity."

The waiter delivered, and Hall found himself being scrutinized, one female eyebrow raised, while two brown eyes took him in. She nodded. The waiter returned. "She accepts and will join you presently," he said.

She appeared shortly, and settled in across from him. "You're Mister Hall, and I'm Miss Anonymous," she said.

He discovered no ring on her left hand. "Anonymous?"

"That's how it will be, but you may call me whatever name you think might fit."

"I will call you Queen," Hall said, "because that is your station in life."

She laughed. "The Virgin Queen, like Elizabeth of England?"

For once, Hall was tongue-tied.

"I am here unescorted, which raises questions about my reputation, which you have probably already resolved," she said.

"I, ah, was merely speculating. I believe you are here because of the session."

"No, I'm looking for a man. My intention is semi-honorable."

"You, ah, I am lost, Queen."

"I wish to be kept by an appropriate man. One with adequate funds to make a beautiful lady very happy. This is entirely the proper spot for that, so you could say I am surveying the terrain."

Hall was entirely flummoxed. In all his years of toil in the news profession, he had never encountered such candidness.

"Have you any prospects?" he asked, delicately.

"Not you," she said.

That was among the most deflating moments of his life. It made him wish he had not been stuck with parents who misnamed him.

"Well, Queen, politicians are an impoverished lot. No one with means ever indulges in this hurly-burly. I'd suggest that you come to Butte, where mining men are making more money in a week than beautiful women can spend in a lifetime."

"I'll probably take you up on it," she said. "Thanks for the wine."

With that, barely two minutes into an interview, she abandoned him and returned to her own table, there to review the prospects.

It annoyed him. He planned to treat her badly in a story about Helena's morals, but it would take a few days to figure out how to do it.

Meanwhile, there was the annoying struggle filling the columns of every paper in Montana.

The Democrats had a thin majority with the help of the Populists, but the stiff old Republican vigilante Wilbur Sanders came close to carrying the legislature. Most of the Democrats favored Clark, but Daly's faction supported William Dixon, who was Daly's attorney. Then the Republicans ditched Sanders and supported Lee Mantle, editor of the *Butte Inter-Mountain,* who might get the votes of the Daly Democrats, except that the Daly contingent continued to back Dixon. And it was plain that both Daly and Clark boodlers were attempting to break the deadlock with thousand-dollar bills.

By early March, Clark had 32 votes, Mantle 25, Dixon 11, and old Tom Carter 1. Clark needed 35 for the majority, and waited in Helena with his acceptance speech in hand, only to fail. A Daly ally, Senator Matts of Missoula County, made it plain: he said that Clark's tombstone would someday read, "Here lies the man who thought he could buy up the legislature of sovereign Montana and got fooled."

The Daly Democrats then joined the Republicans to force adjournment. The legislature had elected no man senator, which meant that Governor John Rickards, a Republican, could call a special session, or appoint someone to fill the vacancy. He chose to appoint the Butte editor Lee Mantle, but the United States Senate wanted no part of it. Montana was without a second senator, and Rickards continued to refuse to call a special session, knowing it would result in a Democrat being elected, so the state drifted along without two senators.

Daly didn't get his capital. Clark didn't get his seat in the Senate. But a lot of Montana's politicians were suddenly affluent.

{ SEVENTEEN }

The snazzy young man stepping off the railroad coach was no stranger to Butte. He'd been in town twice, but this time he intended to stay. In his portmanteau he had a miraculous money machine. It would take a while to crank it up, but soon it would make him, his brothers, and his backers, rich. He had no large ambition other than to make a fortune for the fun of it, and then squander it in bedrooms and restaurants. If he could rattle a few financiers along the way, that would be entertaining too.

The city was cold that March day of 1893; but when was Butte ever warm? It hugged the Continental Divide. Minerals were wherever they had been laid down long ago, and in this case, the richest hill on earth was perched on a high western slope of the northern Rockies.

He got a hack and directed the driver, Fat Jack, to find him some excellent rooms preferably in the downtown area. He was used to great comfort back East, and knew he would soon enjoy such comforts in Butte, but not just yet. The driver, it turned out, knew just the place, and deposited him at the Butte Hotel, in the heart of town, surrounded by saloons and eateries.

F. Augustus Heinze gave the gent a generous tip, asked him to pick up his black leather trunk from the express car, and bring it also. He rented a suite by the month, deposited his portmanteau, and set out afoot for the eastern reaches of the hill, Meaderville in particular, to take a close look at the site of his new smelter, which would be called the Montana Ore Purchasing Company. The smelter was the culmination of years of planning, education, capitalization, and evaluation of the many independent mines operating on the hill, mines that shipped their ore to the great mills and smelters of the Anaconda combine, or the Boston and Montana Company's reduction works in Great Falls—and paid more than they should.

F. Augustus Heinze was not inclined to work any harder than he had to, and would have taken a hack to Meaderville but for his wish to pace every foot of Butte once again, letting the city settle itself in his mind. He had ventured West while still in his teens, with degrees from Brooklyn Polytechnic and the Columbia School of Mines, intending to make a princely living at mining. When he had arrived in Butte the first time, he was swiftly hired as a mining engineer, and spent his days deep underground, reading the way the veins went, mapping copper and silver veins indelibly in his mind. He had an uncanny grasp of what lay under the surface of Butte, and he knew it. In time he returned East, wrote for a mining journal, took additional courses in geology and mining in Europe, and returned well schooled to begin his adventure.

His father, an importer who had created a modest family fortune, had resisted.

But now his father was dead. And his brothers, Otto Charles and Arthur, were willing to venture the family's modest capital in this big plunge. Fritz Heinze—he hated the name Fritz, avoided it and asked others not to use it, but it stuck anyway—owned 51 percent of the new company, which would reduce ore cheaply for the dozen or so independent mines on the hill, thus saving their owners large sums. It was all there in his portmanteau. He had much the sense about mills and smelters that the Guggenheims did: lodes come and go, mines give out, but a smelter remains profitable for long periods, drawing upon one or another mine in the surrounding mineral belt for its sustenance. But Fritz had a larger vision than the Guggenheims: he knew where the veins lay thick and fat and rich, and he planned to claim them, and feed his own ore into his smelter. Somehow, in his head, he had a map of the richest veins on the hill, and he intended to use his knowledge to get very rich.

Meaderville lay upslope and east, and was a favorite recreational quarter of Butte, known for its choice restaurants, cheerful nightlife, and sedate Italian neighborhoods. That was perfect. Fritz would mine the ore, smelt it, and mine the saloons and eateries all at once. Fritz stood five feet ten inches, and weighed two hundred pounds, and was lithe and thick and muscled. He was not handsome but made up for it with a lively eye for a curve, and a great deal of suave cheer. He wore a bowler and well-cut coat, in accordance with his class. His mother was a Lacy, from a family both Irish and Episcopalian, while his father Otto was a German immigrant who had prospered at once in the New World. Fritz Heinze had not known a day of hardship and intended never to know one.

He had been born in December of 1869, which made him twenty-four on this cold day in Butte. In his portmanteau he had the incorporation papers, the deed for Meaderville land, the blueprints, and the contract with a Butte construction company to begin work on the smelter. He hiked to the site, noted that the contractor had staked the ground and was ready to go. Within sight were various independent mines, whose owners would relish the chance to turn their ore into copper and silver and maybe some gold for a tariff well below what the giants were charging, and he'd do it right there on the hill, too, saving them the cost of hauling.

He eyed the city below him, bustling and busy now,

dominated by Clark and Anaconda but with a dozen or so powerful independents, such as the Boston and Montana Consolidated Copper and Silver Mining Company, and the various mines operated by the Lewisohn brothers. These men owned the Leonard and Colusa mines, the Mountain View, West Colusa, Pennsylvania, Liquidator, Comanche, and Badger State, while the Butte and Boston Company operated the Mountain Chief, Silver Bow, Grey Cliff, LaPlata, Blue Jay, and the Belle of Butte. Most of these mines were shipping ore clear to Great Falls, but F. Augustus Heinze had other plans in mind for that ore, hauled at such cost so far away.

Everywhere he looked, he saw the shine. The hill glittered. The money trees were growing fruit. He wasn't one to toil, and didn't intend to. Hire others to do that. Hire good men to run his smelter the way he intended, using the best fluxing and milling processes in the world. Hire good men to wrestle the raw ore from deep down, and crush it and bleed it and heat it until it yielded treasure. There was the itch in him to apply his unique knowledge, hard-won at American and European universities. There was every need to examine prospective mining properties himself; his knowledge of geology and mineralogy would suffice. There was no particular need for him to bother with the rest.

His late father would not approve; his mother's wish that he would pursue the arts or a profession didn't matter. He doubted that his two brothers entirely approved, but they had reluctantly anted up the family inheritance. He studied the Meaderville site, satisfied with it, and then hiked back to the central city, having had enough of cold and thin air and smoke.

There were more important things to occupy his time.

He attended to his grooming, washing up, combing his somewhat rowdy hair, and then descended to the street, in search of a good chop house. He was ready for a tender steak, some roulette, and a few ladies, preferably of the demimonde. He could always find such establishments in Meaderville, but his purpose this eve was to find cheerful establishments near his hotel. That proved to be easy. He had a way of knowing instantly whether a hostelry suited one of his several moods.

Park Street proved to be a cornucopia of such places, so he ducked into one, found it amiable, and settled himself at the mahogany bar. A barman in a white shirt and bow tie soon supplied him with some good Glenlivet on ice, and he sipped gratefully while surveying the clientele. There were several accountant types on the bar rail, which was fine. Fritz liked accountants. Yonder, pushed against the flocked green wallpaper were couples, one probably married, another consisting of a bewhiskered and portly old gent with a thin blond lady who looked nervous and kept fingering a keepsake at her breast; and a third couple who looked bored with themselves and their world. None appeared to be hurting for money, and all were dressed to the nines for an evening on the town.

"I wish to send drinks and compliments to those couples," he said, pointing them out to the barman. "Tell them, courtesy of Augustus Heinze."

The barman was skilled, or else a quack, because he set to work on the libations without further inquiry, and a waiter soon delivered the goods. The couples craned around, nodded and smiled, and lifted their glasses in salute.

It didn't take long. Before the evening was well mellowed, he had met portly old Agamemnon Bulwer and his young vamp Alice Cronsnoble. He was a private banker capitalizing mines, and she was, well, the object of his attentions. The married couple proved to be Salmon and Tootsie Hogarth, he a mining engineer with the Clark group, she a drunk who made eyes at Fritz. And the bored couple proved to be a hotel owner named Higgins, celebrating his birthday, along with his lady friend Esmeralda, who was hoping the evening wouldn't last long.

"I say, fellow, come tell us about yourself," said Bulwer.

"A new man in town, sir. F. Augustus Heinze, from various quarters of Europe and the East Coast."

"Ah, so? You have a specialty?"

"Why, women are my specialty, sir. I have a graduate degree in women, and I am a doctor of female philosophy."

The old boy's eyes lit up. "I'll want to read your dissertation."

"It involved a great deal of research," he said. "Paris, New York, Istanbul, Buenos Aires, Sumatra."

"What does the F stand for?" Alice asked.

He sighed. "A name I got stuck with, and which I wish to bury in the bottom of the shaft."

"Fess up now, Heinze."

"Fritz, sir. It is painful to me."

"Well from now on, Heinze, you're Fritz."

Heinze sighed. This was not new to him. But he would suffer what he must to make the acquaintance of an investment banker.

"Your trade? Your trade, sir?" Bulwer asked.

"Predator, sir. Shark. Barracuda. I plan to eat a mine a day."

"By Gawd, Butte's the place of destiny," the old goat said. "Well, Alice, shall we go start an earthquake?"

"I have a headache," she said.

"My pleasure," Fritz said. He rose, and soon was making other friends at other tables.

Heinze enjoyed them. Esmeralda was making eyes at him and Tootsie was pushing her knee into Augustus's thigh. He was off to a good start and the evening flew by amiably. From Salmon—they got onto a good professional basis swiftly—he learned that the Rarus mine had some timbering problems, and water trouble on the seventh level; from the hotelier he discovered that Butte's city water supply was precarious and tainted, and the Clark interests were not inclined to improve it. But it was old Bulwer who intrigued him the most. Give a banker a drink or two, and suddenly the world opens up. He learned the names of half a dozen mines seeking development capital, and why Bulwer wasn't going to accommodate four of them, and why he called the vamp his secretary and installed her in her own suite.

Heinze picked up another round of drinks, conferred his best wishes upon his new friends, gave them his business card, and drifted to the green baize tables in an adjoining room, where a thin, tubercular croupier was operating a clattering roulette wheel and another fat one was operating a faro game. Heinze studied the lacquered wheel a bit, spotting a slight wobble and a halting conclusion to each spin, and decided not to waste his money there. Instead, he bought into a faro game, bucked the tiger, lost a few dollars, and abandoned the parlor.

He dined on filet mignon and mashed potatoes plentifully smothered in gravy, and then headed over to his hotel, content with the evening. He had six new friends, a heap of valuable and confidential information, three women who were inclined to be accommodating, and several new business connections, most particularly an investment banker.

He entered the lobby, cast aside an impulse to hike down to Mercury Street, and headed toward his suite. Business was always fun. He did his best work evenings, and this evening had been just capital.

{ EIGHTEEN }

Alice Brophy found employment as a laundress for a dollar a day, which was more than she expected. Her employer was the Florence Hotel, which was a vast rooming house rather than a hotel, close to the Anaconda Company mines. Marcus Daly had built it to accommodate his miners. It was a rambling structure, with rooms containing two iron cots, and it was home to over six hundred, mostly off the immigrant boats from Ireland.

Her task was to give each miner a pair of fresh sheets once a month, take in the old, wash and mangle them in the steamy and miserable basement, in an endless cycle. Some of the women who had been in service longer were chambermaids, looking after the lobby, billiard room, library, and the toilets. There were eight porcelain stools and a trough in the basement, always foul, and all over-used. Residents didn't stay long: the Florence served as a way station for the flood of men arriving in town daily. As usual, Marcus Daly had seen the need, and built the edifice. It was called the Big Ship, after someone noted that enough whiskey was consumed there to float a big ship.

A dollar a day was good money; most hotels paid seventy-five cents a shift, so Alice took it gratefully. And it was only a short walk to her cottage, so she was never far from her children. The boarders were young, single, and poor. They paid thirty-five dollars a month and got big breakfasts of oatmeal gruel, stirred in giant pots, which nourished them during their long stints in the pits. Alice considered being a cook, but decided instead to wash sheets. She liked the faintly burnt smell of sheets as they emerged from the mangle, and she liked to carry them up to whatever floor was being serviced.

She felt relatively safe there, mostly because these men

were Irish, and they would treat a colleen good and proper. But not always, and especially not when their brains had been loosened by a little whiskey. So it was always a risky thing, taking sheets up and bringing sheets down, and sometimes she had slapped a galoot or howled for help. But so far it was working out.

She worked harder than the miners, who took home three dollars and fifty cents for a nine-hour day, and that annoyed her. In fact, the more she thought about it, the more she steamed at the very thought. It was bad enough being a woman and getting bounced upon by a randy man when all she wanted was to sleep. But they were getting much more money. She lifted tons of sheets each day. Wet sheets, stinking sheets, dry sheets. Sheets that made her want to puke. She lifted more weight each day than any mucker in the pits. What she could do for three dollars and fifty cents a day! The things she could have! The comforts she could give her children! The world lacked rightness.

Maybe she would tell Marcus Daly about it. This was his ramshackle hotel; this was his way of keeping labor coming to Butte. But he was treating men a lot better than women. Not that this was much of a hotel. It stank. No one cleaned it regularly. There wasn't much air. It just hung in the rooms, wet and stinking and without any oxygen in it. She swore there wasn't a vent in the building. The place had a "dry" room where miners could doff their sweat-soaked mine britches and put on some dry clothing. But that changing room was airless and stank too, and it was said half the miners of Butte either had miner's lung or consumption, and none more so than in Dublin Gulch, sprawling close to the great Anaconda mines of Marcus Daly. Maybe she'd get it, and then her lungs would quit, and she'd cough red into the sheets, and quit working, and die in her cottage, and she'd leave orphans behind, who'd run on the streets and probably die of consumption too.

This Florence was just a big warehouse for men who drank and puked and went somewhere else. So what if Marcus Daly thought he was doing the Irish a favor. He wasn't. He was sending them to an early grave.

The more the widow Brophy toiled, the hotter she got, and as she trudged the stinking dark halls of the stinking building, she built up a head of anger as strong as the steam in a boiler. Her brats were running loose, and when could she see them? No school for them; just out in the smoky cold air, doing whatever they did out in the city. That was a woman's lot to have to break her back scrubbing sheets and stirring the tubs and abandoning her babies.

At least she didn't have to get married and have a miner bounce on her every night. At least she didn't have to fend off Big Johnny Boyle who thought she was some sort of cow he'd sell for a price. Those union bosses, they were something, full of talk about making the world better for men—which was only half the human race.

Alice Brophy, widow of Singing Sean, discovered Feminism and Socialism at the same time, and knew she had found the stairway to heaven.

One winter's day she was straightening the library at the Florence and came upon a tract, in the form of a folded sheet of newsprint, lying on a table. It was called *Justice*. It also said "free." So she took it. She could read some; her ma had insisted, and she had gotten a little more in church schools and rude Butte public schools. A woman needed to read. She couldn't be seen wasting time, so she hid the tract in her bosom and continued through the day's chores, all ten hours of them, and didn't read her free tract until she got home and lit the coal oil lamp. Even then she had to feed her clamoring yowlers, who were turning into little outlaws she had to yell at.

But at last she read the pamphlet, which sounded a lot like the Bible, full of things like "Oh, my brethren, we must fight for justice, so that every man can partake of the fruits of his labor equally with the others, and so the poor and humble will be rewarded, and the rich shall have their ill-gotten gains plucked away from them."

There was a program in it. Let the means of production be owned by the government, and let workers receive the fruits of their labor according to their need and contribute their labor according to their ability. She settled deep in her sprung-cushion chair, a vision upon her. These people didn't say anything about women, and how women worked and didn't get paid much, but at least this was on the right track. She liked the idea. Maybe these good people would extend their thoughts and programs to women someday. But maybe not.

She studied the sheet, looking for its source. It was produced by the Socialist Labor Party, and seemed a lot like the union literature she was familiar with. It talked about a lecturer named Daniel DeLeon, who would visit Butte soon. There were other names in a masthead, people who sure had odd names, like Eugene Debs. That sure was no Hibernian as far as she could tell. And Samuel Gompers. Now what sort of name was that? This was all the work of foreigners. But maybe it didn't matter. The Butte Miners Union was Irish. So was almost everyone in the Florence Hotel. So were most of the people in the Anaconda, Neversweat, and St. Lawrence mines.

She thought and thought about what she had read, and the more she thought, the better she liked the whole idea. If the government owned everything, and paid equal wages to everyone, the rich wouldn't get rich and the poor wouldn't be poor. And the poor wouldn't have to work such long hours, or get so tired, or get so sick and broken on the job, because the government would make sure that everyone was treated right. Maybe it wouldn't work out perfectly, but it surely would be an improvement on what existed there, on the raw hill, where she was surrounded by thousands of desperate people barely hanging on, and a few fit men with gold watch fobs and silk top hats riding around in carriages.

She couldn't find out any more. She scoured the Florence library. During the rare moments when she had some freedom, she hunted for reading rooms or rental libraries. But the Socialist Labor Party had been nothing but a chimera. Then one day she decided to ask Big Johnny Boyle. He'd know. And she wasn't afraid of him, either. She'd defeated his designs, and found means to support herself.

Getting to see Big Johnny wasn't easy. She needed to trade hours with another laundress, and get their boss to approve. That was Mrs. Murphy, and she was the head laundress, and she was beholden to the hotel not to let any working woman feign so much as a headache, much less the vapors. But Alice got it arranged. She traded hours with Agnes Boxleiter, and Mrs. Murphy reluctantly agreed, even if she sniffed something wrong with it.

So the widow Alice Brophy walked the long way over to central Butte, and headed for the Butte Miners Union, which was Local Number One of something, but who cared?

Sure enough, there was Big Johnny parked in a chair, with Eddie the Pick, like always.

"Do I know you?" Boyle said.

"Not if I can help it," she retorted.

"I think you're Brophy's widow lady," Eddie said.

"Oh, yah, you want a husband now? Quit work?"

"No, it'd be more work, marrying. Now I get off after ten hours."

"In a house, it ain't work. What's work about it? You want a husband?"

"No, I want you to tell me about something. What's the Socialist Labor Party?"

"Oh, them. They're horning in on the unions. Piece of trouble, keeping everyone unhappy."

"I read their program. They're going to make my life better."

Eddie the Pick grinned. "Everyone's got a program. I can make your life better."

"I get enough of that at the Big Ship," she said. "And I also have a hat pin and I know where to stick it."

"What do you want to know about the Socialists?" Eddie asked.

"Where I can join, and where I can read up."

"Why? They don't care about laundresses," Eddie said. "They might care about your husband and his wage and his hours, and who hires him. But not a woman."

At least Eddie had a sense of her mission, which was more than she could say for Big Johnny Boyle, who was sitting there grinning.

"How much you making?" Eddie asked.

"A dollar a shift."

"What do you want to join for? That's as good as it gets for a woman."

"A mucker shovels twenty tons of rock a shift and gets three-fifty. I wash more tons of wet sheets, and carry them up, and bring the dirty ones down, and I work harder than a mucker and no one pays me the same."

"Yeah, well, that's tough," Big Johnny said. "Wish we could help."

But Eddie motioned her over to the window. "That's the hill up there. That's how it is. No one's gonna change anything. No United States government's gonna take over them mines. No bureaucrat's gonna pay you the same as a mucker down in the pits."

"I have to start somewhere," she said.

"Fly the red flag?" Eddie asked.

"Is that the color?"

"Socialist color." Eddie headed for a table groaning with stuff no one wanted to read, and shuffled through some of it. "Here's some talks by DeLeon; he's their current hot shot. And Debs. Here's all about Debs, good union man until he turned red on us. And Gompers. I never had much use for Gompers. But here, dig around in here."

"I'll return it."

"Keep it. It just gets us into trouble. When they see red, they send in the National Guard."

"Any of this going to help women?" she asked.

"Just get married, sweetheart," said Big Johnny. "I'll fix you up so you never have to work a day in your life."

"Bullshit, Johnny Boyle," she said.

That stopped him cold.

"I'd work twenty hours a day and not get a dime, and have nothing but babies out of it."

It turned oddly quiet in there.

"You'll want to read everything that Susan B. Anthony has written, and maybe join the Woman Suffrage Movement," Eddie said.

"Suffer what?"

"Get the right to vote."

"What good would that do?"

"Oh, maybe vote for better wages. Maybe vote for better hours. Maybe vote so women can hold property. Maybe vote so women get equal pay."

"Are they Socialists?"

"Beats me," said Eddie.

But then he produced a miracle. There was some suffrage stuff in that unkempt pile, tracts, a booklet about the Feminist movement, a portrait of Susan B. Anthony, and other stuff.

"Thank you," Alice said.

"Good to get that stuff out of here," Boyle said. "Goddamn biddies."

Alice hauled all of it in her apron, since she didn't have a bag, and after that she studied everything she could find, and read by the light of her kerosene lamp, and ignored her brats, and kept on reading. Now that she knew where to order the tracts, she spent money on postage and let her lousy brats starve, and when they whined she told them to boil their own potatoes, which they did, and when they complained that she didn't join them, she told them to go out and make their own living; she was tired of them.

And somewhere along in there, someone started calling her Red Alice.

{ NINETEEN }

Slanting Agnes sure didn't like the man. But he had become a regular, and he left amazing tips, and those tips kept her going and got her a knit shawl for Christmas, so she tolerated him. Sort of. She always let him know it. He was a rotter, that's what he was. But at least he showed up very early in the morning, and not when she had a dozen others waiting to see her. He came early because he didn't want to be seen by anyone.

J. Fellowes Hall was his three-button name. Definitely not Hibernian, which she held against him. He ran that paper, but it took her a while to figure it out. He came every few days to sit at her table, sip her tea, and ask questions. He hardly ever asked about himself or his future, and she was grateful for that. She hoped he'd stumble into a mineshaft someday. He peppered her with all sorts of questions, sometimes things she knew nothing about, and that made her grouchy.

She didn't know he ran the *Mineral* until she saw her own words on its front page. He had asked her if there would be a mine accident the next day, and she said yes, two Boston and Montana men would die when they fell into a smelter furnace. He had stared at her greedily while she closed her eyes and summoned word from beyond the present, and then the future arrived like a flash of lightning, and that's what she saw, and she mumbled it to him. He had hurried away and written her words in his newspaper, so the paper was predicting that there would be an accident at the smelter, and the *Mineral* published that, and then it happened. And after that, Clark's rag sold twice as many papers as before.

She felt bad, like she had exposed those grieving families to the glare of words on paper, so everyone knew that the deaths had been foreseen.

She had made one demand of J. Fellowes Hall, and that was to keep her name out of it. If he published her name, he would never sit at her kitchen table and get the future from her again. He had agreed, but she distrusted him. One of these days he would betray her, and then she would have hundreds of angry and bitter people at her door. Not that she was such a big secret. She had put her card into several papers over the years, and most people knew she had been given powers.

She still saw Andrew Penrose, for example, and he was still looking for mine disasters, and still trying to find some way to keep them from happening. But most of the bills and coin that filled her little jar on the table came from J. Fellowes Hall, so it didn't do much good to despise the man. Since that first vision of the smelter accident, he had published a dozen more visions. But sometimes when he was urging her the most, she went blank or some little tendril of contempt rose up, and she told him it wasn't his business, and she'd seen enough of him. She didn't care whether she was polite or not. You couldn't be polite to someone like J. Fellowes Hall all the time and keep your head on straight.

The *Mineral* was full of sensations, publishing things before they occurred, and it was the best-read paper anywhere around there. That man liked to know whether there would be something bad on Mercury Street, like a murder or a suicide, and once she had a terrible white vision of a girl being knifed by her pimp, and she had told Hall about it, and he had run the story before it happened, and the Butte police wanted to know how that could be. The rag sold an extra five hundred papers that time.

Now, J. Fellowes Hall was perched on her rickety chair sipping her good tea, and he wanted her to look ahead and say where the state capital would be. Helena? Butte? Great Falls? Somewhere else?

"How should I know? And who cares?" she snapped.

He pulled out a five dollar bill and laid it on the table. She hated that. It was a bribe. "I won't," she said.

"Will Tammany win?" he asked.

She liked that. Everyone in Butte knew about Marcus Daly's great horse. Tammany was the pride of Daly's stock farm. A portrait of Tammany was enshrined in the parquet floor of Daly's Montana Hotel in Anaconda, and anyone who stepped on the large image of the revered horse had to buy the house a drink. Tammany ran in all the great stakes races back East, and made a lot of money for Marcus Daly. And Tammany was just one of several great Thoroughbreds raised right there in Montana.

"I don't know and I won't try," she said. "You'd just go bet on it. I won't abuse what's come to me. It wouldn't be a proper bet."

"I wouldn't bet; I want to say it before the race, so the *Mineral* sells a lot of papers."

"I won't try," she said.

He seemed faintly annoyed. Twice she'd refused him this early morning. That suited her just fine. There was something about the man that made her want to stick a hat pin into him. He sat there, plainly disappointed because he didn't have any fancy item to put on his front page. He eyed her door, as if thinking to go.

"Who's going to win Butte?" he asked. "Daly and his Anaconda Company, or Clark? They've been wrestling with each other for years. So, look and see."

"I don't know if I feel like it."

"There's unending wealth down there, beneath our feet. Copper and silver and gold. Enough to make someone the wealthiest man in the world. Someone's going to get it. Who?"

She eyed him, guessing at his motives. What could he put on his front page? "All right," she said.

She closed her eyes, hoping nothing would happen, hoping no white light would fill her vision, hoping she wouldn't be transported to some place in the world to come. But her hopes failed her. She saw a man she had never seen before, and he was well dressed, too. And he was here, right now, and a name came to her. She didn't like the name. What kind of man was that? He wasn't a Hibernian, and he wasn't even Catholic. But he was holding the richest hill on earth in his soft hand. And laughing at the world.

J. Fellowes Hall was watching hawkishly.

"So?" he said.

"No one you know," she said.

"Of course it's someone I know. Did Daly sell to someone else? Clark, he's the king of the hill, right?"

She shook her head.

"No, this one is a newcomer, sort of. He sees the way the veins go. It's like he has magical vision. He knows how the ore got laid down."

"A geologist."

"I wouldn't know that. He's got a lot of learning in him, I know that. And he's not like me, not like people who've been born dirt poor. His pa, his pa sent this man off to schools, lots of schools. And now he's got it all in his head."

"Are you just making him up?"

"You can leave this instant."

"I'm sorry; that was uncalled for. Who is this man?"

"I can't pronounce it. But he's half your age. He's barely out of school."

"There's no boy genius in Butte."

"Fritz, that's his name. Heinze, or something like that, his last name."

"I've heard of him. He's building a smelter in Meaderville. Sorry, madam, but he's not about to take over the richest hill on earth."

She sighed, tired of all this, and wished the man would leave. She had dishes to scrub. "All right then," she said. "You asked. I told you." She rose, wiping her hands on her apron.

"No, wait. How will he take over Butte from two of the most powerful men in the United States?"

"He's smarter. He doesn't need to work. That F, it could stand for Fast instead of Fritz."

Hall lit up, and she knew why. Anything scandalous in Butte ended up on the front page of his rotten paper.

"Is he the playboy of the western world?"

"How should I know? I'm fey, I see things. That doesn't mean I know anything."

"Will he start his own paper?"

"You would ask it, wouldn't you? You'd sell yourself to him if you thought it might get you something."

"Madam, you do carry on. I'm a faithful man. I'm under obligation to Mr. Clark, who hired me, and I have no other plans."

"Except ditching him at the first opportunity."

She didn't know how she knew it, but she was certain of it. He looked uncomfortable.

"He doesn't like your paper and you don't like him. He never gave you a raise. He blames you for not being made a senator. He thinks your paper's not up to Daly's paper, right?"

"I don't know where you got such absurd ideas," he said.

"Because I saw it."

Hall didn't run, but neither was he asking more questions. "I want you to know," he said quietly, "that I esteem William Andrews Clark as if he were my father. I have built his paper into a fine, well-read daily greatly admired by all newspapermen in Montana. The loss of the Senate seat was not my doing. He was a little careless. I have no plan to depart from Mr. Clark's hospitality, or employment, nor would I ever permit myself to be disloyal."

"We'll see," she said, relentlessly. The man probably would be working for F. Augustus Heinze as soon as that dapper little porker started looking for an editor.

"You misread me. In fact, you're not fey, you're just scrounging a living from guesswork. I ought to be more careful about my news sources."

"You'll be taking Heinze's coin soon enough," she replied.

He eyed the five-dollar bill on the table, plainly itching to pocket it, but then changed his mind at the last, and left it there. It had the look and feel of dirty money.

"Take it back if you're not happy with me," she said.

He let it sit. "I don't think I will permit my paper to ventilate your random thoughts. A mistake on my part," he said. He dropped a soft hat over his locks and departed, shedding ice and disdain like a calving glacier.

The poor dearie, she thought. He doesn't know what he's in for.

It was turning into a rare spring morning. The boys had been off at dawn to fish in Silver Bow Creek. No one caught any fish there, but that didn't deter the boys. That's what spring Saturdays were for.

The five dollars on the kitchen table disturbed her. Hall had disturbed her. He made her feel like she wasn't fey at all, just an old biddy with an imagination. She untied her apron, got into her old cloth coat because it was still chill, and in spring Butte could be anything from bitter to sweet. She headed toward Meaderville, which was a goodly hike, but she needed the air. Phantasms! Is that what he thought? It was an uphill walk, but she never slowed. She knew intuitively where to go, a stretch of level ground that was all torn up. A building was rising there, and laboring men were swarming over it, as if its owner wanted it in operation tomorrow. But it was a long way from being done. Even though the building was just walls, some black iron equipment was being anchored inside, and she knew those would crush ore and mix it with fluxes and then fire it in big furnaces being built there. This is what she had seen, this place.

He was there, medium high, dapper, in a loose black suit coat, an open collarless shirt, and a black bowler, looking rather out of place among the workmen in their dungarees and brogans. She stood watching this man she had seen earlier, in one of those sudden, shocking transports into another time. The sight of Fritz Heinze assured her. He was the very one she had seen. If she asked him his name, it would be that name. There was something assuring about all this. It made her mad at J. Fellowes Hall, who had questioned her gifts. She peered a while more at the young man, barely old enough to shave, she thought, and then walked back to her cottage in triumph.

oyal Maxwell felt the world was passing him by. The rich got richer and people like himself, honest and circumspect tradesmen, struggled. Here he was, surrounded by wealth. It lay beneath his feet, incalculable and endless, enriching only a handful. The Maxwell Funeral Parlors were not profiting from it. That was the trouble with death. You had to wait for it. You couldn't hurry it along, except now and then. You couldn't have a big sale or a closeout or a special. There were dry stretches when the world seemed to stay alive and defy the inevitable.

What annoyed him most about Marcus Daly and his Anaconda Copper Mining Company was that it was taking over the entire economy. It wasn't just mining copper and silver; it was running a railroad, operating sawmills and lumber companies, mining coal, running utilities and water companies, generating heat and electricity, and operating hotels and rooming houses. Marcus Daly and his henchmen were making a killing, but undertakers weren't.

That was his frame of mind as he hiked up Galena to the Butte Miners Union for a little talk with the bosses. He found Big Johnny Boyle there, but not Eddie the Pick. Johnny was reaming earwax with a paper clip.

"Who died?" Boyle asked.

"Not you, I see," Maxwell replied. "A big pity. I'd have to charge extra to have a long box made. You'd earn me a little more than typical."

"You're here for something bad."

Maxwell drew himself up to funereal dignity. "Well, if you call making some money for the union bad, or burying your members and their families with dignity and peace of mind, then maybe you're right."

Big Johnny grinned. "Like I say, here for something bad."

"That's the way people think about death," Maxwell said. "I think about comfort and peace. I think there's something the union can do for its members. Provide a funeral benefit for every member and every family member."

"I knew it," Boyle said. "I just knew it."

"Twenty-five cents out of every pay envelope. Just two bits. You keep a nickel for the bother of it all, I keep twenty cents. For that, every member gets a good burial, and so does his wife and children. It won't cost them a thing, except for flowers and the wake. The union makes a nickel more each week. I take the twenty cents, times your eight hundred members, and I'll be ready day or night, weekdays, Sundays, holidays, to be of service, all paid for."

"I just knew it," Boyle said.

"That way, when the time comes, the widows and children will be protected. No unexpected bills. And you won't have to pass the hat anymore. A member dies, and it's all covered. Guaranteed wooden casket, best pine in Montana, fresh varnished, and everything arranged."

"So, twenty cents times eight hundred times fifty-two weeks, right, Maxwell?"

"Yes, and twenty, thirty, forty, fifty dignified funerals all taken care of; no heartbreaking bills sent to the widow."

"And the union gets a nickel a week per member, right?"

"Well, of course, that would be up to you. Perhaps you'll wish to forgo that, and just charge your members twenty cents a week."

"We usually pass the hat to give the widow a start somewhere," Boyle said.

"Well, you could make it fifty cents a week and begin a widow's fund."

"What party are you, Maxwell?"

"Oh, why, I lean this way and that."

"Just tell me yes or no. You ain't a Democrat."

"I'm with the Democrats on silver, you know. I'm a true-blue silver man."

Boyle grinned. "Yeah, if the silver bill passes, Butte maybe shuts down."

"I'm against corruption."

"Yeah, aren't we all. Look, Maxwell, there's a lotta stiffs trying to make a buck off of workingmen's backs. Including me. I live on their dues, right? But they get three and a half a day if they're lucky, and there's not a nickel left over, you get me? Not a nickel. Two bits out of each paycheck, that's taking food out of mouths. That's how tight it is."

"Sure, one less mug of ale," Maxwell said.

Boyle stared at him. "It figures," he said. "Here's the scoop, Maxwell. I'll talk to Eddie. I'll talk to my men. And we'll do some arithmetic. But offhand, I'd say forget it. The owners got a piece of each man; they get rich and no one else does. You want to do some good? Get the owners to foot the funeral bill. Go talk to the whole lot. Maybe start with Clark; he's running for Senate again and maybe he'd make a gesture or two."

That was about what Royal Maxwell supposed.

"Well, sure, Johnny. I'll check back."

But Johnny was leering at him.

Clark, then. Royal Maxwell headed for the Clark bank, hoping to corral the man himself. This would be an easier sell, with the 1894 elections looming.

The strange thing was, Clark's svelte secretary herded Maxwell straight in, and there was the dapper man himself, not a hair out of place, his bold, intelligent eyes raking Maxwell.

It was easy for Maxwell to make his case: Clark wanted votes and here was a cheap way to get a lot of them from workingmen.

Clark listened intently, those blue eyes unblinking.

"I operate for a profit," he said. "You'd have me buying a sort of funeral insurance for my thousand-some employees. That would be another expense against my income from the mines and smelters and other businesses."

"It would win you a lot of votes, sir. Death benefits for all workers."

"Would it? Might it not imply that people perish in my employ? That it's a way of solacing my workers for unsafe conditions? Buying them off perhaps?"

"I think they'd rejoice, sir."

"I can scarcely imagine a miner voting for me because I've promised his widow I'd foot the funeral bill, Mr. Maxwell. Good day."

That didn't take long. There were many other, lesser mines and smelters to see about. He hiked toward Meaderville. The new smelter was well along. Maybe the new firm would want a funeral benefit. The fellow's name was F. Augustus Heinze, and he was so young he probably hadn't thought about death, which might be good.

Sure enough, there was the fellow in a black cape and hat, braving the cruel Butte winds, immersed in some talk over some blueprints. Maxwell waited discreetly until he could approach the new man.

"Maxwell here, Maxwell's Funeral Home," he said.

"I'm not planning on it," Heinze said. "Come back when I'm seventy."

"A benefit for your employees, sir. It will help retain loyal workers."

"A free pint of beer would do it better," Heinze said. Nonetheless he let Maxwell spell it out.

"I've never met a mortician," Heinze said. "Meet me for a drink at the Chequamegon. My treat. You can tell me your business plan and I'll tell you whether I want a share."

Sure enough, when Maxwell penetrated the watering hole later that day, Heinze was waiting for him and promptly bought drinks.

"Now, Maxwell, tell me about your business operation," Heinze said.

"Well, the whole secret of it is to get people to pay in advance," Maxwell said. "It costs almost nothing to stage a funeral and burial, save for the cost of some grave diggers and a preacher. I have boxes galore. I can get a carpenter to make me a utility coffin for five dollars. A little stain turns pine into hardwood, sort of. So the trick is to get people paid up beforehand, and then wait it out. Here's the thing. People move away and forget they're paid up. I bury only about two-thirds of the paid-up people. The rest I never see, so I profit from it far more than you might expect. If I got the mine owners or the mining union to provide free burial, I'd be almost as rich as the copper kings."

"You're a man after my own heart, Maxwell. But I can't do it. I can't offer my employees paid-up funerals. I'd get old men, and I don't want them. What I have to offer to get the men I want is safe working conditions. So we're at cross purposes here. We're on opposite sides of croaking. You're for it, and I'm against it. But here's what I'll do. If one of my employees is a hardship case and he departs from this world, let me know. It's always good business to treat a widow well. It makes hiring easier."

"I think we're kindred souls, Heinze," Maxwell said. "Now you tell me your business plans."

Heinze shrugged. "It's perfectly simple. I'm building the best smelter in the area. It employs the latest reduction techniques gotten from the University of Freiburg. It's close to a dozen independent mines which ship their ores to costly smelters run by Clark or Daly. I'll earn them a much larger profit by milling or smelting at lower cost. And I'll plow my profits into the best mines that will feed my smelter. I'm a geologist, Maxwell, and I spent a goodly time in the pits here, and I know where the ore is and how to stay a few jumps ahead of the owners."

"You think you can tackle Daly and Clark head-on?"

"Not at all. My plan is to ignore them entirely. There's a bonanza here, and I'll have it before long. I know where the veins go, which is more than most of the owners do. They've hardly been in the pits, but I spent a year down there. Making a fortune here is almost child's play, don't you know?"

"I suppose there's more money in copper than in funerals," Maxwell said.

"There's money in anything, bodies or bodies of ore."

The pub seemed empty that night, and Maxwell was contemplating dinner, drinks, and who knows what? It was cold outside, and he dreaded the long walk to his funeral home and its suite at one side. But there was no escaping Butte's brutal weather.

"Say, Maxwell, you up to a lively evening?"

"I really should check at the mortuary; who knows what happens and when it happens?"

"You know of some club or saloon where a man can have a fine old time?"

"Not here?"

"Oh, I have a fine time here; I've met half of Butte's upper crust here. I've already cut deals with seven independent mines to reduce their ore. And I've entertained the wives, too. Nothing like a bottle of cologne for a lady. But Maxwell, I'm not resolutely single."

Illumination lighted Maxwell's cranium. "Well, I know of a fine place, amply stocked with wine, women, and song."

"Ah, now you're talking. Lead the way, Maxwell, and I'll be the dog at your side."

They bundled up against the bitter wind, and Royal Maxwell led his new protégé to the edge of the famed district where miners squandered their payday cash. He headed for the Clipper Shades, on Wyoming and Park, a saloon and dance hall, with a bevy of ladies at hand, and a trade that never ceased night and day.

That was all that F. Augustus Heinze needed. He surveyed the motley crowd as if he knew the secrets of them all. A gent with a sleeve garter was selling dance cards. A rude combo with an accordian and fiddle was generating some sour music now and then. The barkeeps in grimy aprons were peddling rotgut at fifteen cents. The ladies were either dumb Doras off the farms or worn-out hussies with faces of India rubber, blue varicose veins mottling their calves, just visible under bedraggled flounces. A rude oil painting of a lusty nude hung over the bar.

The laughter was an artifice. The music was a bandage. The smoke in the air barely concealed the sweat of the miners, and the perfume of the dancing girls scarcely hid the stink of desperation.

But none of that fazed Fritz Heinze. He bought a two-dollar card, good for twenty dances.

"Looks just fine, Maxwell. I'll have a whirl," he said.

"I'll drink," Maxwell said.

"I always tell the ladies I can't dance, and they love to teach me. I'm a very good student," Heinze said.

"Yes, well, I'll see you down the road," Maxwell said. He had a rendezvous on Wyoming Street, and he hoped it wouldn't lead to another round of mercury pills.

TWENTY-ONE

The election of 1894 was looming, and J. Fellowes Hall girded himself for the annoying task of interviewing his annoying employer, William Andrews Clark. The man was loathsome. His grotesque whiskers and cold blue stare raised Hall's bile. Hall had thought a hundred times about quitting, but in fact he rather liked editing his yellow rag, and liked the long vacation he was taking from his family. He dutifully sent Amber a hundred dollars a month and advised her to stay in the East because Butte was not suitable. Hall continued to live in the servants' quarter of the Clark mansion, which he accessed by a rear stair, and thus enjoyed free rent in the house of the man who made his flesh crawl. He thought that was entertaining, living up there for nothing while loathing his host.

The feeling was mutual, of course. Clark loathed him, and made no bones about it, but kept him on because the *Mineral* was solidly in the black, which no other editor had succeeded in doing, and it dominated Butte. Profit trumped scruple. But the outwardly pious Clark squirmed at the thought of owning a paper whose front pages were devoted to scandals and Mercury Street murders.

Hall approached the Clark bank with some amusement. This would be entertaining. Clark made him wait a half hour, staring at a Tiffany electric lamp, before deigning to see his own editor, but at last Clark's shapely brunette receptionist bade him enter, and Hall discovered Clark armored behind his desk, and unwelcoming.

"Time to do an election story," Hall said. "We need your platform."

"My platform is to elect every Democrat on the ticket."

"I mean, your program. What you stand for."

"My program is to elect every Democrat who will elect me to the Senate."

"No, I mean, what improvements do you have in mind for Butte and Montana?"

"That's nothing I would share in advance, Hall. They'll all see it soon enough."

"Well, sir, getting elected to the Senate requires legislators who are favorable to you. So the public needs to know what you're thinking."

"You think I don't know that, Hall? You have no grasp of politics. I am running entirely on my virtue, and on my loyalty to the Democrat Party, unlike Daly, who spends his every waking hour making alliances with Republicans."

"Ah, Mr. Clark, what about taxes?"

"I'm against them."

"Ah, what about President Cleveland's silver bill in Congress?"

"I'm against it."

"Where do you want the state capital?"

"Helena. Anywhere but Anaconda."

"But Anaconda's convenient."

"Hall, you go back to your rag and make no mention of me. You just attack Daly and the people tearing apart everything we've built here."

"I really need to publicize your program, Mr. Clark."

"You'll soon call me senator. Refer to me as the prospective senator in the news. Never again call me mister. You may also call me the owner and proprietor of any of my businesses. Or president or chief executive. You may not refer to my origins. I don't want them known. Daly, he imagines being an immigrant off a boat gives him virtue, but it doesn't. It only makes him presumptuous. He's too big for his britches. You may say that I am from a good family."

The interview limped along in that fashion, with Hall

getting little to work with, and Clark being as cagey and uncommitted as he could be. And all the while, Clark glared at him, dared him to object. Hall came away, after a brief while, feeling that Clark had no program and didn't want a program, and didn't want to be pinned down to anything except that he was the man for the Senate.

It was odd, what Butte did to people. Maybe it was in the air. Here was a man of boundless ambition and achievement, but he wanted only one thing: the title of Senator in front of his name. Senator Clark of Montana. Senator Clark! Nothing more. Of course he had self-interests in mind. A Senate seat would enable him to oppose legislation he thought might damage him, and push bills that might improve his business. But nowhere in all of this was a program for a commonwealth, a vision, a dream of Montana or the nation beyond his small life in Butte, Montana.

Not that Daly was any better. His two political objectives were to defeat Clark and put the state capital in his backyard. That was it. Toward that end he bought costly newspapers, hired costly editors and reporters and cartoonists, gave extravagant gifts to politicians and newsmen, and curried the favors of powerful men in other parts of the state. When it came to ambition, or achievement, Daly's greatest ambition was to see his racing horse Tammany enter one winner's circle after another. Not even defeating Clark or snatching the capital from Helena was so great a prize as a victorious racing stable. The man had no more political vision than Clark, and maybe less. So there they were, two titans locking horns.

Was it something about Butte? The endless bone-numbing cold? The arsenic in the air? What was it about the richest hill on earth that turned titans into squabbling boys? Yet, Hall thought, that wasn't quite fair. Daly had a vision of sorts: an Irish Valhalla, a place of refuge and prosperity for his fellow Hibernians. That was more of a public vision than Clark had in his well-groomed noggin.

Yet, at bottom, Hall admired Daly far more than Clark. Daly was the more honest and earthy man who was incapable of snobbery, who would never conceal his origins, who mixed with people of all stations, who had a keen vision of a world that welcomed and nurtured those who struggled to gain even the smallest comfort and security. Yes, Daly was a better man. And Hall's task was to assail him for it. He laughed. The world was an odd place. By day he would write scathing editorials about Daly; by night he would salute him in the nearest pub. By day he would support the campaign of Clark for the Senate; by night he'd laugh at his boss, and find out anything damaging that he could worm out of Clark's domestic servants, and gossip about it. It was fun, this life in the worst, cruelest, most generous, and amusing city in the United States.

It had been an odd interview, about what one might expect from William Andrews Clark. The strange thing about it was that it was forcing Hall to think about himself; who he was, what he aspired to be, what he believed. He had not walked far into the bitter day, with Butte's smoke choking the streets, when he came to a decision. It was purely impulsive. He had not given it any thought. He turned westward, into the wind, and began looking at window signs. What he wanted was one that said FOR RENT. Housing was tight in Butte, even though the city had recklessly risen on every spare lot developers could snatch up. Housing for the poor was shortest, which was why Anaconda Copper Company had built vast dormitories, amusingly called hotels, for all the drones in the mines. The miners got decent wages, but the costly city snatched them away, and they were no better off than poorly paid common laborers back East.

He found a promising rental sign in a promising three-story apartment on West Park, and swiftly negotiated the eighty-dollars-a-month rental from a harridan with a distrusting look in her face.

"What's your line?" she asked.

"Newspaper."

"Which?"

"The *Mineral*."

"Oh, shame on you. Gossip and things no one should ever see. I never miss an issue." She eyed him. "You work for Clark, right?"

He shrugged.

"He's a piece of work. I could tell you a few things. Next door, he's got a little blonde stashed away."

"How do you know that?"

"Aren't you the nosy one. I don't think I'll rent to you." She eyed him.

"I'll take it anyway. Here's my eighty. I'll move in this afternoon."

She counted the cash and nodded. "What are you gonna stash in yours?" she asked.

"Just myself."

She looked disappointed.

It took a while to get a cartage man to meet him at the Clark mansion, and to get his few items together, but by evening he was settled. He didn't plan to tell Amber about it, and he'd just let her write him at the paper, as always.

He had just increased the cost of living by the price of rent, and yet he didn't mind. For two years he had worn Clark's collar, living there in the big redbrick mansion. He felt almost giddy, his own two-room suite enfolding him now. He had no kitchen; just a parlor and bedroom and a water closet. It was all he wanted. He couldn't boil an egg, but there were plenty of all-hours eateries in Butte, catering to each shift. The landlady furnished sheets and a weekly maid, but he had to buy his own bagged coal for the parlor stove.

He sat on the edge of his bed, relishing all this. He hadn't realized what life in Clark's servant quarters was doing to him. He had been turned into Clark's dog, and had a dog collar on him, but now he was J. Fellowes Hall once again, the crème de la crème of his profession. He had thought he was keeping an eye on Clark, back there, but just the opposite was true; Clark's staff had been keeping an eye on him. All his comings and goings had reached Clark's ears. Maybe Clark's uncanny ability to recite everything someone else was thinking had more to do with his staff, and less to do with any occult skills.

The windows faced west, squarely into the blank wall of the next apartment building, with no view at all of Butte or the distant snow-wrapped peaks or the sprawling valley. Well, at least he would have whatever entertainment lay in those blank windows across a twenty-foot alley.

He knew suddenly that he would take the *Mineral* in whatever direction he wanted to take it, without paying heed to Clark. He didn't worry about being fired; getting axed by Clark would be an honor, not a crisis.

He wrapped a scarf about his neck and dove into his topcoat and made sure his new skeleton key was in his pants, and then set out for the paper. He was actually two blocks closer to it than he had been, which would be valuable as winter set in. But it was only September. In Butte, September could be wintry, as it was now, with snow collecting on the surrounding peaks. He found no one in the newspaper, and that suited him fine. He lit the lamps and stirred up the stove. Then he collected some foolscap and set to work.

"The *Mineral*," he began, "is pleased to record an exclusive interview with Butte's premiere citizen, William Andrews Clark, who is seeking to represent Montana in the United States Senate. Mister Clark's program is to elect true-blue Democrats to office, his definition of a true Democrat meaning not the weaseling Daly variety, which he regards as renegades who have sold their souls to rival factions. Mr. Clark's great ambition is to elect Democrats of the true-blue variety to every office in Silver Bow County and Deer Lodge County and the government of Montana. He proclaimed his support for this program, and his willingness to back it with all his resources. If elected to the Senate, he promises to work for the benefit of Montana's business. He has declined to name the planks of his platform, but is desirous of being understood to be a man devoted to his party, his good reputation, his integrity, and his acumen.

"Mr. Clark is desirous of establishing the state capital in Helena, and is unalterably opposed to settling it else-where or allowing the state to come under the thumb of any entity or organization or person who does not have the interests of the entire state at heart.

"Toward these ends, Mr. Clark has opened his purse, supporting the election campaigns of those who favor his program. His door is open always; let any man who supports him stop by and make his acquaintance, and hear in Mr. Clark's own words what lies in store if he is elevated to high office."

Hall smiled. The next issue of the paper would make some entertaining reading.

{ TWENTY-TWO }

They mobbed him in Helena. No sooner did William Andrews Clark alight from the parlor car than they hoisted him into an open carriage and started to haul him through town. Then they unhooked the draft horses and pulled the carriage themselves, these roistering citizens of Helena. Clark smiled, settled into the quilted leather seat, drew his cape tight, and settled his silk stovepipe tighter, against the November cold.

Helena would be the state capital. Clark and his powerful allies across the state had whipped Daly's forces by a narrow margin, even though Daly had spent extravagantly on cigars, five-dollar gold pieces, rallies, advertisements, and bottles of good whiskey. It was said he had squandered over two million dollars of his own cash on the Anaconda campaign. But it wasn't enough.

Clark was mildly pleased. The 1894 elections had actually gone to the Republicans, largely because Clark's and Daly's campaigns had torn the Democrats apart. So Montana would have two Republican senators, Lee Mantle and Tom Carter. And Clark would not have the title in front of his name. It annoyed him to spend so much and get such poor results.

Still, he was being drawn through Last Chance Gulch by a mob of cheering citizens who would be grateful to him always. There were plenty of people in the state who preferred Helena, which was more central, and wasn't in the shadow of the Anaconda company, and Clark had welded them together, in all their diversity, on this issue— and won.

He turned to his man, Bitters. "Drinks on Clark tonight. Tell the saloon men to send me the tab."

With that, the crowd whooped its way to the nearest watering holes, where the bartenders were instantly overwhelmed and took to tossing full bottles into the crowd rather than pouring. Clark knew he would foot a formidable bill, but what was victory for, if not a little celebration? And in the process, he would gain a few thousand votes next time he placed his name in the Senate race.

Oh, it was a fine eve, even if it chilled him. They pulled and hauled him everywhere, and from every alley more Helenans erupted to cheer him, even children who escaped their beds. Clark didn't much care for children, and preferred that they stay out of sight and not crawl all over him with their sticky hands. Children were an annoyance.

It was an odd thing, though. He felt no great elation. Whipping Daly wasn't as much fun as buying a splendid new mine or building a smelter. It wasn't on a par with outsmarting half the financiers in New York. But even if he lacked much feeling, his mind was busy every second calculating the effect of his great triumph. Daly was through. Clark knew the man well enough to know it for a fact. Daly's heart had been focused on the capital fight, and he'd lost in spite of his open purse, and that was the end of it for the Irishman. Clark knew exactly what Daly would do next. He'd retire to his Bitterroot Valley stock farm and raise great racehorses and win a great many of the races in which he entered one of his Thoroughbreds. Clark knew such things. He'd always had an uncanny way of reading people. Daly's defeat was, in a way, mortal. From this day forward, Daly's spirit would wander, his body would slow and sink, and his interests would scatter. Clark supposed he should be exultant about it, but he wasn't. He didn't see how this great victory would change his own plans much.

In the morning he took the train back to Butte, feeling oddly hollow. He had won, hadn't he? He was the king of the hill. He had defeated the octopus. He had preserved Montana from a terrible fate, a state in the thrall of a private corporation. Maybe he was feeling low because there were no more battles to wage. He sat in the parlor car attached at the rear of the train for him, all alone, the whole luxurious car his for the short ride. The rails carried him south, through a winding foothill country, and finally across a high plateau that was already wintry. The cattle that grazed on those pastures in summer had long since fled, and Montana had returned to its primal estate, which was wilderness.

Butte was an odd island of city life high in the emptiness. He thought it was the emptiness of the state that was eroding his spirits now. He would do better among his colleagues in Butte. He enjoyed the city life there, the club, the dining, the deals, the politics. He thought of his late wife, Kate, who had fled Butte for warmer and more civilized climes. She had died in 1893 in New York. She hovered at the back of his mind, a ghostly figure, along with his living children, Mary Joaquina, Charles Walker, William Andrew, Jr., and Paul Francis, who seemed as distant as strangers and usually living as far from Butte as they could manage. He didn't blame them.

The scenery was majestic, yet it made no imprint on him. He puzzled at those who said they were lifted upward by natural beauty. There were great peaks in sight, and alpine meadows, and black pine forests, and crystal creeks, and yet it meant nothing. Nature was hollow. A good painter might produce something interesting, but there was nothing in the natural world except lumber and copper. Maybe water. That was a resource too.

Getting and spending. Was that it? No, respect was the thing. Millionaire Clark, the richest man on earth was less important than Senator Clark, the most respected man on earth.

He stepped off of his parlor car two hours later, and instructed his coachman to take him directly to his newspaper. He hadn't set foot in the place for a year or two. As long as Hall was making it pay, there was no need. And Hall was doing that. It was the best-read paper in Butte, with the most ads and the most street sales. Nothing else mattered, not Hall's obvious animosity, not Hall's sensationalism. If Hearst did it and Pulitzer did it, then a paper belonging to William Andrews Clark could do it.

The horses' breaths were steaming from the uphill climb when Clark emerged from his black cabriolet and pierced the ink-stained interior of his paper. He found

Hall, eyeglass perched on his nose, in his little cubbyhole at the rear.

Hall looked up, startled.

"We beat Daly. It's over. From now on, not a word about him, not a word about the Anaconda company, not a cartoon, not a sharp editorial, not an innuendo. He's done. I know the man. He'll spend the rest of his life at his stock farm raising racehorses. You get that?"

"Have you reconciled with him?"

"What's there to reconcile? There's nothing left of Daly. His heart got cut out of him."

Hall stared.

"You aren't accepting my instruction, Mr. Hall. Are you sure you wish to continue in my employ?"

"I'm only trying to understand. Yesterday we were opposed to Marcus Daly and the company; today we're silent."

"Exactly, Hall. And keep me out of the paper too. Not a word."

"Have you given up the Senate?"

"Let people think so if they wish. It'll be real politics now, Hall."

"What do you mean, real politics?"

"That which is never seen, never heard, never felt."

"Are you running for the Senate or not?"

Clark sighed. "When have I stopped?" Hall looked bewildered. "There are public politics and private politics," he said. "There are public campaigns and there are private agreements between people of like mind. I am switching from one mode to another, and abandoning nothing."

That, at last, seemed to penetrate the thick-skulled editor. And it was also a veiled threat. If Hall didn't keep Clark out of the spotlight, Hall would be looking for work.

"The *Mineral* is now a pussycat," Hall said.

That annoyed Clark. "It is nothing of the sort. You will

be vigilant to protect the interests of the company. Or companies. You know exactly where to stand on radical-ism, wage increases, unions, strikes, taxes, regulation, and anything else that comes between the right of a company to make the best of its resources."

Hall stared, comprehension at last in him. Clark could read the man perfectly. He knew all about Hall's loathing for him. All about Hall's vanity, his imagined reputation as a fine newsman, his itch to operate a paper without the control of its owners. He knew why Hall had fled the coop, taken an apartment. He knew that Hall would have trouble finding another position. He knew that Hall was making no provision to bring his wife and children to Butte, and it wasn't hard to imagine why. The man had gone from John Frank Hall to John Fellowes Hall to J. Fellowes Hall, as if each new name was a step up the ladder.

Clark smiled. "See to it, Mr. Hall."

He wheeled away, dodging the inky chases and forms, keeping his white cuffs well away from the Linotypes and pots of sticky black ink, and finally made it to his cabrio-let unscathed. He wouldn't need to charge the *Mineral* for ruining his French cuffs.

Newspapers were worth a lot less than he had imag-ined. Poor Daly had sunk a fortune into the *Anaconda Standard,* brought in first-rate reporters, cartoonists, printers, and a fine editor, Durston. And what did a mil-lion dollars get Daly? A death blow. It would have gone better for Daly if he had no noisy paper at all, especially one that was brilliantly edited. It would go better, Clark thought, to keep the *Mineral* bland, keep his name out of the news, keep his dealings private, and line up the legis-lators who would send him to Washington with cigars and claret and quiet dinners rather than public pronounce-ments. Let all the papers howl and opinionize; it all came to nothing. He only wished he had realized it sooner. He could have saved the investment. He was stuck now, and the rag was earning a good profit, so there was no point in selling it off. But the Clark press would never again trumpet and bellow.

In two years he would have another crack at the Senate. Meanwhile there was money to be made, and pleasures to be bought. His brain teemed with schemes. He had an eye on California, and a killing in Los Angeles real estate or California sugar beets or maybe orange groves. He thought to have himself a plantation in South America, and there were always mines to buy, smelters to build, and maybe a railroad or two.

It was grand to spend everything he could. He fancied himself a connoisseur of art, and planned to buy Rembrandts wholesale. He had a New York mansion in mind, one that would tell the world who he was, and the more gargoyles the better.

He was young and lusty, and well formed, and rich enough to have whatever he wanted, and just now he thought a lovely lady would fill the bill. There were always ways, especially a trip to Europe. He had lost a fine cultivated wife. He would have more. And not just anyone, either. He knew his prowess. He had always been drawn to brunettes. No, that's not what he meant. Brunettes had always been drawn to him. Yes, that parsed it better. And France. The worldly dark-haired women of France made him weak at the knees. And so did his young American ward, Anna Eugenia La Chapelle, who was studying art in Paris. He would go to France, enjoy women and art and fine wine and look in on Eugenia. He could have anyone or anything he wanted. There were a few in Butte who turned his eye, but he had mostly evaded all that. Not anymore. It all was so easy. A lady could be had for a pearl or a sapphire.

The first step would be to fire all of his political operatives. The less people knew about William Andrews Clark, the better. Mark Bitters, who knew him best and conveyed mountains of greenbacks here and there, would be the first. There would be others departing, and when he was done, William Andrews Clark would enjoy a life of such obscurity and mystery that he would live in perfect liberty. This election had taught him a few things, and one of them was to disappear from public view, except under circumstances he would control. The thought elated him.

{ TWENTY-THREE }

F Augustus Heinze was having a fine time day and night. Fritz, as he was known in Butte to his displeasure, had his Montana Ore Purchasing Company smelter up and running, coining money from the start. The smaller independent mines swiftly found out he could process their ore faster, at less cost, and with greater efficiency than the major smelters. Heinze's education at Columbia University and in Freiburg, Germany, was paying off. The investment of the limited inheritance originally opposed by his brother was returning a fine profit month by month.

And so far, the big operators scarcely noticed. They were good businessmen, aggressive operators with a sharp eye on costs and opportunities, and he respected them. But they also amused him. Imagine wasting millions of dollars trying to get into the Senate or move the state capital. That, to Augustus, the name he gave himself, was entertainment. And so was Butte. He began collecting copies of all the mining claims and patents on the hill, legal descriptions, boundaries, the names of those who filed the claims. The boundaries fascinated him. He had never seen such a hodgepodge of borders careening this way and that, turning claims into trapezoids, rectangles, notched squares, angled pieces, and forms beyond classification. How could anyone belowground know exactly where a property ended and a neighbor's began? Of course no one knew, and few were paying close attention to boundaries. He arranged to have a look himself, and soon found ample evidence of skulduggery deep below the grass.

He found himself in a dizzying world of data. There were the veins themselves to consider, and the directions they lay at various levels. He wished he could build a three-dimensional model of Butte's hill, with copper rivers running this way and that. Then there were all the lawsuits about claims, the piracy of ores, the exact boundaries of various mines, as well as stockholder suits, and indeed, who owned what. He was a quick read, and somehow examined all these cases and filed them away in his copious brain.

The boundaries were a mess. The law was a jumble and the courts jammed up. The surface rights were a mess. It was all just the sort of milieu that F. Augustus Heinze thought was delightful. He loved a good tangle. What enchanted him most of all was the federal 1872 mining law, with its famous apex rule. If a vein apexed, or reached the surface, on one claim, its owner could pursue the vein into neighboring claims. He had a right to the whole vein. That so enchanted Heinze that he thought it was a gift from heaven.

His evenings were just as devoted as his daylight adventures into the dusty warrens of clerks and courts and real estate offices and surveying companies. By lamplight, he was planning to meet and enjoy the entire population of Butte, and set about it with great gusto. One could scarcely get ahead in a rowdy place like Butte without knowing everything from mistresses to ambitions.

It was a peculiar old gent's ambition that fascinated F. Augustus Heinze. For one evening he became a brass-rail companion of a certain slovenly gentleman who was downing whiskeys at a regular clip. The man had an untrimmed gray beard to match his untrimmed hair, along with a soup-strainer mustache. There appeared to be as much food as hair in the man's beard, and still more caked across the gent's suitcoat and pants.

He was explicating a Populist view to anyone who might listen, and no one was. Heinze, always looking for fresh zoo animals, lent the man an ear.

"Augustus Heinze here. And you, sir?"

"William Clancy by birth name, son of a bitch by any other."

"You're a man after my own fashion," Fritz said. "A Populist, are you?"

"A man of the people, sir. A man opposed to the great powers, the high and mighty, the moguls and their mistresses, the nefarious and crooked banks, all politicians, and any capitalist who owns a utility or monopoly."

"I guess that leaves me out."

"Not if you quench my thirst, sir."

Heinze swiftly ordered another whiskey and branch for the man. When the barkeep set it next to Clancy, the old man didn't deign to notice it. But somehow he knew it had arrived, and Heinze surmised that pretty soon a gnarled hand would snap it up and pour its contents through the soup-strainer that entirely hid the man's mouth.

"I'm opposed to the whole lot, Mr. Clancy, but I confess to owning a little smelter in Meaderville."

"Well, we see alike then; the little fellows against the big bastards."

"What have you against the big outfits?"

"They are slavers, sir. They enslave us. They rob the honest yeoman of his rewards. They buy entire legislatures. They connive to steal a fair wage from labor. I ally myself with any mortal who is a friend of the poor and oppressed."

"Are you running for office, Mr. Clancy?"

"You insult me, sir. I am not a politician feeding at the trough. I am running for district judge. I will be the first Populist judge in Montana, and strike out for liberty, justice, fairness, and an even distribution of wealth."

"Judge! You're a lawyer, then."

"Don't insult me, you whelp. I am no more a lawyer than I am a barber. And barbering is the more noble profession."

Given the condition of the man's locks, the statement had force.

"If I succeed to office in eighteen and ninety-six, I will bring the malefactors of great wealth to heel."

"How would you do that?"

Clancy strained an entire tumbler through his soupstrainer, and eyed Heinze malevolently. "The law is an ass, sir. I will ignore it as much as possible. My goal is justice, sir. I will restore equity, punish the greedy, slap the fingers of the avaricious."

"What do you do now, sir?"

"Not a thing. I am reduced to cadging drinks from suckers. On good days I enjoy the luxury of a union hall, where I read papers and sign petitions. On bad days, I freeze half to death. But I am also a participant in a great cause, sir. The Populists are the light of the world, and we will illuminate the city on the hill."

That was a little too much metaphor for Heinze, but he was struck by something. Clancy was a man of passion, and however he looked at the world around him, he intended to do something about it.

"You are what I call a justice man, then," Heinze said.

Clancy's eyes burned like coals. "I will manufacture it. I will invent it. I will impose it. I will spread it. I will divide it up and give each humble person a piece of it."

"This is when you become a district court judge?"

"There is a slight filing fee and paperwork, Heinze. Maybe you could look after it for me."

"I will do that," Heinze said. He pulled out his fountain pen and made a note of it, while Clancy filtered another bourbon through his mustache.

"And don't confuse me with Big Mutt Clancy; we are no relation."

"Who's that?"

"I wouldn't know, sir."

"Consider yourself elected, Mr. Clancy."

The old man eyed the younger one. "That in itself would be an act of supreme justice, young fellow. In the blink of an eye, a man felled by injustice would be restored to justice. Coin of the realm would flow into his empty pockets. A regular guaranteed salary commensurate with my faithfulness and ability, sir, is something the titans of Butte haven't seen fit to offer me, no matter how fine the services I offer. Yes, arranging that for me would be justice so profound and bright that your light would illuminate the heavens."

More metaphor, Heinze thought. The man was a metaphor machine.

It wouldn't hurt to have a friend on the bench. Especially that district court bench, where mining cases were heard all day, every day. All those companies with mines cheek by jowl were at each other's throats, and those cases were stacking up in Butte's district courts.

"Judge Clancy, I see your tumbler is empty, and it is my pleasure to refill it," Heinze said.

"I believe in progress," Clancy said. "We move from the dark past to the bright future. We move from aches and pains to euphoria. We move from the pain of bad luck to the highlands of joy. Why, yes, that is a gracious gesture on your part. Now what was your name again?"

"Augustus. Call me Gus. Augustus Heinze, a man of modest means and a bright future."

"Then we are brethren," Clancy said. "Indeed, I'll match you drink for drink."

"You've already outdone me, Your Honor, but I will make sure you are well supplied."

"You are a daisy, sir."

"Your Honor, I'll arrange matters with the barman, and henceforth, you may expect a libation at any time, courtesy of Augustus Heinze."

"Ah, you are a Progressive, a Populist, with a great sympathy for the oppressed."

Clancy's breath was rank, and Heinze thought to escape, but considered the hour well spent. He made certain arrangements with the proprietor, and departed. The air outside carried more than the usual burden of sharp-edged smoke. Was there no fresh air in Butte, a city surrounded by wilderness and mountains?

It might be a trick to get Clancy installed in office, but if that could be managed, everything would be in place. An ambitious man in Butte needed a sympathetic judge. Heinze resolved to work on it. Meanwhile, there were things to do.

There were a couple of lackluster mines that had interested him, the Glengarry and Estella. He had prowled them carefully, applying every bit of geology he had mastered at the University of Freiburg, seeing which way the veins ran, and seeing also how the managers obtusely ignored the obvious. He planned to lease them if he could. His Montana Ore Purchasing Company smelter was on precarious footing, depending on ore from the independent mines. He wanted some ore of his own, a guaranteed flow for his smelter. He owned 51 percent of his company; his brothers the rest, and it was up to Fritz to make it pay. His mind wrestled with that ceaselessly.

He had leased the Estella from a savvy old mining man, James Murray, who had been in Butte from its early days. It was a simple enough deal. As long as the copper ore was low grade, Heinze would retain most of the profit; but if high grade, Murray would get a much larger share of the profit. Heinze knew exactly where to go for the high grade, and sent his foremen into the pit with certain instructions: add waste rock to the high-grade ore so the resulting mix going into the smelter would be low grade. There it was in the official reports: so many tons from the Estella, so many pounds of copper gotten from it, and the Heinze brothers kept nearly all the profit. The mine proved to be a dandy, and Heinze had been coining money from it. Even Murray ruefully joked about how he had gotten suckered. Heinze's company was now in the mining as well as smelting business, and the cunning Fritz was enjoying a few winks and smiles. If Fritz was enjoying the con, Butte was enjoying it even more.

And there were more prizes awaiting Heinze's attention, not least of which was the splendid Rarus, just east of the Anaconda company's great Anaconda and St. Lawrence mines. Heinze laid out three hundred thousand cash for it, and was soon running high-grade copper ore into his smelter, simply because he knew where to pry it out. All of his earlier years working as a geologist were now paying off. With the flood of cash from the smelter, he bought a half interest in the Snohomish mine, and large interests in the Glengarry and Johnstown mines. His smelter was soon turning out over twenty million pounds of copper a year, and earning the family a dividend of over 30 percent a year. In two years, he had converted the family's original investment of a million and a half dollars into twenty million. And he was just beginning. The 1896 elections were looming, and it was time to help his bibulous friend Clancy into office. A friendly judge would help the Heinze brothers even more than Augustus Heinze's skills in geology ever would.

TWENTY-FOUR

Red Alice knew she was in the right place at the right time, doing the right thing. There she was, in a giant Anaconda boarding house for new miners, slaving away for one dollar a day. But all that toil didn't matter. Dragging grimy sheets off beds and putting new ones on didn't matter. Stirring sheets into cauldrons of boiling water, and then pulling them out didn't matter.

What mattered was that she was among the poorest, sickest, weakest, and most hopeless men on earth, and that was what she liked. They were mostly immigrants from the old country, who'd come steerage class and got sent west by Marcus Daly's recruiters who were offering a miracle: steady work, three and a half dollars each day, six days a week. There would be a boarding house, two meals a day included. Money enough for room and board, money for a little whiskey, money to send back across the seas for the rest of the clan. Money enough to laugh a little, and money enough not to feel a hollow in one's belly. But not more than just enough.

She got some help from Eddie the Pick, who drafted a letter for her to mail to the Socialist Labor Party. Please send pamphlets. Send literature. She'd take great care to get it to the right people. Send it to the Butte Miners Union and she would pick it up there. She enclosed a dollar to help them with the cost. Much to her surprise, a bundle arrived, and Eddie the Pick even delivered it to her cottage, and she snatched it before her brats burned it all in the parlor stove to make some heat.

"Workers of the world," it said. "There is a bright promise awaiting you. Better times are coming. You don't need to suffer and starve. You can prevent men from stealing your valuable labor. You can stop the rich from using you, squeezing life out of you, exhausting and sickening you until you die, so the rich can drive around in carriages and butlers can open their doors."

She sure liked that stuff. She pored over the tracts until light failed, ignoring the brats who wanted food. She gave them the evil eye. They were Singing Sean's brats, not hers. He made them, and she was nothing but Singing Sean's cow. Let them fix their own food; let them earn their own keep. But sometimes she relented, and drew them to her and smoothed their hair and cried, and then got mad at them for wasting her time.

So this was it! She counted three hundred twenty. The brats had burned some, but she had a lot. One apiece for most rooms. Some of the workers off the boat couldn't read. The Finns and Bohunks and Italians went to their own boarding houses, but the Florence was Irish and Mr. Daly made it so. She remembered him kindly. He had personally got Sean buried proper. Maybe he'd become a Socialist someday. She'd get a pamphlet to him if she could.

The next day she took the first hundred with her, and when the time came for her to take hot, dry sheets up to the top floor, she added some Socialist Labor Party pamphlets, and whenever she left sheets in a room, two for each iron cot, she also put a pamphlet on the dresser. Let them see it. Let them think about whether they wanted to be slaves all their lives. Let them know there might be a better way!

That afternoon she delivered sheets to fifty rooms, and left Socialist pamphlets in each. The next day she spent scrubbing and mangling, and didn't get into rooms. The day after that she collected used sheets, and carried tons of them down to the laundry. But the day after that, she delivered clean sheets to the second floor, letting herself into each smelly room with a passkey, and leaving a Socialist Labor Party pamphlet wherever she went.

That's how it went for a while, so she wrote the party and sent them another dollar, and asked for more tracts, preferably something new. No one talked with her about them. The men came and went, and she wondered if anyone read them. She didn't see any lying around. There were none in the library. None in the toilets. They sort of disappeared. Maybe some men couldn't read, but others could, and maybe they talked about what they had read when they were in the pit, or lunching down there. Or maybe they talked about all that in the saloons, where some of them went for a double drink of ale and whiskey commonly called a Shawn O'Farrell.

She wished she had fierce pamphlets to give the worn women in the laundry room, but she only had pamphlets for men, for those who could vote, for those who lifted rock all day. But at least she could talk to the women as she stirred the great kettles and pushed the sheets around in the steaming water.

She couldn't say much because Mrs. Murphy was always watching, ready to dismiss anyone who slacked off or caused trouble. Mrs. Murphy wanted sheets to be brought in on schedule, cleaned and mangled on schedule, and carried up to the hundreds of rooms on schedule. And to achieve that, Mrs. Murphy simply handed a pink slip to any woman who failed to do her work.

So Alice Brophy kept quiet, worked a little harder than most, smiled at anyone she thought might be eyeing her, and laundered hundreds of sheets each day.

One day when she was hurrying to the top floor, a coughing man in the little library waylaid her. She eyed him warily; half the newcomers had consumption, and half the ones leaving the Florence had silicosis, miner's lung. This one was gaunt, had wire-rimmed spectacles, and was wrapped in an ancient khaki army blanket.

"You're the one putting out the tracts," he said.

She refused to acknowledge it. She wasn't going to buy trouble if she could help it.

He coughed gently, his fist against his mouth. "It goes against God, you know."

She couldn't identify his accent. Was it Irish? English?

He smiled. "Belfast. Irish father, English mother. Church of England."

"Bloody rat, then."

"No, I'm curious what you know about Socialism. Do you really believe a government should steal everyone's wealth and then hand it back according to its own politics?"

"It's in the Holy Bible," she said. "Everyone possessed everything in common in the early church. It says so."

"Voluntarily," he said, "and it didn't last. What you do voluntarily, in a commune, is different from a government confiscating everything by force."

"I don't know about that, but it makes no difference who does it. Everything's got to be evened out."

He coughed again. "Only that's not what happens."

"I've got to work," she said. "Wake up and help other workers."

He wheezed horribly. "Thank you for the visit," he said. "I'll be here tomorrow, same time. You intrigue me. Tell me your story. How'd you end up doing this?"

She started to tell him she didn't have time for a heretic, but she simply lifted her load of clean sheets and fled. Church of England was he? Marcus Daly must be daft, letting the likes of him in, him that bled Ireland white, him that let everyone starve in the famine. He'd have an Irish name, and who'd know the difference?

She had a new tract they had sent her, this one calling for a general strike, a big strike everywhere, in every county and every state, until the capitalists caved in and treated working people better. Labor would flex its muscle. The rest of the tract was devoted to the Socialist

Labor Party, its leaders and its platform. She left one in each room, on the dresser next to the sheets.

He was there the next day, huddled in that worn chair, a blanket around him, coughing and pale.

"So, you want to talk a little?" he asked.

It seemed an effort for him to talk at all, and he wheezed horribly. "You should be in bed," she said.

"It doesn't matter. This is my last day here."

"Last day?"

"Rent costs money."

"Where are you going?" she asked.

He ignored her question. "What do you earn?" he asked.

"What business is it of yours?"

"Seventy-five cents?"

She shook her head. "More."

"How many tons of sheets do you carry each day?"

She stopped, and set down her load of sheets. "You don't know what it's like to be a woman," she said.

"That should be your cause. Not Socialism."

"What do you know about it?"

"I have a wife in Belfast. I won't ever see her again."

"Have a wife, do you? That makes it worse. Wives are for your pleasure and bringing up babies for free."

"Exactly. It needs changing."

She stared at him.

"You're a Feminist too?" he asked.

"I've been reading Susan B. Anthony."

"Tame," he said. "Much too tame. Try Victoria Woodhull. Free love. Try Elizabeth Cady Stanton."

"Free love is it? Now I know what you're after. I should charge for it."

"Free, I mean unfettered."

"I don't want anything to do with you," she said, plucking up her sheets.

He coughed and grinned. She wondered what he was reading.

"I'm William Ward," he said. "And you're Red Alice."

She ignored him and started up the long mean stairwell that would take her to the top floor. Every step was a burden, with fifty pounds of sheets in her basket. Her heart was pounding by the time she got there, so she set the load down and got her breath. The narrow corridor stank. Men stank. Their rooms stank. She wondered why the Florence bothered to change their sheets.

She opened one room with her passkey, left two sets of sheets and one pamphlet on the dresser, and locked. She did the same with the next three rooms. In the fifth room she left the sheets, spotted two quarters on the dresser, and ignored them. That was a lot of money; half a day's pay. The room stank like all the rest. The men would change their own sheets and leave the dirty outside their door to be picked up. She left a Socialist Workers Party tract and locked.

When she got back down to the basement, Mrs. Murphy was waiting for her. Mrs. Murphy was a big woman, almost six feet and gray haired and heavy.

"Out," she said. "You're done here."

"I do a good job!"

"No you don't. You steal."

"I do not! Search me!"

"Out."

"I want my pay."

"Out."

"It's not stealing. It's something else," she said. "Why are you doing this?"

Mrs. Murphy paused, if only for a second. "Leave, right now, and don't come in, and don't ask for a recommendation."

"It's because I'm Red Alice."

"It ain't anything the company wants in its rooming house."

"How'm I gonna feed my babies?"

Mrs. Murphy thrust an arm out and pointed at the door.

"You owe me," Alice snapped.

The boss lady grabbed Alice and propelled her out, and up the basement stairs, and out the side door of the Florence. She spotted Big Benny Brice, the flatfoot who usually kept the peace in the Dublin Gulch area, and headed his way.

"They just fired me," she said.

"What for, Alice?"

"They said I was stealing."

"Nah, they fired you for the pamphlets. They were going to have me pinch you for stealing, but I just laughed."

"I'm about ready to steal. Not from the boarders but from the hotel. They owe me two and a half days."

"Alice, don't. You can't beat the company. They own the politicians and judges and me. I'm a company man even if no one says it."

"How'm I going to live?"

Big Benny turned real quiet. "You could get married," he said. "I know two cops looking for a woman."

"I'd rather sell it," she said. "At least I could quit."

"Stay outta trouble, Alice," he said.

"I'd go from a dollar a day to nothing a day if I got married."

"Your choice," he said. "But don't come whining."

"Big Benny, you're a shit," she said.

She was thinking about her empty stomach, and the brats and what her options were.

TWENTY-FIVE

William Ward wasn't in the Florence. She hunted for him, dodging the laundresses and Mrs. Murphy, but he wasn't there.

"Where did he go?" she asked the desk clerk.

"No idea."

"Well he had to go somewhere."

"Try the hospital. Try the cops."

"Is there a poor farm, an asylum?"

"Not as far as I know, Alice."

"It's cold outside."

"Yes, freezing, ma'am. He can't live outside."

She gave up, angry at the world, angry at herself. Why did she care? A Belfast Orange Irish with consumption. To hell with William Ward. She headed into the bitter air, choked on smoke, and headed for the union hall. A cruel wind whipped her skirts, and icy air pierced her thin coat.

The miners' hall was well heated, with a coal stove radiating warmth. Big Johnny Boyle was sleeping on a bench. She stabbed him with a finger, and he erupted.

"What are you doing here?" he asked.

"Where do sick broke miners go? Like consumption?"

"Beats me. Try the saloons."

"He hasn't got a dime. William Ward."

"We've got a sick fund," Boyle said. He studied a list. "Not on it. What's it to you?"

"He's got a wife in Belfast and he's dying."

"That's not our kind."

"Does anyone take care of them?"

Boyle hesitated, and came to some sort of decision. "They go into the pits and die. It's warm down there. Abandoned drifts, worked-out places. Some are seventy, eighty degrees."

"Without help?"

"They get help. The brothers bring in food and water."

"And when they die?"

Boyle shrugged. "Mostly buried back in there, rubble over them."

"Is he comfortable in there?"

"Bad air, filthy water, piles of crap, rats and vermin, typhoid, and dark except when someone comes to help. Dark, black, inky, stinking."

"Can you get him out? I'll keep him at my house until he's gone."

"What do you want him for?"

"Because no one else does."

"You've been fired, so how are you gonna feed him?"

"A little gruel, if he can get it down, isn't going to sink me."

Boyle stared out a grimy window. "Yeah, I know where he is. The St. Lawrence, in a worked-out area. I heard it this morning."

"Have them bring him to me."

"You don't want him. He's sick, your children—they'll catch it."

"Everyone in Dublin Gulch has con or miner's con already."

The hardness in his face seemed to soften. "All right, all right. We'll get him."

"And put him on your dole."

"We don't have anything for him. Half the miners in Butte are on the sick dole."

She headed into the bitter air and coughed. At home she found all three of her babies, waiting for her. "Eloise, make some oat gruel. Timmy get a fire going. Tommy, sweep this place."

"There's no coal," Timmy said.

"Go down to the tracks and get some."

"It's cold out."

But he slid into a worn coat and got a burlap bag and left.

"We've got a sick man coming. His name is William Ward, and he's dying. He'll be in my bed."

"It's about time you got slept with," Tommy said, smirky.

"Go wash your ugly mouth."

She wrapped herself in a scarf and coat and felt hat and plunged outside, under an overcast sky. The only good thing about cold wind was that it took the smell away. On a summer's day Dublin Gulch stank. That's when every privy behind every house stank. When the slop dumped in the mucky streets stank. When the hogs and dogs and hens and rats and cats that ate the slop stank. When the sweaty miners and worn women and little thugs who filled the streets stank. She thought the cold smoky air was better than foul summer air.

Dublin Gulch was jammed, four or five or six souls in two-room shacks, the winding street seething with life night and day. Red Alice turned in at Baldwin's grocery, begged some pasteboard from an old box, and a crayon, and made a sign: HELP A SICK MINER EAT.

That was all she needed. She toted the ragged cardboard up the gulch, got a chipped crockery bowl, and headed toward the St. Lawrence. If she hurried, she'd get there just when the shift got out. They'd know. They'd all know about William Ward down there, expiring in the foul air, the toilet smells, and the heat.

She arrived just in time, half frozen because the wind never quit sucking heat out of her. The miners poured out of the triple cages, their dungarees soaked with sweat, steaming suddenly in the bitter air. Some mines had changing rooms. The dry rooms, as they were called, helped miners avoid pneumonia. The union was working on it. The miners eyed her sign, mostly ignoring her, and hurried toward their cottages or a pub and some ale, wanting warm before their soaked duds froze stiff.

"It's for Ward," said one.

"Yes, for him," she said.

He dug into his britches and dropped two bits into her bowl. She gave him a Socialist Workers Party tract, which he stuffed into his pocket unread. That's how it went for half an hour, until the last man reached grass, as they called the surface even if there wasn't a blade of it. She didn't see Ward. They didn't bring him up. Maybe Big Johnny Boyle was full of beans again. But she had given out twenty tracts and gotten two dollars and forty-five cents. She would keep it all for Ward, and feed him until he died and went to hell.

The icy wind drove her off Anaconda Hill, and she hurried down to Dublin Gulch, glad she had handed out all those tracts. No one had chased her off.

She entered her cottage, and it still was cold. Timmy hadn't gotten anything to burn. Eloise and Tommy stared at her, half afraid. In her bed was a man, ashen cold, shaking under his khaki army blanket.

"It's you, is it?" she said.

"You should have left me alone. It's cold here."

"It's also better air. I got enough to buy some coal, and you'll be warmed up."

"You're kind, madam, but misguided."

"What I do is my business, and I'm keeping you until you go to hell."

She found some ragged blankets on her children's cots, and heaped them over the sick man. He looked awful in the autumnal twilight, pale and yellow. His lungs rumbled. His eyes had sunk into their sockets, and his face had not been scraped for days.

"I'm obliged," he said, suddenly clouding up. For all his bravado, he was living out a horror. She dipped a rag into a pail, and sat down beside him.

"This'll be cold," she said.

She washed his face, cleaning away mucus, dried tears,

the cake of silica dust and ash, and fear. She gently washed his forehead, and his cheeks and neck, his ears, his shoulders, and his forearms and arms, and then rinsed the grimy rag and smoothed his hair with it. His eyes followed her, and once in a while he wheezed, his lungs convulsing against the cruel disease eating them away hour by hour.

Timmy returned with a few sticks and two small lumps of coal. It would start a fire. She handed him fifty cents. "Go buy a bag of coal, fast, or I'll fix you good."

He eyed the quarters, eyed the strange gaunt man in the bed, and scooted out the door. Tommy built a niggardly and heatless fire in the stove, while Eloise mindlessly stirred rolled oats in some water. The house didn't warm much. Alice fussed around too much.

"It doesn't matter whether it's voluntary or the government takes it from rich and gives it out equally," she said. "It's all the same to the poor."

William Ward tried to laugh, but all he did was convulse horribly.

"People are too cheap to share it without a shove," she added.

Timmy returned with a burlap sack of coal, and this caught swiftly, sending acrid fumes through the cottage but some heat too. The open stove door allowed flickering orange light to wobble across walls and the floor and ceiling.

"Where are you gonna do it with him?" Tommy asked, and snickered.

"Get your skinny ass outside," she said. He ignored her.

Eloise had the gruel heating, and was stirring it occasionally, her eye on the strange man in her ma's little bed.

Ward stopped quaking as the warmth reached him. His gaze followed the children and her as she busied herself.

"I suppose you'll tell me I remind you of your wife in Belfast," Alice said.

"Not a bit," he replied hoarsely.

"What is she like?"

"I don't know anymore," he said.

"Do you have children?"

"I haven't seen them in two years, and never will again."
He coughed cruelly. Even a few words were too much.

She ladled some thin gruel into a bowl. "I'll spoon this
into you," she said.

"I'm not sure I can swallow it."

She sat on the edge of the worn-out bed, and gave
him a tiny sip, which he downed with difficulty. She fed
more, and he had to dare himself to swallow it, working
up courage each time he faced the howl of his ravaged
throat. The children stared.

She turned to see them gawking. "You'll die of it too,"
she said. "The Irish all die of it."

It was true. For some reason, most of the denizens of
Dublin Gulch were perishing of consumption, while other
groups, in other places, weren't stricken so much by it. No
one could explain it. The priests said it was because of sin.

"It's not sin," she said. "The priests, they don't know
anything."

"It's caused by a germ, a microbe, Mrs.—Red Alice."

"It's caused by selfishness," she said. "If we had equal
incomes, hardly anyone would get sick like this."

No one argued with her. She didn't really believe it. But
she wasn't going to let William Ward die without turning
him into a Socialist, so she thought to start early and keep
right on until he died. He'd end up in Socialist heaven.
What she wanted was a deathbed confession. I have
sinned, please forgive me, because I was not a good Socialist, but now I am.

Boy, would she like to get Big Johnny Boyle to hear that
with his own ears.

He pushed her hand away. "I can't manage," he said.

"You hardly ate."

"What does a dying man need to eat?"

"I buried Singing Sean a few years ago. He got hit by an ore train on the street. No, that's not right. He tried to jump a car for a ride, and fell and got his legs cut off."

"Were there benefits?"

"Mr. Daly buried him, and they gave me a little."

"You've held things together," he said, coughing again.

"Don't talk about it," she said.

He didn't. The warmth and gruel seemed to subdue his restlessness, and even as she watched, he slid toward oblivion.

She didn't know where she would sleep. Share Eloise's trundle bed, she thought. It was a sin to have a strange man in her house, and him married, but she was tired of sin. She was tired of all the old rules and understandings.

She watched William Ward slide into sleep, and was glad that his color seemed a little better. He was gray or yellow when they brought him out of the worked-out part of the St. Lawrence copper mine. She never saw who brought him here but Big Johnny had made it happen. Somewhere, some of the brotherhood had cared, and brought him out. She found a stool and sat beside him, while her children watched her, half afraid to talk, puzzled by this intrusion. The house turned dark as twilight faded, and the stove cooled down, and the night sounds of the rowdy gulch amplified as the small tight world of the immigrants from the old country ignited into good humor.

She sat on her stool, watching the shadowed face in her bed, listening to his hoarse breathing, listening for the failure she knew would come soon, the moment when the con had eaten up the rest of him. She heard shuffling behind, as her babies found nooks for themselves, but she sat quietly, almost as if she were sleeping instead of keeping a vigil. She would vigil all night every night until the end. And it would be a vigil against the world, the system, the beliefs, the arrangements that had torn him from his wife and family, brought him here, and killed him. After he died, Red Alice planned to tell it to the world.

{ TWENTY-SIX }

It was the best of times and the worst of times for Marcus Daly. The Anaconda Copper Mining Company, newly incorporated, was earning fabulous wealth for its shareholders, paying fabulous dividends, and reinvesting its fat profits in new ventures. It owned a goodly portion of the richest hill on earth. Daly lived quietly in Anaconda, driving his handsome carriage from his Sixth Street home to his offices in the largest smelter on earth each day. He and the company's president, James Ali Ben Haggin, effectively controlled the company. After George Hearst had died, his wife, Phoebe, had sold her shares to the Rothschilds, who soon sold out their shares, which were now divided among many stockholders.

There were few crises. The fabulous Anaconda, Neversweat, and St. Lawrence mines poured out copper, a little silver, and a bit of gold. So did the adjacent Rob Roy and Nipper mines, in which the company had an interest. Daly's railroad hauled the ore twenty-five miles to the smelter. The company owned whole forests for mine timbers and fuel, Anaconda coal mines to fire boilers, an Anaconda foundry supplied by Anaconda iron and Anaconda quarries, the Anaconda water works and electrical plant, one of the best newspapers in the country, banks in Anaconda and Butte, the Florence Hotel for the single men pouring into his works. He had built the Montana Hotel, the best in the West, with a splendid kitchen and saloon. And over in the Bitterroot Valley he had acquired twenty-two-thousand acres of lush, well-watered meadow-land, and had built his handsome stock farm there to raise Thoroughbred racehorses. It had become the best stock farm in the country. It had miles of fence without a wire in it, rows of poplar trees lining the graveled roads. It had lush emerald paddocks. His horses trained in the thin mountain air, and did all the better running at or near sea level.

His great horse Tammany had won and won, and now was memorialized in the floor of the Montana Hotel sa-loon. Tammany's noble head and neck were rendered with pieces of hardwood, variously colored, all within a yard-square frame in the floor. Daly thought it was a suitable memorial for a horse that had won nine firsts, one sec-ond, and one third in fourteen races, and had won a leg-endary match race against Lamplighter, with forty thousand dollars riding on the outcome. People stared at that wooden rendering with respect, if not awe.

Marcus Daly stayed close to his wife, Margaret, and his four children, Margaret, Hattie, Mary, and Marcus II, finding time for them and for his church. They were quiet young people, not given to excess, and they pleased him. His rival in Butte, Clark, had taken to shipping his wife and children to Europe for long sojourns there, and then to California's orange groves, so that Clark lived largely alone, pursuing whatever were his fancies in deep secrecy. Those fancies were another reason why Daly was repelled by his rival. It was no secret that Clark had an eye for the women. But there seemed to be a peace between them now; Clark's gaudy paper, the *Mineral,* barely mentioned Daly or the Anaconda Company, and all its nefarious practices; and Daly's own *Anaconda Standard* was con-tent to agitate for the silver standard, and ignore Clark.

Superintendent Daly found time to sit and visit with his smeltermen and miner. They were his people, and even though fortune had favored him, they were still of his blood and bone and heart, and he would lunch with them in cafeterias, drink with them in saloons, stop to talk with them as they rested on their shovels and picks, look after widows, contribute to their charities, see to their comforts. For anyone in the sprawling company, it was never a surprise to have Marcus Daly stop and visit. He knew many by name, not because he was currying favor, but because he actually enjoyed them, called them friends, and shared their joys and sorrows.

He was well into his fifties, and feeling his years, but life was so good that he barely noticed the weakening of his body. He loved horseflesh, and racing became his passion. He built racetracks in Butte and Anaconda, and sponsored festive racing meets, which were often dominated by stock from his own stables. That summer of 1896 another of his great horses, Ogden, won the Futurity back East, and a purse totaling $43,970. That tickled Daly; his trainers had said the horse wasn't mature enough to run, but Daly had overridden them and sent him East anyway.

Could life be any better? Well, yes. Politics were intruding on it once again. Silver and gold were tearing political parties apart, and pitting the creditors in the East against the debtors in the West. The Sherman Silver Purchase Act had not survived, and the value of silver was in free fall. That was affecting most of the mines of Butte; the silver mines high up the slope suffered the most, but the rest of the mines, where silver was an important byproduct, suffered as well. The Populists were becoming a major force, a third party capable of defeating either of the traditional ones. An alliance with the Populists was the only way for either party to win in Montana.

Daly openly supported the Populists and wrote checks. Their candidate, William Jennings Bryan, was eloquent and tireless, and framed the issues in terms of fairness; the poor needed help against the rapacious rich. He was a good candidate, well attuned to his rural auditors, able and charismatic. Marcus Daly liked him, and his appreciation for Bryan went far beyond looking after the price of silver. Bryan and his party wanted the free and unlimited coinage of silver at a ratio to gold of sixteen to one. He wanted to increase the money supply by fifty dollars per capita, which meant cheap and abundant money, some inflation, and opportunity for debt-ridden Westerners to set their economies moving.

Daly was wary of some of the Populists' program, with Socialist planks. But that didn't stop him. He saw in the Populists, and Bryan, a chance to unyoke the West from its Eastern masters, and he applied his resources to the task. The Republicans were running William McKinley, a gold man, and they had a lot of cash in the till for their campaign.

The Populists wanted government ownership of all transportation and communication companies, a national currency, a graduated income tax, direct election of United States senators, the secret ballot, a postal savings system, and a shorter work day for laborers. Some of that was welcomed by Daly and his wing of the state Democrats; some not. He knew that Clark was a silver Democrat also, and might be open to a fusion ticket with the Populists. For a change, they were both on the same side.

So Daly wrote large checks, sent his emissaries to the conventions, and out of it all came the fusionist ticket he had hoped for. If victorious, the Democrats would send two electors and the Populists one elector to Washington to select the next president. Bryan campaigned mightily, and made a speech that resonated in every rural corner of the republic. "You shall not press down upon the brow of labor this crown of thorns, you shall not crucify mankind upon a cross of gold," he said. And many heard him.

That hot political summer paid off. The Democrat-Fusionist ticket, garnering support from rural ranchers and industrial magnates and miners and businessmen swamped the divided Republican party, and gave William Jennings Bryan three electoral votes. But nationally, the Republicans did much better. McKinley won easily.

That meant Butte would face austere times, Daly thought. Less expansion, fewer jobs, maybe the demise of some of the older silver mines, which were played out anyway. And there would be less credit, costlier money, making it tougher to start up new businesses. The Eastern moneybags with their sacks of double eagles had won.

What was there to do but return to his tasks? His mines probed deeper and deeper, and the ore was there. Two thousand feet, three thousand feet under the surface there was still good copper ore everywhere. The nation was electrifying itself, and the demand for copper for wires never slackened. Copper prices edged higher, and copper became the most-sought-for metal, its price inspiring a global hunt for new deposits.

Daly turned to his stock farm, buying the great sire Hamburg, and the dam Lady Reel, and soon had another bonanza, this one of sleek, young, well-bred horseflesh that conquered the whole world. This, then, was the dream. Copper was the means; the stock farm was the dream that pierced back to his youth and the horses he knew as a boy in Ireland. He shared his joy with his employees, who enjoyed days off to see the races at the racetrack on the flat below Butte, or in Anaconda.

Still, he worried, though it was not in his nature to worry. He was not an anxious man, and his bouts of anxiety surprised him. By design, the Anaconda Company was Irish. His successor, when the time came, would be William Scallon. There were others waiting in the wings, including John Ryan and Cornelius Kelley. Its hiring officers, shift bosses, and foremen included James Higgins, "Rimmer" Con, Dan O'Neill, Mike Carroll, John Crowley, James and Pat Kane, John McCarthy, "Fat Jack" Sullivan, and on and on, in every department. They gave preference to Irishmen like themselves, promoted men like themselves, made sure that the company remained Irish to its core, to its soul, if a company had such a thing. It was more than a corporation; it was a fraternity and a refuge for all the refugees from the emerald isle. Butte was New Ireland, its Irish population outnumbering all the other groups combined.

His lawyers were Irish. His accounting men were Irish. The company's friends and associates in Butte, such as Dan Hennessy, saw to the food and clothing and fuel consumed there. Most of the men in the pits were first-generation Irish. They were doing a good job, and the Irish Anaconda Company was minting money for its stockholders. It was paying enormous dividends, and still had ample cash to reinvest, expand, improve operations, so the company was growing, acquiring new properties, discovering still more copper and other minerals. It was also creating new markets for itself, supplying copper for brass, copper for plumbing, copper for anything electric. That was steadily raising the price of copper, and also raising the price of Anaconda stock. Owners of Anaconda shares not only reaped amazing profits, they enjoyed the appreciation of their investments.

It was a prize as glittering as John D. Rockefeller's Standard Oil, and that was what gnawed at Marcus Daly's heart. Ever since Phoebe Hearst had sold George's shares, nearly half the stock of the company was in other hands, in the open market, available to pirates and raiders and scavengers and get-rich-quick hustlers.

And that's what troubled Superintendent Daly. There were rumblings in the bourses of New York. There were adventurers quietly buying shares, working their way in, threatening upheavals. And some of those adventurers were Rockefeller men. There wasn't much Daly could do, and it troubled him.

The lawsuits were chafing him too. The richest hill on earth had generated scores of lawsuits, as corporations wrestled with one another for the incredible prizes that lay under the surface. The company had the best of the copper mines, but there were other mines, some of them silver outfits, clawing wealth from the rock. Clark had widespread interests. So did young Heinze, who was buying shares in independents. So did the Boston financiers, like the Bigelows and Quincy Adams Shaw who owned Calumet and Hecla. So did the Walker brothers, and the Lewisohn brothers, Sam Hauser, and A. J. Davis. There were the Butte and Boston Company, and the Boston and Montana, and the Montana Copper Company. And they were heaping up lawsuits against one another, suits that would be decided in Butte's overworked district court, presided over by an eccentric judge named Clancy.

Daly and Hearst and Haggin knew what lawsuits could do to fabulously wealthy mines. They had been on the Comstock, in Nevada, the biggest silver strike ever known, and had watched the Nevada courtroom wars bleed powerful companies white, while aggressive litigators pocketed the silver fortunes that lay there. The trouble lay in United States mining law, which permitted the owner of a vein that apexed, or surfaced, on his claim to pursue the vein beyond the boundaries of his claim. That guaranteed fortunes for Nevada and California lawyers. Geology is not an orderly world. Faults move veins. The deposit of minerals is complex. Acidic groundwater shifts minerals from one site to another. That gave experts all the leeway they needed to testify in Nevada courts. They built models, opined about faults, guaranteed that such and such a vein did not really vanish; it simply had been moved eighty yards to the left and up forty yards as well. The courtroom dramas in Carson City and San Francisco were all that counted. Men who had found bonanzas and developed great mines ended up with empty pockets. Clever men got rich in the courtrooms.

From the onset, Daly and Hearst and Haggin determined to avoid lawsuits at all costs, and that meant buying every mine that neighbored their bonanza mines, or at least purchasing as much stock as they could in the neighbors', which would give them some control over what the other managements did. But now Daly wondered whether buying the neighboring mines was enough. That unkempt, garrulous clown named Clancy on the district court bench in Butte seemed to favor anyone who wanted to share the wealth. Other men's wealth.

{ TWENTY-SEVEN }

Business was drying up. Royal Maxwell was in dire straits. A rival mortuary, Sullivan, had opened in Meaderville, and another rival, O'Fallon Brothers, had opened in Anaconda. Butte was expanding daily, hiring newcomers daily, yet no grieving person entered Maxwell's black-enameled double front door seeking his services.

He wasn't earning enough to keep his doors open, much less to support his habitual forays to Mercury Street, or occasionally to darker and meaner Galena Street when he was in a reckless mood. He felt as though he were an outsider in a town he had lived in for a dozen years. Maxwell's Mortuary had been there when Butte was small and rough. Maxwell had buried more miners than he could remember, and the carriage trade, too. He'd planted financiers, moguls, mining engineers, rich widows, rich mistresses, and the sickly children who imbibed too much arsenic from the smoke.

While he had rivals now, the plain reality was that people weren't dying fast enough, and he could do nothing to encourage them to die sooner. He was faithful to his

Republican party, which opposed regulation of business, which probably helped him a little, but not as much as he hoped. He was secretly a gold Republican, favoring sound money, but that was anathema in Butte, so he made all the noises of being pro-silver, pro-inflation, pro-easy borrowing. But it didn't get him any more business. A little more arsenic in the air would help, or a little more rock dust in the mines, but everything was going the other direction. The companies were inspecting the cables on their lifts. They were settling the dust in the pits, and building higher stacks to carry the smoke away from town. They were adding changing rooms to cut down pneumonia. The denizens of the most pestilential streets in town, in Dublin Gulch, all went to Sullivan, which was costing Maxwell a body a week. Well, it wasn't much of a loss. Who over there could afford a fine, first-class, dignified funeral, a parade, and burial in Mountain View, with a crypt and a headstone?

One day a story he chanced to read in the *Mineral* started him thinking about other prospects. Two frails had died the same day, one of suicide—she imbibed carbolic acid, which was the poison du jour—and the other had been killed by her pimp supposedly for keeping more cash than she was entitled to. Of course the *Mineral* made a front-page item of it, but that was the yellow press for you. Both of the ladies had been buried in a potter's field, by Silver Bow County, because no one had volunteered to pay for a burial.

Maxwell studied the report, and thought there might be opportunity in it. Virtually all of the ladies in the restricted district were being dumped in unmarked graves at the back of the cemeteries, alone and unremembered, with no one picking up the tab. They had become the county's burden and responsibility. They died frequently and young. They perished from syphilis and other diseases, especially consumption. They died of heartbreak. They died of loneliness. They died from wear and tear after losing their attractiveness and their income. They died when they had varicose veins marring their legs. They died of violence by all sorts of men. Some were beaten to death. Some perished after their faces had been slashed to bits with broken bottles wielded by males. Some died of opium or heroin or anything else that numbed their bodies. They flocked to town, joined their hundreds of sisters, and did not lack trade from thousands of bachelor miners. A few got married and escaped.

All of that intrigued Maxwell. There might be a fortune in it. He might also enjoy any lady's favors in return for the promise of a good burial. He could become the one to bury all the frails and sports. They had money; they just didn't care enough about one another to blow any of it on a fine, bright funeral with a parade and drummers and a good crowd of spectators. But he didn't quite know how to approach anyone. And he didn't know how to get himself reimbursed for a good gaudy funeral. He could propose monthly payments in advance, but he knew how that would work out. He could approach the madams and try to get them to pay in advance. Or the pimps. But the more he puzzled it, the more difficult it seemed. And yet he had to try. Funerals for the demimonde might yet be bonanza ore for Royal Maxwell.

He scarcely knew where to begin. But he thought he could make progress. He was naturally unctuous, and had a dripping and buttery sympathy he could call up for all occasions. He preferred the tony parlor houses when he could afford them, so that seemed the place to begin.

And where better than Chicago Marlene's Parlor? He rehearsed his little talk, while trotting down there one afternoon—he wanted to make his pitch before business heated up—and soon opened the red-enameled door that let him into a tiny reception hall. No one wasted a square foot in the district. Chicago herself met him with an oozy smile.

"A word about business, Chicago," he said.

"Everything's for sale," she said. "At a good price."

"Well, if you have five minutes, I want to make a proposal."

She puckered up, and then eyed him warily. He followed her into a tiny side room.

"I charge twice as much as my girls, Royal," she said. "But if your tastes run toward sagging knockers, I'm here."

"Actually, I want to talk about the unmentionable that happens to us all," he said.

"I take sulphate of mercury," she said.

"I mean passing away, Chicago. The ladies here—well, they don't last long, and almost in the springtime of their lives they end up in a potter's field, planted there by Silver Bow County, forgotten. They don't even have markers. Just a little lonely patch of earth."

She looked ready to explode, so he hurried along. "You know, I feel such a great sorrow when I see those lonely mounds of earth at the back row of the cemeteries. I think, there was a life lost. No one cared enough to bury them properly. No family came to collect the remains or buy a coffin."

She was smiling. "You've come to sell funerals."

"Well, no, I have a better idea. Most of the ladies don't have a nickel to their name. It all goes to the Chinamen. I thought to myself, here's a public service I can do. I can offer free funerals to the suffering people in the district. Of course, if people wish to pass the hat and pay me what they can, that would be fine. But even if I don't receive a thin dime, I would be pleased to give all the people here a proper send-off."

She eyed him. "And meanwhile you want a free screw."

"Well, that too. I was thinking, a two-hundred-dollar

funeral ought to be worth a hundred little moments with your nymphs. The bookkeeping should be easy."

She held out her hand. "Two dollars right now, or get your ass out."

"I don't have—ah, if the girls will service me, I'll service them at the appropriate time, in a gentle and dignified and entirely appropriate manner."

She didn't speak. She just stared, faintly amused. Then she thumbed him toward the door.

"Think about it," he said.

"I already have." She jerked her thumb.

That didn't bode well. The next parlor house, Twice Around Mary's, featured fat women, and he tried that. Twice Around listened silently, sighed, and said "No one here croaks."

He tried an obscure, dark place called Sam's next. No one knew whether Sam was a man or a woman, but she wore skirts.

"Don't you feel pity for the girls who perish by their own hand?" he asked.

"What are you, a preacher?" Sam asked.

"No, I am a man who cares about the lost. They drink carbolic acid, burn out their insides, and die in anguish. Then what? The county comes for them because no one else will. Not even the other girls will. And thus they end up alone, unlamented. Isn't it sad? Here I am, in the business, and no one ever calls on me. I'd gladly offer my services free if only to make the world a little kinder."

"What's your angle, Maxwell?"

"Well, I thought maybe I could exchange a few delights for the solemn promise to bury them well . . ."

Sam smirked. "I knew it."

"But really, the funerals would be free. All I'd ask is that you all pass the hat, and whatever comes my way, why, I'd be able to keep my doors open, pay for the hearse, serve the public."

"You sound like a carbolic salesman," Sam said.

Carbolic acid was the poison that the ladies of the night seemed to favor because it produced more agony than anything else they could drink. Who could explain it?

"I assure you, Sam, I am earnestly trying to uplift the spirits of those caught in the sporting life."

Sam giggled.

Next was Galena Street, a place loaded with cribs. His first stop was Cockeyed Louis, a famed pimp, who sometimes forced a customer into his joint at knifepoint. But Louis just grinned. "You pass the hat and I get fifty percent," he said. "Me, I'd just as soon knife a girl as pay for a funeral. They ain't worth it."

Royal Maxwell toured the district, mostly meeting silence and bleary stares. But wherever he went, he promised a fine, free funeral for the sports, with the hope they'd pass the hat.

The next day Cockeyed Louis croaked. An irate person unknown sliced his throat from ear to ear and left him in the gutter. Maxwell read all about it on the front page of the *Mineral,* which never varied from its sensationalism.

Ah, what a dilemma. He had promised a free funeral to the sports, and now one was thrust upon him. Not a girl, but a mean pimp, well known throughout town. He decided that his whole enterprise was on the line, so he volunteered. He headed for the Silver Bow sheriff's office, claimed what was left of Cockeyed Louis, who was lying in a cell until he could be planted, and took the deceased to his mortuary.

The first thing was to send word to the district, so he hired Watermelon Jones, the messenger, to stop at every parlor house in town with the word. There would be a parade and a planting at Mountain View on Thursday at three. That would be a good hour. He needed to be sure the sports were up, but wanted the ceremonies to be over before business picked up. He tipped Watermelon an extra dime for his hard work, and then set to work. He cleaned up Cockeyed, put him in a fine oaken box with satin lining, polished up the black hearse with the glass sides so all the world could see the fine coffin within, got some fall flowers, put on the black pompons, and got the black horses he regularly rented from Willis's Livery, and then he was as ready as he could get. He would make a small, kind graveside oration in lieu of a cleric. He also hired a couple of drummers, one with a bass drum and the other with a snare drum, and a bugler to play taps.

He felt mighty fine about it. No one would show up to bury Cockeyed. But surely the whole sporting district would enjoy the show and pass the hat. Just to make sure, he brought a spare hat along to start the coins rolling.

Promptly at three on Thursday, Maxwell drove his shining ebony hearse from his establishment toward the district. The casket was heaped with flowers. There were black pompons; the horses were in nickelplate harness. A small black sign next to the casket announced the presence of Cockeyed Louis. And just ahead of his hearse the drummers tolled the hour, snare drum and bass drum in measured cadence. All in all, Cockeyed would get himself a fine send-off. Royal drove straight down Galena Street, and was rewarded to see eyes peeking through curtained windows even if there were few people on the street. Then came Mercury, and finally Silver, a fine display for all to see. Miners in boots and worn britches stared. He thought maybe the miners might pass the hat, so he paused, handed a black silk top hat to them, and whispered that he would be grateful if they would collect on behalf of the much admired Cockeyed Louis.

"Jesus Christ," said one of them.

"Yes, yes, just right. Collect a little to bury the dead," Maxwell whispered, and set his hearse in motion again. Just to sweeten the odds, he drove Mercury, Galena, and

Silver Streets once again, but the miners were lost to view. He finally headed south on Main Street, drawing lots of stares and even stopping traffic. What a fine funeral! Well worthy of a swell. But no one followed. It would be a long ride down to the cemetery, but his drummers marched resolutely, and at last he turned in, past the graves and trees, to the rear row, where an empty grave awaited. The crowd he had hoped for didn't materialize, and he finally recruited the drummers to settle Cockeyed in his grave. There was no one about; only the cold November air shivering his horses and the men.

He looked for the miners on the way back, thinking they would dump a handful of coins into his lap, but no one showed up, and he finally realized he had no coins and no hat. Well, it had been a fine trip; everyone in the district had seen Louis pass by. They might not have liked Cockeyed—no one had ever said a good word about him—but that didn't matter. The whole district knew he meant it; he would give them free funerals, and keep only what was in the hat.

That evening, he discovered he was on the front page of the *Mineral*. "Notorious Citizen Gets Fancy Send-off," read the headline. "Our fair city witnessed a strange sight this morning. An elaborate funeral cortege rolled through town without a single mourner present. The two-hundred-dollar planting party for a certain scoundrel was rumored to be given for free by Maxwell's Mortuary, and it was also rumored that Maxwell was paying off a debt."

TWENTY-EIGHT

No matter how Katarina Costa dressed, it was never enough to conceal the heat inside of her. In fact, the more demure her attire, the more it seemed to advertise something within her that stirred long glances. She understood that perfectly. On this evening she occupied her usual corner seat at the Chequamegon, the rare unescorted woman who seemed to understand she was welcome if she adhered to certain clear standards.

This evening she wore a dignified gray gabardine suit with a frilly blouse buttoned tight up to her neck, with a string of pearls. This contrasted somehow with her unruly jet hair and high cheekbones and Latinate features, and ember eyes whose gaze burned whatever it touched, which was usually men of substance. The heat of her face combined with the schoolteacherish clothing was what made her so fascinating to men, which is why she dressed as she did. In spite of her demure clothing, the lush shape of her figure was somehow invisibly present. She couldn't help it and didn't want to help it.

She didn't lack money, and spent it casually. A brief marriage to a mining engineer had left her in comfortable circumstances. What interested her far more was conquest. She met plenty of gents who turned weak at the knees the moment she addressed them, but they weren't copper kings, and barely interested her. Butte certainly had its rich men, most of them newly minted, but the rich were as common as hen's eggs as far as she was concerned. Butte did not have many powerful men, men whose wave of the hand or signature or command changed the course of stars and destinies.

There were only three now, though she had looked at various powerful gents like the Lewisohn brothers and

Albert Bigelow and found them wanting. Marcus Daly was beyond reach, happily immersed in a good marriage and oblivious of other possibilities. William Andrews Clark was a more entertaining prospect, in spite of a cruel beard that surrounded a pursed little mouth. She could scarcely imagine kissing the man. All the other signals were just right. Clark was a widower, and in recent times he had sojourned in California, avoiding cruel Butte winters. Indeed, Clark's children were rarely to be seen at his redbrick mansion, where he entertained steadily. He was a dandy, getting himself up in luxurious clothing intended to wallpaper his humble origins. He had started to collect bad art and put on all the airs of old wealth, even if his was desperately new.

That all seemed perfect, and Katarina had discovered where the man dined and wined. That was mostly at the Silver Bow Club where she was not welcome, but the Chequamegon saw him occasionally, sometimes with two or three mysterious women. He never came with a single woman, never as a couple. He seemed utterly loathsome, which delighted her. She enjoyed her triumph over herself. The more she recoiled from some man, the more she was drawn to the gent. And Clark was the sort who set her teeth on edge and made her itch to head for the nearest exit.

She contrived to meet Clark by sending a waiter to him with a bottle of wine she had purchased for him. It was a gesture so unusual that it immediately attracted his attention, and he had excused himself and came over to meet her.

He had eyed her carefully, missing nothing. "You have sent a gift to a man who needs none. Is there a sentiment in this? Something on your mind?" he asked.

"You," she had said.

"Then I'm afraid you'll find yourself adrift," he had replied.

Nonetheless, he sat with her, ignoring his own table for half an hour, the conversation almost entirely his questions about her and her background and her demure replies.

He seemed more stimulated trying to guess her intent than attracted to her plentiful charms. Still, a man with a living brain and dead private parts might be entertaining so she had retained hope that the encounter would lead somewhere. But it hadn't. They encountered each other a dozen more times at the Chequamegon, and whenever he had women in tow, they were very different from Katarina. He always stopped at her table, exchanged a word or two, but it became plain that he wasn't examining her with bedroom eyes.

She understood it gradually. To him, the rural Pennsylvanian with English roots, she was the Latin firebrand. The ladies in his various parties were drawn from the same stock as himself. If any of them were his mistresses, enduring the scrape and tickle of that dreadful shrubbery around his lips, they were English or Welsh or Scots or perhaps Scandinavians. She thought the man might go for a French woman, but that would be as exotic as he got. Meanwhile, he shuffled his family from the Pacific to the Atlantic—anywhere but Butte. There was one woman who looked to be more daughter than mate, and she had a sneaking hunch that.William Andrews Clark had a lust for seventeen-year-olds.

Katarina had trouble one night being seated. A new waiter refused to serve an unescorted woman, especially one with smouldering eyes. But he was swiftly overruled by Barney Scallon, the proprietor, who knew that most evenings Mrs. Costa ordered from the top of his menu. He had even set aside some wine for her. Butte was a whiskey and beer town, and wine drinkers were scarce, but he found a way to accommodate her, charging a fancy price for the small stock he kept on hand for her.

But soon she was settled in her usual corner, quietly waiting for whatever happened that evening to happen. She was always alone when she arrived, but not always alone for long. Women in the Chequamegon avoided her, sensing a plague upon their evenings. Men eyed her contemplatively, and she regarded each gaze as a triumph.

She had heard of F. Augustus Heinze and regarded him as a sort of young beaver, not in the same class as Daly or Clark. The gent was younger than herself by several years; somehow living life broadly while still in his twenties, and getting moderately rich. He had eyed her on several occasions, but this particular night she seemed to capture him, and he sat at his own table with half a dozen others, a mixed group of swells and ladies, maybe some of them a little racier than most. But he kept turning to glance at her, and she met his gaze.

He wasn't the most attractive of males, but was solid and cheerful. She didn't much care for him; she had higher standards than meaty twenty-nine-year-olds trying to build copper empires. She watched the party at that table, all of them lively and reordering whiskeys from the ubiquitous waiters. She mostly ignored them, and toyed with her own filet mignon, which she sawed into slivers and ate delicately. She enjoyed well-done meat, which she thought had something erotic about it.

Heinze was trying to follow the conversation at his table; but he looked bored. They were talking about the mines. That's what people did in Butte. He had bought the Rarus mine, a flagging producer that wasn't showing much promise until he steered his crews straight into spectacular ore. It lay east of the great Anaconda and St. Lawrence lode, and Heinze had discerned just where that mighty ore burst into the Rarus, and how it might be mined at a huge profit. He had bought interests in other mines, and seemed en route to becoming more of a mine operator than the manager of an independent smelter. A well-trained geologist, but not good for much else, she thought.

Katarina listened carefully. Most of what she knew of matters in Butte she had gotten by listening to table talk at the Chequamegon. On this particular night, though, Heinze wasn't interested in all that. Then he glanced at her again, and this time the look was so starkly and nakedly purposeful that she smiled. She didn't know where the heat in her came from but it infused her, and radiated outward, and once a man was caught in it, he was the prisoner of his loins. As young Augustus was.

He arose and approached.

"I noticed you're alone, and that's no way to enjoy an evening eating out. Would you join us?" he asked.

"Oh, I think not, but it's lovely of you to inquire," she said.

"I'm Augustus Heinze."

"I'm Mrs. Costa. Katarina Costa."

He was too much the prisoner to pay much attention. "Perhaps some other time?" he asked.

"Perhaps," she said. "I'm here most evenings."

That was invitation enough. He would be back, and alone.

"So I have seen," he said.

"I will send a dessert your way," she said.

He gazed, startled, and smoothly nodded. "I enjoy gallantry," he said.

He passed her tests. Maybe he would be worth an adventure even if it was demeaning to arrange something with a fledgling copper king rather than a lord of Butte. He certainly was a pleasant young man, well spoken, civil and polite, and endlessly cheerful. She might enjoy a minor conquest, though he wasn't half what Marcus Daly or William Clark were. She was opposed to nothing much; it would be easy to put the foundling on the doorstep of the love orphanage if it came to that.

Sure enough, he appeared at the Chequamegon at just the same hour the next night, and didn't hesitate a moment.

"I would be honored to have your company for dinner," he said gallantly. "If your husband wouldn't mind."

"My husband vanished years ago, and has not been seen since. Poor dear. He may be in Argentina, but I'm never sure. Last I heard, he was taking the waters at Marienbad."

"Ah, then we have much in common."

She waited for him to say what they had in common, but he didn't pursue it, and in fact he was referring simply to the reality that both were unfettered.

"What are your designs?" she asked.

"Copper is a handsome metal. It shines red. Its salts are lovely shades of blue and green. It is malleable. It conducts electricity better than anything else that doesn't cost much. It is fashionable to make roofs out of it now because it doesn't rust. It is the perfect utility metal, good for most everything. I should like to become a utility investor, good for whatever is required. And now, what are yours?"

"I am Diana the hunter," she said. "I like trophies."

He waited for more, but she had said as much as she chose to. He directed the waiter to bring whatever the chef thought was suitable, and they turned to banter, each testing the other, which sent the evening by in a rush.

His heat was upon him, but she thought to resist. "I will take you to dinner tomorrow night," she said.

"But I have plans."

"Break them."

He smiled, nodded, and that was that.

It was too easy; she was already bored with Heinze, and resolved to call him Fritz, the name he despised. He was virile and adroit, and she would enjoy all that when the time came, but she really wanted to pocket Clark, who it was whispered was overtaking John D. Rockefeller as the richest man in America. Now that would be something to set her cap on. This one, across from her, was still a boy.

The next evening he showed up promptly, this time in black tie; a dinner jacket with a black satin shawl collar embracing his ample frame. He carried a bouquet, and the waiters swiftly produced a vase for the table. She might be buying, but he was doing the romancing. The formal attire surprised her. He was an engineer and geologist, after all. Scarcely the background to put him in a dinner jacket. Still, it oddly matched her own dress. Perhaps they were both putting on the dog a bit.

She wore something less schoolmarmish this evening, a silky pearl gray dress with tiny cloth-covered buttons down her front, buttons he would wrestle with when the moment came. She read him instantly, and knew where this evening would head, and it amused her. As much heat radiated from Augustus Heinze as did from herself. Much too easy, she thought. But the bouquet was lovely.

{ TWENTY-NINE }

William Andrews Clark sat in a mauve velvet wing chair in a small white parlor, waiting. Sometimes his cheeks itched, but they were so encrusted with wiry hair that he simply had to endure the itch. That was the price paid by men of substance.

The Silver Bow Club, on the fourth floor of the Lewisohn Building, annoyed him. It was not suitable for a man of his stature. Butte deserved better, but so far the club's directors had not seen fit to build an edifice suited to the eminence of its members. The one thing about the club that still won Clark's allegiance was all its quiet parlors, where substantial men could do substantial business in private. That was exactly what Clark wanted, and the club was better than his dining room, with all its snoopy servants, or his bank, where his desk was on a dais that placed Clark several inches above anyone on the other side of it.

So it had to be the Silver Bow Club, seedy by Clark's increasingly grand tastes, in spite of its quiet elegance. No one else seemed to mind, but Clark was always a man for appearances, and the club didn't measure up.

He could build a suitable clubhouse fifty times over, but then it would be his, not the club's, and that wouldn't do. He wasn't quite sure whether he was the richest man in the United States. There was always John D. Rockefeller to consider. But a single Clark mine, the United Verde, in Jerome, Arizona, was netting him four hundred thousand dollars a month. That mine was even more fabulous than his holdings in Butte, and appeared to be almost inexhaustible. He owned dozens of other mines, a Mexican plantation, and real estate in Los Angeles and Santa Barbara. He was making a killing in sugar beets. If he wasn't yet the equal of Rockefeller, he was a close second and catching up by the minute. It all amused him. Rockefeller lived in the East, and his every move was noted in the press. Clark lived obscurely in the West, unknown, and about to become the richest American.

That's why the Silver Bow Club annoyed him.

John B. Wellcome materialized, shed his gloves, topcoat, scarf, and hat, and sat in the other mauve wing chair, a faint smile on his lips. The man was Clark's chief lawyer, accomplished and genial, and a shrewd judge of character. The amusing thing was that most everyone liked Wellcome even when Wellcome was skinning their hide off.

"Cold," he said.

A steward appeared with a bourbon sour, unbidden. Wellcome nodded and sipped. Clark rarely touched spirits when he was dealing with weighty items because they clouded his mind, which was the worst thing that could happen to him.

"It'll be worse in January," Clark said. "I have the first endowment here." He motioned toward a black pigskin satchel. "There will be more endowments, as needed."

"Have much more ready."

"The session will be unruly," Clark said.

The Democrats had a large majority in the Assembly, but most of them were Daly Democrats, not unalloyed Clark Democrats. The Daly Democrats were little more than weasels, allying with Populists and silver Republicans to control the state. Clark would have trouble getting any votes from them, unless . . .

"Who can we get and what will we need?" Clark asked.

"I haven't the faintest idea," Wellcome said. "But most men have a dream."

"Don't speak of such things," Clark said. "Spend it all on virtuous Democrats. I will say it for the record. Let it never be said that I sought less than to reward loyal Democrats."

In Clark's eyes, Daly's brand of Democrat was worse than Republicans. The Senate term of Republican Lee Mantle was expiring, and it would be up to the legislature to elect a new man. And the Democratic legislature would elect a Democrat. But there were real ones, like Clark, and bogus ones who compromised and weaseled, like the whole Daly battalion.

Clark hadn't intended to run, having taken his lickings in the past, but in August, just ahead of the November elections, Wellcome and others had persuaded him to give it a try, especially with Daly's Anaconda juggernaut threatening to swallow the whole state. Daly had been operating quietly far from Silver Bow County, buying distant papers, forging alliances with businessmen, funding the campaigns of local politicians, yet almost invisibly. The old feud wasn't in its grave after all. Clark had swiftly produced a hundred thousand dollars, and his minions had also been out buying newspapers, and the result was that political democracy was going to Helena for the 1899 session.

All of which had revived old man Clark's feelings. The lust uncoiled in him once again. The prefix, Senator, ahead of his name mesmerized him. He would be more than a businessman, more than an entrepreneur, more than the richest of Americans. He would be the most influential and honored and powerful man of all. He was a reflective man, constantly questioning his own motivation and belief and understandings, and he had asked himself whether being a senator was what mattered, and whether life in Washington, and on the floor of the Senate suited him, and whether it would add anything to his happiness. He concluded that it wouldn't but he would do it anyway.

The title would soon bore him. The deliberations would soon bore him. The company of the powerful would soon annoy him. The business of fending off seekers and pleaders and lobbyists and logrollers would irk him. His time could be better spent in Europe, Paris in particular, where life was lived with panache, than in steamy and sordid Washington. But he would do it anyway. He would enter the sordid world of politics. He would suffer the abuses of rivals and editorialists. He would endure the calumnies. It wasn't anything he wanted, which was why he would proceed. The day would come when he could tell people he was elected in spite of his contempt and revulsion of politics and politicians, who were all worms. Ah, yes, he would do it because he had not the slightest interest in it, and would enjoy his secret.

The meeting with Wellcome went quite simply. They hadn't spoken another word about politics or money or whose vote might be required, or what the Daly men might do. It was all beneath Clark, and boring too. When he won the Senate seat he'd celebrate, of course. There was nothing like a victory to get his juices flowing. But even a Senate victory would be nothing compared to one month's profit from the mines.

And it would likely bury old Marcus Daly. That's what he'd celebrate, when the time came. The old man wasn't well, but he was still the bulldog of Anaconda, and needed a final lesson. In fact, that was the whole of it. If Daly weren't on the other side, Clark wouldn't care about the Senate one way or another.

Wellcome vanished into the bitter December night, toting a black bag filled with green paper bearing the image of Grover Cleveland, and Clark permitted himself a glass of spirits now that business was complete. There would be two or three agents working the legislature, including Clark's own spindly son Charlie, a young boodler making his way in a hard world.

Clark waited some more; another guest was coming. Clark had debated whether to let this one through the front door, but decided there was some advantage in it. The man should have stayed in the servant quarters in the Clark mansion. He ordered a sherry and settled into his wing chair, knowing the loathsome man would be late. Being late was J. Fellowes Hall's leverage over people; it delighted the man to keep busy people waiting.

All of which was exactly what one would expect of a man of Hall's vanity. Clark had seen a lot of vanity in his day, and none more blatant than Hall's, which was written all over him, from his gaze to his posture. Clark had been so repelled at first he thought to fire the man, but on consideration he thought he could put such a vast buggyload of vanity to work. Vain people could be valuable on occasion, such as now.

So he sipped his sweet sherry, smiled at the oil portraits of members on the parlor walls, and waited until the editor blew in, his coat flapping.

"I fear I'm a bit tardy," Hall said, without apology.

"It is the way you deal with people," Clark said.

A steward accepted Hall's flap-eared hat, greatcoat, gloves, and scarf. Beneath all that was a tidy gray suit and a florid bow tie of a sort that was offensive on sight to Clark, which was exactly the intended impression. Like most toadies, Hall had contrived a list of items Clark liked and despised, and used it as needed. This wintry eve, Hall was running through his list of capital offenses.

"A drink?" Clark asked.

"Bourbon and branch," Hall said, settling in the opposing wing chair.

"You've kept me here past my bedtime," Clark said, "so I'll compress it all into a few words. I've kept quiet about it, but if the Democrats should decide to pack me off to the Senate, I wouldn't object. Politics have little interest to me, but I wouldn't resist the charge if it were laid upon my shoulders. As you know, I've strongly supported real democracy, and not the mongrel variety Marcus Daly has been promoting. Some people will do anything to hold office, but I'm not among them. I have my scruples, as you know."

Hall was smirking, which is exactly what Clark expected. There was nothing about Hall that Clark could not anticipate. The steward returned with Hall's drink, and Hall lifted it in a gesture of good fellowship.

"Cheers," Hall said.

Clark grunted. Toasts didn't come more banal. "Well, now, Hall, you've followed my instruction to keep me out of the spotlight, and that makes my life much easier. You are to continue with that, excepting only to say that I am a reluctant candidate for the United States Senate, and if a better man is selected, I shall be all in favor of it, so long as he is a true member of the party. Do you have that clear?"

Hall sipped and nodded.

"Now, Hall, I have it on good authority that Marcus Daly intends to influence this selection by any means, fair or foul. He and his powerful company have their own candidates, and would accept even a silver Republican. That's how unprincipled they are."

"Yes, sir, pragmatism is all that runs in Mr. Daly's head."

Clark wasn't sure what pragmatism meant, but it sounded like consumption or syphilis or dementia, so he nodded. "There are good men in Daly's company who see the folly of smothering Montana under Anaconda's corporate influence," he continued. "There are sage men, whose views reach my ears in a steady drumbeat now, whispering that this time, Daly will go too far, and will seek to influence the legislators with illicit offers. These will take all sorts of shapes and forms. It might be cash. It might be a financial partnership. It might be a sudden opportunity to purchase land, enlarge the ranch. It might be a contract to buy all of a man's cattle or produce or lumber. Boodle, Mr. Hall, comes in all shapes and conditions, and you spot it by noting a legislator's sudden prosperity. Is the man in the worn suit now sporting a new one? Is the fellow with a small farm now tripling his acres on the county tax rolls?"

"Boodling can't go undetected, Mr. Clark. It is always found out by an alert press."

"Ah, now you have the general idea, Hall. There will be an invisible link between every burst of prosperity one discovers among legislators and the bottomless pockets of Marcus Daly's company. Your task, sir, is to focus a ruthless eye on this crime against the commonwealth of Montana, to trace the threads back to their source, which will be the Anaconda offices of Marcus Daly. And when you have the evidence, you will shout it from the rooftops. Do you know what I mean? The headline, the front page, sir. The *Mineral* will devote itself to exposing every misdeed and foul bribe flowing out of Marcus Daly's pockets."

"I have it exactly, sir."

"See to it. Say little about me, other than that I remain on the sidelines, willing to serve if asked, but otherwise busy with my operations. If those truly loyal to the party want a true loyalist, they know where to find me. I won't be in any rush to travel to Helena when the session opens. I'll simply stay here, avoiding the circus, my reputation untarnished and without the slightest blemish. Got that?"

"Got it, Mr. Clark."

"Well, good, finish your drink then. I'm going home."

Hall looked amused, just as Clark supposed he would.

{ THIRTY }

J. Fellowes Hall was having the time of his life. Who would have thought it? The 1899 legislature was vaudeville. Never in all his career had news been so amusing and bizarre and ludicrous. And never in all his years as an editor and senior editorialist had Hall engaged in more buncombe, more hokum, more yowling and howling. He had become the most avid bunco steerer in the state. He surpassed every confidence man operating out of every saloon. The *Mineral* was not simply sensational; it was the most unreliable and mendacious in the nation, daily printing a sober-sounding account of what wasn't happening in Helena, while exaggerating or twisting what was happening. And of course the paper's finger wagged only one direction—straight toward Marcus Daly.

Hall didn't know it would be so rich. The legislature met in dark January, divided several ways. The Republicans were the minority, and divided between the silver and gold factions. The Democrats had a large majority, divided between Daly and Clark forces. And then there were the Populists, leaning toward the Democrats, but not anchored anywhere. The task was to elect a United States senator to replace Lee Mantle, whose term was expiring. The law required the legislature to meet and vote daily until a senator was elected and sent packing off to Washington. Each day's ballot differed from the previous ones. Favorite sons garnered courtesy votes and sank away. Coalitions bloomed and faded. The reluctant candidate William Andrews Clark ran nearly last, but gained a little ground week by week. He kept his silence. It served him to be the wallflower this time. The legislators met officially in session, and in hotel saloons, and behind doors, and in caucuses, and in the black of the night, and nothing much changed except that Helena was fattening from the sale of food and drink and hotel rooms and loyalties.

January faded into bleak, dark February without much progress, and it looked as though the state might once again fail to elect someone to send to Washington. The Republicans blamed the Democrats, and the Democrats blamed each other and the Republicans, and the Populists played hard to get and professed their virginity. And in the midst of the clamor, there were whispers of wealth changing hands, boodlers handing out stuffed envelopes, thousand-dollar Grover Cleveland bills being pocketed. There were rumors of mortgages being paid off, new business partners, farms with vast new additions, silent partners, fancier homes, fattening bank accounts. But still the diehards didn't budge, and the voting scarcely advanced in any direction.

Of course the editor of the *Mineral* had a fine explanation for all this: the company—no other name was necessary—was playing its own powerful game. Marcus

Daly's minions, with satchels full of bills, were cutting deals everywhere. That's how Hall's paper saw it, at any rate. Marcus Daly was the spider, and he was spinning a web around the government of the state. As for the *Mineral*'s owner, he was sitting aside in quiet dignity, keeping his manicured hands clean, awaiting the solemn hour of his calling, if it came.

Daly's own editor, John Durston, was spinning other tales, and the *Anaconda Standard* was broadly hinting in cartoons and editorials that Clark was bribing the entire legislature. That was fine with Hall, who ridiculed his rivals in print. A good newspaper fight would only increase circulation. The entertaining thing about it was that Durston and his Anaconda paper were right: they had Clark pegged, and knew how to portray him. Their cartoons depicted Clark as an odious tycoon and swine, which pretty well fit. They had Clark pitching bundles of greenbacks through hotel transoms. Every issue of the *Standard* that hit the streets of Butte was a delight to Hall, and he drew inspiration from the rival paper. There was nothing good to be said about William Andrews Clark. That added a certain spice to his task. How best to defend and promote the indefensible? They should give him a journalism prize. It was like being a Confederate writing editorials for a Union paper during the recent war. That took skill and patience and a sense of the absurd. He was very good at it, and did not underestimate his skills.

Day after day, the tally in the state legislature teetered this way and that, and it was getting tiresome. Clark continued to obscure himself, an invisible wraith minding his business in Butte. But slowly, he accumulated votes until he had collected most of those in his party. But that wasn't enough. The Daly holdouts didn't budge, and it was beginning to look like this legislature wouldn't elect anyone before adjournment. But then things shifted once more, and a few Republicans began to show up in Clark's ménage, which seemed most unusual, given the insults and calumnies each party had visited upon the other. But there they were, a few Republicans who had seen the light, reached for the holy grail, and were about to elect William Andrews Clark to the Senate.

Until a Republican from Missoula cried foul, and waved an envelope with ten one-thousand-dollar bills in it. The envelope bore the initials w. a. c. on its flap. Fred Whiteside, the archfiend, also added that two of his Republican colleagues had been bribed.

Nothing could have delighted J. Fellowes Hall more. The whole show was idiotic. What boodler would put the evidence on the envelope? W. A. C.! Right there, in script, for cops and prosecutors to pick up! Proof of guilt. Except that it was a good joke. A Daly joke. Even the most stupid boodler in Helena would not put thousand-dollar bills into an envelope marked with anyone's initials on it, especially those of Clark. So Hall set to work, as he always did. Another Anaconda trick. Marcus Daly's machinations. Anaconda, the crookedest corporation in the state. This time, Hall had something he believed in. Not for an instant did he think Clark would pen his initials on a ten-thousand-dollar bribe of the sort that could put Clark in the Deer Lodge prison for a few years.

But the funny thing was, everyone else believed it. Here was the proof! Clark had corrupted everyone and everything in Helena. Legislative committees set to work. Prosecutors set to work. Witnesses were paraded. Lawyers pled. Editors ranted. The nation's press was titillated. Reformers insisted on the direct election of senators. But nothing came of it. The evidence was lacking, just as Hall knew it would be. It didn't matter that some legislators' bank accounts waxed fat, and property expanded, and new homes were purchased, and some got shares in new businesses, or sweetheart contracts. It might be that some legislator inherited something from his deceased aunt, and another legislator had won a startling jackpot at poker. No one could prove a thing. But that was only fodder for every cartoonist in the state, including those of Hall's, who busily laid it all on Marcus Daly. It didn't really matter who bribed whom. The reluctant candidate was going to Washington, on the tide of Democratic, Populist, and a few Republican votes.

But that wasn't the end of it. The Senate Committee on Privileges and Elections began hearings as to whether it should admit Senator Clark to full-term membership, and once again the lawyers declaimed, witnesses testified, accusations swirled this way and that, and the stench of Helena soon threatened to engulf the Senate of the United States. Marcus Daly, then fatally ill, was not a good witness while Clark, still vigorous, was impressive. But the evidence ran against him. When it became plain that Clark would not be accepted, in May of 1900, he withdrew his name from contention, saying he didn't want his honor besmirched. Clark would not remain a senator this time around. The whole debacle had played out on a national stage, keeping editorialists occupied coast to coast.

But it wasn't over. Even as Clark resigned, his pals were hard at work. In Helena, they concocted a scheme that would put Clark back in the Senate, this time as an appointee of the governor, who would be filling the vacant Senate seat. But Montana's governor Robert Smith was a Daly man, and had to be drawn out of state so the lieutenant governor, A. E. Spriggs, a Clark man, could make the appointment. Smith was enticed to California to examine a mining property for Miles Finlen, the Butte mining entrepreneur, to whom Smith owed some money that could be repaid by performing this expert service. No sooner was Governor Smith in California and incommunicado, being miles from any telegraph, than Spriggs hurried to the capital and announced that the people's choice for senator should be allowed to stand, and appointed Clark senator from Montana, which at least on the surface seemed a legal appointment. But Smith hurried back, revoked the appointment, and appointed Martin Maginnis Montana's next senator, while all the world howled. It would be up to the Senate to choose between Maginnis, whose appointment was legally valid, and Clark. In the end, it did nothing. The session ended without a decision, which in effect kept Clark out of the Senate.

J. Fellowes Hall sighed, sorry to see the vaudeville come to an end. It had all been so entertaining. It had filled his news columns for months, kept his cartoonists busy, sold papers, and stirred Butte as nothing else ever had. Clark complained publicly that he had been persecuted and besmirched, which Hall dutifully printed word for word, but it was over. Clark had lost the election and his reputation. The copper town slid back to quietness, which meant that Hall would have to draw his news from the police dockets again. He hardly knew what do put on his pages, now that the show was over.

The integrity of the state's entire government lay in ruins. The integrity of its legislators was wrecked. The editorial independence of nearly every paper in the state was compromised. Both Clark and Daly had bought any papers they could get their hands on, and attempted to influence those they couldn't buy, often by lending them money, or making political alliances with their publishers, or threatening them with a competing paper if they didn't toe the line. Indeed, wherever papers continued to oppose one man or another, competing sheets bloomed, financed obscurely, and devoted to polemics and stealing away advertising.

Now, with the turn of the century, things had slid back

to peacefulness. Some of those phantom papers vanished. The larger dailies continued sedately. Marcus Daly took the waters in Europe, hoping to prolong his failing life and health. Montana became the watchword for corruption, unbridled graft, and the domination of public affairs by powerful corporations, most plainly the Anaconda company.

How corrupt everyone was! J. Fellowes Hall marveled that a good newsman like John Durston could let himself become a mouthpiece for the Daly interests, without any compunction about his paper's independence. Rumor had it that Clark had simply paid the owners of the *Bozeman Chronicle* twenty-five-hundred dollars to switch their support to him for the duration of the election. Daly, on the other hand, had bought papers all over the state. And what of those editors? How easily they had been bought. What were their considered views beforehand, and what had they become when a little cash changed their minds? It amused him.

He was the best newsman in Montana, though Durston might give him a run for his money, and he had maintained the integrity of the *Mineral* through thick and thin. It never varied. It was a Clark paper. It opposed the octopus corporation gradually choking Montana. Yes, he had never wavered, the paper had never weaseled, the editorials had never shifted ground, and the paper's integrity was intact. Now that was an achievement in a state when almost no newspaper had gone unscathed by the money flowing into politics and elections. It was said that Clark had spent a million, and Daly had spent a couple hundred thousand, but not a nickel had flowed to the *Mineral*.

That knowledge intoxicated him. He was the only newsman left in Montana whose integrity and virtue were intact. He was true to the highest calling of his profession.

He was the survivor. His conscience was intact and unchallenged. Everywhere else, there were editors and publishers who could not look themselves in the mirror each morning. He thought he would celebrate with a dinner at the Chequamegon, or maybe an adventure a little father down the slope.

{ THIRTY-ONE }

There wasn't much time left. Marcus Daly knew that. The doctors had opinions, but no cures, and there was little to be done. He knew it when he arose in the morning, knew it all day long, knew it when he went to bed, knew it in church, in his dreams, at the dinner table, and when he shaved each morning, knew it when he eyed his daughters.

The real questions arose from his business. The company he and James Haggin had built over many years was suddenly under siege, and from two parties. The first was the abominable Fritz Heinze, whose staff of thirty lawyers, led by his brother Arthur, were attempting to steal the most lucrative mines in Butte, using apex litigation and bought judges. It was theft pure and simple. The courts would decide who owned what, and Heinze owned or influenced the sitting judges.

All his life Daly had avoided litigation as much as possible; he and his partners well knew that mining litigation enriched only the armies of lawyers that bled the profit from mining corporations. But now the Anaconda Company was under assault from every direction, flimsy lawsuits, frivolous lawsuits, absurd lawsuits, all designed to bleed the company white. They were rising from Fritz Heinze's army of buccaneers.

But there was worse trouble brewing, this time in the cozy warrens of East Coast capitalists who had suddenly discovered that the Anaconda Copper Mining Company was one of the richest prizes in the United States. There, a cabal of financiers was scheming to own Butte Hill by one means or another. They had first focused on the two mining and smelting companies operated by Boston's copper men, the Boston and Montana, and the Butte and Boston, but Heinze had tied them up with various lawsuits, mostly dealing with apex issues. So the financiers turned, instead, to the main prize, the Anaconda company. These were no ordinary Wall Street financiers. These were men whose own fortunes derived from Standard Oil, and indeed one of them was William Rockefeller, John's brother, and their colleague H. H. Rogers, a man as powerful as the Rockefellers themselves. It might not be Standard Oil that was eyeing the richest hill on earth, but it was the same cabal. And they were slowly, carefully, and furtively buying every share of Anaconda stock they could get, at any price, and were edging toward control of the company.

Daly and Haggin had watched it closely, and with a certain foreboding. For Haggin, in California, it might mean profit. But for Marcus Daly, it might mean loss of control of the company he had built from his initial purchase of the lackluster Anaconda mine, which he had turned into an incredible bonanza just by steering his miners toward the ore that lay in plain sight within.

Rockefeller and Rogers were not Irish. Anaconda was Irish. Its future executives would be Irish. Its hiring men and accounting men were Irish. Its miners were Irish. Its managers were Irish. Daly had made it so. He wanted the company to stay Irish. He wanted to limit the influence of others. He especially wanted to keep Rockefeller out. The brothers were not noted for their acceptance of the Irish, or for treating their employees gently. They were ruthless, and their vision didn't extend beyond making the fattest profit they could. They would not be good for Butte.

But Augustus Heinze would be worse. Already, his injunctions had thrown five hundred miners employed by the Boston companies out of work when the mines were forced to shut down. Heinze was simply a shark, devouring whatever he could eat.

The Rockefeller interests were buying shares of Butte mines and placing them in a giant trust, called Amalgamated Copper Company, capitalized in New Jersey at seventy-five million, with seven hundred fifty thousand shares outstanding at a hundred dollars each. Into this vast holding company would go every Butte mine and smelter that the financiers could snatch. Daly saw it all coming, saw the financiers move closer and closer to control, and knew that the days of his independence were numbered. If Standard Oil was created at just the right time to fuel horseless carriages and lamps, Anaconda had come at just the right time to wire the cities of America and bring electricity into every home and business. Both had ridden a sudden upswing of demand; both had glowing futures.

Daly thought about all that, talked to his friend James Ali Ben Haggin about it, and both knew the time had come to bend. For Haggin, there would be cash to invest in South American mining ventures. For Daly, control of the new company for as long as he lived; maybe time enough to keep it Irish. So they sold out. Haggin got fifteen million dollars. Daly got shares in the holding company in exchange for his Anaconda shares, and remained president and manager of the Butte company, while William G. Rockefeller became secretary-treasurer and Henry H. Rogers became vice president. Anaconda had been swallowed by one of the largest holding companies in the world. Anaconda was owned in New Jersey. The directors were Wall Street financiers, except for Daly. Suddenly, Easterners owned Butte, Montana. Swiftly the

holding company acquired the Boston mines and anything else it could snatch.

Marcus Daly knew he was merely a figurehead, but he
would use whatever power he had, for the rest of his days,
to protect his Irish associates and workers and their families, and to protect Butte. Even as he struggled, the holding
company shares skyrocketed and plummeted as specu-
lators bought and sold at huge profits. Daly's Anaconda
Company was buffeted month in and month out by rising
value, dropping value, collapsing value, regained value.
And each day Marcus Daly felt the worms crawling
through his body, eating life away.

And there were all those lawsuits in Montana's district
court, each intended to bleed some of the company's
wealth. Heinze had gone from brilliant mining genius
with the best eye for ore in the business to a buccaneer.
And nothing illustrated that better than his outrageous
Copper Trust.

Daly fumed every time he thought about it. Heinze's
brother Arthur had been going through the countless
claims that covered Butte Hill, looking for flaws in them
all, looking for anything the Heinzes could exploit. And
in the course of his close study, he found a tiny patch of
land, irregular in shape, squarely on top of the Anaconda
hill, bordering the company's great mines, including the
Anaconda and St. Lawrence. The total unclaimed area
was only nine one-thousandths of an acre, only a couple
hundred square feet, only the size of an average parlor in
an average home. But it was not claimed, and Augustus
Heinze claimed it, and named it the Copper Trust, with
his own brand of perverse humor. And then the Heinzes
filed apex suits against the greatest Anaconda mines,
proclaiming that all the surrounding veins surfaced, or
apexed, on his patch of land. It was so brazen, so ludicrous, so bizarre, it might have been dismissed—except
that Augustus Heinze owned one judge entirely, and

influenced another. And all of Daly's efforts to have the suits dismissed came to nothing. Heinze was a menace, not just to the company, but to Butte.

Daly had his trap brought around. There had been a day when he would have walked from his great Washoe smelter to the *Anaconda Standard,* but that day was gone now, and would not return. He threw a scarf around his throat and ventured out. The trotters were waiting for him, sleek and ready. His heart always lifted at the sight of his own fine horseflesh.

At the newspaper, he slid out, dropped a carriage weight, and entered the newspaper he had founded and built up from nothing. A gust of cold air swept in on his coattails. His old friend John Durston was in his lair, looking grayer now, but still lean and alert and keen-eyed. The man had stayed with him through everything.

Durston eyed his visitor with pleasure, and nodded toward a wooden swivel chair, and Daly settled gratefully into it. He couldn't stand up for long anymore.

"I've been reading what I can find about the Standard Oil Gang," Durston said. "I always like to know who owns me."

Durston laughed, but it was tentative.

"They own me, too," Daly said. "But I own a piece of them."

"I like the name Anaconda better than Amalgamated," Durston said. "Anaconda is poetry. Amalgamated sounds industrial."

"It's all consolidation," Daly said. "They consolidated a lot of small oil producers into Standard Oil. They're consolidating a lot of copper companies now. It's supposed to be for the good of everyone."

Durston smiled. "I'll know it when my paycheck improves."

"You've fought my battles, John. They may be wanting you to fight theirs. Not just now, but soon." He was referring to his demise, but wasn't sure the editor understood that.

"Scallon will replace you?"

"I've arranged it. There's some others, like Con Kelley and John Ryan ready. Scallon's doing my legal work against Heinze. He's ready. Are you?"

The surprise question baffled Durston.

The editor finally asked whether there would be a shift in viewpoint.

"You know the score better than I do," Daly said. "We don't think much of Heinze, and he's already paralyzing the city, throwing people out of work with his legal maneuvers."

"He's not an uplifting influence," Durston said.

They laughed at Durston's delicacy.

"Amalgamated may not be a good influence on the state," Daly said. "The company passes from local hands into East Coast capitalists—and with it, the state government."

Durston didn't say anything, and sat waiting.

"You'll have less independence, and probably less budget. The new board of the company sees the press differently; a mouthpiece, not a news gathering organization. Not that I am so different, but I've stayed out of your way mostly."

"We're a company paper, and I'm prepared for that," Durston said.

"You may not be when the time comes."

Durston stared into space. "I'm old enough to retire. We have a fine country place near Bozeman. There are lines I don't cross, and at the same time, I'll usually find ways to put my employers in the best light."

"They'll be saying that Montana's about to be owned by the Standard Oil Gang."

"I'll be saying that Heinze's ruining the court system of Montana and corrupting its government."

"They'll be saying the company's Irish and shouldn't be, and Montana should welcome others."

"I'll be saying the state already has and always will."

"Maybe you could talk about Heinze's thirty lawyers and pliant judges."

"I have libel laws to watch out for, Mr. Daly."

"They'll want to shrink your editorial staff, fire some of your cartoonists, spend less on syndicated material, hew the line. They might send a man into the newsroom to check a story in advance, or pull something, or hide something. They might want to keep the company's acquisitions secret, its profit and loss secret."

Durston settled back in his chair and gazed upward, not quite focused on his visitor. "I've been a loyal company man from the beginning, fought your wars, struggled with the whole sordid business of electing William Andrews Clark. I've been all that not because you told me what to do here, but what you didn't tell me to do. I've never been forced to violate the integrity of the *Standard,* or myself, and you've never cornered me with such demands."

Daly smiled. "I'd hire you all over. And when you retire I'll try to find a man to fill your shoes."

"There are several here, Marcus."

"I would need to do it soon, John."

The two stared at one another.

"Soon?" Durston asked.

"A few months, a year, maybe two."

"Then I am lucky to have you in the president's chair for as long as you wish to be there."

"We'll whip Heinze good and proper, John. He's overstepped, and soon he'll be wearing a ball and chain at Deer Lodge."

Daly rose, unsteadily, and Durston eyed him closely, perhaps only then registering what Daly knew about his health, and his future. Change was coming.

THIRTY-TWO

The consumptive Orangeman lived on, damn him. William Ward actually rallied, which annoyed Red Alice. Some color returned to gray flesh. He downed his gruel, and his throat didn't torment him as much. He lay abed, day after day, without the strength to stir. He barely made it to the stinking outhouse behind her cottage.

The children annoyed him and he annoyed them, and they all annoyed Alice Brophy, but there wasn't anything she could do about it, and besides, being annoyed by the Protestant in her bed was more interesting than not being annoyed. The con killed everyone, if miner's con, silicosis, didn't kill them first, but William Ward was making fate take a vacation.

She knew why he still lived. Some men, and he was one, were domestic. Men were supposed to be wild hares, barely able to endure the cottage and kitchen and a wife and children, but it wasn't true. Some men were just the opposite, wanting nothing more than a snug haven from the world, and a mate who might be a friend and lover. Ward was like that. Once he escaped the big boarding-house and got settled in a cottage, with rambling roses in front, his eyes grew less desperate, his breathing got better, the wheeze subsided, and he even slept through the nights instead of coughing himself to death. Singing Sean Brophy wasn't like that. Singing Sean could barely stand to be in the house; give him a saloon and other males, and he was in heaven. But not William Ward the heretic.

She hated it. She had counted on him croaking so she could get on with her life. She had pamphlets to pass out and a mission to fulfill. She intended to turn every working stiff in Butte into a Socialist, and get rid of the corporate system, get rid of it all, string up the rich capitalists at the nearest tree—which would be far away from Butte because arsenic smoke had killed them all. But weirdly, William Ward was still her income. She still took her sign to the mine headframes, asked for coins for a sick miner, still passed out tracts and collected her dimes, and still made enough to feed her family from it. That made her even madder. William Ward's sickness was her piggy bank.

If keeping an Orangeman alive wasn't bad enough, Augustus Heinze was worse. Red Alice couldn't master the whole of it, but it was all bad, and it peeved her. Heinze owned a good mine called the Rarus, which was next to some mines owned by the Boston and Montana Company, with all those rich Boston financiers behind them, and they were throwing lawsuits at each other, and claiming that the ore apexed on their own properties, and they were accusing each other of hauling ore out of the mines that didn't belong to them, and a lot more. Heinze's top men owned some shares in the Boston mines, and that enabled Heinze to file stockholder suits against the management, alleging this or that. It didn't matter what. The whole business was intended to throttle the other side, steal ore, and defeat mining in Butte. That was capitalism for you. Heinze was a courthouse miner. That's how he stole his ore. He had a judge named Clancy there who saw things his way, and never wavered in helping Heinze along. And the other judges helped too, and Heinze was becoming a fatter and fatter capitalist in the courtrooms, rather than by building up productive mines. And the more all these capitalists did this, the madder Red Alice got. This was what was supposed to be the way to make the world prosperous? Ha!

The only one she felt a little kindness toward was old Marcus Daly, who buried Singing Sean, and didn't like lawsuits. But she didn't excuse him, either. He starved his workers and raised Thoroughbreds. His racehorses were treated better than his miners. It was the system, rotten and greedy, that needed replacing, and she was trying hard to get people to do just that.

Then the day came when all the courtroom struggles spilled over into the streets. Heinze got an injunction shutting down the Boston and Montana mines until ownership of the ore could be settled, so the Boston-owned mines complied, and suddenly there were five hundred miners out of a job, and a lot more grocers and saloon keepers and clothiers and coal merchants feeling the sudden loss of income all over Butte. Red Alice hoped the whole rotten system would tumble down, but it didn't.

William Ward was amused. "You can't make over the world," he said from his bed.

"I'll make over you, if you don't shut up," she said.

"It's not the system. It's the bad law."

"The system made the bad law."

"Congress made it. Apex law doesn't exist anywhere else. In other countries, the boundaries of a mining claim are the limits. No one goes chasing a vein into the next mine—at least not legally. So they don't have all these lawsuits."

She seethed at that. "You can get up and leave," she said.

He stared, and slowly got to his feet, and clung to the edge of the bed, and then caved back into the bed.

"You will have to help me, madam," he said.

Stricken, she pushed him into the bed, not out of it, her eyes averted. "You wouldn't be sick in a Socialist world," she said.

"In a Socialist world everything is divided equally, the good and the bad. I'll be glad to share my consumption with you, with your children, with everyone. Everyone gets an equal share."

She glared at him, full of retorts, but he was coughing

again, and she whirled away. Equal share! She'd had more than an equal share of the bad. She'd be glad to share a few things with him, if he wanted.

He was eyeing her with fevered eyes. It had taken only one sharp exchange to set him back by weeks. He weakly tugged the worn blanket over him and turned away. What had been a fragile little companionship had withered in an instant, with abstract ideas tearing them asunder. She had her beliefs; he had his. They had ended up torn, and he was growing gray again, as if every bit of progress had fled him.

She was damned if she would apologize to him. He was just trying to make Socialism look foolish. He didn't like the capitalists any, but he wasn't sold on her views either. She edged up to him, and ran a hand along his shoulder, and squeezed. He coughed, and gazed upward at her, and almost as fast as the color drained from his gray face, it returned to him. He needed only a little love to live.

She was dependent on him. He was the source of the dimes and nickels she collected each day at the mines, at the gates of a different company each time. She hated that. Hated that William Ward had a wife far away, and children far away.

"You will see them someday, William," she said.

It took him a moment to catch her train of thought. "Not bloody likely," he wheezed.

But over the next days he got better again, and she began to think that he would be one of the few who stopped the consumption, who drove it back, who lived on.

She returned to the mines, choosing the Rarus the next day, wanting nickels from Heinze's lucky miners, who were busily at work in the pits. She carried her tin bucket and her hand-lettered sign and her sheaf of SLP pamphlets, and hiked up the well-worn trail to the mines east of Butte, and braved a bitter wind. She wondered how she would survive in midwinter, when subzero cold and whirling snow would engulf her. She would, somehow. She was Butte tough, and that meant she could weather anything.

As usual, men coming off shift eyed her sign, those who could read, and a few dug into their britches while their damp clothing steamed in the cold, and pitched pennies and dimes and a quarter or two into her little tin bucket, and gamely accepted her pamphlet. "Workers Arise!" That's what the headline read. Every few weeks she got a different batch in the mail. But this day her vision was suddenly darkened by two big men, each in a black bowler and a tight striped suit.

"Beat it," one said.

"I have a right to be here."

"You heard me," he said, and knocked her down, a giant shove of the shoulder that sent her sprawling. The metal bucket sprayed her few coins. She scrambled up, started collecting the coins, when the other goon flattened her, sent her sailing several feet. She hit the frozen ground hard. He yanked the bucket from her hand, stuffed the Socialist tracts in his pocket, and kicked her in the ribs. She howled. That toe shot pain clear up and down her chest, and into her hip and out her arm.

The first one laughed. "You got the lesson, sweetheart? No more. Not here, not anywhere, got it?"

"You big goons, you get out of here!" she yelled.

She got another toe in the rib, which hit so hard she felt pain shoot through her whole body. The ground was cold. Her chest hurt. The big galoots above her grinned. One tipped his derby, and they hiked away, carrying her money and her pamphlets and her tin bucket.

Several miners stopped, stared, and hurried away, not wanting to get into trouble.

"Chickenshit," she yelled at them.

Red Alice managed to get to her feet, felt her bruised

rib cage, and decided she could make it down the long dirt trail to Dublin Gulch. Every step tormented her.

She neared her little cottage in the gulch when she spotted Big Benny Brice, the flatfoot whose beat included the gulch.

"Benny, I just was robbed," she said, and told him the story.

"It's because of your politics. You're a Socialist," he said.

"Is that supposed to be bad?"

Benny sort of cackled. "Not for me it isn't."

"I'm going out tomorrow. Will you come along and protect me?"

He hesitated, eyed her, and nodded quietly. "I'll come along for a bit, Alice. Maybe I'll crack some heads."

He sounded worried, but game.

"I'll go to the St. Lawrence tomorrow," she said.

"I'll be there."

She limped into her cold house. The brats hadn't built a fire in the stove. William Ward eyed her, taking it all in. "I can guess," he said.

Now, at last, she sank into the ratty chair, exhausted.

She hurt all that night, but that wouldn't slow her any. She painted a new sign, found a glass jar for the coins, and scavenged a few older tracts she had salted away, and then she wrapped herself in her ancient cotton coat, and headed into the bleak dark dawn. The shift started at seven; in winter, in Butte, that was still dark. No one noticed her. She would be going to the heart of the Amalgamated mining complex this morning. She discovered Big Benny waiting for her, a fine figure of a man in his blue greatcoat and earflap hat, a nickelplate badge on his chest.

"Thanks, Benny," she said, and watched the miners drift by. They eyed her silently, and mostly slid by, wondering about the cop standing off a bit. But a few picked up her tracts and dropped coins into her jar, and she thought things would be all right.

But then the two goons in their derbies showed up, headed straight for her, their meaty fists clenched and ready. Big Benny beat them to her, clobbered one and sent him staggering, but the other slugged Benny in the groin, and Benny whoofed and folded, even as the pair of them unloaded on Benny. She saw one slide brass knuckles onto his fat fingers and start some serious work on Big Benny, who fought back impulsively and bravely, but was no match for two hooligans who knew exactly what they were doing. When Benny went down, they didn't quit. They kicked his ribs and kicked his face, even though Benny got a leg and yanked one down on top of him and let the hooligan have an elbow and a bite or two.

Red Alice screamed. This time miners rushed up, saw that the flatfoot was down, and pulled the hooligans off and held them at bay while Big Benny lumbered to his feet, weak and dizzy, and put his cap back on.

"I'm taking you in," he said.

But one of the hooligans slid a shiny little revolver from his breast pocket, and laughed. "Go tell the sergeant all about it, flatfoot," he said. "He'll sure be interested in your sad story." The other one worked free of the restraining miners, dropped his brass knuckles into his greatcoat, and retrieved his own little snub-nosed. The miners retreated. One of the goons snatched her jar and her sign and her pamphlets.

"Lady," he said, "next time you hand out this crappola, you won't be around to cry."

THIRTY-THREE

F. Augustus Heinze wondered whether Katarina would show up on a bitter day. But she did. She was attired in a wine-colored woolen coat with Persian lamb cuffs and lapel, and a muff to match. It paid to be fashionable when genuflecting before the money machine. He smiled. The lady knew exactly how to appreciate what she was about to see.

"You came after all," he said.

"Why shouldn't I, Augustus?" She always remembered to call him that. Everyone else in Butte called him Fritz, much to his annoyance. That was worth a smile, so he took her elbow and escorted her up the Anaconda hill, past shanties, along worn dirt trails used by the miners, past sheds and eventually past the headframes and mills and boilers surrounding the Anaconda company's greatest mines, the Anaconda itself, the St. Lawrence, the Neversweat, and various outlying ones including his own Rarus. Her attire was so out of place it shocked the eye in that grim world of iron, rough-sawn wood, silvery rails, brick chimneys, black iron, and humming hoists.

The day only improved the scenery. It was bright and cold and not a cloud troubled the sky. It was also numbing cold, mitigated only by a lack of wind. But on any hill crest, such as this one, cold air moved constantly, no matter whether the air gusted through the works.

"I'll be the first lady to see the Copper Trust?" she asked.

He smiled. "I don't know of any ladies in my life. I'm taking you to show you how rich I am; it will inspire your gold digging."

"I'll clean you out of it," she said.

He laughed. If anyone was exploiting anyone, he was working her for all she was worth, which was plenty.

He threaded through the factory jumble atop the hill, and finally stopped at an odd patch of barren clay, marked by raw wood stakes in no particular pattern.

"The Copper Trust," he said, with a gentle wave of his kidskin gloved hand.

She stared, not quite grasping it. He intended that she shouldn't grasp it. The total surface of the Copper Trust came to nine one-thousandths of one acre.

"It comes to a couple hundred square feet or so," he said. "Welcome to my parlor."

"It's too small for my taste. I'd want a larger parlor," she said, eyeing the odd collection of surveyor's stakes.

"My brother, Arthur, and one of my engineers located it," he said. "Unclaimed land atop the richest hill on earth. So we claimed it. I own it. The Montana Ore Purchasing Company has it."

"What's that?" she asked, eyeing a small hole where someone had shoveled away the thin clay topsoil down to the bedrock a couple of feet below.

"That's where all the veins of these mines apex, and that's what permits us to follow the veins wherever they may go, straight into all these great mines. That hole is the Pearly Gate. The ore is ours, not theirs, according to mining law. And we shall have it, and have payment for all they've stolen from us for years."

"Your brother found this?"

"Arthur, yes. Lines get drawn, boundaries are defined, and sometimes not every corner or piece is accounted for. I have a very gifted brother, a man with a sharp eye, a man who reads deeds and descriptions with a magnifying glass."

She yawned. "We're done now?"

"Ah, Katarina, how little your imagination is achieving at the moment. Inflate your brain to the size of your beautiful bosom. We are standing on the greatest bonanza in the history of mining. We are standing on wealth that dwarfs anything the world has seen. This little hole is the doorway to heaven. It requires reverence, a bowed head. You need to stand before that hole and receive a wafer on your tongue."

"I think you're daffy. It's too cold to make jokes."

He sighed. "I see through rock. I see ore radiating from right here, rich veins of copper, spreading into those mines over there, ore they are eating up each day. See how busy they are, steam hissing from their boilers, cages running up from the pits, with my ore loaded onto them."

"Let's go. I'm not buying it. You don't even have enough land here to sink a shaft or put up a works."

"No need. All the law requires is proof that the vein apexes here. That hole will do nicely. Two feet down, solid rock and copper ore, and I have discovered the apex of all those veins in the Anaconda and Neversweat. It's like finding the navel of the universe."

"You're a dope, Fritz Heinze."

He laughed, and escorted her away from that brown hilltop. "My attorneys are preparing the cases; we'll file soon. The newspapers will howl. The moguls will gnash their teeth. The opposing lawyers will yowl and whine and rage. The politicians will cluck. The financiers will recognize a new player. And in a while, we'll shut down the whole hillside. Anaconda's miners will be out in the streets. They'll put heat on Daly and Scallon and their new owners, Rockefeller and Rogers. I've never had so much fun."

He steered her along the clay trail, past cesspools, past yellowish water that smelled of urine, past rusty rails, with loose ore lying everywhere it had fallen.

"Why did you show me this?" she asked.

"Gold digger, meet copper digger," he said. "No, it's

better than that. I'm a courthouse miner. That's what they call people like me."

"I'm a bedroom miner," she said, "and I'll own all of you. You're my slave."

"You're also a witness. You saw the claim. You saw the shaft and the vein in its bottom. Just in case Anaconda has notions of pulling up the stakes, filling the hole, and posting armed guards, I can always call on you," he said.

That amused her. "If William Rockefeller pays well, why would I stick with you?"

"I make ladies happy," he said.

He walked her to her flat, kissed her on the cheek, and headed for the Silver Bow Club, where his brother would update him on the lawsuits. Arthur was a genius. He could find a good lawsuit in anything. It was Arthur who advised that his subalterns purchase shares in all neighboring mines, which opened the door to all sorts of stockholder lawsuits that Augustus found valuable and amusing. He was clogging the district court with them.

Arthur was waiting for him at the brass rail. "Here's to our success," he said. "I filed about an hour ago. It'll probably be assigned to our friend Clancy."

"Oh, my, Vesuvius will soon erupt."

"I suggest you preempt it. A little story in the press. You are about to stop the Amalgamated Copper Company's massive theft."

Fritz Heinze smiled. "We'll give it to the *Mineral*. Hall's a pompous ass, but he'll fill his paper with it if we approach him."

Arthur sighed. "Sometimes, Augustus, you disappoint me."

Heinze grinned. He loved to cross swords with his wily brother, who was just as responsible for the Heinze fortune as Fritz was. He simply cocked an eyebrow. This would be Arthur's show.

"You need a paper of your own," Arthur said. "And I just happen to have one."

"Why should I need a paper? The less I'm visible, the better I like it."

"Some battles are fought in public, and elections are among them, and this state elects its judges. Issues before the legislature are another, and both Amalgamated and Clark have ways of making their views and agendas loud and clear. That's why they win."

"I can spend my money better on other things," Augustus said. "Papers are rat holes."

"Follow me," Arthur said.

F. Augustus Heinze downed his whiskey, wrapped himself in his greatcoat and silk scarf and kid gloves and flap-eared hat, and plunged into an icy late-winter night. His brother seemed to know just where he was going, and turned in to a gloomy Irish pub, and headed straight toward a massive, shaggy, ill-kempt, red-nosed, watery-eyed boozer who was scowling at the world.

"You, is it?" the man growled. "This better be good. I don't come cheap, pastyface."

"Augustus, meet Mr. Pat O'Farrell, a printer and founder of great enterprises."

"My enterprise is foundering all right. I can't sell enough ads to keep a flea in food," he said.

"Mr. O'Farrell has founded a weekly paper he calls the *Butte Reveille,* but it is overmatched by the big dailies and resting stillborn in his bosom."

Augustus Heinze was not impressed. The man was a drunk. He lurked here in this sleazy dark saloon downing ales and muttering to himself and any fool who'd listen.

"Mr. O'Farrell is a phenomenon," Arthur continued sedately. "He needs four ales, or at least two shots of Irish, to reach manhood. Anything short of that, he's a beaten-down dray."

"I'll buy the man some Jameson's and we'll see," Augustus said. He signaled the beefy barkeep. "Pour the man the best Irish whiskey in the house."

"You'll be paying in advance," the keep said, narrowly. "I don't know you."

Heinze laid a greenback on the bar, which the bartender scrutinized carefully, and reached for his prized bottle. He poured an exact, measured ounce in a shot glass, and handed it to O'Farrell, who sighed, downed it in a swallow or two, and smiled. Heinze nodded, and the keep poured another, and O'Farrell sipped that one at a leisurely clip.

"It takes a minute or two to catch hold," Arthur said. "And then he lights up."

It did take a minute. O'Farrell inflated. He sat taller. He stuck his chest forward. He eyed his drinking partners with a steely gaze. "The *Reveille*'s for sale," he said. "Fifty dollars a week will give you the loudest and most sublime and elevated and noble voice in this loathsome city."

"Can you spell?" Heinze asked.

"Infallibly, when I am writing papal bulls and royal edicts. More fallibly with names."

"Why should I pay you fifty dollars a week? For what?"

"I am a rottweiler, a terrier by profession, sir. I am a hangman by vocation."

"Who would you hang, and what would you hound?"

"The Anaconda company, now in the hands of the Amalgamated Copper Company, an infernal holding company, operated by nefarious pirates and vomiting dogs."

Augustus turned to Arthur. "Did you prime him?"

"Nope, this is his natural and infernal nature."

"And what do you think of me? Of the Montana Ore Purchasing Company, Mr. O'Farrell?"

"It was fashioned by saints, sir. It arrived to free us from the tyranny of bankers and rich crooks and scoundrels. It arrived to keep the richest hill on earth from falling into the hands of a single greedy cabal, men who intend to suck the lifeblood from our fair city."

"Have you samples of your elegant and noble prose for me to examine?"

"Ah, sir, I have yet to publish, but I will make an arrangement with you. Finance me for two or three issues, and weigh the evidence, and if I don't fill your needs and expectations, we'll part company in peace and fellowship."

"Pour another Jameson," Fritz said to the keep. "The tab's on me."

They toasted the arrangement, and toasted it a few more times.

"Now, O'Farrell, I have just filed suit to stop the Anaconda Company from stealing any more of my copper and silver ore. Those rich veins apex on my property, the Copper Trust, right there on Anaconda Hill, and I intend to pursue the latter under the mining law of the land, and stop the theft, and win royalties for every ounce of ore that has been stolen from me."

O'Farrell licked his lips. "I'll drink to that," he said.

The next afternoon, the first copy of the *Butte Reveille* hit the streets and was instantly bought out. O'Farrell had poured it on: "Lawsuit Stops Plunder," the headline read. It went downhill from there. "At long last, the corrupt financiers and malefactors of wealth, in their whited sepulchers of the East Coast, will be brought to their knees by a new suit in Montana District Court alleging that these culprits have engaged in stealthy theft of such proportion as the world has never before witnessed," it said.

Augustus found it entertaining. O'Farrell was a genius of invective, and needed only a few facts to turn an event into a morality play. Augustus read O'Farrell's thunderous story with something like awe. Never had he seen words strung together in such biting cadences, such vast disdain, such eloquent indignation. The man might need a little guidance now and then, but Augustus Heinze now had his own rotten little tabloid, which would perfectly obfuscate his real designs, and make him all the more beloved among the ordinary people in town. He wished he had thought of it earlier, and was pleased that Arthur had seen the need. Butte had a new rag.

{ THIRTY-FOUR }

Marcus Daly died a few days after the November election of 1900. When William Andrews Clark read it, he had his servants bring him several hot water bottles to allay the chill spreading through him. He knew he ought to rejoice, but couldn't. The Senate seat was awaiting him now.

But he felt a chill, and set the hot water bottles about his person, tucked between the chair and his robe. The chill did not go away, but seemed to drain him of bodily comfort. Maybe that was Daly's last jest. There was no aesthetic pleasure to be found in a rubber bladder.

The man had been ill for some while, certainly ever since he collapsed while putting together the sale to Amalgamated. And after that, the man had declined steadily. Bright's disease, it was said, along with heart trouble. Daly had gone with his physician to one of the great spas of Europe, Carlsbad, to take the mineral water, but hadn't gained from it. By the time he got to New York and took rooms at the Netherlands Hotel, it was plain that he could not manage the trip back to Butte. And there he lay, life ebbing, his own staff tightly silent about Clark's huge victory at the polls. He and Heinze and the Populists had shattered the old man's grip on Montana.

Clark rang for the servants. The bottles were cooling

much too fast, and he wanted them refilled, hotter. His imported London manservant and two Liverpool maids scurried to work. Clark had them build up the fire in the parlor stove as well. It was late November, not yet bitter, but much too cold for Clark.

He said nothing to Hall; he knew exactly what the editor would do. A bare-bones report of Daly's death, a modest eulogy, and a lot of silence. Let Daly's *Anaconda Standard* fill its pages with Daly's squalid life and death. The *Mineral* would be decently quiet.

The refreshed hot water bottles arrived, and Clark tucked them in, but they didn't allay the cold crawling through him. He told himself he should rejoice: nothing stood between him and the United States Senate. Rogers, Rockefeller, and the Standard Oil Gang didn't care one way or another, and probably thought Clark could be useful. A fellow capitalist and mining magnate might be an asset in Washington. The company's new president, William Scallon, wouldn't care either. It had been Marcus Daly's private war, and now Daly was dead.

For some reason, Clark didn't rejoice. What passed through his mind was some aphorism he had heard somewhere: the death of anyone diminishes us all. The death of his enemy, the man who had frustrated, angered, insulted, and embarrassed him, only diminished everyone. It made no sense to Clark, but he was not used to thinking about lofty matters. The accounting ledgers were his home.

For the next days Clark lived in his own parlor, barely seeing anyone. It was almost as if he were grieving, though of course he was not. The Daly funeral finally took place in New York, at Saint Patrick's Cathedral, attended by three thousand, with Montana's and New York's bishops presiding. There were similar masses in the great churches of Montana. There were eulogies that annoyed Clark. There were tributes and toasts and remembrances that set

Clark's teeth on edge. Everything Daly had done to make Clark's life miserable had been forgotten.

Except by William Andrews Clark. This 1900 campaign had gone better than the one in 1898 but it was more complicated. The unions were stirring. The Populists were fading. The Amalgamated Copper Company was a Wall Street shark worrying a lot of people. Clark had allied himself with the ever-entertaining Fritz Heinze, and between them they defeated Amalgamated without great difficulty.

It was said that Henry Rogers and the Standard Oil Gang had set up a war chest of a million and a half dollars, worried that Clark would carry an anti-Amalgamated government into office. That and two pro-Heinze judges in the Butte district court that oversaw the mining suits were ample to make the East Coast moneymen nervous. But Daly was listless, and not even present during the latter part of the campaign, off in Europe. And his lieutenants lacked the forcefulness of Daly. The one question mark was the unions, which had always been in Daly's camp. But now the working people were uneasy about the Standard Oil Gang, and its expanding presence on the Butte Hill. Heinze exploited that, even bringing in vaudeville acts to draw crowds. The whole thing had cost Clark a bale of hundreds and five hundreds. There were still votes to be bought, papers to be influenced, and legislators to be pocketed. But by the time the election rolled around, the Clark and Heinze forces were unbeatable, and so it had proven to be. He'd won. He'd whipped Daly. He'd whipped all the money that Wall Street could toss at Montana. He and Fritz now enjoyed the esteem of two of the three district court judges that heard Butte's mining suits, Edward Harney and William Clancy; both the city and county government; and they had a solid command of Montana's government, too. Won. The trust spreading its octopus arms into Montana was whipped.

And then Daly had died. Some said he died upon hearing the bad news. The gossip was that those surrounding him at his deathbed in the hotel never spoke a word about the election. But maybe that was all the news that Daly needed to die in defeat. It was an odd thing: in the space of a year, the Anaconda Copper Mining Company had been swallowed whole, and Marcus Daly was gone. Clark shifted the hot water bottles around, trying to get some last heat out of them, but they were listless lukewarm bladders now. Nothing was a comfort anymore.

So, Washington it would be. That wasn't a comfort either. He'd be stuck there for six years. He couldn't imagine spending much time in that damp and sticky city, listening to the drone of bores, attending dreary banquets, shaking the limp hands of limp ambassadors, changing sweaty clothes three or four times a day. He wondered suddenly why he had campaigned so hard, spent so many months of profit to capture that seat. Now that Daly was dead, the seat didn't matter. The awful truth hit him hard: he had run to oppose Daly, and now that Daly had perished, there was nothing to his victory except a title. He would be called Senator, and that was all he would get out of all those dollars.

He arose, leaving a welter of water bladders behind him. There was still the legislative session ahead, in January, and he would prepare to buy his way through that if need be. He wondered whether to bother. His mind had focused on the United Verde mine down in Arizona, and its rich promise. He was building a model workers town, improving his reduction works, finishing a railroad between the smelter and mine, and he was exploring other mining properties. He thought about more trips to Europe, buying art in Paris, sampling fine French wines, building a home or two elsewhere. Butte annoyed him. With Daly dead, what reason was there for him to stay on in the cold, mean, smoky, arsenic-laden iceberg of a city?

After he had groomed himself for the day, taking great pains with his wiry beard to properly conceal his thin mouth, he retreated to his bank offices and dispatched a note to Anaconda's new president and manager, William Scallon. Clark barely knew him, but did know that Scallon was a gentlemanly Canadian lawyer who'd fought the company's legal battles. A quiet man, it was said; a man who listened and weighed all he heard. A perfect lunch companion. So Clark invited Scallon to a little lunch in a private parlor at the Silver Bow Club. It was time for some quiet talk, far from the ravenous ears of the mob.

Scallon arrived at the club promptly, almost as if he was responding to a command performance for a king, which was not far from the reality of the moment. Clark was king of all he surveyed, the ruler of Butte, Montana. But Scallon wasn't exactly kowtowing, either. Behind him were the most powerful financial men in the nation, men who could make or break companies, states, and even pocket-sized nations.

"A victory celebration," Scallon said, settling into the plush wing chair opposite Clark. The lunch would come later, after a fireside chat.

"Oh, yes, a perfect triumph," Clark said. "I'll sail right in when the legislature meets. But of course there might be opposition . . ."

Scallon declined a drink, and settled into his armchair, patiently. "Perhaps you are wanting some idea of our intentions," he said.

"Well, I was wondering whether Mr. Daly's interests spread through your company, and continue even now."

"Yes, there are some," Scallon said. "Mr. Daly was much loved, and his interests lie in the hearts and souls of those who served him."

"Yes, he commanded great loyalty," Clark said, and let it go at that.

"You want to know something of our intentions, and I

don't mind telling you," Scallon said. "Will we attempt to impede your ascent to the Senate?" he asked. "No, it doesn't really matter. Neither will we agitate against you when you are seated. Why bother? We have other things on our mind. Fritz Heinze's various lawsuits hang over us like a guillotine blade. His friendly judges are fully capable of doing grave damage not only to Anaconda Copper Company, but its parent. There are many millions at stake, and also the company's effort to consolidate all the holdings in Butte, to create an efficient, prosperous producer not plagued by a swarm of lawsuits. That, Mr. Clark, is what absorbs us. Fritz Heinze absorbs us. His various lawsuits, shareholder suits, apex suits, ownership suits, intended to enrich himself and weaken or destroy us—that's what's on the mind of William Rockefeller, and I should say, myself."

"That's capital, capital," said Clark. "Shall we dine? I have oysters on the half shell, expressed in on ice, and a few other little treats."

Indeed, the Silver Bow Club outdid itself. There were Limoges tureens of soup, delicate filets of beef, candied yams, all in such abundance that the two men could barely taste each serving. They devoted themselves to exclamations, and small talk, while Clark evaluated what he had just heard. Scallon was known to be true to his word. There would be no impediments this time. Amalgamated would not pour Rockefeller boodle into defeating him when the legislature voted; Amalgamated would not take its grievances to the United States Senate and buttonhole senators about ethics, the thing that so embarrassed him the previous round.

Scallon declined a cigar afterward, which pleased Clark. Cigars were noisome, but seemed to be a fixture of dining at the Silver Bow. Port and cigars never quite appealed to him.

"You know, Mr. Scallon—may I call you William? You know, I have nothing against consolidation. It's rational business."

Scallon raised an eyebrow. "You and Fritz Heinze certainly voiced another viewpoint during the election campaign. Rather vigorously, I must say. In fact, in rather black-and-white language."

"Oh, that. That's when Marcus Daly governed Anaconda. His appetite for expanding the company simply knew no bounds. It had a, shall we say, negative impact on the honest yeomen farmers and independent businessmen, and politicians of our fine state. But that was then, and this is now, and we are looking into the future."

"So you have no objection? You don't believe the company is bad for Montana?"

"Well, I think Fritz Heinze always exaggerated. It doesn't bother me. In fact, I could easily side with you on various issues. I'm also committed to Arizona, where my operations are several times larger than here. No, William, I have no difficulties. I think there might be some advantage to a state government dedicated to keeping its mining operations profitable. And in the hands of experienced men."

"I knew this lunch would be a delight, Senator," Scallon said.

"It's just common sense," Clark said. "Make it all work. Consolidate. Give a firm a continuous supply of good ore for its reduction works, give it freedom from frivolous lawsuits, give it a retailing operation, offering the world wire and brass and finished copper. Give it stability. Give it a steady and economical supply of labor. Give it a good reputation among moneymen in the East. Oh, it makes a lot of sense, sir, and it's the way to go."

Scallon stared. "I think I'll have a drink after all," he said.

In moments, a steward brought two glasses of bourbon over ice.

"Cheers," Scallon said.

"Cheers and success," Clark replied, and they sipped.

{ THIRTY-FIVE }

Watermelon Jones brought word from the bank, as Clark's offices and headquarters came to be known. J. Fellowes Hall tipped the fellow a nickle, and opened up the sealed envelope. It was in Clark's hand, but unsigned.

"Lay off Amalgamated," it said. Nothing more.

Hall studied it, vainly seeking a clue. But there was nothing to explain the directive. Hall headed into the composing room, looking for proofs of pages going into the afternoon edition. There was a front-page cartoon, in which Amalgamated was depicted as a giant octopus with its tentacles wrapped around a virginal lady with a sash labeled MONTANA. It actually was a revised version of an older cartoon in which Anaconda was the octopus, and resembled other cartoons depicting Marcus Daly as a harness-racing driver running over a prostrate lady labeled MONTANA.

Lay off. Well, all right, Hall would lay off. He instructed the compositor to yank the cartoon and fill the hole with something else. He studied the headlines of the stories in the galley trays, and found another about Anaconda's slavish papers across the state, and the coordinated propaganda issuing from them. He was tempted to let that stand, but decided to kill the story—for now. He needed to know what Clark was thinking before he made any decisions on his own.

What an odd thing. Ever since he came to Butte, he had kept the Anaconda Copper Mining Company in his gunsights. Daly's vast, swaggering, domineering company must not be allowed to capture Montana. The capital of the new state should never be the captive of Marcus Daly and his minions. The vast combine of copper mines, timber companies, rail and haulage companies, utilities, and allied stores posed a threat to every other business, every farm and ranch, every shopkeeper, every toiler and workingman in the state. He had published every detail of the company's grope and grasp, every earnings report. He knew the company better than he knew Clark's. He could write anti-Anaconda editorials in his sleep. He could commission new cartoons and remember a hundred old ones. His pay and his job depended on keeping the transgressions of the company, and Daly, and now Amalgamated, before the public.

Until this moment.

It puzzled him. He didn't even know whether to keep the change a secret. Neither did he know whether this was temporary, and he'd be back at his old stand soon enough. For the time being, he would talk to no one. Fritz Heinze was sometimes a good source; maybe he would find out what he could.

And then it struck him that Clark had yet to be elected a senator, and might wish to keep the opposition subdued until the legislators put him in office. Yes, surely that was it. The old man didn't want to stir up the hornets this time. Lay off the company. That made sense. Sometime after the first of the year, William Andrews Clark would become Senator Clark, and the wraps would be off.

But that didn't make sense either.

In truth, Hall couldn't fathom what was happening or why. He headed for the ancient desk where Grabbit Wolf was scribbling, his sharp pencil occasionally scrawling cursive letters into foolscap. Wolf had been his right-hand man, his assassin, his hatchet man, all these years. Wolf had been the bulldog who sunk his canines into Anaconda. Wolf had been the one who turned a routine earnings report into something sinister. Wolf had been the only reporter in Butte to ferret out Marcus Daly's expansion plans, and expose them. The man was a genius.

"What do you make of this?" Hall asked, dropping Clark's note before the reporter.

"Clark's sold out," Grabbit said.

"I doubt it."

"Of course he did. He's a rich man, and he's got the same worries as Amalgamated."

"But they're business rivals."

"Daly's dead. As long as Daly lived, Clark would be on the opposite side. Now there's no need."

"But what about Heinze? They're tied together."

"Clark has just kissed him off." Wolf was relishing the idea.

"That's unthinkable."

"Heinze's no use to Clark anymore. The election's over. Amalgamated lost."

"Clark wouldn't do that."

"Clark doesn't give a damn. He's going to be an absentee senator. He'll live in New York, show up in the Senate now and then mostly for show, and devote himself to running the United Verde in Arizona, between trips to Paris."

Hall had the distinct feeling that Grabbit was right. "What are you working on?" he asked.

"Amalgamated insider trading. Rogers and Rockefeller bought a lot of Amalgamated stock, driving up prices, sold it off suddenly dropping prices, and now they're buying up shares again at bargain prices."

"I'm not supposed to run that stuff."

Grabbit was grinning at him.

"But I will," Hall said. "When'll you have it?"

"For tomorrow."

"It'll be on the front page."

That's how Hall crossed the Rubicon.

He couldn't help but feel the world was shifting beneath his feet, chasms were opening, ready to swallow him whole. He thought he knew Clark, but now he was less sure of it. Did the man have any purpose in life other than to oppose Marcus Daly? And with Daly gone, where was Clark heading?

Hall abandoned the newsroom, climbed into his great-coat, scarf, gloves, and flap-eared hat, which he hated but nothing else was practical in Butte's cold months, and braved the sulphurous air affronting him every step of the way to the Chequamegon. He wanted a drink among fashionable people; mining engineers, capitalists, shift bosses, society. He resisted an impulse to crawl into a dark corner of McGinty's and drink himself into oblivion. But drink he would do, whether in a classy joint or a hole.

He ordered double bourbon on the rocks, and settled into a lonely corner. He didn't want company. He wanted to taste and rub a terrible thought that had been creeping into his head. Was he a journalistic whore or not? He had been a Republican back East, proud of it, before he became a Clark Democrat in Butte. But he switched parties, and lambasted the Republicans of Montana, telling himself they were not the same as the ones he had known. He had enthusiastically fought Daly's efforts to move the Montana capital to Anaconda. He had fought the Anaconda company, now Amalgamated, because it threatened to own Montana, dictate state policy, decide state laws, and operate the state as a fiefdom. But now his employer was telling him to lay off; the burgeoning company was just fine. Hall could readily obey, but what would that make him? What of his principles? What, at least, of his beliefs? Was he ready to trade them in for another set? Was tomorrow's paper going to tacitly disown everything in yesterday's paper? And what did that make of J. Fellowes Hall?

He could not answer that conundrum, so he sipped his bourbon and watched the rest of the people chatter and laugh through the dinner hour, untroubled by who owned their souls. Most of them worked for a copper company and remained loyal to it. What difference did it make to a mining engineer? Hall peered about, seeing people whose main preoccupation was money; the more the better.

He envied John Durston, over in Anaconda, faithfully advocating whatever Marcus Daly advocated, and faithfully laying out Anaconda's case on every issue, and faithfully pummeling Daly's opponents. Durston had never had to switch since coming to Butte, though Durston, too, had started as a Republican and a progressive before heading West. But even now, Durston's paper was faithfully carrying water for its new masters, the Standard Oil Gang, and it didn't seem to bother Durston any that these financiers were among the most ruthless ever seen.

But Durston didn't work for a man like Clark, whose views and politics were whatever suited him at the moment. Hall suddenly loathed Clark, the dapper little man who hid his pursed lips behind a wall of shrubbery, so one could never quite see Clark himself, but only a lot of wiry hair that even seemed to hide his eyes from view.

Hall sipped the last of his double, and ordered another. He had large decisions to make, and these decisions needed lubrication. Some people he knew eyed him tentatively, but Hall glared at them until they retreated. He would not advertise for company this night; he would deal abruptly with anyone who tried to join him.

He eyed the throng sourly. The Chequamegon was usually crowded. He was the one who didn't fit. The rest sold themselves for money or acceptance or high status. But he was a newsman, and a good one, at least he used to be before the devil bought his soul. Newsmen were different.

Newsmen tried to be the conscience of their communities. It didn't always work that way, but it was present, lurking inside of Hall's mind like a headmaster's ruler.

Was he a newsman or not? Were his opinions convenient to the day, or were they grounded in something larger? Was he the rottweiler of his master, or was he something more?

He sipped and knew that the truth was complex. He had ideals and he had betrayed his ideals. He had tried to be loyal to Clark, and now it was Clark being disloyal. He had come to Butte in a fit of vanity, and his own vanity had betrayed him.

He didn't excuse himself. He thought of his abandoned Amber and children, still back East, where he had kept them far from sight with a monthly check. He thought of his own bleak secrets. Who was he to rebuke Clark's slippery ethics? What of his own?

He sipped steadily, but felt absolutely no effect from all that whiskey. His mind was awhirl, and no mere alcohol could slow it down. If anything, he was more alert than he could ever remember, full of loathing not just of himself, but of Butte, and Clark, and Heinze, and every newspaper in town, and every floozy he'd ever dallied with. Butte was rotten; no, he was rotten and every one of those greedy mining moguls was rotten, twisting every ethic they could turn into a pretzel.

He drank steadily but got no further along toward oblivion, and finally quit. He wasn't hungry. He went to his flat, prepared himself for a sleepless night, and fell into a dreamless night. He awakened knowing his life would change, though he couldn't say how. He was tired of being a mouthpiece, ever-shifting, for whoever paid his wage. It was a bitter day, so he bundled well and walked to work, his breath steaming.

Grabbit's story rested in a galley tray, set and ready to be nestled into a page. Hall read it closely. It was all about the way the financiers had milked other stockholders of Amalgamated for all they were worth, driving the stock up, collapsing it, and buying back in at lower prices. These were the games played by the big boys, the Standard Oil Gang, for whom Montana was a spot on a map, and the subsidiary Anaconda Company was simply a grape to be squeezed. A lot of Amalgamated's small-time shareholders had been bamboozled into selling, and the rich got richer. Grabbit had done his job.

"Headline it," Hall told Wiley, the compositor, "right across the top."

He didn't feel like killing the story. He felt good not killing it. He felt he was performing a public service by headlining it. He was ready to take his chances with the boss. Some stories needed to be told. Some papers needed to renew their integrity. Some owners needed to be told to back off.

He found some newsprint and scribbled a note with a proofing pencil. "Good one," he wrote, and placed it on Grabbit's desk. It dawned on him that it was the first time he had commended Grabbit Wolf for a story. He hadn't commended anyone at the *Mineral* since he joined it. Maybe it was time to celebrate good journalism.

He penned a brief introduction, simply saying that his reporter had written an outstanding story, worthy of wide attention, and that the *Mineral* was happy to publish it. He added his name to that, had it set, and dropped it into the page at the top of the story.

"Moneymen Make a Killing," ran the headline. The old press clattered, the copies piled up, and the newsboys hauled them into the bitter air. He wondered how long he would have to wait to get the response he was expecting.

Not long, he thought, as he settled into his office swivel chair and waited.

THIRTY-SIX

They wouldn't leave Red Alice alone. She was out daily with her scrawled HELP A SICK MINER sign and her pamphlets and her money jar. She steered clear of the mines because the goons chased her off and stole her pennies and shredded her pamphlets. So she tried the miners' favorite saloons at shift time, when the men in the pits thirsted for a Shawn O'Farrell. That worked for a while because the miners remembered her, and opened their purse strings.

But then the administration changed, Clark and Heinze ran the city from their offices, and soon the cops were chasing her away, smacking her with their billy clubs, busting her collection jars, and pitching away her pamphlets. When she saw a bluecoat coming she usually tried to beat a retreat, but they often caught her. They knew where to look and what hours she'd be on the streets, and they lurked in waiting.

"You're a bunch of crooks!" she yelled, but they only laughed and pounded on her with their nightsticks. The money in her jar always disappeared.

But Butte was a big, messy city full of neighborhoods, and she survived by randomly picking saloons in unexpected places. Her flatfoot friend Big Benny Brice not only turned a blind eye, but helped her now and then when hooligans showed up and wanted to steal from her or punch her. She loved that copper, but he was the only one.

Somehow she survived. William Ward, her unwelcome guest, neither got better nor worse. He would die in a week if she put him out; he survived indoors, and even was able to help a little. Each day he got up long enough to perform some small service for her, and then fell exhausted into his bed. Whenever she wished he would go, she was reminded that he had become her livelihood. The miners remembered William Ward, who had gone into the worked-out pits to die, and that remembrance was worth a nickel or a dime; enough to keep Red Alice's household afloat.

It would end someday soon. The goons would find her and pound the life out of her. The mines increasingly had their own police, even if none of them wore a badge or was a sworn peace officer. There were rumblings in Butte. There were rumblings in every mining town in the West, including Coeur d'Alene, Leadville, and Cripple Creek. Big trouble was brewing.

One bitter day, when the light gave out at four in the afternoon, she found Ward sitting up, with an ancient blanket over his legs. She thought of him as an intruder, and an Orangeman at that, stuck in her house, ruining her life.

"Twenty-two cents," she snapped.

"It's below zero," he said in that gravel voice that bespoke a ruined throat.

"Maybe you should try it," she said.

"I've overstayed. I will go," he said.

"No, no, no, you're stuck with me," she said. "Stuck with a Green."

"A kind woman."

"I don't care what you believe," she said. "It's all hoodoo."

"What do you believe?"

"I don't believe in anything. It's all somebody's way of controlling the rest of us."

She was worn. It was cold and she had her frail heat blown out of her, and the air stank of sulphur.

"I've got to leave you," he said. "You've helped me more than anyone should expect." The last of his words dissolved into that barking cough again. He couldn't talk much without a rebellion in his throat.

She was weary of him, and didn't reply. Politeness could only cover so much.

"I'll be gone in the morning."

"You go to hell, Orangeman."

"The air is bad. I'd do better in Arizona, place like that."

She didn't argue. She set aside her cardboard sign, emptied her bottle, and stared at the kitchen drainboard.

He stared mutely from his bed, and she read his thoughts. "No, they won't take you down the shaft. I won't let them."

"It's a good place to die."

"No! You shut up."

She wondered how many dozens of sick miners had wandered into the abandoned levels and hid themselves until they died of the con.

He looked feverish. The confrontation had set it off again. "Alice Brophy, you're barking up the wrong tree," he said.

"Just shut up."

"You're trying to start a political party. Socialist Workers Party. You're competing against the old ones here. Republicans, Democrats, Whigs, Federalists, Populists. There's a better way. It's got a weapon, strikes. The Western Federation of Miners."

He fell into another spasm. She knew all about the WFM. They'd been around for years. The Butte Miners Union was Local Number 1 of the WFM, but different, more cautious. The WFM was radical. When they struck in Coeur d'Alene in 1892 company guards shot five strikers. The strikers disarmed the guards and marched them out of town. Governor Willey asked for help, and President Harrison sent General Schofield, who declared martial law and threw the strikers into a stockade without right to trial, bail, or information about charges. In Cripple Creek there'd been another one, triggered by the mine owners' effort to increase the workday from eight to ten hours. The union won that one. Another strike, in Leadville, in 1896, sought an increase of fifty cents in the daily wage, restoring the wage that had been cut earlier. The strike resulted in a lockout, violence, and the National Guard once again. Blood on the streets. Men fighting for a decent life.

Butte miners had been sympathetic but none of that had happened locally, and there was one reason. Marcus Daly was one of their own. His deep pockets had paid their passage to Butte. He listened. He drank a beer with them. He had mucked ore himself. He knew what a day's pay meant to them. And now he was dead, and neither Clark nor Heinze had much sympathy for the men in the pits who broke their backs and ruined their lungs and died young while the moguls turned their labor into private fortunes. With Daly gone, anything could happen, and would. Both Clark and Heinze made a great show of fraternizing with the miners, but it was all for appearances. Only Daly could pour a beer with them, speak their language, share a yarn out of the pits.

"So?" she asked.

"Red Alice needs a new sign. WESTERN FEDERATION OF MINERS. WFM. That's all. All miners will understand. The Butte union may be Local Number 1, but it's not really WFM. And new pamphlets. And a crack at a union job. Secretary, or clerk, or whatever."

"Why not a Socialist party?"

"Parties can't strike. Parties can't shut down a company."

"One by one by one," she said. "Little strikes, big strikes, national strikes."

"See what happens tomorrow."

She felt so giddy she cooked up some eggs. They were costly, but she had two and she fried them and gave them to him, and he nibbled at them, tiny pieces that would stumble down his ravaged throat. The brats could have some oat gruel, like herself.

She found some pasteboard over at Malone's Butcher Shop and crayoned her new sign. All it said was WESTERN FEDERATION OF MINERS NOW. She made the letters big, and used red crayon and outlined each letter with black crayon until the sign seemed to shout. She didn't put anything else on. Let them ask her. She'd tell them Butte needed a real union. She would take her money jar, but she wasn't sure anyone would drop a nickel in. They knew she collected for a miner with the con.

She headed out late in the afternoon, at shift's end, and steered clear of the mines. She'd try the saloons, especially O'Mara's, where there were plenty of men, half with miner's con, who'd like to string up the mine owners one by one. It was over near the union hall, where talk ran hot, even when the air was bitter. O'Mara's was the place for dying old miners whose lungs were quitting. Younger miners avoided the saloon. They believed it was like signing one's own death warrant to drink there—and maybe they were right.

It was so brutal outside she wondered how long she'd last. She had only a thin blue cotton coat, but she had an old gray sweater and scarf and mittens and she'd make do. The wind pushed the smoke from the seven Neversweat stacks down on the town, choking anyone who was outside. It wouldn't be a good day, but she needed cash, and she had no choice.

She stationed herself in the lee of the battered saloon vestibule, and waited out of the gale.

"What's this about, dearie?" asked a wiry man whose clothing was frosted because he hadn't changed to dry after his shift. "Where's the regular sign?"

"I'm pushing the WFM. Start a new local. Get something done around here," she said. "Fair wages. Better hours."

"What's Big Johnny got to say about it?"

"I don't care what he's got to say. We need a real union, not a kept one."

"That's tough talk, Alice."

"Help me feed a sick miner?"

"You bet. That's the Orangeman, eh?"

"I don't care what he is. He's sick."

The man pulled a dime out of his britches and dropped it into her jar. "I don't know about this," he said, and headed inside. A sharp shot of warmth struck her, and then the door closed.

That's how it went for a while. Once in a while she stepped inside, even though women weren't welcome at O'Mara's, but no one tossed her out. One time when she was warming, a bearded stranger approached. "Why the WFM?"

"Marcus Daly's dead," she said.

He nodded. "I'll vote for it. We need more muscle around here." He eyed her jar. "That's for Ward, like before? I'll keep the damned Orangeman alive." He dropped a whole quarter in, two drinks' worth.

She headed into the bitter air again, lest they get restless about her being there, and collected a few nickels more as miners studied her sign. Most didn't comment at all, but eyed her sharply. That was fine with her. She had almost three dollars in her jar, an amazing amount that said something about her new sign.

Then Big Johnny Boyle showed up and eyed her sign.

"What's this?"

"I'm pushing WFM. New local. It's better than your chickenshit union."

"The hell you are. Get out of here."

"I've got the right. It's a public street."

"You heard me."

"They want a new local. They want a real union, with balls."

That wasn't the right thing to say. Big Johnny yanked

the sign from her and ripped it up. "Now get out, or I'll take your jar, too."

"It's a free world. I'm staying right here."

He grabbed her jar, poured the coin in his pocket, and smashed the jar. The glass shattered into bright shards.

She refused to budge. "You treat me like you own me. You don't own me."

He pushed her away from the door, but she refused to budge.

"You tried to sell me when Sean died. You lined up men who'd pay your price. So sell me now. Sell me, Boyle, sell me to the highest bidder. I'll choose my man if I want one, Johnny Boyle."

He gave her a shove. She dodged and fled into the saloon, where twenty men stared and grew quiet. The sudden heat shocked her.

"Boyle tried to sell me," she said. "After Singing Sean died. I'm not for sale. Now he's stolen my money."

Boyle came through the door, carrying the cold with him. "Out!" he yelled.

"He's got my money," she yelled. "Everything you gave me for the sick man."

"That so, Big Johnny?" said the bearded one.

Boyle ignored the miner and manhandled Red Alice toward the door.

"Hold up, Big Johnny," the old miner said so quietly it barely carried through the saloon. He headed straight for the union boss.

But Boyle kept on dragging her toward the door.

"Big Johnny, listen hard. We're all for a new local here. We weren't until you started pushing her around. We just voted. And we'll keep on voting."

"Fat chance you've got," Boyle said.

"Put her out," the barkeep said. "No women in here."

"Never another beer for me in this stinking place, then, O'Mara," another miner said.

The barkeep retreated.

Boyle dragged her into the cold and left her there and headed back in. The cold whipped her thin coat. She fumed. She had three dollars in that jar. Now she had nothing.

She headed back to her cottage. Lousy damned idea, William Ward! Now look at us!

But the bearded one caught up with her and held out his hand. Clenched inside of his hand was all the change that Big Johnny had taken from her.

"Word gets around," the man said. "We'll vote ourselves into a new local real quick."

She stood in the cold, a handful of coins in her hand, watching the big miner retreat into the sulphurous wind. She knew she had already won, and could hardly believe it.

{ THIRTY-SEVEN }

B ad news from gruff Doctor Cockburn.

"Nothing more I can do, Maxwell," he said. "Wish I could help you."

Royal Maxwell absorbed that bleakly. The doctor had just concluded that Maxwell was suffering from several diseases, including syphilis, gonorrhea, consumption, St. Vitus' dance, trichinosis, corruption of the liver, jaundice, diabetes, piles, enlarged prostate, and bloody flux.

He'd been feeling worse and worse. His flesh had yellowed and grayed, and his hair was falling out, and his eyesight was going.

"How did it happen?" Maxwell asked.

"Messing around with bodies will do that to you."

"But they were dead."

"That's what everyone says about the girls. Actually, they were little kettles of microbes."

"Could you supply me with a date?" Maxwell asked.

"I could supply you with a bill. You owe me for eleven visits. And I don't want any more brass tokens."

Doctor Cockburn was referring to parlor house tokens, Good For One Lay, handed out by the various establishments on Mercury Street. They had become Royal Maxwell's cash. He had more than he could use, even when he was more vigorous, so he sold them at half price for cash.

"I could pay you with a spare coffin. I've some fancy ones left over."

"Greenbacks, Maxwell. Or a draft on your bank account."

"I need some laudanum for pain, sir. A great deal of it, to subdue a great deal of pain."

Cockburn peered at him through wire-rimmed spectacles, and nodded. "Tokens will do for that," he said. He shuffled through his shelves, filled with mysterious carafes and bottles, some blue, some brown, found what he was looking for, filled a smaller blue bottle, penned the contents on the label, and handed it to Maxwell. "Ten tokens will do, Royal," he said.

"Ten tokens!"

"Opiates cost. I should charge you double."

Grudgingly, Royal Maxwell emptied his pockets of brass tokens, some to Minnie's, some to Chicago Marlene's, some to Paradise, some to Shorty's Bathhouse. He knew that Cockburn was coining a fortune, but there wasn't anything Maxwell could do except grumble.

"You got the last laugh," he muttered.

"Repent, Maxwell," Cockburn replied, rattling the brass tokens. "Repent of your virtues."

That's how it always ended. Maxwell figured he had no virtues to repent of.

Clutching his bottle of painkiller, Maxwell hobbled into the street, and was blinded by sunlight. He normally worked nights. The restricted district had more or less accepted him, though not easily, and with occasional rank hatred. His decision years earlier to make himself the undertaker of the whores and pimps and madams and opium eaters and saloon men had gotten some sort of results, but not what he'd hoped for. He'd buried a bunch. The denizens of the restricted district were very good at dying. Some committed suicide, especially the older ladies with varicose veins and puffy faces. Others got married and escaped. There were a dozen miners ready to marry any lady who wanted a man.

His offer to bury anyone for free, or whatever came from passing the hat, still stood. It was the only way to bury some of those bozos like Stucco the Pimp. It turned out that the district had its own favorites, and Maxwell pocketed a lot of cash when one of them croaked. But the district had even more skunks, people so rotten that the whores gloated when one croaked, and then Maxwell ended up giving a free send-off, in spite of laying out cash for coffins, rental of draft horses, flowers, and the rest. All in all, he staggered along, collecting hundreds of brass tokens. But he could always sell tokens at half price, so they were as good as greenbacks. He should have guessed that once he took up with the outcasts, his regular business would drop off, and now he had no respectable customers at all.

But that wouldn't last long. He shuffled his way to his establishment, which had fallen into ruin. The syphilis had gotten to his nerves, forcing him into a halting walk, and making it hard for him to move muscles the way he wished. It would only be a short time now before he cashed in. But he already knew what he would do if he could manage it. He would stage his own funeral. He would witness it, too. That's what the laudanum was for.

He entered his peeling-paint building, and headed toward the rear room, where the prize awaited. It was one glorious coffin that had never sold, with smoked-glass walls, walnut and brass furniture, and gold-plated handles. He would bury himself in it.

He would stage the biggest, best funeral ever seen in Butte, black horses with black pompons, his ebony hearse, the casket with the oval of smoked glass in the lid, permitting him to see out but not permitting spectators to see in, and then the planting in Mountain View. He'd watch them lower him into the hole, listen to the last words above, stare up at the teary faces of all the ladies of the night, and then hear the rattle of clay as the grave diggers began to shovel. And then, as light diminished and earth rained down on top of his coffin, he'd swallow his laudanum, enough to send him off in peace, having gotten the pleasure of his own perfect, magnificent, memorable planting.

He felt so nauseous he wondered whether he could manage it. He wondered why he wanted to try. He'd lost all his former friends, especially all the Republicans, since everyone in the district was a Democrat. He was simply washed up. He was broke. He'd enjoyed nearly every dolly in the district, but what did it get him but a lot of festering sores? It was mad, this scheme. Butte had led him into perdition. Anything could happen in Butte. Some men tried to corner all the money; other men wanted every woman.

He wondered who would be pallbearers, and marked it down as something to work out. He thought he'd ask Augustus Heinze and William Andrews Clark for starters. He could publish a list of the people he had asked, no matter whether they turned him down. He wondered who might get his estate, and then realized there wouldn't be any. Everything would be sold off.

It wouldn't work. He slumped in his morris chair,

feeling his innards surrender hour by hour, and knew the whole idea of witnessing his own funeral was a fantasy. He would need confederates. He would need friends. He would need Republicans. He had nothing. He lacked a single friend. He lacked family. He lacked colleagues. He didn't belong to any church or fraternal organization. Once he had contributed to a home for unwed mothers, but that was forty years earlier, and he thought he was doing himself a favor. But now he was all alone. He was damned sick and headed for a pauper's grave at the rear of the cemetery.

He thought about the bottle of laudanum, with Cockburn's scratchy label on it, and thought of drinking the whole thing then and there. They'd find him eventually, even though hardly anyone entered his funeral home anymore.

He rested a while; it was hard to hike around Butte now, and bitter cold, too. Maybe he could beg. He struggled into his black topcoat, couldn't find gloves or a hat but set out anyway. Maybe Chicago Marlene would help him. She had always liked to give her dead girls a good send-off; that meant something to her. Once, when typhus swept through her parlor house, and seven of her ladies turned blue and life left them, he had buried them all. Most didn't have names, but Chicago Marlene had paid, and he had put the girls into a single plot with a biblical verse on it: LET HIM WHO IS WITHOUT SIN CAST THE FIRST STONE.

He scarcely made it half a block when he felt the nausea flood him again, and he sat down abruptly on the street.

"Here, now, you'll get run over by a trolley car," said a copper, who lifted Maxwell up and brushed him off.

Maxwell knew the man. It was Big Benny Brice; the one copper who didn't pound on everyone with his billy club.

"Say, Maxwell, you ain't well," Big Benny said.

Maxwell shook his head.

"I'll take you back to your parlor."

Maxwell didn't resist. Benny's big paw held the mortician upright, and soon enough Maxwell was slumped in his morris chair, still in his coat.

"You been drinking, Maxwell?"

Maxwell shook his head.

"Something wrong?"

Maxwell just stared, and slowly shook his head.

"Yeah, something's wrong; you're looking like a puked-out dog," Big Benny said. "Someone stick a shiv into you?"

"I'm dying. Cockburn just told me so. I've got more fatal diseases than there are in Equador or Madagascar. I was trying to get to Chicago Marlene to see if she'd bury me."

"Dying? You? Funeral directors don't die." Big Benny stared. "Well, I guess they do."

"No friends, no family," Maxwell said. "All alone. Maybe Chicago Marlene would."

"You want a planting? I'll do that for you, Maxwell."

"You, a flatfoot cop?"

He was insulting Big Benny, but he didn't care. He didn't want to be buried by a beat cop. He wanted a copper king to bury him. William Andrews Clark would do. Fritz Heinze could deliver the eulogy. An important man needed important mourners.

"That's right, me boy, a flatfoot with a billy club. And I get to see the world, and I get to see things that people do. You done them a lot of good in there, with your fancy send-offs."

"Good? What are you saying?"

"Maxwell, those girls, they're mostly off the farms. They got treated bad. Bad husband, bad father, rotten mother, and they fled marriages, fled parents, wanting anything but the life that was put on them, got me?"

"What's that got to do with it?"

"They come to the district by the hundreds, mostly hating themselves, blaming themselves, alone, ready to swallow a bottle of carbolic acid and burn themselves to death, eh?"

Maxwell nodded, unwilling for this to go further.

"Alone they are, Maxwell. Buried in a potter's field without a headstone, forgotten. Until you came along. Sure, my boy, you wanted some boodle for it, but for them it was a miracle. Someone cared. You put on a show every time, driving that old hearse around, letting the world know that whoever was in there was special. I saw it myself, boy. I saw the ladies weeping, like your send-offs were the most important thing in the world to them. You were remembering them. They wouldn't die alone. Even their pimps paid respect when you drove by. Call me a flatfoot, boy, but I've got eyes, and I saw the good you did around there, getting the gals buried proper."

He drew himself up. "Me and all the other coppers, we all saw it, and we all think you did a lot of good, boy. So we'll bury you proper, and we'll be proud to do it."

"Bury me?"

"We'll march on either side of you, sir. We'll be a line of blue, escorting you. We'll make sure all of Butte knows it, too. We'd be honored to do it, sir. We saw what you did down in the district. A girl could dream of a good send-off. That meant she was someone, not just a nameless female dumped in a corner of the graveyard. Yes, Maxwell, we saw it and we'll be proud to send you on your way—if you want it, sir."

There was a question in it.

Maxwell felt so dizzy he could scarcely stand.

"Big Benny, I think I'd like to be escorted by your men in blue," he said. "I hope they're all Republicans."

"We'll all be Republicans for the occasion, Mr. Maxwell."

"You will, won't you? Bury me?"

"I think I can arrange it, sir. Should I be taking you to the pesthouse?"

"No, Mr. Bruce. Just leave me here, and maybe in the morning you can check in. The door won't be locked. You can see if I'm a bit better."

"Count on me, Mr. Maxwell."

"You won't let me down, will you?"

"Should I find someone to sit with you, sir? I can find someone, I think."

"No, no, my friend. I'll just sit here and sip some medicine I got."

"Well, good night then, Mr. Maxwell."

Royal Maxwell nodded, watched the copper retreat into the night, and pulled out the laudanum, which he fondled as delicately as he would a woman's cheek.

{ THIRTY-EIGHT }

Nothing happened. J. Fellowes Hall waited for the doomsday notice. Waited for a pink slip. Waited for a visit from Clark's lawyer. But in the wake of the *Mineral*'s new assault on Anaconda, no rebuke issued from up high.

Maybe Clark didn't care. Maybe Clark didn't see the story. Maybe Clark simply planned to give Hall more time, probation as it were. Whatever the case, Hall remained on the payroll, for the moment. It wouldn't last, of course, and Clark would eject him eventually. But Hall felt almost heady thinking about it.

As long as Clark was holding off, maybe Hall could

redress the wrongs the paper had done, mostly crimes of omission. It had failed to report all the news, or it had colored its reportage to fit Mr. Clark's objectives. That was the paper's offense against the people of Butte. It wasn't the thunderous editorials Hall wrote on behalf of the owner; it was twisting or hiding the news on behalf of the owner. The news didn't belong to anyone; it was something different, something attached to the public good, something that ought not to belong to anyone, not even the owner of the paper. Hall didn't condemn himself. He was simply no different from all the other editors of all the other kept newspapers in Montana.

The next day nothing happened, and the day after that nothing happened. J. Fellowes Hall remained the editor of Clark's premier newspaper. Well, then, maybe it was time to produce the sort of paper that Hall might be proud of. But how could he even start if the Damocles sword was dangling over his neck?

He burrowed into his topcoat and braved the sulphurous cold air, something he had never gotten used to. He hiked east, finally turning on an obscure lane that would take him to Slanting Agnes. He had not visited her for years, and wondered if she even existed. Consulting a fey woman about the future was not the way J. Fellowes Hall now did things, but what did it matter? He was desperate for a peek, a clue, a snatched moment from times to come.

The cottage was still there, unpainted, worn, looking ready to cave in, or slide into the nearest gulch. He knocked and waited impatiently, the wind harrying him mercilessly. She opened and stared.

"You is it? I shouldn't let you in here, Clark's paid liar, but I will. Don't expect a thing from me, you who spread lies."

He was expecting something like that, and didn't try to argue. He just nodded and stepped into a cold kitchen. She looked more worn and thin than ever, and he doubted she was getting enough to feed herself and her two boys.

"I don't know about you," she said. "I don't know if I want to."

"Your house is cold," he said, leaving his greatcoat on.

"What do you expect it to be, me a widow lady with no money?"

"The mines should pay a pension or a death benefit," he said.

"Now is that something William Andrews Clark told you to say to me?"

He saw how this was going. "I would like to learn about my immediate future—if you're inclined."

She busied herself, stirring up coals in the firebox of her stove, adding wood, and starting some water heating. All the while she was eyeing him as he sat, waiting and wondering if this was a fool's mission. She would not be hurried. He needed fast answers.

"I don't charge for it. I don't have a gift. Some people have a gift, but I don't. I just have moments, little flashes, that's all, and only when I'm unwilling. I don't want this gift. It's from the devil. People shouldn't know the future. But there's nothing I can do about it. If you want to know when you'll die, then maybe I'll tell you, maybe I won't."

She fussed around her kitchen, brought water to boil, steeped tea, and finally poured some amber fluid into a chipped cup and saucer.

"How are your boys?"

"You're making polite talk. You don't care about my boys. They're just more hooligans, aren't they? Now if you'd asked me what county I'm from, maybe then I'd answer you. It's Clare, County Clare, you know, but you wouldn't know and wouldn't care."

"Madam, I'm sorry I came. Thank you for the tea— I'll leave now."

"Sit down, you jackass."

But he didn't. He only wanted to escape. He started to get back into his greatcoat.

She paused suddenly. "Mr. Clark doesn't like you," she said.

"That's not news."

"Do the things you have in mind. You've got time."

He paused. "What do I have in mind?"

"How should I know? Do them."

"How much time?"

She sighed, annoyed. "You think I have answers. I don't. Things come suddenly to me, and then the peek ahead closes off again."

That was it. A totally unsatisfying encounter. He thought to give her a dollar. She glared at him. Five, then. He reached into his pocket, and pulled out some greenbacks. There were three singles and a ten. He gave her the ten.

"Filthy money," she said. "Clark money."

"You told me what I needed to know."

"I wish I didn't have the gift," she said. "Now things'll be worse."

He left thinking she was crazier than ever, and wondering why he laid a lot of cash on her. She could live for a week on that. He stepped into the choking air, the smoke from the seven Neversweat chimneys lowering over town again. A man couldn't breathe in Butte, which is why so many died young, and not just miners.

He had time. He should do what he needed to do. That had cost him a sawbuck. He was nuts, visiting her.

He coughed his way back to the paper, pulled out some foolscap and began a list.

1. *Clean up air. Higher stacks.*
2. *County poor farm. Shelter for the homeless and helpless. Tax the mines.*
3. *Pension. Widows' fund. Support for old miners and widows.*
4. *Clean air in mines. Fight miner's lung. No rock dust.*
5. *Better water. No arsenic in it. Keep it cheap. The poor need it.*
6. *Cobble the streets, less dust and mire. Slow down disease.*
7. *County rest home. Refuge for sick men and children.*
8. *Mining law. End apex law and litigation. Stop underground theft.*
9. *Tax mine profits for schools.*
10. *Clean up the courts. Impeach crooked judges.*

There were many other reforms that came to mind, but these ten would be a start. He found Grabbit Wolf hammering at a typing machine, and summoned him.

"We've just become the reform paper," he said.

Grabbit started laughing. "Let me guess. You've been bought."

"Sure, William Rockefeller forked over."

"I'll want some whiskey money."

"A quart a story," Hall said instantly. "I'm serious. We're selling reform. We're going to be the paper that cares about everyone in Butte. Choose any one of these to start with. Do a piece on the problem. Get some quotations. Talk to someone who's hurting. Then write the story. New story every couple of days."

Wolf looked over the list. "You want to get us all fired?"

"Clark's too busy to notice."

"What's the one that gets us fired? I'll do that first."

"That would be a widows' fund, a pension, something for men with miner's con."

Grabbit lit a cigar. "I guess you're asking for it," he said. "I can write that one off the top of my head."

There were two younger men on the staff, both gifted cartoonists. "I want some tough cartoons," Hall said. "Tax the mines. Build a hospital. Start pensions. Start a widows' fund. Kick out the crooked judges. Start a poor farm for the needy. Clean the water."

"You trying to get us fired?" asked Potter.

"Yes," Hall said, and walked away.

He settled into his swivel chair and found himself actually shaking. He seethed with some sort of feeling he had never experienced, something so piercing and urgent that he couldn't name it. There was pain, yes. What he was doing scared him. But there was something else, something heady, something that filled him with pride. For the first time since he arrived in Butte, he felt what, what? Honorable. Honorable! He didn't know how much time he had before Clark pitched him out, and the rest of his staff too, but from this moment on, he would run the only reform paper in Butte. And there was a lot to reform. And after he had tackled these, he would have another ten, and another ten after that.

Grabbit vanished from the grimy office, as if shot out of a cannon. The old souse looked inspired. By midafternoon, just in time for the evening edition, he was turning in copy for typesetting. He started with widows' funds. He interviewed three miners' widows in Dublin Gulch, all living hand to mouth after their men had perished from miner's con. He quoted all of them as saying they needed a widows' fund; miners' widows should be cared for by the mines. The mines had ruined the bodies of their men, and left the widows penniless, with children, and nowhere to go for help.

"Those rich men, they feasted on Mike's body, and

won't give me two cents to feed my wee ones," said Margaret McCarthy. "In the Silver Bow Club they don't eat all the food set before them, and my boys wait for the scraps."

There was more; homeless widows, sick children, suicides.

Hall published the story and waited for whatever would happen, while Grabbit set to work on the next. He tackled the apex law next. The 1872 mining law was a license to steal, and that was exactly what was happening deep under the streets of Butte. Grabbit found plenty of lawyers willing to talk, and not just Anaconda's lawyers trying to defend its mines from the onslaught of Fritz Heinze.

Not everyone thought the law was pernicious, and Grabbit collected some good quotes from a few who favored it.

"Apex law keeps me in business," said Gerald Jones, Esq. "It keeps most Silver Bow lawyers in business. No mine is safe in anyone's hands so long as it's legal to follow a vein into the next man's mine."

That made a fine story, which Hall discreetly featured on the bottom of the front page, where no one would miss it. It was sure good business. The edition sold out an hour after it hit the streets, and Hall cranked out some more copies just to gild his profits a little.

And still, no rebuke from Clark. It dawned on Hall that Clark tacitly approved. It enhanced his stature and inclined the legislature to vote him into the Senate. But what Hall enjoyed most was a sense that at least he was pursuing the mission of any good newspapers, which was to enhance the public weal. One might argue about what the public good might be, but one could surely seek to improve security, health, sanitation, wages, retirement, and medical progress.

Grabbit Wolf turned himself into a whirlwind, and developed stories that struck at the heart of Butte's neglect of its humbler citizens. Hall made a point to avoid sensationalism, and published each piece with a quiet headline that would inflame no one.

Opposing papers took notice and began jeering at Hall, accusing the *Mineral* of going batty in its rush to reform a world that could never be changed. The *Anaconda Standard* took issue with any reform that might raise the cost of labor, such as pensions, and Heinze's little weekly, the *Reveille,* heaped coals of scorn on Hall for suggesting there was anything wrong with apex law and litigation.

For the first time since coming to Butte, he began to feel like a man at the top of his profession. Even his perception of Butte seemed to shift. He had come to love the battered, filthy, chaotic, ugly city, the city that killed its own, the city where typhus and silicosis and tuberculosis lurked at every corner, the city where desperate children stole anything they could, just to get food. This was his Butte, ugly and shameful, and laden with vices. The *Mineral*'s voice would be drowned out by the greedy and calculating, but still it was a voice of reform. And that inspired Hall, and his bright employees, to wrestle even harder with the evils at every hand.

"My dear," he wrote Amber. "We've been parted a long while, and now I wish to bring you here, and make Butte our home. I was uncertain about it; Butte is raw and cruel, and unhealthy too, but it is also a place where determined people might prosper. Things get better. There are now pleasant places to live. Begin making travel plans and disposing of what you won't ship, and you will find funds forthcoming in the mail."

He couldn't imagine how it had happened.

THIRTY-NINE

The private railcar, discreetly enameled maroon, rested quietly on a siding below Butte, supplied with steam and electricity by an idling steam engine. It didn't attract notice. It was owned by William Rockefeller, and was furnished in the family tradition of great quietness. There would be no gold-plated faucets within.

But it was luxurious, nonetheless, with walnut paneled walls, a rear parlor with a cut-glass chandelier and overstuffed chairs, two bedroom suites, a galley and quarters for servants, and three water closets equipped with showers. From its curtained windows one could gaze upward upon a turmoil of seedy buildings, a solid brick-and-stone shopping area, and a forest of headframes and boilers, a hodgepodge of mining and smelting sheds sprawling over the crests of the slopes.

Rockefeller, John's brother, occupied one bedroom; Henry Rogers occupied the other. The richest men on earth had come to view the richest hill on earth. The enclosed ebony Rockaway parked discreetly near the private car belonged to William Scallon, president of the company, and Marcus Daly's successor. In due course, they would all climb into the Rockaway and see the sights, but for the moment they convened in the parlor where they could gaze out upon a hill that was not quite yielding itself to them, as planned. For some years, this trio, and its allies, had pursued consolidation, the euphemism for driving rivals out of business and combining all their assets into a single company, of course owned and operated by the three who were sitting in the parlor, enjoying whatever their hearts desired. William Rockefeller was being abstemious; Rogers toyed with a scotch, and Scallon sipped a bourbon.

Rogers was the most striking of the three. He was sixty-one, graying, jut-jawed, handsome, robust, hale, command-ing, and amiable. He spoke in flawless cadences, well-honed by a careful upbringing and improved by wealth. Rogers, rather like the Rockfellers, was a devoted churchman who endowed public buildings and congregations in his home-town, Fairhaven, Connecticut. His geniality was legend. His host this trip, William Rockefeller, operated in his brother's shadow but was a forceful man in his own right. Scallon felt vaguely diminished by two of what the pop-ular press called the Standard Oil Gang.

Matters had come to a head. For some while the Amal-gamated Copper Company had been buying Butte mines. Famous names fell under the company's direction. Those owned by the Lewisohn brothers were gradually being eaten up, as were the famous mines of the Boston people, the Boston and Montana Consolidated Copper and Silver Mining Company, and the Butte and Boston under the control of Albert Bigelow, and many smaller mines as well. There were scores of mines and reduction works on the hill, stretching to Walkerville and beyond, and far to the east and west. Many of these independents still shipped their ore to the Heinzes' Montana Ore Purchas-ing Company, which reduced their ore more efficiently and at less cost than any of its rivals. The ore flowing into it was crucial to its profitable operation. Bit by bit Rogers and his colleagues had brought the smaller mines into Anaconda's orbit, or at least control, steadily diminishing the rich copper ores that the Heinzes could process and send away for final refining in the East. But Rogers's noose failed to tighten entirely, which was an increasing annoy-ance to him, and to the rest. If Standard Oil could dis-tribute two hundred fifty million dollars in dividends to its lucky few owners over several years, the copper trust could yield even more. The potential was there, before their eyes. But what had stymied this great strangle of the industry was F. Augustus Heinze's staff of legal beagles, who fought the chokehold with a variety of lawsuits.

William Scallon eyed the other gentlemen in the private car with some reserve. He might be the president of Anaconda, but he had never encountered men like these. He was a Canadian and a lawyer, and a gentleman. These two visitors to Butte had conducted themselves in a manner almost beyond his imagining. They had induced panic selling of Amalgamated stock, and then bought back in at bargain prices, making tens of millions in sheer profit. They had capitalized their trust with stock that was grounded in thin air, and made many more millions out of nothing. At will, they could make Amalgamated stock rise or fall, sell out or buy into it, and pocket the loose change. But their absolute mastery of the Butte mines was less certain now, thanks to the machinations of F. Augustus Heinze and his vest-pocket judges. That is what brought them in their private car across the continent to this ugly place. Scallon was perfectly familiar with mining magnates like Clark and Daly, but he had never understood men like this who gave little thought to consequences.

"Well, then, gentlemen, let's proceed," he said.

The visitors nodded. The October day was mild enough, but for some reason the East Coast men bundled up before descending the iron stairs and climbing into Scallon's elegant Rockaway, where Scallon's liveried coachman waited patiently.

The Rockaway, a square, enclosed coach with large glass windows, would be a perfect vehicle to see the sights. It would at once insulate the passengers from the rawest smells, while affording them a perfect view. Its black lacquered exterior bespoke quiet elegance. Spectators would not mistake the eminence of those within as it passed through the streets of Butte.

Scallon's coachman knew the route and the schedule,

and without direction he turned the handsome drays up the long slope to the great hill east of town where the Anaconda mines clustered as well as Heinze's Rarus mine, and the Boston and Montana group.

"We'll begin with the comedy," Scallon said.

The driver would take them to that patch of land in the midst of the great mines that Heinze had christened the Copper Trust, and where, according to his lawsuits, the rich veins all apexed. It was a good joke. Heinze's suits had languished in Montana courts for years, too frivolous even for the friendly judges to cope with. But the site would entertain these calculating men from the East, in their black coats and monogrammed silk scarves.

The Rockaway gained the hill, and the city fell away into a chaotic and unpaved district, jammed with rails, dirt paths that took miners to the pits, sheds, flapping laundry on lines, headframes, great stamp mills, hoists, boiler rooms, and heaps of industrial debris, all grim against a bright blue heaven and serene mountain slopes. That was the paradox. So much beauty just beyond this junk pile perched on the hill.

Scallon's coachman took the coach as far as he could, and then opened the door to the substantial men within. They stepped daintily into the grassless mire, eyed the smoke lowering from the Neversweat stacks, and edged gingerly toward the offending claim, which was marked by iron stakes and a NO TRESPASSING sign, as well as an elegant masonry edifice that supported a gilded sign that said COPPER TRUST. It was amusing on sight. The Copper Trust commanded land barely large enough to support a two-hole outhouse.

Henry Rogers stared pensively. William Rockefeller smirked. Neither said a word. This was a sideshow. They looked vaguely annoyed by the waste of time visiting here. Scallon hurried them back to the Rockaway, and the coachman drove the lurching vehicle toward a nearby cluster of rough buildings lying farther east.

"That's the Rarus," Scallon said. "And that's the Johnstown. And beyond, the Boston and Montana's Pennsylvania."

These gentlemen were familiar with the case. Heinze's apex suit against the Boston and Montana declared that the veins being mined there apexed on Rarus ground. The suit had been heard by Judge Clancy and had bounced up to the Montana Supreme Court and back even as Heinze's miners were feverishly gouging the disputed ore out of the ground and shipping it to Heinze's smelter. The courts had forced Heinze to post a bond in the event that the case should go against him. Heinze, in turn, had invented a phantom East Coast finance company with ghostly assets that bonded him, and persuaded the gullible courts to accept the arrangement. If Rockefeller and Rogers could conjure something out of nothing, so could Fritz Heinze.

"Here's the boundary line. Unless you wish to enter the pits, you'll want to observe that beneath our feet, Fritz Heinze is cleaning out the disputed ore as fast as he can, and lifting it over there." Scallon pointed to the works at the Johnstown. "The ore from here's being lifted there."

"We'll stay aboveground," Rogers said. "It's our ore. Amalgamated ore."

"Correct, sir," Scallon said. Amalgamated had not yet folded its newer acquisitions into its subsidiary the Anaconda Company.

He steered his guests a little farther, to the line separating the Rarus from the Michael Davitt mine, another of the Butte and Boston properties. The Bostonians had claimed that Rarus veins apexed in the Michael Davitt; the court had eventually shut down all operations in both mines that involved the disputed veins. But that was all the opportunity Heinze needed to gut the veins and smuggle ore out while awaiting the court to decide. He had sent hundreds of miners into the forbidden ground, where they were hollowing out the rich veins, sealing off the depleted chambers, and feeding the contraband into the Montana Ore Purchasing Company smelter by lifting it from adjacent shafts. Now Heinze's theft was Amalgamated's problem because the trust had bought a controlling interest in the Boston mines and had pushed their primary owner, Albert Bigelow, out the door.

"Somewhere, at several levels under our feet, sirs, ore from here is flowing to the Heinze smelter."

"He's violating the Ten Commandments," Rogers said.

Next they drove to Meaderville and viewed the Minnie Healy mine, which was at the heart of an apex suit with the various surrounding mines, especially the Piccolo and Gambetta, owned by the Boston and Montana firm. The gifted Heinze had discovered rich new veins in the Minnie Healy, and argued that they apexed there and ran into the Boston property, so he had filed suit to claim the ore. The Minnie Healy was thus one of the keys to controlling the veins in several surrounding mines. It was this suit that had drawn Henry H. Rogers and William Rockefeller to Montana that mild afternoon. It would be decided in Judge Clancy's courtroom that day of 1903.

Rogers and Rockefeller walked the boundaries, felt the earth shudder beneath their feet, studied their works and Heinze's, and climbed into the ebony Rockaway once again, while Scallon's driver took them to the next locale. That proved to be Heinze's Nipper Consolidated, which lay next to the Little Mina, which was owned by Amalgamated's subsidiary, the Parrot Silver and Copper Company. Heinze's favorite judge, William Clancy, had put the Little Mina into receivership, further threatening the Standard Oil Gang's copper trust.

Rogers and Rockefeller paced the boundaries, eyed that cluster of headframes and hoists, and examined the bright black foothills of the Rockies, not far beyond. Pockets of snow had collected in the upland valleys, and purple shadows crawled with the sun across the high country.

It was time to go to court. The impending verdicts were so important that they had drawn these princes of finance west. The trust was under siege, and might fail under Heinze's endless assault, which was tying the trust into knots. Stockholder suits filed by Heinze's lieutenants, Lamm and Forrester and MacGinnis, who held shares in opposing corporations, had prevented the Amalgamated Trust from absorbing the Boston properties, and threatened to unravel the entire consolidation of mines in Butte within the Amalgamated holding company.

Scallon's man drove the Rockaway to the ornate courthouse, which looked more like a church than a public office, which may have been intended. Judge Clancy would deliver his decisions at four this twenty-second day of October, 1903. These were simply two more in a string of them issued by the district court in Butte, but these intelligent men well understood that companies crumble under the weight of such edicts, empires collapse, dreams shatter.

They found Judge Clancy's courtroom nearly empty. Scallon nodded briefly at Amalgamated's lawyer, Dennis Jones, and Heinze's lawyer, Albert French, and settled on a bleak bench at the rear. Heinze was not present. It was quiet. Four o'clock came and went and the room remained muffled in silence. Clancy enjoyed doing that. He no doubt knew who were sitting on his pew-like benches, and a little discomfort was in order for all the litigants. He had kept them uncomfortable for years.

Then at last, the clerk of court appeared, and the bailiff, and the handful of men rose as his honor emerged. Judge William Clancy was as disheveled and grimy as ever; food stains darkened his unkempt gray beard. He peered about, his cunning gaze settling on the visitors, and he let them all remain standing. He smiled slightly while the court was called to order, and settled into his chair.

Rogers started to sit down, but Clancy rebuked him. "You will respect the court," Clancy said, gesturing Rogers to return to his feet. And so they all stood, while the judge yawned, shuffled papers, and waited for the clerk to ready himself. Clancy scratched his beard. Scallon thought it must itch, and was probably teeming with vermin. It showed no sign of having been washed. A faint odor drifted through the hushed courtroom, and Scallon thought that none of the rest of Clancy's person had enjoyed the comfort of soap and water, either.

And so they stood, while Clancy enjoyed himself by doing nothing. Then at last, he invited the opposing counsel to step forward.

"Gentlemen," he said, leering slightly. "Let us begin. In the matter of *Forrester and MacGinnis v. Boston and Montana Consolidated Copper and Silver Mining Company* and *Lamm et al v. Parrot Silver and Copper Mining,* I find as follows."

He droned on for a few minutes. The upshot was that the Amalgamated holding company could not legally absorb the Boston or other properties in Montana; that the trust itself was an attempt to create an illegal monopoly; that the holding company would be prohibited from owning stock in the Boston companies or their subsidiaries. In essence, Clancy was ruling that the holding company could not consolidate mines in Montana.

That brought the slightest of frowns to the faces of the Standard Oil men.

But there was more. Judge Clancy licked his lips, which were largely hidden beneath his soup-strainer beard, and continued. The Minnie Healy mine, whose ownership was disputed, belonged to the Johnstown Mining Company, which was a Heinze property. Thus was ten million dollars of ore passed to Heinze, plus the opportunity for Heinze to file more apex suits against all the properties adjacent to the Minnie Healy.

The Standard Oil Gang heard its empire collapse.

"And there you are, gentlemen. The court so rules. Tomorrow I'm heading for the woods to hunt for elk and jackrabbits."

{ FORTY }

William Ward finally died of consumption. Alice Brophy knew it was coming. He had turned waxen, was coughing up blood constantly as his lungs surrendered, was struggling to breathe, had turned feverish, and stared at her from onyx eyes that sometimes seemed to hide the flicker of life itself within him.

He had been a long time dying. The con had waxed and waned. There were months when he seemed on the brink of recovering, only to slide back into desperate coughing, spitting up pieces of his lungs, and utter weakness in which he could not even get out of bed.

Her bed. He had been the unwelcome visitor for three years. Her family had adjusted itself to his presence, sleeping anywhere, or not sleeping at all. He'd been the Orangeman among the Greens. Not that she believed any of that religion stuff, but she felt a special loathing of the Orange Irish.

He had left a family behind and she didn't know how to contact them. Maybe the union would know. In his healthier moments he had tried to help out; cook, clean, anything to ease her life, but it had come to very little. Butte lacked places to die. No one wanted a consumptive, because they infected those around them. Maybe she had the con now. Maybe Tim and Tommy too. They weren't exactly in the prime of health. They looked like ghosts. They were mostly stealing, and were good at it. So far no one had caught them. They saw opportunities, sometimes to trade one stolen item for another; a coil of rope for an apple. They were a part of gangs, lifting anything they could and then trading it for whatever they needed. The gangs roamed freely from Meaderville to the flats below the hill, and their shifting membership was drawn from all over Butte. Timmy often returned to Dublin Gulch carrying something odd, something he said he'd found, but he wouldn't say more, and that odd item would vanish the next day. She didn't like that, but mostly because she feared he would get pinched.

Alice Brophy stared at her still, cold guest, not knowing what to do. Then she decided he was a union man; let the union bury him if they would. Big Johnny Boyle wanted nothing to do with her. She was too radical for him, though radical wasn't the word she used. She wanted justice. She eyed Ward, oddly tender about him. He had given her good ideas. He had tried to help. He had at least been a friend. But now he lay still and cold and green of flesh.

She donned her worn coat and braved the cold, hiking slowly toward the union hall, the headquarters of Local Number 1, Western Federation of Miners. Only this union wasn't like the other locals. Big Johnny and mine management were tight as could be, so this local alone, among all the locals, was actually silent about all the red-hot issues burning through the miners of the West. There were a few firebrands, mostly stirred up by people like Red Alice, who demanded more: mine sanitation, cleaner air, better hours, better wages, a sick fund, a widows' fund, a pension. And Big Johnny had made a show of getting these things, and so had the managements, but it was only a show. The union's sick fund simply paid the hospital to care for the miners who walked in. The widows' fund paid brief death benefits—and then nothing.

Big Johnny wasn't in the union hall, so he had to be next door at the bar. She invaded that all-male sanctum and found him nursing a mug of ale.

"Who let you in here?" he asked by way of greeting.

"I let myself in. William Ward is dead and needs burying."

"So? Bury him yourself."

She was afraid of that. "He was a brother. He paid his dues for years."

"Not for the last three, he hasn't."

"You owe him one."

"Alice, you butt out. Get your skinny ass out."

"I'll make sure the whole town knows about it, Big Johnny."

That gave him pause, if only for a moment. "He wasn't a member," he said lamely.

"You wouldn't even know that. You don't know who's a member. You got three thousand members and you don't know who's one and who isn't. You need a clerk. Like me. I keep track. I'll make sure your dues are in."

For an answer, Big Johnny turned his back on her and sipped ale, and started nudging his neighbors, as if it was all a joke. The barkeep started frowning at her, meaning he was about to pitch her out on her ear.

"Guess lots of people gonna hear about this," she said.

"I don't give a rat's ass," he snapped.

"We need a new union," she said, just as the burly keep started to round the far side of the bar to chase her out.

She ducked into the street, thinking she was clear, but the man followed her outside and booted her in the butt.

"Some friend of miners you are," she snapped.

She stood in the cold wind, letting it cut through her thin coat and chill her heart. Lousy, whoring union. Maybe women should run it. At least women cared. It was said that Big Johnny was in thick with Anaconda's management. He never lacked any beer money, that was sure. And he lived fancy, too. After Marcus Daly died, they kept up the game. Once in a while some bigwig in the company would buy a little brick house for a miner's widow, and make sure it got talked about. Heinze and Clark did the same thing. Tame union, no strikes, no pressure to have pensions or sickness benefits or money for miner's con. No sanitation. The pits were cesspools, full of human waste, every puddle down there teeming with sickness. No wonder so many miners died of dysentery. The miners didn't get poorer; they got dead. The rich got richer and lived long lives.

She needed that job. She hated to say it, but William Ward had been her livelihood. Every day for these years she had handed out tracts and collected cash for the sick miner. The miners knew about Ward, chipped in dimes and nickels, and she had survived. And now he was lying stone cold in her house. She thought maybe she could bury him herself. She had half-grown children now, big enough to help her wrap Ward in a winding sheet and take him somewhere. Maybe drop him off in front of the Episcopalian Church, the damned Church of England, and let them plant him.

She felt a new sadness wash her. She liked William Ward, and she liked him because he wasn't so full of shit as the rest. Sometimes when she was mouthing away, he just smiled at her, as if to say cut out the crap, and she knew she was talking a lot of hot air. But now he was dead, and he was filling up her house. She sure as hell didn't know what to do, and the wind was howling. She wished she could burn him in her stove.

Then she remembered her flatfoot friend, Big Benny Brice, and thought she knew where he'd be skimming along, twirling his billy club they way he did. He'd be over on East Broadway. So she braved the sulphurous smoke and headed into the commercial district, looking for some flash of blue.

She found her flatfoot standing on a grille that vented boiler heat, while a forlorn mutt waited to return to his favorite spot.

"Well, if it isn't Alice Brophy, and how are you?" he said.

"I need a little help," she said. "William finally, well, quit."

"Quit?"

"Died. I always have trouble saying it. He's lying in my bed. No one wants him. The union won't bury him."

"Ah, I see. Well, let's go have a look, Mrs. Brophy. There's a few things need to be done."

She was startled. It was the first time anyone had called her Mrs. Brophy in many years.

They hiked toward Dublin Gulch, and Alice had trouble staying even with Big Benny.

"Now I've been meaning to have a word with you, and about that boy of yours. Timothy is it? That boy's heading for trouble."

"Then let him get into it," she replied.

"Could it be, madam, that he's a bit starved?"

Red Alice started to rub her eyes.

Big Benny Brice said nothing more as they slipped from commercial blocks into humbler ones, and finally into the gulch, with its crowded cottages and endless odors. They turned to Alice's decaying cottage, and the flatfoot stood aside while Alice opened. The room was stone cold. She drew a curtain aside to let in some light, while the copper studied the remains lying in the alcove bed.

The cop touched Ward's face and neck, and nodded.

"Let's walk over to the courthouse, madam, and we'll do what needs doing. Silver Bow will lay him to rest, and I'll see to it. And I'll come with you, if you choose to see him to his grave."

The flatfoot studied the barren kitchen, the lifeless stove, and the lampless interior before he stepped into the smoky winter air.

"He was a good man, I imagine," the constable said.

"He was an Orange—yes, a good man. A miner. When he first got sick he tried to die down in the pits. It's warm there."

"There's a lot of bones down there, Mrs. Brophy. They fed a lot of rats."

They trudged into town, pushing against the bitter wind, until they got to the station house. "This'll do," he said.

She made her report. Time of death, name, next of kin, cause. She couldn't give them an address. Wife and children in Belfast. Cause of death consumption. No estate that she knew of.

"We'll send a man, madam," the desk officer said.

"That's it? That's the end of William Ward?"

"I'll take you home," Big Benny said.

She followed him as he trudged back. He stopped at a coal dealer and paid for a small bag of Montana coal, and carried it with him. When they got to her place, he built a small fire from kindling, and then added some coal. It would take a long time to heat up the cottage, but the flatfoot settled easily in a shabby armchair and waited. She was colder than ever, but had nothing to pull over herself.

And there wouldn't be anything soon, she thought. Her only source of money lay in that bed. And she couldn't find a job, and likely never would, given that she was Red Alice.

It took an hour before a man with a black hearse showed up. By then, the cottage was finally starting to warm.

She didn't know the funeral man. There were more undertakers in Butte than there were preachers.

"We'll head straight out to Mountain View," the man

said. "I put two diggers on the grave, and all we need to do is wrap him. I take it you're not a relative."

"He's my brother," she said, wondering why on earth she said it.

"Kin?"

"In a way. In a way."

"You are welcome to ride with me, madam."

She wondered about it. The cottage was just starting to be warm, heavenly warm.

"I guess I will," she said.

"I'll be going with you," said Big Benny. "Seems the best thing."

The mortician expertly wrapped William Ward in a white winding sheet and tied it close and tight, while Alice and the flatfoot watched. Then he nodded, and the mortician and copper carried the Orangeman out to the ebony hearse.

So they sat in the open seat, while an ancient dray clopped down the long grade to the flats, hastened along by the wind at their backs. True to his word, the funeral man had a grave ready for William Ward. It was nowhere near six feet deep, though.

Big Benny and the two grave diggers lifted William Ward from the hearse and set him gently in the shallow grave, a long white bundle.

"Anything you wish to say? A moment's reflection?" the mortician asked. "A prayer? A verse of scripture?"

Alice couldn't think of a thing. "I'll have a mass said for his soul," she said. "He was a good man. And don't be billing me because I don't have it to give you."

So the grave diggers shoveled, and Alice and Big Benny rode back, into the bitter wind.

And Alice wondered why she missed Ward so much.

FORTY-ONE

Victory called for a party, and F. Augustus Heinze knew how to create one. That evening at the Butte Hotel he threw a corker. There were gold rosettes for the women at the long table; there were gifts of stock shares for the gentlemen, who were dressed in dinner jackets. The women were drawn from the demimonde as well as society, and the ladies eyed one another cheerfully, as if to acknowledge they were not so far apart.

Fritz Heinze knew how to celebrate, and this evening there would be much to celebrate. So the bubbly flowed, the whiskey glasses were filled and refilled, and the ladies glittered in their finery.

It was time for a toast. He stood, an impressive figure, muscular and trim, still youthful. He eyed the assemblage, his gaze pausing at Katarina Costa, wearing scarlet this evening in wanton celebration of her status, and then he lifted a hand to quiet them all, which actually took some while because no one was very sober, and he raised a glass.

"We have something to celebrate," he said quietly. "We have slain the anaconda. We have slain the giant constrictor, the snake that grows fifteen feet in length and devours its prey, including mortals, by squeezing them to their death. We have slain the trusts, the monopolists, the holding companies. We have slain the Rockefellers, Standard Oil, and all their legions of lawyers and kept judges. We have slain them all. Let us drink to that!"

He downed a glass of whatever he was holding; it didn't matter.

"Hear, hear," someone yelled.

"We have spared Montana from becoming a vassal of

Standard Oil! We have protected the integrity of our government and our courts! Anaconda is finished!"

He wasn't quite sure of that, but what did it matter? They drank to that, drank to Heinze's gaudy staff of lawyers, drank to Heinze's Montana Ore Purchasing Company, and drank to drinking.

The evening passed in heady pleasure, and Fritz Heinze refrained from excess. Tomorrow would be a day of last-minute appeals, hurried injunctions, and legal maneuvering as the great constrictor snake writhed to free itself from the court's decisions. He knew just what the company would seek. A change of venue on the ground that Judge Clancy was prejudiced. A new Montana law empowering the company to reject the jurisdiction of biased judges. And of course a hundred petitions that would pile up on Judge Clancy's desk. No wonder the judge decided to go elk hunting. If he stayed around town, he was likely to be the elk.

The gala broke up in the small hours, and he summoned a hack for Katarina, and then accompanied her out to the mud-splattered vehicle. The horse's breath steamed in the silver lamplight.

"Good-bye, Augustus," she said.

"Good-bye? What do you mean?"

"You have another mistress," she said.

"I'm lost, my dear."

"Her name is Standard Oil, and she has captured you. Thanks for all the lovely times. You'll do in a pinch."

He was puzzled, but her wry grin illuminated the moment.

"Well, good-bye then," he said.

He opened the door of the hack, she pecked his cheek, and slid in, adjusting her cape. Then he watched the dray clop away with his prize.

She was right. He had another aphrodisiac.

He returned to the banquet room and found his party had dissolved. It was late. A yawning servant in a white apron toted glasses and napkins away. Empty bottles littered the tables. He had whipped the most powerful combine in the world, and now life was empty bottles and a weary waiter. He didn't feel elated. He had imbibed, but was cold sober. It was odd, how hollow he felt at the moment of his greatest triumph.

He decided to stay at the hotel. He headed for the desk, awakened a sleepy clerk, and took a room. He found his coachman outside and sent him off, telling him to bring a fresh suit of clothes in the morning. He told the clerk he didn't wish to be disturbed. He would get up whenever he got up.

He headed up the stairs to a corner suite, quite at home. He never had been interested in showy palaces, and could enjoy himself anywhere. He was amused by Clark's thirty-six-room brick pile a few blocks west. The man wanted to be important and show it. Heinze didn't want to be important; he wanted to enjoy life. So he let himself in, doffed his tuxedo and undid the rest and plunged into a cheerful summing up of this notable day. His particular pleasure was comparing himself with great figures. He admired Alexander the Great, he sometimes thought of himself as Hannibal, he decided he was occasionally Napoleonic, but more likely he was like Frederick the Great, which reminded him that people still called him Fritz despite his best efforts. Augustus was fine, as in Caesar Augustus, the finest emperor of them all. Or maybe he was Genghis Kahn, sweeping the world before him.

The only thing that worried him was that he had triumphed too young. He had a lot of life ahead, and no more Matterhorns to scale. That meant he would fight boredom the rest of his life, which wasn't the most palatable way to squander his days. And so he drifted through the wee hours, and finally slept. And the new day came and waxed and still he slept, until a furious and unaccustomed knocking awakened him. That made him cross.

It was Arthur, his brother.

"What?" Fritz asked.

"You fiddle while Rome burns," his brother said, mysteriously.

"I'll meet you in the dining room. Order my breakfast."

As good as his word, Fritz settled into a dining room chair, still attired in the evening's glad rags, and began sipping coffee, eyeing his nervous brother.

"Amalgamated's shutting down," Arthur said. "They've laid off everyone here and in Anaconda and Great Falls, the only exception being the pumping crews in the mines. Six thousand five hundred men laid off so far. And they're shutting down the smelter furnaces. They've locked the gates. You know what that means. This isn't short term. And the layoffs are falling cards. Everyone's laying off people or shutting down. We may have trouble getting supplies for our own mines. The lumber camps are shutting down and laying off. The coal mines are shutting down. The railroads are laying off men. It's the whole state."

"It's just a ploy, Arthur. The snake's angry."

"Not a ploy. They're lifting the mules out of the mines. The mules are delirious. The mules are coming up, Fritz, rolling on the grass, dancing in the light."

"So what?"

"I don't seem to get you to understand that this is dangerous."

"They can't stay closed for long. They own businesses, and you've got to operate your business or lose it."

"They've told the papers they have no choice. They can't do business here."

"Well, this is fun," Fritz said, digging into eggs Benedict.

"There are crowds gathering. They know you're here."

"Why here? I didn't lay them off."

"Don't make foolish arguments."

F. Augustus Heinze was not intimidated. "They're playing their aces, but it's still a game. The Standard Oil boys are showing muscle. Give in, or we'll shut down Montana. Look, Arthur, they've got surplus copper. Thousands of pounds of it, and it's depressing prices. This is a slick way to keep prices up and reduce their stockpile by a hundred thousand pounds. You have to give Rogers credit. He knows how to stay profitable."

Arthur didn't much like that. "Try telling that to all those men out there with no paychecks and winter coming on."

"Oh, I'll do that in time. But we'll need to see what's happening in the courthouse."

They slipped out the back door of the hotel, in cloaks, and headed for the Silver Bow County Courthouse, hoping Judge Clancy would not be anywhere in sight. The wind was blowing. There were knots of surly men outside the ornate building. But Judge Clancy was there, with armed guards.

His court was in session. He was hearing motions from Anaconda's lawyers, one of them being that he vacate his earlier decisions because of prejudice.

Judge Clancy yawned, revealing yellow teeth. "I have a prejudice, all right," he said. "It's lawyers that offend me."

He lifted a newspaper in his bony hand, and waved it in front of the crowd. It was a Helena paper, and the headline was "Fair Trials Law," and the kicker above it was "Special Session." Heinze couldn't see the text, but he didn't need to.

Clancy licked his chops. "Your people have been busy," he said, staring at Anaconda's legal talents. "Call a special session, pass the Fair Trials law. That means if you think a judge is biased, all you need to do is certify it and you get another to try your case. Now that's entertaining."

It was more than entertaining. It was blackmail. Amalgamated wanted to pitch out any judge it didn't like and choose its own, and only then would the mines reopen and the miners and smeltermen go back to work.

The courtroom was jammed. One of those present was Big Johnny Boyle. There were other union men listening too.

"I'll take it into consideration, gentlemen," he said, and vanished into his chambers. The mob of unemployed men stirred darkly. A wall of policemen stood between the judge and the mob. The room was stifling. The bench was empty. The guards carried shotguns. The mob stared helplessly at the closed chamber door. The union men studied the Heinze brothers, and Fritz could not fathom what was in their heads.

"We'll lick 'em," he said.

But the remark seemed to fall to the floor somewhere between himself and Big Johnny Boyle.

"The mules are up," Boyle said. "The mules are up."

F. Augustus Heinze wished he weren't wearing last night's glad rags.

That was the sum of the troubles for that day. The Heinze brothers passed through the silent multitude, and headed for the relative safety of the Butte Hotel. Augustus wanted only to get out of his tuxedo, which hung forlornly on him now.

Back in his hotel suite, he found a change of clothing and freshened himself. There was work to do. The hotel seemed deserted, and the streets of Butte seemed empty. The streetcars had quit. The provisioners who supplied saloons and restaurants and stores were not present. It was as if an economic knife had fallen, severing Butte from its commerce. It was quiet, much too quiet, even as the storm clouds hovered over the town, threatening to bring winter down upon it.

He could weather this. He knew what to do which was nothing at all. This would be a waiting game, but the waiting was between Amalgamated and its miners and suppliers. Let them sweat it out. Let one or another crack.

"What are you going to do?" asked Arthur.

Fritz smiled. "Let them stew."

"Is that a good idea?"

"A few thousand miners can bring the most powerful holding company in the world to its knees. All we have to do is watch."

"But isn't it the reverse? The holding company's bringing Butte to its knees. And sooner or later, Fritz, those miners you think you've got in your pocket are going to turn on you. You can bet that Amalgamated is working on it. You can bet that Johnny Boyle's listening to them."

"Then we'll deal with it when we have to. Good afternoon, Arthur."

The evening passed quietly except for the thundercloud hanging over the city. Fritz Heinze had a fine time in the hotel's barroom, listening to the gossip. The worse it sounded, the better he liked it. When the rumors were catastrophic, he thought for sure he had won. He headed to bed early, feeling quite chipper about it all.

But the next morning before he had even finished his eggs Benedict and coffee, a peculiar delegation sought him out. They were men he knew, bankers and union men. There was a man from Senator Clark's bank; and John D. Ryan from Daly Bank and Trust, and A. J. Davis, II, banker son of a banker and mining father.

Fritz invited them to coffee, and they settled around him. Ryan apparently was the delegated speaker. Ryan was Daly's man, and deep in the Anaconda hierarchy.

"Fritz, the union miners met last eve, and agreed unanimously on a simple matter. The union would be pleased to purchase your stock, and that of your colleagues, in the companies in the stockholder lawsuits, the Boston and Montana and the Parrot. We've agreed to lend the Butte Miners Union the means to do so. Then those shareholder suits can be dismissed by Judge Clancy."

Fritz Heinze was startled. He hadn't expected that. The stockholders' suits filed by his lieutenants were what had paralyzed the Amalgamated holding company. Rogers and Rockefeller could do little or nothing with their Montana properties, including the Parrot and all the Boston and Montana mines and smelters, so long as Clancy's verdicts stood and Heinze's men could paralyze the managements of those companies.

"The union would be pleased to resolve this conflict. Isn't that the case, Mr. Boyle?"

Big Johnny nodded. "This is one hell of a winter coming on," he said.

If the union owned the stock it would agree to whatever the Standard Oil Gang required to put the men back to work. Rockefeller and Henry Rogers would win, and win spectacularly. There would be champagne corks popping on Wall Street. And Fritz Heinze's mining empire would fall apart under the pressure of the monopolists.

"No," said Fritz Heinze. "I won't sell out myself or my company or my colleagues or the people of Butte, or Anaconda, or Great Falls, or the state of Montana. I won't sell out."

"That's set in concrete?" asked Ryan.

"It is," Fritz Heinze said, sensing what lay ahead.

FORTY-TWO

The crowd stood silently waiting for Fritz Heinze to speak. There were more people jammed into the courthouse area than Heinze had ever seen in Butte. More people than lived in Butte. They stood there in a deep quietness that might be despair or might be anger, but wasn't indifference. The quietness stretched to the quiet mines, the quiet boilers, the quiet smelters, the quiet trolley cars, and the quiet mountains rising in virgin grace not far beyond. Someone thought there were ten thousand who had come to this place.

Heinze was not fooled by the quiet. He had guards behind him. Before him was a mass of desperate humanity, people out of work and facing winter and starvation. They waited with solemn faces, wrapped against Butte's mean air, which for the moment was free of sulphur and ash and arsenic.

It was not just the working stiffs who waited. The business people listened intently. The newspapermen listened closely. The captains of industry and mining moguls listened from their carriage seats. Lumber barons and railroad men listened. Heinze hoped he was up to the task. Somehow, he had to make his fight their fight, and he meant to try.

And how better than to go on the offensive?

He began with history; his struggles to get a foothold; the efforts of the Anaconda Company to drive him out, which he resisted in all ways and by all means. He talked of all the ways he had been pressured and browbeaten and threatened. He had a fine, sonorous voice and a command of the language, and he put these to good use. He knew he was well liked in Butte, especially by his miners, and he put that to use too.

"They fought me in every possible way. They have beaten me a dozen times in one way or another, and I have taken my defeats like a man. I fought my own battles, explaining them to the public when I had the opportunity, and asking their support at the polls . . .

"My friends, the Amalgamated Copper Company in its influence and functions, and the control it has over the commercial and economic affairs of the state, is the greatest menace that any community could possibly have within its boundaries."

He talked about the cases just decided, but knew he wasn't gaining much traction with these silent auditors. They wanted their jobs. They wanted to be able to buy coal for their stoves, and food for their tables. But he was not yet done with them. He knew their fears and the things they were struggling to avoid.

"It is true that I am deeply interested in the outcome of this struggle. My name, my fortune, and my honor are at stake. All have been assailed. You have known me these many years. You are my friends, my associates, and I defy any man among you to point to a single instance where I did one of you a wrong. These people are my enemies, fierce, bitter, implacable, but they are your enemies too. If they crush me today, they will crush you tomorrow. They will cut your wages and raise the tariff in the company stores on every bite you eat and every rag you wear. They will force you to dwell in Standard Oil houses while you live, and they will bury you in Standard Oil coffins when you die. Their tools and minions are here now, striving to build up another trust whose record is already infamous. Let them win and they will inaugurate conditions in Montana that will blast its fairest prospect and make its name hateful to those who love liberty. They have crushed the miners of Colorado because those miners had no one to stand up for their rights.

"In this battle to save the state from the minions of

Rockefeller and the piracy of the Standard Oil, you and I are partners and allies. We stand or fall together."

He saw the softening in their hard gazes, and swiftly laid out the conditions of a settlement: his lieutenants would sell their stocks to the union at cost if Amalgamated would turn over its claim to the Nipper mine. The rest could be arbitrated. And as a capstone, he demanded the company guarantee a three-dollar-and-fifty-cent daily wage for three years, which surely would please the miners who worried about wage cuts.

The crowd drifted away thoughtfully. He could not tell if these people were really persuaded or were just waiting. They didn't get their wish, which was to go back to work to feed their families. Their thoughts didn't go much further than their empty cook pots. But he had made an offer, offered arbitration, and given them hope. But even as the vast crowd broke into knots and slowly trudged into the cold, he knew he had only delayed the next stage of the crisis.

He made his way back to the hotel, still under guard, and waited. The city of Butte waited with him through the night and day, its shops doing little business, its homes without sustenance, its saloons empty.

Then word came: Henry Rogers, and his head of Montana operations William Scallon, turned Heinze down flat, and demanded a special session of the legislature to enact their pet "fair trials" law, giving them the power to choose the judges who would hear their suits. That was what they had been after all the while, and had not bent an inch. They did not seek a change-of-venue law; they sought a law permitting them to select the judges of their choice. And so the shutdown continued day after day, while miners pinched and starved and moved out of state.

Governor Joseph Toole tried to put together an arbitration committee which included Senators Clark and Gibson, Congressman Joseph Dixon, and the railroad man

James J. Hill. But these worthies failed to bring the two sides together to talk. And so it failed.

Amalgamated had all the advantages. It alone could put the thousands of unemployed back to work. The next weeks saw the wars of the press release, the cannons of propaganda, but there was no progress. Governor Toole refused to call the special session. He would not give the holding company the power to choose its judges merely by certifying that one or another was biased. He would not let a powerful Wall Street company rule the sovereign state of Montana. Fritz Heinze had a point, and everyone knew it. It was shaping into a hard, cold, bitter winter, and as it deepened the unions ramped up their pressure on the governor, along with interested parties across Montana. People were starving.

Then Toole surrendered and called a session to begin on December 1, 1903. And the trust responded by reopening some of the mines and smelters. By the tenth of that month, the legislators enacted the "Clancy Law," as it was being called. The haunting reality of fifteen thousand men across Montana being jobless as winter closed in was too much even for independent legislators.

"They got it," Fritz complained to his brother. "Not even a change-of-venue law. They got the right to pick their favorite judges," he complained. "That's what being a Rockefeller gets you."

"We've got forty or fifty lawsuits that are about to drop down the outhouse hole," Arthur said. "And they'll have the judges to push us out the door."

It was odd how swiftly everything changed. Fritz Heinze was a courthouse miner, and now the courthouse had changed hands. The craven legislature had knuckled under. Amalgamated had just bought the sovereign state of Montana.

But he was determined to gouge out whatever he could. The struggle wasn't over. There was rich ore lying in disputed veins along the edge of his Rarus mine, ore whose ownership had not yet been settled, ore both sides were forbidden to mine until the apex suit was settled. He would go after it.

"It's simply retribution," he told his dubious brother. "It will repair some of the injury they've done us."

"And put a ball and chain around our ankles," Arthur replied. "They own the courts now."

"Aw, Arthur, you keep on being a lawyer, and I'll keep on being a geologist. I know where the ore is."

"And between us we'll practice law and geology in Deer Lodge," Arthur replied.

Fritz Heinze grinned. Adversity simply got his juices flowing.

He sent his miners to the forbidden zone and they were blasting out the ore night and day, and were bringing it to the surface far away, up the Johnstown shaft, thanks to the interconnecting crosscuts and drifts. But it was not a secret for long. Amalgamated miners heard the blasts, and sneaked into the Rarus mine through a dismantled bulkhead and saw for themselves the feverish removal of rich ore. Amalgamated attempted to stop the plunder in court; Heinze defied the court, dodged injunctions and summonses, and dug harder and faster.

"Quit worrying, Arthur. We're fast; they're slow. We'll have it; they'll never touch it. By the time they get in, they'll find empty cuts." But he wasn't sure of that. There had been brawls deep underground. Rival crews had fought with their fists and steam hoses and even with dynamite. It had been worth it; the Montana Ore Purchasing smelter was reducing some of the richest ore ever, hundreds of thousands of dollars of rich ore.

"What if someone is killed? That's dynamite they're tossing down there. That's steam hot enough to scald a man to death. What about that, Augustus?"

"This is the richest hill on earth. The richest hill on earth! So quit worrying. The prize is worth the risk."

But Arthur Heinze couldn't shake his foreboding. Over in Helena, the fury of the courts was exploding.

"Looks like we'll be hauled into federal court," he told Fritz.

"It won't matter. By the time that happens, I'll have the ore out."

It took sixteen days for Amalgamated geologists to gain access to the disputed bodies of ore adjacent the Rarus. For that length of time Heinze had defied Federal Judge Hiram Knowles and dodged summonses. But Heinze's crew hadn't been idle. When the geologists did gain entry, they found the cuts loaded with waste rock. It would be all but impossible to ascertain how much ore Heinze had stolen without massive effort to open the drifts and crosscuts.

The war continued underground even while the litigants were duking it out in federal courts. Then two Amalgamated miners died when Heinze's men were blasting out a bulkhead. But not even that stopped Heinze's gang from disemboweling a disputed vein in the Pennsylvania mine. And even as the battles raged around the Rarus, Heinze's men were pouring into Amalgamated mines adjacent to the Minnie Healy and looting ore over there. Heinze's miners were swarming through the richest hill on earth, cleaning ore out of obscure corners with breathtaking speed and audacity. Any ore was Heinze ore. Any mine was a Heinze mine.

Injunctions had no effect. It was war in the bowels of hell, and crews were employing any tactic at hand, including flooding crosscuts, burning trash and fouling the air, and dynamiting barriers perilously close to opposing gangs. The war raged through the rest of 1903 and into 1904, but finally abated when large numbers of miners were almost trapped by flooding. The judges dragged

Heinze and his lieutenants into court, fined them for contempt, and dressed them down.

Fritz Heinze didn't really mind. He just smiled. He had, in the space of a few months, carved a fortune out of the disputed lodes. The whole escapade had cost Fritz Heinze only twenty thousand dollars in fines, and his foremen got off for a thousand apiece. And in that time he had lifted half a million dollars of ore out of the disputed lodes. Maybe more; he wasn't even sure himself how much ore he'd snatched.

It was time to throw more dinner parties at the Butte Hotel. He had money to spend, and friends to spend it on. He had lady friends to invite; he had colleagues to thank. There were businessmen whose patience he had tried, and now he wanted to restore all those bonds of friendship and obligation that had buoyed him through his life in Butte. He had come to town as an obscure geologist and had parleyed a nose for ore, and some advanced knowledge of smelting, into a fortune. He had taken his licks, but now he survived, still a major independent, still a man with several mines, a giant smelter, a web of contracts with suppliers of fuel and mining timbers and chemicals. He was still in tight with the union men, still a man to drop down the shafts and visit the stopes and crosscuts and enjoy the company of those sturdy men who braved the bowels of the earth each shift.

He might not have a whole victory, and the great snake writhed and threatened, but did not strike him dead. He had more millions than he had ever dreamed of possessing. He had taken modest family wealth and parlayed it into one of the nation's greatest fortunes. He enjoyed that. He enjoyed the thought of good wine, good Havanas, and luscious ladies. He thought it was time to toast everyone who sat at his tables. He was bloodied, and the holding company owned the courts, but he would celebrate no matter.

FORTY-THREE

If Red Alice had believed in God, she would have thought the great lockout was heaven-sent. But she settled for the idea that it was fortuitous. It proved she was right. Socialism was the answer. If capitalists could put thousands of hardworking and loyal men out of work on a whim, then it was time for the nation's industries to be publicly owned.

She took heart. After years of being ignored, suddenly she had plenty to say, and a finger to wag, and an audience to hear whatever she said. She hadn't made any progress with Big Johnny Boyle, but plenty of miners and smeltermen were listening.

She had sold pencils and distributed tracts for years, occupying a certain patch of street in the heart of Butte where a steam vent released heat. She shared the prize ground with a yellow dog, which made its living from the local restaurants. They both stayed warm, at least on most days, but there were subzero times when not even a grille releasing warmth could make her sentry post bearable.

Most days she sold five or six pencils for a dime each. She had her regulars, who dropped a dime into her bowl, took a pencil, and a tract. Big Benny, the flatfoot, kept a benevolent eye on her, and sometimes chased hooligans away when they threatened to clean her out. He was equally solicitous of the nameless one-eyed yellow dog who shared the patch of warmth, and protected the mutt from cruel kicks. It was said that a bratty boy had poked a stick into the dog's eye.

She rarely got enough cash even to keep her in food, but it somehow didn't matter. Her boys, Tommy and Timmy, were geniuses at snatching whatever was needed, or bargaining what they had for what they needed. Somehow there would be a meal each day, if only gruel or soup made from bones gotten at the butcher shop. If Timmy lifted an item or two now and then, what did she care? It was all part of making an unjust world more just, and distributing what had been taken by the predatory and giving it to the needful.

Big Benny didn't turn a blind eye to all that. Sometimes when Timmy or Tommy slithered by, carrying something, Big Benny would corral the boy by the scruff of the neck, confiscate the loot, and return it to the shopkeeper, saying he had relieved some punk of his boodle.

"I caught a brat, turned 'im upside down, shook him until it rained out his loot, and here it is, ready to put back on your shelves," he would say.

That kept him in good stead with the shopkeepers, and it also allowed Big Benny to ignore the boys on other days, especially when it was cold and the parlor stove was empty. If the shopkeepers thought that Big Benny was just fine, Red Alice's boys thought he was even finer. Most days Big Benny never saw a thing.

And somehow Red Alice and her boys received their daily bread. She hadn't seen Eloise in years, and had stopped wondering about her. She had heard that her girl was a rich man's household servant in Great Falls, but she couldn't say.

She viewed the shutdown more positively than anyone else in Butte. Now the miners would see! Now the miners would fight! It was chilly, but she harangued anyone who was willing to stop and listen, often arguing with people, usually under the benign eye of Big Benny the flatfoot.

"This proves it! The only way to keep your jobs safe is government ownership. You'd get your pay from Uncle Sam, not the Standard Oil Gang. You'd be getting paid right now, and working right now, if the government owned the mines."

They were listening this time. Before, they usually nodded, eager to escape the cold and wind, and eager to lift a pint in the nearest pub. Then one day a miner she knew, Star McSorley, approached.

"Come along now, Alice. I've a bunch waiting to hear you."

"Buy a pencil and I will."

"We'll buy all your pencils, Alice; come with me."

"If it's to a saloon you're taking me, I'm not allowed in."

"It's a saloon, and if Gold Tooth Scatt objects, we'll throw him out."

She liked that, petted the no-name dog, and abandoned her post. He led her down Broadway, and then right three blocks, to a little pub she didn't know existed.

He ushered her in. There were twenty, no thirty, miners there. Anaconda men; somehow she knew that. Maybe Anaconda men tipped their hats a little differently. They were nursing their beer and studying her. They were just off-shift. Most had gotten out of their wet work clothes in the dry rooms; it was fatal to head into a cold evening in their brine-soaked work duds. They were pale, not having seen much sun, and some coughed constantly.

Scatt was actually smiling and rubbing his hands on his grimy bar apron. An invasion by a female was fine with him.

"Tell us what you think, Red Alice," McSorley said. "I brung her to talk to us."

It was warm there, and she was warmer than she had been in a long time. Butte was never warm except maybe in July, but this saloon's heat caressed her and pierced her coat.

"We've got to make a better world," she said. "We need a better world, where a man can count on a job and a decent wage, and count on it in the summer and winter, and in the best of times and the worst of times. We need a world where there's a fair wage for hard work, and hours that don't grind a man into his grave before he's lived half a life, and a safe place to work, and a safe place to retire.

"We need a world where a man gets a pension, where they don't just use you up and spit you out to die. We need a world where a man can open his brown envelope and take out enough money to feed his wife and children and keep them in a little place of his own and give them a chance to live. We need a world where there's help if we're injured on the job, where a man who loses his limbs, or his eyes, or his breath while mucking ore for rich men can get help.

"We need a world where we've got someone watching out for us. We're the poor, the forgotten, the ones down in the darkness who drill and shovel and lay up timber and cough our life away; we're the ones who are forgotten when the rich men fight to steal mines from each other and never think of the stiffs two thousand feet down in the earth who are shoveling their ore into cars and sending it up the shaft so that they can make still more money.

"We need a better world than the one we've got," she said.

She felt the warmth of the saloon pierce her clothing, and she unbuttoned her coat and let the warmth reach through her skirts. She hadn't known such warmth since the times when Singing Sean Brophy lived and worked.

They weren't skeptical, these tired men. They weren't arguing with her. They seemed as thirsty for her message as they were for their mug of ale after a hard day's toil deep underground. If the beer in its way was release, so were her words, so was her message. They too wanted a better world than the one they were trapped in.

"There's a way," she said.

No one responded, and maybe they would all discard whatever she said.

"It's the one big strike," she said. "It's when we all strike at the same time, and the rich men who have used us discover that they need us, need our labor, and that without our labor their own wealth falls apart."

Now she did see some skepticism. Who could imagine one big strike across America?

"We get there one by one, local by local, trade by trade," she said. "Not all at once, not tomorrow, but soon. We get there by taking over our own unions. We get there by putting fighting men in office. We get there by tossing out the ones who ride on our toil, who are cozy with the fat cats, who cut deals instead of defending us."

"Like Big Johnny Boyle," one man said.

She didn't reply, didn't even nod. But she knew they all absorbed that and agreed with it, and that from this moment on, Big Johnny would be on his way out of Local Number 1, Western Federation of Miners, and that soon, soon, the Butte Miners Union, as it was called, would lead the howling pack across the West.

She liked the warmth. It had been so long since she had been warm in winter. One of the men handed her a big pretzel from a bowl on the bar. She nibbled on it, licked the salt on it. She hadn't had a pretzel in years. There were boiled eggs, too, and they encouraged her to take a couple and put them in the pocket of her cloth coat.

"What's a better world?" she asked. "A fair wage and a job you can count on. You've just been out of work for many days, all because the owners are fighting, and bribing judges. You were put out of work so that the company could put the heat on the state. You were put out of work and no one cared about you. They knew you'd be starving, they knew you'd not have anything to spend in the stores, they knew that putting you out of work would build up a lot of pressure everywhere to put you back in the pits.

And they were right. They got what they wanted by starving you, by throwing your job aside, by forcing you to live without your wage day after day. And now you want a better world, and you know how to get it."

She wondered where the words were coming from. She wasn't educated, but the words came from somewhere, like a stream of hot water flowing from her, and the heat and warmth made her almost dizzy.

She was suddenly tired. These days she barely had strength to walk from her Dublin Gulch cottage to the grille where the heat was, the place she shared with the yellow dog. She wished she could have the ordinary privileges of any man, and sit in a saloon like this and sip a beer that would dull the pain and ease the weariness of her muscles. A better world for women would be that much further away than a better world for men.

She rose to leave, and they watched her. McSorley escorted her to the door, and pressed his hands over hers, but no one said anything.

She braved the cold, glad of the hard-boiled eggs in her pocket. She carried her pencil jar, but the pencils were gone and a lot of silvery change lay in the bottom. She would buy more pencils, a cent and a half each, fifteen cents for a box of ten, and sell them the next day. The cold didn't bother her this evening because she was warm in the center of herself.

By sheer luck, both Timmy and Tommy were in the cottage. They stared at her, aware that she was somehow different. They looked sullen. She didn't much like the way they looked, mean and ungoverned and cunning. Maybe that was her fault. She'd never liked her children, and they had always known it. She suddenly felt stricken about that; a rush of motherhood bursting in her this odd autumnal eve.

She handed each of them a hard-boiled egg.

"Where'd you nip that?" Timmy asked.

"They were given to me. Some men in a saloon, they gave me the eggs and a pretzel. There's good things for workingmen who go there."

He immediately cracked the shell and peeled pieces off the egg.

"You're good boys," she said. "Now it's time to be a man."

"You been drinking?"

"No, you're fine strong boys, but now you'll get a regular job."

"You crazy?"

"In the pits. They let boys work. You can be nippers."

Those were boys who ran supplies into the mines. Boys could do that, even if they weren't old enough to be mucking. They brought in tools for the drillers, blasting caps for the powdermen, new shovels to replace broken ones, sometimes hay for the mules. They took worn drills out of the mine to be sharpened topside. And they hauled debris out of the pits. They did whatever a half-grown boy could do, and were vital to the smooth operation of any mine.

"What if I don't want to?" That was Tommy muttering.

"You will," she said, iron in her voice.

Timmy looked at her, and at his brother. "I think we're nippers," he said. "We get to nip what's in there." He started cackling.

"You're good boys," she said, and they looked bewildered, never having heard the like. "Big Benny's going to miss you. He won't have much to do."

{ FORTY-FOUR }

The summons from Clark and Bro. Bank startled J. Fellowes Hall. He hadn't heard from William Andrews Clark in years. The *Mineral* had been profitable, and that had seemed all that Clark cared about. But now Hall faced a trip up the hill to the bank, and who knew what?

Clark wasn't even in Butte very much. He was in Washington off and on, occasionally attending to Senate business. More often he was in Arizona, or California, or France. But here was a green-uniformed messenger boy with a brief note:

HALL, BE HERE AT HALF PAST TWO. WAC.

Maybe it would be a raise. Not only was the *Mineral* profitable, but it had the best circulation. His coverage hewed carefully to solid ground through all the politics that swirled around Butte. He had been wary of the Anaconda Company and the Standard Oil Gang, and had said so carefully. He had been wary of Heinze's courthouse gambits, stealing mines via lawsuit, and had stated the case. He had largely avoided discussion of Clark's senatorial career, where Clark was setting records for absenteeism. So if Clark wished to see him, it couldn't be anything bad.

But Hall wasn't sure of that. Clark was unpredictable. And Clark could take exception to anything at any time. It had been a good run. Hall had upgraded the staff, modernized the plant with a rotary press, produced a paper that consistently outsold the rest, and had won acclaim. So he wasn't really sure why the summons made him nervous, but it did.

Hall had finally imported his family from Pennsylvania, actually overriding their own wish to stay East. They had heard awful things about Butte and had no wish to plunge into such a poisonous and bleak world. But Hall had found a comfortable west-side house for them, sent money to ship furnishings and pay their rail fare, and had installed them in the two-bedroom house with a good view southward. The ugly mines were out of sight behind them.

He had welcomed Amber, who frowned for a month as she examined Butte, and welcomed Nicholas and Stanley, who promptly scorned Butte's wild and sleazy schools stuffed with children with foreign names. But now, a year later, they had settled in, and found delight in the rowdy and scabrous city. All of which meant that J. Fellowes Hall was in Butte to stay; he had no plans to move on, and wasn't restless the way he had been during his first years, when each day brought a new affront to his dignity.

He eyed the sky, found it clear, and decided a suit coat would suffice, so he clamped his felt hat on his graying hair and set out on foot, soon arriving at the well-worn stairs to the second floor of the Clark bank. Upon presenting himself, a luscious raven-haired receptionist promptly ushered him into Clark's sanctum. The little man was perched, as usual, behind a vast well-polished desk, and bristling his whiskers in all directions as if each hair was a howitzer.

"Well, Hall, I've sold the *Mineral*," he said abruptly. "I thought you'd like to know."

"Sold?" The news astonished the editor.

"The whole thing. I'm not keeping a piece. I got a good price for it, a nice gain, and it's done."

"Ah, who's the buyer?"

"Why, who else could afford it? John Ryan of the Anaconda company. They prefer not to own the papers outright, so the papers are usually owned by someone high up. Word is, he'll replace Scallon soon. But behind Ryan is some real strength."

"Amalgamated owns the paper?"

"As of yesterday, yes. Thought I'd let you know."

"Are they planning any . . . changes?"

"I haven't the faintest idea. That's all, Hall. You may go now."

"Ah, am I still the editor?"

Clark smiled. "Haven't the faintest idea. I told them I'd tell you this afternoon."

"Well, thank you, Mr. Clark. Is there anything else I should know?"

"They're fine fellows over there, Hall. Scallon, Henry Rogers, Rockefeller. Just fine fellows, personal friends of mine, good God-fearing businessmen who love a good dividend."

Clark waved Hall off, so the editor retreated, slipped past Clark's cheerful assistant, clambered down the creaking steps, and into the smoky streets of Butte. His heart was racing. He was trying to think what he knew about the papers owned by the copper trust, and what sort of copper collar they wore, and whether there was any editorial leeway.

Durston's *Anaconda Standard* relentlessly hewed to the company's view of things, trumpeting whatever needed trumpeting. Durston didn't need guidance from above; he was usually a step ahead of the owners when it came to defending and promoting the Amalgamated holding company. Hall didn't know much about the rest, the company papers in Missoula, Billings, Livingston, and Helena. Neither did he know how various weeklies round about Montana fared. Often those papers weren't actually owned by Anaconda; the company had simply lent operating funds to the papers when they needed cash. That was all it took to influence the editorial direction of those editors.

So Ryan was the man. Ryan was a Daly protégé, a lawyer from Canada, a banker now, a company executive, and the heir apparent whenever Scallon left the firm. Ryan was tougher, harder, meaner, colder than Daly or Scallon; more like Henry Rogers, all piety and family and civility on the one hand, even while he was demolishing rivals and destroying or buying out opposing forms.

And Ryan spent much of his time at the Daly Bank. Well, good enough, Hall thought. He should find out at once where he stood. It all probably would be fine.

He found the Daly Bank up a way and marched in, hoping to meet the new owner.

Ryan was in, it turned out, surrounded by a sea of hair-oiled men in wire spectacles and black sleeve garters whose desks formed a phalanx that protected the great man from the public. He had heard these were Ryan's own legal assistants, all of them looking for loopholes and exceptions and badly drafted clauses.

"J. Fellowes Hall here to see Mr. Ryan," he said to a cadaverous fellow with a sleeve garter on both arms.

"Yes, he's expecting you. Mr. Clark rang up moments ago."

That was Clark, Hall thought. Still reading minds. He knew where Hall would go.

Hall found himself in the most orderly office he had ever seen, devoid of paper, or folders, or motes of dust in the sunlight. And behind an orderly desk was an orderly man, with chiseled face and cold, assessing eyes, all belied by a hearty smile.

"Sit," Ryan said. "Pleased to meet you. A most illustrious editor indeed."

Hall settled into a chair that looked virgin, as if no one had ever sat in it. It was an illusion, of course. Many a bottom had pressed the cushion, and yet Hall had the feeling that he was the first.

"Well now, we have the paper, and we are pleased with

it. We have the best circulation and the best advertising in Butte."

"Yes, sir, I've worked hard to bring it to that level."

"And the most profitable paper, too. Our dear friend Mr. Clark always insists on it."

"Yes, sir, and that comes from selecting stories that draw readers to us." ·

"Well, Hall, we're going to make some minor changes, with your approval, of course."

"I'm sure I'll be happy to adjust the paper to your needs, sir."

Ryan smiled, or rather his lips did; the rest of his face didn't, and his bleak gaze didn't change at all. "You know, Hall, this is a deeply ethical and moral town, with many happy families and warm hearths. Yes, with churches on every corner. We have delicate and gracious women, embued with their duties as mothers and wives and exemplars."

Hall saw where this was going, and nodded.

"I think, Hall, the paper is a bit racy, shall we say, for Butte. This is a sober and quiet place, with neighborhoods suited for children, and high standards of conduct."

Hall nodded.

"So, we shall proceed without coverage of certain unfortunates and without sensationalism of any sort. We want the people of Butte to understand that their town is a haven for the upright and industrious and virtuous, and not a place for unbridled conduct."

"That can be arranged, sir."

"Good. I'm pleased that you are flexible. Some people in the press are difficult."

"I am always flexible, sir."

"Now, as for the paper's editorial opinions, there will be some changes. Henceforth, your opinion page should reflect what appears in the *Anaconda Standard*. Durston knows exactly what is good for the state, the industry, and of course for Amalgamated, and we wish our other papers to reflect his viewpoints, or reprint his editorials so that we may magnify our opinion statewide."

"Yes, sir," Hall said.

"Now, of course, if you are tempted to digress, check here first. You need only bring a draft of what you are planning to say to any of the fellows just outside the door here, and they will approve it or not, or make certain suggestions. We want to speak with one voice, of course, and not have diverse opinions rising from our company newspapers."

"Bring it here, sir, yes, it's just a few blocks."

"Good, Hall, you catch on quite handily. Now, Hall, we're going to change some of the content, also. We've found that some of the stories dealing with the mining industry are less than accurate or enlightening, and we plan to make some changes. There's to be no original reportage about the mining industry. We'll send along an occasional piece for reprint, or make suggestions. And oh, yes, there's a fellow in your paper that you'll discharge. He seems to get things wrong so often that I question his ability. Wolf's his name. I believe he has the odd nickname of Grabbit. Let him go at once, Hall."

"Ah, he's got no pension, sir."

"He should have thought of that before engaging in irresponsible journalism."

"Very well, sir, I will let him go. With a month's pay?"

"No, Hall, just out the door."

Hall wrestled with that and chose stillness. Life was sad.

"Oh, yes, the cartoonists. You have two, I believe."

Hall nodded. He had two brilliant ones whose favorite sport was taking shots at Ryan's colleagues.

"We'll be discharging them, Hall. You can use the ones that Durston employs. We can send over the plates for your press."

"They have families here, sir."

"We all have families, Hall. Now, the newsboys. You're paying them a penny more than other papers do. We'll stop that."

"It inspires them to sell more papers, sir. They're the best in Butte."

"Anyone can do it. You just stand there and wave papers at people. Sorry, but they should go into more productive work if they want higher piecework wages."

"Yes, sir."

"Now then, we'll have you back in a month to review your progress, Hall."

"Yes, sir."

Ryan rose, rounded his spotless desk, caught Hall's elbow, and ejected him, smiling all the way.

Hall stood in the street, breathing smoky air, thinking about quitting, knowing he couldn't, and that he would kowtow to his new masters. Meanwhile there was the immediate problem of carrying out Ryan's commands.

He headed for the paper, sucking sulphurous smoke from the gray air, bracing himself for the tasks ahead. But when he got back to the paper he was no more prepared than when he had left Ryan's office. Inside, he steeled himself to fire Wolf, but couldn't find his star reporter, so he slumped in his chair, relieved for the moment, and then took the sleazy way out. He penned a note and left it on Wolf's typing machine.

The cartoonists would be easier. He found them scratching out new burlesques and paused at their tables. "New owners, boys. Amalgamated. They're making some personnel changes."

Stoltz, one of the cartoonists, sighed, tapped the dottle from his pipe, and started collecting his stuff. Bertrand, the other one and younger, stared, and followed suit. Hall had the sense that this was quite ordinary for political cartoonists. He watched silently as the pair suddenly whooped.

"We'll buy you a beer, Hall," Bertrand said. And moments later the pair vanished into the smoke.

He decided he'd let the newsboys find out about the wage cut when they turned in their daily collection and the circulation man, Stu Billings, totted things up and paid them. Company policy, something like that.

Hall returned to his warren, and stared at the walls. He was no longer an independent newsman. But he still had a job for the rest of his life if he conducted himself in the approved manner. He would not have another.

{ FORTY-FIVE }

enator Clark avoided the New Year's Eve frivolities as being unseemly and beneath his station. He paid close attention to seemliness now, and cultivated dignity as carefully as he trimmed his bristly beard.

The occasion that he wished to avoid was the opening of the Silver Bow Club's grand new quarters on Granite Street, which occurred that first night of 1907, when two hundred fifty or so of the club's members began with a drink in the old fourth-floor quarters, and then carried their glasses the short and wintry distance to the new structure.

Not that Clark disapproved. He had fought for the new building for years. He had been one of the founders and the club's first president in the early eighties. He had railed at the old club because it wasn't suitable for men of station and achievement. So he was delighted to celebrate the opening of the new club, but had chosen to do it his own way, with the first banquet to be held there. That was the best way to avoid all the drunks and reprobates he didn't care to run into.

So the club had been christened without him, christened with Chinese firecrackers, and a waterfall of spiritous drinks that enabled the celebrants to maneuver from 1906 to 1907 without pain. By all accounts it was a rather inebriated crowd that toasted the new club and its grand future.

The new building was a marvel, the finest gentleman's club between the two coasts. It was clad in golden sandstone quarried in Columbus, Montana, and was fitted with the finest furnishings and appointments that money could buy. The building rose four floors and had an Otis birdcage elevator to lift people to their destinations. The servants lived in the basement next to the boiler and coal bunker. The top floor contained bedroom suites for guests or members who wished to stay over. Below that was the grand ballroom. Below that were the club rooms and the saloon and dining room. There were reading rooms, and a separate parlor for the ladies. Members entered through their own grand doorway up slightly from the street, while servants and service people had their own entrance around the corner. The hidden stairway system was intended to shield servants from view as they moved from place to place. It was all just and fitting, and William Andrews Clark heartily approved of it all, including the quarter-million price tag.

The club was ready for princes of industry and commerce, kings, queens, presidents and senators and politicians of all stripes. Senator Clark certainly would entertain there, and enjoy the company of his peers there, and maybe do a little business there. But his exuberance at the completion of the Silver Bow Club was tempered by something else: he didn't plan to stay in Butte. Now that his Senate term was concluding, he was not bound to

Montana in any particular way, and could reside anywhere he chose, and that choice would be New York City, where he would build a mansion, collect art, collect accomplished friends, and sojourn in California or Paris if he felt like it. But all of that he set aside for the moment. He had finally gotten a gentlemen's club in Butte worthy of members and guests as prominent as himself.

He had acquired real estate in Los Angeles and Santa Barbara, plantation property in Mexico, assorted urban lots in places he visited. His Arizona mines drew him there, especially the United Verde mine, which was a fountainhead of new wealth. And even as his properties expanded, so did his family. In 1901 he had secretly married his beautiful young ward, Anna La Chapelle, whose Paris education he had been funding. They had a girl in 1902, but they did not announced the marriage until 1904, which created a great stir and a few raised eyebrows. In 1906 a second girl was born. So there was a young second family residing in Senator Clark's Butte mansion, at least some of the time.

It wasn't that Clark disliked Butte; it was that he was drawn into a larger world from coast to coast, and was embarking on the life offered only to the very rich. He enjoyed the city that made his fortune, and bestowed upon it Columbia Gardens, a beautiful trolley park in the foothills east of town, and delighted to host great parties there for all of the people of Butte. But Senator Clark simply had other interests that stretched farther and farther away from Montana.

Now it was his pleasure to celebrate the opening of the Silver Bow Club, and to celebrate Butte itself, which had finally transformed itself from a raw frontier town into a great brick-and-stone metropolis. It really was his city. He had nurtured it and still employed a large part of its labor force. He wasn't at all disturbed by the reality that it was owned by the Standard Oil people. Or that those people dominated the state government, Silver Bow County and Butte government, most of the newspapers, and many of the state's other businesses.

He chose his guest list carefully. There would be all those fine fellows over in Anaconda, including William Scallon, Cornelius Kelley, and John Ryan. And of course, Henry Huddleston Rogers and William Rockefeller, if they cared to come out to Butte. There would be one person who would definitely not be on that list, and that was F. Augustus Heinze, now a resident of Manhattan, and not welcome at such an event as this.

Fritz Heinze had sold out in early 1906. He had taken his time about it, and probably had tried to keep options open for himself through the long negotiations. But in fact, soon after the election of 1904, and the enactment of the "fair trials" legislation demanded by the trust in December of that year, Fritz Heinze had seen that the end was approaching. He no longer had friendly Montana judges available to keep the Amalgamated Copper Company at bay. He continued to engage in boisterous politics and legal maneuvers, even while he began cloistered talks in Butte hotels with the trust, most especially John Ryan. Eventually the talks were moved to New York because of Heinze's fear of discovery. He did not want to be seen as selling out to the very trust and monopoly he had assailed so virulently all those years.

And in fact, when the deal was finalized, the whole thing was an elaborate ruse. Heinze sold his Butte copper properties to a brand new trust, which in turn was controlled by Amalgamated people, so the nature of the transaction was well concealed to everyone—and no one. The swashbuckling Heinze walked away with ten million dollars for nearly everything he owned or controlled on Butte Hill, and also for the dismissal of his hundred and ten lawsuits against Amalgamated. Heinze still had mining properties in Canada and Utah, and he kept an interest in the Pennsylvania mine in Butte, but in truth he was out. His acerbic little newspaper, the *Reveille,* died too. He was gone.

And now, Senator Clark was hosting a banquet. It wasn't a large one, but it would include everyone who was someone in Western mining. It would be exclusively male, of course. The Silver Bow Club's discreet servants greeted the gents as they arrived, helped them out of their topcoats and silk hats, and directed them to the ballroom, which was fitted out for the banquet. The gents were uniformly attired in dinner jackets for the gala affair, and had snowy starched shirtfronts on display beneath their black bow ties. The senator greeted them and eyed their attire critically. Nothing annoyed him more than slovenly attire or grooming. Not even William Rockefeller would be seated if his glad rags weren't up to snuff.

Fortunately, on this fine winter's eve of early 1907, the assembled princes of mining and commerce were perfectly attired, and therefore welcome to Clark's soiree. He would, following a spiritous hour devoted to camaraderie and a sumptuous dinner of roast duck and truffles, address these captains of industry and finance. Just briefly. This was, after all, to be a celebration, an acknowledgment. He simply wished to make it known that Butte was the most important place on earth.

The senator surveyed his guests benignly. He was especially pleased to see a fine contingent from Amalgamated. These splendid gents were the wave of the future, and the suppliers of copper to a nation that was even then gradually electrifying its cities and in great need of the wire to do so. It was strange, Clark thought, how timing could be everything. The Rockefellers had built Standard Oil on the kerosene that lit the lamps of the nation, but now Standard Oil was fueling the horseless carriages that were crawling across lands once traversed by horse. And copper entrepreneurs like himself had arrived just in time to make electrification possible.

The banquet proceeded decorously, and after crème brûlée and port and cigars, Senator Clark had himself introduced by Henry Huddleston Rogers, and proceeded to address the brilliant assemblage.

"My purpose this evening goes beyond introducing you to the finest gentlemen's club on earth," he began. "The Silver Bow Club is a place of unparalleled comfort and privacy and distinction. Its opening symbolizes something else. The rock beneath our feet, often called the richest hill on earth, has recently become a lot richer.

"This is not the result of vast new discoveries, although we continue to find copper in endless quantities, but in the new efficiencies of extraction. It does us little good to sit upon the most fabulous body of ore since history began if we cannot get a decent profit from it. And only recently have we achieved our goal to get a splendid return on our heavy investment in machinery and labor. As of now, there is nothing to stop us from getting undreamed-of returns out of our investment here."

They were all listening carefully. Clark noticed that some of those starched shirts were well stained by the evening's imbibing, which he duly noted. Such men would likely not be invited next time. He checked his own starched bosom, which harbored not the slightest speck of disorder.

"I am talking, of course, about the consolidation of the copper industry here. At long last, the mine operators are not at war; the courtrooms are nearly empty. The countless apex suits and minority stockholder suits have been dismissed. The lawyers making a living from this heap of litigation have gone elsewhere. The great flow of ore moves uniformly and efficiently to smelters whose very size makes them more efficient and profitable than before, when there were numerous smelters competing for ore from dozens of independents. All this, in short, is the way to wealth. We have ended the litigation and rationalized our production," he said. "Every pound of copper is cheaper than ever to refine."

There was a polite scattering of applause.

"I haven't the exact figures, but the litigation was taking several million a year out of our pockets," he said.

"But things have improved in other ways. First, the government of Montana, on all levels, has become far more accommodating to business, and by keeping taxes and regulation to a minimum, and by giving mining corporations access to a fair and unbiased judiciary, the prospects of greater profit are very bright. We are in constant contact with Montana's officials, advising them and assisting them to help build the state's economy.

"Likewise, the industry and state are benefitting from a friendly and cooperative press at last, a press eager to present the public with the best available understanding of mining and its needs. This ensures that the government will treat copper producers with some equanimity. I am pleased to say that as a senator I was able to influence the federal government along the same lines, and this is already reflected in our profits.

"Of course," he said, delicately, "consolidation is not yet complete, but perhaps someday it will be, and meanwhile there is nothing but amiable relations among the proprietors." That was signal enough for the moment that someday, if the price was right, he would abandon his own holdings on the hill. But that was for the future. He knew that Henry Rogers would take note, and make plans.

"Now, my friends, take it from me: the opening of this splendid Silver Bow Club signifies the beginning of the most profitable mining on earth, a time when copper is the true gold. The richest hill on earth has only just begun to yield its treasure. If you think you've seen a lot, I'll leave you with this. You haven't seen anything yet."

That was it. They saluted him. They toasted him. They toasted the Silver Bow Club, and headed out into the wintry night.

He was among the last to leave, and happened to depart with Anaconda's John Ryan.

Outside, in the cold of the eve, a wraith of a woman stood, with a hand-painted sign pressed to her bosom.

Clark examined the sign, which read CAPITALISM IS THEFT.

"Who's that?" Clark asked.

"That's Red Alice," Ryan replied. "She's nothing to worry about."

{ EPILOGUE }

After selling out to Amalgamated, F. Augustus Heinze established himself in the Waldorf Hotel, where he entertained lavishly while expanding the Heinze brothers' empire to include banking as well as their own shaky trust, United Copper Company. But in New York he was in over his head, and his empire collapsed, in part because of the shareholder maneuvering of his old adversaries, the Standard Oil Gang. That collapse triggered the recession of 1907 and inspired bank reform, in particular the Federal Reserve System.

He married Bernice Henderson in 1911, and they had a son, but she died of spinal meningitis in 1914, ending a brief, bitter marriage. He died soon after, from cirrhosis of the liver, having shortened his life through high living.

William Andrews Clark died in 1925 after a long life devoted to expanding his business empire into one of the nation's major fortunes. He sold his Butte holdings to the Anaconda Company in 1910, but continued to pursue mining and other enterprises on a global scale.

The Anaconda Copper Mining Company gradually consolidated its holdings in Butte, absorbing the Heinze and Clark properties as well as virtually all the remaining independent mines. Eventually it owned the twenty-six copper mines on Butte Hill, along with transportation and reduction works. By 1915 there was no longer a need for the Amalgamated copper holding company, and it was dissolved. The Anaconda behemoth reigned supreme until the late twentieth century. It owned most of Montana's daily press and had an outsized influence on Montana's state government and several local governments. It was brilliantly managed, enormously profitable, and politically powerful. In the late fifties it sold its daily newspapers, which were no longer needed to promote the company's well-being. By the 1960s Montana finally had a vigorous independent press. The company moved most of its operations to Chile where labor was cheaper, but was eventually bought out in 1977 by Atlantic Richfield Company and no longer exists as an independent company.

In the period following this novel, Butte was riven by labor unrest and radicalism as well as managerial arrogance. The Industrial Workers of the World, better known as Wobblies, arrived in Butte to agitate for better working conditions. And the Pinkertons arrived in town, hired by the Anaconda Company to do its dirty work. One of these was Dashiell Hammett, who wrote a vivid novel, *Red Harvest,* depicting the period.

There is still abundant copper underlying Butte, and it is being mined on a small scale even now. Much of the city has vanished into the Berkeley Pit, but enough remains to retain its character.

AUTHOR'S NOTE

Historical novels come in many forms, ranging from the dramatization of actual events and characters and history at one end of the spectrum to novels in which an entirely fictional story is set within an historical period and place.

I have chosen a middle ground here. The copper kings and their minions are drawn from history, while actual events form the narrative spine of the novel. I have dramatized conversations and events that could well have happened and are consistent with history. On the other hand, most of the other characters, such as miners and shopkeepers, are entirely fictional. My intent was to portray people in all walks of life as they struggled with the maneuvering of the copper kings. William Andrews Clark's paper was actually the *Butte Miner,* but I have fictionalized it to the *Butte Mineral* for story purposes.

There is an abundance of superb literature about the rivalry of the copper kings and life in Butte in the last decade of the nineteenth century and first decade of the twentieth. Preeminent among them is *The Battle for Butte: Mining and Politics on the Northern Frontier, 1864–1906* by Michael P. Malone. I have quoted F. Augustus Heinze's famed speech to the miners directly from this outstanding history. Another valuable source is *The War of the Copper Kings* by C. B. Glasscock. *Copper Camp: The Lusty Story of Butte, Montana, the Richest Hill on Earth* is another fine resource rich in anecdote. It is a Writers Project of Montana work with uncredited contributors. Butte is remarkably Irish, and that aspect of the city is exhaustively covered in *The Butte Irish: Class and Ethnicity in an American Mining Town, 1875–1925* by David M. Emmons. The domination of the press of Montana by the Anaconda Company is superbly examined in the splendid, award-winning *Copper Chorus: Mining, Politics, and the Montana Press, 1889–1959* by Dennis L. Swibold. Mining town sociology and tradition is examined in *Tracing the Veins: Of Copper, Culture, and Community from Butte to Chuquicamata* by Janet L. Finn.

These were my primary sources, but there are many other fine resources in magazines, newspapers, and academic papers. I wish to acknowledge the assistance of my wife, Professor Sue Hart, and a distant cousin, Jack Gilluly, in supplying me with valuable research material.

—Richard S. Wheeler